# The Spirit Hunters

# The Spirit Hunters

## A Novel of Prehistoric Fiction

Shirley G. East

**To order additional copies of this book, contact:**
Xlibris
1-888-795-4274
www.Xlibris.com
799163

# CONTENTS

## PART 3

### THE FULFILLMENT

# FOREWORD

At the close of the Pleistocene Era many of the large animals became extinct, at least in North America. No longer did the mammoth, horse, camel and Bison latifrons roam the Great Plains. The giant predators such as the plains lion, smilodon and dire wolf were gone as well. A new form of bison, Bison antiquus spread throughout the area, but after a thousand years of rainfall and good grazing a drought brought their numbers to dangerously low levels. This is the time of Spirit Hunters. A culture called Agate Basin lived along the eastern edge of the Rocky Mountains and throughout the area of Texas, New Mexico, Kansas, Nebraska, Montana, Colorado and Wyoming.

They hunted the few remaining bison, but depended more heavily upon the elk, deer, bear and turkey of the mountains. They also probably harvested the wild plants both as food and medicine. We know little about them beyond the few artifacts they left behind and the bones of the animals they killed. There are indications of cannibalism, which I hope I have treated tastefully. Beyond that, most is speculation based upon comparable cultures. Agate Basin sites tell us they were obviously more sedentary that the Folsom Culture they followed, but they still depended predominantly upon hunting. The wolf was probably the only domesticated animal and seeds were not yet purposefully planted for a dependable source of food. The sites show deeper layers of deposits, indicating that they stayed longer in one place, but they still probably traveled, either seasonally, or when the game in their area became depleted from over hunting. They traded among their groups, and probably exchanged ideas as well. Archaeology has not turned up any signs of organized religion, or burial habits; these are strictly the creation of the author. However, the oldest remains, that of Kennewick Man[3], a Caucasian skeleton found in Oregon, shows signs of injury, indicating that life was difficult for these early Americans. They did not face the dangers of their earlier ancestors from the giant predators, but their life was none-the-less difficult. Finding enough food to feed their group would be a challenging prospect in the face of lasting drought and changing plant and animal distribution. Forest fires would also be a danger. There is clear evidence that forest fires were no strangers to the Rocky Mountains. But our story is about one special group of fictional Agate Basin people. They are led by a powerful strong man, Running Bison and by an even more powerful woman... but let the story tell itself...

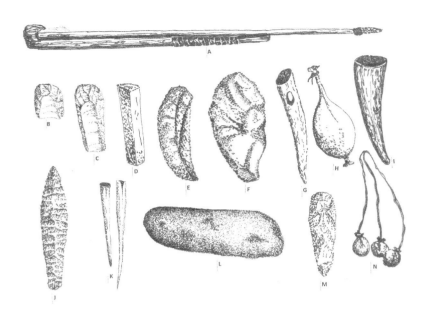

**A.** Atlatl holding Dart **B.** Thumb-nail Scraper **C.** End Scraper **D.** Blade **E.** Side Scraper **F.** Chopper **G.** Shaft Straightner **H.** Water Bag **I.** Horn-core Cup **J.** Agate Basin Point **K.** Awl's **L.** Mano or Grinding Stone **M.** Knife **N.** Bolas

1   The Pleistocene Era ended with the ending of the last glacial period, around 12,000 to 11,000 years ago. With the end of the Pleistocene a long period of drought swept across North America, bringing an end to many of the Pleistocene animals.
2   Bison antiquus was somewhat smaller than B. latafrons. It has short straight horns rather than the long curving horns of latafrons. It was this species of bison that predominated during the Folsom and Agate Basin periods of American pre-history
3   Kennewich Man is a 9,000 year old skeleton discovered along the Columbia River. In the hip of the skeleton was an ancient-looking projectile point. **Malcomson, Scott, L.** 1998

# INTRODUCTION

"What do you make of it?" The small group of archaeologists were crouched around the newly exposed layer at the Blackwater Draw site. "More of the 'spring sand?'"

"It looks like a large pocket. Just like the rest of the artifacts, those we have uncovered so far, all are water polished. Look at these, we just recovered them," he handed the several artifacts to the others. "Look at that Agate Basin Point (Tool Plate)," he pointed.

"It's broken, so?"

"Now look at this," he handed the woman another piece of 'Spanish Diggings Jasper'.

"The other half!" the visiting archaeologist exclaimed. "I am beginning to think you are right Professor. They must have been purposefully breaking these artifacts and throwing them into the spring, but why?"

"Maybe we will know more when we have had time to study them in the lab," the field forman remarked. "Right now, it is too early to speculate. It's too bad we don't have time to excavate this properly. Sanders is threatening to bulldoze the entire area tomorrow. Have you heard anything from the governor's office?"

"I put a call in first thing this morning, but he was at a meeting and I couldn't get through. It doesn't sound good for us though. I'd better get back to the University and bring out more people to clear this area. We can't take a chance on Sanders good will. He is going to get nasty about these hold-ups in his gravel operation. Sooner than later we are going to get kicked out and I'm not depending on the Governor to come to our aid. I'll be back as soon as I can," the professor rose, dusted off his hat and headed toward his car.

"What do you think about the artifacts?" The visiting archaeologist asked the field forman as they watched the professor leave.

"Well, so far we have recovered over 100 artifacts from this pocket They are all pretty much like those," he nodded to the pieces of the Agate Basin point she still held. "Lots of Jasper, and of course Alabates Flint, but there is even a good representation of Edwards Plateau chert. So far almost every Paleo-Indian culture is represented, and the strange thing about it is that all of the artifacts are broken, but all the pieces are there, mixed up in the sand. It almost looks like someone has been purposefully breaking those artifacts and tossing them into the spring; but why?"

"Could be a religious thing," the visiting archaeologist mused. "Like the professor said, we will know more after the lab analysis. Do you think there is any relevance in the location within the spring sand?"

The field forman shook his head; "these things have been tossed around inside that spring for possibly hundreds of years. I can't see that there is anything to be learned from their relative location. No, the lab work might tell us something, but it's too early to say anything more. Right now, our priority is just getting the artifacts out of the ground before Sanders dozes them into small pieces and we find them embedded in the main street some day." He glanced around, "I'm going to get these kids working faster, want to join us?"

"Might as well, the professor left me here and I either have to wait for him to come back or catch a ride back with you. Lead the way!" The visiting archaeologist followed the field foreman toward the dig. She shivered as the November wind of New Mexico swept across the exposed raw earth, lifting a haze of dust and finding its way inside her jacket. It was warmer in the excavation hole.

It couldn't be called an organized excavation because they were struggling to retrieve as many artifacts from the white spring sand as quickly as possible before the gravel pit owner forced them out and carried out his threat to bulldoze the remainder of the Blackwater Draw Archaeological Site. The professor returned just after noon with more students and hot food. After a quick lunch everyone returned to the excavation and all afternoon worked their way through the pure white sand, sifting the artifacts free and collecting them in bags. By dark everyone was freezing and hungry, but the spring had been cleared and the artifacts all collected. Sanders had already informed them that at dawn he would begin working that area of the gravel pit. They had gotten the artifacts out just in time.

Later the visiting archaeologist pulled off her jacket and tossed it on the chair in her motel room. Then she dug into the pocket and pulled out the two halves of the Agate Basin point. Settling on the side of the bed she turned them over in her hands. The stone reflected light from its polished surface. And curiously she fitted the pieces together. *Why?* She wondered...

4    **BLACKWATER DRAW LOCALITY #1**
Ridgely Whitman of Clovis, New Mexico first recognized the importance of Blackwater Draw in 1929. The site is located within Blackwater Draw near Portales, N.M. and is one of the most well known and significant sites in North American archaeology. Early investigations at Blackwater Draw recovered evidence of a human occupation in association with Late Pleistocene fauna. Since its discovery, the Blackwater Draw Site has been a focal point for scientific investigations by academic institutions and organizations from across the nation. The Carnegie Institute, Smithsonian Institution, Academy of Natural Sciences, National Science Foundation, United States National Museum, National Geographic Society and more than a dozen major universities have either funded or participated in research at Blackwater Draw. Additionally, due to the site's tremendous long-term potential for additional research and to public interest the site was incorporated and declared a National Historic Landmark.
The Blackwater Draw Museum was developed under the direction of the author and opened its doors to the public in 1969. The museum displayed artifacts discovered at the Blackwater Site. Artifacts and displays describe and interpret life at the site from Clovis times (over 13,000 years ago) through the recent historic period. It closed its doors in 2017. *Department of Anthropology and Applied Archaeology*
5    The Spanish Diggings Jasper is found in Glendo State Park, outside of Casper, Wyoming
6    Wormington first described the Agate Basin point type in 1957. **Wormington: 1957**

## 7    ALIBATES FLINT QUARRY

Located near Amarillo, Texas in outcrops from Permian Aged rock in the Canadian River Breaks, this fine-grained chert is very distinctive. For more than 13,000 years pre-Columbian Americans dug agatized dolomite from quarries here to make projectile points, knives, scrapers and other tools. Archaeological traces of prehistoric Indians-homes, workshops and campsites- dot the entire Canadian River region of the Texas Panhandle. Few sites are as dramatic as the Alibates Flint quarries. Where for 13,000 years or more people quarried stone for toolmaking. Unweathered flint was obtained by digging by hand or with sticks or bone tools. Chunks and pieces lying around these shallow quarry pits are the tailings or waste pieces. Flint was gathered and used by nomadic peoples for most of the quarry's history.

Archaeologists find tools made from Alibates Flint in many places in the Great Plains and Southwest. Distinctive for its many and bright colors, this flint comes from a 10-mile square area around Lake Meredith. *Geology Fieldnotes: Alibates Flint Quarries National Monument: Texas*

8    The Edwards Plateau region of West Central Texas is commonly known as 'hill country'. It is bounded on the east and south by the Balcones Fault. And to the north it extends to and grades into the Great Plains. The Pecos River and eastern edge of the Stockton Plateau define the western extend of the region. There are pockets of fine-grained gray chert throughout much of this region, and Native Americans from their earliest times until white settlement utilized it. *Texas Parks & Wildlife: Edwards Plateau.*

9    In 1963 The owner of the Sam Sanders Sand and Gravel Pit; Sam Sanders began to protest at having his gravel operation constantly held up so that archaeologists could remove the remains of extinct animals and the artifacts associated with them. Sanders was a businessman, and the constant interference with his operation finally forced the closure of the gravel pit. During the last few months of his life, he struggled against the state and Eastern New Mexico University to keep his operation going. During this time the author worked at Blackwater Draw as part of the crew and later assistant to the Department of Anthropology to rescue what remained of one of the finest archaeological sites in North America. We uncovered the remains of an ancient spring, its vents filled with sparkling white sand. Within this sand were retrieved hundreds of artifacts, from throughout the Paleo-Indian period of prehistory. They were all polished as though they had been passed through a tumbler, and the most intriguing part of the puzzle was that many of them although broken; were complete. They represented materials from as far away as the Spanish Diggings in Wyoming to the Alibates Flint Quarry in the Texas Panhandle and the Edwards Plateau region of south-central Texas. It is obvious that these tools were carried here from long distances, then purposefully broken and tossed into the living spring. Today the site is owned by the State of New Mexico and is under the control of Eastern New Mexico University in Portales, New Mexico.

# PART 1
## THE FLIGHT

# CAST OF CHARACTERS

Chapter 1:
**Sage:** Age 11. The Chosen One, grand daughter of Clover Blossom
**Clover Blossom:** Old one. Has kept a secret for many seasons. Dies leaving her grand daughter with dire instructions to flee for her life.
**Running Bison:** 20. Already a powerfully built man. Sent by the Bison Camp to bring back the Sacred Relics stolen by Clover Blossom and Gray Coyote many seasons before. Known as Dipper as a child.
**Prairie Grass:** 19. Sent with Running Bison. Called Shadow as a child.
**Obsidian:** Dog belonging to Sage, really a wolf, big and black.
**Moon Maiden:** Sage's mother and daughter of Clover Blossom. Murdered.
**Gray Coyote:** Mate to Clover Blossom. Died just after fleeing the Bison Camp.
**Whispering Wind** 14. Young woman of the Bison Camp. Taken captive by Others. Rescued by Sage, called Sunbird as a child. Her spirit is Prairie Dog.
**Thunder Cloud:** 32. Father of Whispering Wind.
**Crooked Spirit:** 40. Dreamer of the Bison Camp.

Chapter 2:
**Whispering Wind:** Age 14
**Sage:** Age 11
**Obsidian:** The protector, a wolf

Chapter 3:
**Whispering Wind**
**Sage**
**Obsidian**

Chapter 4:
**Running Bison**
**Prairie Grass**
**Water Carrier:** 22. Hunter of the Bison Camp
**Walks Far:** 23. Hunter of the Bison Camp

Chapter 5:
**Whispering Wind**
**Sage**
**Running Bison**
**Prairie Grass**
**Hunting Badger:** 45. Headman of the Bison Camp.

Chapter 6:
**Sage**
**Whispering Wind**
**Running Bison**
**Prairie Grass**
**Obsidian**

Chapter 7:
**Running Bison**
**Prairie Grass**
**Raven:** 21 years old. Hunter of the River Camp. Has been seeking the Bison Hunters for several seasons
**Bull Elk:** 23. Traveling companion of Raven.
**Quenquil:** 24. Dreamer of the Savage Camp.

Chapter 8:
**Sage**
**Whispering Wind**
**Running Bison**

**Prairie Grass**
**Raven**
**Bull Elk**
**Obsidian**
**Thunder Cloud**
**Hunting Badger**
**Crooked Spirit**
**Water Carrier**
**Walks Far**
**Angry Bull:** 33. Hunter of the Bison Camp. Suck up to Hunting Badger.
**Jumping Antelope:** 26. Hunter of the Bison Camp
**Blue Butterfly:** 22. Unmated woman of the Bison Camp
**Rain Water:** 30. Woman of the Bison Camp
**Winter Snow:** 25. Unmated woman of the Bison Camp
**Sand Catcher, Juniper Smoke, Pine Cone, Old Badger, Talking Shadow:** hunters and their families who chose to go with Running Bison.
**Crying Coyote, Mesquite Branch, Singing Water:** three youths sent to contact the other camps of The People.
**Cricket:** 10. Sole survivor of an attack by raiders on a Gatherer camp.

Chapter 9:
**Sage**
**Crooked Spirit**
**Running Bison**
**Whispering Wind**
**Hunting Badger**
**Angry Bull**
**Calling Wolf:** 25. Hunter of the Antelope Camp
**Eagle Stalker:** 27 Hunter of the Antelope Camp
**Running Antelope:** 23. Hunter of the Antelope Camp
**Swift Fox:** hunter of the Deer Camp
**Black Bear:** hunter of the Deer Camp

Chapter 10:
**Running Bison**
**Crooked Spirit**

**...g Wind**
**...rie Grass**
**Singing Water**
**Crying Coyote**
**Raven**
**Talking Shadow**
**Calling Wolf**
**Hunting Badger**
**Tall Bear:** hunter of the Bear Camp
***Great Thunderer:*** *leader of the raiders. Sacrificed by Quenquil*
**Iguana:** headman of the Savage Camp.
***Humming Bird:*** *Daughter of Green Parrot. Sacrificed by Quenquil to keep his secret safe.*
**Bending Branch:** hunter of the Savage Camp
**Antler Dancer:** hunter of the Savage Camp
**Horned Owl:** hunter of the Savage Camp.
**Standing Bear:** takes over of leader of the late raider's camp.

# CHAPTER 1

The gnarled hand reached out from under the tattered bison hide cover and grasped the slender wrist of the young girl lying curled up within a bed of deer hides beside the old one's sleeping furs. The long fingers were twisted with age and painfully misshapen, but they had strength enough to waken the girl with a bothersome pinch.

With a startled gasp, the sleeping adolescent jerked into a sitting position and peered through the dark toward her aged grandmother. "What is it?" She asked sleepily. "Are you in pain? Can I get you something?"

"Listen to me, Granddaughter." whispered the old one in a weak yet urgent voice. "I have not much time; I fear I have left this too late. The sky fires beckon and I am ready to go, but before I leave you, I must tell you . . ." the old one coughed and her breath rattled in the cold night air. "Those men, who came into the camp this afternoon, they are looking for me and they are a danger to you. You must flee, this very night, under the cover of darkness." The old one moved weakly within the soft furs, plucking their worn surface with agitated fingers. "I should have told you before." she fretted. "But we seemed safe enough. I didn't think that after all this time they would still be searching . . ."

"Danger! Flee? What are you talking about, Grandmother? Those men are strangers! I have never seen them before, how can they mean me harm?" The girl withdrew her hand and stirred the coals in the fire pit as she added more wood. Soon the warmth began to spread within the cramped shelter. Still she shivered as the wind moaned and whipped about the fragile refuge, shaking it with a blast of rain-laden air. She returned to her place beside the old woman.

The flames ate hungrily at the firewood. Their glow cast a ruddy light over the features of the old woman. She pulled the robe closer under her chin and her mouth hung open just enough to show the stubby remains of one last tooth within her otherwise defenseless mouth. Her face reflected more than just her age. The surface was patterned with so many wrinkles that her eyes were only deep pools within its landscape. Her nose was a hooked beak and the scraggly hair on her nearly bald head stuck out in every direction, an unruly halo, accentuating her features. But her voice was still strong enough to carry the urgency of her concern.

"Listen to me, Sage. I will tell you why you must flee." The old one squirmed into a sitting position and in a voice of utmost seriousness began her tale. "Many years ago, on the very night your mother was murdered and you were born, I saw the signs in the night sky. When your mother, Moon Maiden gasped her last breath, I took my sharpest blade and removed you from her dead body and then I took you up into my arms and with the sacred relics fled the danger of our camp."

"Whatever are you talking about, Grandmother?" Sage's voice was tinged with fright. "My mother died right here in this village when I was just walking. You told me this yourself!"

"These people among whom you have grown up are not your people. I lied to you and I lied to them and claimed a kinship which made us welcome, but I have always known that one day 'they' would find us. My days are gone, I am too old and sick to flee from here, but they must not find you and they must not get the Sacred Relics."

"I have dreaded this day for most of my adult life. The danger is so great, that I dared not even tell you of it, for fear that you would let slip and say something to draw attention to us. That is why I told you that your mother was still alive when you began to walk. Now they have found us and it is too late for me to run. You did not understand their talk and it was hard for the elders to comprehend them, but I grew up with that camp and I understood their every word. We were lucky in that they were asking for a pair of adults. They did not know that your grandfather died soon after we fled the camp. Nor did they know of your birth. We left a bundle buried with your mother, indicating that she died before your birth. Before we reached this camp, we came across a pair of Gatherers with whom we spent several days. It was through them we claimed the kinship. Only these things have saved us. But those men will soon get to the truth. And by then you must have vanished." Again, the old one coughed and phlegm dribbling down her wrinkled chin. With an expert wipe of a rabbit skin fur, the noxious slime was removed and the girl handed her a horn of fragrant tea dipped from the tea skin suspended over the fire. The grandmother drank greedily and then with a sigh continued her tale.

"The tall one, he was called Dipper as a child. His adult name is Running Bison. He and Moon Maiden were as close as a little brother could be to an older sister. He is your cousin. The other, the one they called Prairie Grass, was named Shadow as a child. They are probably good men and have come here on an honest task, but you cannot trust that."

"Our people live to the east of here, across the mountains and beyond the river. There on the Great Plains and Llano Estacado they make their homes. Your people are not as these gatherers, who hunt only deer and elk and antelope, but are hunters of the great bison that live upon the vast plains. This sleeping fur is the only thing which remains of that life and I was foolish to keep it." Her ancient fingers plucked restlessly at the tattered edge. "But I have been prepared to flee for many years. Always I have kept everything ready. You need only load the travois and harness the black dog called Obsidian. Follow that trail I showed you last summer into the mountains; keep going all night and in the morning walk into the rising sun. You know the pass through the mountains, use it and once beyond that find a place to hide. Stay there, safe and hidden until the spirits contact you. I know they will, for you are the last of the line, the spirits dare not allow harm to come to you."

"Grandmother, you are not talking about things of this life!" Sage protested as she tried to settle the agitated old woman more comfortably into her sleeping furs.

"Whatever you do, do not allow those men or others like them to capture you. When you are ready, the spirits will guide you." The old one sighed and sagged backward upon the furs.

"Grandmother! You make no sense! What is all this talk of spirits and hiding?"

"I do not have time to tell you all, but while you load the travois, I will tell you what I can." Sage rose and began, reluctantly, to follow the instructions snapped out by her grandmother, as the old one continued with her tale. "We are of the Bison Hunters, the ones you have heard about from time to time. 'The People', they call themselves. The storytellers weave tales about the Ancient Ones and the Great Beasts who protected them. These beasts were their animal spirits and 'The People' were great. Always there has been one woman of each generation, who was marked by the animal spirits. These women have been the 'Keepers of the Sacred Relics' and it has been their responsibility, not only to keep these relics safe, but offer 'gifts' to the spirits for the well-being of 'The People'. You have seen the bison mark upon my shoulder. Often in the past you have asked me about it, now I will tell you. The mark of the bison is found only on 'The Chosen One', the 'Keeper of the Ancient Relics'. This role came to me because I am one from the ancient line of 'chosen' as are you. Your mother also carried the mark and because of it she did not die a natural death. Someone within the camp murdered her, someone who did not want the line to continue. I do not know who killed her, but you are in danger until the spirits safeguard you. Soon you will reach womanhood. Then the spirits will contact you and give you their protection. Until then you must hide."

"Grandmother, I have no such mark!" Sage protested.

"Of course not." the old woman snapped. "It doesn't appear until you reach womanhood. But it will!" She sagged back against the furs her fragile strength suddenly spent.

"But how will I survive?"

"I have taught you well. You are proficient with the bolas and the woman's atlatl. (Tool Plate) You know the plants to eat and how to prepare them and meat. Obsidian is as good a hunting dog as any among these people. She will serve you well."

"She will probably bite my hand off the very first time I get near her!" Sage protested. "She is not at all tame, more wolf than dog and she particularly doesn't like me! Besides, the hunters will surely run me down if I steal her!"

"She belongs to you." the old woman sighed. "I traded a great deal for her during the winter. You will just have to show her that you are in charge.

I have encouraged you on a number of occasions to get to be friends with her, now you have no more time to do so. Is that travois loaded? Did you pack that deer-hide-covered packet? Guard it with your life. That bundle is the only thing which will protect you, but only if you have it."

"Yes Grandmother, I have packed that packet which you describe. Why have I never seen it before, if it is so important?" Sage sighed, rising and wiping her hands on the sides of her tunic.

"Then there is no time to waste, the wind is rising and the rain is getting harder. You could not ask for a more perfect time to make your escape." The old one ignored her questions. "It is as if the spirits are already protecting you." the old voice held a ring of satisfaction. "Go now and get the dog!"

"But Grandmother! I cannot leave you! Who would take care of you?"

"I will be gone to the sky fires before morning, child. You are on your own. If my spirit can follow and protect you, feel me beside you. Always remember my words, but go now." Suddenly the old woman gave a jerk and her body sagged. With a sighing sound her spirit departed and Sage was left holding the empty shell. With tears, she straightened the aged body tenderly in her sleeping robes and with a final glance went, reluctantly, out into the storm to find the black dog called Obsidian. This task was not hard in the least, for she nearly stumbled over the animal as she stepped from the shelter. With inner trepidation she called the dog, which, to her amazement, followed docilely and stood quietly as she attached the harness with quivering fingers. Then Obsidian, with a flash of blue fire from her eyes, led the way from the camp as if she knew exactly what they were about. Sage followed, frequently glancing over her shoulder for signs of pursuit. Her grandmother's ominous words had thoroughly frightened her and she now gladly followed the big dog through the icy rain, as it led her ever farther away from the only home she had ever known. The rain came down hard now, washing away their tracks almost as soon as their feet vacated them.

Sage struggled after the travois for hands of time as the wind shrieked and rain and sleet beat into her face and soaked her deerskin tunic turning it into a sagging, unshapely, heavy and wet encumbrance. Finally, with a shivering sigh, Sage pulled the garment over her head and calling for the dog to stop secured it atop the travois. She was shaking with cold, but with the burden of the tunic gone she had more freedom of movement and was better able to keep up with the already rapidly disappearing travois. Her moccasins were in little better condition and finally she called to Obsidian to stop yet again and sitting on a boulder, removed them as well. Now clad only in her apron she scrambled along the faint path the dog followed. Soon the exertion warmed her, and she did not feel the cold so much. Upon reaching the mountain trail they took shelter beneath a huge pine for a short time and Sage wrapped her sleeping fur about her shoulder. Shivering she stuffed a piece of dried meat into her mouth and fed another to the dog, amazed as the sharp teeth took it from her gently and left every finger intact.

The wind cooling her body urged them back onto the trail and dawn found them on the far side of the pass through the mountains, a trail that her grandmother had shown her the summer before and had not shared with anyone else. At the time Sage had found this behavior strange, but now she understood it, or at least she thought so. As the sun rose high, Sage stopped the dog and they rested in a sunny glade hidden within the forest. Here she spread her sleeping furs and settled down for a few hands of needed rest. Obsidian settled beside her, alert for danger, as Sage slept.

*    *    *

Running Bison emerged from the shelter and stretched to his full height. He was a big man and his full bushy beard made his figure even more impressive. Prairie Grass still snored within their shared travel shelter, but with the birds' first sound, Running Bison was awake and ready for the day. He added wood to the fire and finally got the damp tinder to take flame. With a grunt of satisfaction, he settled the cooking skin on its support and began heating rocks to drop into the waiting skin of food. This mission to the gatherers of the northwest mountains seemed like a great waste of time to him, but Crooked Spirit had urged that someone make the journey. He insisted that his 'spirit' had assured him that the 'Chosen One' and the Sacred Relics were among these people. How Crooked Spirit could possibly know this was beyond him. Old Coyote and Clover Blossom had disappeared many seasons ago and no one had any assurance that they even had the sacred relics with them.

Perhaps whoever had murdered Moon Maiden took them! Running Bison didn't have a clue how he was to discover if in fact, Old Coyote and Clover Blossom had even lived among these people. He sighed and dropped a hot rock expertly into the waiting skin. A satisfying sizzle and the aroma of the cooking food greeted his nose. So, he sat and waited: waited for Prairie Grass to wake up, waited for the camp to come to life for the day.

Prairie Grass finally emerged from the shelter stretched and finding a turtle shell plate scooped a healthy portion of hot food from the bag. Running Bison had already eaten and was enjoying a last horn of tea before starting the day. A shout from the far side of the camp alerted them that something unusual was happening. Running Bison hurried to join the group of people clustered near a shelter. The language was different from that of 'The People' but close enough that he could make out the general conversation. Sometime during the night an old woman had died, and her granddaughter was nowhere to be found. Even their dog was gone. It seemed that the old woman had died a natural death, but it was strange that the granddaughter had vanished. Prairie Grass muttered at his elbow, "What's going on here, can you make it out?"

"An old woman died in her sleep. It seems there is a girl who is missing."

"Oh! Nothing to get all this excited about," muttered Prairie Grass. "Old people die all the time."

"Yes," agreed Running Bison. "But I'd like to see this old woman, just the same. I have an uneasy feeling . . ."

"Not again!" protested Prairie Grass. "The last time you had an uneasy feeling we were attacked by raiders and barely escaped with our lives!"

"Well we can hardly get into a lot of danger from a dead woman. I just want to see her, that's all. If it is Clover Blossom, we have completed our journey. We can request to search her belongings and if we find the Sacred Relics we can return to our own people and be treated with great respect."

"But what if it is Clover Blossom and this granddaughter has stolen the Sacred Relics again?"

"Clover Blossom had no granddaughter, remember?" Running Bison reminded him, uneasily. "Moon Maiden was murdered before her child was born. If this old woman is Clover Blossom, then she is the last in the line of the 'chosen'. The relics belong to 'The People'. These gatherers would be unwise to keep them from us. It would be either a very foolish camp or a very brave one to go up against the Bison Hunters. Their future would be very shaky."

"Well, I don't like this. If you must see this old woman to assure yourself that she isn't Clover Blossom, then do so quickly and let's get out of here." Prairie Grass muttered. "There is only a pair of us and things could turn nasty if these people turn on us."

"I will try not to upset anyone as I make my request. Remember Clover Blossom was my Aunt. I have a relative's right, to make sure this woman is not she and to claim her belongings if it is."

"How can it be? You yourself said that she had no granddaughter."

Running Bison frowned. "I have never been so sure that Moon Maiden died before giving birth, or if she did, that Clover Blossom could not have saved the child. Moon Maiden was nearly at the end of her carrying time. Clover Blossom was very clever and wise in the women's medicines. She was also of strong character. I do not think she would hesitate to do what must be done to save the child."

"Well, get done what you must and please hurry. I want to get out of this camp as soon as possible. I don't like the way people are looking at us."

"You worry too much!" Running Bison remarked. "I'll take a quick look at this old woman and we will go." He turned as the headman approached and with hand signs and words, he did get the idea across that he wished to see the dead woman and reassure himself that she was not his missing aunt. The headman frowned, then shrugged and led the way inside the cramped shelter. Once inside Running Bison's spirits dropped. Clearly, he could see the old woman and the mark on her shoulder was plainly visible. In fact, he had found Clover Blossom.

It took Running Bison a considerable time to explain that this was indeed his lost aunt and he wished to take her things and return them to her family. He did not explain that he was the only family she had and the only thing he wanted was the Sacred Relic Bundle she had stolen. The headman was hesitant to comply, stating that the girl, Sage, would be returning to the camp from wherever she had gone, probably to do a death prayer and surely she would have a greater claim on the possessions of the dead woman than he. Running Bison sighed and was forced to wait.

Night came and still the illusive Sage had not returned. By morning Running Bison insisted and the headman, tired of all the questions. He was also nervous about having a dead body within the confines of the camp when the spirit would soon be leaving, suddenly approached the pair of men and gave them permission to take the old woman's belongings, provided they took the body as well. Running Bison nodded and very soon they had loaded everything, including Clover Blossom onto their travois and quickly left the camp. A hand of time later they found an acceptable place not far from the trail and there, laid old Clover Blossom out to walk the wind, as was the tradition of 'The People'. Then they went through the entire contents of her belongings, disappointed, but not surprised, to find no trace of the Sacred Relics. Now Running Bison was sure that the absent granddaughter was indeed Moon Maiden's child and that she had the missing relics. Grudgingly they agreed that in all probability they belonged to her and that they were also, more than likely, lost to 'The People'.

"We could circle back around that camp and pick up her trail," suggested Prairie Grass unenthusiastically.

Running Bison shook his head. "With all the rain that night, there will be no trail. Clover Blossom knew what she was doing. She might have been unable to escape us, but you can be sure that she made certain we would never find the girl."

"But why? After all she would be your cousin. You would be responsible for looking after her and protecting her. It doesn't make sense! Why would the old one send her away from the only people who would be willing to protect her?"

"Clover Blossom evidently had no idea who killed Moon Maiden. It could have been me, or you, or anyone. She would not have taken that risk. Beyond all else she would protect the 'chosen' and now the spirits will protect her and if she is meant to return to us, she will. We can only go back to the Plains and hope that one day she does return and has the relics and can perform the offering before it is too late and we are all dead." Running Bison shouldered his pack, discouragement plain in the set of his shoulders and headed down the trail.

\*      \*      \*

Many hands distant to the north, Sage sat on a big mossy log, dug into the food pack and shared some dried meat with the dog. Then they drank from the wide stream they had just reached. Sage studied the valley and surrounding mountains and finally decided to follow the stream up the valley for the present. It was well after sun- high. They had traveled all night and most of the previous pair of days before stopping to rest. Rising with the sun they had pushed hard all this day as well. Surely by now they were safe from pursuit. She followed the stream up the valley and then for many days as it became smaller and smaller, they climbed higher and higher into the mountains and passed through one canyon after another. She had seen no signs of anyone else for nearly a hand of days. Then they crossed through a high pass and down into yet another valley. Still they kept going, deeper and deeper into the mountains. The moon became full and then shrank to a mere sliver, but day after day Sage kept going. Finally, she was forced to stop. They had eaten the last of the dried meat. Sage looked about and picked out a large pine under which she raised their small hide shelter. She unharnessed the dog and picked up her atlatl. (Tool Plate) With a 'woof' Obsidian leaped into the air. Her feet had barely touched the earth before she began sniffing the ground in ever-larger circles, then with a bark she headed up a trail, Sage hot on her heels. In short order they had a grouse and a pair of rabbits for their evening meal.

"Here, my friend," Sage handed the black dog one of the rabbits she had brought down with her rabbit stick. "You have certainly earned a meal of fresh food." She ran her hands through the thick fur along the dog's back, checking for sore spots from the harness but found none. Obsidian wagged her tail and accepted the rabbit. Sage spitted the grouse and cooked it over a small fire, sheltered beneath the tree. She was nonetheless wary, even though she had seen no signs of people of any kind. Her grandmother's parting words still rang through her mind.

The next morning Sage began looking for a place to live. It was mid-summer; they would need to gather food for the winter and build a shelter to keep out the cold. It would take a number of deer hides to cover that shelter. Over the next hand of days, they explored the low valley in which they found themselves. They had traveled far to the east and somewhat to the north from the village of the gatherers. This valley was much lower than the one that she had called home, but winter would still be severe. There were numerous streams to provide them with water. Plants were plentiful as well. If tracks were anything to go by, animals were abundant also. This valley would make them a good home. The signs she had seen of other people were all very old. No one had been in the valley for many turnings of the seasons. This suited Sage very well. Obsidian seemed content with the place as well. She explored even more extensively on her own while Sage was busy gathering rushes and nimbly weaving them into storage baskets of various shapes and sizes. It was Obsidian who found their home. She was off chasing rabbits one afternoon and when she returned, she leaped and whirled and barked until Sage put her half-made basket aside and followed. Obsidian led her directly to a small opening in the canyon wall, an opening completely obscured by a large bush. Once through the opening, however, Sage found herself in a cave. It was taller than her head and deep enough that she could not see the back. Instantly she knew this was far better than a hide-covered shelter. Hugging the big dog, Sage praised her and was amazed to find that her fear of the animal had completely gone to be replaced by a growing love. They quickly moved into their new home and with the expert use of her fire-starter, she soon had a cheery fire crackling in a hearth a short distance inside the opening. Natural drafts drew the smoke upward and to the back of the cave leaving no tell-tale trails to give their location away.

Over the next few days, Sage gathered more rushes and soon had a whole row of storage baskets waiting to be filled. Then one morning she hooked Obsidian up to the empty travois and tossed an old deer hide and a large reed-woven container onto it. They headed to the high end of the valley where the pinyon trees were thick and drooping with cones. Here she spread the hide beneath first one and then another of the trees and with a stick knocked the ripe nuts from their cones and onto the hide. She filled the container completely full with nuts before returning to the cave. This task was repeated, again and yet again, until Sage was confident that she had an entire winter's supply of pinyon nuts. Their rich flavor made excellent cakes and flavoring for stews and pemmican. She dug the tuberous roots of the cattail as she gathered the rushes for baskets. These roots were stored in the cool region at the far rear of the cave. She found other tuberous plants, coltsfoot, amaranth and many different kinds of seeds and berries that she dried and stored as well. Before another turning of the moon, she had a plentiful supply of plant food. There were rose hips and herbs for flavoring tea. Dried flower leaves and other selected ingredients would provide her with a selection of herbal teas all winter long. She had carefully gathered mushrooms and dried nutritious leaves and stems of numerous plants with which she was familiar. She had also stripped the outer willow bark and collected the pain-killing rich cambium. She gathered nettle roots and other medicinal plants, just in case she had need of them. Many other food plants had found their way into her storage baskets as well. There were the tart plums and apples that grew in the valley, as well as blueberries, raspberries and blackberries. She had been too late for the strawberries and other early fruits, but still she had a good supply to provide a variety of vegetable foods. They were, however, still bringing down only small game. She had many rabbit skins ready to tan into winter clothing and feathers enough to make a warm cloak as well, but so far, she had been unsuccessful in killing any deer. They were shy and kept to the deep brush where it was nearly impossible to dart them.

If they were to survive the harsh mountain winter, Sage knew that she and Obsidian would have to kill at least several deer or elk to provide themselves with enough meat. She also knew that she had not the strength, nor the experience to bring down so large an animal with the woman-sized atlatl and darts she carried. As they had fled, Sage had gathered nodules of the natural Obsidian after which the dog was named. She had a plentiful supply and had fashioned crude, but usable knives and scrapers from some of it: now all she needed was the carcass of a large animal to use them on.

The leaves were falling from the summer trees and a trace of snow had covered the ground with a lacy layer of white several times, still they had no meat supply beyond a few rabbits and birds. Sage was becoming truly worried. She sat outside a short distance down the cliff from the cave, enjoying the warmth of the sun as she worked on a stack of rabbit skins. Obsidian had disappeared somewhere on her own earlier in the day. A sound from above caused her to jerk her head around and her mouth fell open in amazement as an entire hand of elk tumbled over the cliff into the valley only a stone cast from where she sat. A woof behind them told her who was responsible for this 'gift'. Sage gave a yelp of glee and ran for the cave to get her atlatl and tools. One cow lay still, her neck clearly broken. The back of another kept her from getting to her feet and running away. A pair more had broken legs and the bull lay on his side kicking his last. Sage lost no time in dispatching the wounded cows. The bull was already dead by the time she returned from the cave. Obsidian joined her several fingers of time later and they had a spur-of-the-moment celebration and thanked the spirits of elk for this gift, both of them leaping and cavorting about with abandon. Then Sage got down to business. Luckily it was a cold clear day. She skinned the first cow quickly and cut it into quarters, giving Obsidian the lungs as her share, a treat the big dog thoroughly enjoyed. The internal organs were carefully removed and set aside to cool. The travois was quickly brought into use to drag the quarters into the cave. Here in the back of the cave the warmth of the fire never penetrated. The icy chill would let the meat cool and Sage would have several days to process it. The next cow went slower; and nightfall came before she started on another. With fingers trembling with fatigue she spitted a few strips of meat over the skewer and sank exhausted beside the fire to rest while they cooked. She munched on a roasted cattail tuber while she waited. Obsidian sank beside her and laid her head on Sage's lap and sighed in contentment while Sage scratched her ears absently. Sage spent the night huddled beneath her sleeping furs, feeding a large fire. Obsidian paced the immediate area and growled and threatened the slinking shadows of wolf, coyote, fox and several other smaller opportunists as they sought to steal some of the meat from the yet-to-be butchered carcasses. The sun rose to find them already hard at work. Before noon the other pair of cows were stashed safely in the cave. After a well-earned rest and a meal, they started on the bull. Sage used a good-sized rock to break the skull at the base of the antlers, saving them to make tools from later. Her arms shook with fatigue as she dragged the final quarter onto the travois and she and Obsidian hauled it into the cave. She rolled up the hides as her last effort and loaded them onto the travois for the final trip to the cave. Night shadows were creeping across the valley floor as she surrendered the remains of the butchering to the impatient carnivores.

Sage settled beside the fire with a moan. Every muscle in her body screamed in protest against the efforts just demanded of them. She was too exhausted to even move. There beside the fire she fell asleep. Deep in the night the cold wind freezing her back wakened her and she patted the big dog curled up against her and struggled to her sleeping furs.

Birds were singing merrily in the bright sun when, with a groan, Sage wakened and struggled to her feet. Obsidian lay at the mouth of the cave making sure no scavengers entered. As Sage moved about the cave, her muscles loosened and soon she didn't feel too bad. A crackling fire drove the chill from the air and soon they were eating a hot meal. Afterwards Sage erected the drying racks and began slicing the elk meat into thin strips with her knife (Tool Plate). Before the sun was overhead, the racks were groaning with meat. She had a pile of tendons set aside to dry for sinew. The supply she had found on the travois which her grandmother had packed, were nearly gone. Now she had one less thing to worry about. She went out and cut green wood for the smoking and spent the rest of the day keeping her fire going and setting up more drying racks. By evening she had plenty more room to hang her strips of meat.

For the next hand or so of days this was the pattern of their life. Then one rack at a time, the elk meat made its way into storage baskets and the racks were disassembled and stored against the far wall. She had fat sausages of rendered fat, an ample supply of tendons, hoofs for glue, antler for tools and the hides to make into robes and clothing. Sage had missed the first deep snowfall. She was surprised to go to the entrance of the cave and see that the world had turned from brown to white.

There was no trace of the elk butchering. Scavengers, large and small had cleaned up the remaining bits and pieces of the carcasses. The heads had been taken into the cave to salvage the brains for tanning the hides. Snow had covered the blood-soaked ground and the cold had removed any remaining trace of odor. As Sage stood staring down the valley, Obsidian growled and nuzzled her back inside the cave. Sound, carried on the breeze, alerted Sage to the danger. Men were in the valley. She could hear them shouting to each other. They certainly weren't hunting. Any game would be far away from all the noise they were making. Then she heard children and women as well and realized that an entire camp had entered the valley.

She dampened the fire with shaking hands and crouched low at the entrance and watched. These people spoke a strange tongue. She could not understand any of their words. The men trod out before the rest, leaving the women and children to pull the heavily laden travois. Sage frowned and then sighed in relief. They had no dogs. Even if they loitered for several days in her valley, she could escape detection, an impossible feat if they had dogs. Her heart still sank as they halted and began setting up camp in plain view of the cave. The sounds of their voices were a pleasant change from the constant silence, but for her own voice, which had availed her for the past three moons. Still they represented a danger she could not ignore. As their camp settled more and more permanently into place she began to wonder if they might not be meaning to stay the entire winter. That night she lighted no fire. Instead she and Obsidian huddled together at the mouth of the cave and watched. She debated if she shouldn't try to leave during night and relocate elsewhere.

Disturbing shadows began to creep along the canyon wall and she watched in amazement as human figures emerged from the shadows and crept toward the sleeping camp. She stuffed her fist into her mouth as the first screams ripped through the valley. Then flames began to brighten the night sky. Men, mostly naked, emerged from shelter, only to be brought to the ground with darts. The smell of blood spilled on the smoldering fires began to drift on the breeze, a nauseating stench. Women and children screamed only to have the sound cut short. One small figure crawled from beneath a shelter hide and quickly melted into the deep shadows of a nearby bush. The butchers did not detect this one. Soon silence once again drifted over the night. The flames died down as the exulted yelps of the attackers faded into the distance. Sage did not move for a long time. Dawn tinged the sky before she gathered her courage and crept from the cave followed by the nervous Obsidian. The dog whined and growled as she sniffed the wind and shifted nervously beside Sage.

The attackers had been very thorough. Bodies lay scattered everywhere, most lying in pools of blood, their faces still twisted in the final scream. Eyes were staring sightlessly into the sky and already the ever-vigilant buzzards were circling. Sage picked her way from body to body. It was a slight sob that alerted first Obsidian then reminded Sage that there was one survivor. Obsidian sniffed and bounded toward a thick cedar shrub and found the girl crouching within its sheltering branches.

Sage called out softly and inched to where the girl could see her. Seeing only another girl the frightened one rose and eased from the branches, looking cautiously around all the while. She was a bit taller than Sage and obviously older as well. She was thin and showed signs of repeated abuse on her bare arms and legs. One eye was swollen shut and her lip was split; yet she had escaped the attackers. Sage took her hand and motioned for her to follow, then quickly left the grisly camp of death. She took the caution to find a branch and carefully erased their tracks away all the way back to the cave. Once there she motioned the other girl to be seated and handed her a horn of hot tea.

"Who are you?" Questioned the newcomer. "You live in this cave?"

Sage strained to understand but failed. "My name is Sage." She replied in an effort to keep the conversation going. Seeing no understanding, she pointed to herself and repeated 'Sage'. Then she pointed to the dog and said "Obsidian, my dog."

The strange girl nodded and pointed to herself. "Whispering Wind." She offered.

Sage nodded and offered food. They sat eating until Obsidian began to growl again, deep in her throat and moved to the opening. Sage and Whispering Wind were right behind her.

Buzzards flew and squawked angrily as they rose in clouds from the carnage. Into the camp trotted a double hand of grim-faced hunters. Whispering Wind began to shake and with a quiet sob dived back into the cave and vanished into the dark recesses. Sage smothered her tiny fire and then watched with interest as the hunters went from corpse to corpse and then began to assemble the bodies in a burial arrangement. Some of the hunters dug shallow graves in the frozen ground while others lowered the waiting bodies into them. When they were finished, they all piled large rocks over the tops of the graves. The buzzards would feast no more on these people. Then the grim-faced men turned and vanished as quickly as they had appeared.

Sage was puzzled. Surely these were Whispering Wind's people. They had buried the slaughtered strangers, yet Whispering Wind seemed as frightened of them as of the attackers. Sage shook her head and called. "Whispering Wind, it is safe, they are gone." Something in her voice if not her words, must have communicated, because Whispering Wind cautiously emerged from the darkness. Still they did not leave the cave that day, or the following. The valley was quiet and then another storm swept in and covered the broken and burned camp with a coat of white. Winter set in for certain then, one storm after another sweeping down the valley, closing the three of them off from the outside, sheltering them in a little world of their own.

Over the next turning of the moon they learned to communicate and were soon at ease chattering with one another in their respective languages. Whispering Wind related that she had been a prisoner in the slaughtered camp, stolen from her own people during the early part of the summer. She had been treated badly by the camp, beaten and abused by all. When the first screams had issued, for a split second she had been sure that her own people had finally found her, but the language shouted by the attackers had not been one she recognized. She had taken the opportunity to slip under the hide of the shelter as the man abusing her had run from the shelter. Still, the slaughter of the camp had been a horrible sight. The second group of hunters had been the ones to trade her into that camp. She had no love for either group.

"Who are your people?" Sage asked.

"My people are the Bison Hunters," replied Whispering Wind. "We live on the Plains and are a great, strong, people. It was by poor judgement that a new and unfriendly woman led me astray. She and I were out picking berries when the raiders found me and carried me away. They are awful people! They are dirty and stupid and don't even know about dogs. The women do all the hard work and the men use any woman for their own pleasure, even the ones with child. These people are lower than dogs!"

"You say that you are of the Bison People? Do you mean the ones which call themselves 'The People'?"

Whispering Wind nodded, "You have heard of us?"

Sage nodded, "My grandmother mentioned 'The People'." she replied cautiously.

"You have a grandmother?" Whispering wind questioned. "I thought you were all alone like me!"

"I am now," Sage replied. "Grandmother died just before I left the camp of the gatherers."

"It is strange that you always refer to the camp as if they were stranger to you rather than your own people."

"They were strangers to me, even though I grew up in that camp. My grandmother and I lived with them, but we did not belong to the gatherers. Grandmother claimed a kinship bond for us."

"Then who are your people?" Whispering Wind frowned.

"Grandmother did not say," Sage lied. "She died before she had a chance to tell me. I guess that makes me a girl without people."

"Then we will travel together to my people and you will be welcomed with open arms. My father, Thunder Cloud will welcome you as a daughter of 'The People' for saving my life," Whispering Wind stated with satisfaction. "We will become as close as real sisters," she tossed another piece of wood onto the fire. "It is settled. We can spend the rest of the winter right here in this cave and I will teach you all about my people. I will teach you the language and tell you all our legends. My grandfather, Talking Shadow, is the storyteller of our camp so I know all the stories by heart. We have little enough to do during the evenings after we have eaten the last meal of the day. I will turn you into a woman of 'The People'. By the time spring arrives, no one will ever know that you were not born one," she grinned at Sage.

Sage felt an uneasy shiver run up her spine, but she did not protest. Perhaps the spirit of her grandmother had led this girl here to teach her the ways of 'The People'. She did not know, nor did she really care. Winter would be lengthy here in this valley and learning about 'The People' was as good a way to spend the long evenings as any other. She was grateful to whatever spirit had brought this girl here to share her winter. Still Sage did not say that her grandmother had been of 'The People'.

They developed a routine. Each morning the girls checked carefully before leaving the cave on their snow walkers. Since the turning of the last moon they had been alone. The snow was now so deep that it was unlikely that any other people would venture through it just to come to this remote place. They began to relax. Sage and Whispering Wind found that they had a lot in common. Whispering Wind was a pair of seasons' turnings older than Sage, she had already become a woman and had enjoyed her 'becoming a woman' ceremony. This she described in detail to Sage.

"When you have your first passing of blood, it is time for the ceremony. The whole camp is involved, from the headman down to the newest unmated male. There are gifts and feasting and celebrating. A girl's father goes out and kills for her, a special animal. Of course, since we are bison hunters, a cow or a young female bison is the usual offering. The hide is tanned by the women of the family and treated in a secret way, known only to the women of The People, so that it is pure white and so soft that it is an absolute pleasure even to touch it. Of course, that is all a girl can do with it until she is mated. That is the first time she can use the hide. It is made into her mating tunic by the women of her family, but back to the 'becoming a woman' ceremony." Whispering Wind grinned.

"There is more to it than just celebrating!" she stated importantly. "The girl must take a 'spirit journey' and discover her protective animal. She must have already gathered enough mourning glory seeds to make the drink. Then on the morning of the ceremony, she goes out alone into some secluded place and using the things that she carried with her, prepares for the 'spirit journey'. First; she must have washed herself and cleaned and braided her hair in the traditional manner. Among the things she takes with her are the white ash of a hot fire and the black ash of a cool fire. Yellow ochre and red ochre are also used and if she is lucky, the ground colored stone which signifies her heritage. I am of the Antelope Camp from my mother's side and the Bison Camp on my father's. This means that I decorated my body with the traditional symbols. Once she has prepared her body and is seated upon the rabbit hide blanket, she is ready to drink the mourning glory drink and wait!" Whispering Wind grinned, "I had to wait for many hours until I had a vision. Then after I was chosen by Prairie Dog, I was ready to cleanse my body and carry the remains off into a secret spot, the same place where I buried my first blood flow. After that I returned to the camp and was greeted by all and was given many gifts. I was given my adult name at this time. No longer was I Sunbird; but Whispering Wind. It is the first time that a female has the attention of the entire camp. After this time, the unmated men court and offer presents. Until she chooses a mate, it is the best time of a woman's life."

"There are similar customs in the camp where I grew up," Sage nodded. "I wonder if at some time both groups were one?"

Whispering Wind frowned and then shrugged, "It is possible, I suppose. There are stories that in the ancient past groups split off from The People and went in all different directions. Perhaps that explains the similarity between our ways of speaking."

"I don't see anything which would indicate that our ways of speaking are at all alike!" Sage protested. "It took me a long time to understand even the simplest things you were saying."

"Well I have heard other people speak and they are a whole lot more different. You really didn't take long to begin to understand me. And we have many words that mean the same thing. For example, take the name of your dog, Obsidian. In our tongue that name means a black shiny stone. It is much prized for the making of tools. And the name for the spear thrower is also the same, as are the words for the darts. Travois is also in our tongue. So, you see, there are a lot of words we share."

"That doesn't prove anything," Sage replied. "These words are the same in numerous tongues. It only means that these tools have been used by many people."

"Well, have it your way, for now," Whispering Wind refused to give up. "Sooner or later you will agree that there is a relationship. Anyway, you might as well begin getting to know your new people. Each night I will tell you one more of the stories that my grandfather has been telling the children of our camp all my life. I cannot begin to tell them as well as Grandfather for he uses his hands and voice to tell the story, not just words. But by spring I will have you acting and speaking like one born to 'The People'!" She grinned. "Once the snow has melted, we will begin our journey to find our people!"

Sage frowned a bit at this, not at all sure that by spring she would be ready to join the very people who had murdered her mother, but she held her silence and went along with Whispering Wind. "Since we are going to make our winter clothing, we will fashion it after that of 'The People'. Of course, elk-hide is a long way from bison-hide, but we will just have to do the best we can." Whispering Wind hummed happily, "Our winter tunic is longer than yours, for it reaches clear to the knee, but we always cut fringes for the last hand's length. I will cut out the shapes and you can make the holes for the lacing, all right?"

"That is fine with me," Sage agreed, much happier to punch the lacing holes, an easier task than cutting the hide with a sharp blade. Whispering Wind selected a burned twig which she had removed from the fire and casting an appraising eye at Sage began to lay out the shape of a tunic on the elk hide spread on the cave floor. In a very short time, she had the outline drawn and was expertly cutting out the shape.

"Here you are!" she handed the front piece to Sage, who took it and began punching out a neat row of small holes along the edges of the shoulder, under the arms to the bottom of the tunic. (awls Tool Plate) "Be sure to stop before you reach the bottom," Whispering Wind reminded, "For we will fringe that." Sage merely nodded and kept on making her precise evenly spaced holes. By the time Whispering Wind had the back finished she had the front ready to lace. They took a break and had a bowl of herbal tea before completing the back. While Sage punched holes for the back of the tunic, Whispering Wind began the pants. They were equally loose and reached well below the knees to cover warm leggings wrapped around feet ankles and legs. The pants had an open seam at the rear, so that one could pass waste without freezing. The tunic covered the area anyway, so modesty was maintained. Men wore two pieces held in place by a waist thong for their personal comfort. Each of them took up their bone needles and with gut sewed the pieces together. Before they retired to their sleeping furs, one complete set of winter clothing was finished but for the decorating. Both girls were well pleased.

"Look!" Sage pointed, "This game trail must be used regularly by the javalina family! I have not eaten javalina meat in a long time," admitted Sage. "It would be a nice change from elk."

"I don't think I have ever eaten javalina meat," Whispering Wind replied, "We usually ate bison; and rabbit and quail if we had to." She reached into a pouch at her waist; "These fruits and nuts are wonderful though. I hadn't realized that there were so many plants one could eat. On the plains there is not so great a choice and the Bison do not go into the mountains, so we seldom get the opportunity to have elk and for some reason the hunters disdain the plains' deer."

"I cannot imagine eating the same thing day after day!" Sage wrinkled her nose; "It must get awfully boring."

"I never really thought about it before, but you are right!" Whispering Wind replied. "I have enjoyed not knowing what we were going to eat for our next meal and the variety has been pleasing. Perhaps this is something you can offer to 'The People'."

"I can't see that is much to offer!" Sage replied hesitantly, "Everyone knows what plants can be eaten and which ones are poison and which ones make medicine."

"You know what plants make medicine?" Whispering Wind stopped in her tracks.

"Not all of them of course," Sage admitted, "But my grandmother was a renown healer. She taught me a great deal about the healing plants before she died."

"Our only healer is Crooked Spirit, the dreamer. He is a kind man and he means well, but he hasn't much knowledge of healing and none at all of woman's medicine. We really need a healer, so if you know it well, you will indeed be made most welcome."

"While you are teaching me the ways of your people, I could be teaching you the healing plants," Sage offered, "It is knowledge that can always come in handy."

"You would do that?" Whispering Wind stood with her mouth hanging open is surprise. "No one shares that kind of knowledge among 'The People'. The healers are treated with special respect. They are not at all anxious to share their secrets. If everyone knew the healing techniques, they would not be able to ask for so much for their services."

"That is silly!" Sage sputtered. "What if they are gone from the camp and someone has need of their services?"

"That person must wait until the healer returns or do without," Whispering Wind answered thoughtfully. "There was a woman last winter who died in childbirth, because the healer was at a neighboring camp. You are right, if there had been someone else who understood the medicines; she need not have died. As it was, she bled to death for the lack of a blood stanching herb."

"I can remember a number of similar instances when people died because the healer was away from the camp, or just too busy to bother!" Whispering Wind sighed. "My own mother was one of them. I was very young, but I can still remember, she cut herself on a sharp branch. The wound became filled with evil spirits. Her arm swelled and by the time the healer returned to the camp it was too late. She died a few days later, in terrible pain. Again, the healer was gone from the camp. Besides, she was merely a female!"

"I agree that it would be very good to have someone else in the camp who knows of healing. A woman would be wonderful! Besides, she would know more of women's ailments. The biggest problem would of course be that a man would not use her services. But then, the men have their own healer. Yes, I would learn these plants and remedies. It would give me a secure place in the camp; a place that no man could strip away."

"Not everyone among the gatherers knew the healing ways, but there was at least a hand of women who were very proficient, some knew one plant, some another. You went to whichever healer suited your problem. Hush!" suddenly Sage stopped, tipped her head and motioned to the dog. Obsidian sniffed the wind, flicked her tail and melted into the brush beside the trail. "Find a place to hide, where you can jump out and dart a javalina," whispered Sage. "Quickly! Obsidian will have them running right into us if we don't hurry!"

Both girls ducked into hiding and almost before they were settled, the javalina, squealing and snorting, came hurrying down the trail toward them. Sage rose and darted the lead javalina, the rest stopped and then scrambled over the carcass of their fallen leader and wild eyed, plunged down the trail directly into Whispering Wind. She rose and cast her dart, by which time Sage had darted another javalina and was nocking yet another dart into her atlatl. Within a few heartbeats, the girls had a full hand of javalina lying still along the path while the rest vanished in a crashing of brush. Obsidian loped into view, almost smiling as she reached the girls.

"How are we going to get these javalina to the cave?" Whispering Wind questioned, "They are far too heavy for us to carry."

"Not at all," Sage replied. "We will skin them, lace the hides together and fashion a pair of traces. That will do for a temporary travois and then we can dump the carcasses onto it and drag them back to the cave. You will see. It doesn't take long at all." Already Sage had her blade out and was cutting the first javalina down the brisket. Whispering Wind quickly followed suit. Within a hand of time they had fashioned their makeshift travois and were underway, back toward the cave.

"You know," Whispering Wind remarked thoughtfully, "You may be younger than I, but you know a lot of sensible things that I would never think of. This makeshift travois for example, makes good sense."

Sage shrugged, "The gatherers were not stupid people. They did not always have everything right at hand when the opportunity showed itself. So, they were quick to make do. I knew how to catch fish single-handed, make fine nets from my own hair or from plant fibers and make snares as well. These skills are probably not of great importance on the open land, but in the woodland they can be essential. All children before the age of a double hand can do these things."

"We have women's chores and work and the men do the hunting," admitted Whispering Wind. "A woman must respect the male taboo and the men have no use for the women when they are unclean, but no woman would think of hunting as we just have. I really am enjoying living free and doing the things which ordinarily I would be forbidden."

Sage grinned at her new friend, "Perhaps we should not be so quick to find your people!"

Whispering Wind nibbled thoughtfully at her lower lip. "You know; I find that I am not in such a hurry after all. What difference does it make if I am returned this summer or the next? I am sure that already my father has given up on finding me and his new mate would be pleased never to see me again. I have had thoughts that she arranged for me to be captured and sold to those raiders. It is strange that she suggested we go out together when she disliked me and even stranger that when the raiders appeared, she was nowhere to be found. No, I am not in that great a hurry."

"Then we will see what happens," Sage grinned. "I like living in the cave and answering to ourselves. As long as we have our health and Obsidian, we can provide for ourselves, so I see no need to be in a hurry to find 'The People'." She agreed.

"When first I left the gatherers, I was afraid of every sound. It was particularly scary at night. But I soon realized that if there were any real danger, Obsidian would let me know. She can sense things long before I am aware. For example, she knew that people were coming into the valley and told me. I was able to put out my fire and hide all signs of our cave long before I could hear anyone coming. And she always knows where the game is," Sage grinned. "Come on, the cave is just around the bend in the trail."

10  A meteor shower.
11  **Llano Estacado:** Also known as the Southern High Plains, or the Staked Plains. The Llano Estacado is a large plateau some 20,000 square miles in area, surrounded on all sides by steep escarpments. It is a hot, dry area with average January temperatures of 40E F. There are no flowing streams on the Llano Estacado and surface water is confined to a few large saline lakes or playas. These playas and the numerous smaller, but almost always dry deflation basins, are a characteristic feature of the Llano and its principal source of topographic variety

in an otherwise monotonously flat, featureless landscape of seemingly unending grasslands. **Wendodrf** 1962:159-171.

**The Llano Estacado** is an area of elevated plateau or tableland. It may well be one of the oldest land surfaces of the American continent. In nearly its present shape and probably at its present actual surface, this land surface has received no new material since being isolated as a tableland. It has suffered little from ordinary water erosion. It is watered entirely by rains, between twenty and thirty inches per year. A six-inch rain that would cause a flood elsewhere will soak into the ground here over night. Only an occasional pond will survive for a week.

It breaks off in a sudden, almost vertical escarpment along the north and west margins. This 'caprock' is more a residual mass of broken fragments of stone, basically chert. The down-percolating waters have continuously dissolved away the lime from what was once a thick limestone layer, leaving the insoluble flints and cherts behind. In various places along the edge of the escarpment springs emerge from the water trickling down from above.

There are no rivers or streams on the Llano, leaving the ponds formed in depressions where the water table extends above the surface as the only available water from natural sources.

Extending from approximately Perryton, Texas on the north to Odessa on the south and Ft. Sumner, New Mexico on the west, the roughly triangular shaped Llano Estacado covers thousands of square miles.

12  A hand equals 5. Measurement of time: A hand of time equals an hour. A finger equals 6 minutes. Measurement of distance: A hand of distance equals the distance one could travel walking in an hour. A finger of distance is the distance equal to how far one could walk in 6 minutes. A season equals a year. A span equals ten.

13  A horn: a container equivalent to a cup, made from the horn sheath of a bison. Paleo Indians used materials from animals for many of their containers. A horn sheath was tough, it didn't break easily and it could be used for a multitude of purposes. In historic times horn sheaths were used to keep gunpowder dry.

14  Noon.

15  *Amaranthus* species: The leaves and stems are tasty when cooked or eaten raw. The seeds were gathered by many Native American groups and were an important food source. **Telford:** p 14-15.

16  *Amaranthus* species: The leaves and stems are tasty when cooked or eaten raw. The seeds were gathered by many Native American groups and were an important food source. **Telford:** p 14-15

17  *Rose* species: The rose 'hips' are very high in vitamin C and are delicious made into herbal tea. **Telford:** p 162-163

18  Snow shoes. Made by bending a supple sapling into a rough circle. The inside was webbed with leather strips cris crossed and attached to the feet with leather straps. It was clumsy, but serviceable.

# CHAPTER 2

Shadows cast by the hearth fire sent shadows leaping and dancing up the walls of the cave. Whispering Wind sat, cross-legged, just beyond the fire, weaving her tale with the use of her voice and hands, much as her grandfather would have done. She held her audience of Sage and Obsidian spellbound with her words and gestures. The fire sent sparks of hot sap into the air, accentuating her story with their own sounds and lights.

"She was not a big woman or so the legends say," Whispering Wind began. "But she must have been very close to the spirits. The storytellers claim that she actually walked among the Great Thunder Beasts, animals higher than a pair of tall men, one standing on the shoulders of the other. These monsters were known to kill a man with only a single stomp of their huge feet, but the 'Chosen' walked among them without fear, and they protected her. She was only a child when her camp left her to walk the wind, alone but for her dying father, during the bitterest part of the winter, on the cruelest part of the Llano Estacado. But she did not die. These powerful spirits cared for her, guided her and led her to a special place. Lightning, her father's totem, provided her food and a sacred spring her water. The spirits led her through a land filled with ferocious carnivores, bigger and meaner than any living today. But she went unharmed, so strong were her protectors."

"She discovered a cave at the very western edge of the great Llano escarpment. Here she made her home and grew to womanhood. She learned to hunt and to provide for herself. She discovered which plants were good food, and which made medicine, and her only companion a huge wolf which she stole as a cub from its mother's den, so desperate was her loneliness. She was but a double hand of years when she devised her daring plan. For days she stalked the great wolf-mother, finally locating her den. While the she-wolf was away, the 'Chosen' crawled into the den with only an old hide within which to wrap her captive. As she backed out of the den the female wolf returned and threatened to tear her limb from limb. The angry wolf sent her fleeing naked with only a torch to protect her from the attack, but she grimly held her stolen cub imprisoned securely in the old hide. She trained it and soon it was her best and only friend. When she reached womanhood, for her celebration animal she killed the meanest, biggest, and most-feared animal on the plains: a cat, larger again than the cougar, with canine teeth so long that they extended more than a hand length beyond the lower jaw. She killed this animal with only her atlatl and dart. She kept the canine teeth to prove to 'The People' how brave she was. Once she became a woman, she set out to find 'The People'. She and her wolf traveled for many hands of days searching for the trail which 'The People' followed each summer to the Great Gathering."

Whispering Wind grew excited, "This was a marvelous celebration and a time when girls could choose mates from other camps, and meet friends living in other camps. The dreamers led the celebrations. New women and men were recognized; babies were named, and matings celebrated. Every camp of 'The People' met at the Great Gathering to exchange news and ideas, visit with others living in camps beyond their own. It was a wonderful time!"

"The 'Chosen' found a camp to travel with, our very own Bison Camp. The leader of that camp was a wise and fearless man. But the dreamer was evil!"

Whispering Wind dropped her voice to a mere whisper, "This evil dreamer created a ceremony which ordered 'The People' to kill the Sacred Beast and feast on its flesh, a great taboo, even then!"

"What happened?" Sage questioned eagerly.

"The 'Chosen' challenged the evil dreamer and they fought right there at the Gathering. The dreamer injured her, but he did not kill her, and she called upon the spirit of the Great Beast for help. The spirit of the Great Beast caused those very animals to charge right into the camps, killing many people, and injuring countless more." Whispering Wind sighed, "It is very sad, we do not celebrate the Great Gathering anymore. 'The People' do not even remember where it was held."

"Then what happened?" Sage directed her storyteller back to the subject.

"Oh! Well the camps of 'The People' were scattered in every direction. But some followed the evil dreamer and they became very powerful. Others followed the 'Chosen' and they also became very powerful. Of course, it was inevitable that they clash again, and of course they did. Many seasons passed, while the camps grew and became powerful. They met; the dreamer and the 'Chosen' at the place remembered as the Sacred Spring. It is said to be a beautiful place where fresh pure water flows into a huge pond providing water for animals and people alike, the same Sacred Spring which provided for the 'Chosen' when she was a child."

"The 'Chosen' stood on a rise and watched helplessly as the evil dreamer slaughtered the very last of the Great Thunder Beasts. She became so enraged; she called Thunder and Lightning down to destroy the dreamer. They fought a horrendous battle there, the ground shaking with the fury of their thunder and the sky lighting up with their lightning bolts. The dreamer's lightning bolt struck the 'Chosen', killed her wolf and mortally wounded her. But before she died, the 'Chosen' caused a lightning bolt of her own to strike the dreamer, disintegrating the huge boulder upon which he stood, and exploding him into as many pieces as there are night-fires in the sky."

"She died? But what about her protecting spirits?" Sage protested.

"You see, the evil dreamer had just slaughtered the last of the Great Thunder Beasts. Now she had only the spirits to protect her, and they called her to join them. At dawn the next morning, her mate and daughter laid her out to walk the wind, her great wolf still at her side. The daughter became the next 'Chosen' and she in turn gave birth to a daughter. Each had the sign of their spirit somewhere on their body, and so continued the long line of 'Chosen' women; given by the spirits to guide 'The People' and help the women understand and grow in strength. There are many secret women's ceremonies, but we are not allowed to practice them. I doubt anyone even remembers them anymore. Over the generations, the women have lost the place of equality that they held when the 'Chosen' walked among 'The People'. However, every so often another powerful woman of this line is born, and she again leads 'The People' back to the path they were meant to follow. Always, nonetheless, the men have resented these women, and many have been killed just because they carried the mark. In spite of this, somehow, the line has continued. One female in each generation has been the 'Keeper of the Sacred Relics', but now no one knows whom these women are, because if their identity were discovered, the men would surely kill them."

"Why?"

"They are seen as a threat to control by the men. Every time a 'Chosen' rises in power, she turns 'The People' back to following the proper ways, and the men lose their total control over the women. You see; the 'Chosen' led the women to a position of equality. Women then hunted with the men and shared in the ceremonies. Inevitably there have been powerful men, and these men have hated and feared the 'Chosen' ones. They have even tried to steal the Sacred Relics from them!"

"Why would they do that?"

"Why?" Whispering Wind exclaimed, "For the 'power', of course!"

"But how can these relics contain power? They are only the remains of dead animals! What is this 'power' you talk of anyway?"

"The Relics are links to the spirit world. Whoever holds them can call upon the spirits to help them. The spirits will answer the person holding the Relics. This is 'power'. If you have never seen 'power' then I cannot explain it to you. I have only seen it once myself, but it was an experience I will never forget!"

"What happened?"

"A child in our camp was dying. A very powerful dreamer came to the camp and with the strength of his spirit helpers drew the sickness right out of the child's body. You could feel 'power' vibrating all over the camp. The next morning the child was outside playing with his friends just as if he had never been sick."

Sage frowned, "I have heard of such healing. My grandmother always said it was trickery used to impress, while the real healing came from the medicinal potions given to the sick person. But Grandmother always said such trickery convinced people that the healer was better than he really was so that he could demand more for his services."

Whispering Wind struggled angrily to her feet, "You just refuse to believe! Maybe someday you will see 'power' first hand, and then you will not scoff at me. I am tired and am going to bed," she lurched angrily off to where her sleeping furs lay and climbed into them muttering angrily under her breath.

*     *     *

Sage sat in the flickering light from the hearth fire, watching the shadow fingers dance against the wall of the cave. Hands of time had passed while Whispering Wind was fast asleep, merely a vague hump in the receding darkness. Obsidian lay just inside the cave entrance, listening to the wolves howling in the darkness beyond. Sage had been too restless to sleep. After so much talk about 'power' she couldn't bring her mind to fasten on sleep. So here she sat, just within reach of the deer hide packet, which she knew, contained the very Ancient Relics that Whispering Wind had just spoke of. Ever since they had come into her possession, Sage had resisted the urge to open the packet. Now, however, curiosity had gotten the best of her and she was shaking all over, whether with fear or excitement, she couldn't say, but the urge was greater than her resistance.

She lifted the deer hide pouch from its storage place and gently lay in on her lap. With shaking fingers, she untied the leather thongs which secured it. Then almost as if in a dream, she spread the deer hide. The wolf skin that held the inner bundle was very old, she could tell at a glance. But whoever had tanned the hide had been an expert. The fur was exquisitely soft and supple, almost as if the wolf still lived within it. The hairs glistened in the firelight, and she could feel slight warmth spread from her fingers through her hand and up her arm with each stroke of the wonderful fur. A feeling of peace permeated her and all stress seemed to flow from her body, leaving her relaxed and enshrouded with a sensation of well being.

She sat, merely stroking the wolf fur, for a long time, letting the feelings engulf her and penetrate all the way to her inner spirit. Then, reverently she unwrapped the hide. They lay shimmering in an eerie light of their own, the ancient ivory a deeper color than any teeth she had ever seen. At one time someone had drilled holes through their bases so that a thong could be run through them, probably the 'Chosen' about whom Whispering Wind had told her. There was no thong anymore, only the teeth, and a pair of small figurines. Careful not to touch the teeth, Sage reached for one of the little figures. It was of a bison, according to the description she had from her grandmother and Whispering Wind, but neither had mentioned so huge a hump, nor so long and lethal a set of horns. The figure was exquisitely carved, right down to the tiny eyes. Just holding it in her hand sent tingles up her arm. Sage lay it gently back on the hide and picked up the other figure.

This one was larger, yet no bigger than the end joint of her finger, but the detail was marvelous. She had never seen such a creature, and if Whispering Wind was right, neither had anyone else in countless generations. This could only be the Sacred Beast of her ancestors. She could feel a pull at her very soul when she held the figure. Indeed, it held 'power'. The animal stood on sturdy pillar-like legs, its' huge sloping, humped back ending in a wispy tail. The head was set on a sturdy neck, and its domed forehead bulged above the eyes. She could almost feel the animal looking deeply into her mind. The nose on this curious creature was long, extending all the way to its feet and on either side were teeth such as she could not even imagine. They stretched to the feet, then curved and swept upward, nearly touching at the tips. If this creature stood as tall as Whispering Wind had indicated; tall enough that a big man could walk beneath its belly and not touch it, then indeed it was an awesome creature! Gently she lay the figure back on the wolf hide.

Now, finally, Sage turned her attention to the teeth. They were huge! Each one extended from her fingertips half way to her elbow. Any animal that had carried them in its head was not one that she would care to face with nothing more than atlatl and dart. Reverently she reached out and touched one. "Ouch!" she pulled her hand back. A tingling ran all the way to her shoulder. Yet it hadn't been painful, only surprising. Again, she reached out and this time was prepared. She ran her fingers down the length of the tooth. The feeling vibrated through her body; 'power' surged through her. Sage gasped and pulled her hand back. Gradually the feeling subsided. Again, she touched the teeth, and again the marvelous feeling radiated through her. Obsidian nudged her shoulder and ran her tongue up Sage's face, whining softly as she did so. Only then did Sage realize that she was enshrouded in a pulsing blue glow, one that extended to include the dog.

Sage sighed and carefully wrapped the Relics back up in the wolf hide and again in the deer hide. Obsidian wagged her tail and returned to her vigil. Sage returned the packet to its hiding place and made her way to her sleeping furs. Suddenly she was exhausted. Almost instantly she slept.

Or did she?

*      *      *

*The figure emerged from a mist and walked toward her. The woman was not tall, nor was she particularly striking to look at. She was dressed in the manner of 'The People', as Whispering Wind had described their clothing. But she wore her hair in a single braid down her back, and attached to the end of the braid was a white owl's feather. She carried an atlatl and darts, and around her waist was a thong from which hung the sacred teeth. She carried a staff, the top of which strangely resembled the head of the Sacred Beast carving. By her side walked a wolf, again, the like of which Sage had never seen. The animal was half again as tall as Obsidian, and a silver-gray color, the ends of the fur tipped with black. Its legs were very long, and it had powerful muscles in its shoulders. The long slender muzzle was tipped with a very sensitive nose. Then the pair turned and looked directly at Sage. Their eyes, both woman and animal, were as blue as the sky. The only person whom she had ever known with sky colored eyes was herself. Those eyes had set her apart from the gatherers and had made some people nervous. Whispering Wind also mentioned them as unusual. She had not met anyone with blue eyes before either, but at least she had heard of them. Now Sage understood the strange glance Whispering Wind had given her upon making that statement.*

*The woman walked toward Sage and upon reaching her extended her hand. Sage could feel herself reaching out to this stranger. Their hands touched. It was just like when she stroked the teeth; a marvelous thrill of feeling invaded her whole body.*

*"I am Yel, your grandmother many, many generations past. I have come to you to help you understand who you are and what role you are to play in the lives of 'The People'. Throughout the generations, there has always been one of our blood-line. Always a female, not always with a task, but always the 'Keeper of the Relics' as you name them. When I lived, the sacred animal of 'The People' was called mammoth. You have seen the figure, now I will take you to see the real animal. Take my hand and we will be off."*

Sage again took the stranger's hand and suddenly she was whisked high above a broad plain. Below her were animals of many kinds, animals she had never seen, but the ones which caught her attention were the huge beasts trumpeting to one another. They were truly magnificent. Their domed heads touched the sky fully more than the height of three tall men. When they called one to another, it was like unto thunder, and when they ran across the plain the very earth shook beneath their feet. There were other strange animals as well. Sturdy dun colored animals with flowing tails and stiff hair along the crest of their necks ran like the wind across the grass. Others with long necks and big feet wandered through the grass as well. There were antelope with strange horns roaming among them. Then Sage noticed huge cats, with deep ruffs of long fur about their heads and shoulders. They stalked the other animals. There were animals such as the one that had provided the teeth as well. These creatures hid in the tall grass and pounced onto the backs of the fast running animals, sinking their fang-like canines into the throats of the hapless victims and bringing them down. Also, there were wolves such as the one that walked beside the woman, and they too were predators.

"This was the past," ancestor Yel said, "'The People' refused to follow the directions of the spirit animals, so these you see no longer walk the land. There are others as well. 'The People' are stubborn. Once they followed me and learned to eat plants and give thanks to the spirits for their bounty. But soon they forgot! For a few generations, women walked beside their men, but then, gradually, were forced once again into submission. The angry Spirits brought a great storm, and when the storm was over, no longer did these animals walk the land. Still "The People" did not learn!"

Ancestor Yel sighed, "So it has been time and time again. The One has given 'The People' chance after chance, and always, for a time, they return to the proper ways, and prosper. The circle is open and all is well. Then, *again, powerful men take away their equality, and 'The People' suffer. Death, disease, starvation, catastrophe! But they forget. They ignore! Now, once again The One has threatened to close the circle and remove 'The People' from the land forever. Once again, The One has allowed them but a single chance. The ceremonies must be revived, the spirit offerings made, the women given their rightful place beside; not behind, their men. The women's ceremonies must be returned to them. Food must not be squandered, ignored, or wasted. Proper veneration of the spirits must be returned. These proud and stubborn hunters must take the spirits into their hearts, not just make empty word prayers to them. This then, is your task, Bear Claw Woman!"*

Slowly the mist began to swirl about the woman's figure and then she was gone. In her place stood a great wolf. She looked deeply into Sage's eyes and spoke...

\*     \*     \*

*I am Spirit Wolf. I have 'Chosen' you and tested you and found you satisfactory. I have provided you with the wolf dog, Obsidian. She will protect you and guide you, and I will walk with you as well. But you must heed my words and follow them! The One, the greatest spirit of all, has given 'The People' only this one last chance. If you are unable to complete the task, the circle will be closed and The One will wipe 'The People' from the face of the land. When the time is right, you must go among 'The People' and teach them the proper ways. The women have forgotten their secret ceremonies; the men have once again pushed them into a place of submission when they were set to walk beside their mates.*

*You have been given special talents, your grandmother has given you the knowledge of the plants, I will lead you to the sacred 'power' places, and I will show you the ceremonies, lead you to discover the use of 'power'. Now I mark you!*

The spirit wolf reached forth her paw and touched Sage on the breast. *I claim you as my own, Bear Claw Woman, woman of 'The People'!*

Sage tossed in her sleeping furs and called out softly in her sleep. Obsidian came and lay beside her, yielding comfort.

\*     \*     \*

"I am sorry that I upset you last night," Sage offered Whispering Wind a peace bowl of tea. "I did not mean to scoff at what you told me. I just did not understand."

Whispering Wind pushed her hair from her face and smiled, "I know that you just did not understand, but sometimes you can be so stubborn. Just because you cannot see something or touch it or eat it doesn't mean that it doesn't exist."

"I know that," Sage sighed, "It is hard to explain. I have so many fears, and so little understanding. My grandmother died before she could tell me everything. Sometimes I think her spirit sent you to me."

"Why would you think that?"

Sage shrugged, unwilling to commit further. She was still not completely at ease with the things she knew. This was a woman of 'The People'. What would she do if she knew that Sage was in possession of the Sacred Relics? What if she knew that Sage's own grandmother had been one of the line of the 'Chosen'? Would she help Sage or would she hand her over to 'The People' and claim the status such a feat would award her? At least Sage was free of any mark on her body, for this she was thankful. Her grandmother had always been very careful to conceal that mark, the perfect image of a bison.

"You look awful," Whispering Wind remarked, "Do you feel sick?" she took the bowl and shrugged her sleeping furs aside.

"Now that you mention it, I do feel rather sick," Sage remarked. "Perhaps I am coming down with something," she shrugged and turned to walk away.

"Look!" Whispering Wind exclaimed, pointing to the floor of the cave, "You have started your bleed!"

Sage looked down, noticing the trail of blood spots leading from the fire. Then she realized that the insides of her thighs were wet and slippery. "Oh!" she remarked, suddenly at a loss for other words. She just stared at the blood spots, slowly their meaning filtering into her brain.

Whispering Wind was not at such a loss. She scrambled up and taking Sages hands began to dance gleefully about the cave, all but dragging the dumbfounded girl with her. "You are now a woman!" Whispering Wind exclaimed, "This is wonderful! We can have our very own 'becoming a woman' ceremony."

Sage withdrew her hands and went to sit beside the fire, biting her lip in consternation.

"What's wrong?" Whispering Wind stopped dancing and frowned at Sage, "Don't you want to be a woman?"

"I don't know," Sage admitted. "It has always been something in the future. I guess I just never thought of it actually happening to me."

Whispering Wind began to laugh again, "Well it has, and we are going to celebrate! We are going out and kill a proper animal and we are going to follow every step of the ceremony. And when it is done, I will give you presents. I realize only Obsidian and myself will not make a very big 'camp' but we will do the best we can. I saw mourning glory plants just yesterday, up on the ridge where the snow has blown clear. I will go and gather the seeds while you wash and do your hair."

"Shouldn't we kill the animal first?"

"Oh, that is for your family to do, which means me and Obsidian." You get prepared. We will find the animal. Come on, dog! We have a job to do!" she and the tail-wagging Obsidian left the cave.

Sage looked around, finding herself alone with a wad of cattail fluff clutched in one hand and a soft strip of rabbit hide in the other, placed there by Whispering Wind as she talked. With a sigh she rose and searched out the soap root and a clean rabbit fur, then stripping naked, left the cave and hurried to the stream. Luckily it was a sunny warm day, but the water in that stream would still be icy cold. Snow covered the ground as deep as her knees and she would have to break the ice in the stream with a rock, even to get water to wash by.

She was not disappointed. She was shivering almost uncontrollably before she had finished, and although it was only a dash to the cave, she was freezing by the time she reached the welcoming warmth of the fire. Here she hurriedly dried off and wrapped herself in a warm robe. Gradually the cold receded and she turned to follow Whispering Wind's many instructions. First, she located a frazzled twig and began combing the tangles from her waist long hair. This done, she clumsily braided it in the fashion they had practiced a number of times. It was much easier however, when Whispering Wind had done it for her.

Sage then searched out an appropriate rabbit skin to serve as her 'blanket' and a tortoise shell to hold the water and another to contain the various pigments she would need as well as the animal fat with which to mix them. This done she settled back to wait. It wasn't long before she heard Whispering Wind chattering to the dog as she returned to the cave.

"These seeds are old and dried," she protested, "But that only makes them more potent, which is just as well, for I could only find a few." She handed a small bowl to Sage, "Are you ready?"

Sage nodded, "As far as I know, I have everything you said I would need."

"Good! Then off you go. Remember; find a spot that feels right to you. Obsidian and I are on our way to kill your 'animal'," Whispering Wind collected her atlatl and darts and she and the dog left the cave and headed toward the high end of the valley, her snow walkers leaving a lacy trail in the snow.

Sage gathered up the various things she needed, and as an after thought added her atlatl and darts as well. She dressed again and wrapping the robe closer about her, she wandered across the valley, seeking a place which 'called' to her. It was hands of time later before she found such a spot. She was far up the valley herself and settled beneath the spreading branches of a huge pine. Here the ground was bare and it was a little sheltered from the biting cold of the wind. She cleared some broken branches and lesser twigs to make a place. One branch; as big around as her arm had a viciously pointed splintered end where it had broken from the tree. She arranged her things against it. Then beside it she spread her rabbit skin, removed her clothes, mixed the mourning glory drink and settled down to have her spirit journey. She waited . . . and waited . . . finally a mist began to form before her eyes...

The great blue-eyed wolf waited in the meadow. Sage walked slowly toward it, unafraid. As she approached the animal began to speak.

*       *       *

*Welcome, Bear Claw Woman! Again we meet. Last night I claimed you as my own. Today I give you the first of my gifts. Understand the meaning of it and protect it and it will protect you and channel 'power' for you. Soon it will be time for you to return to 'The People'. But first there is much you must learn, not the least of which is how to control 'power'. Listen to the woman of 'The People'. She has been sent to teach you the ways, help you to understand the task.*

\*　　\*　　\*

Mist began to swirl and soon there was nothing but a dense fog. Slowly Sage became aware of her surroundings. Birds were chirping in the trees and the sun was far-gone. A flicker of movement caused her to look upward. High above her, a white owl flew from the topmost branches of her tree, and as it took flight, one of its tail feathers drifted gently down to land just in front of Sage. Her head hurt and her stomach threatened to discharge its contents. Sage groaned and quickly turned away as she became very sick. Afterwards she felt better. She was freezing so she washed quickly, saving the residue to bury later, and donned her 'new woman' clothes, gifted by Whispering Wind, welcoming their warmth. Then she picked up the feather, frowned and shrugged. If she had taken a 'spirit journey' she had no more memory of it than of her dreams the night before. She knew that she had dreamed, for she had wakened with a sense of unease, but had no memory of any actual dreams. She twirled the feather absently in her fingers, then opening her waist pouch she carefully tucked it inside. It was possible that this could be a message from her guiding spirit. Perhaps white own had 'chosen' her for her own!

An angry bellow and a snapping and crashing of brush sent her grabbing her atlatl and darts as she whirled toward the sound. Bursting from the brush just beyond the great pine charged the largest, angriest grizzly bear she had ever imagined. In the split second afforded her, she registered that the animal was injured, but not mortally so. From its side projected the shaft of a dart. From beyond she recognized the voice of Obsidian, raised in a frenzy of barking, and beyond that the shouts of Whispering Wind egging the dog on. There was no more time, Sage could only cast her dart and quickly grab the broken branch which she braced against the base of the tree and aimed the splintered end toward the charging bear. With a roar the bear lunged directly at her with blood from her dart frothing from its mouth, its deadly sharp teeth and claws reaching out to embrace her. The impact jarred her whole body as the huge animal impaled itself on the broken branch; its one paw raking across her arm painfully as it twisted in its final death throes.

Then Obsidian erupted from the brush and launched herself full-force onto the carcass of the great bear. Whispering Wind was not far behind. Breathlessly she stumbled into the clearing and came to an astonished halt. Twigs and branches decorated her wildly disarrayed hair, her face was scratched and dirty, and her clothes showed signs of rough usage. The dart holder was askew and she had nearly lost one moccasin.

"I'm not sure if you two are trying to help me or kill me," Sage managed to say shakily. "If this is your idea of a proper ceremonial animal for a 'becoming a woman' rite, you must be crazy!" She swept her hand toward the bear.

"We were after a doe," Whispering Wind stuttered, "The bear came after our kill and all we did was try to drive it away. Then it came after us and we ran. It kept chasing us so I darted it, thinking it would go away. But it didn't. Instead it treed me and finally Obsidian worried it until it chased her. I got down when it finally turned and began to go away. I sent Obsidian after it just to make sure it kept going and then the next thing I know, here we all are. And you killed it yourself! What a magnificent 'kill' the spirits have brought to you!"

"Spirits!" Sage gasped, "The only spirits that brought this bear are standing right before me?" Then she sat shakily on the ground. "I just cannot believe this. I come out to find a quiet place to have a simple spirit journey. All I get is sick when I finally come to awareness, half the day is gone and the only thing I have seen is an owl! Then suddenly that bear all but kills me, and all you can say is, 'spirits'!"

Whispering Wind was no longer paying attention to Sage, however. She was walking around the bear admiring it. Obsidian seemed to be of the same mind now that she had finally assured herself that the bear was indeed dead and she released her death grip on its throat. Sage watched as Whispering Wind heaved and shoved until she finally removed the branch from the carcass. Then she pulled back the lips and admired the teeth, picked up the paws and turned them over in her hands, mumbling all the time under her breath. Sage, giving up finally went to help her and they did manage to heave the bear onto its side.

"Well we might just as well skin the creature out," Sage grumbled, "At least it will make a warm sleeping fur!"

"We will do more than that!" Whispering Wind responded. "We will save these claws and make you a necklace of them. The teeth can serve as the centerpieces. I have never seen even the strongest of hunters wear a bear claw necklace!" A shiver went up Sage's spine.

"Just the sort of thing to make me welcome in your people's camps," Sage mumbled but began skinning the animal. It was dark long before they completed the chore. In the end Whispering Wind built a fire and they spent the night hunkered beneath the tree. Sage had only the robe beyond her change of 'new woman' clothing' and Whispering Wind had nothing at all. They cut pine boughs and spread Sage's robe over them, then pulling the heavy bear hide, fur-side down on top of the robe, they crawled beneath. Sage wondered how many fleas would have taken up refuge on her person before morning, then yawning hugely, drifted off to sleep. Oddly Sage slept very well.

The better part of the next day was spent butchering the bear and moving the carcass back to the cave. Once the animal was quartered; Whispering Wind and Obsidian took the first load, while Sage stayed to protect the remaining meat from carnivores. They returned by mid morning and the girls switched places. When Sage and the dog returned, it was to find hot food ready for the mid day meal. After that the only remaining thing to move was the skin. They both heaved it onto the travois and removed all traces of their occupation. Even though they had seen no one in the valley for turnings of the moon, they were always careful to leave no traces for anyone to follow to the cave. Wolves could be depended upon to clean up the remains left at the butchering site. Sage even loaded the branch that had actually killed the bear onto the last load. It would end up in their hearth fire. Just before they left, Sage looked the area over with a critical eye. The branches from their bed rested on the travois to be added to the smoking fire for the meat. Now the place was obviously a kill site of some sort. There were bear tracks, and Obsidian's of course, but they were indistinguishable from wolf tracks. Sage was satisfied that no trace of human presence could be detected.

Once back at the cave the girls dragged the bear quarters to the back of the cave. They were tired, and the meat would be fine until morning. The hide still had to be stretched and scraped before it began to rot. Whispering Wind prepared the pegs for the hide while Sage rolled it out and they decided where to process it. They decided on the wide flat area at the back of the cave. It took them over a hand of time to get the hide stretched and the pegs driven into the hard dirt floor of the cave.

Now it was ready to start. The girls sharpened their side scrapers and one on either end they began scraping the bits of flesh remaining on the hide and continuing to stretch it as they worked. It was hard, back braking labor, but as women they didn't even think about that, it was just part of their daily lives.

They took breaks from time to time and had tea and a few bites to eat, but did not take time out for a real meal. It was well into the night when they finished. Now the hide was left to dry before the next step in its preparation. Finally, they crawled into their furs and slept.

Birds were singing in the valley, and the sun was well up before they wakened. Sage began preparing the meal while Whispering Wind checked the hide. The skull was setting beside the hearth, a grisly sight to-be-sure. Whispering Wind took it and with a good-sized rock began whacking at the upper jaw.

"What are you doing?" Sage frowned, "We only need the brains."

"I told you. We are making you a necklace from the teeth and claws," Whispering Wind replied.

"I won't be able to wear it once we leave this valley. That is a lot of work for something that must remain hidden."

"Of course you can wear it!" Whispering Wind protested, "You killed that bear; it is your right!"

"Well, it will only end up causing a lot of trouble, just you wait and see," Sage replied.

Whispering Wind rocked back onto her heels where she squatted beside the skull, rock still in hand. "That was the bravest thing I have ever seen! I intend to tell everyone about it. You could easily have been killed, and it would have been my fault."

"But instead you were quick thinking and used that broken branch to cause the bear to impale itself. Like I said, the 'spirits' provided this bear. It was supposed to be your ceremonial animal, not the doe that I killed. It is really unwise to disregard spirits. You don't want to anger them. Why, this bear is every bit as dangerous at that cat creature the 'Chosen' killed for her ceremonial animal," Whispering Wind grinned, "Wow!"

Sage could feel icy chills run up her spine and a sharp pain just above her heart caused her to draw in her breath. She must have gone pale for Whispering Wind asked, "You all right? You look kind of funny."

Sage nodded and said, "I must have injured myself when the bear attacked, I sort of got a pain here." She touched the spot, "Ouch!" She pealed back her tunic and squinted at the area. Sure enough, there was a small bruise there.

"We need to check those scratches again as well," Whispering Wind remarked. "The poultice you put on it seems to be working wonderfully though. There were no evil spirits this morning and it doesn't seem to be bothering you at all."

Sage glanced at her arm, "I have forgotten all about it," she admitted. "It doesn't hurt at all. We can check it later. You had better get those teeth knocked out if that is what you are determined to do. I will work on the claws." Actually, upon thinking about it she rather liked the idea of the necklace. Whispering Wind was right, she had killed that bear, and she did have the right to wear the symbols of bravery that attended such a kill. Bother if men didn't like it!

She took up a sharp blade and began opening the bear paws. It did not take long to sever the connections and she had a nice sized pile of bear claws. By the time she had finished Whispering Wind had succeeded in removing the canine teeth from the skull. She gathered up all the parts and wrapped them in a rabbit fur. "I will make the necklace," she stated. "It will be my 'gift' to you."

"That will be a wonderful gift," Sage smiled. "I promise that I will wear it with pride."

"You had better!" Whispering Wind grinned. "It will take me hands of time to drill and string it on sinew. At least I will not have to polish them. The bear did a fine job of that. By the way, I didn't even get a chance to ask you, what is your spirit guide animal?"

Sage frowned, "I have no idea. I can't remember a thing from my 'spirit journey' if I even took one. I woke up sick and was emptying my stomach when the bear came bursting in on me. The only thing I saw was a white owl, when it flew away it left a feather behind."

"That's it!" exclaimed Whispering Wind, "White Owl is a fine spirit animal! Did he call to you, give you any advice?"

Sage snorted rudely. "The bird just flew from the upper branches of the tree I was sitting under. It was probably sleeping there, and it was merely wakened by my vomiting and decided to go hunting. The loss of a feather was probably just by chance."

"Nothing is by chance in the Spirit World."

"Well I can assure you. The bird did not speak to me! I have never had any kind of animal speak to me, not counting Obsidian when she whines and I understand what it is that she wants." Sage protested.

"Well . . . I am sure the feather was a sign, none-the-less. You are probably not listening for the spirits. That is why you do not hear them," Whispering Wind stated with satisfaction as she wrapped the rabbit skin expertly about the teeth and claws and tucked them away to work on later. "You really need to begin listening, Sage, or you will not know how to call upon them when you have need of them."

Sage thought guiltily of the packet not a hand's span from where Whispering Wind stood, and she could vividly remember the 'power' which surged up her arm from merely touching the teeth. She understood very well what Whispering Wind was telling her. In fact, even though she had felt a bit silly doing it, she had listened for the owl to communicate with her. But it had merely flown off and then the bear had crashed into her life and she had forgotten all about her 'spirit quest'"

"What did you do with the feather?"

"I have it right here," Sage patted her carrying pouch.

"Well at least you had sense enough to keep it!" Whispering Wind replied. "We also need to find an Adult name for you. No longer can you be Sage, for that is a child's name. But we have until you join 'The People' to select that.

19   Black Water Draw. The Paleo Indian site from which the Clovis culture draws its name. Located between Clovis and Portales, New Mexico. During the 1962 excavation by Eastern New Mexico University, a spring was uncovered. It contained pure white sand and hundreds of artifacts, all broken, and both parts found within the sand. All of the artifacts as well as the sand were highly polished by sand and water action. Personal experience.

20   Horses. During the Pleistocene, horses roamed the whole western part of North America. They died out at the end of the Pleistocene.

21   Camels: There were two species of camels roaming the plains during the Pleistocene. One was the ancestor to the Llama and Alpaca, the other to the Bactrian and Dromedary camels of Asia and Africa.

22   Lions: similar to African Lions but much larger. A full-grown male plains lion could weight over 500 pounds.

23   *Smilodon:* Saber Toothed Tiger: An animal larger than the African Lion, equipped with a set of canines nearly 10 inches long. The teeth of this fierce animal are the Sacred Relic teeth

# CHAPTER 3

Sage woke up to find Whispering Wind hunkered over an old basket, emptying her stomach. She groaned and vomited again, then sank limply to her furs. Sage tossed back her furs and hurried to where her friend lay. "Wind, are you all right?" she questioned

Whispering Wind moaned then shoved a tangle of hair from her face. "I don't know what it is," she admitted. "I feel fine when I wake up, but the first move I make, up comes everything, and I haven't even eaten. My head hurts and my stomach is churning. It goes away after a hand or so of time, but still, it is irritating."

"This isn't the first time?" Weakly the other girl shook her head. "How many days have you had it?"

"Since the turning of the moon," Whispering Wind admitted. "Nearly a hand of days."

"Every morning?" Sage persisted.

"Yes, every morning!" Whispering Wind replied weakly.

Sage sat chewing her lip thoughtfully for a short time, "When did you have your last blood flow?" She asked quietly.

"What?"

"Your blood-flow? I don't remember that you have had it since you came to live in this cave with me. That has been well over a pair of moons' turnings ago, nearly another beyond them."

Whispering Wind sat up turned very pale and flopped back down again.

"Wait!" Sage shook her head. "Stay there, I will make you a drink that will help." She hurried to the fire and poured water from a storage skin into the water heating skin suspended above the fire. Then she added wood to the coals and quickly a fire began to crackle, driving the cold from their immediate area of the cave, and adding a cheery sound as well. Very soon rocks were hot and in the meantime Sage had sifted through her store of medicinal herbs and found the one she was seeking. She added it to a bowl and poured hot water over it. Soon it had steeped and she carried it to where Whispering Wind lay watching her.

"Here, this will settle your stomach. Drink it and I will make some grain cakes. You can nibble on them as well. I promise you when you sit up, you will feel fine."

"You are right, I have not had my blood flow since The Moon of Harvesting," Whispering Wind admitted. "Do you think . . .?"

Sage shrugged. "You show all of the signs of early pregnancy. You admitted that the man who owned you raped you repeatedly, it is not really surprising."

"No, not Angry Bear!" Protested Whispering Wind, tears in her eyes. "He would not be the father. I had just completed my woman's cycle. He had not mounted me yet. It would be the child of another, a young man who was kind to me. He wanted me to run away with him. We had slipped off that very morning of the raid when I was left unguarded while gathering nuts. He promised to return me to my people and we planned to be mated then. This child would be fathered by Deer Stalker." She sniffed, wiping her eyes, "He was killed in the raid also."

Sage was running her hands over Whispering Winds flat stomach and rounded breasts. "Do you feel any added sensitivity in the breasts?" She questioned all the while checking for other signs.

"Some," Whispering Wind admitted. "But I attributed it to the nearness of my cycle. Do you really think . . .?"

"We will know shortly one way or the other," Sage replied. "I cannot say for sure, but I would suggest that you take things easier until we can be sure. For now, you can probably get up without undue unpleasantness."

"You mean no more climbing trees and chasing grizzly bears?" Whispering Wind grinned as she sat up. "You are truly a fine healer, Sage, I feel wonderful!"

Sage nodded, "I will make up a packet of the herb and so long as you drink it before trying to get up, there should be no more morning sickness. Besides it is good for you any way, I will get our meal started now, you think about . . . things . . ."

Sage busied herself with preparations for the meal and Whispering Wind wandered around the cave, a wistful, happy smile on her face. Occasionally she stroked her still flat stomach and hummed a little song.

Their days settled into a routine. Another storm struck that day, erasing any signs they might have left anywhere in the valley. Day after day winter drew up and cast its full fury at the valley, but they were secure and warm in their cave. The Moon of First Snows passed, as did the Moon of Permanent Snow. The wolves called to one another at the far ends of the valley, but they did not dare come closer. Obsidian had attacked one that had foolishly ventured into her territory, Whispering Wind planned on making a hood from the hide and since, none other had challenged her. One moon passed, the Moon of Shortest Day, then another, the Moon of Deepest Snow.

"Those wolves sound much closer," Whispering Wind stated nervously one evening as they were settled beside the fire. "I think they are losing their fear."

"If they get too close, Obsidian will remind them, whose territory this is," Sage assured her, silently worrying about the very same thing. This was the Starving Moon! The wolves had been moving closer every night, their calls louder and braver. Obsidian was one. They were many. Sage only hoped that the fear of fire would keep them from actually venturing into the cave. She was getting restless herself. The many frequent storms had kept them mostly inside the cave for more than a moon now, she was ready to get out and move about and breath the fresh air. She needed exercise.

Whispering Wind was most definitely pregnant. But she lived in a kind of daze now, smiling and dreaming happily about the baby. She did work on the necklace for Sage, and by the end of the next moon cycle had finished it. Sage felt uncomfortable with the strange weight about her neck at first, but soon adjusted. Now she would feel naked without the necklace.

There had been no more conversations about 'spirits'. Now Whispering Wind could talk of nothing but the child she was expecting. She ate enough for a pair; that is for certain. Sage was amazed at the quantity of food she consumed yet she did not get fat. But the baby grew, rounding out her stomach making moving about the cave more and more difficult for Whispering Wind. The morning sickness had vanished and the girl was blooming. Her cheeks carried a rosy glow, her eyes a sparkle, and her skin and hair glowed with health. The Month of the Newborn Animals arrived, yet still the valley was held in the grip of deep snow.

"Whispering Wind, come and smell," Sage called one morning just after rising.

"What is it?" the other girl questioned, as she sat up in her furs.

"Spring!" Sage answered, "I can smell it on the air."

"Oh," the girl answered, "Are you sure?"

"What is wrong with you?" Sage protested, "Haven't you had enough of winter? I know that I have. Besides, we are almost out of plant food. It is a good thing we have had the bear meat, for without it the elk would have been eaten long ago."

"I know, and you are right, I am as tired of winter as you are, but spring means the snow will melt, and without snow this valley isn't as safe. This might not matter to you, but I am in no shape to try to escape raiders."

"We will have to be extra careful of course, but without snow our tracks are much harder to follow as well. There were only very old signs of anyone coming into this valley when I arrived. Chances are good there will not be any others. Besides, with the remains of that camp and the burials, no one will venture any farther. I really do think we are safe here."

A few days later Sage came laughing into the cave. She and Obsidian had been out most of the morning and she had a basket filled with shoots. "Look!" she grinned, "Cattail sprigs!"

"That is very nice," Whispering Wind replied, "But why are you so excited?"

"Don't you see?" Sage dumped the basket beside the fire. "They are the first sign that spring is really here, and besides, to be practical, they are good to eat. I, for one, am ready for some fresh plants, and these are the first to appear!"

"You can eat them?" Whispering Wind asked in astonishment.

"Of course, do you think I would have collected so many otherwise?" Sage shook her head.

"I will prepare them while you cut up some of that rabbit Obsidian just dropped at your feet. Just toss the pieces into the cooking bag and soon you will learn about eating cattails. Tomorrow I intend to see if the ground is softened enough to dig for tubers again. I know where there are bunches of them which I located last fall. They should still be good, providing others haven't gotten to them before me."

"What others?" Whispering Wind's head snapped up from her task with the rabbit.

"Animal others," Sage replied, "Not human." Deftly she stripped the tender green shoots into a bowl and then transferred them to the cooking bag. She rummaged through her dwindling supply of herbs and added a small handful. Whispering Wind finished the rabbit and added it as well. Obsidian crunched happily on the head and innards of the rabbit and soon a wonderful aroma began to fill the cave.

With the arrival of the Moon of New Plants the wolves moved away from the valley floor and went in search of easier game, the elk and deer would drop new fawns. The snow began to melt and brown patches of earth appeared and spread. Spring rains started to fall, and soon the ground became a quagmire of mud. The snow level receded and new green growth appeared on the trees.

*     *     *

Sage sat up in her furs. "Wind, do you hear that?" she whispered loudly.

"What?" Whispering Wind answered sleepily, "Is something wrong?"

"I don't know," Sage replied. "Something isn't right. I don't hear any night sounds for one thing. It's too quiet." The spot above her heart pained her, sharp darting pricks of pain. This is what had wakened her. The big dog was moving restlessly at her usual place at the mouth of the cave, ears flicking back and forth, and soft whimpering sounds further troubling Sage.

The words were no more than out of her mouth than the whole valley seemed to move. A distant grumble became louder and louder. The earth quivered beneath her feet, and Obsidian moved back away from the mouth of the cave, tucked her tail between her legs and growled low in her throat.

"What is it?" Whispering Wind whimpered, sitting up in her furs, arms wrapped protectively around her bulging belly. We're going to die!" she began to wail nervously. "I knew it! It's an earthquake, and we are going to be crushed to death!" She scrambled from her furs and wound her arms around Sage, shaking with fear. "I don't want to die!" she whimpered, "I want to have my baby and return to 'The People'. Quick! Before the cave collapses, let's get out of here!" She scrambled clumsily to her feet and began to lurch toward the mouth of the cave. Sage grabbed her and pulled her back.

"Don't be silly!" she snapped, "This cave is the safest place we can be. It isn't an earthquake!"

"How do you know?" Whimpered the frightened woman.

"I have lived through one. This isn't an earthquake."

"Then what is it?"

"I don't know," Sage replied. "I will take a torch and see." She rose and pulled on her clothes and moccasins in preparation for leaving the cave. She took up a torch and headed to the mouth of the cave. Obsidian met her there and placed herself across the entrance blocking Sage from leaving. The big dog whined but refused to move.

"Don't go?" Whispering Wind pleaded, "I don't care what it is. Morning is soon enough to find out!"

"It's a flood," Sage replied with a relieved sigh, "I can hear the water."

"Now that you mention it, I can hear the water also. There is no sense in going out and getting washed away and drowned. Morning will be here in a few fingers of time. It can wait until then surely. We are in no danger here in the cave, are we?"

"Obsidian doesn't seem to be worried about inside, but she certainly doesn't want me to go out there." Sage stood at the cave opening, running her fingers through the thick fur on the dog's back. "Go back to sleep, Wind. I won't leave the cave."

She added wood to the fire and began a skin of hot water for tea. Whispering Wind was right. It would be foolish to venture out into the dark. Water was dangerous, and it could come from anywhere during a spring flood. She had no idea how much water had been released above the valley, but she was certain their friendly little stream would be an angry, muddy flow when the light of day arrived. Whispering Wind settled back into her furs and was soon fast sleep.

Sage sat beside the fire drinking her tea and rubbing the spot above her heart. Gradually, what she had first thought to be a bruise had refined and defined, until it was clearly what she had begun to fear, but it was not a copy of her grandmother's birthmark. No, it was no bison, but rather a perfectly formed wolf.

She had watched her grandmother, rubbing the mark she carried, in just the same way from time to time. Often, she had wondered why: now she knew. The mark was a channel to the spirits. It had alerted her to danger. It had wakened her from a deep sleep. Begrudgingly she went to the basket and retrieved the deer-hide wrapped packet. She added wood to the fire and unwrapped the packet. Even since her first bleed, the packet had sent out fingers of power to her, usually late at night. Now it called strongly. She laid back the deer hide and settled her fingers into the wonderfully soft fur of the wolf pelt. A sense of perfect wellbeing permeated her entire body. Time passed and the fire burned down to just faint crackling of pitch and red-hot coals. Reluctantly she added more wood. Slowly she unwrapped the wolf hide and revealed the Relics in the light of the fire. With gentle fingers, she took the tiny bison figure and opening her amulet bag she dropped it inside. The other figure followed.... The spot on her breast now pulsed with a warm pleasant feeling. She realized that this was why the packet had been calling her. She was to carry these tiny symbols in her amulet, perhaps to aid the Ancestor Spirits to find her. She sighed, remembering the tiny wolf already there, appearing as if by magic the morning after her 'spirit journey'.

Sage could not remember her 'spirit journey' but even without it she knew that the spirits had chosen her. There had never really been any doubt. She knew who she was, a direct line from the ancient 'Chosen One', of the blood, selected to protect the Relics, carry on the line and return the Relics to 'The People'. Her grandmother had told her this much. Now she reached out and sealed her fate. She took one of the teeth up into her hands and brought it to rest against her breast. The object pulsed in her hand, sending surges of 'power' coursing through her body, bringing her concentration, calm, and purpose. So, she sat, until the faint tinges of light outside heralded the dawn. Then she calmly wrapped the teeth again in their wolf skin and deer hide and returned them to their storage place. She felt wonderfully rested and filled with strength. Serenely she walked to the mouth of the cave and looked out.

The devastation that greeted her eyes took her breath away. The entire valley was a raging mass of churning muddy water. Entire trees had been uprooted and were rolling down the valley carried by the angry, greedy water. There were other victims there as well. Bodies of drowned elk and deer, wolf and smaller creatures had been gathered up and captured by the raging cascade. The edge of the river was but a short dart cast from the mouth of the cave. High above their valley, a beaver dam had held an entire lake of water captive, until finally, the overpowering mass of the liquid confined there had ripped the dam away and came down the streambed in a single unstoppable wall of water. It had devoured everything in its way, sweeping all into its ravenous torrent.

A short time later Whispering Wind joined Sage and they both watched silently. Later they fixed a meal and gradually adjusted to the sound of rushing water just beyond. All day long they worked about the cave, by unvoiced agreement not mentioning the flood outside. Well after dark they retired to their furs. Some time during the night, the bulk of the water passed and by the dawn the valley was returned to its former proportions. It was, however, forever changed. Where once a clear little stream had bubbled over pebbles and moss-covered rocks, now a deep raw gash slashed down the valley. Gently sloping valley sides had been gouged and scoured. Spreading meadows, which had supported lush grass the summer before had been replaced with deep deposits of mud, over which, lay the cloying stench of death. The only living thing in their valley now, were the myriad of vultures circling to settle on the bloating carcasses left behind as the water receded. There was no sign of the death camp, and the burials had been washed away as well. As the girls looked around, they realized that they were safe in this valley, for no one would come here in search of any thing. There was no food for grazers, therefore no grazers for meat eaters. The entire valley had been scoured into a sterile nothing. This also left them with a pressing problem: food!

"What are we to do?" questioned Whispering Wind.

"I don't know, perhaps there are still elk on the ridge above the cave. Obsidian ran them over the edge last fall. It might work again. One thing is certain. You are in no shape to go anywhere. That babe is about ready to be born. I don't even like leaving you here alone for as long as it would take for me to look for meat."

"Speaking of Obsidian, where is she? I haven't seen her since we got up."

Sage frowned, "I have no idea. You are right; she was gone when I got up. I didn't think much about it because she frequently goes out early, but she should have returned by now. I think I will go out and see if I can locate her."

"You won't go far?"

"No, just a short way," Sage took up her atlatl and darts out of habit as she passed and slipped from the cave. She was about to whistle for the big dog, glancing up the valley, when she realized that she could hear her barking frantically nearby. Sage frowned and then laughed as she nocked a dart in her atlatl and headed for the dog at a run. Obsidian had driven a pair of deer into the thick mud layering the valley floor. The animals were floundering in the mud. It took only a few heartbeats for Sage to reach her and barely longer for her to dart the deer. Pulling the carcasses from the mud wasn't easy but she finally got them onto shallower mud. Sage sat down to catch her breath and hugged the big dog. "Thank you so much," she ruffled her fur. "We could not have survived this winter without your care and devotion. You are truly watching out for us." The spot on her breast throbbed once, and Sage realized suddenly that Obsidian was exactly what she had just said, a guardian sent by the spirits to guide and protect her, just as her wolf had protected the ancient 'Chosen' one. A shiver ran down her spine and she quickly got to her feet and dragged the first deer the rest of the way to the cave. The mud was slick and clinging, but the deer slid easily on it. Then she returned for the other one.

"Well at least we will not lack for meat for a while," Whispering Wind stated as she finished loading the drying rack with strips of meat handed to her by Sage. The main hearth was roasting one of the hindquarters of the first deer, but the remainder was being dried for future use. With the arrival of the Month of Warm Breezes, warm weather there was a far greater chance of the meat spoiling unless it was dried, either smoked or with a thick coating of salt. Salt was plentiful, but the girls were doing both, just to have a change of taste.

The marrow from the leg bones had been collected, and it would be used to make tasty broth for a pair of days. The remainder would be cooked and used to mix with bits of dried plants and meat to make a long storing food in the intestine tubes from the deer. This was commonly used as travel food among most peoples. The sinew had been removed and laid out to dry. Sage sent Whispering Wind to her furs when the other girl began to look stressed. Soon she was snoring softly and Sage sat beside the fire and drank her tea. Then she took out the relic teeth once again. She wished they could talk and tell her what was expected of her. From what Whispering Wind had told her of the stories of 'The People' and from the little her grandmother had imparted before dying, Sage knew that she was the 'keeper of the relics' and was responsible for their safety. This probably also meant the return of them to 'The People'. Whispering Wind had also said that the women responsible for the relics were also responsible for making offerings to the spirits at some sacred spring from time to time. The tool knappers crafted special tools which were ceremoniously 'killed' at the spring and their parts thrown into the water by the 'chosen'. This would insure good hunting and healthy lives for 'The People'. It didn't sound too difficult. Finally, late into the night she returned the relics to their place and went to her furs.

\*     \*     \*

A blood-curdling scream ripped through the darkened cave. Sage jerked upright and with trembling legs lurched to where her atlatl and darts lay. Grabbing them she stuck a pitch-ended torch into the dying coals of the fire and when it lit turned to search the cave for danger. Obsidian pranced beside a wildly thrashing Whispering Wind who released yet another scream. Sage dropped the weapons and hurried to Wind's side.

"What is it?" She questioned, trying to untangle the girl from her furs.

"I'm being killed!" wailed Whispering Wind, "Ripped apart from the inside!" She thrashed onto her back and Sage was able to jerk the furs off of her. The first thing she noticed was that the hide beneath Whispering Wind was a little wet. Having gone on numerous occasions with her grandmother to births and helped with many of them Sage realized that the birth had begun. Whispering Wind was suffering labor pains, nothing more.

"Try to lie still and let me see if I can see the head," Sage said steadily, while helping the other girl onto her back. Sage squatted and holding the torch looked for the baby's head. "You are not ready yet," she stated. "It will be some while before the baby is ready to be born. We have plenty of time to get ready."

Whispering Wind quieted some, trying to breathe slowly and get her nerves under control. "Here, drink this." Sage handed her a bowl of tea. "It will help calm you and make the pain easier to abide. While you rest, I will get the birthing place set up, just as we planned. I have everything ready."

"How can you be so calm?" Whispering Wind questioned. "Aren't you scared at all? After all, how many babies have you brought into the world?"

"I helped my grandmother with any number of them, "Sage replied, "And on several occasions, when she was not available, I managed on my own, so you see, this is not 'my' first baby. Just relax Wind; I do know what I am doing. I accompanied my grandmother from the time I was a hand old."

But what if there is a problem? I remember a woman who died because they could not get the baby delivered. It died, rotted in her body, and killed her."

"Well. This baby is very much alive," Sage replied as the child kicked strongly. "It just is in no hurry to join us. You might as well try to get some sleep"

"Is that all you have to say? Get some sleep!" Whispering Wind Screeched.

"You are going to need all your strength for this, Wind. I don't promise it will be easy. Births usually are not. It could be a day or more easily before you begin to have real labor pains."

"Real labor-pains!" Whispering Wind sputtered, "What do you call what just about ripped me apart now if not real labor-pains?"

"False labor-pains, if you must know," replied Sage evenly. "Now, like I suggested, get some sleep, I know I am going to." She turned and extinguishing the torch crawled into her furs and yawned before snuggling down and falling instantly to sleep.

The sun was bright and the birds calling outside when she woke. Whispering Wind was still snoring lightly, sound asleep. Sage smiled, the drink she had given Whispering Wind was meant to calm and relieve pain. Evidently it had done its job. She heated water for tea and began breakfast. The food was nearly ready to serve before Whispering Wind wakened. Sage carried her meal to her and sat beside her to eat her own. "How do you feel?" she questioned.

"Like a fool for waking you up like that," Whispering Wind replied. "I guess it just took me by surprise. You have explained what to expect, and I have certainly seen enough births to know what to expect. It just seems different when it is you."

"Well just take things easy today," Sage suggested. "I have more of the pain killing drink for when you need it."

"I hope that I won't need it," Whispering Wind smiled. "I will try to work with you, I promise. I have seen what it is like when an expectant mother doesn't try to control herself. She makes things that much more difficult for those trying to help her and makes it harder on herself and her baby as well. I will not cry out again."

Sage smiled and drank her tea.

They spent a quiet day, and Whispering Wind obediently drank the painkilling brew when she was told to. She slept the night through.

"I think I need to check your progress," Sage suggested early the next evening. "I have an idea that tonight might be it."

Whispering Wind obediently lay back on her furs and Sage checked the opening. In doing so, she went pale. It was not a head that her questing fingers encountered, but a foot. The baby was turned the wrong way. Something must be done, and quickly. The opening was as wide as it would get. The baby would be born before morning, but it would die in the process if it tried to come out feet first. Sage rolled back on her heels.

*     *     *

The labor pains had been steadily growing all day, both in intensity and nearness. Whispering Wind, true to her word, had not made even the smallest protest of discomfort, even though Sage knew the pain was getting intense.

Once, only moons before her grandmother died, this same thing had occurred. Sage was a small person, her bones delicate and fine. It had been her chore, under the direction of her grandmother, to turn the child around still inside the mother. Of course, there had been a number of strong women to hold the struggling woman so that she did not move. Now there was only Sage.

She sat for a short while frowning, and deep in thought and then making a decision, she sighed. "I am going to make you a special drink," Sage rose to her feet, "And I want you to drink every drop of it."

"What is wrong?" a thread of fear, feathered through Whispering Wind's voice. "I know that something is, just from looking at your face, so don't try to fool me."

"The baby isn't turned right," Sage said calmly, "I am going to have to reach up inside you and turn it."

Whispering Wind just stared at her, not speaking for some time. "What do you need for me to do?" She finally asked.

"First, drink this," She handed Whispering Wind the brew.

"What is it?"

"A pain killer," Sage replied, "A very strong one. Once it has started to take effect, I am going to drive stakes into the floor and tie your arms and legs so that you cannot move. Then I am going to reach inside and turn the baby. Once the head is right, I will cut the bindings and help you into the birthing rack, but it will be extremely painful for you, even with the drink."

"What if you can't . . .?"

"I will."

Whispering Wind looked her right in the eye, calmly took the drink and swallowed every single drop then handed the bowl back and lay back and extended both of her arms.

Sage bit her lip and gathered soft rabbit skins to pad the wrists and ankles. Then she looped rawhide thongs around the wrist padding, tight enough that Whispering Wind could not pull her hands free, but not so tight as to cut. The thongs she attached tightly to pegs that she positioned and pounded into the floor with a large rock. She repeated the process with the legs. By now Whispering Wind was barely awake, the powerful drink dulling her senses. Sage returned to the hearth where she had a small bowl of animal fat waiting. It had been heated to boiling and allowed to cool enough not to burn Sage's hand and arm. She scrubbed both hands and arms all the way to the shoulder with soap-root, then rinsed completely. Glancing at the waiting woman, she began covering her right arm with the animal fat. *Please, Grandmother, if you are there, help me!* She prayed. Then she was ready. She also took a stick and wrapped rabbit hide around it. This she gently inserted between Whispering Winds teeth. She didn't want her to bite her tongue in pain.

Sage positioned herself in a squatting position between Whispering Wind's thighs, she rubbed her amulet bag, calling to the spirit of wolf for aid, then, again, calling to the spirit of her grandmother, slowly, carefully, she began to insert first her fingers, then her hand into the birth canal. Whispering Wind taunted, her hands twisting in the bindings, her legs straining as well, but she made no sound. It seemed that Sage's every move caused her friend excruciating pain, and every move took forever. Something guided her hand, whether the spirit of Clover Blossom, or some other, for slowly, she made progress. She located the baby's head, and pain running up her arm, began to turn the small body. The baby kicked, and she almost lost all feeling in her arm so great was the pressure from Whispering Wind, but then suddenly the baby slid into position and with a sigh, Sage carefully withdrew her arm. With her other hand she cut the bindings and helped Whispering Wind into the birthing rack. She was white with pain and her entire body was shaking but she stumbled with Sage and sank into the squatting position. Then her whole body jerked and with a mighty thrust, the baby slid out and Sage grabbed it. It was over!

Sage closed her eyes and gave a silent *Thank you!* Whispering Wind sagged into the frame totally exhausted. Sage wasn't finished yet, however swiftly cleaned out the infant's mouth and blew into it. She filled the tiny lungs with air, and with a light slap on the backside, smiled as the enraged infant, cried out in protest. She tied the umbilical cord in two places with sinew and cut it between. She carried him to the fire and with a soft rabbit skin washed the squirming body clean of the birthing juices. Then she wrapped him in another rabbit skin and laid him on the sleeping fur. Now she turned once again to Whispering Wind, relieved to see that she had passed the afterbirth. Sage cleaned her expertly, packed the area between her legs with absorbent shredded bark and helped her to her furs, where upon she handed her the infant, snuggling him to his mother's breast. The baby sighed and then grasped the nipple and began to suck lustily. Whispering Wind winced and then smiled happily as she drifted into an exhausted sleep.

Sage still had things to do. She had set aside the umbilical cord. Now she cut it so that she had a pair of sections. These she set aside. The remainder of the birthing tissue she set in a basket for Whispering Wind to take out and bury. It was nearly dawn before she was able to crawl into her own sleeping furs; satisfied that she had completed a difficult task successfully. Her arm throbbed painfully, and was swollen and red. She had applied a poultice and wrapped it, when she treated the abrasions on Whispering Wind's wrists and ankles, but she knew that it would be bruised and painful for days. It was a small price to pay for a new life. She settled comfortably and fell into a deep peaceful sleep.

The angry squeal of the infant woke her. It was morning; Whispering Wind was yawning as she changed the soiled padding for her new son. Sage quickly rose and got the hearth fire going. Then she prepared the ever-ready tea that they always had upon waking. Left over cold roast and small grain cakes was all they had to eat, but there would soon be plenty of fresh plant food available. As soon as Whispering Wind was recovered sufficiently to travel, they were leaving the cave and looking for another similar place to spend the next turning of the seasons. Sage had already separated things in her mind. If they found a place not too far, once Whispering Wind was settled, she and Obsidian could return for the remainder of their possessions. She had not yet informed Whispering

Wind. For now, she removed the soiled packing and replaced it with fresh, she took the soiled baby packing and put it with the other. Then she helped Wind sit up and brought her food. The baby was snuggled down into warm furs asleep.

"Have you thought of a name for him?" Sage asked.

"Among 'The People', babies are not given names until they have passed their first turning of the seasons. Until then they are merely called the son or daughter of their mother, so this child will be Wind's Son until he begins to walk. Then we will have a naming ceremony, and I will decide what to call him as a child."

"It is hard for me to get used to the way 'The People' change names. Among the gatherers a person was named at birth, and they died of old age with the same name. It seems strange that your people give so many different names to a person."

"Why? A person is not the same as a child as they were as a baby, and certainly as an adult they are far different. Even in old age they may have earned a special honor name. I certainly would not wish my son to be an old respected elder and still answer to the name, Wind's Son. It would be disrespectful toward a lifetime of achievement."

"I would say a lifetime of achievement would give respect to the name."

"You were given the name Sage at birth?"

Sage frowned, "I have no idea what I was called as a baby, I suppose that I was called Sage then, for this is the custom of the gatherers. I have seen some people however, who were certainly wrongly named. There was one woman called Gentle Breeze, and she would have been better named Angry Storm, for nothing that anyone did ever seemed to please her. She complained constantly about everything. Perhaps there is some merit in your system after all."

"When we reach 'The People', you will have the opportunity to choose a name more to your liking," Whispering Wind reminded.

Sage shrugged, "I am quite content to answer to the name that I carry now."

"We will see," Whispering Wind smiled, "I think 'Bear Claw Woman' would be a fine adult name."

Sage merely snorted rudely and went about clearing the remains of their meal. Yet, inside there was a tingling. After settling Whispering Wind comfortably, she checked the poultices on the other woman's wrists and ankles and removed the one she had concealed beneath her tunic. Her arm was darkly colored with angry bruises, but it was not particularly painful, merely rather sore. She flexed her fingers and then began the task of sorting through the belongings they had accumulated over the turnings of the moon. These turned out to be quite impressive. She didn't remember producing so many storage baskets, nor filling them with such an array of odds and ends. She set one basket aside and tossed all the scraps of leather and fur which had been left over from the making of their garments and other items. Most of these pieces were far too small to be of any use. Into other baskets she shifted the things which would be essential while they traveled.

"What are you doing?" Whispering Wind called from her resting-place on a robe from her bed comfortably supported by the cave wall. "Surely preparing for the 'spring ceremony' can wait until I am able to help."

"What spring ceremony?" Sage replied. "I am sorting out things to throw away. Have you any idea how much useless stuff we have?"

"So what?" Wind shrugged. "You never know when you might need some of that stuff you are throwing away! Don't the gatherers celebrate spring?"

Sage shook her head, "Not unless you call to gather new fresh food, a celebration."

"Well, 'The People' do! We make new summer clothing and new foot coverings proper for the warmer weather, and we have a special feast, with all fresh food."

"The gatherers make lighter weight clothes and new foot coverings as well, and they certainly feast on fresh plants, but no special meal is prepared."

"You have missed out on a lot living with those people," Whispering Wind replied.

"I have also learned a lot which you haven't, so don't be so condescending. Just because the gatherers were not exactly like your precious 'people' it doesn't make them inferior, merely different. I for one do not think eating a singular diet of bison meat for an entire lifetime particularly enlightened!"

Sage tossed another empty basket toward the back of the cave and pulled another forward.

"You're not just cleaning up, are you?" Whispering Wind questioned, "You're preparing to leave aren't you?"

Sage nodded, "That's right. This valley no longer provides enough food for us. It is time to move on. As soon as you are strong enough to travel, we are leaving."

"You did intend to tell me this eventually, didn't you?" Whispering Wind frowned.

Sage sighed and turned to the other woman, "I intended to tell you, yes, when you were in the proper mood, which evidently isn't now."

"I'm sorry," Whispering Wind apologized, "It seems that you are making all of the decisions any more. I guess I have been so involved with myself that I haven't been much help in doing anything, much less helping make decisions. You are right of course; we cannot stay here any longer. Where did you have in mind?"

"I came through a valley not far from here. We almost stayed there, but I was so used to running away, I just didn't realize that I had run so far. It affords better hunting, and I found absolutely no signs of anyone ever having been there. Best of all, it is not all that far, merely a pair of days easy travel."

"When do we leave?"

"As soon as you are able. There are far too many predators here for my comfort. Once the easy pickings are scavenged, they will come looking for us. I'd just as soon we weren't here."

Whispering Wind shuddered, "I will be ready to travel tomorrow!"

Sage shook her head, "I couldn't possibly be ready so soon. Besides, you still need an infant carrier, and we did not think of that. It will take me more than one pass through all this stuff to sort out what we take and what is left behind. I can always come back for some things, but not food. We must take all of it with us or the predators will have moved in here before I can return. Obsidian can pull a travois, as can I, leaving you only the infant to worry about."

"Nonsense! I can pull a travois as well. With the baby in a carrier, I can do my share. Women of 'The People' are strong! We are used to long days of walking, even with new babies!"

"Well, it won't be necessary for this particular 'woman of The People' to prove how strong she is. The things that I am leaving are not particularly valuable. It is possible that I won't even bother returning for them. So long as we have the essentials, the rest can easily be replaced."

Whispering Wind rose and began rummaging through a basket, coming up with some leather straps and a pair of rabbit skins. "I will start on the carrier right now!"

"Are you sure that you feel well enough to be doing anything so strenuous? You lost a lot of blood, and although I have been giving you blood replacing herbs, they cannot have had enough time to be effective. We have a few days. There is no immediate hurry."

"I want to leave this valley!" stated Whispering Wind. "I will feel much safer, and happier, elsewhere. Truly, I am feeling very well. It has been a hand of days since my son was born. I have gained strength daily."

"When I am ready, we will leave," Sage insisted, "I still have a lot of baskets to go through."

"I can help," Whispering Wind replied, "See, I will go through this basket while you check that one." She followed suit and began emptying the basket. Sage tried to stop her but it was too late. "What is this? I haven't seen it before," she turned the deer hide packet around in her hands.

"It is something my grandmother left me," Sage tried to take it from her. Whispering Wind pulled the packet back out of her reach. "What is in it?"

"Just something . . ."

"Well, I cannot remember my grandmother. I am curious as to what sort of things a grandmother thinks are important," deftly she untied the cords and the packet opened. She stared dumbfounded as the wolf skin came into the light. She stopped, drew in her breath, and carefully lay the packet down on the lid of a basket. "What is it?" She whispered her breath caught in her throat, "I could swear it has 'power'!"

"I told you. My grandmother was a healer," Sage quickly replied.

"No! This has nothing to do with healing!" Whispering Wind glared suspiciously at Sage. "And don't try to convince me that you don't know what is inside. I am right, aren't I? It is some kind of 'power' packet or something, isn't it?"

Sage sighed, "I suppose you won't let go until you have wormed it all out of me." She flung down the food packets she had been sorting through and came and picked up the wolf hide packet. "You tell me!" she flipped it open exposing the pair of teeth.

Whispering wind squealed and leaped back, "The 'Sacred Relics'!" she grabbed her throat with her fingers. "You have the Sacred Relics of 'The People'! But how, I don't understand? They vanished long ago. No one knows where they are?"

"Well now you do," Sage wrapped them again and deftly replaced the deer hide and thongs.

"It is a long story."

"Well I have the time!" Whispering Wind snapped. "All these moons, you have been lying to me, pretending that you knew nothing about 'The People,' when all the time you have been hiding their most sacred treasures. You are just a common thief and I think I deserve an explanation!"

"I haven't been lying to you," Sage explained. "I didn't even open that packet until the night of my first blood. Something powerful drew me to it, probably the Spirits. How should I know? I'm just now learning about 'power'. We lived a peaceful life with the gatherers. I didn't even know they weren't my people, although I never really felt accepted by them. I attributed it to my eyes."

"I should have guessed," Whispering Wind mumbled.

"Why? It was certainly a surprise to me when my grandmother, on her deathbed, tells me this fantastic tale about me not being the person I always thought I was. About my mother being murdered, and she and my grandfather cutting me from the dead body and fleeing with me. She was always nervous when strangers came into the camp, she always insisted that I hide and stay away from the camp until they left. I never understood why, but she was my grandmother, so I merely did as she told me, to the point that I just made a habit of leaving the camp whenever someone strange entered. I thought she was a bit peculiar about it, but the night she died she insisted that I flee and take the Sacred Relics with me. That was the first time I was even aware there was such a thing. I was so scared I just did as she told me."

"You are Moon Maiden's child."

"That was my mother's name," Sage admitted.

"But you don't carry the mark!" Whispering Wind protested, "I have seen your shoulders, both of them. It isn't there!"

"No, it isn't," Sage admitted, "It is here." She undid the front of her tunic and revealed the small mark.

"But how? I have seen your breast and I even examined the bruise you got when the grizzly bear attacked."

"That wasn't a bruise, but the beginning of the mark. It developed gradually after that, until one day it was recognizable as a wolf. My grandmother had a different mark and she called it a bison. She was always careful to keep it covered. I doubt that any among the gatherers knew of it. In fact I am probably the only living person to know she bore that mark."

"That explains a lot!" Whispering Wind said with satisfaction. "The bear, brought by the Spirits! Of course! The 'Chosen' could not have a common doe as a ceremonial 'gift'. Just like the Ancient Yel, you were given the most powerful spirit offering possible for your, 'becoming a woman' ceremony. You are probably going to do great deeds, like fight evil dreamers with lightning bolts!"

"I sincerely hope not!" Sage protested. "I might be able to make the offerings at the Sacred Spring which you described, but I have no way of fighting evil, dreamers or any other kind."

"Obsidian is your protector, isn't she?"

"I think so," Sage admitted. "I sort of asked that question myself and the wolf spot sent warm feeling through my body."

"The spirits communicate with you, don't they?"

"I am beginning to believe so," Sage admitted reluctantly. "I certainly feel something guided me to turn your baby. But they have also directed us to leave this place. I know because the spot throbbed with pleasure when I made that decision, and I have put it off, because you were so heavy with child and the feeling has become almost painful. But don't get me wrong, no 'spirits' actually talk to me. Nor do they guide me, other than the feeling of right or wrong that the mark imparts. It is hard to understand what these spirits want of me."

"How can that be? It is so simple! You are to return the Ancient Relics to 'The People', of course! And I have been sent as your guide."

"I am not at all sure of that. First of all; my mother was killed by one of The People. My grandmother fled to save the Relics as much as to save me."

"But that was a long time ago! The danger is probably long gone, with whoever killed your mother."

"I don't think so. Those men, who came into the camp, they were looking for Grandmother. They asked for her by name. I am sure that they came for the Sacred Relics. She was certain, as well, that is why she forced me to flee. She had the travois packed and ready, even to the dog. She paid dearly for that animal. She was always prepared, all of my life, to flee at a heartbeat's notice."

"Who were the men? Did you get names?"

"One was called Running Bison, the other Prairie something or other." Sage shrugged. "I could not understand anything of their conversation. All I recognized were their names and Grandmother's, but she understood every word. They were looking for her. It so agitated her that this is probably what killed her. She was so upset and so insistent that I did exactly as she instructed. I ran! I loaded the travois, hooked up the dog and in a downpour of rain fled the camp. I didn't stop until I reached this valley. I knew nothing of ''The People', the 'chosen', or the Ancient Relics until that night. I put the whole thing to the back of my mind. Then I discovered you in the death camp and you were able to fill me in on the whole legend of the 'chosen' and the Sacred Relics. This is why I have said that I felt the spirit of my grandmother brought you to me. Now however, I am more inclined to feel that the spirits of our ancestors or rather, their spirit helpers have brought us together, so that I might understand the significance and of course the danger of being in possession of these Relics."

"But Running Bison would never be a danger to you," protested Whispering Wind.

"You know of him?" Sage stared at her open mouthed.

"Know of him! I spent months trying to gain his attention. Running Bison is the finest person I have ever met. When his mate died in childbirth I was hopeful that he would look my way, but then I was stolen soon after. Anyway, Running Bison would protect and defend you to the death. He would never be part of a plan to kill anyone. If he was seeking your grandmother, it was because someone else was a danger."

"Maybe he was only interested in returning the Sacred Relics to 'The People'," Sage suggested.

"Well, that is possible; after all they do belong with 'The People'. They are of no use to the gatherers, and you are under obligation to return them anyway."

"It is not yet time," stated Sage with finality.

"How can you know that?"

Sage shrugged, "I don't know the answer to that question; I only know it isn't time for me to return to 'The People'. I have asked the spirits and they have answered painfully. That is all that I know. We are leaving this valley and going to the other one, and until they guide me otherwise, that is where I will stay. You are of course free to do whatever you wish."

"That is unfair!" Whispering Wind protested. "You know that I won't leave you. You are closer to me than if you were born my sister. Besides, I owe you my protection."

Sage grinned at this, "I feel honored, but just what do you think I am in need of protection from?"

"Perhaps your own stubborn decisions," Whispering Wind grinned back. "Any way it is getting late, let's go to our furs and finish this packing tomorrow. I do find that I am getting tired."

"I will make us some tea," Sage dumped the rest of the food she was sorting and picking up the water bag poured some into their bowls and added the tea to steep.

# CHAPTER 4

Running Bison tossed the last branch onto their fire. Most of the other men were sleeping, but he was feeling restless. This whole thing regarding the Sacred Relics had the entire Bison Camp unsettled; soon it would be time for the Spring Ceremony and one more year without an offering at the spring. *One more year of bad hunting and starvation for 'The People'*, he sighed and looked toward the Ancestor Fires in the sky. *Where can she be? How can I find her? We came so close, only to be thwarted by Clover Blossom. The old one was very clever. It has taken me seasons to unravel the clues. The gatherers were my last hope. Where do I search from here?* He asked himself.

They were camping just beyond a long narrow valley where the recent spring rains had gouged a deep narrow channel onto the spreading plain. His group was spreading out along the entire area. If she fled from the gatherer camp, it would be deeper into the mountains. There were as many places she could hide as Ancestor Fires in the sky. It was an impossible task that he had set himself and his men, but they were desperate. The girl had to be found and forced if necessary, to make the offering this spring. Others had tried but The Spirits refused to listen. Each season the hunting had become poorer, until now, there was barely food enough to keep 'The People' alive. Some camps were talking of splitting away and moving into the mountains and making a different way of life. But they were bison hunters! They had always been bison hunters. Somehow it seemed wrong to even think of another way of life. Running Bison just didn't know which way to turn. He was a leader among his people. They all looked to him for direction. If he couldn't find the girl, perhaps they would no longer listen to him. It was even possible that they would look elsewhere for leadership.

He still hadn't figured out who had killed Moon Maiden. Even if he located the girl, he could not guarantee her safety. He could do his best to protect her, but not knowing the enemy made even that difficult and he was unsure that he could even win her trust if he did manage to find her. Finally, late into the night, his head aching he retired to his furs.

\*     \*     \*

Whispering Wind loaded the last of the supplies that she insisted on dragging on a light travois. She was busy checking on all the securing lines and didn't notice that the braided band that she wore around her wrist had become untied and fallen to the ground. Sage had secured the lines to Obsidian's travois and was easing into the straps of her own. They seemed to be taking an awful lot with them, but a new baby required a lot of things. What was left behind in the cave was not worth returning for. It could all be replaced. Sage signaled the dog and just as the sun was rising above the mountain to the east, they set off.

\*     \*     \*

Just beyond the mouth of the valley, the hunters of the Bison Camp were rising. Prairie Grass was heating water for tea and Water Carrier was dropping hot stones into the cooking hide. Running Bison was checking the dogs for signs of sores and repairing worn parts to their harnesses. The others were breaking camp. The men had been out searching for more than a turn of the moon. Some were starting to grumble. They did not like being separated from their families for so long. "What makes you think she will be in this area?" Water Carrier questioned.

"This area would be safe," Running Bison replied. "If I were looking for a safe place to hide, these mountains would certainly be my choice. Hardly anyone ever comes here, for one thing."

"But what makes you think a girl, not yet even a woman, would know that?"

"I don't think she would, but powerful spirits protect her and they would certainly guide her to the safest place possible. That just happens to be this area of mountains."

"There have been tales of raiders in this area," Walks Far remarked.

Running Bison frowned, "I have heard those tales also, but we have had no proof of raiders, at least not since Whispering Wind was stolen."

"Yes, but you found the men who stole her and they didn't have her."

"I still don't believe that they didn't know where she was. But I had no luck finding out anything further. They weren't telling all."

"Well, since they are now all dead, there isn't much we can do about that!" replied Walks Far. "Perhaps if you had been less quick to put them to death . . ."

"They deserved to die! What else would you have me do after they killed a full hand of our women and children?"

"Well I think we are wasting our time. We have been scouring these mountains for over a moon. So far we haven't found a single trace of anything," protested Water Carrier.

"We will quit if we find no sign soon," Running Bison replied.

"How soon?"

"Running Bison frowned; he did not like anyone challenging his decisions. "When I say," he stated abruptly and began harnessing his dog. The conversation was over and the other men were not so stupid as to press it. Grudgingly they fell in line behind him and they all entered the scoured valley. Running Bison's big black hunting dog ranged out before the men, sniffing for signs of game. It was nearly mid day when the black dog barked and Running Bison raised his hand to halt the group. The dog stood beside a bush, just about the only thing still alive after the flood. Running Bison hurried to the dog and knelt beside him. He lifted a bit of brightly colored leather, woven in a fine braid. Instantly he recognized it, a thrill of fear, or hope, feathered down his spine. He had crafted the bracelet himself and gifted it to Whispering Wind on her 'becoming a woman' ceremony.

"Quickly men, spread out and look for signs!" Turning back to the dog, he caught sight of the cave entrance. Quickly he slipped in and frowned. The place was deserted, but had not been so for long. The coals in the hearth still held a faint trace of heat. He searched through the scatter of baskets and discarded bits of food and fur. Picking up one of the smaller baskets, he frowned. The pattern was not one used by The People, but rather by gatherers. Evidence also indicated that not a single person, but rather a very small group had been living in the cave. He studied the dusty floor. There were prints of at least two different people, probably both women. Other tracks told him that they had at least a single dog. Still searching, he found evidence of an infant as well. So now there was probably a pair of women and a dog, plus an infant. He frowned. If one of the women was Whispering Wind, who was the other? He knew of only one other it could be and she was with a large dog. The size of the dog tracks indicated a large dog.

One of the men outside shouted, Running Bison tossed down the basket and left the cave.

"They went this way!" Water Carrier shouted. "Up the valley, toward the pass to the west!"

"It is Whispering Wind," Running Bison joined the others. "I found this just before the cave. I recognize it. I gave it to her at her 'ceremony'."

"You can't be sure it is she," reminded Prairie Grass. "It could have been taken from her and another lost it."

"You are right," Running Bison's heart fell. "I was just so encouraged."

"We follow the trail, yes?"

"Yes! We follow the trail. It is the first hope we have come across. Whoever lost the bracelet was not alone, however. There is a pair of women, an infant and a dog."

"How do you know all that?"

"I studied the evidence inside the cave. And they are not even a day ahead of us. The fire still held faint traces of heat."

*     *     *

"Why?" Whispering Wind sat on the rock, tired and cranky. Sage was being totally unreasonable. Wind was in no mood for her silly safeguards. First of all, she had lost her prized bracelet and Sage wouldn't hear of her going back for it. Wind was nearly in tears, for Running Bison had gifted it to her. It was the only thing she still had to remind her of her former life. Now it was gone and Sage was determined that they were to lay a false trail to the north, then double back and go to the west.

"All right," Sage gave in, "You stay here and rest, Obsidian and I will lay the false trail. I will be back in no more than two hands time." Quickly she unloaded both travois and stacked the contents in a pile beside Whispering Wind. Then she loaded a number of large rocks in their place. They had left the valley behind early in the day, crossed another valley to the west of it and now Sage was determined to leave a false trail clearly leading through a wide passage into another valley. They were to go up through a very difficult and narrow pass into somewhere to the west. It made little sense to Whispering Wind, who now sat nursing her son and watched Sage and Obsidian disappearing through the brush. Who was there to follow their trail?

She rested and waited beside the pile of belongings heaped beside the path. Sage and Obsidian, with fully loaded travois of rocks made only little effort to cover their trail. If someone were following, she wanted them to find it, but not too easily. Once through the passage she led the dog onto a rocky ledge. Here she unloaded the travois and smiled as she carefully placed the heavy load of rock in natural looking places. Then she picked up the poles and strapped them to her back. It did not take them nearly as long to return to where Whispering Wind waited for them. Sage made sure there was no signs of the return trip. If anyone came upon their trail, even by chance, they would follow it into the valley and lose it among the rocky slopes. Then Sage reloaded the pair of travois and with Obsidian in the lead, Whispering Wind between and Sage following, she made absolutely certain there were no traces of their passage. They spent the night huddled beneath the sheltering branches of a huge pine.

\*      \*      \*

Running Bison and his group camped on the rocky slopes of another valley. They had lost the trail, but he had hopes of picking it up again once it was light. At dawn both groups broke camp and moved on, going farther and farther apart. By nightfall Sage and Whispering Wind were settling into a small cave where Sage had sheltered for a short time the previous summer. Running Bison and his hunters were traveling farther away as they vainly searched for a trail.

"What do you think we should do?" Prairie Grass questioned, as the men sat huddled around their fire drenched by drizzling rain.

"What can we do, except return to where we last absolutely recognized their trail?" Running Bison answered.

"That was near the mouth of the valley, almost an entire day's travel," protested Water Carrier.

"What would you suggest, then?" Running Bison asked.

Water Carrier shrugged and pulled his shelter hide more closely over his head. "I think it is a disgrace that an entire group of seasoned hunters has been tricked by a pair of females, barely women," he muttered.

"A pair of females didn't trick us," Running Bison reminded him. "The Spirits which protect the 'chosen' one tricked us."

"I thought you said we were following Whispering Wind," Prairie Grass said.

"I have reason to think they are together," Running Bison replied.

"Well if they are and Spirits are protecting them, we are hardly likely to find them. But why would the spirits keep the Sacred Relics from us? That doesn't make any sense. We need them, or at least we need this girl who can offer the prayers," Walks Far offered.

"I would like to know the answer to that question myself," Running Bison replied.

The men scoured the area where they last found traces of the girls, but they finally gave up and with much grumbling and protest recognized that there were a hand or more paths that the pair could have taken. The rain would have completely washed away any path even for the dog to follow. With great regret, Running Bison turned his hunters back and they returned to the main camp, many hands south. For the remainder of the spring and all through the summer he puzzled the mystery. Hunting was poor. Rain did not come. The bison were thin, sick and wary. The People ranged farther and longer and found less to sustain them.

\*    \*    \*

In their new home, the infant thrived. He was a good baby, seldom crying and never ill. There was a bounty of food in the new valley and the girls soon had a good storehouse begun for the coming winter. The mark on Sage's breast sent her no signals. She almost forgot about it.

Obsidian was out hunting with Whispering Wind, Sage babysitting to give her friend a break. Sage had no idea where he came from. She was all alone in the cave playing with the baby, the next thing she knew, a violent pain surged through her head as her hair was cruelly jerked and a sharp blade held to her throat.

"Make a sound and you are dead!" Hissed a guttural male voice, in a language she did not understand, but the general idea was plain enough. Sage froze in terror. A pair of other shadows entered the cave and she was shaking with fear now. They pawed through the stores of food, joking to each other as they either stuffed their bellies, or stuffed the supplies into their backpacks. One eyed the infant, but so far none had offered him any harm. The first man eyed Sage's bear-claw and tooth necklace. He frowned, said something to the others and then grabbed the necklace. Sage gasped as the thong brutally cut into her throat and cut off her breath. Gagging, she struggled against the man. His response was to twist the thong even tighter. Gradually Sage began to lose consciousness. The man shoved her sagging body against a log and untied the thong, releasing the pressure. Sage gasped for breath and in a fog watched as the hunter tied her necklace about his own neck. A black rage began building inside her, but she realized that she was helpless to alter the situation. Her throat burned, but she could, at least breathe again.

"Get us some food prepared!" the first man shouted at Sage. She may not have understood his words, but the meaning was fairly clear. She quickly set about fixing them a meal. The hunters watched her carefully, but not quite carefully enough. Inside an angry rage against these brutal hunters began to build. She rubbed her amulet and sent a silent prayer to whatever spirits might be out there. Nothing happened. The filthy, smelly, unmannerly men merely set about stuffing their food slovenly into their mouths, making bets as to which of them would spend the night with the woman. Sage wondered where Obsidian and Whispering Wind were, they should have returned long ago. She hoped that they would come soon with one thought and then with the next that they would stay away.

"Come here, woman!" The leader-hunter demanded of Sage. She was feeding the infant and did not put him down quickly enough to suit the leader. The hunter reached out and grabbing the baby by his heels swung the small helpless body around and around, then he flung the baby hard against the back wall of the cave. A dull, squashing thud was the only sound the baby made and with a sinking heart, Sage knew that Whispering Wind's son was dead. Then the hunter dragged Sage screaming and kicking to where she had only that morning rolled her furs. He shoved her painfully down on the furs and when she bit him on the arm, he struck her so hard across the face that her head snapped and for a heartbeat she feared he had broken her neck. Blood oozed from a cut on her lip and her right eye quickly swelled shut. Then the man was ripping the lacing of her tunic, roughly pulling it from her. Cool air rose chill bumps on her exposed flesh. Painfully he pinched her small breasts, then spitefully bit one hard. Sage screamed and tried again to free herself. The hunter only laughed, her bear-claw necklace dancing mockingly at her from around his neck. The more she fought, the better he liked it. He was an animal, getting pleasure from inflicting pain. Sage had no strength left. She lay still, her mind reeling. The hunter groped between her legs, finding her most private place. She was outraged as he thrust his fingers up into her. He shoved his knees between her legs and spread her legs wide. Then he pulled aside his breechclout and with a savage thrust drove into her. Her whole body thrust up in protest. Sage nearly fainted as the hunter forced into her tortured body again and again. She turned her head away, only to see the crumpled remains of the infant. Bile rising in her throat, she closed her eyes and her whole body, one strumming band of pain, suffered the hunter's thrusts. She was too small to fight him. Finally, he grunted and his body taunted, then relaxed. He withdrew from her and with a grunt of satisfaction, rose only to be replaced by another and that one was, in due time, replaced by the other. Time seemed to pass very slowly. The first pair of men had fallen silent and Sage could see them sprawled beside the fire, snoring loudly. The remaining hunter was getting angry. He pumped into her again and again, but without success. His man part was not hard. With frustration he grunted, then turned to say something to the others. Sage saw his eyes bulge open in surprise, then with a grunt he fell across her and moved no more. She could smell the scent of urine and feces and realized with surprise, that he was dead. Sage squirmed and shoved at the horrible inert mass, finally heaving it off her. She sat up. The other hunters were lying in pools of their own blood. A dart had passed directly through the heart of one; the other's throat had been ripped open by sharp canine teeth.

The sleeping potion she had put in their food had taken effect. Whispering Wind and Obsidian had done the rest. The filthy hunters hadn't known the face of their killer. Already Whispering Wind was cradling the body of her son, tears streaming down her face. Sage crawled to the fire and collapsed beside it, sobbing. Pain ripped through her abused body, she tried to rise, but had not the strength.

Obsidian lay growling deep in her throat. Whispering Wind wrapped the body of her infant son and without a word went out into the night with him. Sage lay for hands of time beside the fire, to hurt and tired to move. Finally, late into the night Whispering Wind returned and helped Sage to her own bed. Here she ministered to the injured one as best she could. Finally, the painkilling potion she administered took effect and Sage knew no more for a time.

\*       \*       \*

Sage opened her eyes and for a heartbeat wondered why only one eye responded. Then the abused flesh of her body painfully brought the events of the horror filled day clearly back into focus. Slowly she sat up. The cave was neat, everything in its place, no sign of violence visible. Silence however, was the only answer to her soft calls. She was alone. There was no sign of Whispering Wind or of Obsidian. Then groggily, she drifted off again, sleep claiming her.

"Here Sage, wake up," Whispering Wind gently laid her hand on Sage's forehead. Sage opened her eye. She frowned and then tried to rise. Pain took her breath away. "Don't try to move too much," Whispering Wind said evenly, "You have broken ribs and probably your arm as well. I did the best I could for you."

"Are you all right?" Sage questioned, worried at the strange behavior of her friend.

"I will live," Whispering Wind replied grimly.

"The baby?"

Tears filled her eyes and Whispering Wind began to weep, "I took him . . . out to . . . the big rock," she whispered, "He always liked . . ."

"The men?" Sage questioned quickly.

Whispering Wind stopped crying. It was as if the troubled waters of a lake had suddenly smoothed. "They will murder no more babies, nor rape another woman!" She handed Sage a bowl of broth, then rose and walked back to the fire. "We dragged their bodies to the deep crevasse and dumped them in, then shoved rocks on top of them. No one will find them, even if they do come looking. From the looks of them, they were outcasts." Whispering Wind reached into her waist pack and withdrew something. "here! I removed this from one of the bodies." Sage took her bear-claw necklace and nodded. Whispering Wind took it and placed it on a ledge until Sage's neck had time to heal.

"We must leave here, just as soon as I am able to travel," Sage tried to sit up again and when a sharp jab of pain slammed through her chest, slumped back onto the furs.

"Where will we go?" Whispering Wind questioned. "Danger seems to follow us wherever we go. We are not safe hidden in this valley; we would not be safe with the gatherers, not since they know someone is seeking you, nor according to you, with 'The People'."

"Perhaps we were not careful enough here," Sage whispered, "We became careless, felt too secure. Spirits do not always use the gentlest of ways to communicate. You have said so yourself. Perhaps this was their warning."

"That is it, Sage!" Whispering Wind jumped to her feet. "Blame it on the spirits! Perhaps it is you who are to blame! Did that idea ever come to you? Have you ever doubted the decisions that brought us to this place? Maybe the spirits have called to you and you have just ignored them. Maybe that is why my baby had to die!"

Whispering Wind flounced angrily from the cave.

Sage felt awful! She could understand the pain that her friend was suffering. She would gladly have died in the infant's place, but the spirits had chosen otherwise. There was nothing she could do to ease Whispering Wind's distress. With a soft moan she curled onto her side and tried to ease the hurt of both mind and body with oblivion. For a time it worked.

Sage slept most of the next hand or so of days. Whispering Wind kept giving her the pain killing drink. She did not again mention the death of her child or anything else that could cause suffering. Gradually Sage's body began to heal. Obsidian refused to leave her side. From the whining and woeful expression, Sage knew the big faithful dog blamed herself. By now, Sage was able to sit up and move about the cave some, but she was still too weak to go far. The bleeding resulting from the rape had been profuse. She had several broken ribs and her right arm was still strapped to the branch. Bruising had turned from dark angry to yellow and finally disappeared. She rummaged through her medicines and found the blood builders. She took them. She also took the last of her secret 'medicine' which her grandmother had instructed her about. She had forgotten all about it, but the rape brought it to the forefront of her mind. This plant could prevent her conceiving a child

The moon made a full turn, passing the Mid-Summer Moon before Sage felt more or less her old self. It was now well into the Burning Grass Moon. Whispering Wind had spent most of her days gathering food plants as they came into season. She had dried berries and plums and many plants that Sage had taught her were good food. The deer meat had long ago been eaten, but Whispering Wind was an excellent cast with her rabbit stick and Obsidian brought in a consistent collection of rabbits and other smaller animals. They had not gone hungry. Now it was time to seriously consider their future.

"If you want to seek out 'The People', I will not try to stop you," Sage said quietly.

"But you would not go with me?" Whispering Wind questioned.

Sage shook her head, "The time is not yet."

"Then I will stay," Whispering Wind replied softly. "We have shared too much to be parted."

"I feel the same," Sage wiped a tear from her eye, "But I would not hold you back."

"I think it is time we did some serious hunting for winter meat," Whispering Wind rose. "Do you feel up to it? I would go out with Obsidian, but the wretched creature refuses to leave you and I cannot hunt elk alone."

"I feel fine," Sage smiled. She did feel fine. She had wakened that morning with cramps in her stomach and a slight trace of blood on her thighs. She was greatly relieved. She was not pregnant from the rape.

They gathered up their atlatls and darts and left the cave. It was a hot humid day, with clouds piling high in the sky. Thunder rumbled from afar and lightning flickered beneath the clouds.

"That storm will strike before dark," Whispering Wind sniffed the air, "I can smell rain!"

"I hope the lightning does not set the forest on fire. It is so dry that the whole thing would go up like a newly tindered fire."

"You are right," Whispering Wind sighed, "But I still hope it rains. We have had so little since spring." She did not look in the direction of the big rock as they passed. Sage knew that the scavengers would have long ago devoured the pathetic remains she had so lovingly laid out to walk the wind. It still hurt Sage to remember the happy laughing baby. It enraged her sense of right and wrong that those evil filthy hunters had held the right of life and death over them. Suddenly the spot over her heart throbbed, not pain, not pleasure, but somehow a sense of rightness. Sage stopped in her tracks. Was this another dubious message from the spirits? Then she shrugged. She was tired of trying to figure out what these spirits were wanting. She was not even sure she really believed in them.

They worked their way up the side of the valley until they were on a high ridge. They could see the entire valley from here and Sage realized this was probably how the hunters had spotted her when she went to the stream to fill the water skin. They had missed Whispering Wind and Obsidian because the pair had left much earlier, but Sage had gone late in the day to fill the water skin.

"There are tracks here!" Whispering Wind called excitedly, "A number of elk have been by here, not long ago; see!" She pointed to still-steaming droppings littering the trail.

"Fine, let's go after them. I only hope we do not have to follow them too far; I have no desire to have to carry that much meat all the way back to the cave."

"Then maybe we should consider moving," Whispering Wind said in all seriousness. "I would not miss the memories of that place."

"Nor would I," Sage replied. Once again the spot on her chest gave a throb, this time of pleasure. Sage knew their time at the little cave was almost over. They followed the elk along the ridge and into a deep valley. The brush was so dense they had a hard time finding the trail. Then suddenly the black clouds rolled in and the lightning boomed, flashing along the underside of the clouds and forking down to the earth. The crash was earthshaking and the hair on their arms and heads actually stood up. Obsidian whined and circled, tucking her tail between her legs and looked about for somewhere to hide.

"That was close!" Whispering Wind shrieked, grabbing Sage by the arm. "Look!" she pointed to a tree slowly toppling down. They leaped out of danger, at least of the tree, but it crashed across the trail, cutting off their retreat. Greedy flames flickered from the charred trunk, quickly igniting the surrounding brush. "Run!" They both shouted together and took off down the trail as fast as they could go, crashing noisily through the brush, no longer caring if the animals ahead of them were frightened or not.

They continued on their helter-skelter route until finally they were out of breath and forced to stop. They looked back over their shoulders and the sight there gave them reason to run again. Black billowing smoke rose in angry spirals on the rising wind. But flickering flames and heat were only a short dart cast behind them. The fire was spreading nearly as fast as they could run. Again they set off, this time trying to find a clearer path. The barking of the dog well ahead of them alerted the girls and they hurried toward Obsidian. She kept barking and leading them, first onto a narrow path which was much easier than crashing through the brush, then onto a wider path where they could actually run.

And run they did! The fire was almost literally on their heels. Smoke began to smart their eyes and seeing clearly became difficult. Soon they were coughing as well. Then Sage stumbled and catching Whispering Wind off balance, they both tumbled over an embankment and splashed into a sizable stream. Obsidian was there as well, barking and splashing in the water as she lead them up the stream. It did not go far and a solid cliff of rock blocked their way. The cliff was high, soaring nearly vertical and the stream magically sprung right from its base. Obsidian barked once again then disappeared into the wall of rock. The girls looked at each other, then as one they dived headfirst into the water. It was deep enough that they could feel their way forward. A short distance farther and they were able to stand up. Obsidian was barking wildly. Sage called to her and the big dog stopped barking.

"Where are we?" Whispering Wind looked about.

"I am not sure, but the fire isn't here," Sage replied. "I think it must be one of those crevasses we saw earlier. The wind is blowing the fire the other way. We should be safe here."

"Safe, I doubt anyone could possibly find us in here!" Whispering Wind laughed, "We actually had to swim to get here." The girls gave one another a startled glance and then as of an accord, said, "Let's look around."

They scanned the narrow vertical walls, there was no way out from there, but Obsidian was wagging her tail and splashing through the stream. The girls followed. After a few fingers of time the crevasse opened into a high walled box canyon. The far end narrowed and there was a game trail leading upward. Milling nervously in the canyon meadow was at least a double hand of cow elk and their young. Sage and Whispering Wind and Obsidian were all down wind, so something else was agitating the animals. Sage glanced upward. The sky was now an angry black. Rumbling thunder reverberated down the canyon and the girls realized that shelter was soon going to become very important. Already they were wet to the skin, their scanty aprons little protection and now the hot muggy air was being replaced by much cooler air.

"Over there!" Whispering Wind pointed. "I think that dark spot in the wall could be a cave. Even if it isn't, we had better find some kind of shelter. Here comes the rain!" She yelped as not rain, but ice pellets began to pummel them. The hail only lasted a few heartbeats and by then they were nearly to the wall where the dark area beckoned. Obsidian dived into the cave ahead of them and they heard a cacophony of angry barks and screams and pandemonium resounded from within. The elk heard moved to the lower end of the canyon where they had entered. Soon an angry, spitting, snarling cougar streaked from the cave, Obsidian right on its tail. Sage and Whispering Wind grinned wetly at each other and hurried into their newly claimed abode. They could hear the dog barking as it chased the big cat toward the upper end of the canyon.

They looked curiously around. At one time, for a long time, pack rats had called the cave home; an enormous midden of sticks was piled against one wall. The rats had probably ended up as food for the cat. It didn't take them long to pull some of the dry branches out into the middle of the floor and with a quickly constructed fire drill, took turns working to start a fire. The temperature had fallen from hot to very chilly in a matter of heartbeats. Obsidian came rushing into the cave and shook water all over them. Sage and Whispering Wind wore nothing but moccasin and apron. The fire soon warmed the air in a small area and the chill finally went from their bodies. They felt warmer once they were dry and hands of time later the rain finally stopped. If they hurried, they could make it back to the other cave before dark. It was decided that bare footed was better than soggy foot coverings so they were discarded as well. They scrambled quickly after Obsidian. She led them not toward the stream where they had entered the canyon, but the opposite direction, up a very narrow twisting trail. Once up on the ridge, they found the path they had traveled after the elk. The rain had drowned the forest fire but a vast area had been blacked in the short time the fire had burned. They did not stop to examine the damage but hurried on. They were glad to get back, even without meat. It was a pleasure just to pull on warm tunics and pants. Then they ate a few bites of cold food and tumbled tiredly into their furs.

The morning was cool and clear, a fresh breeze sweeping down the valley. It did not take them long to load their travois for the first trip. By mid day they were approaching the new cave. Obsidian growled and raised her hackles. Sage quickly unharnessed her and the big dog shot like a dart into the cave. An outraged yowl greeted her, but the cat had learned its lesson the day before, with a screeching of protest it abandoned the cave and shot up the trail to disappear over the top. Sage and Whispering Wind unloaded and strapped the travois poles over their shoulders. One more trip and they would be moved. By dark they had settled roughly into their new home.

"Tomorrow I think we should go back and make sure that we did not leave anything behind which we might need," suggested Sage. "Then we can wipe our trail completely away. It looks to rain again soon, probably tomorrow after the heat has built. The rain will wash away any last traces we might have left."

"You know, I have been watching those elk," Whispering Wind said as she chewed on a rabbit leg. "I don't think they leave this valley. There are water and plenty of food for them. The only way out is the way we came in . . ."

"I see what you are getting to, if we blocked the trail leaving the canyon, the elk couldn't get out. Food all winter."

"We can take our time killing a single animal and processing it completely before taking another. Besides, they are tastier in the fall after fattening all summer."

"When we have all we want, we can remove the barrier and let the rest leave when they want."

"And if anyone comes down that trail we will see them and can escape the same way we came into the canyon the first time," Whispering Wind nodded her head happily.

\*     \*     \*

Running Bison stood on the ridge where they had lost the trail of the women in the spring. This time it was only he and Prairie Grass. He was determined to figure out where they had been tricked, even if it was moons later. There were only so many paths and he was determined to search each and every one of them, if necessary. He was desperate. There had been no rain on the grasslands. There was little food for the bison. The people had been hungry all summer. There had been considerable talk of replacing Angry Badger as headman. So he had left Water Carrier to keep an eye on the camp and he and Prairie Grass were once again, trying to find the answer to the puzzle.

"If it were me and I were trying to lay a false trail, I would do just as they did, but I would take the most unlikely path."

Running Bison nodded, "Just what I was thinking. I would go that way," he pointed to a narrow, difficult and steep path leading to a narrow pass between a pair of steep cliffs.

"What are we waiting for?" Prairie Grass grinned back.

Running Bison whistled to his hunting dog and soon they were scrambling up the steep path. It led down into a small valley and onward toward the west. "I would not stop here," Prairie Grass stated, "This valley is too small."

"Agreed."

So they continued into the next valley. "This feels right!" Running Bison stated. "It is large enough to supply easy game hunting and there are plenty of places to shelter. They took refuge in a cave before; let's see if they did so again."

The hunters spent a hand of days searching the valley before they came across the cave. They were disappointed to find it empty, but heartened that they had guessed correctly. "They haven't been gone for long," Prairie Grass stated, "This rabbit skin was removed only a few hands of days ago."

"Then they cannot be far ahead of us. Come on man!"

"We can get a better look from that ridge up there," Prairie Grass pointed, "We can see the entire valley from there."

Running Bison frowned, "Perhaps that is why they left."

"Well if they stay true to their past movements, they will have gone to ground in some place impossible to find. These women know they are being hunted."

"I don't think so," disagreed Running Bison. "But if we are correct, spirits are guiding them. We must convince the spirits that we wish to protect the women, not harm them."

"How do we do that?"

"I am not sure," admitted Running Bison, "But I spoke to Crooked Spirit before we left and he gave me a packet and very strict instruction on how to use it."

"So what are you to do?"

"I think now is the time to go on a spirit quest of my own," Running Bison stated firmly. "I will do so this very night."

"Is that why you have eaten nothing all day?"

Running Bison nodded, "We will make camp just below this ridge. I must wash and purify my body as well as my mind."

Running Bison made his way to where a small stream trickled from higher up. Here he washed thoroughly with soap-root, even his hair and bushy beard. He used a frazzled twig to clean his teeth and rinsed his mouth out with a bitter tasting herb, careful not to swallow any of it. Then he built a small smoky fire and cleansed himself with smoke. Now he had followed Crooked Spirit's instruction to the smallest detail. When he returned to the camp, he went to where he had already set up his shelter. Here he untied a hide and carefully unrolled it. Inside was another hide: a very special hide, lent to him by Crooked Spirit. The faint light of the moon reflected from the white fur of the Sacred Bison. It was very old and rather shabby and tattered. Much of the hair had already fallen out. Carefully Running Bison spread the fur and seated himself cross-legged upon it. He had set the spirit drink to steep with hot water before going to bathe. Now it had cooled and he took a deep breath and drank it all. Then he waited . . .

*     *     *

A mist formed, deep and quiet. Running Bison looked all around, but he could see nothing but the fog. But he could hear something, far away and he called out. Slowly the figure of the white bison emerged and came to him. *You have called my name.* The animal stated. *Why do you call me?*

"I am Running Bison, hunter of the Bison Camp of 'The People'. I have called you because we are desperate. There has been no rain. There is no food for the bison and no food for 'The People'. All creatures are starving."

*Your people have not made offerings to the spirits in many seasons. Why should we hear you?*

"We have tried."

*You have not made proper offerings.*

"We have no one to make them. The Sacred Relics have been stolen. We know not where they are"

*Evil ones killed the Keeper. The Relics were taken before they were used against 'The People'. The keeper was not protected. The Relics were not protected. The spirits took them from you.*

"We need them back and we need the new Keeper as well. I know that she lives. She was raised among the gatherers, but now it is time for her to return to her own people and take her place."

*Then it is up to you, Running Bison, to convince her to do so. It is up to you to protect her and see that the evil does not touch her.*

"I know not where she is."

The white beast shook his head and the mist parted. Running Bison gasped as he looked just over the ridge from where he sat and down into a deep hidden canyon. Here in a cave protected from view, sat Whispering Wind and another, one with eyes as blue as the sky.

*Remember, if you fail, the Sacred Relics will be taken from 'The People' forever. The People will vanish as the mist on a hot morning. Listen to what she has to say. Follow her and she will lead 'The People' on the spirit path. She has much power, but she knows not how to call upon it. She must learn before she can be returned to 'The People'. The time is not yet.*

"The People' need to have the offering at the Sacred Spring."

*Go from this place! Return in the spring, when the snow has gone from the mountains. Then she will be ready!*

"But how will I find her?"

*She will be where you see her.*

"And Whispering Wind?"

The mist swirled and the bison faded and vanished. Running Bison was alone.

# CHAPTER 5

What do you think?" Whispering Wind held up the tunic she was decorating, "Should I add more of the red quills along the edge, or maybe around the sleeves only?"

Sage studied the garment for a time, "Why don't you do both? It would even be nice if you put it around the bottom edge just above the fringe. I don't understand why you are going to all that trouble to begin with. There is no one to see it but you and me."

"That doesn't mean it can't be pretty!" Whispering Wind said in disgust, "If it were left up to you, our clothing would be just plain, unadorned, hide."

"What is wrong with that?"

"Don't you want to look pretty?"

"For whom? As I have already pointed out, there is only the pair of us. Obsidian doesn't care."

"Well I do! It makes me feel better to be dressed nicely. I enjoy looking at well-made tunics with designs on them. If I am willing to go to the trouble to do the design, then that is my choice."

"Well, I suppose we have enough quills to do a hand of tunics. I had no idea that porcupine quills could be dyed with plant juices. The colors really are quite nice and the porcupines were delicious as well."

"What did the gatherers use for decoration?"

Sage frowned, "You know, other than my grandmother, I don't believe any of the women bothered decorating their clothing. I never thought about it before, but when I was a child, I was the only one with designs on my tunics. The other girls made fun of me for being vain. After a while I refused to wear a tunic unless it was plain. Grandmother got angry, but she gave in. She still decorated her own though, right up to the end. I just wanted to fit in, not stand out."

"Well I am going to make your tunic really nice. We have all of these elk teeth and what better way to use them than to make our tunics pretty," Whispering Wind beat steadily on a dry tendon with a rock until it separated into fibers. Then she selected sinew that suited her and rolled it onto a twig. When she was finished, she returned to her tunic decorating.

"I am far more pleased with the supply of meat we have," Sage admitted. "We have enough to last the entire winter and into the spring if necessary. We have tubers and berries and fruits and plenty of small game as well. There are enough dried plants and grains to provide an interesting variety of foods. Even if the snow gets very deep, we will not starve."

"We certainly should not freeze. I cannot believe that we didn't think of making a closure for the mouth of a cave before this. It makes so much difference and with all the wood we have stored in the side cave and the food in the back one. We will be very comfortable. Your idea of putting a hide between this cave and the other keeps this part of our shelter nice and warm. We do not even have to wear our heavy clothing in here."

"And the hide across the entrance keeps out the snow and cold wind."

"Not to mention cougars and bears!"

"Actually, when I came up with the idea it was to discourage skunks if you remember!"

Whispering Wind laughed, vividly remembering the female skunk that had decided to move her family into the cave in spite of them. They had discouraged them in the end but all three had gotten sprayed before the skunks left. They had stunk for hands of days and no amount of scrubbing with soapberries had made the slightest difference. That had been just after they had taken the cave away from the cougar. It had stayed in the canyon for nearly a turning of the moon before finally looking elsewhere for a new den.

The time after moving into the canyon had been wonderful for both of them. Whispering Wind was able to put the death of her son into perspective. The fact that she had avenged him had helped. Sage had been able to put the savage beating and rape out of her immediate mind and concentrate on other things. Now was the end of the Moon of Permanent Snow. They had successfully hunted the elk, taking several of the young bulls and an older cow that had lost her calf to the cougar. The remainder of the cows and the mature bull they left alone. The elk were still in the canyon, the forage there enough for now. They had hides rolled up in the colder part of the cave to work during the winter. They had a good supply of sinew, hoofs for glue, Elkhorn for tools. Whispering Wind had insisted on removing the ivory teeth form all the elk they had killed and several skulls they have come across in their gathering.

Snow had fallen, melted and fallen again. Now there was a scattering of white, but not as deep as elsewhere. The forest above and the direction of the winds had left their canyon virtually snow free. The ridges above were windswept and icy, the burned valley was deep in snow, as were many places, but they had little need to leave the canyon. Everything they needed was here.

"I think we need to make up a stash of supplies and weapons just in case someone does enter the canyon," Whispering Wind said.

"You mean hide them down where the stream goes through the rock."

Whispering Wind nodded, "We could escape that way and no one would think to go into the water to find us. It might mean the difference between life and death. I have not forgotten the attack on you. From the cave we can see anyone entering the valley by the trail. We have learned to listen to messenger Raven. He always alerts us to anything passing along the trail, but if people come into the canyon, we are cut off from escape with the very first foot placed upon the trail. Even if we saw them and hid until they passed, it is unlikely that we could escape unnoticed. But we could easily slip into the stream and they could never track us, we would be under the rock and in the next valley before they even knew of our existence, from there we could escape and they could never find us."

"I suppose that it wouldn't hurt to be prepared. We could bury a cache of supplies, travois and a travel shelter in the burned valley and then if we needed to escape we would be prepared."

"Atlatl and darts sleeping furs: Shelter a dry change of clothes, travel food," Whispering wind named the items off on her fingers.

"We need not be caught again," Sage nodded. "I will start right now preparing. We can carry the supplies over the ridge and have them ready in no more than a pair of days."

"I will make the spare set of clothing and foot coverings. We can use the elk stomach for storing the dried food, wrap it with the sleeping furs and they with the shelter hide. Spare harness and travois poles and as you suggested, atlatl and tools."

They set to work the decorating of the tunic forgotten. Late in the night they retired to their furs, only to be up at first light and back on their project. "I have some branches which will make the atlatls," Sage dug through a stack of branches set aside from the fire food. "Here they are!" she rocked back of her heels, "There are plenty of straight shafts in these tied bundles we set to dry before the last turning of the moon. I think we should take at least one of the bundles as well."

"Set them over there with the sleeping furs that I have sorted out. "Whispering Wind pointed as she continued to cut a tunic to add to the load. "Can you knapp some extra scrapers and blades as well?"

"I already have some spares we can use," Sage dug into yet another basket. She came up with a hide container filled with blades and knives. When she couldn't sleep at night, she used her time to an advantage. She had at least a double hand of extras. "I even have a couple of extra rabbit sticks!"

By sunset the next day they had a pair of travois fully loaded with supplies. They set out early the following day and traveled up the trail, across the ridge and down into the burned valley. The only thing that they hadn't counted on was the amount of snow. Their snow walkers were strapped to their feet and before mid day they were at the cliff where the stream came from the canyon. Although the stream was unfrozen in the canyon, here it boasted a healthy layer of ice.

"I think we could use that crevasse over there," Sage pointed, "We can use those rocks to make it inaccessible to predators and the overhang should keep out the rain."

"Let's hurry!" Whispering Wind shivered, "It is getting colder and colder. If we don't hurry, we will be taking the short way to the canyon."

Sage glanced at the sky, "We will be taking the short way back any way. There is no way we can beat that storm. I would be in favor of a quick plunge into icy water followed by a fast run to the cave, than spending the remainder of the day getting back. That storm will be upon us before we get these buried."

"Then let's get started."

They worked rapidly, but as Sage said, the snow began to come thicker as time passed. Before they were satisfied with the cache, they could barely see their hands before their face. The wind was rising in force and it was getting colder every hand of time that passed. They had to use a large rock to break the ice and then stout branches to make the hole large enough for them to enter the water.

"I do not look forward with pleasure to diving into that stream and then running to the cave naked, but it is preferable to trying to walk against this storm. We cannot even see to find the trail!" Whispering Wind sighed as she began removing her mittens. Once started they lost no time, however, in stripping, making a bundle of their clothes, wrapping them as tightly as possible in their capes and with a stout stick again clearing the ice from the hole they had ready.

"I am going, now!" Whispering Wind took a deep breath and jumped into the ice water. She shrieked from the cold and then ducked beneath the water, dragging her clothing with her and disappeared. Sage, shivering from cold, followed suit. Obsidian whined but followed. By the time Sage emerged in the canyon, Whispering Wind had unwrapped her clothing and was pulling foot coverings onto wet feet as quickly as she could. Already she had her pants and tunic on. Only the outer cape had gotten wet. Only breaths of time later Sage was following her lead. Obsidian had the kindness to shake the water from her coat where it did not wet the girls. They wrung the water from their hair and picking up their wet cloaks hurried to the cave.

The wind was shrieking overhead, trees on the rim of the canyon bent over almost flat from the force. Yet only a light snow fell inside the canyon and it piled up on the opposite wall. They added wood to the fire as soon as they entered the cave and soon enough were warm and their hair was drying from the heat of the fire.

"I hope we do not have to use our escape route when the water is freezing. I am not sure how we would break the ice on the other side and we could not live long in such cold water," Sage was still shivering occasionally.

"I agree," Whispering Wind grinned, "It took all my courage to jump into that water. The only thing that made it possible was that I was already so cold. I just thought of the alternative and that made it easier."

Sage nodded and handed Whispering Wind a hot bowl of stew from the cooking bag. "Here, this will warm you up." She scooped out a portion for herself and another for Obsidian. The big dog was shivering from the cold, her thick coat still very wet. Sage called her over close to the fire and with a pinecone brushed the thick fur allowing the heat from the fire to dry it. It took a long time, but finally the dog was dry and had stopped shivering. Darkness had fallen and they had all exerted a lot of energy. The wind moaned and tugged at the hide cover, but inside the cave was warm and dry.

It was a terrible storm, raging for days. When it was over, the canyon was nearly waist-deep in snow. The elk were having a difficult time finding food now, the grass was deeply buried so they browsed on twigs and small branches until those were gone and then they left.

Meanwhile . . .

"I wonder how far back this cave goes," Sage frowned into the dark corridor.

"You want to explore it and see?" Whispering Wind questioned.

"I think that it would be a good idea. Perhaps there is another exit. If there is, we should know about it."

"How will we keep from getting lost?"

"Obsidian will know the way back. She can follow any trail."

"Just the same I think we should mark the way. I have several charcoal twigs. We can draw on the wall when we come to a place where we could get lost returning."

Sage took a hand full of the charcoal sticks and put them in her waist pouch. She made up a bundle of torches and lighted the first. Whispering Wind attached her bundle to her back and they started out. They had discussed several times the idea of exploring the back regions of the cave. Now, with the storm making them prisoners, it was an excellent opportunity. Obsidian led the way, Sage right at her heels, Whispering Wind bringing up the rear. Any time they came to a place where they had a choice of tunnels to follow they made marks on the wall to indicate the right way back.

The first passage they followed meandered for about a hand of dart casts, there were several rooms off it, and then it abruptly ended. They backtracked and started on another. This one had fresh air drawing the torchlight so they knew there was some sort of exit ahead. They passed several side passages, making their marks and then the floor angled downward and they could hear running water. Soon they found the main channel that their stream joined at the end of the canyon. It had always been something of a mystery that the water volume on the other side of the cliff was so much greater than the water exiting the canyon. Now they knew.

"This is wonderful!" Whispering Wind grinned, "Now we do not have to go out and scoop the snow away and break the ice to get water, nor do we have to melt snow. We have all the water we could possible want, right here."

"It will certainly make things easier. I always worry about leaving foot trails in the snow. Anyone up on the rim could see them and know that we are here."

"I doubt there is anyone up on the rim to see, especially in this weather, but it is still a worry. At least we do not have to break ice in order to wash."

"Let's see where that passage leads. It seems to be where the fresh air is coming from."

"I want to explore the passage across the stream also, but not now, it can wait. We need to know if there is another entrance. I want to make sure that no one can sneak up on us from behind, human or animal. I would rather not share the caves with a bear or cougar."

"Yee! What was that?" Whispering Wind struck at her hair, "Something tangled in my hair!"

"Listen!" Sage tilted her head, "Do you hear that sound?"

"What is it?" Chirping sounded all around them.

"I have no idea, duck!" Sage followed suit and shadows swept into the light of the torch and out again, "There are birds in here!"

"Not birds!" Whispering Wind shuddered, "Bats!"

"Of course," Sage laughed shakily, "Caves are the home of bats. I didn't even think of them. There is no bat dung in our part of the cave," she lifted the torch. The roof of the cave was clear, but for a few bats clinging to the surface and squeaking at the light. "There are only a few of them and little or no droppings here."

"They probably enter where the air exits. Come on, let's hurry!"

"Give me a boost. I can't reach the ledge," Whispering Wind hastened and then suggested that they try to move a large rock over so that they both could reach the ledge. With a lot of shoving, they finally got it placed so that they could crawl onto the ledge from atop it. Obsidian merely backed up and with a short sprint leaped effortlessly up. For another hand of time they wandered within the bowels of the earth and finally could see light ahead. "There it is!" Sage called out, "I can see light!"

They picked up their pace, scrambling steeply uphill now. The bat population was prolific here, guano covered the floor and the pungent odor was rank once they penetrated the area. Then they were able to see the exit. With a sigh of relief they realized that they would not be getting visitors from here, at least none which would survive the entry. There actually were bones of small creatures that had fallen into the crack far above their heads. Even so nothing larger than a small rodent or a snake could possible even fall through. The opening was perhaps a hand width, no more, although it extended for quite a length. Then the passage ended. Bats passed by them squeaking in protest against being disturbed.

"Well, this certainly shows us where this passage ends!" Sage grinned. "We need not fear of danger from here."

"Tomorrow we will explore the one beyond the stream. Perhaps there is another exit that direction," Whispering Wind replied, "I think we could possibly use part of the cave system, but certainly not all of it. I had no idea it was so extensive."

"This place is large enough to shelter an entire camp and still leave each family with its own home. With the game in these mountains and the plant food available, I am amazed that no people live here," Sage replied.

"It certainly is a wonderful place," Whispering Wind agreed. "The winter is gentle in the canyon, at least compared to winter on the plains. When blizzards like this one strike, people always freeze to death. A sheltered place like this with plenty of food stored up, winter would be easy!"

"Well, we had better head back to the home cave. It is probably getting late, although I cannot tell the time of day, except that it is light outside from that crack. I do not relish the idea of being here when these bats go out at night."

"I don't think they go out during the winter. I think they sleep. That is probably why we haven't noticed them before. See, there are only a very few moving about, or even protesting at the light."

They followed their marks and were back at the stream in less time than it took them to explore from there. "If you want to continue, I don't mind," Sage offered. "It is hard to tell if it is day or night inside the earth, but I am not tired."

"Fine, then let's cross on that ledge over there, that way we don't get wet," Whispering Wind pointed to the wall where the stream again disappeared into the earth. Above it a wide ledge led from one side to the other, merely knee-high above the floor.

Quickly they crossed and were soon following yet another passage, this one leveling out and then rising gradually. There were several smaller passages leading from it, but they were careful to mark the way. Finally it opened out into a space so wide and deep that their light did not penetrate. Here they stopped. It would be too dangerous to go farther.

"It must be huge!" Whispering Wind said.

"I want to come back here with more torches and see how big it is. We could move around the sides and stick lighted torches into cracks in the wall every-so-far and see."

"A fine idea. But now we had better head back. We have enough torches if we do not get lost on the way."

"Not a worry. Like I have already said, Obsidian could lead us, even in the dark. Her nose can find the way."

"I would rather do it with the torch light," Whispering Wind grinned, "I am not fond of the idea of trying to navigate this place in the dark."

They retraced their path and were amazed to find that it was very dark outside. They had spent the entire day exploring the cave system.

*     *     *

"I am going to bundle these torches up and take them back toward the stream," Whispering Wind followed suit and hoisted a huge bundle of prepared torches onto her back. She started off down the passage. They had carried about half of their supply of torches on down the passage already. They left piles at regular intervals, so that they could light one from another and move back and forth. It had been about a double hand of days since the storm had abated; yet they had not left the environs of the cave. Every pair of days they would trek to the stream to fill their water stomachs.

The days were spent creating the torches. There was ample pitch from the cones and sap they had collected just for this use. They also had a huge pile of dried grass that they had gathered for stuffing under their sleeping furs to make it softer. These they separated into two piles. One reserved for the original intent, the other they designated for torch material. This they separated into bundles that they soaked in animal fat. This burned slowly. Still, they did not squander their supplies. There were never torches left behind lighted and except for the exploring of the big room, which they had yet to do, such a thing was an unthinkable waste.

"Have you noticed that the water within the cave is not really cold?" Sage asked Whispering Wind one evening as them sat beside the stream filling their water stomachs. "I think I will bring some fat and ash soap and bathe and wash my hair." They were both dirty and their tunics grubby. It was far too cold outside to wash body, hair or tunics. Even though they had scrubbed with soap made of finely pounded ashes and animal fat boiled until it was a thick viscous mass, they were finding unwelcome guests in their hair and furs. Obsidian spent a lot of time lately scratching and Sage had discovered fleas while brushing her.

"You think it would be warm enough? I have though of bringing wood here to warm water for bathing. Wood is not so heavy to carry, but then I never remember."

"Well, I'm going to bring wood tomorrow, but only too warm by after. I intend to jump right in and bathe. It may be quick, scrub fast, but at least the water will wash away the fleas and I will be clean."

"If you do, then so do I!"

The next morning they gathered up the fat and ash soap and each looked like a huge deformed hunchback in the wavering light of the torch as they made their way to the underground stream. Sage, true to her word, started a small fire and then stripped and jumped in. She let out a shriek of surprise and then began to laugh, "Quick, Wind, join me!"

"What is it?" Whispering Wind was nearly undressed, but stopped and looked suspiciously at Sage.

"Nothing!" Sage smiled, "It just feels so good to be getting clean." She was already lathering up her hair. Obsidian was running along the edge of the stream whining. Then with a final glance at Whispering Wind, in she leaped.

Whispering Wind still looked dubious but she continued to undress. Finally she took a deep breath, preparing for the shock of the cold water and jumped it.

"Yee! ..." She yelped, "You could have told me the water was very warm beneath the surface!"

"Why?" Sage laughed, "It would have spoiled the surprise."

"This is wonderful!" Whispering Wind ducked beneath the surface, wetting her hair. I could stay here for hands of time. She reached for the bowl holding the soap. Sage had paddled a short distance upstream and tried to stand. She immediately sank and came up sputtering.

"It is much deeper here and the water is even warmer," she called out. I think I will swim around for a while.

"Be careful!" Whispering Wind shouted, "Do not drown!"

"I learned to swim seasons ago!" Sage answered, "Come on, it is really great!"

"Thank you, but this water is deep enough. I do not know how to swim."

"Really?" Sage looked surprised, "Then it is time that you learned. I will teach you. Swimming is easy and it can be useful if you happen to fall into a river unexpectedly."

"You can teach me to swim?"

"Certainly, it is easy. Look! Here is all you do . . ." Sage spent a hand of time showing Whispering Wind how to move her arms and kick her legs. Soon both women were frolicking happily in the water. After a time Sage crawled out and called to Obsidian. "Stand still!" she ordered, "I

need to get this soap worked completely through your fur. No more fleas
for you!" She finished and laughingly shoved the big dog back into the
water, laughing even more as the animal cavorted about in the water, her
efforts washing the soap and dead fleas from her fur. Sage leaped back
in and continued Whispering Wind's swimming lesson.

"I can't believe it! I am actually swimming!" Whispering Wind
laughed, "But my fingers are getting really wrinkled. I think perhaps we
have been in here long enough."

"You are right. But it was such a pleasure I hate to get out, besides
the air is much colder than the water."

They quickly scrambled out and hugging the fire quickly dried with
a pair of absorbent skins. Then they donned their tunics and sat on rocks
that they had positioned beside the fire. Here they combed their hair and
dried it with the heat from the fire. Then they braided it and smothered
the fire. With torch in hand they retraced the now familiar path back to
the front cave.

Once there they made an attack on the remaining unwanted 'guests'
they worked ash into their sleeping furs, then took them outside and left
them on the ledge for a time. They had lugged most of their supplies more
than a moon earlier into cold storage rooms. With little more than bare
floor left, they took branches and swept the floor clean. Luckily, they
had stored the dry grass in another place. Finally they felt that they had
eradicated their unwelcome parasites.

"I wonder why the water is so warm?" Whispering Wind mused later
as they ate their evening meal. Both women were keeping a sharp eye
out for any surviving fleas. They had shaken the ash from their sleeping
furs and spread them over fresh dried grass.

"I have heard of such places. The older gatherers sometimes visited a
hot spring. They claimed that it helped the aches in their bones. But the
people who claimed the spring demanded a 'gift' to use it. I have heard
the average 'gift' to soak in that spring was a pair of blades, or even a
whole deer hide."

"What?" That is silly. "No one can own a part of the land. Land
doesn't belong to one group or another!"

"Well, the Nut People seemed to think that spring was theirs. It was in
the center of their winter camp, so they demanded a 'gift' of anyone who

came to share it. They claimed that they had to provide protection and sometimes food. It is not much different from the bride gifts, I suppose."

"Well we do not have to pay for our warm bath at least." They both felt much better. They had even scrubbed their spare tunics and spread them out to dry so that they could soften the leather later. Obsidian was lounging sleepily in her usual place and she hadn't scratched once since returning to the living cave.

\*       \*       \*

Sage woke. It was late in the night, but not yet dawn. Something was wrong. She looked about the peaceful shelter. Whispering Wind was a shadowy hump rolled up in her furs. Obsidian lay sleeping before the entrance. Yet something had awakened Sage. Then a sharp pain at her breast caused her to draw in her breath. She frowned. The wolf mark had not alerted her in several turnings of the moon, not since the colored leaves had fallen from the trees.

The dog did not seem concerned. Nothing seemed amiss in their immediate area. "What am I supposed to do?" she muttered to the air. "It is the middle of the night. Surely you didn't wake me up to take a spirit journey?" The spot throbbed warmly. Sage frowned, sighed and crawled back into her furs. It was no good! The spot kept throbbing and keeping her awake. "All right!" She sat up and muttered. She rummaged through the basket where she had stashed the sacred relics and the dried morning glory seed. She poured water into a bowl and added the seeds and with an expert transfer she added a small hot stone from the verge of the fire. In a few heartbeats the water was hot and the brew steeping. She waited, yawning all the while. It was warn and the fire sent finger shadows climbing the wall, occasionally accenting them with sparks of exploding sap. She swallowed the brew quickly and then settled down comfortably. The fire sent fingers of fog swirling, growing thicker and thicker . . . a deep mist formed, wrapping Sage in its embrace . . .

\*       \*       \*

*I have brought you to this place once again.* The swirling mist revealed Spirit Wolf. *You know that you have been chosen to lead the people to a*

*new way of life. It is nearly time for you to begin your task. 'The People'
have been careless. They have not thanked the spirits for their gifts of food
for generations! They brag about their exploits, never giving credit where it is
due. Now The One is very angry with them. The rain does not fall upon the
plains and provide good food. Only bad plants grow and poison the animals.
The bison sicken and die. For 'The People', the life of hunting bison is over.
They must learn now to hunt the deer, bear and elk of these mountains. You
must o go to them and tell them this. Teach them the plants, the ones good
for food and to a select few, the ones good for healing. Soon, with the coming
of spring, it will be time for you to join 'The People'. You have learned the
secrets of this canyon; you have become tempered to face the rejection and
suspicion that will be directed at you. You must rise above the call to be a
part. It is not your destiny.*

"Why must I go to them? They are nothing to me! Why would they
listen to me?"

*They are your people. This is why you must go to them. It is your place
to guide, to offer the prayers and to do what you can to help these stubborn
ones. They are your blood. This is why you must help them. It is what you
were born for. We have given you the most powerful signs we have to give
you position among them. The bear teeth are a sign they will understand.
The elk teeth and the design on your tunic are of special significance. The
dreamers will understand. You will look to the ridge above this valley at
the high of the next moon. There you will see a man named Running Bison.*

"I know of him."

*He will guide you to 'The People'. You must be clever and work through
him to demand a gathering of all the people. There is a valley, far to the
north of here. Your ancestors gathered there and once a year as the 'Tribe of
The People' was united. Use your influence with Running Bison and have
him demand runners be sent to all of the camps! But before you go there with
the Bison Camp, before you even go to the Bison Camp, you must make an
offering. Then and only then, you are to go to the place of the gathering and
tell the people what I have told you.*

"Why should they believe me?"

*Bring thunder and lightning down upon their heads if they do not
believe you.*

"How do I do that?" Sage sputtered in exasperation.

*It is simple. Raise you hands and call out for thunder and lightning. It will answer, as long as you carry the sacred relics and the staff that I will provide. Go in the morning beyond the place you bathe. There in the great room you have yet to explore, is a tree root, growing down from above. You will recognize it. Cut the root and form it into a staff. Carry it with you always. Do not let it be taken from you, or disaster will befall 'The People'. The staff will call all the power of the spirits. You have been provided with the feather of the white owl. Wear it in your hair. The dreamers will understand the message it carries. Your protector will provide the rest.* The mist began to swirl.

"Wait!" Sage called out, "I have many more questions!"

Silence was her only answer.

*     *     *

With a groan Sage was ill. She blinked and looked about. The fire had burned down leaving only faint coals and the sky was beginning to lighten. She vomited again into the basket beside the opening and then crawled back into her furs. She hated these spirit trips. She never remembered a thing and she always got sick from the spirit drink.

"Sage, are you going to sleep all day?" Whispering Wind called. "I have the meal ready and it will spoil if not eaten soon. Are you ill?"

Sage groaned and crawled from her furs.

"You look awful!" Whispering Wind exclaimed. "Perhaps you should stay there, I will bring you something to eat and you just sleep and take it easy today."

"I'm all right," Sage sighed, "It was the spirit drink."

"You took spirit drink?"

"That is what one does to take a spirit journey," Sage pulled her tunic over her head and then pulled her foot coverings into place. She did not bother with the pants. Seating herself in her usual place beside the fire, she reached for a hot grain cake.

"Why did you take a spirit journey?" Whispering Wind persisted.

"Why? Because this miserable spot on my breast wouldn't let me sleep, that's why!"

"Well? What did you learn?"

"Nothing!"

"Nothing?"

"Well nothing that I can remember any way. You know how these spirit journeys are for me. I can never remember any part of them," she grimaced. "That is why I think it is foolish for me to take them. If the spirits want to inform me of something, they should just come out and do so. These spirit journeys are a waste of their time." She finished the grain cake and reached for another. "I thought today would be a good day to explore the big room. We have talked about it and talked about it. Now let's just do it!"

"All right," Whispering Wind looked at her, a bit surprised, for she had been suggesting just such a thing for days and always Sage had provided a reason to put it off yet another day. "I have everything ready. The extra torches are already across the stream and the extra soaked grass is ready."

"Then we might as well get started, hadn't we?" Sage rose pulled on her pants and swallowing the last of her tea picked up a torch and lighted it. She led the way toward the underground stream. Obsidian bounded ahead, barking in excitement.

"She loves swimming in the warm water," Their lives had been much more pleasant since discovering the wonders of the warm water. They were blissfully clean and no more fleas lived with them.

"We haven't time to swim today," Sage called after her, "We are going beyond the stream." The dog merely barked back in return and ahead she could hear the splash where the animal leaped into the water. Whispering Wind merely laughed.

"Bring that bundle of torches and we will follow this wall," Sage called, "I think this crack will do. See, I can jam the base in here and it will stay."

"I'll take the next one," Whispering Wind lighted a new torch and led off.

They followed the wall finding places to hold the torches and gradually the wall turned. "This is at least a dart cast for a strong man!" Sage looked back to where they had started, "It really is big!"

"We are starting to go across the back, but there are many more passages going from this area. I cannot believe how big these caves are. We could get lost in here and wonder for days and never find our way out. It is as well that we have been careful. Ump!" She sprawled flat on her face.

"You all right?" Sage leaned to help her up.

"I tripped," Whispering Wind said rather shakily. "I'm not really hurt. I just got the breath knocked out of me."

Sage cast the light from her torch to see what had tripped Whispering Wind. The roof of the cave had sloped lower here and a tree had sent down its roots. They had reached the floor of the cave and one had snaked out in search of water. This had tripped Whispering Wind. Sage ran her eyes along the root. "Look here!" She held the torch up, "Isn't this an odd root?" She reached out and touched it, meaning to run her hand along the smooth surface. Instead she jerked back and sucked in her breath. 'Power' surged along the nerves of her arm, sending tingles racing the nerves.

"What is it?" Whispering Wind noticed.

"I don't know," admitted Sage, "I think maybe this is some kind of 'power' thing."

"What do you mean?"

"I touched it and it sent the same feelings that the Sacred Relics do. Let me do it again, maybe it was just an accident." She reached out and laid her hand on the root. Again the tingling sensation vibrated through her body. She pulled her hand back. "It has 'power' all right and look here, this knob looks just like . . ."

"The head of a wolf," Whispering Wind finished for her in awe. "Truly, it is a 'power' object. It was probably meant for you to find. Look, we can chop it off above that knob and down here." She pointed lower. "And it will make a marvelous staff!"

"What do I need a staff for?"

Whispering Wind thought for a moment then replied, "All of the 'Chosen' carried staffs. It made them easily recognizable, even a long way off."

"Well I have no desire to be recognized, especially from a long way off!"

"Well, we had better get busy cutting it free or we will end up trapped here in the dark.

"Then no one will ever see me, with or without a staff," Sage replied dryly, as she ignited a new torch from the nearly dead one she held.

They dug their knives out of their waist pouches and while one held the torch in one hand and steadied the root with the other, the other chipped away at the root above the nodule. A second torch had to be lighted before they got it free and by then all their other torches had gone out. The meager pool of light cast by the single torch illuminated the three of them. With a final hack, the root separated and they were quick about severing the lower end.

"Let's get out of here," Whispering Wind whimpered, "We have only this torch and one more to get us back to the stream."

"Lead the way, I'm right behind you," Sage grasped the root and followed right on Wind's heels. Obsidian woofed and led them quickly, back to the stream and their stack of torches. They crossed on the ledge and hurried back to the living part of the cave.

"I think you can use a rough rock to grind that area smooth once you have it carved down," Whispering Wind suggested. I can hardly believe how much it looks like a wolf. The head leads right into the handle of the staff. A master carver could not have done it more perfectly."

"All I have to do is carve this area away, smooth it and it will make a perfect place to grasp. And the root is straight and sturdy. I can cut it here," Sage said with more enthusiasm than she had earlier.

"Do you think I dare touch it?"

"I don't know. You helped chop through the root."

"But I was careful not to touch it below the nodule."

"Well it isn't finished, so it really isn't a 'sacred' thing yet, I don't know though if it will harm you or not. I would not wish you to get hurt. What do the legends suggest about other people than the 'Chosen' using the sacred things?"

Whispering Wind thought for a time, "I don't think the stories say anything, except that sometimes the sacred things were stolen."

"Well if they didn't harm the thieves, it is hardly likely they would harm you."

"Perhaps you are right. I so would like to touch it," her voice was wistful.

Sage passed the staff over to Whispering Wind. She smiled and ran her fingers reverently along the shaft. Iit almost breathes doesn't it?"

"You can feel it?"

"Oh yes! It makes me feel wonderful!"

"Then I guess it is safe for you to handle the Sacred Relics."

"Any of them?"

"There are only the teeth, and now this," she added.

"The bear claw necklace is sacred and so are the design decorations on your summer tunic."

"The tunic?" Sage yelped is surprise. "You never said anything about that!"

"It was my gift to you. I drew the most sacred of designs, the circle of time. Each of the elk teeth is placed at special places along the circle. The last one is you, for the circle is still growing. You have not yet lived your part of the circle."

"Winter is nearly over. Running Bison will be coming for us soon," Sage said.

"Running Bison? How do you know?"

Sage shrugged, "I just know," she stated dully. "It is more of that spirit stuff. I never know how I know something. I just do."

"Running Bison . . . "Whispering Wind sighed. "Oh, how I wish he would look at me!"

"How long has it been since you saw him last?"

"Nearly three turnings of the seasons, the spring before you rescued me," Whispering Wind admitted "he has probably been mated again for a long time and he probably doesn't even remember me."

"I'm sure that he hasn't forgotten you, no man is likely to forget a woman who looks like you. But he probably figures you are dead after this long. But if he hasn't mated again, I'm sure you will have ample opportunity to get his attention on the trip back to 'The People'."

"We are going to go back to 'The People'?" Whispering Wind had a dreamy look on her face, "It has been so long since there has been more than we three. It will be strange to have others about again."

"Well, we can leave here just as soon as Running Bison arrives with the tools for the offering," Sage frowned.

"That must have been some 'journey' you took last night!" Whispering Wind sighed. "Does Running Bison know he is to come and bring these tools?"

"I certainly hope so! For I will feel all kind of a fool if he doesn't," Sage laughed, "We could sit here waiting all summer."

"If the spirits tell you he will be here, then he will come. They are never wrong!"

"Well you can watch for him. Just as soon as the snow begins to melt I have things to prepare, such as travel food, supplies and medicine. He should be here within a double hand of days."

"So soon?" Whispering Wind began to dance across the cave floor humming happily under her breath.

"Remember, he could already be mated again," Sage called after her.

"Just to look at that man is a pleasure!" Whispering Wind replied. Then she frowned. "What if he looks at you instead?" Her lower lip began to quiver. "You are my dearest friend and I would never protest if it happened that way, but my heart would always . . ."

Sage snorted rudely. "Look at me!" She shook her head. There isn't a man alive who would even know that I am breathing if you are around! Besides he is my blood relative," Sage reminded her. "Looking is forbidden among blood."

"Ah! That is right!" Whispering Wind began to smile again, a dreamy, far away look in her eyes. Sage shook her head.

The next morning Sage awoke to an unusual sound; water, dripping beyond the cave opening. Quickly she threw back her furs and padded barefooted to the opening and loosened the hide cover. Sticking her head out she studied the steadily falling rain. Sometime during the night it must have begun. Nearly half the snow covering the floor of the canyon had been melted. The air outside was moist and warm. The snow would be gone quickly at this rate.

"I think that perhaps I should prepare for us to leave while you finish that staff." Whispering Wind stated as they munched on seed cakes and drank their morning tea.

"You are certainly anxious to be away from here," Sage remarked. "I could begin to feel that you have been unhappy with my company, or is it perhaps the thought of Running Bison which makes you impatient?"

"Perhaps," was Wind's smiling reply.

"Well, I have nearly finished the staff. It only requires a bit more rubbing with a fine stone."

"How can that be? You only started working on it yesterday!"

"I found sleep difficult," admitted Sage. "I worked on it during the night."

"Then you must be tired."

"No," Sage shook her head, "I feel wonderfully refreshed, actually. It must be the effect of that staff. The teeth do the same thing."

"I wonder if your summer tunic will have the same effect?" Whispering Wind mused.

"I certainly hope not!" Sage protested. "I really have hesitation about that tunic, Wind. I hate the idea of standing out among others. I would much rather blend in."

Whispering Wind began to laugh. "Only you, Sage, could come up with so ridiculous a statement. There is no way you will ever blend in. You are of the line of the 'Chosen'. You have been marked by Wolf Spirit, carry the Sacred Relics and wear the teeth of the most savage beast known to 'The People'. Now you carry that staff as well. We have only to attach that white owl feather to your braid and you will be recognized in a breath."

"What if I don't want to do this?" Sage questioned. "What if I just want to hide the teeth, the bear claws and not wear that tunic? What if I hide the staff? Why can't I walk into the camp merely as your friend?"

Whispering Wind studied her for several heartbeats of time. "You are serious, aren't you? You really don't want all the attention which your station will bring to you?"

Sage shook her head, "Look at it from my point of view, Wind. I don't know these people; they don't know me. I would really resent some stranger walking into my camp and proclaiming to be the answer to everyone's prayers. I would refuse to believe in the truth of her claims. In fact, I would be inclined to drive her from the camp!"

"I see what you mean," Whispering Wind said thoughtfully. "Perhaps you are right. We will see what Running Bison has to say. He will council us wisely."

Sage merely snorted. She finished her grain cake and handed the staff to Whispering Wind. "What do you think? Will a little more rubbing on this area finish it?"

Whispering Wind ran her fingers over the area, "It is nearly as smooth as the rest," she remarked. "But I do agree that it wouldn't hurt to rub it more." She rose and went to the mouth of the cave. "Do you think it will rain all day?" Sage had left the tie loose. Whispering Wind stuck her head out and watched the steady downpour. "Every trail in these mountains will be a mudslide. It would be impossible to travel."

"Spring is always wet. This rain has just melted the snow faster than it would have other wise. But we don't have to travel the trails, so what is the worry?"

"Oh, nothing . . ." Whispering Wind replied wistfully. "I just wondered if . . ."

"If Running Bison were on his way yet?" Sage finished for her.

Whispering Wind smiled, "do you think so?"

Sage shook her head, "I have no idea. According to what I said yesterday, it will be at least a double hand of days before he arrives. I have no idea where he is coming from, so I have no idea if he is under way yet. You have waited three turnings of the seasons so surely you can wait another half turning of the moon!"

"I will try."

*　　*　　*

Running Bison sat hunkered over a small fire. It was all he could afford. There was not fuel to squander. The people had suffered greatly this winter. The bison had traveled south earlier than usual; robbing them of the opportunity to have a last hunt just as the ground froze. Crooked Spirit had advised them to hunt earlier, but as usual the headman and hunters had ignored him. Now a hand of infants and children had died. Nearly as many adults had walked the wind. They had holed up in a valley at the edge of the plains, but even there they had not been treated kindly by the weather. It had been suggested that they travel south following the bison to a kinder place, but the headman had decided to stay. They had been trapped by deep snow right from the start. Hunters had found a few straggling bison. These had kept them from total starvation. A few deer and elk had helped and in the end they had eaten most of the dogs. He had gone out alone with his pair of dogs and provided food for the camp, or they would have eaten that pair as well.

Hunting Badger may have been a great hunter in his prime and Running Bison knew that he had been, for he could remember the headman as such. Now, however, Hunting Badger refused to heed council from anyone. Running Bison had made suggestions from time to time, it had gotten him the task of seeking out Clover Blossom and Coyote the first time and on the next he had been sent to find the 'Chosen' himself. Actually, he had not told Hunting Badger that he in fact knew the location of the young woman. He had instead, sworn Prairie Grass to secrecy. Running Bison could not say just why he had done this, but some inner feeling had urged him to do so. When he had returned from the mountains, he and Prairie Grass had traveled far beyond the camp to the 'place of stone', a place he had only vaguely heard of and here they had gathered enough stone to craft a plentiful supply of the finest tools 'The People' could remember. Crooked Spirit had selected a hand of the finest and Antler Dancer, the most talented knapper of the camp had been instructed to make from these, some of the most beautiful tools Running Bison had ever seen. The point, a ceremonial killing tool, was crafted with finer flaking than any he had ever seen. The knives and blades were equally wonderful. He had them now, carefully wrapped in a special hide, tanned from a really fine wolf pelt. It was packed away on his travois.

He studied the sky. It would rain soon. That at least would melt the snow. Then it would be time. He glanced around the camp. Everyone was asleep. He had sat here musing for far longer than he realized. With a sigh he rose and went to his shelter, Traveler, his trusted hunting dog and Brown, the one that pulled the travois by his side. He took the pair of them everywhere he went, for fear of some desperate member of the camp killing them for food. He pulled his sleeping robe about his shoulder and happily let his mind drift, as he always did just before sleeping. "Whispering Wind . . ." he sighed.

# CHAPTER 6

Whispering Wind, you are going to wear your eyes out!" Sage protested. "You have been watching that trail all day long for over a hand of days! All the watching in the world will not bring them any sooner. Brother Raven will alert us to anything entering the canyon. The racket he makes could be heard clearly all the way to the burned valley"

"I know," Whispering Wind sighed, dropped the hide back into place and returned to the fire. Her woe-begotten expression was mixed with anxiety. "But it seems to be taking him ever so long to find us," she settled on a log across from Sage. "You don't suppose he got lost and missed the canyon, do you?"

"I am sure that the spirits will bring him straight and true. The ground has barely had time to dry enough for a person to travel over the trails. If there are any streams of any size between him and this canyon, he will have to wait until they can be crossed."

"Listen! Do you hear that? Raven!" Whispering Wind leaped to her feet and rushed to the cave opening. "It's them!" She yelped, "There's a pair of dogs with him and one other man, I think it is Prairie Grass, yes, that is who it must be. Come on!" She ran from the cave and shot up the trail to meet the men. Sage froze; suddenly a cold chill ran through her body. Her wolf mark began to throb painfully and she began to shudder. Something was terribly wrong. She leaped to her feet, cleared the cave entrance with a single bound and chased after Whispering Wind, but she was too late. Whispering Wind realized her mistake and skidded to a halt a long dart cast from the men. She wheeled around and fled back down the trail, the pair of hunters right on her heels. They captured her in a few quick leaps and knocked her to the ground. Sage watched helplessly from concealment and Obsidian, growling, tugged her deeper into hiding. Right now there was nothing she could do for her friend but hide and wait for an opportunity. Stealthily she inched back up the path to the cave, slipping inside just as the hunters, shoving Wind before them, passed from sight beneath the ledge.

Quickly Sage grabbed her sleeping furs and the Sacred Bundle, staff and a hand full of torches. Calling softly to Obsidian, she slipped beyond the rear hide and deeper into the cave, letting the dog lead her through the dark. She hoped that the men hadn't killed Whispering Wind and that she had enough sense to realize that Sage had removed all traces of her own presence and that of the dog. If they presumed Wind was alone, Sage would have a much better chance of helping her. She tightened her grip on the sleeping robe, containing her atlatl and darts and some food. When she could hear the underground stream, Sage halted and dumped her burden. In the dark she felt about for what she needed. With a knowing grip her hand closed automatically around the familiar shaft of the atlatl. She found the darts next to it.

She held tightly to Obsidian's fur and softly urged the big dog back along the passage they had just traversed so quickly, only this time they barely crept along. Finally she could hear the hunters laughing and joking in a language she could not understand. In the background she heard Wind's soft sobs. Clearly these were not Running Bison and Prairie Grass. Whispering Wind had made a terrible mistake, Sage only hoped she was not about to pay a heavy price for it.

Sage silently pressed her body against the cold rock of the cave wall and peered through the crack between the hide and the wall. Whispering Wind lay in a whimpering heap on her sleeping furs. Already her face was swelling from the brutality of her capture. The hunters were gorging themselves on the remains of the women's mid day meal. These were not hunters in the true sense. They were dirty and smelled strongly of body odor, a state in which no hunter went in search of game. They were also disgustingly unmannerly, hardly chewing their food. It dribbled down their chins and they just kept stuffing more into their mouths. At least they had left their dogs outside. Sage signed silently. Dogs would have smelled

Obsidian for certain and probably Sage as well. So far luck was on her side. She clutched her atlatl and darts tighter. One man had finished eating now and turned his attention to Whispering Wind.

"No! Please!" She pleaded, "I am no threat to you! Take the food, take the supplies, but please, make me no harm."

The hunter merely laughed. Even badly battered, Whispering Wind was beautiful! He reached out and grabbed her by the front of her tunic. With a mighty yank he burst the lacing and Whispering Wind was suddenly exposed to the pair of men. They both were upon her now, all thoughts of food swept from their minds by her tender beauty. Outside dogs began to bark, but the men either did not hear them or simply ignored them. The first man had Whispering Wind by the hair now, kneeling above her head with a sharp blade at her throat. The other was hastily avoiding her kicking feet. They were laughing lewdly as they wrestled to subdue her. Finally the one at her feet got hold of her pants and jerked them off, following through by forcing himself between her legs. He grunted and pulled aside his breechclout, exposing an erect and ready male member. Whispering Wind moaned. Outside the dogs became quiet. The men were breathing heavily now. The one astride of Whispering Wind was facing Sage. She watched steadily as he started to lower himself onto Wind. Obsidian was ready to attack, held back only by Sage's hand on her head. Slowly she brought back her arm, aiming her dart at the man's heart. She was poised to cast.

The man made a soft gurgling sound; a look of utter surprise crossed his face and then was slowly replaced by the blankness of death. He slowly crumpled onto the prone woman; a dart driven directly into his back. A pair of men appeared in the cave opening and the other man quickly let Whispering Wind free and began inching away from them. In a breath he also was dead.

Whispering Wind alternated between struggling to free herself of the burden of the dead hunter and to cover herself from the sight of these new men. The bearded one stepped quickly forward and with hardly any effort jerked the inert body off Whispering Wind. She pulled her sleeping fur around her nakedness and sat weeping. Her eyes were both blackened and her lip was cut and swollen, but otherwise, she had been very lucky.

Sage had no doubt as to the identity of the bearded man when Wind threw herself wailing into his arms.

*     *     *

"Sage! Are you there?" Whispering Wind finally called out softly, "They are here. Come out and meet Running Bison and Prairie Grass."

Sage pulled the hide aside and stepped into the living area of the cave, Obsidian at her side.

She and the big man studied each other for several heartbeats and then Running Bison nodded and turned to Prairie Grass. "Our search is at an end." He returned his study to Sage, "You are the grand-daughter of Clover Blossom, are you not?"

Sage nodded.

"You could have saved us all a lot of trouble had you not fled from the gatherers camp. I am sorry that you did not get the opportunity to say a proper goodbye to Clover Blossom. I am sure that you were very close to her."

Again Sage nodded.

"Are you sure this is the one?" Prairie Grass whispered to Running Bison. "She doesn't look like much."

"On the contrary, she looks exactly right," Running Bison replied and then turning back to Sage, continued, "You know why we are here?"

"We have been expecting you. That is why Whispering Wind went too hastily out to greet you. She should have waited to be sure of your identity first."

"We have been following that pair for some time, hoping to reach them before they discovered this canyon and the pair of you. We knew we were close and it is just as well that we left caution to the wind and came running the last few fingers of time."

"I had better go check on their dogs," Prairie Grass excused himself, "Don't want them to die of the clubbing I gave them. We need all the dogs we can get." He backed, ill at ease, from the cave and disappeared. Whispering Wind had located her summer tunic newly finished and modestly turning her back to them dropped the bed fur and pulled it over her head.

Sage went to the fire and filled a bowl with water, then added some medicinal herbs to it and a small hot stone from the fire. The stone sizzled as it touched the water and soon the bowl smelled of the herb. Then Sage got a soft rabbit skin and began to carefully treat Whispering Wind's injuries.

"Who were those men?" She asked.

"I think they were outcasts," Running Bison replied, "There was only the pair of them. I sneaked up on their camp one night, but I could not really understand them. They were making a lot of effort to hide their trail. My Traveler kept on their track, however and I did become anxious when I realized they were headed straight toward you. That is when we threw caution to the wind and began to run."

"It is a good thing that you did," Whispering Wind said in quivering voice. "Had you not I know what my fate would have been."

Running Bison shook his head, "it would have been no different." He stated evenly. "Your friend here and her helper," he nodded toward Obsidian, "Were already in position to eliminate those men. We merely got there ahead of them."

Whispering Wind looked at Sage and then smiled, "Yes, Sage would have saved me." She said evenly, "she is . . ."

Sage frowned.

"Powerful?" Finished Running Bison.

Sage snorted rudely and turned, "I might as well go and get my things. I left them beside the stream." She took up a torch, lighted it and quickly vanished behind the hide, Obsidian by her side. She trotted down the passage turning over the events of the day so far. It had gone from peace, to terror and now to an uneasy feeling she couldn't quite place. This man made her feel uneasy. Not in any way related to trust, she was certain he would give his life to protect them, but something about him . . . it was almost animal magnetism. "Huh!" She muttered. "I have been listening too much to Wind. If I am not careful, she will have me looking at the man! That can't be!" She shuddered and turned her mind too more pressing issues.

She found the bundle of furs where she had hastily dumped them. Scooping them up into her arms she started back then stopped. She lowered the bundle to the passage floor, removed the Sacred Relics and the staff and tucked them into a dark niche a short distance from the stream. Then she returned to the living cave with the remainder.

Prairie Grass was leading a pair of dogs into the cave as she arrived. They cowered from him and whined, pulling away as far as possible in their harnesses. Obsidian went over to them and both sank to their bellies and tucked their tails. The big dog sniffed and then touched each of them and then lost interest and wandered over to check on Whispering Wind. Prairie Grass led the animals to a place on the far side of the cave and tied them to a stake he drove into the floor of the cave. Already Traveler and Brown were settled near the fire.

Prairie Grass also fetched their backpacks and the supplies from their travois. He handed Running Bison's gear to him and settled his own over near the new dogs.

Meanwhile, Sage had made hot tea and was warming up the remainder of the stew that the raiders had left in the cooking hide. There was enough for a meal. The men were hungry. They had not stopped to eat for fear the raiders would reach the girls before them. Both nodded in appreciation as they ate the stew and hot grain cakes. Sage had added salt to the food, realizing that people living on the plains found it a treat. Whispering Wind had been amazed that she used it in almost every meal, for The People hoarded it and used it quite sparingly. She also added other things for seasoning. There were tubers, mushrooms and wild carrots and wild celery in it as well. She had also included some dried leaves of sage.

"I have never tasted better stew!" Prairie Grass smacked his lips, "These cakes are excellent as well."

"Sage constantly prepares food in wonderful ways!" Whispering Wind commented. "I am always amazed at the taste. For example these grain cakes; she has added ground up nuts to them as well as honey to make them sweet."

Both men nodded and continued to eat. "There is more tea if you want it," Sage offered, "And I can give you dried fruit as well."

"What is that?" Prairie Grass asked.

"These are small fruits that grow on trees. They are tart, but sweet. They also save well. I also have a few dried berries from last summer, but they have lost most of their flavor. These fruits will surprise you." She went and found the basket containing the dried apples and scooped some out. She added them to a skin of boiling water to which she had already added honey. Soon the whole cave began to smell of the cooking fruit. When it was done, she served the men and Whispering Wind, then sat and joined them.

"My father," Whispering Wind asked haltingly, "He is well?"

Running Bison nodded. "His mate did not survive the winter however for she died in childbirth along with the baby. Thunder Cloud will be glad to see you. He has missed you dearly and it was difficult for him, not knowing if you were alive or dead. He was much relieved when I was able to tell him that you were alive and safe. He is waiting anxiously for your return."

"He knows that I am with Sage?"

Running Bison shook his head. "No one but Crooked Spirit knows of Sage. I only told the camp that I had discovered where you were and was fetching you from the people you had been living with. I made no mention of Sage." He looked at her a bit uncomfortably. Sage stared levelly back at him and finally he said. "I did not know how to tell them how I knew about you."

"Sage wants to live with the camp for a time before letting them know who she is," Whispering Wind sighed, "She is not at all happy about this 'Chosen' thing."

"I don't blame her," Running Bison replied, "I would not care to be in her place. It is a fine thing when the spirits smile on the people and all is well, but the first sign of trouble and they forget. It is all someone's fault and Sage will be the one to blame. I just hope the spirits accept the offering and bring the bison back and begin to make life easier for 'The People'."

"The bison will not return, at least not in their lifetime," Sage said quietly, "No number of spirit offerings will change that."

"No bison?" Prairie Grass questioned open mouthed.

Sage shook her head, "Bison are not for 'The People' any longer."

"But . . .! Without bison, what will we eat?"

Whispering Wind answered him. "What you have just finished eating. They are to move into these mountains and learn to use plants and to live on small game and plants."

Both men shook their heads. "That will never happen!" Prairie Grass stated emphatically. "Not as long as Hunting Badger is the leader of the camps! 'The people' will never leave the plains and eat plants!"

"They will," Sage replied softly, "But it will take time, more time than some of them have. There will be death before they understand the ways of the spirits."

"This is the message you bring?" Running Bison questioned.

"I don't bring any message," Sage protested, "Words just come from my mouth. I have no idea what they are until I say them." She frowned, "It just happens! I don't hear spirits!"

She rose and walked into the shadows. "I will make the offering for you. You take Wind back to her family. I am perfectly happy right here. Obsidian and I can make it on our own."

"I can't do that," Running Bison replied evenly. "We need the offering, yes, but it is just as important that you return to 'The People' with the Ancient Relics. They belong to 'The People'."

"According to my grandmother, they belong to me. Well, not exactly belong to me, but I am responsible for them. Someone killed my mother to get them. They are safer here."

"There has been nothing but one disaster after another ever since Clover Blossom stole the Relics and vanished. Nothing is going to change until they are back among 'The People'!" Running Bison stated stubbornly.

"What makes you think their return will make things better? Perhaps the spirits are angry with 'The People' for killing the Keeper! Just maybe, no number of Relics would change anything for 'The People'! It is possible that if the spirits are sending messages that it is 'The People' who need to change. If the spirits starve them long enough, plague them with enough sickness and bad luck, maybe then 'The People' will listen to their dreamers. Maybe then the spirits will smile upon 'The People' again. Either way, it has nothing to do with me!" Sage backed deeper into shadow.

"You will return with us," Running Bison stated firmly. "You will bring the Ancient Relics and you will show them to The People."

"You may take me back as a prisoner, but not willingly!" Sage grated out.

"Let's stop arguing!" Whispering Wind rose. "I am tired, my head hurts and I am in need of rest. Can't we talk about this in the morning?"

"There is nothing to talk about," Running Bison said stubbornly. "Sage will make the offering in the morning, then we will leave this canyon and return to The People'. I will agree, she need not disclose that she is the 'Chosen' until people get to know her, but that is as far as I will go."

"You can go as far as you want to," Sage muttered under her breath. "No matter how far it won't be too far to suit me!"

"Did you say something?" Running Bison smiled.

"Only 'good night'," Sage replied. She gathered up her furs and spread them near Whispering Wind. Running Bison spread his near the opening to the cave. Sage glared in his general direction. He was making absolutely sure she did not escape during the night.

The sun was just rising above the mountains to the east when they finished the quick meal the women prepared. "Now we will go to the place where you intend to make the offering," Running Bison stated. "I have the tools right here." He patted a well-wrapped packet that he retrieved from his backpack.

"Where do you suggest the offering be made?" Questioned Sage stubbornly.

"I am quite certain that you are aware of the proper place," He replied evenly.

"Not at all," she shrugged, "Why would I know?"

"Sage, stop being difficult!" Whispering Wind stomped her foot, "You know as well as I do that they should be made at the underground stream!"

"Underground stream?" Prairie Grass repeated. "You mean we have to go deeper into this cave?" He shifted nervously from foot to foot. "It is dark in there!"

"Of course it is," Sage smiled to herself, "And there are bats!"

"Bats!" He shuddered, "I hate bats!" He looked hopefully toward Running Bison. "No reason for all of us to go there is there? I would be more than happy to stay here and guard the dogs."

Running Bison frowned, "If you wish," he nodded. "But the rest of us had better be on our way. Is it far to this underground stream?"

"Not far," Whispering Wind replied. "Merely a short walk."

"Fine, I will take the torch, you lead the way," He took Sage by the arm and started to urge her toward the passage. Obsidian growled deep in her throat and bared her teeth. Running Bison was momentarily taken back and released Sage. She in turn jerked her tunic sleeve back into place and glared at him. Then sticking her nose up in the air, she stalked after Whispering Wind down the passageway. Running Bison frowned and then sighed. *This woman is going to be more trouble than I have anticipated.* He thought to himself. Sage merely smiled with satisfaction.

Whispering Wind trotted with assurance toward the underground stream. Sage and Obsidian followed. Sage was taking note of everything along the way. She smiled to herself and took a better grasp on Obsidian's fur. She had a plan!

"Listen! Do you hear the water?" Whispering Wind called to Running Bison.

"I hear it," he replied, "It sounds to be a good sized stream."

"Oh, it is more than that!" Whispering Wind replied. "It is the most wonderful place! The water is actually warm, even in the coldest of weather."

"A heated spring?" He stopped.

"Oh, I don't know if it is a spring!" Whispering Wind considered, "We thought it comes from deeper in the mountain."

"Perhaps it does. I have heard of such places. They are wonderful for the old ones the water just seems to pull the stiffness out of their bones."

Whispering Wind led the way to the edge of the spring. Here Running Bison knelt and carefully unwrapped the special tools for the offering. He had a rabbit skin and an antler baton as well. These he handed first to Sage. She nervously grasped the rabbit skin and then accepted the unfamiliar baton. She turned the tool over and over in her hands anxiously. Then he handed her the first of the sacred tools for the offering. Sage accepted the tool. She almost dropped it! A warm tingling ran up her arm from the smooth stone. She held it closer to the torch and admired the wonderful workmanship of the tool. No knapper of the gatherers had the ability to craft anything close to the beauty of this. It was as long as two joints and as wide as a pair of fingers and nearly thin enough to show light through. (Agate Basin Point-Tool Plate) The flaking on the stone was so finely accomplished that it seemed that only a single flake crossed the surface. Along either face a long thin flake had been struck from the base. She turned it over in her hand and against her will slowly stepped to the edge of the stream. She lifted the tool into the air and closed her eyes. Words seemed to flow effortlessly from her lips. The prayer was so beautiful the others held their breath. Then with a fluid move she wrapped it in the rabbit fur and gave it a single swift rap with the baton. A dull 'clink' sounded as the object broke in two. She opened her eyes and removing the pieces from the skin cast them into the stream. Other tools followed: more Sacred Points, scrapers, blades, knives, awls and gravers, all the finest material and craftsmanship. Sage made sure that she took her time. She kept a knowing eye on the torch. Just at her feet lay the only extra torches, a hand of them. When she judged that it was about to flicker out and they need light another, with a quick kick she sent them into the stream. She grasped Obsidian's fur and urged her toward the bat area of the cave.

Whispering Wind yelped, "Sage! Why? We cannot find our way back in the dark! Obsidian will have to lead us."

Running Bison was a quicker thinker, he understood exactly what Sage was doing, but before he could grab her arm, the torch flickered out and they were plunged into darkness. Whispering Wind moaned; Sage smiled to herself and nudged Obsidian around them and toward the ledge. Without a sound, or at least one which could be heard above Wind's fretting, the pair of them crossed and Sage let the big dog guide her deeper inside the cave. Obsidian seemed to understand exactly what she wanted. With sure steps she led Sage all the way to the big room. It seemed that something beyond the big dog urged her on. The spot on her breast had changed from a gradually mounting pain to a warm gentle throb. Gradually the sounds of Whispering Wind and Running Bison muted and faded away.

Sage had investigated the big room on two separate occasions without Whispering Wind. She knew exactly where she was going. They would never find her here and she had stashed enough food for a hand of days if necessary. "Take me to the tree root," She whispered to Obsidian. The dog whined and stepped forward. When she stopped, Sage reached out in the utter darkness and felt the smooth surface of the root beneath her hand. She knelt and wrapped her arms around the dog. "Lead them off," she whispered. "But do not go far. Come to me when it is safe." Then she reached up and felt for the handholds she knew to be along the root. Up and up she climbed. When she reached the ceiling, she inched along the root and then up again as the roof rose. Near the high ceiling the root had developed into a large knot, one which was hollow on the upper side. From beneath, with only torchlight it would be impossible for anyone to see the knot, for it blended with the rock surrounding it and within its nest, she was totally hidden. Here in this safe place, she had stored her cache of food and several spare torches. There was even an extra sleeping fur. With a satisfied smile into the friendly darkness she settled down to wait.

Back at the stream, Running Bison swore soundly. She had outsmarted him. He had expected her to try to bolt, but not now, not deep inside the earth, trapping them all in darkness. "You can quit your game now!" he called angrily. "You are frightening Whispering Wind and I am not amused with your childish pranks!"

"She isn't here," Whispering Wind whimpered, "Sage knows these caves as well as I do and with Obsidian to guide her, she can move anywhere without our knowing where she is. It will take us hours to return to the living cave in this darkness, even if we can find the passage way."

"Are there no more torches?" Running Bison asked in exasperation.

"No," Wind whimpered, "We did not wish to waste them, so we only had a small supply and as you saw, Sage kicked them into the stream."

"Where does it go?"

"What?"

"The stream. Where does it go from here? Does it exit the mountain any where near here?"

"I . . . I don't know," Whispering Wind whimpered. "We never thought to try to follow it. It joins the stream from the canyon in the burned-out valley, but that is some distance from the mouth of the cave."

"Then there is no way we can follow the stream out of this cave?"

"I don't know . . ." she replied sniffling.

"Then we had better find the passage leading back. Here, take hold of this strap," he took her hand in the dark and placed a length of leather in it. "I am going to get down on my hands and knees and feel for the stream until it meets the wall. From there I can lead us to the passage and we can follow it to the outside. Then I am arming myself with a large supply of torches and I promise you, when I find her, Sage will get the sharp edge of my tongue for this trick." He followed his words with actions and within a few fingers of time later he grunted and rose to his feet. "Here is the passage we entered from. Can you lead us out from here?"

"I....I think so," Whispering Wind responded.

As they moved, painfully slowly along, feeling the wall of the passage with their fingers, Running Bison called out in a loud voice, then whistled, then called again. Finally, far ahead, a bark answered his call and in mere heartbeats, his hunting dog, Traveler, reached them. The remainder of their journey was much quicker.

"What happened?" Prairie Grass exclaimed, "Where is the other one?"

"She escaped!" Running Bison grated through clinched teeth, "But not for long! Is there another exit from this cave?" He looked to Whispering Wind.

She nodded, "But nothing larger than a bat could escape that way."

"Then she is still in there," he nodded back into the darkness. "We have a choice. We can set Traveler to track her, or we can wait here until she gets tired of playing her childish game and comes out."

"I'd rather wait!" Prairie Grass paled. "We aren't in any big hurry, are we? I mean, what difference does a few days make for our return?"

"You are right, of course, but I would prefer action to waiting. You two can stay here, but I am going to go back in there, well armed with torches and Traveler. You watch, we will find her and she will regret her actions. It is time she realized that her wishes are not the only ones to be considered."

"Let me fix you a packet of food," Whispering Wind offered, "You will get very hungry if you plan to explore the whole cave. It will take you a number of days to do so."

"You are right," Running Bison sighed and sat glumly on the rock he had more or less taken as his seat. Traveler whined and licked his hand. "Why did she do it?" he questioned Whispering Wind. "You know her better than anyone. Why did she run away?"

Whispering Wind considered. "Sage is afraid," she replied. "She is very nervous about standing out in a group. Ever since she was a small child she has tried to blend in and disappear amongst the crowd. To expect her to actively step forward and assume a leadership position is not practical. She will not do it! She would rather live the rest of her life alone."

"But 'The People' need her!" protested Prairie Grass.

"'The People' are strangers to Sage. Remember it was one of them who killed her mother. She has no reason to trust them. I am the only person she has ever known besides her grandmother who lived as a member of The People. She took a long time to tell me that she was actually born to them. No, that approach will not convince her."

"Then she can hand over the Sacred Relics and go her own way!" Running Bison was getting irritated with the whole undertaking. "She made the offering. Perhaps that will be enough. Maybe we should let her stay here alone and when we need her to make an offering, we could come to her. It is far better knowing where she is than having to scour these mountains every time we need her."

"But I don't want to leave her here alone!" Whispering Wind protested. "She is my friend, why we are closer than blood sisters! If she is to remain, then I will stay with her."

"What of your family?"

"My father has gotten along without me for this long. He will just have to find another mate to do the women's chores. Regardless, I would not return to his shelter. He allowed his mate to abuse me. That wipes out any obligation on my part to look after him."

"So what are we going to do?" Prairie Grass asked.

"We will give her some time to consider her position. She is alone in the dark that cannot be pleasant for her. The only way out is through this opening. Eventually she will get tired of playing games, or will get hungry. So I guess the answer to your question is that we will wait!"

"You are sure this is the only way out?" Prairie Grass frowned.

"No, I am not sure, but what other choice do we have? Whispering Wind has assured us that these caves are quite extensive and Sage knows them better than we do. She has that 'dog' of hers and I'm sure 'she' will lead quite ably in total darkness."

Whispering Wind nodded, "Obsidian is very protective of Sage."

Running Bison seemed to understand, "The dog is her protector. Every 'Chosen' has had such an animal, although until now they have always been wolves."

"Obsidian is a wolf, she was just raised as a dog," Whispering Wind replied. "But you are right all the legends speak of these animals. I do not see, however, what good waiting for Sage to come out will do. She will not change her mind. Besides, what you are asking her to do would take a lot of courage from even the bravest of hunters. What you really need to do is win her confidence. I think that if you proved that you would protect her, she would be more agreeable with accompanying us all back to the camp."

"How do I do that?" Running Bison asked in exasperation. "She hasn't given me much of a chance to prove any thing!"

"Well for one thing, making demands of her before you even let her get to know you isn't going to help." Whispering Wind sighed, "We will just have to take things slowly. But first of all, we will just have to wait until Sage comes out of the cave. That could take days. She could even get lost in there!" Wind fretted.

"Not with that dog!" Running Bison snorted. "I'll bet anything that while I was crawling about on hands and knees trying to find our trail, she was holed up somewhere snug just laughing at us!"

"Sage wouldn't do that!" Whispering Wind protested.

"Well she certainly would and did, leave her best friend alone in the dark, unable to find her way out."

Whispering Wind shook her head, "No, if we had truly gotten in trouble, Obsidian would have led us out. We have talked many times about what we would do if we got trapped in the dark."

"Oh and what answers did you come up with?" Running Bison leaned forward. "Think, Whispering Wind! It could help us understand where to look!"

"I would look in the big room," Whispering wind replied. "We explored it some, but not completely."

"Big room?" Running Bison frowned, "Where is that? You have not mentioned it before."

"No, well you hardly gave me a chance!" Whispering Wind replied. "It is beyond the stream."

Running Bison shook his head, "She couldn't have gone there. We would have heard her in the water."

"No. There is a ledge. It would have been quite simple for her to simply walk around us and cross. We practiced crossing the ledge in the dark, from the other direction, several times."

"Wonderful!" Prairie Grass muttered, "Now what do we do?"

"Nothing different," Running Bison replied. "We sit here on our backsides, growing increasingly irritated and wait for her to get tired of her childish prank." He frowned, "In the meantime, however, we can search for the Sacred Relics. She will be much more agreeable to going with us if we have them," he grinned.

"She keeps them in that basket over there," Whispering Wind pointed, a twinge of disloyalty bothering her.

Running Bison quickly searched the basket, finally dumping the contents onto the floor. A number of items tumbled out, but not the distinctive, familiar packet.

"That's funny, she has always kept them there," Whispering Wind bit her lip, then winced in pain. "What could she have done with them?" She mused . . . "Oh!" she smiled, "I'll bet when she hid from 'them." She nodded toward the dead bodies. "She probably took them with her. I would say they are stashed somewhere beyond." She nodded toward the yawning black opening of the inner cave.

"Well, at least I intend to make an effort to retrieve them. She couldn't have had much time. They weren't at the stream, which means that she stashed them somewhere between here and there. Traveler, come here," he called his dog. "Take a good smell of the container. That's it!" The dog looked at him, wagged his tail and began sniffing. The trail led directly to the passage. Running Bison grinned at the others, picked up a hand full of torches, lighted one and followed Traveler encouraging the dog on the trail.

\*     \*     \*

Obsidian had difficulty getting her teeth to grip on the deer hide packet. It was wedged far down into the crack, just about beyond her grasp, but with some effort, she succeeded. She trotted down the passageway toward the front of the cave and then detoured down one side passage, whipped around and down another, cris-crossing the corridor back and forth. Then she made her way toward the bat room. Finally, she backtracked again and careful to keep the packet above water eased into the stream and let the water carry her beneath the wall, beyond where any human had explored. There she climbed from the water and lay the packet beside the staff. Then she waited and listened.

Traveler led Running Bison down the passage. Then he stopped, whined and turned down a side corridor. He stopped, raised his nose and sniffed. Puzzled he returned to the main passage. He smelled again, wagged and led off down a different passage. Again, and again he stopped, turned and backtracked. Finally, he sighed and lay down. He could not follow the trail. "So, she is smarter than I thought!" Running Bison muttered. "It's all right, boy, you have just been bested by an expert. There is no way Sage could have laid such a trail, but that blasted 'dog' of hers could!"

Not far away, Obsidian thumped her tail silently against the stone floor and smiled into the darkness.

"Now I'm really mad! I'm going to search that big room until I find her!" Running Bison muttered to himself as he headed back toward the mouth of the cave. Almost before he was beyond sound, Obsidian was back in the water. She paddled under the stone wall and crawled onto dry rock beyond the stream. It took her only fingers of time to reach the root. She didn't bark, but she scratched at the root to get Sage's attention.

Soon the root vibrated as the girl climbed down. "What is it?" she whispered. Obsidian took her arm and tugged. "No, it is safer here!" Again Obsidian tugged. "All right, let me get my things." Sage scurried back up the root dumped everything into the sleeping robe and eased sure-footed back down. "I hope you know what you're doing!" she whispered.

Obsidian thumped her tail against Sage's leg. When they came near the stream, Sage stopped. "We are too close!" she protested. Obsidian merely led her to the water and nudged her. "Oh, all right! Just let me bundle this stuff so it doesn't get wet." Sage quickly knotted a thong securely around the opening of the bundle, then trusting Obsidian she entered the water, one hand secure in the dog's fur, the other holding her things above the water. Obsidian let the current carry them a short distance, then led Sage from the water.

"It is pitch black in here!" Sage muttered. "I suppose it would be safe to light a torch." Obsidian licked her face. "All right but just so I can see what this place is like." Quickly she found tinder and soon had a torch lighted. She sighed. I didn't think the dark would be so scary." She admitted. "Wow! Would you look at this place?" she lifted the torch. It was a small area, just over head height and about the same size as the living cave, but the walls glittered and sparkled back at her, the light faceted, reflected and intensified by a thousand glittering crystals. The spot on her breast throbbed with pleasure and Sage nearly dropped her torch as 'power' surged through her.

"You were right to bring me here. This is truly a place of great power!" she said in an awed voice. "My staff and the relics!" She exclaimed, "You have brought them here!"

Obsidian wagged her tail, grinned wide and looked around. "Well, I had better put out the torch!" Sage said regretfully. "It would not do to burn it completely up. But first I'll lay out my sleeping furs and food so that I can find them in the dark." Quickly she followed actions to words and then snuffed the torch. The blackness that descended was darker somehow than it had been before. The silence was not nearly so overwhelming for she was seated beside the stream.

Time dragged. There was nothing that Sage could do but wait until either she gave up and gave in to Running Bison or the other three got tired and left. Somehow, she did not see giving up as a part of Running Bison's make-up. Later, she couldn't tell how much later, she heard him return, with the dog leading the way. They crossed the ledge and she was certain went all the way to the big room. She smiled to herself. *Just try to find me! That dog can follow as many false trails as Obsidian left, but not even he can follow a trail in water!* She could tell when they returned even before she heard them, the light of the torch filtered through the water. "What is he doing now?" She frowned. *It is taking him a long time to check out this area. What if he decides to follow the stream? I will be trapped!*

Obsidian licked her hand. Sage hugged the dog, drawing comfort from her nearness. Finally the light shifted and she could hear him crossing the ledge. "I know you can hear me!" Running Bison called out. "This childish game will not gain you anything but a few days' time. I am in no hurry! You can hide and sit alone in the dark until your food runs out. I will still be waiting, in comfort, with pleasant company and light and heat and good food, although not as good as what you prepare. I am going now. Think about what I say."

Later Sage ignited a tiny wick in a bowl of oil. It made a great deal of light to her starved eyes. The oil took a long time to burn and she had more. So she studied the crystals lining the walls of this room. Finally though, even this began to pall. She sighed, snuffed the flame and rolled up in her furs. Sleep was a long time coming.

*    *    *

*"Sage! Sage!"* A distant voice called. Sage listened as the voice approached. *"Oh, there you are! I have been looking all over for you!"* The woman who now spoke to Sage was a stranger to her. She was a plain woman of slight build. She wore her hair braided down her back and from the end fluttered a white owl feather. She was dressed as a woman of The People. Her age was indeterminate. *"Of course, you don't know me. I was called Basket. We have met, but perhaps you do not remember."*

"You seem familiar, but no, I do not know you."

*"Well, no matter."* Basket seated herself on the log beside Sage. *"We must talk."* she sighed, *"Your grandmother did not find time to tell you all."* She began. *"I am here to help you understand. I realize that you are confused and frightened, as well you should be. The task which faces you is not an easy one, but then never is the life of a woman of The People one of ease. My life was no easier. I did survive it, however and so must you."*

"You talk in the past. Have you come down from the Ancestor Fires in the sky?"

Basket nodded. *"The spirits have kept a keen eye on you, Sage, Bear Claw Woman of The People. They saved you from death even before you were born. You have been marked by the spirits. You belong to them."*

"What if I don't want to belong to them?"

*"You have no choice,"* Basket smiled. *"you were born of 'the line'. You are 'Keeper of the Sacred Relics'. See, you have even been provided a Sacred Staff and the bear which supplied that beautiful necklace was a 'spirit bear', these things make you the most powerful individual among The People."*

"They killed my mother."

"It had to be. The Sacred Relics were in danger. Clover Blossom did her part within the circle when she rescued them and you and took both to safety. Now it is time that the Relics are returned to The People. You have been selected for this task."

"Then I can give them to Running Bison and be done with this 'spirit' business?" Sage asked hopefully.

"Not so," Basket shook her head. "You are the Keeper. Only you can make an acceptable offering, just as you did this very morning. The spirits heard you. They have answered. Even now they protect you and those just beyond where you hide. It is not yet time for the group of you to leave this cave. Great danger to all of you lurks just beyond. By the time your food has run out the danger will be gone. Then it will be safe for all of you to join The People."

"Obsidian! Somehow she is a part of this. I just know that. What part does she play?"

"The Watcher! Each off us has always had such an animal. This one has been given to watch over and protect you, even as my own Spirit Wolf protected me." Basket motioned to where the animal in question lay just beyond reach waiting.

"You say there is danger. Where does it come from?"

Basket shook her head. "This I cannot say. The Watcher will know. Trust her with your life."

Sage sighed. "Do I have any choice in the matter?"

Again Basket shook her head. "When it is time, she will lead you from the sacred room. Do not forget this place. It is from it that you will be able to draw strength."

"What good will that do if I am to leave the cave and join The People?"

"You will return to this place. You will understand when. Until then draw strength from your staff, the Sacred Relics and the Watcher."

*        *        *

Suddenly Sage was alone on the log. Her strange visitor had vanished in a single heartbeat. Then she was souring high above the mountains, moving swiftly to the plain. There below her was a huge scourge of people, sweeping along the edge of the plain, killing, burning and completely destroying all human life in their path. Only a few survived. Sage watched as they struggled to follow a big bearded man, this handful of survivors. Among them she recognized herself, Prairie Grass, Whispering Wind and their dogs. Then she wakened, surrounded by the total darkness of the cave. Obsidian lay against her, providing comfort and companionship. Sage had a headache and she knew that she had dreamed, but as usual could not remember the dream.

24  An Agate Basin point made of Spanish Diggings jasper.

# CHAPTER 7

Running Bison, wake up!" Prairie Grass shook his friend, "Listen!"
"What is it?" Running Bison whispered back, "It is the middle of the night!"
"I know," Prairie Grass replied, "Something woke me. I went outside. It was then that I heard."
"Heard what?"
"That is what I'm trying to tell you!" Prairie Grass replied exasperated, "If you would just give me a chance to do so!"
Running Bison tired of trying to make sense of Prairie Grass. He rose and quickly made his way to the mouth of the cave. From the Ancestor Fires it was not yet quite the middle of the night, yet the eastern sky was alight with an orange glow. He could hear sound as well. The steady repeated thump! Thump! Thump! Of drums. The sound came from probably several valleys to the east of the canyon.
"What do you make of it?" Prairie Grass asked.
"I don't know," Running Bison replied, "But I intend to find out. Get your atlatl and darts. We are going to investigate."
"What about her?"
Running Bison glanced to where Whispering Wind was peacefully sleeping. "No need to bother her, we will be back before she wakes." He led the way swiftly from the cave, Traveler at his side. In an hour the two men were flat on their bellies looking down into a large valley, the very one where they'd lost Sage's trail a season earlier. A large band of people was occupying the valley. They were deeply involved in some sort

of celebration. At least three hands of fires were casting the orange glow and groups of people gathered around them and laughed and drank from skin bladders. Men, women and children as well as a welter of dogs ran and intermingled. If anyone in this valley was asleep, they were truly hard of hearing. Carefully the men slipped closer, then closer still.

Suddenly the drums fell silent. From a shelter not far from where they crouched, two men were escorting a third toward a quickly constructed platform a short distance away.

"Look!" Prairie Grass grabbed Running Bison's sleeve, "That is strange the man doesn't even protest that he is being led, completely naked, before the entire camp!" He pointed to the man now being urged up the steps of the crudely erected platform.

"I don't think he is aware," Running Bison replied, "He walks like he was drunk on fermented drink."

"What are they doing?"

"Some kind of ceremony," Running Bison crept closer, melting into the shadow of one bush, then the next. Prairie Grass followed suit. "Look at that man on the platform! Have you ever seen anything like that in your life?"

Atop the quickly erected structure, stood Quinquel, great Spirit Leader of the Serpent People. On his head he wore the feather head dress of his calling. Brilliant feathers glittered in the reflected light of the ceremonial fires. A many-colored feathered robe rested on his shoulders and swept the stone at his feat. On either wrist he wore a wide band of leather, emblazoned with colored stones. His skin had been oiled to glow in the firelight. About his lean waist he had wrapped a long band of woven grass, dyed in beautiful colors. Below it he wore only the ceremonial white breechclout and a wide decorated band around one ankle. In his left hand he held a long, serrated blade of obsidian, hafted to a wooden handle, from which dangled a pair of eagle feathers. The flickering lights emphasized the cruel beauty of his chiseled features.

The assistants dragged the drugged man up the remaining steps and spread him on his back across a wide flat stone. Then they knelt and bowed heads to the spirit leader. The big, burly man made no protest, nor did he make an effort to escape. Running Bison frowned. Clearly, he could see the man breathing. His eyes were open and he was not bound. Yet he did not fight. Something was dreadfully amiss.

"What's wrong with him? Is he drunk?" Prairie Grass whispered.

"I would say so, but I don't like the looks of this. We had better figure a way to get him away from here and quickly!"

"How? There are only two of us. We wouldn't have a chance! What is he doing? Oh! I can't believe it! By the spirits! What kind of people are these?" Prairie Grass nearly lost his meal as his stomach rolled.

Upon the platform, Quinquel had raised the obsidian blade. Then as the drums began again with an insane clatter, he brought the blade down in one smooth motion and cleanly cut the living heart from the man spread out before him. He raised the still-beating heart and drank the vital blood as it dripped into his mouth. A great cheer went up and the entire mass of people began to whoop and dance about. The heart was handed to one of the men who had dragged the hunter up the steps. He in turn raised the organ above his head and spoke at some length to the people gathered below him. They cheered again. Then the flap on the shelter moved and another man was brought forth. The first pair shoved the corpse of the dead man off the back of the structure. It was then that Running Bison realized that he had not been the first to meet so bizarre an end.

"Can you recognize the new man?" Running Bison asked.

"No, I don't think he is anyone I know," Prairie Grass replied, "Let's get out of here!"

"No, not just yet! They may have one of our hunters, perhaps more. I will not just sit here and watch them murder hunting mates and friends!"

"Would you rather join them?" Prairie Grass was scooting back, "We can do nothing for them."

"I don't know that yet. I am going to work my way around to the other side of that shelter. I want to know how many more are inside."

"What if there are guards?"

"Then I will perform a 'ceremony' of my own!" Running Bison began to move. "Are you coming?"

"I'm not staying here by myself!" Prairie Grass quickly melted into the shadows behind Running Bison.

The pair of them inched their way carefully to a position directly behind the shelter from which the victims had been taken. By now the celebration was beginning to lose much of its fervor. Many individuals were showing the effect of the fermented drink. Women had ushered children off to sleep and many had joined them. Men lay down beside the fire and began to snore. Within a few minutes most of the celebrants were retired. The last man was sacrificed and the drums came silent. Clearly the ceremony was over. Now the flamboyantly robed figure stepped down and led his minions off to a large shelter some distance from the slaughter.

"I am going to cut the bindings and see what is inside," Running Bison whispered. "Watch my back!" He followed actions to his words. It took several heartbeats for his eyes to adjust to the light inside. There was one guard, leaning against the center pole, snoring. On his lap was an empty bladder. The remaining people within were breathing gently in sleep. It took only a moment for Running Bison to make sure the guard did not wake up . . . ever. He shook first one, then another of the people in the shelter. None responded. The light was too dim to recognize any of them, but it made no difference. He opened the slit and dragged the first out.

"What's wrong with him? Why are you dragging him?"

"They are all in a sleep from which I cannot wake them. Here, take this one and carry him to the top of the trail. I will be right behind you with another."

Prairie Grass grunted as he slung the inert body over his shoulder and set off.

Now the camp was quiet. The fires were burning down. They had some time before dawn. It took them several trips, but finally they had all the people from the shelter lying on the ridge.

"What now?" Prairie Grass questioned. "They won't wake up and we can't possibly carry them all back to the cave before dawn." Just then one man groaned and began to waken. Soon several were groggily on their feet.

"Come, now, men. We have no time to lose!" Running Bison roused them, "There is no time to waste getting to a place of safety."

The groggy men looked blankly at him. Running Bison realized they did not understand his words. He tried to communicate again, with little better success.

"We know of a place where you will all be safe. Trust us. But we must hurry before they wake up."

"They won't wake up much before mid-day," one of the hunters managed to relay in badly spoken, broken and only marginally understood words. "But I'm not leaving without the others! If we few got free, maybe the rest can as well."

"You mean there are more of you?" Running Bison frowned, finally getting the just of his words.

"Not as many as there were, but yes, there are almost twice as many as you see here. Mostly women and children; They are being held in that big cage over there," he pointed beyond the 'altar'. "Only the ones they plan on sacrificing are brought to the shelter and drugged. The Savages are getting tired. Tonight they only killed a few."

"Are there guards?"

"Two at the cage, but they are probably dead drunk now."

"Then let's make them merely 'dead'," suggested Running Bison. "Then we can get your people away from here."

"They aren't 'my' people. Some of them were taken prisoner far to the south of here. But that savage always sacrifices the strongest first, so most of those left in the cage are women and children."

"It matters not. We will free them."

"Come on, why are we wasting time here?"

Running Bison set off at a run, cutting silently around the carnage and toward where he could just make out a large cage of poles lashed together with strips of rawhide. The guards were still at their post but not for long. Running Bison and another hunter slipped up from behind and without a sound slit their throats and eased the bodies to the ground. If anyone were to check, they looked to be asleep.

Running Bison had given out all his blades and knives to hunters. Several were opening the cage door. It did not take long to waken the people inside. In only moments the cage was opened. Silently, those who could walk were supporting those who could not, as the procession silently exited the valley. Behind them came hunters with branches. A pair of others was laying a false trail the other way. Soon they joined the main group and with utmost care their trail was obliterated.

Thunder rumbled and lightning forked across the sky. The spirits had provided cover. Soon they were all trudging along in a downpour. The storm was short-lived, providing just enough to wipe their trail completely. Not even the best tracking dog would be able to find them. Silently they followed Running Bison toward the canyon.

The sun was not yet up when they reached the pathway down into the canyon. Running Bison did not so much as glance that way as he led the group past. Some distance beyond he bid the hunters farewell, communicating at best he could that they should hurry away. The strangers, grateful for being released took their leave. Silently they passed out of sight. "Well, this has been an interesting night!" Prairie Grass sighed, "I would have been better off to have simply turned over and ignored those drums. We could have been captured back there and killed! Did you ever think of that? And for what? To rescue a bunch of strangers, people we would ordinarily have avoided even having contact with. It makes no sense!"

"Perhaps not; but at least we got out of that cave for a time, and it was a great adventure while it lasted. Admit it. You have been bored with just sitting around day after day."

"I haven't been sitting around," Prairie Grass protested, "I was the one to dispose of the bodies of those raiders, remember?"

"So you were," Running Bison sighed. "Come on, let's get back. I also have had enough excitement for one night." The hunters turned and retraced their path to the canyon. They did not notice that they had a pair of shadows, following silently behind. Running Bison smiled as they entered the cave. Whispering Wind was still curled fast asleep in her robes. She had not even been aware that they had left the cave. The men quietly took to their own sleeping robes for a few fingers of rest before the sun rose.

Outside, huddled against the wall at the base of the trail, two men studied the canyon and the cave.

"What do you make of this?" Bull Elk asked.

"They were hunters of 'The People'. I recognize the tongue. It is the same the slave woman Whispering Wind spoke. I learned a few words of it from her and a general understanding as well."

"I wonder why they set us free?"

"I care not. I am only interested in finding a way to repay them. You know that we both would be dead by this time tomorrow but for those men. I would follow one such at that!" Raven replied.

"You would leave our own people and join them?" Elk questioned.

Raven considered his words. "What is left of our people? Those worth any thing were sacrificed to that bloody Quinquel over the past several weeks. You may not have noticed, but we are all that are left of the River Camp."

"You are right. It is not safe in these mountains, not even in a large group. I would agree that it is best if we can be accepted by 'The People'. They do not live in these mountains. Besides, I have always wanted to see what it is like to hunt bison, first hand." Bull Elk admitted. "I wonder what they are doing here?"

"We will watch and find out," Raven hunkered down against a rock.

"I am hungry. You don't suppose they would share food with us, do you? We have no hunting weapons you know."

"It is also cold," Raven studied the cave. "I plan on approaching and offering friendship. After all, four hunters are safer than two; they might welcome us."

Bull Elk shook his head, "If they had wanted to welcome us, they would have led the whole group here. No, these hunters did not want to deal with a lot of people, but I agree that perhaps they would welcome two," he grinned.

"We will wait." Raven wiggled into a more comfortable position.

So they did. The sun rose and eventually even warmed the place where they waited. But there was no movement from the cave. "Listen!" Raven whispered, "Do you hear that?"

"Savages!" Bull Elk began to sweat. "They have followed our trail?"

"I don't think so, but if one of those hunters were to leave that cave they would be spotted. After they saved us, I cannot let that happen to them. I am going to alert them before the Savages get here. We still have a few breaths of time. Come on!"

The men quickly sprinted toward the mouth of the cave. Just below they called out quietly. A head popped out, followed by the rest of Running Bison.

"Savages!" Raven pointed.

Running Bison squinted, nodded and the pair sprinted into the cave.

"Wake Whispering Wind," Running Bison called to Prairie Grass. "We must move deeper into the cave. Quickly, get the dogs loaded with packs."

The strangers seeing what was under way quickly began to help. The dogs were packed, Whispering Wind wakened and in very short order they were all moving into the darkness of the inner cave. All signs of their habitation had been erased.

"What are these men doing here?" Whispering Wind demanded of Running Bison. "How did they come to be in the cave? They cannot be trusted! They are members of the camp which kidnapped me!"

"You mean that you can understand them?"

"Are you listening to me? I told you these are the men who kidnapped me! Doesn't that bother you?"

"Right now, no. I will explain later. Right now, I am far more concerned with the dangers out there and believe me, they are far greater than a pair of weaponless hunters who are in as much danger as we are."

"What kind of danger? You wake me from a sound sleep, order me to lead you deep into the cave and then proceed to load all our possessions onto the dogs. I think that I deserve an explanation!"

"You will get one, just not right now," Running Bison glanced over his shoulder to verify that Prairie Grass was erasing their trail. "Just now, if you will, tell these hunters that we will be safe here."

"Why should I do that? Why should I help save their worthless hides?"

"Because I have asked you to," Running Bison replied. "Because we are all in great danger and it would be very helpful if I were able to communicate with them. Now can the rest of your questions wait until later?"

Whispering Wind sighed but turned to Raven. "This hunter asks me to tell you that your worthless life is safe here in this cave."

"I thank the hunter, more than he can ever know. And I do most sincerely apologize to you, Whispering Wind, for having any part in your capture by my camp. It was not my idea and I did not participate in the capture, or the mistreatment that followed. You know this to be true."

Whispering Wind frowned, but on thinking back she realized that he spoke the truth. If any thing Raven had given her extra food when her own ration had been bleak.

They went as far as the underground stream. Here Running Bison halted the dogs. "I am going back and keep an eye on the cave. If you hear me whistle, take them into the big room and put out the torches. I will lead the danger away from you."

"But there is no way out!" Whispering Wind protested, "If they come in after us, we cannot hide."

"They have no torches and will not bother with making any. I will lead them away. You need not fear. Now please, just do as I say. Later, if I am alive to do so, I will explain more fully. Now is not the time!" He trotted back down the passage, Traveler at his side. Whispering Wind ushered the three men and the dogs over the ledge and searched out one of the oil bowls and lit the wick. Then she extinguished the torches. The cave was plunged into darkness, but for the tiny point of light. The men crowded closer. Prairie Grass broke into a cold sweat and peered fearfully into the dark beyond the tiny circle of light.

Time seemed to stand still. They waited . . . and waited. Finally, when it seemed they would explode with the need to know, Running Bison returned. "They have gone. Didn't even give the cave a glance. Probably didn't even see it with the hide blocking the entrance. They scoured the canyon, and then returned to the trail above. I think we are safe now, but it would be best if we keep watch, just the same. We can, however, return to the living cave."

"Then are you planning on telling me what is going on?" Whispering Wind demanded.

"Certainly, just as soon as we are settled but I am sure that these hunters can tell you far more, however, than Prairie Grass or I am able. We merely released them. They know the details of the savages who held them prisoners. This is why I am pleased that you understand their tongue."

Whispering Wind followed him back to the living cave. "I don't suppose you can get in contact with Sage?" Running Bison asked.

Wind shook her head, "I have no idea where she is, but when she is ready, or rather, when the spirits are ready, she will return. I am sure that if there is danger out there," she nodded outside, "The spirits have protected her until the danger is over." She smiled to herself, "You might keep that in mind when she returns. It could be that by her actions, your own life has been saved. Now tell me what has been going on."

Running Bison and Raven alternately gave her information, which she translated to the other, so soon everyone knew what had taken place. It shook Whispering Wind to the core that such people as those described, actually walked the land. "Why did you even go to investigate such a thing? And once you understood the danger, why did you stay?"

"People were being killed," Running Bison explained, "I could not sleep at night if I did not try to help them!"

"But how could you know which were in the right? It could be that those killed had committed vile acts against the others!"

"Believe me, even you, doubter that you are, could not be convinced that the savages were innocent. I had never, in my entire life, witnessed such acts of senseless cruelty. That dreamer cut the heart from a man and before it had stopped beating, drank his blood. Does that sound to you like the act of an innocent man?"

"I believe you! It is just that you were foolish to risk your life and that of Prairie Grass, for a bunch of strangers. You should have never taken such chances!"

"I am most grateful that he did!" Raven cut in, "I may not rest very high in your esteem, but I have always prided myself on being an honest and loyal hunter. I can only say again, I had no part in kidnapping you. I did my best to watch over you while you were in that camp and even protect you as best I could. But I had no control over them trading you off to another camp. What I do not understand, is how you escaped the slaughter of that camp. When we found them, I searched all about for you. I finally concluded that the people who killed that camp had taken you with them. I figured that they were either men of your own camp, or you were still a slave, only with a different group. Actually, it was the discovery of that camp which convinced Bull Elk and me to leave the people we had been walking with and seek another group. We were looking for the Bison Camp when the savages took us by surprise."

"Perhaps I have been wrong to accuse you of the kidnapping," Whispering Wind agreed. "You speak truth when you say that you did what you could to make my life more bearable. I have not forgotten the time which you spent teaching me words of your tongue. It made my life among your people much easier. But, could you not have helped me escape?"

Raven looked away in embarrassment, "I was not able to do more than I did. Those who did kidnap you were watching closely. I was merely the guard assigned to keep you from escaping. I don't think they trusted me too well. There was no chance."

"Why did they take me?"

Raven shrugged. "There was talk of a woman of your camp . . ."

Whispering Wind nodded, "The new mate of my father. She hated me."

"What do we do now?" Bull Elk asked, "Are we hiding in this cave or getting out of here while we still claim our lives?"

"We cannot leave until Sage decided to rejoin us," Running Bison replied irately.

"Sage! Who is Sage?"

"She is my best friend," Whispering Wind began.

"She is a relative of mine," Running Bison finished.

"You mean we stay in this place of danger for a woman? Where is she any way?"

Running Bison nodded in the direction of the inner cave. "In there, somewhere. She is playing a childish game refusing to come out and accompany us peacefully."

"You mean she is a slave?" Bull Elk shifted uncomfortably.

"On no! Nothing like that!" Whispering Wind protested, "She is The Chosen! She just doesn't want to be chosen, that is all."

"Chosen? For what?" Raven asked.

"The Chosen One is the woman responsible for the safe keeping of The People's Sacred Relics and also for performing the Sacred Prayers for Renewal."

"Your dreamer is a female? I don't think I want to join a group with a female dreamer," Bull Elk began to shake his head. Turning to Raven he asked. "Why didn't you tell me this? I would never have agreed to seek out people who let a woman be their dreamer. There is no telling how many taboos she has broken!"

"She is not the dreamer," Running Bison assured them. "She is merely the 'Keeper of the Sacred Relics'. She probably does prayers for the women as well. She has no connection with the men of the camp."

"Then she is in there somewhere making female prayers?"

Whispering Wind shook her head, "She is in there, hiding from Running Bison and Prairie Grass. Sage doesn't want to go to the camps of 'The People'. She is afraid of them!"

"Why is she afraid of her own people, her own blood relative, if she is some sort of female dreamer, she should be welcomed by them as special?"

"There is where the problem is. Sage doesn't want to be set apart. She doesn't want to be 'special'. She prefers to blend in and there is no way that the 'Keeper of the Ancient Relics' or the 'Child of the Mother of The People', could ever just blend in. I am the only person of 'The People' she has ever met."

"How can that be?" Raven frowned, "You just said she was a relative of Running Bison."

So Running Bison and Whispering Wind told the tale of Clover Blossom and Sage.

"It was she who rescued me after the camp was slaughtered. We watched you come into the valley and bury the dead. Well, Sage watched you. I hid in the far reaches of her cave quaking in terror that we would be discovered and become slaves again."

Raven was thoughtful for a short time and then shook his head. "You would have been returned to your own people. We do not usually take slaves. There had been an exchange made for you and the agreement was that they take you far away and then release you. The headman, however, saw a chance to enrich himself. Who was to know: certainly not the woman who traded you to him in the first place. If the men of your camp were intending to retrieve you, they would have done so long before then. So the headman benefitted twice, once from the female's trade and again when he traded you to the slain camp."

"So, is this Sage person so important that we risk capture again by the savages?" Bull Elk asked nervously.

"We are not leaving here without her," Running Bison stated with finality. "The luck of The People has been gone from them for far too long. She must return the Sacred Relics."

"There is a 'reason' why we wait here," Whispering Wind added, "We may not know what that reason is, but the spirits do and it is they, not stubbornness, who direct Sage. When it is safe, she will be returned to us, willing or not. Sage has no say in it."

"Is her 'spirit power' that great?"

Whispering Wind glanced beyond them and smiled, "See for yourself!"

The men whipped around and then froze.

Sage stood in the mouth of the passage. Beside her was Obsidian. Around them was a blue glow that radiated from the pair. Sage carried the sacred packet and she held the staff in her right hand. "It is safe now to leave the cave," she said quietly, "The danger is passed."

*     *     *

"So, what made you change your mind?" Whispering Wind walked beside Sage. They had left the cave almost immediately.

"I did not change my mind," Sage sighed. "But the spirits are more powerful than I thought. I could no longer fight them. I lay in the crystal cave and 'power' visited me. Then I understood."

"Understood what?"

Sage sighed, "I cannot fight them. They will, however, protect me from harm. Now is the time for me to join the camps of 'The People'. Besides, I got tired of Running Bison constantly waking me up with all his shouting and threats!"

"You could hear him?"

"I could hear all of you. When you waited, beside the stream, I was not even a dart cast away. I could hear your every word clearly."

"But how?"

"Where the ledge crosses, beneath it, there is an opening into another room. It is most beautiful. I have named it the crystal cave, for the walls are made of crystals. It is a sacred place, filled with 'power'. Obsidian led me there, to escape Running Bison until it was time."

"You knew of the danger?"

Sage shook her head, "I was not ready to face 'The People'. It was not yet time. I can't explain it any more-clearly than that. You know that I don't know these things. Power directs, power decides. It was Power that directed my steps to avoid Running Bison, Power and Obsidian. When it was time, she led me back." Sage laid her hand on the head of the faithful animal.

"But now, you tell me about these two hunters. How is it that they have joined us? And further, how is it that they seem to know you quite well?"

"They were members of the camp which kidnapped me. The tall one, Raven, was usually my guard. He taught me many words of the tongue. It was probably less boring for him to be able to communicate. I also taught him a few words of my own tongue. Since I was with that camp for several turnings of the moon, I learned to understand them quite well."

"Oh and did he ever . . . well you know?"

Whispering Wind shook her head. "We were both closely watched all of the time. I don't think the headman trusted him, at least not alone with me. Believe me; I would have tried almost anything to get free. That camp wasn't so bad. Raven made sure that I was treated well. He may be ugly, but he has a good heart. It was after I was traded that the abuse began. The people of the slain camp were dirty and mean and they got what they deserved!"

"Well you will be back with your father soon. I suppose then I will see little of you."

"Why would you think that? I have told you. You will be welcomed as a sister. I may even insist that you be formally adopted."

"How can you do that?" Sage giggled, "I am an adult!"

"Seriously, I do not think it will be a problem."

"I know that you have talked about the people of the camp many times before, but, please, tell me again. I am still nervous."

"Well, of course Hunting Badger is the Headman. He is getting too old, really, to be the leader. He takes too long to make decisions. The position should go to a younger man."

"Such as Running Bison," Sage smiled to herself.

"Well, yes. Running Bison would be the logical person."

"Except that he seems to spend more time trying to capture me than he does in the camp. That would not be very good for a leader."

"But he has 'captured' you," Whispering Wind reminded, "So there is no longer a need for him to be out of the camp seeking you out. Of course, he was also looking for me."

"And he has found you as well," Sage reminded.

Whispering Wind merely sighed.

"You surely aren't still carrying a special fondness for him? Why the man is a real bully!"

"He is not! Just because he encourages you to do what in your heart you know you should doesn't make him a bully! He is a deeply caring, sensitive man!"

"Rot!" Sage exclaimed, "You are so blinded by the man you can't see him clearly! Well I can and if you are so unfortunate as to draw his interest and find yourself mated to him, well then, I feel sorry for you. You will surely be disillusioned!"

Whispering Wind stopped in her tracks. "If I didn't know you better, Sage, I would say that you are jealous. That is impossible though, I know, for Running Bison is your blood relative. It is taboo for you to 'look' at him!"

Sage shook her head. "I have never 'looked' at him!" she protested perhaps a bit too strongly. In her heart she questioned Whispering Wind's words. Had she 'looked' at Running Bison? She could not answer. "Rot the man! He is too full of his own importance!"

"Don't worry, Sage. Now that you are back among your own people, you will find a man who makes you feel special, in the same way that Running Bison makes me feel special. Then you will understand."

"Oh yes! I can just see it. You go ahead and line up the men who would welcome a mate who claims 'Wolf' as her 'spirit animal'. I'm sure I will be able to make a selection from that group."

"Well, that could be a problem." Whispering Wind admitted. She thought for a moment. "Maybe the new man, Raven!" she smiled, nodding, "He is a very nice man. You could be quite happy with Raven."

"Raven! The ugly one! Just a short time ago you were accusing him of all kind of vile things, from kidnapping you to selling you to others!

Now you can calmly stand there and suggest him as an acceptable mate for your best friend?" Sage all but shrieked at her.

"I'm not standing, I'm walking, which is what you should be doing," Whispering Wind was fast leaving Sage behind.

"That is your way out of answering me!" Sage accused, "It won't work." She hurried to catch up.

"Perhaps I was too strong in my accusation," Whispering Wind replied. "True he was with that camp and it is also true that he was my guard for most of the time that they held me, but he was always kind to me. That is important in a mate."

"Fine, then you mate with him! I keep telling you that I don't want a mate. I just want to be left alone!" Sage screeched in agitation.

"Then I will take myself elsewhere to walk!" Whispering Wind huffed off to walk beside Prairie Grass, leaving Sage to her own devices.

*Don't need her as a friend any way! What kind of friend would treat one the way she has just treated me? Well. Perhaps I did deserve it, but she could have been more understanding and not gone off like that! Well I won't bother her anymore! It is obvious that she prefers the men any way. We got along just fine before she came crashing into our lives. I don't need anyone but Obsidian!* Sage trudged on by herself.

When they stopped and set up camp for the night, Sage began erecting her shelter just as far as she could from Whispering Wind and still be within the confines of the camp. Running Bison walked by and without even breaking-stride said, "Move your shelter back beside Whispering Wind's where it belongs. I care not for your childish spats; the safety of the camp is more important. I will be back this way shortly. I expect you to have complied." Then he was out of sight in the trees.

Sage fumed. She struck her shelter and dragged it over beside Whispering Wind's, but Wind totally ignored her. *Fine!* Sage unrolled her sleeping fur and went to the stream to wash. Whispering Wind was right behind her so she went farther upstream. When she returned to the camp she found trail food in her stores and shared it with Obsidian. Then she crawled into her furs and turned her back to the camp.

*   *   *

Sleep was a very long time in coming . . . *Come on Saaaageee* . . . Whispering Wind called from far ahead. *I have the men waiting* . . . Sage struggled through deep snow, dragging her travois behind. Each step seemed to be more difficult than the last. Far ahead she could see Whispering Wind dancing along on lush grass as she called. *Saaaage! hurry uuuuup we are waaaaaiting* . . . Each step seemed to take Sage farther away rather than closer to Whispering Wind, but finally she struggled free of the snow. The men were lined up for her to choose from. Sage shuddered. The first one looked to have been set out to walk the wind long ago. He smelled the same. The second was missing an arm, most of his teeth, all his hair and probably had a hand of grandchildren. The next was missing a leg and dressed in ragged castoff clothing. And the last was one Sage recognized as one who 'serviced' the dreamers. She shuddered. Whispering Wind and the men all began to laugh . . . Sage woke up, sweating.

It was a long time before she slept again.

\*       \*       \*

Whispering Wind lay studying the Ancestor Fires in the sky. She couldn't sleep. She knew that she had hurt Sage's feelings. She hadn't meant to, but she had. Now she knew that her best friend anywhere lay just beyond, probably as miserable as she. Finally she sighed and crawled from her shelter.

"Sage, are you asleep?"

"No," came the muffled answer.

"Can we talk?"

"That depends. Are you going to try to marry me off to a dead man, or one missing most of his body parts, or the one who services the dreamers? That is what I have dreamed."

Whispering Wind laughed softly, "Poor Sage! You really are having a bad time, aren't you?"

"I am if it means not having you as my friend," Sage's head came from beneath her sleeping fur and Whispering Wind could see wet trails down her face.

"Never!" Whispering Wind shook her head, "No matter what you were to say or do, I will always be your friend. I might get mad at you sometimes, but that doesn't mean I'm not your friend. I know that sometimes I try to convince you what is best for you, but that is only because I love you more than a sister. I just want you to be happy!"

"I don't know where my happiness lies," Sage admitted. "But I don't feel it is with any man. After those . . ." she shuddered. "You know exactly what I mean. You were treated in a like manner. Yet it doesn't seem to bother you, the idea of a man touching you."

Whispering Wind crawled inside the shelter and squeezed between the outer wall and Obsidian. "It does bother me. And when that man was on me the other night is was the same bad dream again. But when Running Bison darted him, I realized that the men who had raped me were dead. All of them. They could no longer hurt me. A woman must have a man, a mate, to survive amongst The People, amongst any camp. What else can we do? It matters not if we care for them or not, a man is vital to our position. Perhaps you will be luckier than the rest of us. You are special. Just maybe, you will be able to establish a position which doesn't require a man."

"I don't see how that is possible. For one thing, I am a stranger to the camp. It doesn't please me that I'm dependent upon Running Bison for my very existence. He has, however, stated that he is my relative, so therefore he must accept the responsibility for me. But someone in that camp killed my mother, what if they try to kill me as well? Will Running Bison protect me? Does he even know where the danger, if there is danger, comes from? How can I feel safe?" Sage worried.

"Running Bison will protect you, even to his own death, you know that! Besides, it was many seasons ago that your mother was killed. It is possible that whoever murdered her is also dead by now. It might not even have been connected with the Relics. We can't know for sure. But I can see why you wouldn't want to go back. I can only assure you that I will always be your friend. Running Bison will care for you and we can't know anything beyond that," Whispering Wind replied.

"But I don't want to share a fire with Running Bison. I don't care if he is my only relative!"

"Well . . . there are an unusually high number of unattached females in the camp. Maybe we could convince Hunting Badger to let us set up our own hearth. Then you and I could share a shelter. The storyteller tells of a time when the camps all had a 'women's hearth' where they could gather, work, watch children and visit without worrying about breaking any male taboos. It seems a reasonable thing to ask. I don't want to return to my father's shelter, not after the way he didn't bother trying to find me."

The spot on Sage's breast thrummed softly. She smiled.

"According to the storytellers, more than once during the lifetimes of our ancestors, women were equal to men. But again and again, the men have changed this. Each generation has taken away a little more of the women's freedom and made them more dependent upon the men." Whispering Wind replied. "The men seem to fear 'women's power'. Each time that a powerful Chosen One appears among the people, they lose power, they are forced to give the women a more equal footing and a say in the running of the camp. Men don't like that! So they gradually take away the equality, little by little, until finally, we are hardly more than slaves. Then another Chosen One appears and restores the balance. Maybe that is why you have been sent?" Whispering Wind tilted her head and nibbled thoughtfully on her lip. "As I have said, there are a number of unmated females in the camp. I think it might be possible to convince the hunters that it would be easier to provide for them all at one hearth rather than individually. I'm sure that the hunters responsible for sisters, or mothers, for example, would favor a single hearth where every hunter gives a share of the kill. It would make things easier on all the hunters. At one time or another, every one of them has been responsible for providing for a female relative. It makes sense as a solution. I will ask Running Bison, if it is all right with you, that is, if establishing such a hearth is possible. I do not wish to return to my father's hearth and he is probably not wanting me there either."

"I don't want to be forced to share a hearth with Running Bison. Maybe you have an idea at that! What about these other unmated women? Do you think they would be interested in sharing a hearth with us? I don't see any male allowing just the two of us setting up our own."

"You are certainly right about that! I think that it might be possible, but I intend to try even if it is just you and I."

"Who will hunt for us? Will your father provide for you if you are not at his hearth? Do you think that Running Bison will provide for me?

Better still, is there any possibility they will allow us to hunt for ourselves? After all, we have been doing so for seasons already." Sage asked.

"They will not let us hunt." Whispering Wind stated firmly, "Even if we have and even if we starve. They will never allow us to hunt bison."

"We need not hunt bison," Sage shook her head, "There are other animals; even on the plain I am sure."

"There are antelope and a few deer, but they still won't let us hunt."

"What about with our bolas and nets and rabbit sticks? Surely there are birds and rabbits!"

"Of course! But would they provide sufficient food to keep the pair of us alive?"

"With Obsidian's help and with my knowledge of plants there would be more than enough!" Sage smiled.

"There is no taboo for women hunting with nets, rabbit sticks and bolas," Whispering Wind smiled back.

A figure came into view out of the shadows. Running Bison materialized, "If the two of you don't get some sleep, you will be sorry come morning," he reminded them. "I have heard part of your conversation. I will speak with Hunting Badger about the possibility of your sharing a hearth of your own, but I can't promise he will agree." The man faded back into the shadows.

The girls grinned at one another and Whispering Wind returned to her own shelter. Both slept soundly until Prairie Grass wakened them to bright sunshine. Running Bison had the cooking fire burning hotly, water heated for tea and several rabbits spitted over the coals, nearly ready to eat. The rest of the camp had been broken down and already packed on the travois. It did not take the women long to follow suit.

\*     \*     \*

"We will be leaving the mountains today," Running Bison stated, "And in another hand of days we will reach the camp. Everyone; keep a sharp eye out for danger and for food. We could use a fresh supply of small game for the evening meal each day. Our supply of dried meat is getting dangerously low and I don't want to take the time to process a large animal. Rabbits, birds, any small animals will do; even perhaps to an antelope but nothing larger."

"We could eat one of those small deer before it spoiled," Raven stated.

"Possibly, but I would prefer not," Running Bison thought for a moment.

The small party moved from the mountains down onto the plain. As Running Bison suggested, they took a supply of rabbits and birds as they traveled and prepared them for the evening meal. As the women walked, they gathered the plants they were familiar with and the evening meals were quite tasty. Sage had an ample supply of salt packed on her travois. She was not ready to give it up just yet. Then late one day Running Bison held up his hand to halt the group. Ahead they could see a large camp spread out below them in a bison wallow. They had arrived.

# CHAPTER 8

You can't mean that!" Thunder Cloud sputtered.

"It has never been done," The hunter, Jumping Antelope replied evenly, "But I do not see that it would create a problem. So long as they do not break the taboos, I see no harm in it."

The council had gathered, late at night, after the camp was settled in sleep. The topic under discussion was Running Bison's suggestion that the camp let Whispering Wind, Sage and the other unmated women have their own hearth.

"But it makes me look bad!" protested Thunder Cloud. "It tells everyone that I can't provide for my own daughter!"

"You have a new mate and three other children to provide for," Reminded Jumping Antelope. "I would think you would be relieved not to be required to provide for yet another. Besides, Whispering Wind is an adult now."

"But her own hearth? It has never been done."

"It has been done, even in this very camp," Crooked Spirit, Dreamer of the Bison Camp spoke, "And when it was done, it worked very successfully. Generations ago, the women had their own hearth, much as the unmated men do today. It was a central place where all the women could gather, work together and watch the children at the same time. I have never understood why it was disbanded."

"Because the women demanded to be allowed to hunt!" sputtered an old hunter, "They demanded a voice in the council of elders as well. In fact they demanded many things. It took generations to get them back in their place."

"For the moment," Hunting Badger rose. "I will allow this pair of females to have their own hearth, attached to Running Bison's hearth, since he is responsible for at least one of them, but they will not be allowed to hunt."

"They only ask to go out with their bolas, rabbit sticks and nets," reassured Running Bison. "There is no taboo preventing that. The women of 'The People' have done so for as long as anyone can remember."

"That brings us to another problem," Angry Bull, hunter, rose, "I have no hunting dog. That woman has an excellent one. I want that dog!"

"That seems a reasonable request," Hunting Badger nodded his head.

"That dog belongs to the woman," protested Running Bison. "Besides, I am not at all sure that you could take her. The animal is particularly devoted to Sage and since this woman is a relative of mine, I have the final say about the dog."

"You already have two dogs!" Angry Bull sputtered.

"Now it seems I have three," Running Bison said evenly, "The dog belongs to the woman! That is the end of the conversation."

"What gives you the right to decide?" Angry Bull rose and faced Running Bison across the fire.

Hunting Badger rose as well, "Sit down, Angry Bull!" he ordered angrily. "I am in charge here, not you and not you, Running Bison!" He turned to each man as he spoke to him. "In the case of this dog, I feel that Angry Bull has a right. I give him the dog!"

"NO!"

The entire council turned. Just beyond their circle stood Sage, Obsidian at her side. Sage had the staff in her hand. Silence descended.

"This dog is mine! No one has the right to take her from me. I did not wish to come to this place, or travel with this camp, but Running Bison insisted. I leave, now!" She turned and began breaking down her shelter. Soon, as the stunned elders watched, she had the dog harnessed and was leaving the camp.

"Wait!" Crooked Spirit rose, "We have been too eager. Let us reconsider."

"What do we care if she leaves?" Angry Bull sputtered, "She isn't even a woman of this camp! We have more women than we need now and she is just one more mouth to feed." He glared at Running Bison. "But the dog is mine! The headman has just said so!" He marched boldly to where Obsidian stood patiently in the harness. The hunter reached out to unhook her.

Obsidian curled back her lips and exposed long sharp teeth. The growl accompanying the action was not lost on the watchers. Angry Bull ignored the warning and cuffed the dog across the head. In one smooth move, Obsidian had the hunter's arm in a vice-like hold, her yellow eyes spitting hatred as she again warned. Angry Bull kicked out; Obsidian sidestepped; but kept her grip. Sage, however was not about to stand quietly by and let anyone abuse Obsidian; she brought the head of her staff down sharply on Angry Bison's head.

"Get away from her!" she shouted, "You bison dung! You are not fit to own a dog!"

Angry Bull staggered back, falling to the ground in a daze and Obsidian released his arm. The watchers stood, spellbound.

Now a serious act had been committed against a hunter. It could not be ignored. A woman had struck a hunter. Even within so forward-looking a camp as this, it could not be disregarded.

"Someone! Hand me a weapon! This woman and her dog die!" Angry Bull staggered to his feet, blood seeping from a wound on his forehead.

"Wait!" Crooked Spirit, Dreamer, spoke.

"For what?" Angry Bull shouted, "You all saw!"

"She is a stranger," Crooked Spirit cut in, "She cannot be expected to know! You go up to a strange dog with an attitude and then complain when the dog takes action to protect her own. The dog acted as any good dog would. She is blameless. The woman merely protected her friend. She cannot be faulted for that. Any hunter of this group would have acted the same."

"She is a woman!" screamed Angry Bull.

Sage balled her hands into fists and closed her eyes, her mind screaming out at the injustice of this! *By the spirits! May lightning strike!*

Overhead black clouds rumbled and built. Thunder grumbled and then suddenly, a bolt of lightning struck, not far from where Angry Bull stood. The hunter leaped away and then turned to face Running Bison, still demanding an atlatl and dart.

"She is my sister!" Running Bison stepped forward, "If you make a move to harm her, you will have me to deal with. She is under my protection and the protection of my hearth. If the Bison Camp cannot make my sister welcome, then it isn't a camp within which I can walk."

"Then go!" Angry Bull staggered to his feet, clutching his arm. It would be bruised, but the big dog had not so much as broken the skin, "You are nothing to me!"

Running Bison said angrily, "If you drive away my relative, I go with her. I go and so do those who came into this camp with me. Can the Bison Camp afford to lose three seasoned hunters? Is one dog worth such a loss? Do not forget, if we leave the other four dogs go with us as well."

"I have just recovered my daughter," Thunder Cloud, spoke. "I owe her return to Running Bison. I and my family go with him if he leaves."

"I also will walk with Running Bison," Crooked Spirit spoke softly.

"Elders! Hunters! There is no need for such haste!" Hunting Badger quickly soothed, "We can work this out. As Running Bison pointed out, this female is his relative. This grants her welcome into the camp. Since she brought the animal with her, I think perhaps it is her dog. These new hunters that Running Bison brings are sorely needed. I see no reason to prevent the two females from having their own hearth, being responsible for their own food and responsible for contributing to the welfare as a whole of the camp as well. But Running Bison is totally responsible for their actions and, THEY DO NOT HUNT!"

Hunting Badger turned to Angry Bull, "We will discuss this incident further. For now, stay away from her and the dog. That is the end!"

Running Bison quickly made his way to where Sage stood, stubbornly refusing to return to the camp. "You see. You have gotten your way!" He stood before her, refusing to let her pass. "The council has been reasonable, now it is your turn."

"I am not wanted here," Sage pleaded miserably, "I told you before we came here, but you would not listen."

"You are wanted here," Running Bison stated, "I want you here. You are my only relative, Sage. I have spent seasons searching for you."

Sage shook her head, "We both know what you were seeking. It was not me."

"Look. I have given in about not letting anyone know that you are Clover Blossom's grand daughter. I have even claimed you as a sister. I have won you the right to keep your dog."

"They had no right to even suggest she be taken from me! Besides, you know that cannot be. Obsidian is the Watcher."

"I know that! But unless I come out and tell them that you are the 'Keeper of the Ancient Relics', I have no real excuse to deny their demands. If I were Headman, it would be different. What I said would be, but Hunting Badger is Headman. The only thing which kept you from being darted on the spot and that dog in your possession was the fact that I and those other hunters threatened to leave the camp if you did."

"Would you?"

"Have left the camp? Absolutely, that was no threat! Hunting Badger knows that his grip as leader of the Bison Camp is slipping. He has made many poor decisions these last several seasons. The whole camp has suffered as a result. I am not the only hunter who is dissatisfied. The reason we have so few dogs is because Hunting Badger chose to wait until too late to follow the bison herds south. The camp got trapped in a blizzard. We ran out of food and had to eat most of the dogs. I chose to go without rather than kill my pair. Now I am resented for having two dogs when others have none. The women complain because they are forced to pull the travois. They have been forced to do so for two seasons now."

"Why?"

"Why! Because we have no dogs, I have just explained that to you."

"It is spring."

"So?"

"There are many wolf dens in the mountains."

"What does that have to do with our problem?"

"You need dogs, right?"

"I have just said so."

"Then steal them! Find the wolf dens and steal the pups. Wolves make just as good a dog as do dogs. Look at Obsidian! Where do you think she came from originally? Even the gatherers have heard the stories of how the Ancestors of 'The People' stole wolves to replace their dogs."

"By the spirits! Why didn't I think of that?" Running Bison began to grin, "See, already. You have made a difference! You wait and see. This idea of yours will change the hunters' opinions of you. Wait here. Promise!"

"I will wait," Sage sat on the ground next to Obsidian.

"Promise!"

"I said I would wait!" she answered angrily.

Running Bison returned to the waiting council. "The woman has made a suggestion which will solve the problem of dogs," he announced. Everyone waited for him to continue. "The dog, Obsidian, seems to be the center of the whole matter. There are others just like her out there, just waiting for us. The solution is simple! We hunters did not think of it, but a woman did. Tomorrow I will lead as many hunters as are interested into the mountains and we will steal pups from the wolves. They will make fine strong dogs."

Several of the men nodded. Others made exclamations. Angry Bull snorted and derided. "Wolves! That is just the sort of an idea a woman would come up with. What good would wolves do us? Can they be trained to pull a travois? Can they be trained to hunt with people?"

"To answer your questions," Crooked Spirit replied, "Yes, they can. You have just observed an example of their loyalty. That animal which walks with the woman is no dog! Open your eyes men, she is all wolf! Wolves make excellent camp animals. They are pack hunters. Once they accept the camp as their pack, they are loyal to the death. I cannot imagine why none of us thought of it. We have all heard the stories of how our ancestors tamed the wolves. If they can do it, then so can we. I will go with you, Running Bison."

"Then it is settled? the woman is welcome? The dog remains hers?"

Hunting Badger rose and looked around the council. "We have much to think about from the workings of this night. Tomorrow Running Bison will take a group of hunters out to capture wolves. The women may have their own hearth and they may use their bolas, rabbit sticks and nets to capture small game. No hunter is to be responsible for them. If they starve, it is their own fault. They will be required to contribute the same as any other hearth to the general welfare of the camp. I have spoken." He rose and left the fire. The council meeting was over.

Sage slowly returned to the place where she had erected her simple shelter. She did not unpack the travois. Instead she simply released Obsidian, pulled her sleeping robe from the pack and curled up beside the travois. She also had much to think about.

\* \* \*

"Where are the hunters going?" Whispering Wind yawned as she poured herself a bowl of tea and watched a double hand of hunters and four dogs leave the camp with two nearly empty travois.

"Hunting," Sage replied with a grin.

"What is so amusing about that? But surely they are not going hunting? They took travois with them."

"They are going hunting," Sage assured her, "They are going out to replenish the dog pack of this camp."

"Huh!"

"Running Bison leads them into the mountains to capture wolf pups."

Whispering Wind began to laugh, "What a splendid idea! Trust Running Bison to think of such a clever thing!"

Sage merely snorted rudely in reply. She then handed Whispering Wind her bolas and net, picking up her own and their rabbit sticks, "If you wish to have anything to eat, come on."

"Wait!" Wind was cramming the remains of one of Sage's seed cakes into her mouth, "Where are you going?"

"Out to get our food," Sage replied. "I will tell you about it on the way." And so she did.

"You mean we must provide for ourselves! Yet we are not allowed to hunt! Well, that seems hardly fair."

"We must also bring in our share for the general food supply. Are you sure that you still want to have an independent hearth?"

"I certainly do!" Whispering Wind said indignantly. "They only agreed because they didn't think we could. Well, they will be surprised. Come on! I'll go around this way; you go that. I'll meet up with you at that outcropping of rocks over there." She headed out at a trot, bolas in one hand, rabbit stick in the other. Sage circled the other way, Obsidian sniffing and heading out to one side. When the girls met, Sage had four rabbits, Whispering Wind three and two prairie chickens and Obsidian two rabbits by the ears, swinging from her mouth. The women attached their game to their waist thongs and made another sweep. This time they returned to camp and dressed out their game. Several women were watching them. "I think I will go down to that stream and follow it up for a way. I am sure that there will be some watercress there," Sage said.

"I will go with you. I think we could find some onion as well. I remember a patch over by the outcropping. There was lamb's quarter as well." So they wandered out again, Obsidian with them. They returned just before noon, well laden with plants.

Whispering Wind set her basket down beside their shelter and frowned, "Where are our rabbits and chickens?"

Sage looked around, "They are gone," she replied. She sniffed, "Someone is cooking our food! I cannot believe that anyone would just take it!"

Rain Water called from the next hearth, "Hunting Badger came to your camp and took the game as part of the common food supply. He said to tell you that you are still far short of your share."

"Communal food supply?" questioned Whispering Wind, "When did the Bison Camp have a communal food supply?

"Today is the first I have heard about it," replied Rain Water.

"Oh? Well how much is our share?"

Rain Water shrugged.

"I will go and ask," Whispering Wind stated, "You might as well get the plant food going, or we will get nothing to eat for our mid day meal." She marched off to find the headman. Obsidian disappeared on a mission of her own and Sage, not even noticing, began getting the watercress and lambs quarter cooking. She cut the onions and tossed them into another basket to be mixed with the cooking food later and then she added salt. Before she finished, Obsidian laid a rabbit at her feet and vanished once again. By the time Whispering Wind returned there was another rabbit beside it on the spit cooking over their fire.

"Well! Of all the nerve!" Wind sputtered, "Can you believe it? We are delegated to contribute the equivalent of a deer each day to the 'camp share'. Not even the best hunter is required to bring in that much!" She sat down discouraged. Then she sniffed, "Where did you get those?" she brightened.

"Obsidian," Sage nodded, "She brought them in after you left."

The big dog lay beside Sage, crunching her own rabbit.

"Well, we will just have to go out again and show those hunters that we can do it," Sage replied, handing Whispering Wind part of a rabbit, crispy brown and dripping juice. She then handed her a bowl of cooked plant food and one of salad.

"What are you eating there?" Rain Water asked, from the next hearth. "Where are your men? Your hearth doesn't look big enough for more than just the two of you."

"That is because the two of us are all living at this hearth and Obsidian, of course." Whispering Wind replied.

"Just the two of you? No men? You got a dog? How can that be? Who will provide for you?"

"We are quite able to provide for ourselves," Whispering Wind replied, "And we are eating plants. Actually they are very good, both to eat and to keep the gum disease which comes from too much meat in the diet away."

"Plants? Well, if you say so," Rain Water lost interest. She cut a healthy slab of bison steak from the hump she had spitted over her own fire.

"Come on!" Sage rose, "If we are to bring in 'our share' we had best get started. I figure that we will need at least twice again what we have already contributed."

They left the camp, collapsible baskets tied to their waist thong and extra leathers as well. It was late when they returned. By then Obsidian was pulling a hastily constructed travois. On it were piled well-over thirty rabbits, nearly as many quail and prairie chickens and three porcupines. Their baskets were laden with plants as well. Both were tired but exulted. They had proved that they could contribute their share. Whispering Wind set out quail and prairie chicken for their evening meal and the morning one as well. The rest she dragged over and dumped before Sand Thistle, mate to Hunting Badger.

This set the pattern of their days. Sage and Whispering Wind were virtually feeding the camp with their contribution. No hunters bestirred themselves to bring in so much as an antelope. By the time that Running Bison and his group returned, they were both disgusted.

"Hello."

Sage looked up to see a young woman of about her own age standing beside the fire. She had a bison hump steak in her hands. "I have brought this to you, as a welcome offering. No one else seems to have thought of it," she smiled, "I am called Blue Butterfly."

"Welcome to our hearth, Blue Butterfly. Please, sit down and join us. We were just getting ready to eat."

"Thank you. I would like that." She seated herself, accepted a bowl of tea and sipped. "This is very good. Actually, all of the food you prepare smells wonderful. I hope that you can use the meat."

"I am sure that we can, provided it is not required as our 'share' to the common food supply."

"There has never been a 'common food supply' until now." Butterfly remarked. "I cannot imagine why Hunting Badger is doing that. Do you really have this hearth as your very own?"

"So far," replied Whispering Wind. "Although, there are times I wonder if it is really worth it. They are really punishing us for having it."

"But I would give anything to live at such a hearth! My father insists on mating me to one of the older hunters. I would much rather work as hard as you do if I didn't have to mate with that old man."

"Then join us," Sage offered, "There is room for one more."

"Really? Do you mean it?"

"If no one else objects, certainly you are welcome. More hands make the work easier."

"I will get my things. I have already asked my father. He cares not, so long as he is not required to provide for me." Butterfly rose and hurried away. Very soon she was back, with all her worldly possessions. They set up her shelter beside their own and soon the three of them were sipping tea and watching the bison steak cook. When it was nearly ready, Angry Bull shoved into the hearth and rudely snatched it away. The women watched helplessly as he carried off their meal. Obsidian growled, deep in her throat.

"Well, it is as well we have other food," sighed Whispering Wind. "I was really looking forward to that steak. I haven't eaten Bison in ever so long."

"Men!" sniffed Butterfly. "They care not if we starve, so long as they don't have to work."

"Excuse me, I saw what happened," a woman of middle years stepped forward. "I may not have much, but I will happily share it with you." She carried over several spitted small birds and a few lizards. "I also have no man to provide for me. This is all I could find."

Whispering Wind dug out another tortoise shell bowl and filled it with cooked plants and salad plants. The small portion of meat was passed around. "This is very pleasant," the new woman said after they had eaten. "I have never eaten plants before, but they were excellent. Do you think it would be all right if I came with you tomorrow and began to learn about these plants? I promise I will not get in the way."

Sage looked at Whispering Wind who nodded. "I am called Winter Snow," the woman introduced herself. "I am sure that you do not remember me, Whispering Wind. I mated into this camp shortly after you vanished. But my mate died several moons ago and since then no man has wanted me. The family of my dead mate wishes me gone. I would like to live at this hearth, if I would be welcome."

"There is room beside me," Blue Butterfly offered, "It you two don't mind."

"There is room," agreed both.

The next morning four women went out with bolas, rabbit sticks and nets. Before mid day they returned to the camp with more than their 'share'. That afternoon they rearranged the hearth and by nightfall another had added herself to their numbers.

"We must do something!" Angry Bull stormed, "They flaunt before us!"

"I have said they could have the hearth," reminded Hunting Badger.

"You said nothing about the others; only the pair of them."

"Why do you complain? They are providing you with all the food you can eat."

"Bah! Rabbits and birds! Not fit food for a hunter!"

"Then go out and hunt!" Crooked Spirit recommended, "I have not seen you refuse the food they provide. Why last night you ate two whole chickens and if my ears did not deceive me, would have eaten more, had not other hunters beat you to it."

"Running Bison should be back tomorrow. Then we will have another 'council'. This can't be allowed to go on," Water Carrier agreed.

The next morning the women's hearth went out seven-strong. Now it was one of the largest hearths in the camp. Soon other women gathered around and during the afternoon, laughter could be heard from that hearth. Children played happily under the stern supervision of adults and much work was accomplished. Women were learning about plants, how to recognize them, prepare them and cook them. Even if the hunters disdained to eat the food, the women and children did so gladly.

Running Bison and his group were due back that very evening. Whispering Wind had prepared a special meal for him. Sage has shown the women how to pack certain plants into the cavity of the birds, then wrap them in clay jackets and bury them in the hot coals of the fire. If placed there in the morning, by night the birds were tender, succulent and wonderful tasting. She had fixed this meal only once before, at the cave and Running Bison had been very appreciative. Now there were nearly a dozen of them nestled in coals. There were also goldenrod greens and tubers dug from the edge of the stream. There were salad and seed cakes as well.

Running Bison's group came into the camp well before dark. Their travois were laden with the big baskets taken along to hold the stolen pups. Yelping from within told the success of their trip. They had found several dens and stolen upward of twenty pups. In a few moons, pulling the travois would no longer be women's work. For now, however, the pups were turned over to several youths to care for. These youths helped themselves to the 'common' food stores to feed the pups.

"How have things been for you while we were gone?" Running Bison asked Sage. "At least I am relieved to see that you are still here."

"Oh, things are wonderful!" she replied shortly, "Every day we bring in rabbits, quail and prairie chickens so that the lazy hunters can fill their stomachs and then complain that the food isn't fit for a hunter!"

"What?"

"You heard her," Butterfly replied. "The woman's hearth is required to feed the entire camp; yet forbidden to take the antelope or deer which we come across. The hunters have not left this camp since you did. Every day we go out and they sit around and make fun of us."

"And Hunting Badger has condoned this behavior?"

"He has done nothing to discourage it," Whispering Wind replied.

"I see," Running Bison replied. "I think it is time for another council meeting. If this thing does not get straightened out tonight, be prepared to leave this camp." He thanked the women for the wonderful food and took his leave.

From the women's hearth, Running Bison visited several more. When it came time for the elder's council to meet, most of the camp was still up milling about, keeping and eye in that direction.

"Tell us about the wolf hunting," Hunting Badger rose and opened the meeting.

"As you can see," Running Bison motioned to where the pups were being contained, "We had significant success. We took only the strong. In a few moons they will be splendid travois animals or hunting partners."

"Did you see any new sign of the savages?" Crooked Spirit asked.

"Some signs, but all were old and none heading in this direction," Running Bison replied.

"But that is not why this meeting was called."

"I want first selection of the pups!" Demanded Angry Bull.

"Everyone will get a pup," Running Bison snapped, "What of the women?"

"What of them?" Hunting Badger eyed him cautiously.

"Why are they supplying food for the entire camp? What is this 'common food supply' which suddenly has appeared? Where are the hunters?"

"They wanted their own hearth, let them provide for it," Jeered Angry Bull.

"I agree," Running Bison answered. "But only for it, not for the entire camp!" He stalked to where Hunting Badger stood. "You not only did not put a stop to the miss-use of these women; but encouraged it. Is this not true?"

Hunting Badger shrugged, "I have more important things to consider than a pair of silly women!"

"Then perhaps you should consider this," Running Bison stated angrily. "If they are miss-used again, I am taking them and all who care to follow me, from this camp, "And not only are they to provide only for their own hearth, I insist that they be allowed to take deer and antelope as well as smaller game, so long as they do so with women's weapons."

There was an angry stir among the men. People watching began to gather in small groups and talk among themselves. Hunting Badger rose. "This is an outrage!" he shouted, "You are not Headman of the Bison Camp. You will not tell me what can and cannot be done in my camp!"

"Then I no longer belong to this camp!" Running Bison rose and left the council. He made his way to where the women and a number of men waited. "You have heard. I am leaving this camp. With me I take any that believe as I do, that the women deserve to be treated fairly. I take my family, Sage, Whispering Wind and the others of the women's camp. We leave at dawn," he stalked to where he had his shelter erected. Raven and Bull Elk waited for him there. Soon Crooked Spirit and Thunder Cloud joined him. Walks Far, Juniper Smoke, Prairie Grass, Talking Shadow, Water Carrier and Pine Cone also joined him. This included half the hunters of the Bison Camp.

"I would join you as well," tottered Old Badger into the group." If you will consider a worthless old man as myself."

Running Bison nodded.

With the dawn, those leaving the Bison Camp were on the move. Running Bison led them from the wallow and onto the plain. Behind, left in the wallow, was a handful of angry hunters and Hunting Badger, along with a hand of women and children belonging to the hunters.

The wolf pups were either carried; or secured on the travois. Hunters helped pull the heavy loads, providing some relief for the women. The first evening there were several hearths set up, the largest among them the newly recognized 'women's hearth'. Around it many women were busy preparing the meal, watching small children and repairing garments, most of which bore the distinct teeth-marks of wolf pups. It was a tired but happy camp.

"Where do we go from here, Running Bison?" questioned Jumping Antelope.

"I have been asking myself that very same question," Running Bison replied. "I have spoken with Crooked Spirit while we travel. He has reminded me that we are in need of tool material. I think I will take this camp to the north. There is a place there where excellent stone can be quarried. It is far superior to that which we now use. Besides it is far removed from the danger represented by the savages. But the savages are a danger to the other camps as well. Most of you have family within those other camps. I think it would be well if we sent runners to them and informed them both of the danger and our destination. It is time The People had a Mid-Summer Gathering! The valley near the place of stone would be an excellent place to hold one."

There was some discussion, but mostly agreement. Three youths were selected to go to the other camps. They were Crying Coyote, Mesquite Branch and Singing Water. Running Bison and Crooked Spirit sat with them for a long time, explaining where they thought the other camps to be and describing the way to the valley for them. Finally the youths nodded and all retired. At dawn the camp watched as the three headed south and a ground-eating lope. Then Running Bison's camp turned north and began to move as well. They were well organized. Their whole lives had been spent in just such activity. A pair of hunters headed out before the camp to bring down deer or antelope for food. The women, following Sage, began walking wide of the camp gathering plants as they went. Meals were much tastier now. Men began tasting, then eating this new plant food. Salt was provided, as were other seasonings. Sage knew many. She showed the women how the women of the gatherers cooked the food. Bison meat was no longer the only choice. At night, however, camps were situated in well-sheltered spots where fires would not easily be spotted. Trackers went into the distance, checking for signs of other people. Running Bison was taking no chances.

Sage watched their new leader. More and more she was impressed with him. Running Bison was a caring and level-headed leader, just as Whispering Wind had said. He made wise decisions. He did not take chances. Each day they stopped well before dark and the wolf pups were worked with by their handlers. Women were allowed to rest and prepare a leisurely meal. They were in no hurry. The pups began to respond quickly. Within two hands of days it was no longer necessary to tether them. They were settling into camp life. Among them, levels of dominance were beginning to develop. Loyalties were being formed. They responded to care with an undying love and bonded. And they were growing, rapidly.

A moon passed. The youths returned from contacting the Antelope and Wind Camps. These, in turn, would contact others, until all the camps had been notified. Gradually 'The People' were converging on the valley for the Mid-Summer Gathering.

Raven watched Sage. He did not do so openly. She was not inclined to notice that he existed. He gave her the prime share of his kills, for the 'women's hearth of course'. Sage and Whispering Wind still shared a shelter, but Blue Butterfly and Winter Snow and the other pitched their shelters around the hearth. The seven unmated women of the Bison Camp had cemented the heart of the camp with the activities of the hearth. There was always something going on there. And to the amazement of the hunters, these women did provide not only for themselves, but for any others in need, as well.

Then Raven and Bull Elk came across the first of the 'trails'.

\*     \*     \*

"Do you smell that?" Bull Elk sniffed the air, as the pair of hunters topped another ridge. They were far from the camp. "Campfire smoke and something else I'm not sure what."

Raven also sniffed the air, "Burned meat." he identified the smell. "I think we should see what it is."

Bull Elk nodded and the men headed toward the smell. They topped a low ridge and stopped. Below them, in a small valley lay the remnants of a small camp of Gatherers. The remains of their shelter were still burning. Scattered about the central camp lay numerous bodies; most being attacked by a flock of buzzards. The only things moving in the camp were the birds.

"Savages?" Bull Elk questioned.

"I don't know. It looks like the camp we discovered when Whispering Wind was a slave. It doesn't really look like 'savages', but more like those raiders. These people were killed, not taken captive for sacrifice."

"How can you tell? There may have been many more than those we see."

"Look at the shelters. How many persons would you say made up this camp?"

Bull Elk studied the shelters, "Perhaps three double hands, maybe more."

"Then let's go down there and count the bodies. That is the only way we can be certain."

Bull Elk grimaced, "I hate buzzards!"

Raven shrugged, "They serve a purpose. If it were not for the scavengers think how badly the land would smell. Even the insects that are such pests serve their purpose. Remember when Walking Man got darted and the wound rotted. He would have died except for the intervention of the healer. Remember how he placed maggots on the wound and in a short while they had eaten all the rotted flesh and the wound healed. We all thought that Walking Man would die."

"What you say is true, but I still don't like those birds. I am sure that other scavengers watch and wait for death, but they are not so visible while doing the waiting. Buzzards circle and sit on trees and wait."

"Well the sooner we get down there and check, the more likely we are to understand who did the killing. Personally, I can't say there is much to choose from between the two. Perhaps the raiders are quicker and the death is less bloodcurdling, but dead is still dead," Bull Elk grimaced.

The hunters silently worked their way down into the death camp. The birds rose in a great noisy cloud of protest. Raven began at one end of the camp, Bull Elk at the other. They counted 28 individuals. Some had been darted. Some had their throats cut. A few had been bludgeoned to death. They decided that the raiders had more than likely been responsible for the slaughter. They noticed that there were no weapons, little food and no dogs, although there were several travois. They were standing near the central fire discussing this when they heard a noise. It came from a partially burned shelter a hand's distance from them.

"What was that?" Bull Elk whispered; the hair on the back of his neck suddenly rising.

"I will see," Raven replied, already making his way toward the sound. His young wolf walked in front of him balanced on the balls of its feet, the hair on its back standing upright. She growled deep in her throat. The shelter was nearly collapsed and it took only a shove by one foot to complete the process. There was a bison-hide-covered object within and it was moving and issuing the noise. It sounded like a child crying. He called out softly as he raised the hide. Only the quickness of his response saved him from a nasty dart wound. The being within the hide, leaped free and, with a quickness that surprised both men and wolf, escaped into the heavy brush covering the side of the stream.

"What was it?" Bull Elk asked.

"I don't really know. But whether a child, or a small female, I could not judge but which- ever, certainly hostile!"

"Probably it thought we were the raiders returned."

"Well we had better decide what to do with these people. Do we just leave them, in case the raiders return? Or do we lay them out and say prayers over them, in which case, if the raiders do return they will know that someone was here?" Raven sighed.

"You aren't going after her?"

"If it is a, 'her' and if she doesn't want found, there is no way we will be able to do so. We don't have time any way. Our best hope is that 'she' decided we are friendly and follows us back to the camp."

"What about seeing if that wolf of yours can trail her? You are always bragging about her. Now is an excellent chance to see if she is really worth all the food you put into her belly."

Raven smiled. He called the young wolf to him and let her get a good smell of the hiding place.

"Woof!" The animal wagged her tail and took off at a fast pace, hot on the trail. A few minutes later, she stopped before a rotten log and wagged her tail again. Raven grinned at Bull Elk, who was reasonably impressed. They could see the top of a head within the hole inside the log. Raven squatted down and spoke quietly for several minutes. Gradually, the head began to move and finally a boy of about a double hand of seasons squirmed from his hiding place in the log. He was bloody and filthy, but otherwise seemed unhurt. Both hunters gave the broken dart he held a healthy respect.

The child eyed the hunters and the wolf, with suspicion, but did not try to run. Raven continued to talk to the boy until finally the child reached out and took the offered hand of peace. By this time it was getting quite late and they still had to remove all signs of their presence.

*     *     *

"There is no way we can make it back to the camp tonight," Raven sighed. They were some distance from the slaughtered camp, but still a greater distance from the Bison Camp. "I think we should camp here tonight and go on in tomorrow, when we can see."

Bull Elk agreed and they began to set up an overnight camp. The child shook his head and gestured. He was so insistent that finally, in exasperation, they let him lead them into a tangle of brush and finally beneath the thick, wide-spreading branches of a tall pine. Here it would be nearly impossible to be detected.

Raven began to start a tiny fire to cook a rabbit he had taken, but the boy kicked dirt on his fire and shook his head wildly. So, they camped without a fire. They ate trail food and the wolf got the rabbit. Finally they rolled up in their sleeping furs and tried to sleep. Late into the night the wolf growled softly, waking Raven. The hunter shook the snoring Bull Elk awake and they crouched in their hidden bower, suddenly thankful for the insistence of the child. The boy squatted, clutching the young wolf tightly to him.

Beyond where they hid, a large company of people were moving through the night. They were making little noise. The brightness of the moon reflected from a face here and there and Raven shuddered as he recognized the beautiful features of Quinquel. The savages were following a trail and it was then that Raven realized they were after the raiders. There was no sleep for the remainder of that night and as soon as it was light enough to see the small party beneath the pine melted into the distance as they made haste to the Bison Camp.

*     *     *

"The news is worse than I had hoped for," Running Bison frowned. "You say that both the raiders and the savages are moving in a line parallel to us?"

"They are both moving north," Raven replied. "I am not sure that the raiders know they are being followed. But if those savages catch up to them, half our worries are over."

"What of this child?" Running Bison indicated the boy, shyly watching him from within a welter of tangled hair.

"I have no idea!" Raven sighed, "I can't understand a word he says. But his camp looked to be gatherers."

Running Bison nodded. "Winter Snow," he addressed the woman working at the hearth beside them. "Would you ask Sage to come here, please?" She nodded and shortly Sage stepped up to the hearth. "Raven has found this boy, much the same way that you discovered Whispering Wind. He thinks the child might be a gatherer."

Sage nodded and said something to the boy. He responded with an outpouring of words so rapidly that one nearly tripped the next. For several fingers of time, Sage and the child spoke, then she nodded and turned to Running Bison. "You are correct in assuming he is a gatherer. He is, or rather was, from the Acorn Camp. The raiders struck suddenly, after dark. He says there were many hands of them, led by a big, dirty, mean, man with a wide scar across his face. The boy's name is Cricket, by the way."

"What are we going to do?" Sand Crawler asked.

"How far are these groups from us?" Running Bison questioned Raven.

"Close enough that they could see our camp fires at night," Bull Elk replied.

"About a half day hard run," Raven replied.

"Sage, would you take this youth to the women's hearth, feed him, clean him up and then bring him to me. Perhaps with your help we can discover more. In the meanwhile let it be known that tonight we camp in a wallow and no fires!"

Once the camp was broken, Running Bison led them away from the mountains. They stopped late in the afternoon and true to his words, camped in a deep bison wallow.

"You were captured by these people also?" Cricket asked Sage.

She shook her head, "You are not a captive. "I was born to 'The People', but I grew up with the Pine Cone Camp. This is why I speak your tongue. But what was the Acorn Camp doing so far from the western mountains?"

"Fleeing!" Was the sad answer.

"From what?"

"Raiders, the strange people from the south who cut out hearts and drink blood, from death and disease. The western mountains are all aflame; fires burn without stopping; the raiders have taken to hitting camps while they sleep. The Acorn Camp slipped off in the dead of night, hoping to find a new and better place to live. Instead they found death."

"But you escaped!"

"I did, but what of the Porcupine Camp and the Badger and the Snake? They are all dead!"

"What of the Pine Cone Camp?" Sage asked sadly. While she had no close friends among them, she had known them all.

Cricket nodded. "They were one of the first. The raiders wiped them out more than two seasons ago. We had hoped to be so far north they wouldn't bother with us. Not so," he sighed. "I was the acolyte to the dreamer, Mud Dobber. The raiders took him alive. I had no other relatives, now I do not know if Uncle is dead or alive." He sighed, "I will probably never know."

"You might talk to Crooked Spirit, the dreamer of this camp. He is getting old and has no one to follow him. The tongue is not so difficult to learn. In a few moons you will feel that you have lived in this camp all your life," Sage reassured him.

"If I am still alive," was his sad reply.

That night and for many which followed, Running Bison held them to the strict rule, no fire which was not completely shielded within a shelter and even then only flame enough to cook small game. He was taking no chances.

On one occasion, only days after rescuing Cricket, the entire camp could hear the faint, but clear beat of drums. Raven, Bull Elk, Running Bison and Prairie Grass could each, visualize clearly in their minds, the ceremony which was taking place. All shuddered. Again, a moon later, they thought they heard the very faint sound of drums, but no one could be sure.

Crooked Spirit welcomed Cricket and in a short while they were able to understand each other well enough for a bond to form. Gradually, the haunted look left the boy's eyes and he settled into his new slot in life. The wolves fascinated him. He spent his every free minute with the animals and finally in exasperation, Running Bison gave him one of the last unclaimed to be his own. He named it Spirit Chaser.

The wolf pups were about five months old now and most were beginning to learn to pull the travois. Their loads were small, but they seemed to enjoy the task. Others accompanied the hunters. They were amazed how quickly the animals learned hunting skills. The blood of their wild ancestors had prepared them very well for the task of hunting.

The seven women of the 'hearth' still brought in a consistent contribution to the larder of the camp. The hunters had not once gone out to hunt bison but so far they had found no fresh sign and hadn't even seen a herd in sight. Then, at last, they crossed a wide muddy river. Now Running Bison visibly relaxed. The ban on fires was relaxed. Hunters went out with their 'wolves in training' and even returned with game. The women were gathering and preparing food as well. Then they headed west.

25  *Allium* : wild onion: **Tilford:** p 160.
26  *Rorippa nasturtium-aquaticum:* Watercress. Grows in fresh water. Excellent in salads but preferably cooked. **Tilford:** p154.
27  *Chenopodium album:* Lamb's Quarter. **Tilford:** p 88
28  The Platte River

# CHAPTER 9

I would speak with you," Crooked Spirit requested of Sage. Most of the women were out gathering, but she had been relegated to the 'blood shelter' and had just emerged. He was waiting for her.

Sage frowned; the dreamer made her feel uneasy. She sensed that he saw more than the rest and understood what he beheld. Running Bison had promised that she would have time to settle in before he told anyone that she was Clover Blossom's grand daughter. So far he had kept his word. She nodded and led him to a log in the shade of a huge oak tree.

"What do you wish to talk about?" She asked.

"The boy, Cricket, he is learning quickly. I thank you for suggesting that he seek me out. It was a thoughtful consideration on your part."

"You are welcome," she replied, then waited for him to continue.

"That is an unusual staff which you carry," he remarked.

Sage nodded and waited.

"Whispering Wind tells me that you killed the bear whose claws and teeth that necklace is made from." When they first entered the camp, Sage had kept the necklace hidden, but once the woman's hearth was established, she took to wearing it openly again.

Again she nodded.

"A grizzly bear is a formidable kill for even the most seasoned hunter. Did it not seem strange that you killed it while on you vision quest?"

"At the time I hardly had time to think at all. I was just coming out of my 'spirit journey' and it burst forth and attacked me. I'm afraid I only reacted. There was a broken branch with a sharp end, I just held it up and the bear impaled himself. As it was, I gained these scars from his 'hug of death'," she raised her sleeve and showed him the marks.

"The necklace carries much 'spirit power'," Crooked Spirit replied. "But you already know that. The staff is equally special and I have been told you own an unusual tunic as well. It also had special decorations. Tell me although Running Bison claims you for a relative, he is very unspecific about the relationship. Could it be that you are the granddaughter of my old friend Clover Blossom?"

Sage sighed and nodded.

"I knew it!" the old man smiled. "Tell me, did she have a good life after she left here?"

"She was not exactly unhappy among the gatherers," Sage sighed, "But I think she missed her friends. She never told me many stories about her young days and but she spoke your name a few times. I think, had things been different . . ."

Crooked Spirit smiled and sighed, "Ah yes, the dreams of youth, and the demands of adulthood. So often they do not agree. Had not my older brother died . . . had not Clover Blossom mated to Gray Coyote; had not Mood Maiden been killed . . . So many things, all out of our control. But you! You are completely in control, are you not?"

"Me?" Sage shook her head, "I have no idea!"

"Of course you do! I knew it the moment you stepped into the camp. You started making changes right then and look at the camp now! The women's hearth has been reestablished, Running Bison is now the headman, we raise wolves to replace the dogs so unwisely eaten and now we go to the Valley of the Gathering. Running Bison tells me that you made the Spring Offering."

"What is it that you really want, Old Friend of my Grandmother?"

"I want to know if you carry the Ancient Relics. If you are visited by the spirits, if you bear the mark of the Spirit."

"But you already know the answers to those questions," Sage replied.

"Moon Maiden died before giving birth. How can I be sure?"

"My grandmother cut me from her body," Sage replied. "I can show you the mark, I can even show you the Relics, but I cannot make you believe, or disbelieve anything."

"Clover Blossom could have gotten you from another camp, raised you as her grand daughter. You would not know."

"Then why do you bother with me?"

"Because, I have prayed to the spirits, I have made offerings and I have hoped, beyond hope that the things which I have seen with my eyes are real and not the desperate longings of an old man. I had nearly given up and then you walked into this camp. It was as if the spirits were shouting in my ears!"

"And yet, you do not trust!"

"Oh, I trust, all right. I just hope the trust is real and not just some cruel trick!"

Sage reached out, "Take my hand."

Crooked Spirit hesitated a moment, then reached out and strongly clasped her hand. Sage could feel the vibration that she sent through the old dreamer. It seemed to come from deep within her and the longer she held his hands, the stronger it became. Finally, a deep feeling of exhaustion spread through her and she dropped his hands. Crooked Spirit sighed and nodded his head. "I feel seasons younger," he smiled. "It is as though you have refreshed my spirit. You are truly a powerful woman, Sage, Bear Claw Woman, granddaughter of Clover Blossom. My prayers have been answered." He rose and walked thoughtfully back to the shelter which he now shared with the youth, Cricket.

Sage stayed sitting on the log for a long time. Then she rose and went about her usual camp chores, but with a subdued air about her. When the other women of the hearth came in Sage exhausted retired to her shelter and slept.

Crooked Spirit found time, well after the camp had settled down, to speak with Running Bison. They walked a short distance from the camp. "What are your plans for this Gathering?" He asked.

"What do you mean, plans?" Running Bison questioned.

"Are you going to tell The People that the Sacred Relics have been returned?"

Bison glanced at the old dreamer sharply, frowned and then sighed, "I haven't decided. It depends upon the way things go after the naming and mating ceremonies and the renewal of the hunter's loyalty to the spirits and if everyone is in a receptive mood, then perhaps. I promised

Sage that she would be given a chance to settle in. After all, hers will be a position of great responsibility. I am not sure she is ready . . ."

Crooked Spirit snorted! "She is ready. I have never met one with as much 'power' as she has. Why just this afternoon I sat with her and I came away from the meeting, feeling at least two hands of seasons younger. I am refreshed and renewed."

"Then she knows that you have recognized her?"

Crooked Spirit nodded, "She is reluctant, as you say, but she is ready. It only needs The People to be ready to receive her."

"That, as you know, may be a problem. If she begins initiating too many changes, they could get very nasty. You know how the hunters are. The idea of a woman, any woman, having the least bit of equality and they feel they are threatened." Running Bison shook his head.

"Why do you think she will start trouble? So far the only thing she has brought back to the camp is the women's hearth and you know yourself, that we have discussed bringing it back many times. I do not see that as a big change. After all, each camp can choose for itself. If the hunters do not want it, then the camp will not have it," explained Crooked Spirit.

"You forget all the plants that we now eat, just as if we always did so. And the wolves which we train, do you not see those as changes?"

"You brought the wolves into the camp. No one need know that it wasn't your own idea. After all, we all know that our ancestors walked with wolves. But the plants could be a problem. Perhaps we could suggest to the women that they stay near the camp while at the gathering and refrain from including the plants in our food while we are there. After all, there is no need to introduce change all at once. Next season will be soon enough to include plants."

"I will speak with the women. Perhaps that is the best suggestion. Once the other camps see how the Bison Camp fares they will be more open to following our lead. We need only have a very successful season and they will listen." Replied Running Bison.

"How many days until we reach this valley?"

Running Bison frowned. "I am not sure. You know it was almost as if the suggestion to go there came from outside myself, but I know that cannot be. I only remember the valley from the tales of old Broken Leg when I was a child. But I am certain we are headed there. Does any of this make sense to you?"

The dreamer nodded, "She speaks to you, directs you through your mind. I have heard of such things. Usually however, this has been only through siblings, or mother and daughter. I have never heard of it through persons related farther than that. Come to think of it, I have never heard a man being involved at all. This mind talking has always been only a female thing."

Running Bison shifted uncomfortably, "I can't believe she communicates with my mind. I would know, wouldn't I?"

"Only if she wanted you to know; otherwise you would just have an idea pop into your head and think it was your own." Crooked Spirit shifted to a more comfortable position. "Tell me, do you think you can control her?"

Running Bison snorted, "So far I have had very little success in that direction. She has a strong mind of her own, but she is unsure and scared. To a degree I think that I can reason with her, but control? No, I don't think I can control her."

"You must be very careful that she doesn't find a way to control you."

"You think she might cause danger?"

The old dreamer shook his head, "She is controlled by spirits, far more than she realizes. If they decide to use her to control you through this mind thing, then I have no idea what might happen. Usually, however, the spirits do not harm The People. But spirits cannot be depended upon. They can do things that make no sense to us when they happen. It is only later, sometimes much later that we understand. I have been feeling uneasy for several seasons, ever since this thing with Moon Maiden. Did you ever figure out who . . .?"

Running Bison shook his head, "It made no sense at the time and although I searched and searched for the killer, I found no clues. I am no closer to understanding today than I was the day Moon Maiden died. I know that Clover Blossom did not trust anyone, not even you and I and there were none closer to her than you."

"It was only great fear that caused her to flee as she did. Clover Blossom was a level-headed woman. Perhaps she discovered something which we did not."

"I have sometimes wondered if Hunting Badger was not somehow mixed up in that."

Crooked Spirit glanced sharply at Running Bison, "I have had the same thoughts," he admitted.

"Well, wondering about it is just a waste at this point in time. There is no way we can be sure of anything. It was too long ago."

"I wonder if Clover Blossom ever said anything to the granddaughter? Perhaps she knows something which will give us a clue?"

"You think?"

Crooked Spirit nodded, "It is possible. She might not even be aware that she knows. Would you like me to speak with her? Perhaps I could get her to talk more easily than you, she seems to distrust you."

Running Bison grunted agreement. The men returned to the camp and retired to their own shelters.

\*        \*        \*

Sage lay in the shelter she shared with Whispering Wind. She had slept for several hours and was now wide-awake. She watched the Ancestor Fires twinkle in the night sky and wondered if one of them was her grandmother's, or possible the mother she never knew. Restlessly she tossed and turned for a time, then with a sigh, rose and left the shelter. She wandered a short distance from the camp and found a comfortable place beneath a large tree, tucked into deep shadow, with Obsidian at her side. She watched silently as the men came toward her and sat, almost within touching distance. There was no way that she could move without being detected, then, the conversation caught her interest. Shamelessly she listened. After they left, she thought about their conversation.

*I wonder??? Could I really communicate with the mind?* She grinned then closing her eyes called; *Whispering Wind! Wake up!*

"What is it? Sage? Where are you?"

*It works!*

"What works? Where are you? I hear you, but I don't see you!"

*Come to the big tree at the edge of the camp. I am there*

"How can that be? I hear you as clearly as if you were standing beside me."

*Come, I will explain.*

"It's 'power', isn't it? I don't know that I want to know!"

*Oh come on. This could be fun!*

"If you say so . . ." Soon Sage detected the other woman making her way to the tree, "What is going on?" Whispering Wind demanded. "I was sound asleep."

"Never mind; you heard me! That is what is important!"

"But how did you do it?"

"I have no idea. I just closed my eyes and called you with my mind."

"Your mind? I knew it? I don't want to know! It is dangerous to play around with 'spirit things'."

"How else do I learn how to control them? I must experiment. Don't you see? And you can help me."

"How?" Whispering Wind asked suspiciously, "Will it be dangerous?"

"I don't think so," Sage grinned, "What could be dangerous about a simple conversation."

"Where spirits are concerned, anything could be dangerous."

"Well, if you don't want to help me, I'm sure that Blue Butterfly . . ."

"I didn't say that!" Whispering Wind quickly cut in, "I just asked if it was dangerous!"

Sage sighed, "You ask questions which I can't answer. It seems that everything in my life turns out to be dangerous. I don't want to bring harm to you though, so perhaps it would be better if I practiced on someone else; maybe Running Bison?"

"You are not serious?"

Sage shook her head, "But I do intend to see if I can communicate with him, but later, once I am in more control. Perhaps I can even talk to the dreamer."

"You wouldn't?"

Sage shrugged, "Any way, it is getting late. I have proved that it works and now I find that I am very tired. Let's go back to our furs." She rose and led Whispering Wind back to their shelter.

* * *

Far to the south, the Antelope Camp was sleeping soundly. A dog wakened, barked once and then yelped and became quiet; shadows poured into the camp, shadows of deadly intruders; and then sounds erupted. Screams, death calls, fire, silence!

"We should have kept going last night!" Calling Wolf said to Eagle Stalker.

"We would have only gotten lost and missed the camp," Running Antelope panted, "These deer did not seem all that heavy when we started back. But mine weighs more with each step. I have no desire to carry it farther than necessary. We started out again very early. With luck we will catch up with them before they are on the move again."

"It should not be much farther," commented Calling Wolf. "They should be just over the next rise. That is where Jumping Bear planned to camp for the night."

"Look!" Running Antelope stopped, "What is that light ahead?"

"That should be the camp," Eagle Stalker stopped, then dropped his deer and began to run, "Come on, something is wrong!"

The other hunters followed suit. A short time later the three burst into the quiet camp. Flames ate greedily at the shelters and furs. Bodies of friends and loved ones were strewn about the camp in pathetic crumpled heaps. Women, children, hunters, all silent, forever . . .

"Who could have done such a thing?" Eagle Stalker stared helplessly about.

"I don't know," Calling Wolf answered, "But I don't intend to stay around and wait for them to return." He began rummaging in the remains of his own shelter, wincing as he found the body of his mate. He had not cared for her, but still . . . this was no way to die.

"We can't just leave them here like this!" Eagle Stalker shouted, "We must lay them out or something!"

"What if these raiders return?" Calling Wolf kept collecting things and packing them on his travois.

"For what?" Running Antelope asked, "They have taken everything they could carry. I am going to set my family out. You go on by yourself if you are in such a big hurry. But think on this, where are you going?"

Calling Wolf stopped. He looked around the camp. "If we had come on into the camp last night, maybe we could have prevented this."

"Or, maybe we would be right here with them," Eagle Stalker stated. "There is nothing we can do for these people. At least make sure who is here. I don't see Drifting Sand anywhere," he said hopefully.

"He is here," Running Antelope replied hollowly.

The hunters worked for hours. The sun rose, became hot and still they toiled, setting one after another of the camp out to walk the wind. When they finished, several were unaccounted for; a double hand from the entire camp.

"I am going back for our deer. We will need the food," Eagle Stalker stood beside the last body.

"What are we going to do?" Running Antelope asked.

"I don't know," Eagle Stalker replied, "I have not had time to think. What suggestions do you have?"

"Search for those missing," Calling Wolf answered, "perhaps they escaped and are hiding nearby."

"They would have seen us and made themselves known," Running Antelope said.

"I think we should try to warn the other camps!" Calling Wolf replied. "They are still behind us."

"I would rather push on and catch up to the Bison Camp. It would be safer," remarked Running Antelope. "Then again, what do I care about my safety?" he frowned. "You are right. It is better we warn the other camps. Come on let's go! Leave the meat!" he called as Calling Wolf stooped to collect his deer. "We cannot make any time carrying a heavy load. We will just have to depend upon what we can find for food."

With a frown Calling Wolf looked regretfully at the deer and then at the travois he dragged. With a shrug he dropped the poles and walked away. The three hunters set out as a ground-eating lope, headed to where they knew the Deer Camp should be. It was nearly dark when they saw a pair of men coming their way. Both groups stopped, then as recognition bloomed, came together. The hunters were Swift Fox and Black Bear of the Deer Camp. They had a chillingly similar tale to tell.

"Three of the other camps were wiped out," Swift Fox informed them. "We are all that is left, except for a handful which are just behind us; women and children. Somehow, a few did manage to escape. One pair who were out coupling beneath the moon, a pair of children who decided to sneak away from their camp and hunt for frogs, that is all. Oh and a couple hands' full of people who are with Hunting Badger. It seems that now Running Bison leads the Bison Camp."

"Then we number about a double hand total," Eagle Stalker shook his head.

"This is all that remains of The People?" Swift Fox questioned.

"We don't know about Running Bison!"

"Who is going to lead us?" Eagle Stalker reached out a hand and stopped him.

Swift Fox shrugged, "Hunting Badger has more or less taken over as leader," he replied.

"I do not know that I wish to follow that old man," Calling Wolf frowned.

"For now, it matters little who leads, so long as we go far out onto the plain and evade whoever is out there, killing The People," Swift Fox answered.

"We don't know that the Bison Camp has been hit," reminded Running Antelope.

"Well, gather everyone together and let's get out of this place!" Eagle Stalker recommended, "The longer we wait, the more danger we are in."

"We have pushed those people as hard as we dare," Swift Fox replied. "We have been walking nonstop for three days and nights. They have no food and very little water. They are dead tired."

"Would you rather they were merely dead?" asked Eagle Stalker.

Swift Fox sighed, "We can perhaps get a little more from them." He led the hunters over the rise and into a small wallow where the pathetic remains of a once great tribe huddled in fear.

Soon they were headed east, out onto the plain, hoping to evade whoever was after them.

*     *     *

Far to the north, Sage lay in her robes. She reached out with her mind, exploring . . .

*Hello . . .*

Calling Wolf stopped. He looked all around. He was ahead of the camp, checking for danger. But he would swear he had just heard a woman's voice. He peered into the darkness. "Hello?" He called out softly.

*Oh! Uh . . .Who am I talking too?*

"Where are you? Come out where I can see you!" There was not so much as a bush, behind which anyone could hide. Chills began to race up and down his spine.

*Uh . . . that would be difficult. You see;* Sage grinned to herself, *I am a spirit.*

The hunter began to shake with fear; he looked all about him. There was no where to hide. No one was playing a cruel joke on him. There could be no murdering savages hiding just waiting to slit his throat. "Go away!" he managed to stutter in a guttural whisper, "There has been too much death. If your spirit has been left to wander, go elsewhere!"

*What do you mean; death?*

"You know what I mean! The Antelope Camp, the Deer Camp, the Bear, the Badger! All wiped out, all dead! Did you do it?"

Sage sat upright and stopped smiling. *Where are you?*

"What do you mean? I'm right here, talking to you!" Calling Wolf replied.

*No! No, you are not. I have no time to explain now, perhaps later. But it is essential that you tell me. You say the camps are all dead? How did this happen?*

"If you are a spirit, then you know. If you are not, then you are trying to trick me."

*I am sorry; I did not mean to frighten you. You see I am new at this and I was just exploring, but wait . . . if there is trouble, Running Bison should know!*

"You are with Running Bison?"

*Yes. I walk with his camp.*

"Where is the Bison Camp?" now the hunter was suspicious.

*We are north of the muddy river. We crossed it two days ago.*

"Then how can you be talking to me? We are at least a double hand of days south of the muddy river."

*You have been attacked? By savages? Lead by a tall beautiful man?*

"I have no idea! I saw no one. We were out hunting. When we arrived, the camp was already all dead; the same thing with the survivors of the other camps. Now we follow Hunting Badger. We are going far out onto the plain."

*I will tell Running Bison. What is your name? I would know the man to whom I talk!*

The hunter thought for a time, then reluctantly answered, "I am Calling Wolf, but who are you?"

*I will talk to you again.* Sage looked up at the sky. It was not yet even close to morning. *Running Bison!* She called out.

"What?"

*We need to talk! I have news!*

"Sage?"

*Yes.*

"What games are you playing now?" Running Bison shrugged his sleeping fur from his shoulder.

*No game; I was just laying here, you know . . . and I spoke to a hunter of the Antelope Camp. They are south of here, a double hand of days. They have been attacked; also the Deer and Badger and other camps. Only a few have survived. They are with Hunting Badger.*

Bison Man leaped from his bed, shaking the whole frame of the shelter as his head struck the support. He rubbed his head, swore in frustration and gritted his teeth. Then he was striding across the camp. "Sage! Get out here!" he hissed just outside her shelter. Whispering Wind mumbled nearly wakened. But Sage scrambled out.

"What is going on? I want an answer and I want it right now."

"I just told you," Sage shrugged, "I was just trying that mind talking thing which you and Crooked Spirit mentioned, just wanted to see if it really worked."

"How do you . . .?"

"I was sitting against the tree just behind you. I wasn't trying to listen, truly! It is just that, well, I didn't know what to do, so it seemed best to just stay where I was until you left. Then I decided to try it! Well, Crooked Spirit was so convinced that I could . . . I just wanted to try."

"All right! I accept that. Now tell me about the camps!"

So Sage sat on the log with Running Bison and told him.

"Do you think you could talk to this Called Wolf again?"

"Calling Wolf, he said his name was Calling Wolf."

"Fine, then Calling Wolf; do you think you can talk to him again?"

Sage shrugged, "I'll try," she sighed. She closed her eyes and wrapped her arms around her.

*Calling Wolf . . . Are you there?*

"You again?" The hunter stopped and glanced all around. No one was near, "what do you want?" He muttered.

*Running Bison is here with me. He wants information. Will you talk to me?*

"Well, all right, but I don't believe this! I am just suffering from tiredness. I'm not really talking to someone who isn't here. Just the same . . ."

*Thank you . . .*

"Well?"

"What do you want me to ask him?" Sage frowned, "Wait, give me your hand."

"What for?"

"Maybe you can talk to him yourself."

Bison Man took her hand.

"Go ahead, ask him a question."

"Ah . . . How many of you are there?"

"No, with your mind!"

Bison Man frowned, then closed his eyes in imitation of Sage and tried again . . .

"There are two double hands plus of us left," Calling Wolf replied, still peering into the darkness. At least he recognized Running Bison's voice. "Eleven are hunters, the remainder women and children. Seven are wounded, one so old he can barely keep up and one woman about to deliver a child." *Where the spirits are they?* He thought to himself.

*We are north of the river, but I told you that,* Sage replied.

"You can hear my thoughts?"

*Your thoughts are the clearest.*

*You really are spirits! What happened to the Bison Camp? Are they all dead as well?*

*No! I told you. The Bison Camp is fine. Really! This is no trick,* Sage replied

*I don't know how she does it,* Running Bison assured the hunter, *but she is as alive as you and I. Perhaps it would help if I told you that this woman is the 'Keeper of the Sacred Relics'.*

*You promised!*

*This is more important than you or I,* "Besides I very much doubt this hunter will tell!" Running Bison said.

*I won't say a word! No one would believe me any way. But what do you want of me?* Calling Wolf asked.

*We have seen the ravage of the savages! We know of what you speak. Be very careful. Do not go near the mountains, have no fires at night, nothing which could draw them to you. If you need to cook, stop before dark, keep your fires very small and put them out as soon as you can. Erase your trail. And move as quickly as you can north across the muddy river. We will talk again.*

*When?*

*If you need me, call.*

*Who?*

*I am Sage. I will be listening . . . good night.*

Calling Wolf straightened his shoulders and strode out strongly. Oddly enough, he felt refreshed and strong.

Sage sighed, "I would go to rest now, if you are finished. I am very tired."

"I, on the other hand, feel wonderfully refreshed," Running Bison rose. He looked at her carefully in the moonlight. "This draws life from you doesn't it?"

Sage frowned, "I just feel very tired."

He nodded, "Be careful how you us this tool given by the spirits. They give nothing without asking something in return. In the future, if you wish to speak to me, unless it is impossible, come seek me out. This tool drains you while it refreshed the other person."

"What are you going to do?"

"I don't know. Tell me, Sage, do you take us to this valley or do I?"

Sage sighed, "The spirits take us both" she answered.

*       *       *

"We will stop here," Hunting Badger looked about. There was little to break the unending flatness. Far to the west, mountains were barely visible in the setting sun.

"I think we should keep going until we find a bison wallow," Calling Wolf recommended, "We are too out in the open here."

"I have said we will stop here!" Hunting Badger replied angrily.

"But we are right out in the open."

"So! That way nothing can sneak up on us. Or did you think of that, hunter?"

Calling Wolf shook his head, "I am still nervous. I would feel more secure if we couldn't be seen, particularly the fires after dark. You can see a fire for a long way."

Hunting Badger frowned and then shrugged, looking around at the group of expectant hunters. "What are you, a band of frightened women? Are you all as weak in the knees as this sniveling excuse for a hunter?"

"I camp here!" Angry Bull thumped down his backpack, "Woman," he pointed to the nearest female, "Get me food!" She scurried off to do so.

Other hunters began to unload and slowly the camp formed. Several small hearths were lighted and rabbits and game birds were spitted. But the people were uneasy. Long before dark their fires were smothered. Everyone was too tired to do much more than tumble into their furs, not even bothering erecting shelters. Outside the camp, a group of hunters quietly took turns watching. Hunting Badger had not selected these, but they watched.

An ear-splitting scream rent the air. People erupted from their shelters, hunters with atlatl and dart to hand, women with anything they could use as a club; again the scream.

"Morning Dew has gone into labor," one of the women explained, "I cannot keep her quiet."

"Did you give her the pain killing drink which the dreamer gave you?" a fretting woman asked her.

"I lost it. It must have fallen off my travois," the other woman explained.

Another scream pierced the night.

"Shut that woman up, or I will," demanded Hunting Badger.

"She is having a baby, Headman!" the woman explained, "It can be very painful and this is her first. She is frightened."

"You have been warned!" the headman stomped off, "Everyone back to your furs. You hunters! What are you doing out there! The noise comes from that infernal woman!"

"We are just keeping an eye out . . ." a hunter explained.

"Go to your furs!" shouted Hunting Badger.

The hunters looked uncomfortably at each other, then regretfully did as the headman bid, leaving the camp unprotected. For the next half-hour the laboring woman frequently whimpered and groaned, but she did not scream out again. This, however, was not good enough for Hunting Badger. He stalked from his shelter and to where the women were doing their best for the mother-to-be. "I told you to keep here quiet!" He shouted at them. Then he took out his blade and before anyone could stop him, stepped behind the woman, grabbed her hair, pulled her head back and slit her throat from ear to ear. The small group of women watched in stunned horror as death clouded her eyes and the woman crumpled to the ground, dead. Hunting Badger did not even glance at them. He turned and returned to his shelter.

It was a greatly subdued camp that followed him the next morning. Hunters grumbled in small groups, careful to avoid Angry Bull and a couple others who were close to the old headman. Calling Wolf was shocked to the spirit. They had lost so many already. He could not understand purposefully taking the lives of still two more.

The only explanation that Hunting Badger gave was, "They would only have slowed us down!"

Calling Wolf walked with Running Antelope. They were far ahead, once again, searching for trouble. *I wonder if she listens during the day?* He thought to himself.

*Calling Wolf?*

The hunter stopped in his tracks. "What is it?" questioned Running Antelope, "Did you hear something?"

"No . . ." Calling Wolf replied, "Nothing."

"You Sure?"

"Of course I'm sure! I'm going to go that way. You check over there!" He strode away.

*I'm here. I didn't expect you to answer. It took me by surprise. I just wanted to let Running Bison know that we are only about a hand of day's walk from the muddy river. We have been pushing day and night with only short rest stops. Then last night, well . . . it is hard to tell, Hunting Badger, he killed one of the women. She was having a baby and he got upset because she was making noises. Any way, I just wanted Running Bison to know.*

*I will tell him. Thank you, Calling Wolf. If I can help in any way . . .*

The hunter shook his head and sighed.

Somehow, they made it to the muddy river. Once across everyone relaxed some. The whole camp was upset about Morning Dew. She had been a friendly, happy woman. There was no reason for Hunting Badger to have done what he did. Resentment was rampant. Too many had already died.

# CHAPTER 10

"What do you think? Is this the valley?" Crooked Spirit lay sprawled beside Running Bison and Raven, looking down into a large peaceful valley. A stream ran through it, weaving its way around scattered stands of trees. The only sounds were those made by birds twittering in the trees.

"I would say that it is," Running Bison replied. "It looks safe enough. We haven't seen any signs of others since crossing the muddy river. Have Prairie Grass and Singing Water returned yet?"

The hunter, Raven, shook his head, "They should be in some time late today. I sent them rather farther out than usual, as you and I discussed."

Running Bison nodded, "Talking Shadow and Crying Coyote should find the rest of the people today or tomorrow. Even taking into account, the slowest, they should all be here in a couple more days after that. Let's go see what this valley offers!"

The three rose and trotted into the valley. A flock of turkeys burst from the brush and took off in a burst of color and noise. A hand of them went no farther. Shortly thereafter, two deer were brought down as well. This game would make a welcome change from the steady diet of rabbit they had been living on. It was good to be stopping for a time. The camp was tired. By evening they were satisfied and the camp had been brought into the valley. Women laughed and children played. The stream was welcome to all. Many bathed, and several women gathered watercress, wild onion and other plants and tossed these into the bladders of heating water. The deer and turkeys were spitted and by dark everyone was ready for food and relaxation. Tubers made their way into coals and berries were wrapped in leaf baskets for after the meal.

Prairie Grass and Singing Water slipped quietly into the camp. Rather than worry the women and children, Running Bison had been careful to send out his men in such a manner the camp was not alerted to the extra precautions.

"People have been west of here," Prairie Grass stated, "But the signs are old; at least last moon, probably the one before and only a small group then. I would say the savages have broken up the camps of the gatherers as well and these few are those who escaped. Their basketry was 'gatherer'. But there were no signs of any large groups; not savages, or raiders. Still, we would be well advised to keep lookouts just in case, at least for a time."

"I think we should still be careful with the fires," Singing Water glanced about the camp. No one had taken any precaution to smother the hearths. In fact, some were casting sparks high into the night. "You know how far a fire can be seen at night."

Running Bison sighed and motioned for one of the nearby hunters to go and suggest the hearths be smothered for the night. "You are sure that our trail is impossible to follow?"

Singing Water nodded, "From the time we became aware of danger, as you suggested, hunters have gone behind the camp and made sure there was no trail to follow." He and his wolf were settled now beside Running Bison's fire, enjoying venison and turkey. Only the glowing coals lingering in the hearth gave off any light, it was dim but enough to eat by. In a short time, the remaining hearths were extinguished as well and the valley settled into darkness.

\*       \*       \*

Singing Water and Crying Coyote lay on their bellies atop a rise, studying the camp spread out below them. It was a very large camp. There were many hearths, people shouting and laughing and dogs barking and playing with children. At one end of the camp someone had erected a curious structure. It looked to be a large pole cage and it was filled with people. Beyond it was a sizable shelter with guards at the opening. Within the center of the camp, numerous men were reorienting huge boulders into a more refined formation. The hunters watched with fascinated dread, for they knew what was to come. They had watched last night.

The pair of them had traveled very rapidly back toward the muddy river. They had made excellent time, crossing that body of water at noon the second day. Then they had been truly unfortunate. They had stopped to eat their noon meal in the shelter of a thicket of trees. The wolf pups had flopped down beside them, out of breath. The punishing speed of the hunters was hard on their still-growing bodies. But they were alert. It was the pups, who raised their snouts, almost in unison and gave a soft "Woof" to forewarn the travelers. Quickly the men scooted deeper into the brush.

Here they remained until they identified the problem. At first they heard nothing, but then they caught the faint vibration of the drums. They were far away.

"What do you think?" Singing Water asked.

"Running Bison said that the savages had drums."

"You think it could be them?"

"Only one way to find out; we follow!"

They eased from their hiding place and motioning the wolves into the now-familiar formation, they headed toward the sound. It was well after dark when they had slipped silently to the top of the rise and observed the camp below. They were downwind, so the camp dogs would not smell them. There, last night, as tonight, they watched.

The routine was the same. A number of people were taken from the cage and led to the large shelter. Once inside something happened to them. When they were led, one at a time, completely naked, from the shelter, they did not protest, fight, or even seem aware. They merely went quietly with the guards and submitted to the grotesque sacrifice carried out by the tall, strangely-dressed dreamer.

"What do you think?" Crying Coyote whispered, "Do you think it will be safe?"

"No, but I don't see another way. If we don't rescue those people, they will all end up with their hearts cut out. If you have any other suggestions, I'm willing to listen."

"No one went near the cage after the ceremony got underway. They were all too filled with fermented brew. If it is the same tonight, I think then that is our best chance."

"What do we do with them once they are free?" Singing Water asked, "Have you thought about that?"

"I only know that I recognized several people in that cage. I tell you, they are of the Bear Camp. I spent an entire winter with them three seasons ago. There is no telling how many others of The People are in there."

"What about the camp with Hunting Badger? We are supposed to be bringing them to the valley. Running Bison will be angry if we just forget about them!"

"I have no intention of forgetting about them. I saw Tall Bear in that cage. He was a hunting brother that winter. I will not leave here without him!" Crying Coyote replied.

"All right! We will wait until the camp quiets down, then go down there and deal with the guards and take Tall Bear from the cage and any other person who wants to go!"

"I doubt any will chose to stay," Crying Coyote reminded him.

"Well let's get ready. We know what is going to happen now. I don't think I could stand to watch that again. We can work our way around toward the cage and wait."

"I want to see whom they take out of the cage first. If any are our people, I'm not waiting. I'm not going to just lie here and watch them be murdered."

"There are more men down in that camp than there are hunters left to The People! Have you lost your mind? There are only two of us," Singing Water sputtered.

"Then we had just better hope that none of our people are chose to be 'offered' tonight.

＊　　＊　　＊

"Sage, I am worried. Are you sure that Calling Wolf hasn't seen Singing Water or Crying Coyote?"

"That is what he said. The camp crossed the muddy river yesterday. They are following the upper branch, which will bring them right by this valley. But there has been no sign of the men you sent to lead them in."

Running Bison frowned, "I wonder where they are? Surely they couldn't have missed the camp. I sent them along the same path."

"Unless something came up," Crooked Spirit offered. "Why not have Sage 'see' if she can find out what happened to them?"

"You mean. . .?"

"I could try," Sage replied, "If you wish?"

Running Bison thought for a time, "I suppose that is the only way to be sure. But I don't like it. Every time Sage tries this mind thing, it drains her. It is not fair to ask her..."

'You didn't ask, I offered."

"Very well," Running Bison sighed, "But only because we really need to know."

Sage nodded. Then she closed her eyes and concentrated. It was becoming easier every time she did this. *Crying Coyote! Can you hear me?*

Crying Coyote stopped dead in his tracks. "What is it?" whispered Singing Water just behind him.

"Did you hear anything? A woman's voice?"

*He can't hear me. Only you can. Don't waste time, please! I am with Running Bison. Where are you? What has happened? Don't try to talk, just think. I will hear you.*

"No, I haven't heard anything. Are you sure?"

Crying Coyote shook his head. "Must have imagined it," he whispered.

*Where are you?*

*Uh...we have found the camp of the savages. They have some of our people. We are going to try to free them, tonight, after the ......*

"They are at the camp of the savages!"

"Give me you hand!" Running Bison followed suit. *Get out of there! Running Bison?*

*Save yourselves, man! Two of you can't possible free all those people and not get captured yourselves! It is foolish to try!*

*You did!* Sage reminded him.

Running Bison frowned at her; nodded and closed his eyes. *All right but be careful. Take them beyond the muddy river, keep in the water on the north side and follow the branch just as we did. Remember, KEEP EVERYONE IN THE WATER!*

*I will.*

"Are you all right?" Singing Water took him by the shoulder.

"I'm fine. In fact I have seldom felt better!" Crying Coyote grinned at him, "Come on man! I've got a plan! We'll take them to the river, keep in the water, just as we did before and those stupid people down there will never know what happened to them!"

\* \* \*

"Did you hear something?" the big guard glanced nervously all around.

The other man took a long draw on his flask and then shook his head, "You're always hearing things! Its moon's ago since those people vanished and the guards were found dead. Stop worrying! Nothing's going to happen. Here, have a drink!"

The first guard took the bladder and drank deeply, "Still, it gives me the creeps! No way they could have gotten away like that without help. We didn't find a trace of them! Almost as if 'spirits' did it!"

The second guard snorted rudely. "You and your 'spirits'! You see spirits behind every bush! If there were spirits don't you think Quenquil would know about it?"

His only answer was a gurgling sound. Then he felt a light pain at his throat, he reached up and brought his hand away covered with blood. His eyes dimmed and his legs gave way. Then all went black.

\* \* \*

"Get the bottom binding, I'll get the top!" Crying Coyote Whispered to Singing Water. "Tall Bear! You in there?"

"Who asks?" A shadow came forward, "Crying Coyote! That you?"

"Yup! Come on man let's get these people out of here!" The bindings gave way and Tall Bear fell into Crying Coyote's arms. "How many of our people are here with you.

"About a double hand. So far we have been lucky. None of us have been sacrificed. The rest of these people followed the bearded raider Great Thunder. He was one of the first to be sacrificed."

"Raiders! I don't know...." Crying Coyote looked at the people. "Well, we can't stop to sort things out now. Follow Singing Water. Keep all in a line and try to step in only one set of footprints. I will follow and leave them no trail."

"They have dogs."

"We have this!" Crying Coyote grinned as he held up a skin flask.

"What's that?"

Scent of a female wolf in heat!" the men grinned quickly and then started ushering the people onto a path. It was explained by those who could communicate with others; to follow closely. None objected. Soon the cage was empty. Crying Coyote settled the bodies of the guards against the cage, took a quick swig of the dropped bladder, shuddered, spit and threw the bladder down. *Fermented blood!*

Before the sun rose, they had crossed the muddy river and were slogging along the shallows. They were a ragged bunch. Several children were having trouble keeping up. Crying Coyote swept a small boy onto his shoulders. Some other men saw him and soon the smaller children were all being carried.

"We will crawl into the brush here and rest," Singing Water directed, leading the way. "But not for long. They may be following! We can't take that chance."

"Where do you take us?" a tall hunter asked with difficulty.

"Just here," replied Crying Coyote. "Now we can decide what to do. We take our people far from here."

"Does that mean we," he swept his arm to include his own group, "Are not welcome?"

"I don't know! Some say that you were among the raiders who killed many of The People last spring. It this true?"

The hunter nodded slowly, "It is true."

"Then I do not see how you can be welcomed."

"We are all that is left of our tribe. You have lost many as well. It only makes sense to band together. Who is your leader?"

"Running Bison leads us."

"Is that him?" He nodded to Crying Coyote."

"No, Running Bison is at the camp."

"But you don't want to take us there?"

"I didn't say that. I will talk to Crying Coyote and see what he has to say. Then we will decide."

\* \* \*

"Let me think about it," Crying Coyote asked. I will let you know before we leave here."

Singing Water nodded and they both settled down to rest, leaving the wolves alert and watching. The men did not fully trust those they had saved. *What do we do now?* Crying Coyote sighed.

*Have you escaped?*

*You again?*

*Yes, well I have been waiting.... where are you?*

*At the muddy river. We have all of them with us. Many were of the camps of the raiders. They wish to join The People! What do I tell them?*

*I will get back to you......*

"They want to join us?" Running Bison frowned, "Are you sure that is what he said?"

Sage nodded, "He is waiting for my answer," she sighed tiredly.

"Give me your hand......

\* \* \*

"You are sure?"

Crying Coyote shrugged. "It seems the logical thing to me. As the man said, we are all weakened in small groups. If the camps have been wiped out, or nearly so, it makes sense. We may not be able to escape these savages any other way. If we end up running out onto the plains, we could get lost and everyone die. We have no way of knowing. No one has ever gone there, or at least no one I know. Besides, the raiders are as weak as we are. Their leader is dead. We could use friends."

"All right. We will take them. I just hope that Running Bison ......."

Crying Coyote shook his head, "He won't. Running Bison is a reasonable man. He will do what is best for the camps."

"I hope you are right," Singing Water replied, "We have really done badly on this task. We were sent out to find Hunting Badger. Now we not only didn't do that, but we bring in half the raider camp back with us." He frowned, "Running Bison will never trust 'us' with anything important again."

"Of course he will! He will be impressed that we were able to think for ourselves and save all these people as well. It is just the sort of thing he would have done himself."

*　　*　　*

"I am Headman of this camp!" Hunting Badger shouted, "How dare you take it upon yourselves to say where we go!"

"You can direct those who are of the Bison Camp, of course," replied Calling Wolf, "but you are not Headman to the rest of us. We are all from different camps. I choose to follow this branch of the muddy river north and west. You are free to lead your people wherever you choose. If other decide to go with us, that is their choice as well.

"What is so important about following that particular path?"

"We all agreed to meet in a valley to the north of the muddy river. I am taking my people and any others who wish to go with me to that valley."

"And you think you can find it; one particular valley in all these mountains?" Hunting Badger snorted, "There is no way! But I know the valley of which you speak. So I will lead you there. Then no one can say that Hunting Badger is not a reasonable man!" He stalked away.

Calling Wolf sighed, "Life can be so difficult?" Hunting Badger had opposed every suggestion he or other hunters had made. Even to walking within the verge of the water. He had set himself up, immediately, as the leader of the entire group. This had not been received well by most of the hunters. It almost seemed that the man called for the savages to attack them. He camped out in the open and refused to have the fires smothered before dark and left a trail that a child could follow. Was it not for the hunters who fell behind and erased the trail and for the level-headed people who did understand their danger, the savages would have found them long ago!

Calling Wolf would be very glad to reach the valley and join Running Bison. He even looked forward to meeting the woman......

*Calling Wolf?* He shivered.

*     *     *

"What do you mean, there is no trail?" Quenquil demanded.

"We have taken the dogs Great Dreamer! They smell the cage. They go to the edge of the camp. There they smell the bushes, but they go no farther. We can find nothing! The guards are dead, just as before, their throats slit. And just as before, there is no trail. It is as if 'spirits' have taken the sacrifices."

Quenquil frowned; he no more believed that spirits took their captives than did the hunters facing him. But he could do nothing about it. He was a dreamer and the mysteries of following a trail were not proper for one of his position. Captives were getting harder to find. When first the Serpent People had headed north, captives were plentiful and if some escaped; so what. There were many more to take their places. But over the last three seasons, not so; they had moved far north of their homeland now and he was disgusted that this last group had escaped. Perhaps to the west they would do better? It had been several seasons since they had traveled to the dry deserts. People there were scattered, but easily captured. He was tired of these mountains. Someone was out there; someone clever enough to leave no trail.

He dismissed the men and settled at his fire to think. A short time later, Iguana, Headman of the camp joined him. "What do you think?" Iguana asked, "We had no luck last time trying to find the escaped people. Whoever did this must be the same person. Do your spirits tell you anything?"

"I have not had time to commune with the spirits!" Quenquil replied angrily, "I need quiet and the lack of disruption in order to talk with the spirits. I cannot get that in this camp!" He rose, "I am going to the top of that bluff above the river. From there I should be able to speak to the spirits. I have no idea when I will return to the camp. Just keep people away from me!"

The headman nodded. Iguana was no fool. He knew what happened to people who crossed the dreamer. He had seen too many, some close friends, find themselves spread across the altar, victim of Quenquil's bloody knife. He had no desire to join them.

The tall dreamer left the hearth, gathered up several packets and bundles and left the camp, his multicolored feather robe dancing in the wind. Iguana watched him go and then turned to more important things. Calling a man waiting a short distance from the hearth to him, he handed the man a strip of meat and motioned for him to be seated, "What do you think?"

"There are still a number of men blindly loyal to him. Sending Humming Bird to the altar was a mistake on his part. Her family was very loyal to him: no longer. Green Parrot has spoken quietly against him as well. But we are still too few. Perhaps this last escape will turn the balance. People do not like it when their family members are sacrificed."

"Still, it will be another moon before we sacrifice again. Perhaps by then we will have more strangers. The dreamer said something about Bending Branch. Perhaps we should talk to him and his family?"

"If Bending Branch were to turn, then we would have a chance. This dreamer has been leading us on a blood bath for a hand of years. I am tired on this constant moving and raiding and taking captives. I cannot say that it has done anything to improve the lives of the Serpent People. I would rather return to my valley home and the way of life we lived before Quenquil had his great vision. Many others feel as I do."

The headman nodded. "I have spoken to most of the people. As you say, many feel as we do, yet those few who are loyal to Quenquil.... they are not to be disregarded. We will wait and see what message he brings back when he returns to camp. Meanwhile, all we can do is wait."

Quenquil followed a game trail to the top of the bluff. From here he could see far in all directions. The land spread out before him, open and empty. The grass was brown and scanty. Only along the river was there anything green. There were no grazing animals in sight. Nothing moved except a pair of circling vultures. The heat radiated from the land in shimmering blankets. Even the water of the river was sluggish. This land was nothing like the rich, bountiful land from which the Serpent People had come. It was time to go home. He shook back the feather robe and laid it, carefully folded, beside him. Then he took out the pouch that contained the peyote buds. Expertly he stoked a tiny fire and heated water in a tortoise shell. Into this he transferred a pinch of the dried 'button' ground into powder. He added another pinch and satisfied, returned the remainder to his stash. While he waited for the drink to steep, he prepared for his 'journey'. Then he quickly swallowed the entire drink and seated himself to wait. It did not take long. Brilliant swirling circles began to form. Inside his head he could hear the drum beat. Then the form of Humming Bird began to take shape. She knelt before him and bowed her beautiful head. Her sad eye looked deeply into his. *Why? I loved you! I would have done anything for you. I even died for you.* Then her form shimmered and dissolved. Colors streaked through his mind, random assortments, but nothing that made any sense. It had been like this ever since he had sacrificed Humming Bird. The spirits refused to visit him. Then the effect of the drug began to fade and he returned to reality.

The dreamer sighed. Humming Bird haunted him, awake, dreaming! It made no difference. Sadly, her death had to be. He could not afford for anyone to realize that he and Humming Bird.... had she not gotten pregnant, things would have been different. But she refused to couple with Striding Snake as he had begged her. She loved Quenquil. She wanted no other. The people would have burned him alive if they knew that he had relations with a woman, any woman! This was the greatest taboo a dreamer faced. So in the end, he had done the only thing he could. He had sacrificed Humming Bird to save himself. He sat there for a long time, thinking. It would not be long before the people turned against him, unless he was very careful. For a hand of years he had held them in the palm of his hand, but no more. He could nearly touch the resentment of some. Strangers sacrificed to his visions were one thing, but when it came to members of the camp.... this was something else.

\*    \*    \*

"Come on Wind! It is getting late!" Sage shifted restlessly from foot to foot.

"Late! The sun is barely above the land!"

"Well, you said you wanted to explore!"

"All right," Whispering Wind gathered up her tools and followed Sage and Obsidian from the camp. They had been in the valley for over a hand of days. Now they were going out to explore the area. Soon people would be coming into the valley to join them and there would be no time. Running Bison had not been enthusiastic, but he had not forbidden them. The pair cut through a canyon to the west and entered another valley. The far end of the valley presented sheer cliffs of red jasper. It was from here the tool knappers were securing materials to craft into blades, knifes and other tools which The People used on a daily basis.

Beyond the valley of Jasper they entered another canyon. The high sheer sides were stained various colors and bands of rich stone blended as well. A stream cut through the middle of the canyon, yielding fresh water and shade. Along its verge huge cottonwood trees spread their canopies. Sage and Whispering Wind headed for the shade. Here they stopped and ate their morning meal. Obsidian bounded up to them, another of her endless rabbits in her mouth. She flopped down and ate her own meal.

"It has been more than three moons now, since you joined The People," Whispering Wind reminded, "Soon Running Bison is going to ask you to explain to the people just who you are. Have you decided what you are going to do?"

Sage nodded, "I'm going to run away!" she said seriously.

Whispering Wind dropped her mouth open in surprise. "You are teasing me, aren't you?" she asked not completely certain.

Sage smiled sadly, "I am teasing," she admitted. I do not know what I will do. Seriously! Running Bison has spoken to me already about this as has Crooked Spirit. They both suggest that I tell those with us, before the others arrive, rather than tell everyone at once. I can't see that it makes any difference either way. No one is going to like it."

"You return the Sacred Relics."

"And how many are going to 'suggest' that I also bring down all the death which had visited the camps. What good are Sacred Relics if their Keeper also brings death to everyone she touches?"

"That is nonsense! And you know it! The savages have been attacking the camps since before you joined them. Even the gatherers were attacked. They can hardly blame that on you!"

"Can't they? You forget; I grew up with the gatherers. It is far more likely they will use the attacks against them as further proof that I am cursed. I am afraid, Wind! These people are all strangers to me. They owe me nothing! Why should they listen to me? Particularly when what I have to tell them is nothing they want to hear."

"So the spirits have spoken to you? You do know how they guide the people?"

Sage sighed and nodded, "I know and as I have said, it is not what The People want to hear."

"What do they say?"

"The One and the spirits have for generations given The People a richness of food. All they could possible eat, all the grazing animals of this great plain, but in return, The People have forgotten the spirits. In their heart, they credit their own skill, not the 'gift' of the spirits for the food. The People have refused to listen to the spirits. For generations they have done so. Now the spirits are unable to protect The People from the anger of The One. Death, disease, hunger, disaster! These are what are in-store for The People if they do not change. The One has already taken away the bison. Rain has not fallen. The snow was slight. Water is drying up and the grasslands are becoming moving dunes of sand. The One has demanded that The People move into the mountains and learn to eat plants and small game. Can you see hunters of bison quietly listening to a woman and leaving this way of life for the one offered?"

Sage shrugged, "I cannot."

"I see what you mean. What does Running Bison suggest?"

"He has said that he will do what he can to protect me, but he cannot guarantee that there will not be danger. But even he has no idea where the danger might come from. He cannot protect me night and day. No one could."

"You have Obsidian and you have me," Whispering Wind reminded, "I am sure that Crooked Spirit and Cricket...."

"An old man and a child and a woman and a dog! This is my protection?"

"I am sure there will be others; Raven and Bull Elk perhaps. They know you best."

"Add to that Calling Wolf and Crying Coyote and maybe I have a chance."

"Who are they?" Whispering Wind blinked. I have not met these people."

"Nor have I," admitted Sage, "But I have talked to them."

"You mean...?"

Sage nodded.

"Oh!" Whispering Wind replied.

"They will be entering the camp tonight."

"Who will?"

"The people with Crying Coyote; he brings some from other camps and many who were raiders. They wish to join with Running Bison."

"Raiders! He brings raiders into the camp?" Whispering Wind leaped to her feet. "Quickly, we must warn Running Bison. The camp must be prepared!"

"Running Bison knows. He is planning to welcome them. They are as broken and splintered as are The People. They seek refuge, not attack."

"You are sure?" Wind still stood, prepared for flight.

"Sit down! There is no need to panic. Running Bison knows what he is doing."

"Oh," Whispering Wind peered suspiciously at her friend. "All of a sudden you have become awfully friendly with Running Bison. When did all this happen?"

"While you were snoring happily in your dreams," Sage replied.

"I do not snore!" Whispering Wind protested, "Do I?"

Sage nodded solemnly, "But very prettily" she added.

"So does Running Bison know about your... you know... talking?"

"He knows. In fact he has joined hands with me and spoken with these men himself. He was impressed!" Sage grinned. "But he still has suggested I do not do it again. At least not unless there is danger," Sage rose. "Well we should be going, we have a long way yet ahead of us."

"You have a destination in mind?"

Sage shook her head, "I have no idea why I said that!" Then she looked around, catching just the tail of the dog disappearing up a trail, "But we will be left behind if we are not quick. Obsidian obviously knows where we are going."

"She could be on the trail of food," suggested Whispering Wind.

"No, she has already eaten. Besides I feel a 'pull'."

"I knew it! You always involve me when you go out on these 'power' searches."

"Would you rather I had asked Blue Butterfly?" Sage stopped.

"You know not!" Wind protested, "But you could have warned me."

"I have, just now," Sage replied reasonable. Whispering Wind merely shook her head and mumbled under her breath. Then she picked up her things and followed Sage.

They passed through the canyon, into yet another valley and followed still another stream. Finally Obsidian wagged her tail and headed for a stand of trees, nearly in the middle of the valley. Sage could feel the 'pull'. Whatever she was being drawn to was there, within the trees. Then, as they approached, Sage realized that the power was truly 'within' the trees. They formed a perfect circle, not quite closed.

Whispering Wind stopped, "I'm not going in there!"

"They won't hurt you," Sage replied.

"But this is a 'power' place," Wind protested.

"Yes, but the power accepts your presence. You will be safe."

"What about you?"

"Me! I had to come. Every time I 'mind talk' I am drained of energy. It takes me nearly a day to recover. And I never do so completely. I have come to this place to absorb 'power'. The spirits give, but they take as well. If I do not find a place such as this, particularly just before I must expand a lot of power, I could not do so. Don't ask me how I know this, I just do. Now go over by that big oak as get comfortable. I must concentrate." Sage made her way to the very center of the grove and climbed upon a large boulder there. Then she took out a hide and spread in upon the stone. Her drink was already prepared, saved in a small bladder. Once settled on the boulder, she swallowed the drink and closed her eyes, opening her mind at the same time. Obsidian settled at the foot of the boulder, Whispering Wind against the tree and the three of them waited. The sun was warm and the twittering birds relaxing, soon Whispering Wind found her eyelids closing. Soon she was fast asleep.

"Where are you?" Sage called out, "Spirit Wolf?"

\*     \*     \*

*I am here.* The animal answered from beside her. Sage jerked about to find she was no longer alone.

"I need to know. What is going to happen?"

*I cannot tell you that.* Spirit Wolf replied. *Not even spirits know until a thing occurs.*

"But I was drawn to this place. It is just as before I joined the camp. I was taken to the crystal room to absorb power. Is that not why I was drawn to this place?"

*It is.* Spirit Wolf closed his blue eyes. *You cannot expand so much power mind talking and not renew it. Your levels are dangerously low. You could die if you use it all up. You have not yet learned how to use 'power' without draining yourself. Until you do and even after, of course, you will have to renew occasionally. Power places are all around you, but you have not learned to recognize them. Until you do, I will have to draw you to them.*

"You mean they are everywhere?"

*More or less; but only a very few can recognize them. You must look!*

"What do I look for?"

*You had no trouble recognizing the crystal cave. This place you understood. Others are out there like them. You and usually only you, will recognize the significance of a thing, be it a special stone, a ring of trees such as this one, or even the staff you carry.*

"You mean I can draw 'power' from my staff?"

*Of course! It works both ways. You can also draw 'power' from your wolf, but be very careful if you do, for although she will give freely, she cannot renew without your help. You could kill her.*

"I would never hurt Obsidian!"

*Basket said the same thing, yet she caused the death of her 'spirit helper' and she loved her more dearly than anything else in her life. She was most fortunate that the spirits gave her back, but not quite.... complete.*

"Will I ever learn...?" Sage sighed.

*All the chosen ones have started the same. It took each of them a long time to learn. Most were as old as you before they realized the special gifts. For example Basket was gifted the mind talking and she could only talk to her twin. You have been given a greater share. You can even talk to men. But you must be very careful. Others listen.*

"What do you mean?"

*There is much evil out there. The evil has ears! That is all that I can tell you.*

"You mean others can hear? Not just those I call?"

Wolf Spirit looked away. *I must go now. Touch the rock. Draw the power. Seek other such places.* Before Wolf Spirit vanished, Sage saw the woman Basket and her wolf standing just beyond. She was smiling. A mist formed and when it cleared, Sage found herself alone. She reached down with her hands, spread them flat on the warm surface of the boulder and absorbed. She slept. When she wakened, she found herself encased in the now-familiar soft blue glow. Slowly it dissipated. She gathered her things, climbed down from the boulder and smiled. She was renewed. Whispering Wind, on the other hand, was sound asleep beneath her tree. It was well after sun-high. Obsidian went and washed Whispering Wind's face waking her.

                    *        *        *

"Ugh!" She wiped the dog slobber away, "I guess that it what I get for merely closing my eyes for a breath," she laughed.

"A breath?" laughed Sage. "Look at the sun! Unless we hurry, it will be dark before we get back to the camp and Running Bison will not be happy with us."

"Then we had better hurry!" Wind was already scurrying back along their trail. Then she stooped and turned back, "Did it work? Do you feel better?"

Sage nodded, "I can even remember a bit. Her name is Basket."

"Who?"

"The woman who guides me."

"Not a spirit?" Whispering Wind sounded disappointed, "Just an ordinary woman?"

"Only if you care to call the twin 'Keeper' ordinary," Sage answered.

"Really? Are you certain? You actually spoke to the twin Keeper?"

Sage shook her head, "Spirit Wolf spoke of her being a twin and she stood just beyond smiling at me. It is the same woman I have spoken to before. Has there been another such?"

Whispering Wind shook her head, "What was she like? I mean...."

"She looked just like you or me. Well not like you; you are beautiful, she is quite plain. She is no taller than I and just as plain. But her wolf was really special. You could almost see through her! Spirit Wolf told me that was because she made a mistake and her guardian was accidentally killed. The spirits gave her back, but did not make her quite complete, although only Basket could tell the difference."

"And I slept through the whole thing?" Whispering Wind muttered in disgust, "And did you absorb the 'power'?"

Sage nodded, "I feel must better; not at all tired."

They hurried along the trail, not stopping until they crested the verge of the valley. Here they paused making sure all was well below before entering the camp. All was quiet. Running Bison had been keeping a sharp eye out for them. He sighed in relief as he saw them slip into the camp.

At his hearth sat Crying Coyote. Sage eyed him with interest. It would not be proper to speak first, so she waited until Running Bison recognized them. As always, every time a man saw Whispering Wind, he was taken aback. Her rare beauty consistently had that affect. Then when it was Sage's turn, he hardly noticed her, his eyes going back to Wind. Sage was used to it by now. She murmured a greeting and went to where Running bison indicated they sit. Obsidian sank beside her.

"Crying Coyote has brought a group of people to join us. They wait just beyond the valley until we decide. Crooked Spirit and I are going out to meet with them now." He turned to Sage, "Are you ready?" she nodded.

Whispering Wind looked surprised, but before she had time to say or do anything, the party was leaving the hearth. If Crying Coyote was surprised that Sage accompanied them, he did not ask. Rather his eyes kept turning back.... toward Whispering Wind.

Crying Coyote led the three to where Singing Water waited with the group of refugees. Once there, Sage separated herself, stepping back and into the shadows. There she did as Running Bison had suggested. She closed her eyes and let her mind search. It touched here, then there, than on another. There were many impressions, but not of anger, violence, or hatred. These people were safe. She stepped forward, caught Running Bison's eye and nodded. Then she and Obsidian slipped away and returned to the camp. Her task was done.

The next morning the Bison Camp watched with mixed emotions as the new people came into the valley. They were ragged, dirty and starved. They had no possessions, shelters, nothing at all. The women of the Bison Camp had gone through their own things and gathered what they could afford to give. These items were set out to share with the new people. Stone knapper offered tools and hunters, spare weapons. The new people were overwhelmed with the generosity offered. They gladly sat and ate the food proffered. Before dark they were clean, settled in some kind of shelter of their own and wearing new clothing, even if missing an item or so. Their stomachs were full and they now again had personal possessions. Most decided then and there that Running Bison and the Bison Camp were where they pledged their allegiance.

"Where is the woman who spoke to me?" Crying Coyote asked Running Bison, "I know that you know her, but I didn't see her when I came into the camp."

Running Bison grinned, "You had eyes only for Whispering Wind, who granted is very beautiful and as others have, you overlooked the one with power."

"The plain one with the ugly dog?" Crying Coyote frowned, "Isn't she the gatherer you brought in with Whispering Wind?"

Running Bison nodded.

"But she can talk with her mind? I haven't ever heard of that before. Can all of the gatherers do that?"

"She isn't a gatherer," Running Bison admitted, "She is the daughter of Moon Maiden."

"Moon Maiden, your cousin, the one.... oh! Does she... Sage, I mean...?"

Running Bison again nodded.

"Do they all know?" A negative answer was returned. "Only a few?"

"It is not yet time," Running Bison shifted to look toward the south. "Once the rest of the people get here; then it will be time to make decisions if all goes well."

"Hunting Badger is with them. How will it go when he comes into this camp?"

"Hunting Badger is an old man. He has lost most of his influence. Only a few still follow him."

"He leads all who remain of The People."

Running Bison shook his head, "Most follow Calling Wolf."

"How... oh," Crying Coyote nodded, "I see."

"Who is the strongest among those people whom you brought in?"

"The one who calls himself Standing Bear is strongest among the remains of the raiders. He is supported strongly by the hunters Antler Dancer and Horned Owl. If you have them on your side, the rest will follow. I think the survivors of the Bear Camp will follow me. They know me from several winters ago. Beyond that I can't say, but that is the greater part of the group."

"You have seen what the woman can do, would you follow her?"

Crying Coyote thought for a moment then regretfully shook his head, "We are hunters of bison. There is not a man among us who would follow a woman." He frowned, "But I would follow you."

"Even if I follow the woman?"

Crying Coyote shook his head.

Singing Water burst into the camp. "They are coming!" he shouted, "Hunting Badger leads them!"

29  *Laphophora williamsii:* Peyote: Cut and dried 'buttons' of Peyote when chewed, produce olor hallucinations. **MacMahon:** p 355.

# PART 2
## THE MESSAGE

# CAST OF CHARACTERS

**(In order of appearance)**

Chapter 11

**Standing Bear**: Now leader of the 'Raider" Camp

**Hunting Badger**: Old Headman of the Bison Camp

**Calling Wolf:** Hunter now of Running Bison's camp

**Running Bison:** New Headman of the split faction of the Bison Camp

**Blue Butterfly:** Unmated woman of the 'woman's hearth'

**Crooked Spirit:** Dreamer

**Angry Bull:** Hunter loyal to Hunting Badger

**Moon Maiden:** Sage's mother, long dead.

**Sage:** The Chosen

**Bear Claw Woman :** Sage's adult name. As such she is from her on.

**Leaping Antelope:** New Hunter.

**Wolf Leader:** New Hunter, stepson of Thunder Cloud, father to Whispering Wind

**Winter Rain:** Unmated woman of the 'woman's hearth'.

**Whispering Wind:** Mate to Running Bison. Best friend to Sage-Bear Claw Woman.

**Obsidian:** Loyal protector of Sage. Large black wolf-dog.

**Bull Elk**: Hunter New to Running Bison's Camp

**Raven:** Hunter new to Running Bison's Camp.

**Young Wolf:** Raven's wolf.

**Basket:** Spirit ancestor

**Yel:** Spirit ancestor

**Morning Star:** Unborn Daughter of Bear Claw Woman.
**Sister Cougar:** Young Cougar befriended by Raven.

Chapter 12:
**Guardian:** Obsidian reborn.
**Quenquel:** Savage Dreamer
**Robe Maker:** Woman of Running Bison's camp
**Flower:** Child of Running Bison's Camp

Chapter 13:
**Crying Coyote:** Second in command of Running Bison's Camp
**Antler Dancer; Horned Owl, Thunder Cloud:** Hunters who followed Hunting Badger.
**Talking Shadow:** Story Teller of the Bison Camp.
**Little Doe; Soft Breeze, Mountain Quail Happy Breeze, Sun Dancer; Willow Woman, Singing Bird, Laughing Water, Dancing Star, Broken Branch Green Moss:** Women of Running Bison's Camp
**Sparrow Squirrel, Fireflower, Snowflake:** Female children
**Speckledfish, Cricket, Crane, Porcupine, Pebble, Pinecone, Badger, Badger:** Male children

**Sycamore:** 11. Seeker of personal glory.
**Gatherer:** 11. Youth who learns a hard lesson.

Chapter 14:
**Wawoo:** Gather-Bear Man's wolf
**Hollow Bone:** Cricket's Adult name.

Chapter 17:
He Man: Self Appointed leader of group going after Hunting Badger
Jumping From: Hunter
Red Fox: Hunter
Laughing Antelope: Hunter
Bear Paw: Hunter
Feather Robe: Mate of Bear Paw
Dancing Willow & Sparrow: Her Daughters

Fire Weed: Mated to He Man
Left Hand: her stepson
Ash Leaf: Mated to Laughing Antelope
Cottontail & Frog: her young children
Laughing Water: Mated to Red Fox
Dancing Willow: mated to jumping Frog
Grasshopper: her stepson

Chapter 19
**Green Parrot: Beaded Lizard; Walking Man: Whistling Elk**:
Hunters of the Serpent Camp
**Iguana**: Headman of the Serpent Camp.

# CHAPTER 11

The valley was beginning to look like a gigantic ant nest. The raider people led by Standing Bear were more or less settled to the north of the Bison Camp, upstream but within easy shouting distance, yet separate. When Hunting Badger led his rag-tag band into the valley, he of course immediately headed for the best area, which of course was already occupied by Running Bison and his camp. So Hunting Badger set up on the opposite side of the stream.

Immediately, Calling Wolf settled his followers lower and closer to Running Bison's camp. He was relieved to be there and away from the constant irritation which Hunting Badger represented. Besides, he was curious to meet the woman...

Running Bison was not there when he arrived at his hearth, so Calling Wolf sat and looked about the camp. The adjoining hearth immediately captured his attention. Here a number of women were gathered, laughing and working. One in particular, caught his attention. She also took his breath away. The other younger women were uninteresting. The one called Blue Butterfly was playing with a young wolf, encouraging it in it's misbehavior and then scolding it for the same behavior. The hunter shook his head. *No way to train an animal.*

Quickly he looked around. He wondered if the woman who spoke to him was at that hearth. The only other young female at the hearth was small, plain and accompanied by the biggest dog he had ever seen. Fleetingly he wondered how, in a camp obviously in need of dogs, a woman was in possession of one such as that. It struck him that many things were not ordinary about Running Bison's camp. Then the man himself arrived and Calling Wolf forgot all about the women, almost.

After several days of unease, the varied group of people began to settle. The three dreamers remaining to the camps were busy, under the tutelage of Crooked Spirit. A large shelter had been erected and a place cleared just beyond it. Here the ceremonial hearth would be built. The dreamers scurried first here and then there, showing people, explaining to them, initiating them in the ways of the ceremony. The dreamers, themselves, had drawn heavily upon smatterings of memory and tales of the story teller. They had the bare bones of the Gathering from legend, but it was their responsibility to make sure that it progressed smoothly. That no one, or anything important, was forgotten. It was a weighty responsibility.

Running Bison was also very busy. He was consulting with other 'headmen' and making sure that materials were available for the various aspects of the ceremony. Such things as bison hide hunting robes, for the new hunter initiation and props for the storytellers tales. There were hunters to be introduced and welcomed into The People. They needed to select names and totem spirits if lacking. So many things... and then there was Whispering Wind. He was ever frustrated that he could not find the time... *should have spoken to her at the cave.*

Crooked Spirit approached the hearth. Running Bison motioned him to sit. It was very late; they were probably the only ones, besides the guards, in the extended camp who were still awake. "Have you had time to speak with her?" The old man sighed as he settled comfortably and accepted a strip of cooked venison.

Running Bison nodded, "She is still being stubborn," he admitted. "But when the time comes, I think she will fulfill her task."

"Then she has the Relics?" Running Bison nodded. "You have seen them?"

"She has them wrapped in a deer hide packet. Inside is the wolf bundle and within that the Ancient Tooth Relics. I have seen them. They are real and genuine. Even at a distance I could feel their power."

"I am worried, just the same. Should she not be preparing in some way?"

Running Bison shrugged, "She left the camp several time to go to some secret place. I am sure that she is gathering her 'power'. I have advised against any more of the 'mind talking'. It could be dangerous, for all of us."

"But you said that she could sense hostility! Would not this knowledge be to our advantage?"

"We already know the source of hostility. Besides, we both know that she is vulnerable to a particular danger. It would be best if she were kept from drawing anyone's attention until the ceremony. After that the danger will be less. Still I am uneasy and she is a very new and untried 'Keeper'. I know that she has unusual powers but she also lacks control over them. I am not sure she even realized their extent. That in itself is a cause for concern. What if she lost her temper with someone? Could she do them harm: or other innocents nearby? I am not all that certain that the incident when Angry Bull was nearly struck by lightning was an accident of nature. She was really furious with him."

"Have you given any more thought to who killed Moon Maiden?" Crooked Spirit accepted another strip of meat. "If it was Hunting Badger and if he should recognize her..."

Running Bison sighed, "I was certain earlier, before the camp split, that he had recognized her. But he has made no move since coming into the valley. Even Angry Bull has been conspicuous by his absence. I was sure he would make more trouble about the dog."

"Dare I bring up another troubling subject?"

"Go ahead."

"The hunters returned this evening and I overhear them complaining. They have not found bison to hunt in over a pair of moons. What will the new hunters do for hunting capes? And what will we eat at the closing ceremony, if no one locates bison?"

"There are only two new hunters and both of them have the hunting capes of their fathers. Not an excellent solution, I agree, but a solution none-the-less. As for the food, venison may have to suffice. I have sent runners out north, east and south. There are no signs of bison."

"Well, I suppose venison will do if it must, but all the same.... have them keep looking." Crooked Spirit yawned and rose, "I am to bed. Tomorrow is a busy day. Must get the fuel for the hearth and get the spirit drink brewing. So many things to see to..." he wandered off toward his own shelter.

Running Bison remained sitting at his hearth, deep in thought. He had hopes for this Gathering and grave misgivings as well. There were the new people they were initiating into the tribe; desperately needed new people. Then there were the hunters who were fanatically loyal to Hunting Badger. Trouble could come from that direction. Added to all of this, Running Bison had an inkling that the message which Sage was to deliver at the closing ceremony of the Gathering, would not sit well with the majority of The People, old or new. He had no idea how he would hold the band together. No one, beyond himself and a hand of other hunters would follow Sage. He was faced with the aspect of deserting her, which he could not do, or losing control over the Camp, which he did not wish to do. Long into the night he pondered, finally allowing the vision of Whispering Wind to slip into his thoughts.

On the first day of the celebration the drums called The People together. At dusk the ceremonial hearth was lighted. New hunters were to be welcomed into The People. First the pair of boys who recently became men, where introduced by proud relatives. Both had lost their own fathers, but that made their welcome even more important. Each new hunter was valued. They were gifted the hunting capes of their fathers, items not considered important enough to be stolen or destroyed by the raiders or savages. They were presented with adult atlatl and dart, new blades, hunting knives and new names. Now Mud Dauber became Leaping Antelope and Jackrabbit became Wolf Leader. Thunder Cloud looked on with pride at his new 'son'. Wolf Leader would be a fine addition to the hunters. Besides he would now be responsible for bringing in some of the food for the family. At least until he set up a hearth of his own or joined the unmated men's hearth. Until Running Bison had taken over as Headman, they had frequently gone hungry. Now, they had plenty of food, no bison, granted, but stomach filling food. And the plants they had added to their diet had actually taken away his sore gum disease. His teeth had even tightened up in his jaw. He really enjoyed the salt. He could hardly get enough of that.

The new hunters formerly belonging to the raider, Giant Thunder's camp, were eagerly anticipating their first bison hunt. All their lives, they had heard tales of the great Bison Hunters. Not one among their number had not thrilled and wished... now they were becoming Bison Hunters. They were, admittedly, disappointed that none had actually seen a bison as yet, but soon, they were certain, they would be among the fearless 'wolves of the plains' as The People were known.

They awaited the call of the drum and leaped into the celebration with atlatl and darts raised and savage screams erupting from their throats. They were greeted with uproarious cheers. As they danced wildly around the hearth, each, in turn, told a story about himself. He embellished the greatness of his valor, the many animals he had killed, the strength of his spirit, accuracy of his dart cast, purity of his heart. As they danced, each drank liberally from the bladder attached to their waist thong.

Women and children watched and cheered. Then the storyteller took over. His grandson helped the old man to a place of importance. "Many, many generations ago, when our Ancestors had not yet been brought from the underworld to walk the earth, The Great Spirit Father of all, Hesa, The One, looked down from the sky. He declared that the land was good. He populated it with animals. Great Animals, Spirit Animals! Among these he named Bison. He gave these plains and the great Llano Estacado to the south to Bison. He told them to multiply and become strong. He placed between the land and the sky, the realm of eagles, of thunder and lightning, of the rainbow, of the sun and the moon. Then from the land below he called First Man and First Woman. They climbed a spider web from the earth below and when they saw the sky and the land and the animals: they were happy. Hesa told First Man and First Woman that they were the guardians of all the animals, of the deer and the bear, the antelope and the elk, the bison, every animal on the land. Then, Coyote and Wolf, Cougar, Lynx and Bobcat were set free to hunt the animals. First Man and First Woman were to care for the animals, protect them from the predators and to spread and multiply. Their children would become The People. Hesa told First Man to keep his heart pure, to remember the spirit of the animals, to give 'gifts' of thanks when an animal gave itself up to his dart, to be food for his family. The animal would return and give food again and again, so long as Man did not dishonor him. Man was to be proud of his mate, kind to his children, a good provider to all. He was given 'dog' to be his faithful companion and hunting partner and so The People spread across the land."

"To each," another Storyteller took over, "A totem spirit was given. When a boy reached manhood, Hesa instructed he was to go on a Vision Journey. On this journey he would meet his 'spirit guide' the animal special to him. Never was he to forget his 'spirit guide'. In his amulet he would carry for the remainder of his life, something significant, given to him by his 'spirit guide'. A special 'kill' was to be made for him and he was to share this kill with all of his camp. Then and only then was he, a Man of The People."

Again the old man took over. "But, as The People spread over the land and they became great, they began to forget about the spirits. No longer did they make 'gifts' and no longer did they thank the spirits. They took credit upon themselves. They praised themselves for the great hunters they had become. Hesa, The One became so angry that he sent Great Dreamer to The People with a message. Return to the ways of First Man and First Woman or he would take away the animals and leave The People to starve. The People laughed at Great Dreamer. So, The One took away the Great Thunder Giant and Swift One and many other animals. And, The One caused a great time of starvation to spread over the land. The People became sick. Plagues and disease, starvation and death came down upon them. The land, once rich with grass and forage became a land of moving dunes. Hesa took away Mother Rain," the old man shook his head. "They sent up cries to The One and promised to return to the old ways."

"The Spirits took pity on The People. They sent Ancestor Brothers, Blue Coyote and Stone Man to show The People the way. The way back to the proper veneration of the spirits, back to the plains from which they had been driven into the Starving Mountains, back to the bison. He showed them how to tame the wild wolf and make him brother-dog. And as then, still today, we are the 'wolves of the plains', Bison Hunters!"

Now the women joined in with the dancing. Not with the men, but in a circle beyond the circle. And they all danced to the beat of the drum until the Sun greeted another day. Thus-ended day one of the Gathering.

The sun rose over the quiet valley. Nothing stirred but the young wolves and the youths responsible for them. The rest of the camp lay in

The Spirit Hunters | 225

their sleeping furs. No one would rise before sun high. Sage had been absent from the celebration the night before, but only one had missed her. His eyes had searched and searched, in vain.

Today would be the ceremony for the women and new children. Winter Rain was flustered with honor, for Running Bison had asked her, as a member of his extended hearth to garner essential information about the women traveling with the raider's band led by Standing Bear. Each needed to be recognized by a totem of The People. Some would require new adult names as well. These were very important tasks and the woman bloomed when she was asked to undertake them. Whispering Wind was dealing with an obstinate Sage.

"No! I appreciate all of the time and effort that you went to making it for me, but I will not wear it."

"Bu," Whispering Wind's lip quivered, "I made it special, just for you. This is the most important time of your life. You are my dearest friend. I wanted so much to do something special for you. Why won't you wear it?"

"Everyone would know."

Whispering Wind shook her head, "Not many would understand. Only the Dreamers and Crooked Spirit already knows. Besides, tomorrow you will be returning the Sacred Relics and everyone will know any way. Please! For me..."

"If I wear the tunic, then no bear claw necklace."

"Why?"

"I have told you time and time again..."

"Oh, that old 'I don't want to stand out' reason!" Whispering Wind stamped her foot. "That is childish and you know it! Besides, if you don't wear the necklace, your adult name won't make any sense!"

"I don't need an adult name! Sage suits me fine!"

"We have been over this before. Sage is not a suitable adult name. It is a child's name. Now you cannot go through a 'becoming a woman' recognition ceremony before the entire tribe and continue to go by Sage. It just is not done! Besides, I have already picked out a suitable name for you and as I am presenting you that is my right!"

"What name?"

"You also know that the name is not revealed until the ceremony," Whispering Wind replied just as stubbornly as Sage."

"Perhaps I just won't show up at all then!"

Whispering Wind's mouth fell open, "You wouldn't do that... would you?" Her lips began to quiver again.

Sage sighed, "It seems to me that ever since we joined this camp it has been one 'don't' after another. You can't do that, that isn't permitted, that is taboo! Every time I turn around! First they try to take Obsidian away from me. Then it is 'no mind talking', then 'don't leave the camp without telling me where you are going' and 'stay with the other women'." Sage shook her head. "I am supposed to be returning the Sacred Relics tomorrow, yet does anyone ask me if there is anything which I might need? Any help I might need? No! It is still 'stay in camp'. How am I supposed to commune with the spirits in this noisy place?"

Since they were the only ones moving in the absolutely quiet camp, Whispering Wind merely raised an eyebrow, "Do you need help?"

"No."

"Do you need to leave the camp?"

"I have managed to do so when I needed to."

"Is there anything which anyone can do for you?"

Sage shook her head.

"Then what are you complaining about? It is obvious to me, at least, that you have everything in order for tomorrow. We finished that white feather robe days ago. That is the only thing that you asked for. I have seen you collecting white ash for days now. If you needed more, I would assume that you would ask."

"I had to do that myself," Sage admitted.

"The ceremony begins at dusk when the drum begins to beat. I expect you to be there, dressed according to your status as a member of the Headman's hearth. Please, Sage. Even if you wish to spite me, do not shame Running Bison. He has many problems that you are not even aware exist. He doesn't need another. If it means so much to you, then don't wear the tunic. It will hurt my feelings, but I will overcome that. It is much more important that you be named."

"I have many things to complete before tomorrow night. I don't know if I will find the time to be here in the camp for the ceremony. I was not able to attend last night. But I will try," Sage conceded. Then she gathered up her staff, a number of packets and calling to Obsidian left the camp. Eyes followed.

Sage made her way to the stream. Here she dumped her burden down and sat. She sighed. She had just condemned herself to spending the whole of today and tomorrow by herself. She didn't have a thing to do, but had been too stubborn to give in. "Well, we might as well go dump this stuff at the tree," she said to Obsidian.

"Woof!"

"You are on her side also, aren't you?"

"Woof!"

"Well, if I don't stand up for myself some of the time, you know as well as I do that Whispering Wind would order me about all of the time. Since we have joined with this camp she has gotten very pushy. I think she must be having success with Running Bison. If she isn't telling me what to do, she has that silly grin on her vacant face and hears no one. That is a sure sign!"

"Woof!"

Sage got up, gathered her packets and wandered upstream to a deep grove of trees. Here she climbed the huge cottonwood and stuffed her bundles into the crotch where she already had an accumulation of stuff. Then she settled in as comfortably as possible. She rested her staff against the curious knot on the tree and felt the tingling begin. She then yawned hugely and was soon sound asleep.

The drum wakened her. She scrambled down from the tree to find Obsidian waiting patiently. They ran all the way back to the camp. Already most of the 'new women' were gathered at the hearth. Her hair was a mess and she was grubby as well. Quickly she brushed her hair and braided it down her back, the quickest style she could think of. She searched all over for a clean tunic, finding only the one which Whispering Wind had laid out for her. Grinding her teeth in frustration she pulled it over her head, shoved her feet into moccasins and forgetting all about the bear claw necklace which she had around her neck, bolted for the central hearth. She was there and walking among the other 'new women' before she realized that she still wore the necklace and that the tunic had been purposefully cut lower around the neck by Whispering Wind, to display the necklace. It was too late to do anything about it now. She shifted back into the shadow, however and tried to undo the lacing. They were stuck fast and refused to release. Grinding her teeth in frustration, she had to step forward when Whispering Wind called her name. As Sage stepped to the front of the group, Whispering Wind took her hand.

"People of the Bison Camp, I, Whispering Wind, Daughter of Thunder Cloud and member of the new 'women's hearth', introduce to you, this new woman of the Bison Camp. As a child she was named Sage. She grew up among the gatherers and is now returned to us. She has made her vision journey and White Owl 'gifted' her a feather. Her spirit animal is the Great Grizzly Bear who has claimed her as Bear Claw Woman." There were many gasps and ah!!!'s. Sage stepped forward and accepted the applause of the few that knew her and stood the curious stares of many others. Then it was over and she was able to escape back into the shadow. *I will get even with you, Whispering Wind!* She silently promised. Whispering Wind simply smiled back, a gleam of victory sparkling in her eyes.

Men rarely attended the woman's ceremony. This one was no different. Running Bison had delegated Winter Rain and Whispering Wind to see that this one ran smoothly. He still had a number of things to attend to before the closing ceremony. They had not found any bison, so had been forced to settle for deer. There were many other similarly frustrating problems. Male eyes, however, did follow her. They narrowed.

Sage, now Bear Claw Woman, danced half heartedly with the rest of the women. They were required to dance until dawn. It was a silly custom. She was anxious to leave the group but could find no way to do so. So she danced until dawn. *I can't believe that silly name!* She moaned in frustration. *Now, I suppose that I must answer to it for the rest of my days.* The necklace bounced up and down, catching the light from the hearth as she danced. Still, eyes watched.

"I am so tired I think that I will sleep late," Whispering Wind chattered as they all trouped toward the hearth. Blue Butterfly and Winter Rain were yawning as well. Sage had no chance to have a private word with Whispering Wind, which she suspected, was just as the other woman wanted. Wind was sound asleep before Sage even made it to the shelter they shared. Obsidian lay just beyond the shelter, watching. She growled low in her throat. The hunter stopped, then backed away and left.

The sun was high before any from the 'women's hearth' wakened. Then they sat around munching on grain cakes and drinking tea. There would be little food consumed until the closing feast. All were eagerly anticipating the feast.

Hunters had been up before the sun. Late the day before, several groups had returned to the camp. None had found bison, not even tracks of bison. But deer and elk had been brought in. They were now slowly roasting in a deep pit, prepared just as the Storyteller said it had been done in Ancient Times. A hand of men had spent the previous day digging the pit. Then it had been filled with wood and lighted. The coals were still red-hot when the sun rose. The deer had been dressed and the hide removed. Then they had been coated with a thick covering of red clay. This was allowed to dry before they were lowered into the pit. Then more wood was piled on top and it was lighted. All day more wood would be added, until the ceremony began. Only then would the fire be allowed to die down. When it was time, men armed with scapula shovels would clear the ashes from atop the carcasses. They would be raised and the clay casings broken open. The meat inside would be so juicy and tender that it would just fall off the bone. Sage had given Running Bison a generous amount of salt for this project.

Sage quietly left the camp during the early afternoon. She and Obsidian made their way to the grove of cottonwoods. Here she began to prepare. There was no time for sleeping. For some time she sat in the crotch of the tree with both hands holding the 'knot' the now-familiar blue aura began to pulsate around her. Obsidian eased back into the brush and watched.

\*     \*     \*

*Sage! Where are you? It is time!* Running Bison glared angrily around. There was no sign of the missing Sage.

Suddenly, the drum beat stopped. A death-like silence settled over the entire Gathering. The crowd swung as if on one neck to watch as the figure entered. She was eerily white in the reflected light from the big hearth. Her hair had been covered with a thick coating of white ash after she had braided it down her back in a single braid from which fluttered the feather of White Owl. Her face and body had been covered as well. Around her shoulders she had wrapped a white feather robe, so long that it swept the ground. Beside her walked the big black dog-wolf, in stark contrast. As she entered the assembly, people fell back, giving her a clear path. No one spoke; all eyes were glued on her. In her hands she carried a deer-hide wrapped packet.

Crooked Spirit, Dreamer, held his breath as she approached. Her blue eyes held his as she stopped before him. There she raised the packet and threw back the feather robe. Beneath it she was naked but for an apron and the thong around her throat which held the bear teeth and claw necklace. The wolf tattoo on her breast was starkly clear.

"Hear me, People of the tribe! I, Keeper of the Sacred Relics, return them to the care of The People. Here and at this time, I give them into the care of Crooked Spirit, Dreamer of The People. Now, I declare the offering on behalf of The People has been made. The spirits have spoken." She lay the packet at the feet of the dreamer and with a flourish opened the protective covering. The wolf skin glowed as if alive in the light from the hearth. She carefully folded back its layers, revealing within the pair of teeth, wretched so many generations before from the head of the great Long Toothed Cat, by Ancestor Yel, Great Keeper of the Sacred Relics. Carefully she picked up and raised the teeth. She and the dog-wolf beside her were encased in a shimmering mist of blue. She held up the teeth and showed them to the crowd. Many gasped. Others stepped back; Hunting Badger clutched his fists together angrily.

"What message do you bring from the spirits?" asked Crooked Spirit loudly. "What words do the spirits have for The People?"

Sage, Bear Claw Woman, returned the sacred relics to the wolf hide and wrapped them again, then again in the deer hide. The packet she handed ceremonially to the dreamer. Then she turned to the crowd. She looked at them, slowly letting her gaze drift from one side to the other. She reached out with her mind and touched theirs. Then she locked eyes with Hunting Badger and spoke. "Look around you! Think back to a pair of seasons ago... What changes have occurred among the people? How many loved ones have gone to walk the wind? Look at how the once great Bison Hunters have been reduced to a few frightened hands of people.

Why? Have you asked yourselves this question? Ever since the murder of Moon Maiden, has the Bison Camp prospered? Why have the Spirits deserted The People? Have you even wondered?"

She glanced around at the silent crowd, hanging on her every word. A cold shiver ran down her spine. "When did you last thank the spirits for the gift of food? Why do the hunters of The People brag of their own prowess? Your actions have angered Hesa, The One! The Spirit of Bison has turned away from you! No more will the Spirit of Bison yield up his kind to the darts of the disrespectful hunters of The People. Their hearts are corrupt. Their thoughts are selfish! They have not kept the hunter's taboos."

Many muttered and grumbled within the crowd. This was not the news they wanted to hear.

"The One," she continued, "Has become angry because The People have broken many sacred taboos. He has threatened to close the circle and wipe The People from the face of the land. There are others, perhaps more worthy of his gifts. The One has allowed the raiders and savages to attack The People and kill many of their number. Yet you do not heed the warning, you do not hear. The Dreamers have told you again and again, the storytellers have informed you of the proper ways. Still, you do not listen."

She turned and faced Running Bison. "One Headman, however, has begun to listen; only one has led his camp along the proper paths, his camp has suffered no loss, yet even he and his camp will be denied! Until the stiff necked, over proud men of The People bow down their heads in prayer to the spirit, not just one day a season, but every day of every season, not just with the mouth, but with the heart, The One will continue to visit upon The People, plagues, disease, starvation and death in many forms!"

"Kill her!" shouted Hunting Badger, "I have heard enough of her false words!"

No one moved; even Angry Bull hesitated.

"The People are to move into the mountains. The mighty hunters of The People are to learn to gather plants and snare rabbits and birds for their food. They are to bow their heads and bend their knees until they have taken the spirits back into their rebellious hearts. Then and only then will The One again give game worthy of the name 'hunter' to The People. Take warning, you proud, stiff-necked hunters! Change, or watch your women and children die before your eyes. Change, or suffer the torture of a slow painful death for yourself and those you hold dear! The Spirits will not return to The People until the very last disrespectful hunter has either changed or died!" She turned and left the gathering as silently as she had arrived.

Running Bison was stunned by her words. He had known that her message would not be happily accepted, but even he had not expected her words to be so harsh. But he knew the words came, not from Sage, Bear Claw Woman, but from the spirits of the Ancestors. Strong man that he was, the future looked very bleak to him. He knew that a deep-burning anger would be filling most of the hearts within the Gathering. Sage was in danger. He and his camp were in danger.

Crooked Spirit stood on shaking legs. He clutched the Sacred Relics to his skinny breast and wordlessly watched the woman walk from the gathering. Already much angry grumbling could be heard. Fermented drink had been flowing freely. He greatly feared there would be blood shed this night.

Eyes watched her leave the gathering, many sets. Most were filled with anger; one pair was filled with something else...

Sage returned to her shelter and removed the feather robe, returning it to its container. She heated water and found some soap root and removed the ash from her body and hair, at least as best she could. The residue was caught in a container to be ceremonially disposed of later in a sacred place. Once again the drum beat had resumed. The people could be seen dancing around the hearth. She could hear Hunting Badger shouting to them. She was very tired. She wrapped her sleeping fur about her and slipped from the shelter. In the cover of darkness she slipped from the camp and made her way to the stream. There she followed it upstream for several fingers of time before reaching the deep thicket of trees. Here she scrambled from the water and up the huge cottonwood and snuggled down into the hollow bowl created at its crotch. Obsidian backed into deep brush nearby and relaxed. Soon the woman was fast asleep, the knob of her staff resting securely against the power knot. As she slept, she absorbed 'power'.

The dancing drew to a close. Hunting Badger shouted to the hunters, "We are going on a great bison hunt! Any hunter is welcome to join us! Let that woman prattle with her spiritual dribble! We will show her just what a real hunter of The People is capable of! We will kill so many bison; it will be impossible to eat all the meat, even in an entire season! Dawn approaches! We go!"

A cheer was raised and many hunters rushed drunkenly toward their shelters where they gathered up atlatl and darts and some, the more sober of them, hunting capes as well. A wildly leaping and gesturing band of men staggered after him and out of the valley.

Crooked Spirit and Raven watched them go with sinking hearts. Many hunters followed Hunting Badger; far more than they had anticipated. Nor had they anticipated this 'bison' hunt. Running Bison was on a short trek of his own, with the beautiful Whispering Wind, his new mate, at his side. He knew the camp would sleep for the better part of the day and little would happen over the next or so after that. He was anxious, perhaps too anxious for good leadership, to spend some time alone with his new woman. He had left Raven in charge of the camp. The trusted hunter knew where he was destined if anything went wrong and he was needed but...in the mean time...

Those remaining in the camp slept until sun high. Then feeling the effects of the fermented drink, they crawled, moaning, from shelters, feeling sorry for their rumbling stomachs and hurting heads. Most found something to settle their stomachs and retired back to their furs. The camp was very quiet.

"What do you mean? She has to be here! I did not see her leave the camp, did you?"

Crooked Spirit shook his head, "I was too busy trying to settle those drink crazy hunters down and stop them from following Hunting Badger. I thought you were watching her!"

"I was!" Raven replied, "Until that fight broke out. I was, if you remember, the one to break it up." He shrugged, "I watched her go to her shelter. I thought she was still there, until I went seeking her, a short while ago. She was gone, the dog was gone and her sleeping furs were ripped and scattered and her things destroyed. I found what was left of her feather robe scattered around the hearth, but most of it had been burned. Whoever was responsible for the attack on her shelter and hearth certainly had less than her best interest at heart. But I found no trace of the woman, or of her dog. They have just vanished."

Crooked Spirit shook his head, "Power has a hand in this. She could not have left the camp of her own free will, for I still have the Ancient Relics. She would not leave without them. I think that we must seek our answer beyond the camp."

"I am going to scout the rim of the valley, perhaps I can pick up her trail."

"And I will see if I can 'talk' to her," Crooked Spirit replied. "Be careful, it will be dark soon. There have been strange things happening."

"I will keep my eyes open," assured the hunter.

*     *     *

Sage woke refreshed. She gathered her things into her sleeping fur and tossed the bundle from the tree. Then she and Obsidian headed back toward the camp. Eyes watched. She stopped at the trail leading up to the camp, found soap root and washed the remainder of the ash and fat from her hair and body. Then she climbed up the bank.

Obsidian growled and began a leap. She yelped and fell to the ground, a dart in her side. The valiant animal tried to rise. Before Sage could move, the hunter was on her. His first blow knocked her to the ground. His big fists closed around the necklace and he jerked hard. The thong did not break. He kicked the unconscious woman in the stomach, the ribs and with one savage stroke, broke her right arm. Then he went down on his knees and struck her repeatedly about the head. He rolled her over and with angry jerks, untied the necklace. As he rose, already he was tying it about his own thick neck. A wide evil grin spread across his face. "She has died too slowly, that is too bad! You," he looked into the blue eyes of the dog, "Will die slowly!" Then he vanished up the stream and out onto the plain.

Raven had checked the entire ridge. He found nothing. Slowly he returned toward the camp. A sound stopped him in his tracks. There ahead of him crawling along the path, he recognized the big black dog. A trail of blood followed her. In a heartbeat he was kneeling beside her, gently cradling her head in his hands. Obsidian whined once, looked back over her shoulder and died. Even as the light of life was leaving her, the hunter gently lay her head down and followed the path of blood. Before he reached her, he saw her body, a shimmering broken pile within the rich green grass. He went down on his knees beside her, a wail of grief distorting his ugly face. Tears ran down his face to drop upon her quiet body, sparkling like dew in the sunlight. Finally he rose and headed back to the camp. He saw no one, but went directly to his shelter. He jerked out the travois, hooked his wolf to it and added a soft robe and his atlatl and darts and hunting tools. No one saw him leave the camp. At the stream, carefully, with great heart-rending sobs, he laid her upon the soft robe. Obsidian was settled beside her and her staff was added. Then the hunter released his young wolf from the traces and, settling them on his own shoulders headed out of the valley toward the west.

He passed through the canyon, then the valley of jasper and on into yet another valley. Here he found what he was seeking. A proper place to lay her out to 'Walk The Wind'. The grove of huge trees almost called to his grief-stricken brain. He pulled the travois into the grove and was amazed to find them growing in a nearly perfect circle. In the center was a boulder. It stood shoulder high and was flat on top. Here he gently lifted the big dog and lay her at the base of the stone. Then he lifted the woman within the robe and laid her on the boulder. He smoothed her hair back from her battered and broken face, found and lay her staff beside her and fell to his knees beside the dog. He sobbed his heart out.

A groan brought his grief to a halt. He rose and almost refused to believe what his ears and eyes told him. She lived! He laid his ear to her breast and faintly, very faintly could hear her heart beating. Carefully he lifted her, robe-and-all and placed her back on the travois. He dragged it to the stream a short distance away and there washed the blood and debris from her. She looked only marginally less 'dead'. Then he found a branch and feeling gently with his fingers, returned the broken bones of her arm to their relative positions. He gently wrapped a strip of robe around her arm then bound it to a branch to hold it in place. He stripped inner bark from the willow tree and over a quickly built fire heated water in a shell bowl he found in her things. Then he added the willow bark and when it boiled, set it aside to cool. Then he smeared soft mud over the scratches and bruises to keep the biting insects from hurting her further.

He discovered broken ribs, so another strip of his robe went to bind her rib cage. By then the willow bark tea had cooled and he forced some of it between her teeth. The remainder he poured into a small bladder he again found among her things. Then he covered her with what remained of his robe and with a last regretful glance at the faithful dog-wolf, left the place. Raven knew not where he was heading. He only knew that she was in danger if whoever had done this thing realized that she was not dead. He headed west and kept going. He stopped late and sheltered beneath the deep branches of a huge pine. His wolf watched as he tended to the woman. She moaned and whimpered but did not open her eyes.

The next morning she was burning with fever. He bathed her body in a stream, cooling the fire spirits. Then he again took up the leathers of the travois and walked. For days he walked. Finally, hunger brought him to a standstill. He could be of no use to her if he were too weak. So he sheltered her beneath the branches of a huge cottonwood. He set her staff beside her, just touching her shoulder and leaned the head against a knot on the tree. He did not see the shimmering blue mist that traveled from the knot down the staff and into her body.

Raven found a deer. He did not kill it. In fact he forced a flock of vultures from it. It was not good meat, but it was not yet rotten. He cut some of it free and took it back to his camp. He roasted it over the fire on a spit and ate. He caught broth and drippings in the bowl and fed it to Sage. She ate a little. Each night she had eaten a little. Sometimes water, or willow bark tea, but in the evenings, always, as much broth as he could get her to eat. The marrow from the leg-bones of rabbits brought in by his wolf was made into healing, rich broth and fed to the woman. Her heart was beating stronger. She moaned from time to time, but still did not open her eyes. He spoke to her, but there was no answer.

*     *     *

Sage saw the dart vibrating from Obsidian's side. A black rage ran through her and she raised her head to see who had done this vile thing. Before she could move, the big dirty hunter was upon her. His huge fist drove into her face and Sage felt a blinding pain, then nothing.

*     *     *

She opened her eyes. She was sitting on a log in a green meadow. Birds were singing all around her and the soft breeze caressed her face. A sound beside her made her turn. The woman, Basket sat beside her. Walking toward them was another woman, accompanied by a huge silver wolf. Sage knew this woman was Ancestor Yel. She approached.

*"What do you suggest we do?"* She asked Basket, totally ignoring Sage. *"Things are completely out of hand. We just didn't foresee such a problem. She has to go back!"*

*"I have failed".* Obsidian crawled on her belly to them, laying her great head at Sage's feet. *"I was the Watcher. I let this happen!"*

*"We must do something."* Agreed Ancestor Basket. *"If she does not return, the circle will close and all will be lost."*

*"Return?"* Sage questioned. *"Where am I?"*

*"You have died."* Ancestor Yel answered. *"Now we must decide what must be done."*

*"Died?"*

*"Yes, died,"* Basket replied; *"but you cannot stay dead! You must go back!"*

*"We cannot force her to return."* Reminded Ancestor Yel. *"She must choose to do so freely."*

*"And if I don't choose?"* Sage asked.

*"But you must!"* A voice piped beside her.

Sage turned and found the most perfectly beautiful little girl, sitting beside her.

*"If you don't return, I will never be born."*

*"Who are you?"*

*"I will be named Morning Star. I will be your daughter. If you don't go back, you will miss much joy."*

*"But, how can you be my daughter? No man has 'looked' at me. None has asked to mate with me?"*

*"You are wrong!"* The child replied most seriously. *"My father has 'looked' he has loved, even now he mourns most deeply for you. His love is like a deep river and it will wash away the pain and will bring you great joy, as will I, but only if you choose to return."*

*"Before you choose, beware, there will be much pain."* Basket cautioned. *"The body you lived in has been badly broken and battered. We can do nothing to alleviate the pain you must* suffer if you choose to return."

*"I failed her! I also must return!"* Obsidian leaned against Sage's leg, her head on Sage's lap.

*"You cannot return unless you are reborn,"* reminded Yel.

*"Then I will be reborn. I will do whatever I must. I have failed! I did not protect!"*

*"You did not fail!"* Basket reassured Obsidian. *"Sometimes these things just happen. It is not your fault. It was unforeseen."*

"What if I choose not to return?" Sage asked.

Yel rose, *"then the circle will close. Those persons for whom you care most will die horribly, of disease, starvation, and murder. Your daughter will never live. The People will be wiped from the face of the land as so many grains of sand carried on the wind. The One will choose others to walk in their place."*

"Please Mother!" A soft hand slipped into hers.

Sage looked around her. The meadow was beautiful. Obsidian was with her. She looked at the child sitting so trusting beside her and remembered Whispering Wind's child. She had been responsible for its death. As if reading her thoughts, Yel spoke.

*"The child will be born again to Whispering Wind. The spirits are not totally unkind. But only if you return."*

Sage sighed, *"I choose to return."* A sharp blinding pain shot through her head and Sage groaned. The hunter, on his knees sobbing at the base of the boulder, raised his head and then rose to his feet.

Time meant little to Sage. Pain ruled her very existence. Every move made jarred her unmercifully; the bouncing of the travois caused constant hurt to lace through her battered body. Her broken nose made drawing breath difficult. The jaw was bruised and several teeth loosened as well. Fractured and cracked ribs made expansion of the lungs painful also. Ache raced through the broken arm that also was a constant throbbing anguish. It seemed that every part of her body protested, but the pain in her head was the worst. Her entire existence was wrapped around that misery. She was unable to move any part of her body, not even open her eyes. Most of the time she was unaware of anything but the pain; still she remembered the words of Ancestors Yel and Basket and the child Morning Star. These thoughts kept her alive and the hope for the future, both her own and that of The People. She could not leave Whispering Wind and Running Bison to die a horrible death when she could prevent it. Gradually even those thoughts however, were driven away by the pain.

*    *    *

Raven had been traveling through the mountains for a full moon. He had no idea where he was heading, but when he mounted the top of a steep rise and found himself on the northern verge of the very valley where Running Bison and Prairie Grass had rescued him from the savages, he realized where subconsciously he had been headed. To the cave!

He had fed Sage, cleaned and washed her, put poultices on her cuts and bruises. He had kept the binding on her ribs, holding them in place until they could heal. The arm was still in proper relation regarding bones, but she did not wake up. He talked to her, as he walked, as he rested, as he fixed their evening meal and as he settled her to sleep. Occasionally she moaned, but she did not speak and she did not open her eyes. It was as though the woman was locked in some kind of inner battle and he had no idea, which side was winning. She was fading away before his eyes.

There were no signs of people in the valley, but he felt the skin crawl up his back as he pulled the travois past the blackened area where once the savage's hearths burned. He was glad when he crossed the ridge and started up the steep rocky trail into the next valley. It was nearly dark when he followed the trail down into the canyon. He settled the travois against the cliff just below the cave and he and the wolf entered the cave. The wolf yelped and leaped past him and he had only time to grab a dart and shove it out in front of him when an angry cougar leaped at him. She raked his arms with both sets of claws, luckily for him the sleeves of his tunic were long and made of deer-hide. He drove the dart directly into the cat's heart.

Mewing at the back of the cave alerted him to the fact that the cat had young. He dragged the body of their mother to one side and carried Sage up into the cave. Their supplies, left behind when they deserted the cave, were more-or-less intact. The cat hadn't liked the smell and had kept her young away from them. Raven spread furs and lay Sage onto the soft bed. The young wolf was barking at the cats that were hissing at her. Raven frowned and sent the wolf outside. He was hesitant about killing the young cougars. They were not yet quite old enough to survive on their own and he regretted the killing of their mother. When he called his wolf in, he settled her beside Sage. The fire he started further upset the young cats. They crouched toward the back of the cave and yowled off and on all night. The young wolf growled and woofed back. Raven got little sleep.

In the morning he decided to take one of the elk in the canyon. He feared leaving the defenseless woman along with the cats so he left the wolf beside her. He dragged the carcass of the cougar out and caped the hide from her body. He was a frugal man so he saved the carcass to feed to her cubs. Less than a hand of time later he had brought down a young bull elk only a short distance from the cave.

*    *    *

Sage sighed. The pain due to movement was gone. True there was noise, but she could tolerate that. Then the voice was back. Always soothing and calming, she had gotten used to that voice. It called to her and helped her move through the canyons of pain in her mind. Gradually it had moved closer, until now it was just on the verge of her consciousness.

*    *    *

The hunter came into the cave with a quarter of his elk. He settled it beside the fire and tossed the pair of cats part of their mother's carcass. They yowled but they were hungry and finally they ate. All day he processed the elk. Finally, close to evening the young cats streaked from the cave. He could hear them calling to each other near the stream. He had left the remainder of the cougar carcass outside. They stayed around it all night and in the morning, both the carcass and the young cats were gone.

He stripped the remainder of the elk meat into thin strips. Some of it he salted and dried; some of it he smoked. He had found coltsfoot and wild onion along the stream. This he garnered and brought back to the cave.

He had recently gotten the woman to chew a little solid food. He knew she favored these plants so he fixed them for her. As on every other occasion he sent prayers to the spirits to help her heal. He had little in the way of healing skills, but he had watched the healer work on many wounded men. He had asked questions and now applied the knowledge to treating Sage. She ate the plant food greedily. He even got her to chew a few bits of fresh elk stew. She hadn't moaned all day. She seemed to be resting more comfortably. But still, she refused to open her eyes. He sighed.

During the next hand of days he settled them into the cave. Buzzards circling on the ridge above the canyon drew him to investigate. One of the young cougars had been killed by a bear; the other watched him from up in a tree and followed him back toward the cave. Late in the night, she came back inside and crouched against the far wall. The next morning he tossed her some raw meat. She ate hungrily. Then she left the cave. That evening she was back again. He had gone out during the afternoon and taken several rabbits with the rabbit stick he was learning to use. This was proving to be a good weapon. His aim was improving. He tossed one rabbit to the wolf and another to the cougar. He shook his head and went about fixing the meal. Later, he fed Sage rabbit stew and cooked coltsfoot. Her eyelids flickered.

The next morning when he went out to hunt, the cougar followed. He watched. When a rabbit bolted he threw the rabbit stick, it hit the animal and broke its back. The rabbit lay kicking. Quickly, looking briefly at the hunter, the young cougar bolted and grabbed the rabbit. She hunkered over it and growled. The hunter merely grinned and shrugged. The cat trotted off with her prize and Raven picked up his rabbit stick. This was a game he frequently played with the young wolf, teaching it to hunt for itself.

Again that evening the cat slipped into the cave. The hunter shook his head and sighed. It was bad enough that the woman did not respond, the young wolf was still learning, but now to have a half-grown cougar share their cave? He wondered what messages the spirits were sending him.

He had gathered more plant food and he cooked it with some of the rabbit he had managed to keep for himself. He added a minute amount of the salt and carried it to where the woman lay. He had a bowl of tea in one hand and her food in the other. He set down the stew and started to kneel beside her. She opened her eyes...

# CHAPTER 12

Raven dropped the tea bowl and spilled in on himself. With a grimace he set the bowl aside. When he looked up, her eyes were again closed. As usual he talked to her, but again she did not respond. With a sigh he returned to the hearth and poured more tea. She obediently ate the food he placed in her mouth. He talked to her as always, but she would not open her eyes again, no matter how much he pleaded with her. Finally he gave up and went about his usual evening routine. The wolf and the cougar had at least stopped snarling and growling at each other.

The next morning, first-thing, he looked at the woman. Her eyes were open. This time they stayed open. Raven was elated. The day before he had removed the chest bindings and left them off. Today he planned on releasing the arm. It seemed strong enough and had been strapped for a moon and half way through another.

"I hope that you are hungry," he said, "For I have fixed you a nice meal."

She made no response.

"I think that today you can sit up. You have been lying flat for far too long." Actually, he had settled her nearly daily for the last half moon, against the wall, shifting her weight from the back, for it was beginning to look red and angry. Sitting her up had helped.

"Here, give me your hand." He reached for the left one, but she did not move to help him. "All right, now, I will scoot you back a bit, there!" Expertly he slid her the short way. "That should feel better."

The woman stared blankly ahead, her eyes not moving at all.

"I hope that you don't mind the tunic which I made for you. I realize that it is not as fine as one made by women of The People, but I am a hunter and not skilled concerning garments. It is a bit big, but it should be comfortable. I did not find a tunic when I found you. I guess that you did not have one."

"The leaves in the canyon have turned. Soon it will snow. I am sure that you are wondering why we are sharing this cave with a cougar. Well, you see I killed her mother and she is too young to live on her own, a bear killed her brother. I know that it is strange."

On and on, he kept talking to her. In the days that followed, he gradually helped her, first to stand and then walk a few steps. He carried her to the stream and floated her in the warm waters. He exercised her arms and legs. Finally he encouraged her to try to stand on her own. She was able to and with encouragement followed his instructions. Still, she did not talk. She did not make any move without being told to. It was most frustrating! Raven was encouraged, however, for he felt they were making progress. As the fall passed into winter, he took her daily to the stream. Gradually her legs returned to their former strength. He took her out and had her throw the rabbit stick to strengthen her broken arm. As always, he talked to her and she did as told. But she never said a word.

The young cougar, however, was learning nicely. He had developed a habit of stunning game with his rabbit stick and letting the cougar complete the kill. Then one morning, he was amazed to see her ambush a young elk and bring it down. He knew then that she was old enough to make it on her own. But his mouth truly fell open when she dragged her kill back to the cave and laid it beside the hearth. Then the young cat retreated to the mouth of the cave, gave a plaintive yowl and vanished into the canyon.

It was a long and lonely winter for the man. Young Wolf made it much better for him. He romped and played with her during the long evenings. The woman sat against the wall and stared vacantly ahead. He had rubbed salve on the bruises on her throat and they had eventually disappeared. In fact, she was normal again in every way, but one.

It was late winter when he noticed that she was paddling a bit on her own in the stream. After that she wandered around the cave occasionally as well. He smiled. Yes! She was getting better.

He returned one afternoon, late, nearly dark and found that she had kept the hearth fire going and had hot tea and a meal ready for him. He was dumbfounded! Gradually she began doing things regularly about the cave. When spring arrived, he took her out to the canyon and seated her beneath a widespread pine where she could enjoy the fresh air. He and the wolf wandered down to the stream to gather the first of the spring cattail shoots. Eyes watched them go.

Stealthily, the animal slipped from her hiding place. She watched the hunter and Young Wolf, disappear from sight before proceeding. Then, quietly she approached the woman. Before her, the creature gently lay down her burden, then, looking deep into the vacant blue eyes she melted back into the safety of the heavy brush and vanished.

The small bundle deposited at Sage's feet began to squirm. It raised an oversized head, at the end of a skinny neck and both ears flipped forward. The creature struggled to its feet. Feet far too big for the long skinny legs they supported. Graceful it was not. It wobbled toward Sage and with great effort climbed into her lap, where it curled into a ball and laid it's big head on her leg. Then with a huge sigh, it closed its blue eyes.

Sage absently laid her hand on the creature and sighed.

When Raven returned he was astonished to find Sage with the curiously ugly animal in her lap. Then it opened its eyes and the hunter stopped. Instantly he understood that, strange though it looked and although he had no idea from where it came, 'spirits' were at work here. Sage carried the pup, for a wolf of some sort it surely was, although none such as the hunter had ever seen.

From that time onward, the woman was always where she could touch the pup. It, in return, was a slave to her. It wobbled on its gangly legs, tripped over its oversized feet and chewed on everything: moccasins, robes, leggings, baskets; nothing was safe from her sharp little milk teeth. But it never left the woman. And it grew! And grew and grew!

Mid summer was approaching. Raven was astonished that it had been an entire season since he had found the woman beside the stream in the Valley of the Gathering. Sometimes he caught a glimpse of 'sister cougar' while out hunting, but she never returned to the canyon. He was glad, however, that she had survived.

They were at the stream, swimming and Raven had just washed the woman' hair. The pup was splashing about and woofing loudly, enjoying the way her voice echoed in the cave. Then while Raven had his back turned, she vanished. He could hear her barking, but she was not to be found. He also could hear her splashing! He took a torch and walked carefully beneath the ledge. There was just room enough for his head and the torch to enter the room. He held the torch up high and sucked in his breath. He found a place to jam the base of the torch into that would hold tight then he quickly returned to the cave.

"Come! There is something I want to show you!" he called to the woman. She turned and he led her toward the ledge. "Be careful that you do not hit your head," he led her through.

Sage looked about then crawled from the water. She stood and laid her hands against the wall, clutching the crystals with her fingers. She sighed, closed her eyes and began a low, slow chant of prayer. As the man watched, a blue shimmering glow began to encase her and the young animal by her side. The hunter could not understand what was happening, but he clearly understood that 'power' was involved. Slowly he backed from the room and waited outside.

*　　*　　*

The pain was not so intense anymore. Sage wandered along one dark passageway after another, searching for the exit, but not finding it. She could hear the voice calling to her, she tried to answer, but she could never reach its source. Sometimes she heard other voices calling as well. Gentle hands, loving hands cared for her. But try as she might, she could not find the exit from the maze of pain. There were times... but then again, she was lost. At first all was darkness, filled to overflowing with agony. Then, gradually the intensity faded, but the darkness remained. She tried to follow the voice. She was too weak! There were times she knew it was very close, but again and again, each time she called out, she was lost. Then light entered her world. But it was not clear light, but rather a misty brightness. Still, it was better. She was reaching about one day, exploring with her hands and found her staff and it pulled her closer, but it had so little 'power' left that it was little help. She hadn't realized when she had chosen to return that it would be so painful, nor that it would take so long. There was no 'power' to help her. Weakness was her keeper. With the help of the staff, she was able, finally, to see her surroundings. But she could not break through the final barrier. She tried, but she was too feeble.

She recognized the hunter, Raven, the ugly one, or so people said. Sage found him beautiful. As he spoke to her, through the pain and the mists of darkness she realized that she was, as Morning Star had told her, deeply loved. Not only did he talk to her, almost constantly, explaining about the day to day happenings, but at times, particularly at night when he lay near her, but never touching, he even said words of love. He did many things, little things, thoughtful things, to make her life more bearable. He made her special food, taking pains to prepare the things that he knew she liked. He brought flowers into the cave and even braided them in her hair. Always he made sure she was clean and comfortable. She watched as he labored to create the tunic that he gently covered her nakedness with. It was soft, supple and warm. The winter chill did not touch her. His big clumsy fingers created soft rabbit-fur undergarments. The best of the sleeping furs went to her. A robe was slipped around her shoulders on chilly evenings. And the cave was kept safe and warm all during the winter months.

Even when he felt she could not comprehend his words, the hunter always told her when he was going from the cave and when he would return. He carried her to the spring, he swam with her he always saved her the best of the food; and he talked to her.

He led her one day out into the sunshine and settled her beneath a tree. While he was gone, she called, as she had many times and finally her call was answered. She could feel the 'power' as something climbed into her lap. Laying her hand on the object, she sighed. Obsidian! But she was so small. Sage knew that if she drew power from Obsidian now, she would kill her. She must be very careful.

As the days passed, Sage realized that soon, very soon, she would be able to break down the last barrier that kept her from returning to the land of the living. She was getting stronger. Soon she would be able to reach out and take, in both hands, the joy of life! Then the hunter led her beneath the ledge and into the crystal room. Sage crawled from the stream and the last barrier shattered. Weakly she clutched the crystal walls of the cave and sobbing, began a prayer of thanks.

The torchlight flickered and went out, but she did not notice. Soon, another took its place and the kind hunter ducked from the crystal room yet again. Sage did not know how long she stayed in the room, but finally, the pup whined and rubbed against her and she realized that she felt wonderful. She was strong and there was no pain. She knelt beside the pup and looked at her.

"Well! We both did it!" she murmured, running her hands over the gangly creature. "You have been born again and I have finally returned. It was a very long journey and I am glad that it is finished. Come, we have much to do," she slipped into the water, followed by the wolf pup and emerged beside the hunter. Whole at last!

*       *       *

Bear Claw Woman looked deeply into the hunter's eyes. "I can never repay your kindness," she said quietly, "I cannot begin to thank you for all that you have done for me."

Raven shook his head, "Thanks are not necessary. Anyone would have done the same." He blushed and suddenly shy before her, his heart quaking in dread and something else...

"You are wrong," she replied softly. "Only a man with a deep love would have continued caring for so long. I do not know how long it has been for you, but for me it seemed to be forever."

He shrugged, "The time has sped by. It has been but a season since I carried you from the Gathering."

"A season?" Bear Claw Woman shook her head, "So long?"

He nodded and handed her the rough tunic he had made for her, suddenly aware of its failings. Bear Claw Woman donned it without remark and reached for her staff. "I have tanned the hide of a mountain lion," he stuttered. "I was planning on making you a new tunic from it."

She looked up at him. "This one is fine," she answered. "I find no fault with it."

He gulped, smiled and led the way back to the living cave.

Bear Claw Woman looked around, as if she had just arrived. "The others, where are they?" She frowned.

"Others?" Raven shook his head, "We are all there is. There are no others."

She sighed, "I thought probably that was so." She looked around. "Although, sometimes I thought I heard other voices. Bear Claw Woman leaned her staff against the wall and settled beside the fire at her usual place. Automatically she dished up food from the bladder heated by the hearth. "So, you have cared for me by yourself for an entire season."

He nodded, taking the bowl from her, "It does not seem that long."

"Yet, it could not have been an easy task; and for one as sensitive as you, embarrassing at times."

"You were not aware...." he stumbled over his words.

"But now I am," she replied softly. "The entire time that I was struggling on my journey to return, only your voice guided me. Only your words gave me hope and strength. They were words of caring, words of love. I needed them. You gave of them freely. And while you cared for something no more responsive than a piece of firewood, I have learned the depths to which a man's love may stretch. I have glimpsed the very heart of a truly great man." She smiled tenderly, "It makes me feel very unworthy."

"I.... I..." he twisted his big hands, at a loss for words.

"Over the moons you have spoken many words. You have spoken of bravery, of pain, of caring and frequently of strength and purpose and even, when you thought no one listened, of love," she said softly. Then she reached out and laid her hand over his. "But I was listening. And desperately I wanted to answer."

"You..." his mouth dropped open and a flame of hope dared to flicker in his soft brown eyes, "You are sure?"

She nodded. "I am very sure. When a man speaks of love to a woman in the many ways which you have spoken to me, it would be impossible for that woman not to realize that the man in question is worthy of only the most loyal love in return."

"But I am not a handsome man!" he flushed red.

"And I am not Whispering Wind!"

"I never...." he shook his head, "Felt anything but kindness toward her. She was a prisoner and I was her guard.

"I know that. Even Whispering Wind, at her most empty-headed, knew that." Bear Claw Woman admitted. But she was right about one thing. She told me that you were a wonderfully kind man and I could do much worse than 'look' at you."

"She... did?"

"And I, foolish girl that I was, told her that I wasn't interested in any man, no matter how kind."

"Oh." He seemed to wilt.

"But, luckily, I have seen the foolishness of my ways."

"You... have?"

She nodded. "I have come to realize that far from being 'ugly', you are the most beautiful man I have ever seen. Not perhaps, on the surface, but where it counts, in the heart; while I, on the other hand, am frequently stubborn and obstinate."

"You are wonderful!" he stuttered and then blushed again.

She shook her head. "I am plain and strong headed and," she sighed, "Unfortunately, marked by Wolf Spirit. What man, in his right mind would want that woman?"

"This man!" he boomed!

She tilted her head, "It that an offer?"

"I.... You..." he fumbled with his hands again, then took a deep breath and looked straight into her laughing blue eyes. "Yes!" he nearly shouted.

"I accept," she replied.

He blinked, "You... do?"

She nodded.

"You... are sure? I mean, it is only just recently that you have come back..." He was nearly afraid to touch her."

"I feel wonderful!" she replied. "It was the 'power' room, you see. I could not tell you, but the reason it took so long is that I needed some kind of 'power' object to help me. My staff was weakened because I drew so strongly on it. It could not replenish without 'power' to draw on. Then Obsidian..."

He cut in, "I tried to ... it was too late. She died in my arms..." Tears ran down his face.

"Oh not when she died," Bear Claw Woman hurried to reassure him, "When she returned!"

"Returned?" He looked around and then his eyes lighted on the gangly pup with the blue eyes. She thumped her tail and grinned, a big toothy grin. His mouth fell open. "You are sure?"

"Very sure; but you see scavengers ate her old body, so she had to be born again. She is still too young."

"That explains how you came by her," he sighed and nodded. "This 'power' stuff is very confusing. It is also dangerous, is it not?"

She shrugged. "Life is dangerous!" she smiled, "But back to my story. I could not reach any places of power. I was dreadfully weakened and until you took me into the crystal room, I had no place from which to draw."

"You mean, if I had found it earlier..."

She nodded. "But now I am strong. As strong as ever I was."

"Then..."

She smiled at him and held out her hand.

"But we have no headman, no one to say the words..." he said in a voice filled with disappointment.

"Certainly we do!" she replied, "We have Raven, Headman of the Camp of the Cave!"

Slowly a wide grin began to spread across his face. "Yes," he nodded, "Yes, we do have him!

"So quickly! Say the words!" she urged.

He rose. "If there is anyone in this camp who finds reason to claim this purposed mating taboo, let them speak now."

Silence.

"Then, as Headman of the Camp of the Cave, I, Raven, declare this pair mated."

The Pup leaped and jumped, "Woof! Woof! Woof!" She barked.

Oooouuuuuhhhhh! howled Young Wolf.

Raven and Bear Claw Woman laughed and with smiles and clasped hands, walked to the bed of furs where Sage had lain for so long. Gently the big hunter lowered her to the bed. Slowly he ran his fingers over the flesh that just recently he had dared not think about. Before the dawn,

Sage, Bear Claw Woman, learned just a little about the joy that Morning Star had mentioned.

"Come, Sage, I have something to show you." Raven called to her.

She laughed, "Sage was a child, my mate. She no longer lives in this body. She died, back at the Valley of the Gathering, beside the faithful Obsidian. You have not matted a child. You have mated a woman of The People. Like it or not, her name is Bear Claw Woman," she laughed.

"Bear Claw Woman?" He shook his head, "That was the ridiculous name which Whispering Wind gave you. Yes, it fits. You are a strong woman." He looked critically at her, "But what happened to your necklace? It was not with you when..."

"Angry Bull!" she shook her fist. "He killed me for that necklace. After all the worry Running Bison and Crooked Spirit suffered; all their fears about the results of the 'spirit message', I was killed for simple greed."

"I wish you wouldn't say that!" Raven frowned.

"What, that he killed me for greed?"

"That he killed you," corrected the hunter. "You were perhaps in the land of spirits in your head, but your body did not die."

"Are you so sure?" Bear Claw Woman frowned, "Because Ancestor Yel and Ancestor Basket assured me that I was indeed dead. I was given a choice. I could have stayed dead."

"But you chose to return?"

"If I hadn't, well many would have suffered; Running Bison, Whispering Wind, in fact all of The People. They would have died horribly of disease, starvation; I can't begin to say all the things they would have suffered. And then of course there was Morning Star!"

"Morning Star, I do not think that I have heard of one by that name!" Raven shook his head, thinking, "No, I am sure of it."

"Not yet, perhaps," Bear Claw Woman smiled to herself, "But you will. You will, indeed! Besides, Obsidian was there as well and she also wanted to return. She just had to travel a different route. I couldn't be born again; there isn't time. But for her, there was; which brings me back to that evil hunter. He not only killed me, but he killed her in such a way that she had a long and painful death. At least mine was sudden!"

"But I wish him to suffer for what he did to Obsidian and me!" She raised her fist and shook it, "If I could I would ask the Wolf Spirit of The People to strangle him with that necklace!"

Far away, on the plain to the east, the thong holding the necklace around Angry Bull's neck shrank, just a little, then, a little more.

"Will you show me 'sister cougar'?"

They were climbing the trail out of the canyon, in search of game. It had been a hand of days since Bear Claw Woman had returned completely to the 'land of the living'. This was the first time that they had left the immediate area around the cave. Young Wolf was ranging out ahead, accompanied by the gangly pup. He was having no luck in flushing any game. Finally he gave up and rejoined the humans. The pup ran to Bear Claw Woman, as though she had been separated for hands of days rather than a few fingers of time. She was nearly as big as Young Wolf, but her feet were still much too large and although she was getting better control of them, she was still very clumsy.

At four months old, her tail now turned down rather than curve over her back. Her legs had grown longer. So had her body, but no matter how much she ate, she was still skinny. Her head was still too big, but at least her ears now stood up like a proper wolf. She had also changed color. No longer was she black. Her coat had changed to a gray, only the tips of the hairs still black. Bear Claw Woman recognized her for what she was going to be. She would be just like Ancestor Basket's, Spirit Wolf and the one which Ancestor Yel, merely called Wolf. This pup would be of a species that had not walked the land since the time of those ancestors. Obsidian was now a Dire Wolf.

Raven shook his head, "We will get no hunting done this day! Not with that one, jumping about and crashing through the brush like an enraged grizzly bear."

"She just needs to learn!" protested Bear Claw Woman. "Just because she is Obsidian returned, doesn't mean she has control yet over this body!"

"You can't call her that!" the hunter protested.

"Why not? That is her name." Bear Claw Woman replied logically.

"Because she is no longer black."

The woman tilted her head, studying the pup; "No she is not and I fear that she will be lighter yet before she is grown."

"Well I hope that is soon," the Hunter grinned. "Already she is as big as my Young Wolf!"

"If I cannot call her Obsidian, then what name would you suggest?"

"Well," the hunter considered, "you could call her Big Foot; or perhaps All Feet!"

"Those are not proper names for my guardian!" Bear Claw Woman protested. "Besides she will grow into those feet soon."

"You mean she will get even bigger?"

The woman nodded, "She is but four moons of age, wolves grow until they are a whole season old."

"But she will be half again as big as Young Wolf!"

Bear Claw Woman nodded.

"Then perhaps we could call her Large Wolf."

"I think perhaps I will simply call her Guardian."

"Guardian," the hunter considered. "Yes, I think that is a good name for her. She certainly does do that. Even before she could get any control over those feet, she did stay beside you and she watched every move I made. Sometime I think she would have tried to attack me had I ever given her cause to think I intended you harm."

"That is her task," Bear Claw Woman nodded. "Perhaps that is why she returned as one of the Ancient Ones; to set her apart."

"Well she certainly stands out, or she will shortly. She will make a formidable protector when she reached full growth. Yes, I agree, Guardian should be her name."

"What do you think?" Bear Claw Woman asked the pup. "Does the name Guardian please you?"

"Woof! Woof!"

AOoooooooaaaahhhhhhhhh!" Howled Young Wolf.

Both humans laughed.

They continued on up the trail. Bear Claw Woman pointed out the stump of the dead burned tree, struck by lightning, which had cut her and Whispering Wind off long ago.

"We ran just as hard as we could and finally fell into the stream in the burned-out valley. Of course it wasn't burned out until then. That fire very nearly burned us up also. That is when we found the canyon. We had walked right by the trail and not seen it. But we were surrounded by fire and Obsidian led us into the canyon."

How can that be? You were beyond the canyon wall!"

Bear Claw Woman grinned, "Come, I will show you. Besides, I think it is time I checked on the supplies we hid in case we needed to make a quick escape. I nearly did that, just to irritate Running Bison. He was just so overbearing!"

Bear Claw Woman hurried down the trail and Guardian led the way. She knew exactly where they were headed. When the pair reached the stream, Guardian leaped in with gusto and paddled straight beneath the wall.

"Woof! Woof! Woof!" she called.

Bear Claw Woman laughed and called her back. "I wish to check on the supplies we left here. There is no telling when we might need them!" The pup paddled back, climbed from the water and shook it all over them, thoroughly wetting them both. They both laughed and shook the water off. Then Bear Claw Woman led Raven to where she and Whispering Wind had hidden their stash.

"We nearly froze to death getting back to the cave," she explained. "We had to break the ice with a branch, strip naked and dive into the hole we had made. The wind was icy and blowing so hard that we had no choice. There was no way we could have returned by the trail. As it was, we lost no time pulling on our tunics on the other side and we still had all the way to the cave to go, wet and freezing. It took most of the evening just to thaw out!"

"This is most impressive!" Raven nodded. "You were well prepared. Had you escaped Running Bison I do not think he would have captured you again easily!"

"He would not, unless I wanted him to," she sighed. "But by then, the spirits had changed my mind. So we never needed this stash. I cannot believe that it is still like we put it there. That could have been yesterday!"

"It is getting late so perhaps you should show me the route back, although I have already guessed that one merely swims beneath the wall. But only because I know that your Guardian just did so and I am familiar with the door to the 'power room'."

So they entered the water and followed Guardian beneath the cliff, emerging, wet and laughing, inside the canyon.

"The stream follows this narrow fissure for several fingers before it widens out to where you are familiar."

"No one could follow a person on this path of escape," Raven nodded, "It is a good route to know."

Later, after the evening meal, they lay wrapped in their sleeping furs, satisfied, for the moment,

"Where do you think they are?"

Raven shrugged, "Running Bison planned to take those who would follow him into the mountains and find a place where they could live and follow what the spirits commanded. There was much discussion in the camp after your words; few of the hunters planned to follow him. They had decided to ask Standing Bear to lead them. Some of course, planned to go with the old headman."

"Hunting Badger?" Bear Claw Woman shook her hair back, "He was not highly regarded by those of his own camp, nor by Calling Wolf and his group."

"That group planned on going off on their own," Raven revealed, "Only the old Dreamer and his own woman would be willing to follow Running Bison."

"How can that be? He is a strong leader!"

"What you say is true, but it matters not how strong a leader is, if the direction of his leadership in not popular. I can only tell you what I overheard. No one was in favor of following the direction of your 'spirits'"

"Then they are all doomed!" Bear Claw Woman sighed, "And it is too late for me to do anything about it."

"There would have been nothing that you could have done any way. They would only have harmed you in the end or driven you from the camp."

"What would you have done? Would you have followed Running Bison?"

"Only if you were with him," Raven admitted, blushing, "I would have followed you, no matter where you led me."

"I would have gone with Running Bison," Bear Claw Woman admitted, "Whispering Wind is my dearest friend. Blue Butterfly and Winter Rain were becoming like sisters to me. I would not have been happily parted from them."

"And now you have only me," he sighed, "One ugly man.

"You are not ugly!" Bear Claw Woman protested. "Not to me! Remember, I am 'spirit gifted' and I can see beneath the surface! You are perhaps plain on the outside, as am I, but inside you are beautiful. It just took me a while to see that," She admitted.

"That you find me beautiful is not I think, much of a recommendation. You think that half grown pup of yours is beautiful as well."

"Ah! But wait until she is grown! Then, you also will admit that she is beautiful."

"I will wait!"

"Why were you drawn to me?" Bear Claw Woman stretched out on the fur, the firelight caressing her bare flesh and inviting the hunter to follow.

"I was sitting here, in this very cave, over there by the entrance and you walked into the room. There was a funny blue glow all around you and I could feel 'power' radiating from you. It was the most profound experience I have ever had, well almost!" He grinned and ran his hand over her smooth stomach, "There was something about you, I can't explain it, but it called to my very soul. For moons Bull Elk and I had been moving from camp to camp, looking for something to cause us to stay at any of them. We found nothing. Then Quinquel and his bloody followers captured us. When Running Bison rescued us, I vowed that I would follow him, no matter what, for he was truly worthy. But when you walked into this room, I knew that you were my destiny. I don't know how I knew it, but I did. It gave me no end of worry. What would a wonderful strong woman like you ever see in me? I know that I am ugly and I am shy and I lack the words."

"Stop! Right there!" she sat up and shoved her hair from her eyes. "You are far too hard on yourself. Yes you are perhaps less than handsome, but that is hardly important. We will all grow old and with age, handsomeness goes! Yes, you are shy, but when you think you are alone, or perhaps forget about your surroundings, your words are like the ripples on a quiet lake. You wooed me for moons with your words of love, promising such joy that I was wrapped in a cocoon of joy. It still surrounds me." She said softly as she lay back and drew him to her. What followed was very private indeed.

\* \* \*

"We should consider leaving this place and finding the rest of the camp," Raven sat drinking tea beside the fire.

"Where would you look?"

He shrugged, "I have no idea. I thought that perhaps you knew where they are."

"Me!" Bear Claw Woman stared at him puzzled, "Why would you think that?"

"Well... you know!" he was embarrassed. "The mind talking thing."

"Mind talking; I hadn't even thought about that. I guess I just wanted it to be 'us' for a while at least. I know that eventually we must find the others and then I will no longer be just a woman in love with a man. I will be that thing which I loath!"

"Which is?" Raven was puzzled.

"The Chosen!" Bear Claw Woman sputtered, "We will never have time for 'us'. There will always be someone needing something. You will see. I just hope that you do not become disgusted with me and decide that you would rather be mated to a 'normal' woman."

"Why would I wish for any other than the one who fills my heart?"

"You say that now, but you have not been forced to share my attention and time. Believe me it will come. We will never be allowed to be alone. Can you honestly say that you would not hate that?"

"I can honestly say that I will not care for it. But to have you for my own, I am willing to suffer any pain, any irritation or discomfort just so long as you do not turn away from me. After all, I am but a hunter and not even a particularly great one. I have never made any spectacular kill or demonstrated a particular skill."

"You are the man I love!" Bear Claw Woman sputtered, "I need nothing more. The life that I will be forced into will only be bearable if I have you at my side."

The hunter reached out and drew her to him, "I will always be by your side, if not in the flesh, always in the spirit. Remember that. I know that there will be times that we will be separated, but so long as I know

258 | Shirley G. East

that you are waiting for me, I will always return." They smiled deeply into each other's eyes and drifted gently down to the sleeping furs. The gangly pup sighed and closed her eyes, a smile spreading on her muzzle.

They spoke about leaving from time to time over the next few days, but as yet made no move to begin collecting their things. Each day Bear Claw Woman went to the stream and wadded under the ledge. In the crystal room she began to gather 'power'. It built up inside her, but she could only take in so much at any single time. Guardian was still growing at an astonishing rate. Already she was taller than Raven's Young Wolf and she was yet only a hand of moons old. They had discussed training her to the travois but decided that she was still too young. She needed her energy for growing. Bear Claw Woman knew that as an adult Guardian would stand half again as tall as the wolves they were used to; just as Obsidian had been the largest dog that anyone had ever seen.

Raven began, finally, to prepare for their departure. He had no idea where they would go, but he was confident that when the time was right, his Bear Claw Woman would show him the way. He went beneath the cliff and withdrew the supplies which Sage and Whispering Wind had stashed there and went through them. He replaced their atlatls and darts with fresh ones and added things of his own as well. They would leave from this place. There was no reason to leave good things behind.

He also began to prepare trail food. Sage had a plentiful supply of salt in the cave. This he placed carefully in water-proof packets and set these against the cave wall. Even though Guardian was too young to pull the travois, she was strong enough to carry a light pack; so, he fashioned a harness and bags to attach to it. She was not happy with this, but after several days of working with her in the canyon, she quit chewing it to pieces. It fascinated him that she had to be taught, just as any other pup, except when it came to guarding Sage. This was so deeply imbedded in her spirit that not even being reborn had changed it. Still, she was a long way from old enough to be a proper protector. For now, that was Raven's job. Before long he had a sizable pile of things ready to pack upon their travois. Bear Claw Woman had not spoken of their leaving again, but she watched the stores assemble.

*    *    *

*Saaaagggggeee!* The scream ripped through her mind!

Bear Claw Woman jerked upright. Her whole body was ridged. The hunter beside her came instantly to alert. "What is it? Is something wrong?"

"Whispering Wind!" she was shaking from head to toe. *She is having her baby. She will die, unless....* Then she wrapped her arms about her and became like a block of stone. Raven watched wide of eye and frightened. He had seen this trance thing only once before and it had nearly killed her then. But now he was ready. He knew that as soon as she returned he must take her to the crystal room. So he began to prepare.

*Wind! I am here!*

*Sage! Help me! My baby! It is coming! I have done what I can...*Pain drove through Bear Claw Woman's body, taking her breath away. She groaned and Raven reached for her, but drew back. It was not yet time.

*Who is with you?*

*Running Bison!*

*"What women? A man is worthless with childbirth!*

*Robe Maker, Flower, Blue Butterfly... we are ready. Flower knows what to do. Guide her, please...* again pain. This time Bear Claw Woman knew what it was. Labor pains *I am with you Wind, just like last time. Relax and go with the pain.* She directed her thought away from Whispering Wind and searched...

# CHAPTER 13

**Previously, back at the valley of the gathering...**

When Running Bison and Whispering Wind returned to the valley of the Gathering, after two wonderful days together, they found that everything had changed while they were gone. Crooked Spirit met them and related a jumbled tale. When he had parted from Raven, the hunter was going in a search for the missing Sage. When the hunter himself did not return, Crooked Spirit called on Crying Coyote and the pair of them went in search of either of the missing ones. They found the travois trail and followed it to where Obsidian lay, dead, at the base of the stone. Already scavengers had consumed part of the carcass. They had buried the rest out of respect for the faithful animal. They recognized the foot prints of the hunter and his dog, so they returned to the camp and checked his shelter, hunting tools and nothing else were gone. They found no sign of Sage, although many people had spent the entire day searching for her. They found blood, along the stream in the grass and something had been dragged for some distance.

The only thing which made any sense what that the hunter, Raven had killed the dog, kidnapped Sage and fled. But that made no sense either. Why would he have killed the dog and then taken her body with him? He greatly admired the loyalty of the animal. And if he were going to flee, why leave the majority of the things he would need along the trail. He had not even taken his extra darts, nor spare knives and blades. Even the hunting cape, given to him by Running Bison and one of his most cherished possessions, had been left. Yet he had taken extra sleeping robes.

The camp was now, nearly deserted. Most of the hunters had followed Hunting Badger out onto the plains; mere fingers of time after Running Bison and Whispering Wind had left. Even Standing Bear, Bull Elk, Antler Dancer and Horned Owl and their fellow hunters had gone, after the elusive bison. Running Bison was amazed that his trusted companion, Prairie Grass had followed Hunting Badger, as had Thunder Cloud, leaving his family behind. Crooked Spirit had no idea when, or if they would be returning. Raven had been left in charge of the camp and now he also was missing. What remained in the camp were two dreamers, three hunters and several double hands of women and children. Crooked Spirit had decided to wait until Running Bison returned before doing anything else.

Running Bison called the men together. "What do any of you know of the disappearance of the woman, Sage?" he questioned. None could help. The women knew little more.

Winter Rain stood up. "I was the first one to return to the hearth. Already someone had been there. The white feather robe we had all worked so hard to make was ripped into many pieces and most of it burned in the fire. The shelter shared by Sage and Whispering Wind had been torn apart and all the contents scattered," she attested to the ransacking of Sage's shelter and the destruction of her things.

The three hunters had gone out and when they returned they had explained to the women what they had found. The women were all upset to hear of Obsidian's death and no one felt that any good would come of this. "She spoke out against the old Headman," Winter Rain shook her head, "I would not be surprised if he didn't have something to do with her disappearance!"

Blue Butterfly rose, "I saw a man moving in the shadows, but I could not identify him. He was only a shadow. I could not name him as the hunter, Raven, or any other. But he was moving toward the stream and he came from the direction of our hearth."

"Would you advise trying to contact Sage?" Crooked Spirit whispered., "You know, mind talk."

"I will try," the headman nodded.

"Let me!" pleaded Whispering Wind. "I would do this; you have other matters to attend to." Running Bison nodded. Whispering Wind made her way to the big tree where she and Sage had first 'mind talked' and settled against it. She closed her eyes, wrapped her arms tightly about her middle and called, *Sage, where are you? We are all worried. Obsidian has been found. She is dead. You probably already know that, though. Please, Sage, talk to me!* Again and again she tried, but she received no answer. Finally, she gave up. She was nearly convinced that Sage, also, was dead. As she returned to the group, tears were running freely down her cheeks. She sniffed and shook her head.

"I will keep trying," she said, "No matter how long it takes. I just can't accept that Sage is dead! The spirits would protect her! She was the last of the line of The Chosen! Surely the spirits would protect her!" she whimpered.

"Everyone was really angry with her words at the closing ceremony." Crying Coyote replied, "It doesn't surprise me that someone killed her. The old Headman even commanded it. Probably one of his men followed her from the ceremony and did kill her and that dog as well."

"But why drag the dog all the way to that valley to the west? That doesn't make any sense, besides; we know whose tracks made that trail," Crooked Spirit objected. "Besides, what did he have on the travois. The load was heavy enough to leave tracks. He did not take any of his own possessions to make so heavy a load; in fact he had no need of the travois at all to carry what he left this camp with. The only explanation is that he had Sage on that travois, but why?"

"She would never ride a travois!" Whispering Wind objected.

"Perhaps she was dead as well when he found her," Crying Coyote replied. "Maybe he took her off somewhere to lay her out to walk the wind!"

"Then where is he? Why hasn't he returned to the camp?" Blue Butterfly asked.

"Even though Sage and her whereabouts, is a problem," Running Bison cut in, "We have other problems just as pressing. It is time to leave this valley. You have all heard the words sent by the spirits. Most of the men have disregarded those words and went out into the plains lead by the headman, Hunting Badger. Do we sit here and wait for them to return, or do we go after them, or do we go our own way?"

"What way do you go?" Crying Coyote asked.

"You know the way I choose," replied Running Bison. "I will follow the dictates of the Wolf Spirit. I take my family and any other who wish to go, back into the mountains and find a place where I can provide food; not bison, or other big game, but plenty of nourishing food. And I will pray that in my heart, someday, the spirits will find a reverent attitude. Perhaps, even in my lifetime, they will return the bison to The People."

Crooked Spirit rose, "I and my acolyte will go with you."

"I know that earlier I said that I would not follow you," Crying Coyote stood, "But a man can change his mind. I will follow Running Bison. Hunting bison may be a wonderful experience, but it is one which will have to wait!"

The other two men shook their heads, "I will not live like a woman!" stated the more forceful of the pair. They turned away and called to their families. Within a hand of time they had left the valley, headed out onto the plains to find Hunting Badger and his hunters.

This left two hunters, two dreamers; a pair of new men and several hands of women and children watching them depart.

"My man went with the old Headman!" one woman, named Little Doe stated. "I must wait here for him to return! I have two children. They need someone to provide for them!"

"And I," added another. "The men might follow that madman for a short distance, but soon they will return. Once the fermented brew wears off and their senses respond: and so on, until at least a double hand of women and half that of children had stepped aside.

"They did not think of you when they left!" reminded Crooked Spirit. "You will be here all alone once the rest of us leave. Think about it! Do you want to take the chance that your men won't return? What if the Savages find you? If you men do not return, who will hunt for you? Who will provide food for your children?"

"What do you offer us, Headman?" Little Doe challenged, clearly rethinking her stand.

"All that I can offer is a place where food is plentiful enough to provide for the coming winter. There are less than a hand of men able to hunt here and it will take everyone, man, woman and child, working together to provide shelter and food for so many. But provide I will. Be warned, however, that all that follow me will be required to contribute their share, be that great or small. I offer just leadership and fair treatment."

The women talked among themselves. Then Little Doe stood up. "You speak true. Our men did not remember us. What is to say that they will return? I would choose to be part of a camp where women are treated as equals! Do you offer this?"

"I do offer that," Running Bison nodded, "The women will have a say in everything regarding the camp, as long as it concerns them. I do reserve the right to lead the camp, decide where we settle for the winter and organize the camp as a whole. However, there will be a representative on the council and I will always be available to listen to complaints and suggestions."

"Then I and my children walk with you."

"You are a fool!" another woman, named Soft Breeze, shouted from the group. How do you know you can trust this man to keep his word? The men have merely gone hunting! They will return! And I will be waiting here for them!"

"You heard the words from the spirit," replied Little Doe. "There will be no bison out there. What promises do we have that all the men won't starve to death out on that plain, lost and thirsty!" They took no food with them, not even proper sleeping robes! My man wasn't that good a provider anyway; we frequently went hungry. He beat me as well! What need do I have of him? I would rather work and be given an honest say in my own life and that of my children!" She marched over to Running Bison, dragging a small boy by the arm and was followed by a slightly older girl, pulling their pitiful belongings on a ramshackle travois. The remainder of the small group looked to her and then back to the other. They shifted from foot to foot but did not move.

Before high sun the camp had been broken. Travois were loaded; some pulled by wolves, others by women and the few men remaining. Everyone had a share either to pull or carry. When they were ready Running Bison led them from the Valley of the Gathering, leaving a milling group of women and children behind.

A squabble broke out in the left-behind group. Shouting ensued followed by a short scuffle. Soon they were scrambling to catch up. One woman, Mountain Quail sported a black eye, but no one asked how she came by it. Before dark they had caught up and the camp was settled in a small valley liberally blessed with trees. Crying Coyote and Running Bison set out as soon as the camp was settled, leaving Crooked Spirit and Talking Shadow in charge and Whispering Wind and Winter Rain settling the families. They returned shortly with a pair of deer. These were quickly portioned out and at least this first night, everyone had enough to eat. Enough was cooked to provide meat for the morning meal and something to snack on during the day, for they would not stop again until evening. Whispering Wind and the women's hearth had already begun showing the other women which plants were good eating. The next morning Wind began organizing the women into small groups. Some watched the children, others kept the travois moving, still others went out parallel, a short distance from the moving camp and gathered plants, while a few, led by her began hunting small game. Nothing was overlooked.

That evening rabbits and birds were spitted and most of the remaining deer meat was cooked before it could spoil. There was plenty of food for the next day, so no one had to hunt. Running Bison had decided to go deep into the mountains and find a valley that would support so large a group through the winter. They had plenty of time to prepare, provided they found a good place soon. He was not happy to be so far north but hoped they could find a large cave or series of caves to shelter in for the winter. By applying the good sense he had learned from Whispering Wind and Sage, he knew they could be comfortable in such a place, but could everyone get along with one another during so long a confinement together? He was still worried about Sage. He was sorely afraid that she was dead. If so, he realized, The People had no chance of survival. He had tried to 'talk' to her, as had Whispering Wind and Crooked Spirit: all to no avail. Finally, after a double hand of days, he accepted that she would not be returned to them. They just had to accept that Sage was dead.

He selected to follow the rivers, where travel would be easier on his people. They moved fast for so large a band and one with so many women and children, but they were organized. When he had reached the mountains and the river turned into streams and then vanished. He carried on until he crossed the mountain pass and in another valley picked up yet another river. They went south and finally turned west along yet another river. He kept the mountains between his group and the last known location of the savages. Finally, he headed once again south into the mountains. He was now seriously looking for a place to spend the winter. They had not traveled as far south as he would have preferred, but they were running out of time. They had to prepare for the winter.

He found just the sort of place he was looking for a moon and a half after leaving the valley of the Gathering. The valley was large, with high mountains on both sides and a number of streams meandering through it. Trees were plentiful and most important; there were three caves along a section of cliff that faced south. They would be sheltered from the wind and warmed by the sun. Water was near; plant food plentiful. A lake provided a plentiful supply of cattail reeds for baskets and many hungry fish. Game trails told the hunters that elk and deer, bear and turkey, were abundant.

Once they left the Valley of the Gathering, he had moved into the mountains and then headed his camp south, into a warmer area.They wasted no time moving in. The men began hunting at once, but Running Bison made sure that they did not forget to thank the spirits of the animals for giving themselves as food. Wolf Leader was proving to be a valuable hunter, clearly able to do his share providing meat. The women began gathering plants, digging tubers, making baskets and locating pine trees from which to gather the nuts later. As they worked; if a squirrel happened by it ended up in a game bag as did many other small creatures. Partridges, turkeys, mountain quail, pigeons and dove were netted and brought down with bolas. Even the feathers were saved, for during the long winter, they could be made into warm robes. Children gathered branches and the larger children dragged sizable ones to the caves. Blackberries, blueberries, raspberries, thimble berries and plums were collected. Elderberry plants were collected as well as berries: the plant was kept for its medicinal uses, as were the vines of the grape. Willow cambium was collected as well. Before the leaves fell, they were well settled in. Each of the three caves had a hunter in charge. The women were organized by one selected from among themselves. She was in charge of making sure the meat was properly processed and stored. She was also responsible for making sure no one took more than their rightful share, at any time. Each of the caves also selected one woman to be on the Elder's Council.

The men brought in more than three double hands of deer, elk and bear. The hides were used to close off the cave openings, providing not only warmth, but a degree of safety as well. The young wolves were full-fledged hunters now and they frequently went out on their own and brought in game as well.

"What do you think headman?" Crooked Spirit asked. "Are we ready for the winter?"

Running Bison frowned, "I cannot answer that, for I have never lived in this area. We are much farther north than I would prefer. If it had not been so late in the season, I would have taken this camp to the escarpment at the western edge of the Llano. I know that we would have survived there."

"But what about the savages?" Crying Coyote asked, "Are you not concerned that they would have located us there?"

"That is one reason we are snug in this valley. There are no signs of anyone ever coming here."

"It is nearly impossible to get into the valley." exclaimed Crooked Spirit, "Only that one steep and dangerous trail in or out at either end."

"Which was one reason for selecting it, yet it is large enough to provide enough food for the winter moons. We have also been careful not to leave obvious signs that we are here. Besides, it would be nearly impossible for anyone to sneak up on us."

"The hard time will be when people are forced to spend much time together trapped by the weather in the cave. We need to provide them with something to do, so that they do not end up fighting."

"A wonderful idea," Running Bison grinned, "I will ask Whispering Wind to organize the women of our cave into designing and making very complicated and beautifully decorated tunics. Perhaps the other caves would do the same. There is still time to find dyes and I am certain that they have enough porcupine quills to decorate a tunic for every female in the camp. She has also removed all of the teeth from the elk and the teeth and claws from the bears, to say nothing of the hoofs of both deer and elk. What she plans to do with them I did not ask."

"We may find ourselves wearing finely decorated tunics as well," Crying Coyote grinned, "But I see the advantage of keeping busy. I think we could also encourage the making of wooden bowls and spoons as well."

"I want to carve a Wolf Spirit," Cricket exclaimed

"I would be more than happy to go from cave to cave and tell the stories," offered Talking Shadow, Healer and Dreamer, "It is important that the new people learn the stories and we have no storyteller."

"Then perhaps we should appoint one of the women as storyteller," Crooked Spirit suggested, "They all know the stories as well as we do. I am sure that Winter Rain, for example, would do an admirable job."

Running Bison nodded. "We have tried to put some of the new women in each of the caves, not only to break up those who do not get along, but to give them all a chance to learn the ways of The People. I am sure that we can keep fighting from breaking out, but it is easier if everyone is busy. At least we should not have hunger to worry about."

"I hope that the same can be said for sickness," worried Talking Shadow. "I do not have a large supply of medicine plants. That is my greatest worry. I think our weakness will come from disease. My hope is that the plants we now have added to our diet will keep away much of the illness. I know from talking to the healers from the gatherer camps, that plants, particularly the dried fruit seems to keep much sickness away."

"There is still time for the pair of us and Cricket here, to go out and search out more medicine plants," Crooked Spirit offered. "But you will have to show us which ones."

"We will begin tomorrow," Talking Shadow nodded. "I know where some are and I am sure that if we look we will find others as well."

"We have prepared the best that we were able," Running Bison nodded. "Now we must organize our camp so that people do not waste or squander the food and keep them busy so that they do not become frustrated with the restraint of the cave for so long a time. You have all offered some excellent ideas. Let's get started selecting the women to organize these projects. It is good to have them in charge. They are better able to keep an eye on what is happening. They have children to consider as well. This will make them even more concerned with how things are organized."

So they did.

*     *     *

Running Bison, Crooked Spirit, Talking Shadow and Crying Coyote were sitting around a small fire beneath a pine tree. The women were selecting their leaders and the men did not wish to interfere. In the west cave, where Whispering Wind was settled against the wall, Blue Butterfly was taking charge... "We are to select one woman to be in charge of the organization within the cave and another to be a member of the camp council. I think we should start with this task before we go on to others. First we should select the Cave Headwoman."

"Whispering Wind is mate to the Headman, isn't that her place?"

"No, she is Headwoman of the entire camp," answered Blue Butterfly.

"Happy Breeze is the oldest and most experienced. I think she would be the best choice as Cave Headwoman," stated Sun Dancer.

"I would rather Willow Woman be in that position," replied Happy Breeze. "It is a position of much organizing. These tasks are not my strength."

Bleu Butterfly looked around the group, "Are there any more suggestions?" There were none. "Then does everyone agree on Willow Woman as Cave Headwoman?" The group considered, talked some among themselves and finally nodded. "Fine, then I hand this discussion over to her!" Blue Butterfly smiled and sat down.

Willow Woman blushed. She had been a second wife to a poor hunter among the raider camp. Now she was being honored with the position of Cave Headwoman. She knew that it had been the right decision, coming with Running Bison. She doubted that her mate even realized that she was gone. She blushed prettily as she rose and took over. "I thank you," she said shyly. "I will try to do a good job and always be considerate." She glanced around at the group. "The next thing we need to select is the member for the camp council." She frowned, "This is a most serious position: one that carries much responsibility. Whoever is selected is charged with bringing our suggestions to the camp council and voicing her opinion on these and any other problems presented to the council. Whom do you think we should select?"

"Well Happy Breeze may not be a good organizer, but she always has an opinion. They are usually sound, backed by a lifetime of experience. I do not think we could do better than have her as our voice on the council," Singing Bird suggested.

"Would you accept the part?" Willow Woman asked.

Happy Breeze considered for a time. "This I could do. As my niece has said, I usually do have an opinion and I like to think that I have thought through things, before I voice that opinion."

"I feel that Happy Breeze is the best choice we could make!" Blue Butterfly nodded.

"Then if everyone is agreed, she is our council voice." Every woman nodded.

"The next thing we need to decide is where the hearths are going to be located in this cave and who will live at each one. Since Running Bison is our camp Headman, I think it is only fitting that his hearth is here in the center of the cave," Willow Woman glanced around. No one looked upset with her suggestion so she nodded and continued. "Laughing Water, you have settled against that wall, if that place suits you, there can be your hearth. I think that Calling Swan can live at your hearth and help you with the girls." Both women grinned, for they were best of friends. Both nodded. "Then that is settled. Willow Woman looked at the other women. "Singing Bird, you and your child seem settled toward the back there. Would it be all right with you to share your hearth with Sun Dancer and Prairieflower?" The women nodded. "That leaves the rest of us to share one hearth, against this wall," she pointed to the only empty area left.

"This is a big cave. There is plenty of room for each hearth to have storage pits and places to put extra things as well, baskets and whatever! Against the far back we can stack the wood for the fires.

By the time the women called to the five men, they were more than happy to return to their respective caves. Running Bison had already called a Camp Council meeting for the evening to discuss settling in and general responsibilities. The cave Headwomen and council members had been invited to attend. He wished to get everything clear from the beginning. He, Wolf Leader and Crying Coyote would be needed to hunt and to train the upcoming hunters. Of the more than double hand of boys in the camp all except three would be becoming men over the next season or so. It was now up to them to make sure these youths were prepared to take their place as men of The People. The women of the camp faced a nearly-identical problem. There were only a pair of very small children and there was a pair of girls of a hand and one a season older. The greatest majority of the children were at least a double hand of seasons. This fact along, proved that times had become increasing hard on The People. But it placed a hardship on the adults of the camp. There was much training to be done.

Whispering Wind met Running Bison at the opening of the cave with a smile. He knew then, that all had gone well. He was even more amazed to find that the women had made exactly the same choices as he would have made. He glanced around, noticing that four hearths were beginning to take shape. He was also pleased to see that the organization of the hearths did not put a burden on any single hearth, or on any one woman. He was even pleased to see that Speckledfish, the oldest of the boys, had been placed at his own hearth. The boy was likable and showed both intelligence and ability. He would very soon be taking his spirit journey and become a man.

\*      \*      \*

"Is everyone here?" Running Bison looked around the group. He mentally counted and nodded. All were here. "As you all know." He began. "We are very short of men in this camp. It is essential therefore that those of you selected to lead, understand exactly what you have been called upon to do. I realize that the leadership role is new to you, for unfortunately, most headmen do not credit the excellent talents that you possess. With the burden of training the boys upon the shoulders of only the three of us hunters, as well as the task of bringing in the meat to the camp, we will have little time to give to the actual running of the camp. This is your task. It is my hope that the camp council can make the majority of the decisions regarding the camp and life within. If you need help, I will give you my best recommendation, but the final decision will still fall to you."

"And if we do make a decision, you will enforce it?" Robe Maker asked.

Running Bison shook his head, "You will enforce it. It must be clear to all, from the very beginning, that your decisions are final. If force is needed, then I will provide that force, but I cannot foresee a circumstance where force will be necessary."

"Then you are really telling us that this is our camp and also our responsibility!" Happy Breeze asked.

He nodded.

"Even if you do not agree with our decision?"

"I could have gone among you and selected the women I felt would best serve as cave Headwomen and Council members and the result would have exactly the same as you have selected yourselves. You are capable! Every cave has made the wisest possible selection. And since you did the selecting, you will be far happier with your choices, even though they are exactly the same ones I would have made. During the coming winter we will all get on each other's nerves. Always this happens. But if we start out early, organize and have plenty of work to keep busy with during the long winter months, the time will go faster and we will not loose patience with each other so quickly."

"But first, I wish to outline the responsibilities for which you have been selected. It is best to be clear about these. Cave Headwomen, you are in charge of the food supplies. Each cave will be stocked according to your energy and ability. If for example, you wish a liberal supply of pinyon nuts, then it is your responsibility to provide them. This goes for every food item. Talk among yourselves; decide what you wish to stock in the cave. If for example, the middle cave chooses to store many tubers and no nuts, that is their choice, but they cannot demand to share the nuts of another cave. Use the talents of your people. If you have children and they are old enough to gather berries and nuts, then arrange so that they may do so. If you have someone skilled at fishing and you wish to add dry fish to you stores, then do so. Discuss among yourselves what it is that you want. Decide how much food you need to put away to last until spring, but remember, gluttony is not to be encouraged, nor is waste!"

"But, how do we know how much is enough?" Dancing Star wished to know.

"You know what is required for each meal during the day, do you not?" She nodded. "Then remember that there are these double hands of days in a moon." He held up three fingers. We are just entering the Moon of Falling Leaves, after it comes the Moon of first Snow, then the Moon of Standing Snow. We celebrate the Moon of the Shortest Day after that, then the Moon of Deepest Snow and the Starving Moon. Food for each of these you must store."

"That is a lot of moons! We know how much food for a single day!"

"Perhaps this would help," Cricket offered the woman a stick.

"What is this? Wood for my fire? How can that help me count food?"

The boy shook his head, "If you look, you will see marks that I have cut into the stick. These are how many days are in a moon. You can set aside food for each day, marking off one mark and going to the next. At the end you will see how much food is needed for an entire moon. Put aside that much for each of the moons which Running Bison has counted out for you."

Dancing Star looked at Running Bison. "This will work?" she asked.

"Absolutely," he replied, "And once you have decided on the days allotment, do not let it change or you will run out."

"May I have this counting stick?"

"Cricket nodded, "I made one for each Cave Headwoman. In my former camp, this was an important tool for the one in charge of the food. It works well."

"So if I tell you, Headman, that my cave requires a hand of elk and deer each for the winter season, you will provide them?"

"As well as a like number of Bear and a number of turkeys as well," he added.

Dancing Star, Broken Branch and Willow each clutched their counting stick very serious expression on their faces. "I did not realize that I would be responsible for my cave not starving. This is indeed a very serious task," Broken Branch murmured.

"And we must decide who brings in which food! How can we decide this? That has always been the Headman's task!"

"Now, in a way, each of you is part Headman," Running Bison replied. "I cannot do it all; therefore, I am depending upon you for help.

I am not worried at all for I know that you are each capable of doing these tasks and doing them well."

"So if I decide that Sparrow, Squirrel and Flower are to collect pinyon nuts until they have a hand of baskets filled with them, this then is their task?"

"It is and it is also your decision as to the size of the baskets!"

"What if we decide that the whole camp is to go pinyon-gathering?"

"Then we do so!"

"What then is our role?" asked Robe Maker.

"If there is a difference of opinion, if there are hard feelings, it is your responsibility to bring those involved together, talk the problem through, come to a solution and see that everyone abides by it! If you see a task that needs doing and no one has undertaken to complete it, then you may ask someone to do so. Just remember to be fair to everyone. Treat all equally. You are there for people to bring their problems to." The three women nodded.

"Are there any more questions? If you need to bring something to my attention, Whispering Wind will be available to listen and she will bring your concerns to me if you do not wish to bring them yourselves. She is Camp Headwoman. Now I have a number of tasks which need immediate attention." Running Bison rose.

"Each cave needs to select one of the boys to learn to knapp stone. The wood supply needs to be increased. The older boys are capable of this task. They are also capable of going out with the wolves and bringing in game. We have noticed tracks of mountain pig, turkey and in the higher elevations, sheep and goats as well. I will lead a hunting group after the sheep tomorrow and Crying Coyote will lead another group after the pigs. Wolf Leader will lead a deer hunting party." He grinned down at the women. "So your first task is to select the boys who will accompany us and tell them. We leave at dawn." With this Running Bison closed the meeting.

Willow Woman and Happy Breeze hurried to their work. "I think Crane would work better with the Headman than Porcupine," Willow Woman suggested. "Porcupine is less likely to listen to instructions. He would best be sent with Crying Coyote. Speckledfish would be a great help to Wolf Leader." Happy Breeze nodded.

At dawn the next day, Running Bison headed toward the upper elevations with Crane, Sycamore and Ram following closely. Each carried their child sized atlatl and darts and bolas. Crying Coyote led Porcupine, Gatherer, Pebble and Pinecone after pigs: Speckledfish and Badger went with Wolf Leader to hunt the deer.

They were not out of sight before the Camp Headwomen had gathered with Whispering Wind to decide their day's task. "Should we split up into groups, or all go out together?" Broken Branch asked.

"We should decide what needs doing first," recommended Willow Woman. "Then we can decide how many and for how long and how much!"

"The first thing we need is containers, regardless of what we decide to do," pointed out Dancing Star.

"Then." stated Whispering Wind, "The first need, is for baskets. Do we have any empty ones?" All three women shook their heads. "Then we should begin by gathering rushes. At the same time we can collect the tubers at their roots and there are many other plants nearby which can be collected. Might I suggest that today, at least, we make this a whole camp project? Once we get to the lake we can decide who will do what."

"I will tell the others to bring rabbit sticks, bolas and digging sticks. They trouped to the lake, laughing and giggling.

"I want to pull the rushes!" Green Moss shouted, "Who will help me?"

"I Will," offered Calling Swan.

"So will I," shouted Fireflower.

"And I," giggled Snowflake.

"I will begin weaving baskets, just as soon as I have reeds," Robe Maker stated. "I am the fastest basket weaver in the camp. Perhaps Soft Breeze will also make baskets. She is nearly as quick as I and her baskets are much finer." Soft Breeze nodded.

Whispering Wind called out, "Anyone wishing to gather plants for drying come with me!" She headed toward the stand of trees nearby. A hand of females followed her.

"I would seek the healing plants," Cricket called. "Those who would help Crooked Spirit and me, we are going to those trees over at the far side of the lake. We saw red alder among them." Cottonwood and Flower followed him.

"Is it proper for a girl to be gathering medicine plants?" asked Robe Maker.

Crooked Spirit nodded, "I have been thinking of teaching at least one of the female children the healing ways. We are in need of a woman's healer. Perhaps Flower will be the one." So Flower went with the dreamers.

Soon the entire camp was busy with their respective tasks. As soon as a basket was completed, it was delivered into waiting hands and soon put into service. As the day wore on, full baskets began to accumulate beside the women weaving. Two more sets of hands had joined them when it was realized that more baskets were needed than they could produce, working at top speed.

*    *    *

All through the Moon of Falling Leaves and the Moon of the First Snow Fall, they worked, becoming a well organized and smoothly functioning unit. The boys going out daily with Running Bison and Crying Coyote and Wolf Leader, proudly returned with mountain sheep, goats, mountain pigs, bear, both grizzly and black, deer, both white tail and mule deer and elk. Every few days a group went out and returned with numerous turkeys as well. The head woman of each cave had given Running Bison her estimate of how much of each type of meat the cave needed. If he felt her estimate was low, he provided more than she requested and if the estimate was high; he tried to provide that as well. Before the first heavy snow, both he and Crying Coyote felt that unless something unforeseen happened, they should make it through the winter without a problem. Wolf Leader was turning into an amazingly competent hunter.

The women in charge of the food supply were especially careful to be sure that nothing spoiled and no varmints sneaked into it. Mice were their first problem. Mice particularly liked the plant food. They chewed holes in the baskets and scattered the contents, leaving it uneatable for the most part. Something had to be done. They were multiplying at an unbelievable rate! So Pebble and his wolf were given the task in cave three. It was the hardest hit. They worked for several nights and the wolf dispatched numerous mice, but the problem continued. Finally Crooked Spirit and Talking Shadow were called in.

"Is there something which we can feed these mice which will kill them?" asked Summer Storm.

"Perhaps I can suggest something," Talking Shadow suggested. "When we were collecting medicinal plants, the children accidentally brought it a number of Death Camus. They thought that these plants were wild onion or the eatable Blue Camus. I have kept them. Perhaps we could feed them to the mice!"

"How do we get the mice to eat them and not the good food?" Pebble asked.

"We will have to coat the containers of the good food with something which the mice do not like!"

"What would that be?"

"Wolf Scent!" Crooked Spirit answered. "Just the presence of the wolf has slowed down the destruction. But this very night we will try this poison."

All afternoon the food supply was gone through and moved. By evening the only thing left for the mice was the food they had already destroyed, liberally seasoned with ground up Death Camus. Within a hand of days, there was not a mouse in cave three. Cave two was next and then cave one: however, the destruction accomplished by the rodents was serious. Now the food supply was stored up off the floor, on specially built racks and it was organized so that at the very first sign of activity by the rodents, they could be eliminated. Still a significant amount of their winter plant supply had been destroyed.

The meat had been smoked or salted and dried. It was now stored in baskets hung from the roof of the cave. Likewise, much of the plant food ended up hung in nets. This however turned out to be better, for so long as it was above heads, it could be placed closer to the hearths.

The Moon of the Shortest Day arrived. People were more-or-less confined to the caves now. There was visiting between groups and now the 'hunters' were making snow walkers. The women also made several sets, for general use.

Talking Shadow was instructing Cricket and to every one's amazement Flower, as well in the arts of healing. Both children were avid students.

The women were gathered in the larger cave working on tunics. They had tanned the hides and were now ready to cut and stitch and decorate. They hoped to make a new tunic for every member of the camp. Whispering Wind was busy giving suggestions and providing supplies. Running Bison was teaching Porcupine, Crane, Pebble and Speckledfish the art of tool knapping.

It seemed that everyone had something to do except Sycamore and Gatherer.

"I intend to go out and practice using my new atlatl," Sycamore followed action to his words.

"Where are you going?"

Sycamore shrugged, "I haven't thought that far." Already he was strapping his snow walkers onto his feet.

"I will go with you. I am tired of staying in the camp. Fresh air would be good. Did Running Bison suggest a place to hunt?"

Sycamore shrugged, "I did not ask him. He was occupied with other things. I did not think it was important enough to bother him."

"We should tell someone where we are going." Already Gatherer was strapping on his own snow walkers and had gathered atlatl and darts as well.

"We will not be gone that long. Nor will we go far. We will be back before anyone has time to miss us." Sycamore was tromping snow to settle his walkers and before Gatherer could protest further, headed out from the cave toward the nearest trees. No one saw them leave the camp.

"I thought that you weren't going far?" Gatherer called. They were already so high that the cave was merely a dot against the cliff.

"That was before you decided to go with me. But we could come back with a sheep and provide fresh meat for the camp. Think how proud our mothers would be! Besides, if I can bring in a sheep, then I will be ready to take my vision journey and become a man! You could do the same, and then we could celebrate together."

"I don't think we should do that without consulting either Running Bison, or at least Crooked Spirit. There are purification ceremonies to be done first."

"You are right. We will just bring in fresh meat. Hay! Look here, fresh tracks! Come on!"

"But.... Those aren't sheep tracks! Those are bear!"

"All the better!"

"I don't think...."

"Then don't!" Sycamore set off following the tracks. Gatherer's wolf began to whine and tucked her tail. Something was bothering her.

"Sycamore, wait!" Gatherer called.

But Sycamore did not wait. Either he did not hear, or he chose not to, but either way, soon he was out of sight among the trees. Gatherer called his wolf to heel and reluctantly followed the snow walker tracks. The wolf continued to whine and she constantly got in front of Gatherer and stood cross ways. Finally, in exasperation, he ordered her back to the cave. He stood and watched as she pleaded, then turned and disappeared through the trees. Then Gatherer turned and began hurrying to catch up to Sycamore.

Sycamore could see blood on the snow. Quickly he moved to the place. A deer had been taken. Part of the carcass was buried in the snow and the tracks told clearly that this had been a bear's work. The youth circled the kill, trying to pick up the trail of the bear. A roar and crashing of brush alerted him.... Too late! The bear rose on hind legs and again roared. Then he came crashing down on all four and like lightning attacked. The youth had not even time to draw his atlatl and dart.

With a single swipe of his huge paw, the bear ripped Sycamore's right arm from his body. With a gurgling scream, the boy fell to the ground. By then the bear was upon him. The second swipe eviscerated the boy, sending entrails and blood in a wide arc across the snow. With a huff the bear grabbed the carcass by the back and dragged it to where he had buried the deer. He dug another pit in the snow and dumped the body inside. Then he covered it with snow, just as he had the deer. The only thing remaining to evidence the boy's presence now was one snow walker and his atlatl, lying in a patch of bloody snow. The bear retreated into the deep brush once again.

Gatherer called out. "Sycamore! Wait up! You are getting too far ahead!" He pushed through the brush. When he came into the small clearing, he stopped. "Sycamore? Where are you, he called in a loud whisper." He saw the snow walker, the blood. He began to shake in fright. "Sycamore?"

A hot huff of breath on his neck and an agony of pain shot through him, then blackness.

The bear dragged this additional food cache to where he had buried the other one. He dumped the body. He was well fed from the deer, so he was sloppy.

Gatherer could feel hot trails of pain running through his back. Blood seeped from the wounds, pooling on the ground beneath him. He opened his eyes and nearly screamed. He was looking directly into the eviscerated cavity of Sycamore's body. Blood and gore everywhere. His stomach emptied and he closed his eyes and awaited the bear's return. He waited.... and waited. Cold was settling around his body. Death was closing in. Then he heard the snapping of a twig...

She followed his trail, well behind, knowing that a scolding was in order for disobeying his direct command. Her ears were back and her tail tucked, but still she followed, nervously sniffing the wind. The smell of bear and blood were very strong now. Timidly, she entered the glade. A roar and crashing in the brush sent her flying back down the trail. The bear did not follow.

Gatherer quivered. The bear stood over his grave and huffed, then pawed more snow upon him and the remains of Sycamore. Then the bear again left.

She circled and came in closer, from a different direction. She could smell the death smell of Sycamore. But Gatherer's smell was still living. She made sure and then streaked away. It was down-hill all the way to the camp.

"Woof! Woof!" she leaped and called. "Woof! Woof!" she whined and circled.

Running Bison looked up, frowned and returned to his teaching. Now was no time to be playing with the wolves.

"Oooooaaaahhhhh!" She howled. "Woof! Woof! Woof!"

The headman set aside his work, frowning and called. "Does anyone know who is responsible for this wolf?"

She leaped into the air, circled several times and streaked back along her trail. Several yards along she stopped and howled again; then waited.

Crying Coyote glanced at the wolf. "She wants us to follow. Something is wrong here. I will get my weapons and snow walkers." He left the cave and shortly returned. The wolf watched and waited. When Running Bison joined Crying Coyote, she whined and led the pair of hunters away from the camp. Running Bison whistled for his own wolf and then called several others as well. The young animal led them as fast as they could travel. Before the hunters reached the clearing, already they could hear the roar of the angry grizzly bear and the snarling and growling of the pack of wolves. They were ready with atlatl and darts as they entered the glade.

The bear rose on his hind legs and roared. Running Bison let fly with his first dart, at nearly the same time Crying Coyote drove his dart into the chest. Then Running Bison sent his second dart into the left eye of the bear, his first protruding from the throat. With a roar of pain and rage the animal came down on all fours. He shook his head and roared again as another pair of darts was driven into his body. Slowly he began to weaken. The wolves snapped and nipped at him, careful to avoid the vicious swiping of his paws as still more darts were driven into his body until finally he grunted and crumpled to the ground, dead.

She did not wait. Already she was digging, sending snow flying, until she had reached the boy. She got his tunic in her teeth and began pulling him from the grave. Her brother soon joined her and they slowly dragged Gatherer to safety. Now, with the bear dead, she called the hunters to him.

Running Bison knelt beside the still form. There was a slight rise of the chest. The boy was still alive. He shrugged from his warm robe and wrapped the child in it. Crying Coyote came to stand beside him. "There were two of them. The other one is dead. There is so much blood and damage to the body I cannot say which of the boys it is."

Running Bison sighed, "This one is still alive. Other than cold and loss of blood, I do not see that he is much hurt. The only wound I find it where the bear bit him on the back. I think that perhaps he was smart enough to let the bear think he was dead. It saved his life. I am going to start a fire and warm him. See if you can rig up travois and we will carry them back to camp."

"What about the bear?"

"If we make a travois from your cape, we can let the wolves pull the boys. We will drag the bear. If this one lives, he will have a bear skin sleeping robe and a necklace from the claws." Crying Coyote nodded.

It was nearly dark when the hunters returned to camp. By then everyone knew that Sycamore and Gatherer had gone out alone. When the hunters returned, Gentle Rain and Basket Woman were waiting. When Running Bison lifted the still boy into his arms and called for Crooked Spirit, Gentle Rain began to whimper and call to the spirits. Basket Woman began to wail a death-chant when the remains of her oldest son were revealed.

Gatherer was carried to Talking Shadow. The dreamer checked the wound. There had been extensive damage to the muscles of the left shoulder. The damage was so extensive that the dreamer was fairly certain that the boy would never use his left arm again. He stitched the muscles back together as best he could, treated the whole area with a cotation of herbs he knew would drive away the spirits of fever. Then he sewed the open gashes together, applying a second coating of herbs. All he could do after that was keep the boy warm and wait.

Shock had taken its toll. The boy lay at the dreamer's hearth, moaning and tossing, but he did not open his eyes. His wolf trembled and stayed at his side, refusing to leave, even to eat. Finally the dreamer sighed and tossed her food where she crouched. She whined, but finally did eat. Outside the older boys were butchering the bear. Pebble cut the claws free and busted the teeth from the head. Gatherer had been his best friend. He planned to make a fine necklace of the claws and teeth, much like the one he had seen the power-woman wear. If Gatherer lived, he would present it to him. If not, he would give it as a death offering.

Speckledfish took the hide of the bear. Already he had pegged it out. This animal hide would not be touched by any woman. If Gatherer lived, it would serve as his spirit animal. Grizzly bear had certainly marked him. If he lived through this initiation, he would become a truly powerful man of spirit.

Beyond the cave a wail rose. It was time to lay Sycamore out to walk the wind.

30  He would lead his camp south along the North Platt River to just west of Ft. Collins, Co. at which point he will pick up the Muddy and follow it to the Colorado. They will follow the Colorado west to the Gunnison and from there south to the Uncamphagire and there will pick of the Animas. The camp will winter along the Animas south of Silverton, Co.

31  *Alnus rubra:* Red alder: Native Americans used an infusion of the bark to treat tuberculosis and lymphatic disorders. The leaf tea, used as a skin wash, is said to be a soothing remedy for poison oak, insect bites and other skin irritations. **Tilford:** p 12

32  *Zigadenus* species: Death Camus: A very poisonous plant. **Tilford:** p 194.

# CHAPTER 14

The camp settled down into an uneasy silence after the incident with the two boys. Running Bison blamed himself for not being more careful. Basket Woman blamed herself for not giving more attention to her oldest son. The result was that she almost strangled Badger with attention. She made his life miserable. She also moved to the hearth of Mountain Quail.

It seemed that the Moon of the Shortest Day was much longer than any before it. Finally, the new moon rose and everyone sighed in relief. Mourning for Sycamore ended. Gatherer was slowly recovering. As Talking Shadow had feared, the muscles tightened and he had little use of his left arm. The scars on his back healed puckered and angry. They were also very painful!

"The dreamer gave me this salve to rub on your back," Gentle Rain sat down beside the boy.

"It is too painful!" he replied sullenly, "Besides why bother, I am useless! I will never be a great hunter!" He kicked the edge of the wonderfully tanned bearskin. "What good it that, or this?" he held up the bear claw necklace around his neck. "Will they give me courage? Will they return my arm?" He snorted and kicked dirt onto the hearth fire. "I am nothing!"

"You are alive!" shouted his mother. "Would you rather that I chopped off my hair and opened my arms in mourning? Have you no regard for Basket Woman! How dare you feel sorry for yourself! You will heal, in time and I hope one day be proud of the scar you carry!"

"Proud! How can I be proud of being a coward? No one understands! I failed my best friend! He walks the wind because I did not keep up. I was not at his side when the bear attacked! I was lagging behind like the coward I am!" he sobbed.

"Coward? You think of yourself as a coward?" Gentle Rain snorted, "You are regarded by the camp as one of the bravest and most clever boy to ever be tested by the spirits! You were smart enough to play dead and allow the bear to bury you. You were smart enough to send your wolf back to the camp for help! You were greatly honored by bear spirit! You were tested by one of his most powerful sons and he found you worthy! He marked you as one of his own! Where, I ask you, is there shame in that?"

"There is no truth in any of this!" Gatherer shouted. "I was not clever! I was so afraid that I dirtied myself and then I fainted! I didn't send my wolf back to the camp! Well I did, but only because she had more brains then I and tried to stop me from following Sycamore! It was lucky for me that she did not obey me. If there is a hero in all of this it is Wawoo! She it is, who saved my life, not me!" At his mention of her name, the young wolf whined and snuggled closer. Unconsciously his left hand closed in her fur.

"Who would not be frightened?" his mother protested. "What makes you think any hunter, no matter how brave, would not be frightened to face an angry grizzly bear empty handed? It is not bravery that counts at a time like that. It is survival! And you, my son, survived! In a few days time, the dreamer will be calling for your adult naming ceremony. I will be very proud to present my son to the camp. I will look each member straight in the eye and name you Bear Man!"

Gatherer snorted, "Then you had better name me One-Armed Bear Man!" he replied.

"Maybe I should name you Sorry-for-Himself!" Gentle Rain retorted!

"I se no reason to get an adult name; for I will never be a hunter; whoever heard of a one-armed hunter?"

"Perhaps you should ask the dreamer that question!" Gentle Rain replied, "I for one have heard of just such a person and a great hunter he was!" She stepped behind him and with his protests ringing in her ears began rubbing the salve into his scars. His face went white, but he refused to make any sound of pain. His left hand clutched in the fur of the wolf.

During the Moon of Deepest Snow, Bear Man joined the rank of hunters. His hand was now working rather well, but the arm was stiff and difficult to bend at the elbow and he could not raise it. Crooked Spirit studied the arm and then made a rope exercise apparatus.

"You place the leather sleeve around your arm. Then with your foot in this loop raise the arm as far as the pain will let you. Hold it there for a few breathes and let it back down. Do this a double hand of times after the first meal of the day and again before you retire to your furs."

"This will return the use of my arm to me?" The young man asked, for the first time daring to hope.

"Do you remember the legend of the Hero Brothers, Blue Coyote and Stone Man?" Bear Man nodded. "Well, Stone Man suffered just such an injury as yours. With an apparatus very similar to this one, he regained the use of his arm and became one of the greatest hunters of all times!"

"I will use it just as you have directed!" Bear Man replied, gratefully.

The Starving Moon arrived.

Whispering Wind tossed aside the furs. Running Bison had risen earlier. She sat up and immediately became ill. With a groan she returned to her furs. Softly she smiled and reached for the dry seed cake she had tucked away near by. Then she ran her hands over her slightly curving stomach.

The Spring Moon arrived and the camp sighed. It had been one of the best winter seasons any of them could remember. The only tragedy had been the death of Sycamore. The women had kept busy making new tunics for every member of the camp. They were wonderful. The women had gone to great lengths to design each tunic special for the wearer. They had made a row of Running Bison across his tunic, dyed with the juice of the walnut. Blue Butterfly's had a bottom boarder of butterflies made of dyed porcupine quills. And so on with each person's name, somehow depicted, on his or her tunic. Bear Man had a truly ferocious grizzly bear standing upright down the front of his tunic. And around his neck he still wore the teeth. Unconsciously he ran the fingers of his left hand over the necklace and then patted the head of his faithful Wawoo. Speckledfish found a flying falcon worked in porcupine quills on his tunic.

Whispering Wind sat beside the hearth marking out the pattern for inserts on a pair of spare pieces of tunic leather. She smiled dreamily as she did so. Soon, very soon she would tell Running Bison.

The camp was busy. Excitement prevailed! Women were clearing out the old, cleaning the caves. New stones were being brought in by the youths for the hearth linings. Girls and women were gathering the first new growth of green plants. In a hand of days they would celebrate the Spring Ceremony. With it several new adults were entering the camp. Crane, Porcupine Speckledfish, Pebble, Pinecone, Ram and Cricket had all become adults since Gatherer. Fireflower had become a woman. There was even to be a mating, for Crying Coyote had finally found the courage to approach Green Moss. There was much to celebrate! Finally, Whispering Wind announced that there was even a new child to be anticipated. Running Bison was both happy and uneasy. Whispering Wind was not his first mate. She had died in child birth. But Wind was so happy; he had not the heart to voice his concern.

The valley had been kind to them. With proper use, it had provided them with a bounty of food. With spring, it had renewed itself. They had taken only what they needed. There were enough animals to reproduce and provide food for the fall. The girls and women were proficient with their nets after Whispering Wind showed them that the nets worked equally well with fish as they did with birds. This she had learned from Sage. The wolves were now a year old. They were well-trained members of the pack. Food was not a problem for the camp. When it came time to decide whether to move on or stay; the women wished to stay, at least another season, in the valley. It was safe here. They were settled and happy here. The hunters now knew the area. They were almost always successful bringing in game. The caves were comfortable, roomy, dry and safe. What more did they need?

The drums called. As the sun traveled behind the western mountain, the people were called to the celebration. It had been decided that each new hunter would be presented his new tunic with the symbol of his adult name, as a part of his initiation. There were no bison hunting robes. It had even been decided to change their name as a camp. No longer would they hunt bison, so no longer would they be the Bison camp, but rather the Wolf Camp! As soon as the ceremony was over, they had located a number of dens that they planned to raid. Before long, every member of the camp would have his or her own wolf!

Crooked Spirit led the celebration, followed by Talking Shadow and Cricket, blowing on the bird leg whistle he had carved during the winter season. Robe Maker beat the drum. Everyone hurried to the big hearth constructed before the center cave.

"We come here this day to give thanks to the spirits which have guided the camp this past season and to offer prayers that they will continue to guide us." Running Bison opened the ceremony. "It is with hearts filled with veneration toward the spirits, not with our own greatness; that we bring to this gathering. During this winter season boys went out into the land; they prayed and were chosen by spirits. Today we honor these spirits and in their name; present new men to the Camp of the Wolf."

Crooked Spirit took over. "During the Moon of the Deepest Snow, the boy Cricket was called by Golden Eagle. He made a whistle from the leg of his spirit bird and now he carries it as a symbol of his guidance. I give you Hollow Bone, Man of The People! Whispering Wind presented the new man with a tunic emblazoned with a Golden Eagle worked in porcupine quills and richly fringed along the bottom edge.

The new man accepted and stepped back.

Happy Breeze stepped up next. "My grandson became a man during the Moon of the Shortest Day. The hunting bird Falcon called him. I give you Swift Falcon, Man of The People. He donned his new tunic, with the flying falcon worked on it. There was in addition, a boarder of blue porcupine quills just above the fringed bottom.

Willow Woman presented Porcupine, now Standing Brave, to The People. Next came Happy Breeze again to present Crane, now Tall Bear. Little Doe brought forth Grouse and presented Looks Far, New Hunter to the Wolf Camp. She was followed by Smiling Sun to present Singing Elk, no longer Ram the boy. Pebble became Stone Killer and Pinecone, Tool Maker, for he had certainly learned to make beautifully chipped tools during the winter. And finally, Fireflower put away her childhood name and proudly became Water Spirit, Woman of The People.

Then Crying Coyote stepped forward and formally asked Running Bison for the mating to Green Moss. The woman dressed in a pure-white tunic and leggings stepped forward and the dancing began. Fermented brew was handed around and everyone drank and ate their fill of the plentiful offering of new food.

"You will be careful not to over exert?" Running Bison asked Whispering Wind, "It would not hurt you to sit and watch the dancing."

"I am pregnant, my mate, not old!" Whispering Wind laughed, "Do not worry; your son will be born a strong healthy baby!"

"A son is it?" he frowned, "Is it not considered bad luck to guess at the gender of a child? Will the spirits be angry?

She shrugged. "Of course, I do not know that it is a son," although in her heart she was sure. "But what man does not want sons?"

"This man would be just as pleased with a daughter, particularly if she is as beautiful as her mother. But I do worry. Childbirth is not the safest of times. There are so many things which can go wrong and although Talking Shadow is fine for a dreamer, he lacks much as a healer."

"Ah! I do miss Sage!" Whispering Wind sniffed, "It still seems impossible that she is dead. I would have her beside me at the birth of this child. She is a truly gifted healer!"

"Sage is?" Running Bison looked at her amazed.

"You forget, her grandmother was a healer. She taught Sage well. She is far more gifted than any healer I have ever seen."

"Do you ever 'call' to her any more?"

Whispering Wind shook her head, "What is the point? She will not answer."

"We don't know for sure that she is dead. We never found her body."

"We found Obsidian! Sage would never have left her, even dead, not like that! I just know it! Do you ever 'call'?"

Running Bison nodded. "Every once in a while, I do," he admitted. "But I never feel that there is anyone out there to listen. I haven't bothered in a long while."

"I think that I will offer up a prayer for her spirit."

"Then I will leave you to prepare." Running Bison rose and walked toward where the new men were gathered and went about once again welcoming each of them.

Whispering Wind stepped back from the merrymaking and settled against the base of a large pine. She ran her fingers over a large knot on its trunk and sent up her prayer. *Sage found a path that drew her closer to living. She called out, but her voice would not rise above a whisper in this land of the dead!*

The new men wanted their own space. It was decided that they would move into a shelter built before the caves with Talking Shadow. In Crooked Spirit's cave, Robe Maker would remain as council member and Basket Woman would step in as the cave Headwoman. Badger would live there as well. Dancing Star's hearth chose to move to Running Bison's cave and the rest to Crying Coyote's cave. Once the shifts were made, everyone settled in happily.

The new hunters made a tremendous difference. Their shelter was lively and with Talking Shadow to direct them, well managed. Young though they were, they carried their share of the responsibility. With the increase in plants in the diet and the fact that the women and children contributed so much of this fare, the entire camp operated smoothly. As soon as they were old enough, the wolves were stolen from the dens. Soon everyone was complaining of chewed shoes and robes. The 'soon to be hunters' were put in charge of the new wolves, along with Fawn, Strawberry and Blueberry, with Calling Swan in charge. She had proved that she was successful in training the wolves to pull the travois and generally behave.

It was the Moon of Spring Full-bloom. Whispering Wind had added the expansions to her tunic. She was blooming and very obviously pregnant. Looks Far was on duty at the upper end of the valley, training his wolf. A movement at the very top of the pass caught his attention. He motioned the wolf to his side and they slipped into the brush. Looks Far peered out and was astonished to see more than a hand of hunters examining the path. Cold chills ran down his spine. He did not waste time, but slithered down into the gully behind him. It was full of small bushes and he had to go down onto hands and knees to follow the trail that his wolf traversed with such ease. He had twigs caught in his hair and dead leaves and other debris caught in his clothing. He rose, shrugged the loose stuff off and followed a game trail at high speed back to the camp.

"Hunters!" he called softly into the first cave and kept going. Running Bison was working with Crying Coyote and the new hunters in the second cave. "Hunters are coming into the valley!" He called gasping for breath, "I saw at least a hand plus. "They were studying the trail!"

Even before his words were finished, Running Bison and the rest of the hunters had grabbed their weapons and were headed from the cave. "Warn the women and then join us!" The headman instructed.

Looks Far nodded, "I have already done so! I go to the lake for the gathering women. He could suddenly see the wisdom of Running Bison's orders that no one goes anywhere without alerting the camp. Without having to waste time asking, he already knew that they had planned to work on the shore." Already he was running again, this time down the valley, keeping to the hidden trails, hoping against hope that none had finished early and was returning by the open path.

There was a group of a double hand of women and children, laughing and splashing in the water. He waved to them and made the sign for danger. Silence descended and they huddled together in the shallows. "Is this all of you?" he gasped.

"Green Moss and Basket Woman have gone into the forest to dig for tubers," Whispering Wind answered.

"I know where they were going." Sun Bird stepped from the water. "I will go for them." She pulled on her moccasins and headed quietly and swiftly into the woods. The rest headed back to the caves, following the path within the forest.

Looks Far nodded to them at the cave and grabbing his weapons set out again, this time following Running Bison and the hunters. He found them hunkered down within brush at the base of the trail.

The hunters were still where he had seen them, silhouetted against the faultlessly blue sky.

"I came down this way." Looks Far whispered, indicating his obvious trail down the gully. "It is not easy to follow, but it leads quite close to where they are and is completely beyond their view."

Running Bison nodded and everyone began rearranging their weapons. Then, on hands and knees they embarked upon following the gully. The brush was thick on either side, but the pigs that had made the trail had followed the easiest path. Carefully, making absolutely no noise, they worked their way upward.

As they got closer, they could hear the men arguing. Running Bison motioned for those behind him to stop and he listened. The wind blew is such a direction that he could catch only an occasional word or so, but he began to grin. Then he continued on and soon the voices were clear to all. The men were also coming closer.

"You are so certain that they came this way! I do not understand how you can know! It has been nearly an entire season, yet you are confident that you are still following their trail." the big hunter just behind their leader protested.

"I tell you, they are here! If I were Running Bison and leading women and children, these are the choices that I would have made. Besides we found discarded foot wear just beside the river only yesterday. It was not even a season old and made in the fashion of The People. I just know we are near," Calling Wolf justified his actions.

"I hope that you are correct!" muttered Bull Elk. "If you are wrong, we have wasted many moons, nearly froze to death during the winter and are lost!"

"I know that I am right!" Calling Wolf replied.

Running Bison rose and called. "I would not want you for an enemy on my trail, Calling Wolf!"

The hunters jerked to a stop, and then Calling Wolf began to grin, "See! I told you!"

Bull Elk stood there, his mouth hanging open, and then he also began to grin ruefully. "Next time I will believe you." Behind him crowded the rest of their group.

Running Bison led his group from the brush and joined the hunters bunched together on the narrow trail. He was surprised to recognize every one of the men. There was Thunder Cloud, father of Whispering Wind and mate to Willow Woman. Singing Wind and Messenger, from the Bison Camp. Bull Elk, the man he had saved along with Raven from the savages and Pine Cone, the storyteller of the Bison Camp and three survivors of other camps. Running Bison did not know their names. There was also, a hand of men whom he recognized as from the former 'raiders camp'. A full three-hands of hunters in all.

"Tell us!" called one of the later. "Are our families with you? We have been searching long for them. If they are not with you, they have vanished!"

"What are the names of the women you seek?" Questioned Crying Coyote.

"My mate is called Laughing Water and I have a pair of daughters, Blueberry and Strawberry." The man replied.

Crying Coyote nodded, "They will be most happy to see you. I know that you have been sorely missed by them."

"Is my Dancing Reed and Robin also with your camp?" hopefully asked another.

Again Crying Coyote nodded. The hunter sighed in relief and began to smile.

"I had a woman named Smiling Sun and a boy, Ram." questioned yet another. Again Crying Coyote nodded.

"They are all with us." assured Running Bison.

"And perhaps the woman Snowdrop?" another asked.

Running Bison shook his head. "That woman did not come with us."

The hunter sighed and then shrugged, "You do have some unmated women though?"

"That we do!" Running Bison replied. "In fact, until you hunters arrived, we had nothing but unmated women, excepting my own mate and that of Crying Coyote that is. I can assure you that the women of the Wolf Camp will find you a most-welcome addition to our camp. I feel there will be celebrating in the camp tonight!"

As the group entered the valley and came within range of the caves, Hollow Bone withdrew his Eagle-leg whistle from his waist pouch and blew a happy tune. From within the caves, faces appeared and people began streaming out into the valley. One woman stopped, then threw back her head and gave forth with a trilling call, instantly answered by one of the men. They ran toward each other and were soon sobbing and clutching and hugging. Blueberry and Strawberry also broke away from the other girls and ran screaming, "Father! Father!" Soon they joined the pair.

Other women recognized long missed mates as well.

Bull Elk looked around a bit confused, "I do not see Raven!"

Running Bison shook his head, "He is not with us."

"The woman Sage, is she not with you either?"

"Sage is dead," Running Bison sighed, "At least we fear she is. The night that you all left the Gathering, I did also; completely unaware that someone killed both Sage and her dog. I returned a pair of days later. We found the travois trail where Raven had left the camp and later found the body of the dog. But of the woman and the hunter Raven, we have found no trace. We have concluded, that probably, someone killed the pair and Raven found them and took the woman somewhere for burial and just kept going. I know that he was deeply attached to her in his heart, although he never spoke a word."

Bull Elk nodded. "He was much attracted to her," he agreed. "But I find it hard to believe that he would go off alone. We were as brothers. That makes no sense!"

"You went off with the bison hunters without him!" reminded Crooked Spirit. The other hunter looked to the ground and turned red in the face.

"Then you would agree that perhaps the woman was not dead and he took her off somewhere to hide her?" Running Bison questioned.

Bull Elk frowned, "I would say that such an action is well within his character. And I know where he would have taken her furthermore!"

Running Bison looked hopeful, "You do?"

"He would take her back to that cave!"

"Running Bison struck his palm with a closed fist, "Of course! Why didn't I think of that?"

"It is at least over a moon hard walking to that place."

"You know how to reach it from here?"

"I am familiar with this area, yes. Just south of here the mountains open up and you can travel west to east. It is not easy, much rough country and a pair or more high passes must be traversed, but it can be done. I would lead you."

Running Bison sighed, "I cannot leave the camp, but perhaps you and Calling Wolf could make the journey. I would not ask you, understand, but if you were to choose to do so..."

"What about the 'talking'?" Calling Wolf questioned from beside Running Bison.

The latter shook his head, "Nothing!"

"Do you have any suggestions as to why?"

"She could be dead. Or she could be in danger and afraid, or the savages could have her." Running Bison replied. "I have thought of all of these reasons."

"She could just be obstinate!" suggested Bull Elk, remembering his first meeting with her.

"I don't think so," Calling Wolf said, "I also have tried. When we first set out to find you, I called and called, to no avail!"

"What are you talking about?" Frowned Bull Elk.

Calling Wolf looked at Running Bison and when that man nodded, he turned to Bull Elk. "The woman, Sage had the ability to 'talk' with her mind. She led those of us with Hunting Badger into the camp that way and also communicated with Crying Coyote when he located the prisoners held by the savages. Those of us with whom she had communicated that way, have all tried, but there has been no answer."

"Well if she is dead, then where is Raven?"

"That question is one for which I also would like an answer. This camp has chosen to remain in this valley for another season. If the pair of you wish to make the journey to the cave to find answers, I would wish you well and provide what provisions the camp can offer."

"I will consider," Bull Elk nodded. "I wish to know what happened to Raven."

"There would be time to reach the cave and return before snowfall?"

"Easily," Bull Elk affirmed.

"Is this something you would choose to do?" Running Bison asked.

Bull Elk nodded. Calling Wolf studied him for a short time and then nodded as well. "I have nothing else to do," he replied, "And I am curious as to the fate of the woman. I never did get to really sit down and speak with her. This I would truly like to do. I think she is a very powerful person and I would explore this power with her. Among my people I was once similar to what you call a dreamer. A shaman deals with spirits, but he also has a family and is part of the camp, not set aside like your dreamer. I think the woman Sage was, much as one of our shaman, in tune with the spirits"

"She was more than 'in-tune' with the spirits," Running Bison replied, "She was marked by them and guarded by the big wolf-dog, a creature sent by the spirits."

"Then we will leave immediately," Bull Elk stated.

"It will take a few days to get supplies together and select the wolves who will accompany you. I think that in a hand of days all will be ready. Until then, relax and get to know the camp. You might be surprised just how well our organization is working. It is amazing how much of the work has been removed from our shoulders by the women and how much happier everyone is. The women have proven that they are every bit as wise as we are at organizing. Time and again I have been amazed that their choices have paralleled my own. This camp has enjoyed one of the easiest winters I have ever experienced."

"This valley looks to be a wonderful place," agreed Bull Elk. "There is an abundance of game and no one could fault the safety! I am still amazed that Calling Wolf found you!"

"I just hope that others, less friendly, are not so clever!" Crooked Spirit muttered.

We left a trail just as easy as yours to follow," assured Bull Elk. "Besides, I do not think Calling Wolf was so much following your trail as deciding, at each point, what choices you would make, Running Bison. He then led us on that path. The only sign that anyone had ever been in this country was the single moccasin we found alongside the river beyond that pass and we brought it with us."

"At least that explains the mystery of Green Moss's lost shoe!" laughed Crooked Spirit.

"She finally accused one of the wolves of eating it. I will enjoy explaining to her that her own carelessness caused her loss. She had the entire camp looking for that shoe at one time or another. It seems that it had special meaning for her. It was a gift from Sage. Green Moss had some sort of feeling that those shoes made for easier walking. I can't see how that could be. They were no different from any other moccasins made by anyone else. But that was her claim!"

Calling Wolf nodded, "I have heard such claims before, about items made by a shaman. They have special powers that cannot be seen, but they are felt."

"Then if we ever find the girl, I'll certainly have her make me a pair of moccasins!" declared Crooked Spirit. "These old feet of mine could use them!"

"If you will direct me to this Green Moss, I will return her shoe," said Calling Wolf. "Oddly, it was in perfect condition. I thought that it had been dropped only recently."

"I will get her for you," Crooked Spirit nodded and ambled off toward the center cave.

That evening began a hand-of-days long celebration. The addition of the new hunters had made them a strong camp indeed. The only thing worrying Running Bison was whether or not they were going to fit in. The spirits demanded that the hunters cleanse their hearts of all self-glory. If these new additions would not comply, they could well loose part of the camp rather than gain. He would not wish this to happen. Only time would tell, but he was sure that there would be some problems before everything smoothed out again.

"We will go out and dig tubers and gather water cress and lamb's quarter." Willow Woman was laughing and had a special sparkle in her eyes. Already she looked several seasons younger and there was a strong lift to her step. "I am Headwoman of this cave," she explained to her mate.

"You?" he asked in surprise. "Is there no man in this cave?"

"Of course, but what has that to do with the organization of the cave? The men are the hunters; they concern themselves with providing meat to the camp. We women are those who do the gathering, preparing, storing of food and making of garments. It is only sensible that we are in charge of those tasks. We do not need a man to tell us how to do our own tasks!" She stood taller than he remembered and carried herself proudly. Thunder Cloud found that he liked this. His arrival had even made a difference to his adoptive son, Porcupine, or rather, Standing Bear. It would take him a while to adjust to the boy's new status as an adult. He hardly recognized little Snowflake; she had grown so much. But his heart was full to overflowing. He had sorely missed his family. Thunder Cloud had castigated himself severely. Upon leaving Wanderer and his group still seeking the elusive bison, he and the other hunters had returned to the Valley of the Gathering, only to find it void of human life.

Calling Wolf had assured them that he could find the Bison Camp. Most of them were ashamed of themselves. They had gone off like a bunch of fools, chasing after that pompous old egotist, Badger. For a double hand of days they had followed, before they realized that they were fools! When they had finally returned to the Valley of the Gathering, their families had vanished. Calling Wolf had declared that Running Bison would have taken them to a place of safety. They had few options, so they had elected to follow him. Until reaching this valley, some had begun to lose confidence, but now they realized that they had followed a superb leader.

Thunder Cloud had learned the hard way that his sense of judgement was not to be depended upon. He realized that Thunder Cloud might be an excellent hunter, but he was now glad to leave the leading to others. He was amazed that his own mate had turned out to be one of those leaders. Willow Woman called to several other women and children and expertly organized them into a work group. Out of curiosity, Thunder Cloud wandered along with them. He justified the trip by telling himself that he was guarding them against danger. In reality he just wanted to watch his mate and the women and enjoy the experience. He had already realized, by the atlatl and darts they carried that they were in no need of protecting. His own Daughter, Whispering Wind, was wonderful as camp Headwoman and her obvious pregnancy also pleased him. The idea of becoming a grandfather was suddenly warm to his heart.

Other hunters were discovering the same thing. Antler Dancer was astonished at the growth of Strawberry and Blueberry. Both girls had not only grown in size, but they had assumed responsibility for the training of the young wolves. This task would never have been entrusted to a female in any camp he had ever lived in, but in this camp, not only did they do the task, but they did it very well. Already the puppies had learned the meaning of the command "no" and a number of others as well.

Over the next few days, the newly reunited hunters were introduced to so many changes that it made their heads spin. Some felt genuinely uncomfortable with the situation. Others found that the changes worked. So long as they were free to hunt and associate with the other hunters and their families were safe, they had little concern regarding who was leading. If the women wanted to be in charge of women's work, they cared not.

Others were uneasy with the degree to which the women hunted. Even with Running Bison's explanation that with only a pair of adult males, someone had to take on the task and that the women hunted no big game did not appease them. They demanded that no female be allowed atlatl and darts. Running Bison sighed and informed them that he was Headman and that decision was his alone to make. They did not like that, but for the moment no one challenged him.

At the end of the celebration Calling Wolf and Bull Elk set out with a pair of wolves and travois heaped with provisions. Running Bison wished them well. It was now The Moon of first berries. The women had added to their supplies a basket of dried mushrooms and a cooking bladder of stew for their dinner over the next pair of days. At first Calling Wolf had looked with suspicion at the mushrooms given him for his evening meal, but he soon became so fond of them that he could eat them at every meal. So Whispering Wind made sure he had a plentiful supply to take with him. After all, he was searching for her best friend. It was the least she could do.

Calling Wolf and Bull Elk had made a drawing on the ground and explained where they were headed and the geographical features they would encounter. If they found Sage and Raven, they would persuade Sage to get in contact with the camp and then they hoped to bring both of them back with them. Spirits were high all the way around as the hunters became smaller and smaller in the distance and then vanished at the far end of the valley.

"Do you think they will find the cave?" Whispering Wind asked.

"I hope so. They certainly seem to think they know how to get to it. At least Bull Elk does. And after the way he led those hunters to this valley, I think Calling Wolf could locate anything," Running Bison answered.

"I hope so," Whispering Wind ran her hand over her bulging stomach. I want her here at the birth of this baby."

"You are worried?" the hunter frowned. "What are you keeping from me? Is there a problem? Are you in any danger?"

Whispering Wind sighed. "I just want Sage here for the birth," she replied. Increasingly over the past moons she had realized that this pregnancy was exactly like her last, but Running Bison knew nothing about that baby. She had never told him, or anyone, about her murdered baby. So now she was almost positive that her little son was being returned to her by the spirits. If this was so, she was absolutely sure that he would arrive in the same manner and if this was so, there was a great possibility that both she and the baby would die.

Later she was sitting with Robe Maker. "Have you ever delivered a baby?"

"Robe Maker looked at her in astonishment. "certainly!" she exclaimed, "I have delivered many and helped with even more."

"Have any been born the wrong way, with the feet coming out first?"

"Not that lived," admitted the old woman. "Feet-first is very bad. Always the baby is born dead and sometimes the mother dies also, for there is so much blood."

"You have heard of turning the baby though?"

"Turning the baby?" The woman shook her head, "How would you do that? It is still within the mother!"

"I saw it done once," Whispering Wind lied. "The healer was very wise. She had the mother staked out on her back, hands and legs tied so that she couldn't move. Then the healer reached up inside where the baby comes out and turned the child around."

"And the mother lived?" Robe Maker stared open-mouthed at Whispering Wind.

"Both lived," replied Wind.

"I have never hard of such a thing! I would say that it is impossible. You say that you have seen it done?"

Wind nodded.

"Where? Who was the woman? What child?"

Whispering Wind bit her tongue, "No one that you would know. Later, the baby was killed, but there was no harm done to either of them. The mother was even able to get pregnant again."

"And the next baby, it was born normally?"

Whispering Wind shrugged, "I do not know," she replied. "But I think there should be someone in this camp who could do such a thing, if there ever is a need for it."

Robe Maker nodded. "I have heard of that happening in other camps. Always though the baby at least, died. But my hands are too big."

"What about me?" Flower questioned, "I have very small hands, but I am strong. Do you think that I could do such a thing?" She moved closer, "I would like to learn this."

Robe Maker studied the child. "You are gifted in the arts of healing," she agreed. "It would be logical that you would be the one to learn, if such a task could be learned."

"It was well into the labor and the child could be seen coming out wrong." Whispering wind replied. "The healer had small hands, such as yours. First she washed them very well, all the way to the shoulder, in hot water with soap root. Then she coated the one arm with bird fat, just cool enough that it did not burn. She had already given the woman a drink to take away some of the pain and then slowly, very slowly, she eased the child back inside the woman and turned it carefully around. When the head was right, the child just popped out into her hands, perfectly all right."

"I will think on this," Flower nodded, "It seems that it would be possible."

Whispering Wind went back to her own hearth, somewhat relieved. She hoped that if needed, Flower would be strong enough to turn the child. There was nothing more she knew to do.

Moon of Early Summer arrived. Whispering Wind was now having difficulty moving about. Her back hurt constantly, just as it had before. She could see the little feet and feel them kick. So far all was well with the baby, lying cross ways. She had spoken to Flower, now double hands plus and just about to become a woman herself. The child did not seem fearful and she certainly understood what should happen. Whispering Wind made sure that there was a supply of pain killing herbs and that more than one person knew how to use them. She had pads and hide cordage to tie her arms and legs to stakes stashed in a handy place. The Moon of Mid Summer arrived.

They had a Mid Summer celebration. There had been some friction, but when the newly-arrived hunters saw how well the camp functioned, grudgingly, they admitted that things worked out well and they certainly did not have to exert much to provide meat for the camp. Running Bison was not at all sure that some of them had the proper spirit veneration but hoped that in time that would develop. He sighed in relief when all the hunters decided to stay. Each of them was presented with a partially-trained wolf pup for their own. With the coming of the hunters, however, the caves became really crowded. So the unmated men elected to live in shelters beneath the trees near the caves. This was fine for the warm moons, but for winter other arrangements would have to be made. Again they settled down to gather food for winter.

Running Bison was expecting the return of Bull Elk and Calling Wolf, or hopefully a contact from Sage, but nothing...

The Moon of Late Summer arrived. With it Whispering Wind went into labor.

The Pains came deep in the night. She jerked up and gasped. Running Bison was instantly alert. "Is it time?" he questioned.

"I think so," Wind answered. "At least the labor has started. But according to Robe Maker, it could take a pair of days before the baby is born after labor starts."

"Then I need not call her?" Running Bison had started to pull on his tunic.

"Come back to the robes." Whispering Wind sighed, "Morning will be here long before this baby."

"You certainly do not seem as jittery as most first-time mothers!" Running Bison shook his head.

Shock coursed through Whispering Wind. Then she gritted her teeth. "I am scared half to death!" she admitted, through shaking lips, *just not for the reasons you think!* "I am just putting on a brave face."

Running Bison grinned and tossed aside his tunic, gladly returning to the furs.

Whispering Wind was not lying, now. The baby had just kicked again, right at the birth opening. She began sweating and shaking in fear. *I don't want to die! Please, don't do this to me! Spirits! If you are there, If you hear me! I beg of you! Do not let my baby die! Sage! Where are you? I need you1 Saaaaaaggggeeeeee!* She silently wailed. Another Labor pain ripped through her.

*Wind! I am here!* Bear Claw Woman answered.

# CHAPTER 15

*Sage? Is it really you? You're not dead? Why haven't you answered me?* *I have called and called! We all have.*

*It's a long story. I'm as alive as you* are. Bear Claw Woman could feel the other woman relax.

*Where are you?*

*We are far to the west, on the other side of the mountains, in a safe valley. Where are you? Calling Wolf thought you would be at the cave. He and Bull Elk went there to find you. They left here over a pair of moons ago. They should be back by now.*

*That is strange! We are at the cave, but they never came here. Perhaps they got lost. But we are leaving almost any day now; we will come to you.*

*We?*

*I am with the hunter Raven. You were right. I am very happy.*

*I am glad.*

*The baby, it is like the last time?*

*Yes!* Whispering Wind was shaking again.

*Relax. You say that Flower knows what to do?*

*I have told her what you did the last time. Everything is ready.*

*I will guide her. When it is time, when the opening is as wide as it will get, then call me. I will be with you through it all, just as I was last time. I promise you; you will have your baby son once again. The spirits have promised this to me.*

*Where were you? Why didn't you answer my calls?*

*I was dead.*

*What?*

*I was dead. The hunter Angry Bull killed me and took my necklace. He killed Obsidian as well.*

*I know. We found her. But how could you be dead then and alive now?*

*I chose to come back. For you and your baby, for myself, for Raven and our child, for The People, those who choose to change. But it has been a long and painful journey. I have heard your calls, but I had not the strength to answer. The hunter did not know about the 'places of power' and without Obsidian, there was no way to reach them.*

*But you are at the cave!*

*Yes, but I had not the strength to even move a finger, much less, go to the crystal cave. The hunter found it, with the help of Obsidian.*

*But you said....*

*She has been reborn. We have named her Guardian. She is a hand of moons old now.*

*And you have a child?*

*Not yet, but one day I will have a beautiful daughter. She will be called Morning Star.*

*The spirits have shown you these things?*

*I have met her and spoken to her. She sat beside me and took my hand. She told me of the love that the hunter Raven holds in his heart. It was with her help that I made the decision to return. She convinced me that there was much joy for me living. And Obsidian! She begged me to return. She chose to be reborn. But I will tell you all when we meet again. For now I must go back to the crystal room. You should feel much better now. I have tried to give you strength. Rest now and call me when it is time.*

*I will. Goodnight Sage.*

*Bear Claw Woman, remember? Good night.*

The woman sagged back onto the furs, so still that, for a heartbeat, the hunter feared that death had taken her once again. The wolf whined softly. "I know. We go now to the crystal room. I will carry her there and settle her against the wall so that the 'power' may flow into her body. We will sit with her," he rose and lifted the limp body, carrying her cradled in his arms, the torch held out before them.

Bear Claw Woman sighed as he settled her against the wall of the crystal room. He made sure that she was as comfortable as he could make her. Guardian lay beside her. Raven returned to the room beyond the ledge and made sure that the bundle holding their clothing and an extra robe to wrap around her was water tight then he held as much of it as he could above water and hurried beneath the ledge. One more trip brought them dry wood and food. He knew that she would be ravenous when she returned.

As he settled her against the wall, Bear Claw Woman sighed. Already she could feel the 'power' surging back into her body. The comforting sounds of her mate starting a fire, then wrapping a warm dry robe about her shivering body seeped into her consciousness. She could smell the wood smoke from the fire and see the flickering light from the flames against her closed eyelids.

Later yet, she smelled the cooking food. When she opened her eyes, he was sitting quietly beside the minute hearth, running his fingers through Guardian's fur, letting the warmth of the fire dry it somewhat.

"The stew smells wonderful!" She said quietly.

He glanced quickly up. "I am getting better at fixing it the way you prefer," Raven smiled.

"You shouldn't be doing 'women's work'," she protested.

"I don't consider the work as belonging to one of us or the other. I am used to doing my own cooking. While you were in the 'land of the dead' I did the cooking for both of us. I do not consider it to be beneath me to prepare the food."

"Still!" She signed and accepted a bowl of stew, nodding and smiling at the first bite. "It is even better than mine."

Raven smiled back.

"I see that you have prepared for an extended stay here. That was clever of you. It will be much easier for me to help Whispering Wind if I am in contact with the 'power'. As you know, babies do not come quickly. This one will be no different. It is just a matter of waiting until the right time and turning the child around. The girl, Flower, is only a youth herself and she will need me to give her added strength in her arm and guide her movements. Until Wind 'calls' we can relax and rest. I am sure that you are tired, for I roused you from a relaxing sleep and you have not gotten back to it."

"A hunter is used to doing with little sleep. I am fine, but I would not protest against lying on the robe with you unless there is a taboo?"

Regretfully Bear Claw Woman nodded. "I fear that you are right. A man's spirit could bring trouble in such a completely woman's task as having a baby. But afterwards..." she smiled.

"You have discovered where they are?" he changed the subject.

"Yes. They are in a deep valley far to the west, on the other side of the mountains."

Raven nodded, "I think I know the valley."

"Really?"

"The area on the west of the mountains is familiar to me. We lived in that area for several seasons when I was a youth."

"How long would it take to travel from there to here?"

"A moon, perhaps a little longer. Why?"

"Whispering Wind tells me that Bull Elk and Calling Wolf left that valley a pair of moons ago, headed for this cave. Yet we have not seen them anywhere."

Just then a voice echoed from just beyond. Both of them jerked upright and then Raven began to laughed, "I think they have arrived. I would recognize that voice anywhere." He grinned and turned toward the opening. Stay where you are!" he shouted, "I will join you shortly."

"What's that?" Bull Elk jumped back, shivers going down his spine. He hated caves!

"Raven? That you?" he lifted his torch, "Where you at?"

Calling Wolf laughed, "You are scaring yourself, man!"

"Well, where is he? I can hear him, but I can't see him, yet I know that he is close."

"I am right here," Raven appeared beneath the ledge.

"We found Young Wolf guarding the cave, but you were nowhere around. We called! It is dark outside and so we came here, thinking maybe you were getting water, or something. Where is the woman? You have her here, don't you?" he questioned, hopefully.

Raven nodded, "She is just beyond there, in a small room where she goes to gather 'power'.

"Then she is still alive?" Calling Wolf asked.

"Very much so, now," Raven answered. "But for a long time her injuries were so bad that she had no strength. It is just recently that she has returned to her former self. Right now she is in there, gaining 'power' to help Whispering Wind deliver her baby. It is coming wrong. I will go and ask her if it is all right for the three of us to be here. It could disturb her. I will be right back." He slipped again beneath the ledge.

"I heard," Bear Claw Woman said. "You are right. It would be better for you to wait in the living cave. Besides, your friend Bull Elk does not like the inner cave. He will be happier where he can see sky. I will be fine here. The baby will come soon and then I will rejoin you. It will not be more than a day, perhaps two. You hunters can get everything ready, for the journey back to the valley. When I can join you, I will. Then we will leave."

Raven nodded. "If you need me, send Guardian."

"I will," she promised, "Go now. Remove the male influence from this area. It is better that way." Bear Claw Woman smiled and hugged the hunter. "You have left me food and oil for my wicks. I have Guardian. For now, all that I need is to gather strength for the birthing. It is better that I am not disturbed."

Regretfully, the big hunter slipped beneath the ledge and soon their voices receded as the men returned to the living cave. Bear Claw Woman drew her tunic over her head, smoothed it to cover her bare shoulders and upper body and settled down beside the fire. It was better this way. She could collect her thoughts and concentrate. But she missed the warmth of the man. She already missed his companionship.

\*    \*    \*

"I was certain that you were here," Bull Elk stated, grinning ear to ear. "I kept telling this stubborn hunter that you would bring the woman here, if she was still alive, that is."

"She is."

"What happened back at the Valley of the Gathering? I can't remember much beyond the dancing. I drank too much fermented brew. That is the only explanation for the stupidity of my actions. I cannot believe that I actually followed that crazy old Wanderer! Bison! I could almost feel my dart sinking into one! So, like a drunken fool I went with the rest! Just because he promised I could hunt bison! Of course we had nearly full bladders of beer when we left, for the last thing we did before he started hollering, was, fill them up. We kept drinking from those bladders until they were empty. Once the headache and rumbling stomachs passed and sanity returned, we had no idea where we were, or even how long we had been stumbling drunkenly across the plains. There was nothing but rolling sand hills, anywhere you looked."

"We left Hunting Badger after a pair of hands worth of days, once we had sobered up, but by then we were lost," Calling Wolf added. "I tried calling the woman, but she did not answer. She has never answered again. I assumed that she was dead, that the savages had attacked after we left and everyone was dead, or that Running Bison was so disgusted with us that he took his people and left. Of course by the time we finally made it back, there was no one left in the valley, but no signs of an attack either. It was then we concluded that they had just left. We found faint travois trace marks on the ridge."

"From then on Calling Wolf led the way and to our surprise, straight to Running Bison and the families. But of course, you were not with him. That is when we discovered that the dog was dead and the woman thought to be dead as well. But that didn't make sense, for you would have been with Running Bison had the woman died. That is when I realized that she had to have been still alive, at least when you left the valley. I knew you would bring her here to this cave. I remembered that it held some kind of 'spirit power' for her. Remember the first time we saw her, she had that funny blue 'glow' about her?"

Raven nodded, "and of course, you were right. I did bring her here and we spent the winter season here. She recovered from her injuries here and now we are ready to leave this place and rejoin the camp. As you can see, we were about to leave."

"Where were you going?"

"To find you. What took you so long to reach us? You should have been here long before now."

"What do you mean, to find us? You did not know that we were coming here!"

"Bear Claw Woman did."

"Bear Claw Woman?"

"You do not remember the adult name given to my mate at the Mid Summer Gathering?"

"Your mate?"

'Yes, my mate; the girl, Sage."

"You are matted to The Chosen One?" Bull Elk stared at his old friend with new respect. "You say that her name is now Bear Claw Woman?" The hunter frowned. "That hunter, Angry Bull, he wore a bear claw necklace just like the one she wore, when we left the gathering."

"The very one which he stole from my woman when he tried to kill her," Raven nodded. "I hope to meet him one day and have the pleasure of slowly strangling the life from him. Then I can return the necklace to its rightful owner. It is not right, that a man like him should wear it. It has 'power'. It belongs to Bear Claw Woman. She killed that spirit bear on her vision journey."

"Then maybe the spirits will kill him," suggested Bull Elk.

"Guided by the hand of Bear Claw Woman," agreed Raven.

"How did you know that we were coming here?" questioned Calling Wolf. "When we were at the valley with Running Bison, he had no idea that you were here, at least not until Bull Elk suggested it. But even then, I do not know how you could know."

"Whispering Wind told Bear Claw Woman."

"Then she is 'talking' again?" Calling Wolf asked.

"Only just recently," Raven admitted, "In fact, only last night."

"Then she is just recently recovered from the 'illness'."

"At the beginning of the new moon," admitted Raven.

"Then why only now... Bull Elk began to question, then grinned and nodded as Raven turned a fiery red. "Ah!"

"The woman is now calling on her 'power'?" asked Calling Wolf.

"Whispering Wind is having her baby. It is coming out feet first. Bear Claw Woman is guiding the hand of the girl, Flower, to turn the child so that it may be born."

"I remember 'talking' to her. Always I felt strong, refreshed. If she can do this for Whispering Wind and her helpers, the child will come safely into this world."

"But it takes a terrible toll on Bear Claw Woman. It drains her completely of strength. That is why she is staying in the 'power' room.

There she can draw strength to replace that which she loses. When the child is born and she has recovered, they will come here and we will leave."

"They?" questioned Calling Wolf. "There is another with her?"

"Only the animal, Guardian," Raven answered.

The pair of hunters nodded. "I remember that dog, big, black and powerful!" Bull Elk replied.

"That animal was killed by Angry Bull. This one is still young, but it is a 'spirit animal none- the-less." Raven answered. "Come now. You have already settled your animals. Eat! There is food enough for the three of us. Then we will rest until morning. We can talk more then."

*     *     *

*Bear Claw Woman?* Whispering Wind called. *It is time!*

*I am ready.*

*Already I have taken the pain killing drink. My arms and legs are staked to the floor. Flower is ready, the baby is ready. I am frightened!*

*No need. Call for Flower to take you hand.*

*I am here, Chosen One.* a young girl answered. *I am ready to do as you direct. Already I have washed with the soap root and used the grease.*

*That is fine. Now follow my directions...*

Bear Claw Woman could feel the pain ripping through Whispering Wind as though it coursed through her own body. She began to shiver as sweat poured from her. She could feel the small hand of Flower as she reached up and pushed the baby farther inside Whispering Wind. It was as if the hand were within her own body. She grasped the crystal wall with both hands, writhing in agony. It was as though the child was within her own body. She felt the child shift, move into the proper position and Flower slowly remove her arm and hand. Then she felt the child kick angrily, just below the heart.

*It is done.* Flower called to her.

*Yes, I know.* Bear Claw Woman replied. *You have done well. Now quickly, take her to the birthing platform, for the child will be born... now!*

Bear Claw Woman sighed and collapsed against the wall. It was done. Whispering Wind had her son again. The spirits had given the promised gift. She was cold, so cold, she pulled the robe around her shoulders and careful to maintain contact with the crystal wall, Bear Claw Woman slept. Guardian snuggled against her, sharing the warmth of her own body. She kept watch.

From far away, a message came. *Thank you, Sister of my Heart. He is beautiful. I feel wonderful!*

*You are welcome; rest now.*

*   *   *

"So, why did it take you so long to get here?" Raven questioned at the early morning meal.

"We got lost," admitted a shamed faced Bull Elk. "I was sure that we were on the trail to the high pass, but I was wrong. And then again I made the same mistake. Finally though, I found the correct path. I cannot imagine how I made such a mistake, for the path was clearly marked by the lightning-struck tree. I just did not see it."

"Well you are here now. Perhaps spirits guided your eyes," suggested Raven.

"What do you mean?" suspiciously questioned his friend.

"Simply that Bear Claw Woman had a task to complete before she left this place. She needed the strength from the crystal room. The spirits guided you upon wrong paths until it was time and then showed you the correct path. You are here now. When Bear Claw Woman returns to us, we will go to the valley where Running Bison and the camp await. And they will know that we are coming. For Bear Claw Woman will let them know."

"But how will she 'mind talk' along the way? You, yourself, said that the 'talking' drains her strength."

"Perhaps she will tell them before she rejoins us. I do not know. I do not ask questions. I just trust." The men finished eating and began going over the wolves. Both had made the journey in fine condition. As they waited for Bear Claw Woman, they repaired or replaced worn harness parts. "No need to pack securely for the first part of the journey," suggested Raven. "We only go to the end of the canyon. Once we are on the other side of the wall there will be time enough for packing."

"You have found another exit from this canyon?" Bull Elk asked.

"Not me. Bear Claw Woman showed it to me. She and Whispering Wind found it long ago. They left a stash of food, weapons and supplies, beyond. It is very clever. No one would ever find it without a guide. But you will see!"

They organized their supplies and by nightfall were ready to leave as soon as the sun rose. They sat late around the fire, talking, remembering past quests, until finally, all three retired to their furs. Sometime during the night, Raven felt the familiar soft form against his body. He rolled over and with a sigh, pulled her to him. Then he drifted into deep, contented rest.

They awoke to find Bear Claw Woman quietly working around the hearth, preparing the meal. Guardian lay beside Young Wolf, enjoying the rabbit she was chewing upon. Both hunters commented upon the strange appearance of the animal but were content with the explanation that she was merely of a breed of wolf, with which they were unfamiliar. Then they were ready to leave the cave. Raven led them down-stream. Both hunters were mystified that they had been instructed to stash everything into watertight bundles. When they reached the place where the water filled the entire canyon, they were even more puzzled. But Raven, Bear Claw Woman, Young Wolf and even Guardian did not even hesitate. They just stepped into the water and kept going. They were all chest-deep in water, the wolves treading, when the solid cliff blocked their way. Bear Claw Woman went first. She took a deep breath and with her bundle clutched to her chest, dived into the water and vanished. Guardian followed then Young Wolf, Raven and finally the astonished pair of hunters and their wolves. When the latter emerged, Raven and Bear Claw Woman were already at the cache, uncovering what remained of it. In a very short time they were heading south toward the pass which would take them west. By going through the stream, they had already saved half a day in time.

They traveled along the same trail by which the pair of hunters had journeyed to the cave. Calling Wolf led the way and Bear Claw Woman followed just behind. Raven and Bull Elk brought up the rear, catching up on the happenings in their respective lives over the past season. As they traveled, Bear Claw Woman garnered plants for their evening meal. They always stopped just before dark and set up the camp. The hunters were self-sufficient but Bear Claw Woman still preferred to do the cooking. The men set up the shelters and dressed the small game. They also provided for the animals. But Bear Claw Woman provided a hot meal, whether it was spitted rabbits or birds, or a stew. And always there were plants and salt. Bull Elk had handed over his stash of mushrooms and Bear Claw Woman added them to her own supplies.

For over a hand of days the weather was perfect. Then a storm moved in and it began to rain. "I think we should stay here, in this sheltered overhang until the storm has passed," Calling Wolf suggested, "We are in no great hurry and I have no particular desire to get soaked to the skin in these high mountains. It is cold, even if it is summer."

"The animals could use a rest," admitted Bull Elk. "Our wolves have been traveling for a pair of moons with only the break at the cave. I would agree. Besides we could take the time to bring in a deer and have a few meals of fresh meat."

"You think the rain will continue for much longer?" Raven frowned at the sky.

"It looks like it," Calling Wolf nodded, "Even if we rest just this day. If by tomorrow the sky clears, then we go on. If not! We stay until it does clear."

"What do you think, Bear Claw Woman?" Raven asked. "Would you rather continue, or could you use a rest?"

"I am not in need of a rest, if that is why all of you have suddenly become afraid of a little wet!" She shook her head and glared around at the men. "Do not try to make my way easier. I can keep up." In fact, she was bone tired. Her season of little activity had taken a toll on her stamina. It was probably showing and the men had noticed.

"None-the-less, I think we rest," Calling Wolf raised an eyebrow at her. If you need an excuse, then make me a pair of moccasins which make my feet feel better as I walk. I have heard that you can do this. Besides I would speak with you about this 'power' which you have and it is difficult when we are forced to walk in a line."

"Very well I will make you moccasins. In fact, I will make all three of you moccasins and myself as well. And I will be more than happy to sit here in the dry shelter of the overhang to do it. But do not blame me if you find that we are caught in snow before we reach this far valley."

So she dug out the materials and began cutting and punching and lacing. Bull Elk and Raven set out to bring down a deer. Calling Wolf sat with Bear Claw Woman. "What is it that you wished to speak of?" she asked.

"In my tribe, before we left, I was apprenticed to become a Shaman. I have seen others with 'power' before, but none like that which you have and none nearly so strong. I would know the source of the power."

Bear Claw Woman shrugged. "There is no secret to the source of my power. It comes from the spirits. I carry the mark of wolf. I am from the ancient line of The Chosen. These women, all born to The People, have a special relationship with the spirits. They also have a special task. Mine is to turn The People away from their self-serving attitude. When first I gained the mark, upon becoming a woman, my ability to even draw on the power was nothing! It had to be learned and I had to grow in my ability to use it. The spirits did not guide me. I had to figure things out for myself. They provided Obsidian as my protector, but that is all."

"I had to seek the power. Draw on it and learn to use and control it. I am still learning. But when the spirits give a gift, they also ask in return. I am not yet certain what it is that they will ask of me."

"But you have spoken to them?"

Bear Claw Woman nodded. "I have spoken to Ancestor Yel and Ancestor Basket. It is through them that I am able to draw on the power. But it is only since I died that I have been able to remember the 'spirit journeys'. Before that words just came from my mouth and ideas popped into my head. I had no idea from where they came."

"You died?" Calling Wolf stuttered. "Not really? I mean, not really dead."

She nodded, "Indeed very dead. But since I am the last of the line of The Chosen I was given a choice to either stay dead, or return and complete the task I had begun. As you can see, I chose to return."

"I have never met anyone who was dead and returned," Calling Wolf admitted. "Your power must be very great indeed!"

"I have no power," Bear Claw Woman corrected him. "I am just a tool for the spirits to use. They communicate with The People through me."

"The 'mind talking' is a powerful tool," protested the hunter, "I know that I have experienced it with you and always I feel refreshed and strong afterwards."

"While I in turn am drained of energy. Without the relics to restore the power which I have used up, I must find some other source or I am all used up. I no longer have the relics, or my necklace. Guardian is too young to take power from her and without a source for her to restore, I could kill her. So you see it is not so simple."

"Then the room at the cave was very important. Perhaps we should consider moving the camp to the area of the cave. Then you would always have a place to go and restore yourself."

"The Ancient Relics do the same thing. But as you may recall, I turned them over to Crooked Spirit at the Mid Summer Gathering. I was struck down by Angry Bull before I had a chance to reclaim them. Without a keeper, they will loose their strength. Without them, I have no strength. It is as the circle of life, always moving, but never closed. If the circle of life should close, either by accident, or intent, The People will die. That is the promise of the spirits. This is why my task is so difficult. The spirits have threatened to close the circle of life and let The People die because they do not respect the spirits anymore. The People take credit for the 'gifts' of meat and heap glory upon themselves. This is why 'Bison' has been taken away."

"I heard your words. Until the men of The People remove from their hearts, the thought that they are responsible for the kills which they make, until they stop bragging of their own greatness, the spirits will not return the bison. It is an impossible task! It cannot be done!"

"Then The People will die!" she shrugged. "The spirits have promised to heap upon them plagues, disease, starvation and misery, until they change. If the men of The People have no consideration for their families, they will watch them die, one by one, until only they are left. If by that time they still refuse to admit in their hearts that any deeds they have accomplished were gifts of the spirits; then in misery, they also will die. This is the promise of the spirits."

"What of those who do change? Do they also suffer?"

"Has the camp of Running Bison suffered?"

Calling Wolf shook his head, "They flourish!"

"Then there is your answer."

"Why then, are the bison not returned to them?"

"That is not what the spirits promised. Not until the very last conceited hunter has called the spirits into his heart. Until he has admitted, to them and to himself, that they, not he, are responsible for the feats of glory that he has accomplished, will the bison be returned. It is unlikely to be in our lifetime."

"If you are the last of the line; who will follow you? Who will be the spirit link for the next generation?"

Bear Claw Woman ran her fingers absently over her flat stomach. She smiled dreamily. "My daughter," she answered.

"You have a daughter?" Calling Wolf asked in surprise.

"Not yet. But one day," she replied. "And when she becomes a woman, the spirit will mark her and she will carry on the task just as those who came before us."

"Always a woman?"

She nodded. "The dreamer is for the men. The Chosen are for all." She finished the moccasins she was working on and handed them to him. Calling Wolf grinned and quickly donned them; testing out the feel on the floor of the rock shelter. He nodded and placed his old shoes in the pack.

"So what does a Shaman do?" she questioned. "I have never hard of such a person."

"I was learning how to channel the power of the spirits. With spirit journeys and special prayers, fasting, sometimes self-inflicted pain, I was touching the spirits with my mind. But my teacher died. There was no one else in the camp that knew the way. That is why I left and began searching for another teacher. I have continued searching until now. I would learn from you, if you would teach me."

Bear Claw Woman considered the man. "I would not know how to teach you," she answered honestly. "But I will share with you any knowledge which I possess. Crooked Spirit would probably be a much more satisfactory teacher. He is a wise and caring man."

"But he does not possess the power which you do," replied Calling Wolf.

"Power is not for everyone. If you are not pure in your heart, power can corrupt and draw you down the dark corridors of the mind. It can twist and tease and fool you, until your mind explodes! It can make you a slave to it. Be very careful, what you wish for. That wish could lead you to your death. I have hard tales of dreamers who have been consumed by power. They were turned into truly evil men, causing much sorrow and destruction within their camp."

"You think I seek power for myself?"

"I do not know. I merely give warning as to the possible results of power misused."

"I will consider your words," the hunter rose and went to meet the pair returning.

They had fresh meat that day. The rain continued all day and through the night. The next morning they wakened to still-overcast skies and a steady downpour. For three more days they stayed at the rock shelter, watching the rain. The meat that they did not eat was smoked and stashed on their travois. Then on the fourth day the sun rose in a clear blue sky. They were glad to get under

way once again.

*　　*　　*

Calling Wolf stopped. He looked up the trail that they were following. Debris, boulders and trees cluttered the way. The path hugged the edge of a steep cliff. In places it was barely wide enough for them to keep their footing. The wolves were carrying packs now rather than pulling the travois, for the trail was far too narrow for the clumsy apparatus. All three men had huge backpacks, but Bear Claw Woman walked free. Raven insisted.

"What do you think?" asked Calling Wolf as the four of them crowded to survey the blocked trail.

"Looks dangerous to me," Raven stated, "All the rain has loosened the mountain side. The whole thing could come down on us. Is there another way?"

"Yes, but it means at least another pair of days travel," Bull Elk replied. "There is another pass to the south, beyond that mountain, but I cannot guarantee that it is problem-free. Can you see the extent of the slide?" He called to Calling Wolf who had discarded his pack and was climbing up into the rubble to see beyond.

"There is a lot of debris, but I think if we are careful, we can get through. I am going to go ahead and scout the trail. The rest of you wait here until I return. If it is not blocked around this cliff, we can probably get through. I will be back in a short while."

Guardian was whining and leaning against Bear Claw Woman her tail tucked between her legs. Bear Claw Woman frowned. "The way is unsafe," she stated. "We should not go through here. Calling Wolf is in danger and so will we be if we follow him."

"I will go and tell him," Bull Elk shed his backpack and carefully threaded his way through the debris, calling ahead to the other hunter. He cleared the landslide and was trotting along the open area of path when a rumbling and shuddering sounded from above. The big hunter cried out as the mountain gave way and he slithered with it over the edge and out of sight. Calling Wolf came leaping back into view. He was totally cut off from the rest; a gaping raw scar was all that was left where heartbeats before, had been the trail.

"Can you see him?" shouted Raven.

"Who?" Calling Wolf shouted and then realizing Raven could only be referring to Bull Elk, peered over the edge. "I can see him!" he shouted. "He is down there among the debris, or at least part of him is. I can only see one leg."

"I must go down after him!" stated Raven. Quickly he was off-loading his pack. "Hand me those lengths of hide. We will knot them together and make a rope that I can use to lower myself over the edge. Once I am below this shelf I think I can slide down to him. Here, hand me that!" He pointed to a stout branch that he had been using as a staff. Bear Claw Woman handed him the staff.

"Please, be careful! It is bad enough that Bull Elk has been injured, or worse, we can't lose you as well."

"I will be careful. But I think it best if you take the animals back down the trail. We will work our way back down to that canyon below. Can you manage?"

"I will, somehow," she assured him. Biting her lip, Bear Claw Woman began dragging the heavy packs of the three men back down the trail. First one and then another and finally the last. She glanced frequently at the spot where her mate was sliding, amongst a welter of debris toward the buried man. It seemed an interminable time, although she knew it was only heartbeats of time before he reached him.

"He's alive!" Raven shouted.

"I will have to go ahead until I can find a way down!" Shouted Calling Wolf. "I will find a way to the canyon floor and follow the stream back."

"We will all meet there," answered Raven. He then turned his attention to digging Bull Elk from the rubble. Bear Claw Woman crept back up the trail and unhooked the makeshift rope. She eased to the edge and let the rope slither over the edge.

"Get back from there!" Shouted Raven, "The trail is unsafe!"

"You have need of that rope!" she shouted back, "I am far safer here than you are there! I am going now, back down the trail with the wolves. I will come up from below and help you!"

"No! Get to a safe place and stay there!" Raven shouted. "You listen to Guardian! Do as she tells you! We should all have paid attention to her." The hunter turned back to his task, sending rubble and dirt cascading on down the slope as he continued his frantic digging. Bull Elk was still half buried in the landslide and his head was in that half. If Raven did not free him quickly, the big hunter would certainly be dead.

Bear Claw Woman dragged the packs and led the wolves back down the trail. A hand of time later they reached the bottom. Here she left the packs, shifting things she was sure to need onto one of the animals, then as swiftly as she could she led them down the canyon to where she judged Raven would be with Bull Elk. The canyon was partially blocked; already the stream was disappearing into a dry bed. She scrambled over the rocks and loose dirt and slid down the other side, taking part of it with her. The animals scrambled after her, barking and whining. Already the stream was backing up on this side of the landslide. She could see that unless they were out of the canyon before night, they would be in as much danger from the water as from the water logged earth itself. Raven was easing the still form of Bull Elk carefully down the rubble, slipping and sliding along beside him. Bear Claw Woman began climbing toward them, calling Guardian after her. She had supplies packed on the wolf that they would need to care for the injured hunter.

"There is a place just this side and a little below your position!" she called up to him. There is a solid ledge where we can treat his injuries."

"I told you to stay out of danger!" shouted Raven.

"I did not hear you," she replied. Already Raven was easing the injured man toward the ledge. Bear Claw Woman and Guardian joined him there.

"His leg is broken," Raven said.

"He has several broken and cracked ribs as well," added Bear Claw Woman. "And this head wound does not look good either. But he is still breathing and as soon as I have bound the head, we can transfer him to this robe and begin lowering him down the rest of the way. We had better get beyond the blockage to the stream, before the canyon becomes a lake. There is no assurance that the landslide will hold the water back for any length of time. The earth is already loose and wet."

"Hello!" Shouted Calling Wolf from up the canyon. Both Raven and Bear Claw Woman called back and within a short time the big hunter came running and scrambling into view. "We have to get out of here!" he panted. "The water is already backing up at an alarming rate. Here, let me have this end. Woman, lead that wolf out of here and leave this rescue to us. Get the animals to a place of safety and we will follow. Quickly, before the blockage gives way and sweeps you away!"

Bear Claw Woman glanced down at the water, amazed to see that the water level was considerably higher than the last time she had noticed. She lost no time in following Calling Wolf's instructions. The remainder of the wolves waited atop the rubble watching and whining. "Come on," she called to them, "Leave the hunters to do their job. We have one of our own!" She scurried to where she had dragged the packs and quickly reassembled one of the travois upon which she dumped the heavy packs. Then she hitched the travois to Young Wolf and led him quickly along a trail that led upward and away from the canyon. She did not look back until she reached a place of safety. Here she stopped and waited. Guardian stayed leaning against her, whining and prancing, her tail tucked between her legs. She watched their trail just as avidly as did Bear Claw Woman, looking for the hunters.

The earth rumbled and an angry grumbling sound informed her that the blockage had been breached. Fearfully she started back down the trail. Guardian woofed at her and then stayed by her side. Bear Claw Woman skidded to a halt at the turn of the trail. Below her, water lapping at their heels hurried the hunters, carrying the wounded one between them. They were safe! She sagged in relief.

They made a quick camp just where they were. Bear Claw Woman began preparing a pain killing drink, as Raven started setting and binding the broken bones. Calling Wolf set up the camp. They lay the injured man on the first sleeping robes laid down. Then Bear Claw Woman settled herself beside the injured one and took her staff in hand. She laid one hand on the forehead of Bull Elk and closed her eyes. Slowly the blue aura began to surround them. Raven opened his mouth to protest, but closed it. She would do what she must. He could not interfere. Guardian sat just beyond the woman, watching her every move. A short time later, Bull Elk groaned and opened his eyes. Bear Claw Woman sighed and opened hers as well. She smiled softly and the blue aura began to fade.

Raven was ready. He had food for her and carried it to where she sat. He could see her trembling from strain and she was white and he knew, cold. "What can I do for you?" he asked, as he wrapped a warm robe around her shoulders and handed her the bowl of food.

She smiled and said, "You have already done much. You have saved Bull Elk's life and gotten the three of you to safety. I do not know what I would have done, had you been trapped and drowned. There would be no reason for me to go on, not without you!"

"I feel the same way," he answered. "Keep that in mind when you insist on one of these dangerous 'power' transfers. Have you the strength to walk to our robes, or may I carry you?

'I would like that," she murmured. The big man grinned and scooped her up, carrying her to their robes and gently laying her upon them. "I must rest for a time and then before we leave this place, I must find a source of power."

He looked around, blinked and then nodded. "What do you look for? I will seek this place out while you rest."

She shook her head. "One day I will teach you what to look for, but now, I can find it best with the help of Guardian. She will understand what I need and locate it."

"Where is she?" Raven looked around the camp. "She was here and now she is gone."

"She will be seeking a place of power," replied Bear Claw Woman. "When she finds it, she will return and take me there. See to the comfort of Bull Elk. The pain-killing drink is ready. It would be best if he could eat something as well. Then look to yourself. There are several deep scratches on your arms which need cleaning and food would do you no harm either." With a sigh she settled onto the robes and closed her eyes.

The accident had happened just after sunrise. By mid way through the afternoon Guardian cam back into the camp, carrying Bear Claw Woman's staff in her mouth. She laid it beside the sleeping woman, nosing it against her hand. Bear Claw Woman sighed and her hand closed around the staff. A faint blue glow spread from the staff. Raven smiled. Guardian had found a place to gather power. Shortly thereafter, Bear Claw Woman opened her eyes. Color had returned to her face and she smiled at the big hunter. "I will return before dark," she said as she gathered up her staff and started from the camp with Guardian.

"Wait!" Raven shouted, "I would go with you! There could be danger!" He grabbed his atlatl and darts and hurried to where she stood.

Guardian grinned, ear to ear, her eyes sparkling with some private joke and then she led Bear Claw Woman and the worried hunter from the camp. Half a hand later they moved into a valley that spread out before them. Guardian led them down the length of the valley to a place where a perfect circle of mesquite trees touched the sky. Within the circle was a slight hollow, where at one time yet another tree had lived; a tree that had given Ancestor Basket and her twin their very own staffs. In thanks, the girls had planted seeds from the old tree as a gift and a promise. The promise had been richly fulfilled. Guardian twisted in a tight circle. "Woof! Woof! Woof!" She barked.

Bear Claw Woman smiled and laughed as the gangly animal leaped and cavorted. Then she seated herself in the very center of the circle, right where the ancestor tree had grown. Already Raven could see the blue mist beginning to form. He nodded and stepped beyond the trees. Nearby there was a huge boulder. On its side were scratching. Someone had drawn a picture here. He squatted and squinted, running his fingers over the faded lines. Two figures stood side by side, each holding a staff. Beside one stood an animal, which he was sure would have been a wolf, just such as Guardian would one day grow into. He could feel the tingling run through his fingers and realized with a shock, that this boulder was also a power place. He smiled to himself. Bear Claw Woman would be pleased when he showed this to her. He settled his back against the warm side of the boulder and waited.

The sun was low in the sky when Bear Claw Woman came from the grove to him. She stood straight, her step was sure and he could tell at a glance that she was refreshed and strong. "Come, see what I have found!" he smiled. "This valley is a good place. Even I can feel the pull of 'power' that is here."

She came to him and squatted beside the boulder. As she touched the marks, sparks of 'power' shot through the air to her fingertips. She laughed. "You have done well, my mate. This is truly a wonderful place. First the Ancestor Grove and now a message sent through time from the Ancestor Basket. She traced the figure beside the wolf. This was she. The other is Star, her twin sister. See. They both carry staffs!"

"I think that in the morning we should move our camp to this place. It will be a pair of days at least, before Bull Elk will be able to sit up. We will have to stay here for at least a moon and half way through another, before he will be able to walk on that leg."

Bear Claw Woman nodded her head, "He will be healed in a moon, perhaps more. But you are right. He must come here. He must come into the circle with me. There the spirits will heal him."

"In a moon only?" exclaimed Raven, "How can that be?"

"Power." Was his answer. She rose again to her feet and they left the valley. It was dark before they reached the camp where Calling Wolf and Bull Elk waited.

As the sun rose, the two hunters carried the third to the valley. Already, before they arrived, Bear Claw Woman had gone ahead and prepared a shelter for the injured hunter, at the very center of the circle of mesquite trees. They lowered him onto the furs she had prepared and then left. While Bear Claw Woman settled Bull Elk comfortable, the other pair of hunters returned and moved their camp to the valley.

For a moon, Bear Claw Woman and Bull Elk stayed within the circle of trees. At the end of that time, Raven and Calling Wolf watched with amazement as Bull Elk walked from the circle, leaning heavily upon a crutch, but strong enough to get around on his own. Bear Claw Woman followed just behind him, Guardian at her side.

"Tomorrow, we go!" Bull Elk laughed, "I have never felt better!"

Bear Claw Woman smiled into the face of her mate. "See!" she said, "He is mended; just as I promised."

"And you?" Raven asked, "How do you feel?"

"I am tired," she admitted, "But we cannot tarry longer. If we do not keep moving now, we will be caught by snow. We are not prepared for snow."

The next day they headed west. But things did not go as they expected.

# CHAPTER 16

**Again, back at the gathering...**

Hunting Badger was furious! How dare that upstart female proclaim such gibberish? She must be stopped. And he was the man to do it. *I was right! I knew it right from the time that she stepped into the camp! I could smell the corruption of Clover Blossom!* He ground the stubs of his few remaining teeth together. *I should have recognized that abomination by her side! It is too bad that I did not let Angry Bull dart them both on the spot!* He stomped from the Gathering toward where his rag-tag camp was settled. Behind him followed nearly all the hunters from the Gathering. They stumbled, staggered and shouted drunkenly to each other as they crossed the stream and into his camp. It took only heartbeats of time before his few women had their belongings loaded onto travois and were following him and the hunters from the valley.

Angry Bull watched them go from his hiding place beside the stream. He licked his lips and glanced back toward the camp. He saw the woman and her dog leave the camp and move toward the stream and grove of trees. He watched the rest of the camp scatter as he made his way to her shelter. He made quick work of searching her belongings, finding nothing that interested him. She had the coveted necklace still around her neck. In anger he ripped the feather cloak to shreds and tossed them into the hearth. They were just beginning to smolder as he trotted toward the stream.

It was mid-morning when he caught up with Hunting Badger. The headman looked at him sharply, noted the necklace and smiled. "Come and walk with me!" he waved, "We have much to discuss.

He mentioned a few trivial things and then got to the main subject. "She is dead?"

Angry Bull nodded, grinning, he fingered the bear-claw necklace. "As is that miserable dog. I made sure that cur knew who killed her. Before she died, she understood it was a mistake to bite Angry Bull! Where do we go?" He looked about the group, noting that most of the hunters were drunk and still pulling from time to time on their flasks.

"Out onto the plains after bison." Replied Hunting Badger. "They must be out there somewhere; can't have just vanished!"

"That woman said...."

"I know what she said!" Hunting Badger cut in, "What can that stupid bitch know? Who does she think she is fooling? She is no more 'chosen' than you or I."

"She was, you know," Angry Bull corrected him. "Her power was amazing. I watched her gather it. So strong was her connection that the air actually turned blue. I couldn't get the sacred relics, but I made sure she was the end of her line."

"If you are in such awe of her, I'm surprised that you have the courage to wear her necklace. It could be dangerous to you," Hunting Badger sneered.

"I'm not afraid of woman's power," Angry Bull scoffed. He stomped off to walk with a group of hunters whom he was sure he could impress with his deeds. Hunting Badger watched him go, shook his head and strode out.

They traveled hard for over a hand of days. On the day they entered the moving sand, most of the hunters had begun to sober up. They complained and vomited and demanded tea prepared. The few women complied too the best of their ability. The moving sand was extensive. They were still within its boundaries when the storm hit.

The wind picked up slowly. Then the sun began to fade into a red haze. By high sun, it was no longer even visible. Sand began to sting the eyes and get into the throat. The women covered their faces with pieces of rabbit skin. This helped keep the sand out. But traveling became increasingly more difficult. By mid-afternoon visibility was almost entirely gone. It was barely possible to see the person walking next to you and the singing of the wind made conversation impossible. Late-afternoon the message was passed along to make camp. With a sigh the women deserted their travois and began to struggle to erect the few shelters that they carried. This was made doubly difficult. The wind ripped the hides from their hands and the poles refused to take grip in the loose sand. Finally, however, they did get them more-or-less up.

Hunters hunkered together filling the few shelters to overflowing. The women were left to do their best in the open. For several days the camp was trapped by the storm. Sand toppled the shelters and they had to be dug free and erected once again. There was no way to prepare food. Water was getting scarce as well. But finally, the wind stilled and quiet filled the camp. When the sand was cleared, three were dead. They were left behind, laid out on a dune to walk the wind. Shadows slipped to the top of the ridge. They watched the camp move away; then they ate well and then they followed.

For another hand of days Hunting Badger led them to the east in a straight line.

Calling Wolf and a group of men sat around their hearth. They had no sleeping furs, no food, water, nor possessions. All they carried were their weapons. Bull Elk had brought down a pair of rabbits and one of the other hunters a badger. These were cooking over a poor fire made up of sticks and grass. The meat would barely suffice to keep hunger at bay.

"What are we doing here?" Bull Elk asked as he tossed another meager offering into the fire. "We have no provisions, nothing but our weapons and daily we draw farther from the others. Are we going to follow that old fool Hunting Badger forever?"

Calling Wolf glanced around the group, "You suggesting that we go out on our own?" He looked steadily at Bull Elk. "What do we know of bison hunting? Have you even seen a herd of bison? Have you any idea how to hunt them?"

"I have heard tales," Bull Ell replied, "We are all hunters here. How hard could it be? We just sneak up on them and dart some; nothing to it!"

"I also have heard tales. Tales involving hunting cloaks, rituals and offerings. The spirits are already angry with The People for lack of proper attitude toward the spirits. What additional harm could we do by breaking taboos?"

"They aren't our taboos," Bull Elk replied logically.

"I know how to hunt bison," Thunder Cloud spoke.

"You do?" Bull Elk turned to the older hunter. "That's right you're from Hunting Badger's band yourself. You have hunted bison before."

"Many times," agreed Thunder Cloud. "But Calling Wolf is right. We have no hunting capes. It could be very dangerous without them."

"How so?" Calling Wolf asked.

"Bison are stupid creatures. Also, they do not see well. But they smell very well. And if one makes a move, the whole herd follows. The reason for the hunting capes is so that the bison do not recognize you as a human. To them you are only another bison. They do not know where the attack comes from. So they merely move away from the dead animals. But if they do recognize you as human, they are as likely to stampede right over you as run away. There is no escaping a stampeding herd of bison, particularly a big one. We would all be trampled to death."

"Oh."

"So far we haven't seen so much as a bison turd," exclaimed a burley hunter. "I am beginning to think the woman is right! The spirits have taken the bison! We wander across these plains starving, without even the most basic of supplies. That crazy old headman is going to get us all killed. Already three have died. How many more will do likewise before we get smart?"

"What do you suggest?" Calling Wolf asked quietly. Already men from nearby hearths had stopped talking and were listening.

"I'm for going back!" the hunter proclaimed, "Only thing is, I don't know where 'back' is any more. It has been many days since there has been any sort of landmark to even know which direction we go!"

"We have been going east, until yesterday," replied Calling Wolf. Now we are going south."

"The river is that way isn't it?" asked another hunter.

Calling Wolf nodded.

"How do you know that we have changed directions? Everywhere looks the same to me."

"The position of the sun," answered Calling Wolf. "Until yesterday we walked into the sum in the morning and away from it after sun high. Now the sun comes up over our left shoulder and sets over the right one. We are traveling south."

"Could you lead us back to the mountains?"

Calling Wolf looked around. Several men had moved to stand at their hearth. He studied them thoughtfully. Then nodded, "I could," he admitted.

"But could we make it alive?"

"Not without food and water. Not without at least a few basic supplies." Calling Wolf admitted.

"You know where we could get these?" another hunter asked.

"Possible at the river; but even then, it could be some distance. I was as drunk as the rest of you when we left the valley. I'm not even sure how many days we have been gone, but by the moon, it must be over half a moon by now."

"Then the rest will have already left the valley," Bull Elk stated.

"I don't care so much about the rest of the camps," admitted the burley hunter. "But I don't like this flat land with nothing in it. I'm a mountain man, born and raised there and at least I know how to find food in the mountains; seems to me there isn't any out here!"

Calling Wolf nodded, "A group of fast-moving hunters could possibly make it to the river before they starved," he said.

"After the rest have bedded down for the night, we will be ready to leave. We will wait at the outside of the camp. Any who wish to go, join us there," the burley hunter stated. "You will lead us?" he asked Calling Wolf.

Calling Wolf studied the men for a time and then nodded, "I will lead you," he replied.

The men moved away from the hearth, just as Angry Bull marched by. He eyed them suspiciously, but no one acted out of character, so in the end he stomped off. Calling Wolf spoke softly to Bull Elk, "That one will cause trouble for us one day."

Bull Elk grunted and reached for the last of the meat. It was still partly raw and tough as leather, but he was still hungry. "Perhaps one day I will kill him," he replied equally softly. Then he gave a big yawn and with exaggerated care curled up beside the smoldering coals and began to snore. Calling Wolf grinned and followed his lead.

Darkness fell, the camp became silent. Then, one by one, like shadows, the men rose from their sleep and crept to the outer edge of the camp. Three hands of them gathered there and when it was clear that no more joined them, Calling Wolf led them quietly away. Bull Elk carried a scrubby branch, saved from the supply for their fire. With it he wiped away their trail. When the sun rose and the camp awakened, they had simply vanished.

*　　*　　*

"I looked!" Angry Bull exclaimed, "They left no tracks!"

"They must have gone one way or another!" Hunting Badger shouted. "You just aren't a good enough tracker to have found them!"

"What you mean? I'm the best tracker you ever knew! You said so yourself, lots of times! It was 'Angry Bull, no one else could have found that track!' or 'you are the finest tracker ever, Angry Bull!' Are you now saying that I don't know what I'm doing?"

"I'm saying that they didn't just vanish into the air!" Hunting Badger stormed, "They went somewhere! And I want to know where!"

"Then find them yourself!" Angry Bull stalked off.

"Perhaps I will!" Hunting Badger shouted after him. "And perhaps I don't need Angry Bull anymore! You are not the only tracker in this camp!"

Angry Bull stopped. His position close to Hunting Badger was very important to him. Status was involved here. Slowly he turned and glared at the canny old headman. "All right," he conceded, "I'll look again. Perhaps you are right and maybe I didn't look closely enough." He went to his weapons and picked them up. "I will make another circle of the camp. He tucked a moccasin into his belt and trotted away from the camp. Once over the hill he withdrew the shoe and made a faint print with it, then erased all but the very minutest trace of the track. Farther away he repeated the action. Then he continued around the camp. He did not even bother to study the ground, or he would not have missed the brush marks. Then he circled back and shouted. Several men came running.

"See here!" he pointed, "Toward the east.

Hunting Badger joined the hunters, squinted at the tracks and muttered under his breath. "We will follow them," he stated. "I will not stand for such utter disregard for my authority! He turned to Angry Bull.

"You are still the finest tracker in this camp!" he pounded the hunter on the back. "Come and walk with me."

Several more times that day, Angry Bull found traces of the hunters. He smiled to himself as he made the prints while scouting before the camp. That night he earned an extra portion of food. Every day he followed the same pattern, always showing Hunting Badger the evidence that they were still on the trail of the group led by Calling Wolf. Gradually they traveled farther and farther to the east. The food gathered as they moved was pitiful indeed. Then a snake bit one of the men. They stopped for a day, but when it was clear that he was dying, Hunting Badger left him. He was not alone for long. One of the women became so weak that she couldn't keep up. No one had the strength to pull her weight on a travois, even if they had such a thing. She also was left. This began a trail of offerings to the foolishness of Hunting Badgers leadership. Before the next full moon, another three hands of people had left the camp, to travel to the ancestor fires in the sky. Now the camp numbered little more than four hands of people, only three of them women.

"They slow us down!" whispered Angry Bull, "And they eat what little food we have. What do we need them for? They are too old and ugly for a hunter to want to enjoy any pleasure between their thighs."

"Once we find the bison we will need them," reminded Hunting Badger.

Angry Bull merely snorted.

Well after the camp slept, the lone hunter crept to where the women slept. Quickly he drove a dart into each of them. They died without a sound. Hunting Badger was angry, but there was nothing he could do about it. After that the camp picked up speed.

They had been gone from the valley of the Gathering for two moons. All were starving, reeling from hunger and weak. They had managed to find water enough to keep them alive, but that is all.

"Look! Angry Bull pointed, squinting toward the horizon, "See that?"

"Where?" Hunting Badger also squinted.

"Over there! I saw that dark patch move. It's bison! We have found a herd!" Angry Bull shouted pointing.

Hunters stopped, stared and then began staggering toward the dark moving shape. "Look!" exclaimed one, "Tracks! Yeee! Aaaah!" he began to chant and dance.

"We haven't time for that foolishness!" shouted Hunting Badger. "Come on before they get away! We can give thanks to the spirits after the hunt!" He began leaping across the prairie after Angry Bull, determined to be in on the first kill. Soon they were running past fresh bison dung and even stepping in it. It was glorious!

Finally they lay panting at the verge of a huge wallow. They watched the animals as they pawed for food and lay chewing their cuds. It was a small herd, they were poor and skinny, but they were bison. To the hunters they were the most wonderful sight they had ever seen.

"What are we waiting for?" whispered one green hunter, named Raptor Feather.

"Don't want to spook them," answered a more seasoned hunter, called Running Antelope. "There is no way we can sneak into the herd; best to wait until dark. Then they can't see us. Come back from the edge and let's find some fresh shit to rub all over ourselves. It will block the smell of human. Then we can sneak right into the herd. You will see."

The green hunter nodded and slipped away from the edge. Others were doing the same thing. Then, as the sun went down, Hunting Badger gave the signal. Four hands of hunters crawled silently down the edge of the wallow and into the herd. Suddenly someone gave forth with a blood curdling yell. In a flash the bison were on their feet, bawling in confusion and then stampeding away into the darkness.

"Who did that?" shouted Hunting Badger. No one answered.

"Well we got over a hand of them!" Angry Bull stated, "Plenty of meat. Besides they won't have gone far."

"I wanted them all!" hunting Badger shouted. "And we would have killed them all but for whichever stupid hunter had to give a victory yell!" He glared around, "I'd better never find out which one of you did it!"

Several men looked at each other and shrugged. No one would ever tell.

Finally they all set to butchering the bison. Several of them gathered up enough dried bison chips to get a fire started. Meanwhile the rest of the hunters were busy cutting the hide away from the carcasses and getting the rich organ meat cut free.

"Ye!" a hunter shook the liver he held in his hand, "What is this?" Several long thin black squirming bodies slithered from the still warm meat. On the ground they flopped and squirmed, until the hunter stomped on them. "Bad meat!" he stated throwing the liver down. He turned to the head and broke away the lower jaw. Then with swift practiced strokes, he cut the tongue free. He smelled it, checked it for holes and finally satisfied, skewered it and started it cooking over the fire.

As the meat cooked, Raptor Feather turned to Running Antelope, "That meat smells strange to me."

"Nah!" replied the other, "You just don't remember the smell right. It's fine. Look; here take a bite of this! I just took it off the spit!" He handed a piece of liver over. The first hunter bit into it, then smiled and nodded.

"You are right. It tastes fine!"

That night every hunter in the camp ate bison meat until he vomited it up and ate more. By morning they lay about the wallow, moaning. A few staggered to the fire and rescued the last morsels from burning. About half the men rose slowly and began stripping meat from the carcasses. Then someone realized that they had no racks to dry the meat, nor smoky fuel for a fire. They began cutting the meat into steaks and suspending these over the small hearths they could keep burning, while others went in search of bison chips to keep the fire going.

Dark shadows circled overhead and the vultures settled along the rim of the wallow to wait. Before dark the meat was beginning to smell ripe. The next morning, regretfully, the hunters left their kill to the carrion eaters. They carried what they could and walked away from the wallow. Angry Bull led the way, following the herd of bison.

That night several hunters complained of stomach pains and they suffered diarrhea. By morning they were feverish. Friends helped them to keep up. By the second night most of the camp was suffering.

"I told you that meat didn't smell right," whispered Raptor Feather. Running Antelope merely groaned in response. "I'm not eating any more of it!" he threw his portion of bison meat away and wiped his hands of the grass. A short while later he vomited his stomach empty. By morning he was feeling marginally better. A pair of hunters had died during the night. His friend was doing poorly.

"Here!" he offered Running Antelope a portion of tea he had brewed.

"What is that?" weakly the man questioned.

"It will make you vomit up the bad meat," Raptor Feather replied, "See, I feel better."

"You did not eat as much as the rest of us," his friend reminded him. "Besides, I haven't anything in my stomach. I have had diarrhea for a pair of days. I am raw and bleeding."

"We all are," the hunter assured him. "Please, drink this. I promise you that it will help.

"All right," replied Running Antelope, "It couldn't possible make me feel any worse!"

Soon Raptor Feather had gone among the rest and made sure that they discarded the tainted meat. He had enough water and found enough plants to make a purging tea for them all. By evening, most were feeling much better. With the morning another man had died and the rest staggered away across the plain. Three days later little more than a double hand of men staggered down into the breaks of a small river. Here Hunting Badger declared they would make camp. They did. There was a plentiful supply of water and several of the hunters recognized edible plants. After a hand of days, the men were more-or-less recovered. One brought in a deer and they cooked it well and ate sparingly of the meat. They gained strength. Over the next few days they moved gradually along the river and when it joined a large river, it was decided to follow this back to the mountains. Hunting Badger blustered and ranted, but to no avail. Finally, grudgingly, he led them back to the west.

They moved slowly, hunting and camping along the river. Sleeping furs were tanned from the deer hides. Rabbits were plentiful and several of the hunters cut their fur into strips and wove these into robes. Turtle shells were turned into bowls; travois poles were cut and put into service. Gradually the hunters assembled the supplies they had left behind. When someone suggested fermenting beer, however, they all shouted him down.

Hunting Badger was leader in name only. Only because the hunters didn't care who led them. Angry Bull stayed close, trying to curry favor from whatever hunter he could.

Late one day the lead man shouted. "Mountains! I can see the mountains! We are finished with this plain! Come on men!"

They picked up pace. The next evening they trotted into the valley of the Gathering. There was not a soul there to greet them.

"We will follow the mountains south!" Hunting Badger declared, "We will winter along the Llano Estacado!"

"What you decide to do is up to you," Raptor Feather rose. "But the rest of us are going on without you and your shadow there!" he pointed at Angry bull.

Hunting Badger stared open mouthed for several heartbeats and then he snapped his mouth shut and glared at the gathering. "So, I lead you to hunt bison. We hunted bison! Then I brought you back to the mountains, just as you asked. Now that we are here, you are saying that you no longer have need of my leadership! This is gratitude?"

"You did not lead us to anything but starvation and death," Raptor Feather replied evenly. "The only thing that you did was to be clever enough to walk in front. From this day forward, this camp no longer recognizes you. To us you are dead! Leave this camp and do not return. If you do, the only thing that will greet you is a dart. Now go!"

The solid wall of hunters stood with weapons drawn. Angry Bull and Hunting Badger backed away, step by careful step until they were safe, then they turned and stalked angrily away from the camp.

"They will regret this!" Hunting Badger stormed, "How dare they treat me like this!"

"Where do we go now?" Angry Bull asked, "We won't be welcome at Running Bison's camp."

"We don't need them!" Hunting Badger snapped, "We don't need anyone. I know where there is a cave large enough for us to spend the winter. In spring we will decide what to do. Right now it is getting late in the season. We need to prepare for winter. There is no way that just the pair of us can travel to the Llano. It would be too dangerous. But we will be fine in this cave I have in mind. There are plenty of deer and elk in the area. We won't starve."

"How far is this cave from here?"

"About a day's walk," Hunting Badger replied.

"Then what are we waiting for?" Angry Bull glared back at the camp rapidly fading from sight. "Let's get going!"

The pair of hunters turned and walked rapidly toward the far end of the valley. In short time they passed through the jasper quarry and into the valley with the ring of trees. Dusk found them some distance to the west. Here they spent the night and started out again at dawn. At sun high they entered a large valley. Part way down the eastern cliff was an opening. A curl of smoke rose from it.

"Somebody is already in the cave!" Hunting Badger stopped and glared at the smoke. "Find a place to hide. We will see how many there are. Maybe they will take us in." They found a place to squat in the shade of a big tree and here they rested and watched.

About mid-way through the afternoon Angry Bull stretched and yawned. "I haven't seen any men come from that cave at all. All I have seen are about a hand of women. I don't think there are any men, besides I think that I recognize at least a pair of those women. One is the mate of He Man and the other is called Laughing Water. I once lay with her. Don't know where the men are, but they are stupid men. We can be assured of a welcome in the cave. Come on, I'm getting hungry!"

Hunting Badger grunted and followed Angry Bull toward the cave.

They heard the excited shouting of the women when they saw them approaching. Hunting Badger gave forth with the trill of recognition and they walked confidently into the small group.

\*    \*    \*

Where do we go from here?" Running Antelope asked Raptor Feather.

"Do you think that we could find Running Bison and the camp?" questioned Badger Tail, "My mate and children probably went with him."

"We were really stupid to follow Hunting Badger," muttered Elk Caller. "Now we may never see our families again and all because we couldn't wait to kill a bison. It really wasn't worth it!"

"What is in the past is done," Raptor Feather replied, "We waste time talking about it. We need to look to the future. Right now it is getting dangerously late in the year. My question is, 'do we have time to move to the south before winter comes, or are we better off finding a place nearby to hole up and get enough meat and supplies to make it through the winter?' We haven't much time to decide."

"Does anyone know enough about this area to know where we could hole up?" Running Antelope asked around.

Several men shook their heads and then Badger Tail offered a suggestion. "We could move into the mountains and look for a place. If we don't find something within, say a hand of days, and then we could head for the Llano. I just don't think we could find enough food there to make it through the winter. I think that the mountains are a better choice, even though they are much colder and the weather far more severe. There is food here."

Hunters studied his words. Several heads nodded. "I agree, this is a good plan," Raptor Feather state, "Do you all agree to this?" He looked around at the waiting faces. Slowly each man nodded. "Fine this is what we will do then. I know the trail to the south of the river. I would suggest that we follow it back into the mountains and find a place to set up our winter camp."

"What of the savages?" Elk Caller asked.

Badger Tail spoke again, "They do not like the cold weather. Probably long gone from this area. I think we are safe. Besides, Great Thunderer was a bigger threat and we know that the savages killed him. That would scatter his band. I think that if we keep our eyes open, we will be safe."

"Then what are we waiting for?" Running Antelope stood up and reached for his back pack, "Let's get going!"

The hunters looked at each other, nodded and picked up their own packs. Within heart beats, Raptor Feather led them from the valley of the Gathering to the south, toward the river. They reached the river in little more than a hand of time, crossed it and began working their way up the southern side. For several days they scanned the area, seeking a place to set up their camp. A hand of days passed, then another.

"Look" shouted Badger Tail, "Up ahead! See that cave? Let's go investigate!" he led the way as the hunters scrambled over boulders and debris. Within a hand of time they were standing inside the cave.

"It is big enough," remarked Badger Tail. "And the opening is small enough that it could be easily shut off to keep out the cold and predators. What do the rest of you think?"

Hunters glanced around and then nodded. "Then this is it!" Running Antelope whooped with glee, "Let's get settled in and go hunting!"

The next day Raptor Feather and Running Antelope brought down three elk. Badger Tail came in with a deer over his shoulders. By the end of a hand of days, the hunters had a hand more elk and several deer, pigs and smaller game. Their drying racks were groaning with meat. But they dared not stop.

"Sh! I heard something," Elk Caller whispered. He and Raptor Feather were creeping along a game trail, following several elk.

"I did too," Raptor Feather replied, "Here, duck into this brush. I don't think it is game."

"What do you mean?" Elk Caller bent double to follow the other hunter into the thick brush.

"Sounded like voices to me," answered the other hunter.

They hunkered within the brush thicket and waited...

"Are you sure?" Cattail Woman asked, "I don't think we should be doing this. What if some hunter comes along? We could be killed for even having weapons."

"Would you rather we all starved to death?" Dancing Crane muttered, "We don't have much choice, remember? We have children to provide for. And so far we are doing a poor job of that!"

"It isn't my fault that I missed that elk!" sputtered Cattail Woman, "I told you that I was not good at the atlatl and dart. But you insisted!"

"We really have little choice!" sharply retorted Dancing Crane, "Either we hunt, or we all starve. Now which is your choice; because if you keep on complaining, next time I'll bring Tuber Woman and you can stay in the camp with the children."

"No! I am sorry," replied Cattail Woman, "I just feel bad because I missed."

"That is understandable. Yee!" Leaped Dancing Crane."

"What is it?" Cattail Woman turned white and began to tremble.

"Look!" pointed Dancing Crane, "Foot prints!"

Cattail Woman crowded to squat in the trail and squint at the moccasin tracks. Then she rose and glanced worriedly around. "Come on Crane, we could be in real danger! Let's get out of here!"

"Not so fast!" Raptor Feather stepped from hiding.

The pair of women cowered in fear.

"Who are you?" Raptor Feather demanded, "Where is your camp? And what are women doing with weapons?"

"We can explain," Dancing Crane licked her dry lips and croaked breathlessly.

"I am waiting," the hunter scowled.

"We have no men," Cattail Woman stepped forward, "but we do have children and more women back at our camp. Someone has to hunt for them."

"Where are your men?"

"A bear killed one of them. Three died of disease and a pair simply vanished, she answered. "Leaving a double hand of women and children without food or protection. We are simply doing our best to stay alive."

"You have a camp?" Badger Tail asked.

The women jerked about, "How many of you are there?" she stuttered.

"Just the pair of us," replied Raptor Feather, "But we have a larger camp nearby."

"You have food?" hopefully asked Dancing Crane, "Our camp is very hungry."

"We have better than that," Raptor Feather replied, "We have a double hand of men without mates, no women at all in our camp."

"And we have a double hand of women without mate," she began to grin.

"Where is your camp?" Badger Tail asked, "We would go and meet with you there. Perhaps we can do something about combining the camps. Raptor Feather is Headman of our camp and I assume that your camp has someone..."

"I am acting as Headman," confessed Cattail Woman, "But before we take you into our camp we would know something about you."

"Were you at the Gathering?" asked Badger Tail, "I do not remember you if you were."

The women shifted uneasily. Then Cattail Woman sighed, "We were once part of Great Thunderer's camp." She confessed. "When the Savages attacked, our group was out gathering. When we returned to camp, everyone was either dead or taken captive, including Great Thunderer. So we escaped into the mountains. We have been living here all summer."

"I see," replied Raptor Feather. "Well, others of your band have joined us, so I see no reason that you should not."

"Others?" questioned Dancing Crane. "I don't suppose the hunter Elk Caller is with you?" She asked wistfully.

"You know Elk Caller?" Badger Tail asked.

"You know him?" she began to get excited. "He is my mate. Please, tell me, is he still alive and well?"

"You will soon see for yourself," Badger Tail began to smile. He threw back his head and trilled a shrill call. It was answered almost immediately. Again he called and then grinned, "He will be here very soon."

Dancing Crane blushed, then began smoothing down her tunic and trying to comb the tangles from her hair. "Oh spirits! I must look a mess!" she wailed.

"You look absolutely beautiful," replied Cattail Woman, "And well you know it."

Just then a man came pounding down the trail. He spotted Badger Tail, "What's up man?" Then he stopped abruptly, stared and leaped forward. He scooped the sobbing woman up into his arms and whirled around and around laughing joyfully "Spirits alive!" he whooped, "I can't believe it's you! I thought the savages killed you!"

Dancing Crane wept also, "I was sure that you were dead. Until just now, I dared not hope!" she sobbed, "Just wait until Cici and Turtle see you!"

"They live?" Elk Caller stopped dead, "Both of them?"

"Of course," Dancing Crane smiled. "They were with me gathering, remember?"

He nodded, "But I was so sure that you were all dead. Oh what a day for celebration this is!" again he hugged the woman.

"Then you think it would be acceptable to bring the rest of the men into their camp?" Raptor Feather questioned.

"Camp," Elk Caller again stopped, "There are more of you?"

"Of course," Dancing Crane replied, "The whole group is still together."

"Come on men! What are we waiting for?" Elk Caller began hurrying down the path with his mate.

"I will go back and bring the rest of the men," Raptor Feather offered, "You go ahead and we will follow shortly. Badger Tail, you go with him and leave a wide trail for us to follow. I am sure that the men will be in a hurry." He disappeared down the trail.

Elk Caller and Badger Tail followed the women back to their camp. There, stunned women and children watched silently, until Cici recognized her father. With a yelp she leaped toward him, followed closely by her little brother, Turtle. Within a hand of time the remainder of Raptor Feather's camp arrived. They brought food with them. All they could carry. In no time at all, it was cooking in stew pots and skewered over open flames. Hungry women and children watched the meat cook. They had lived on plants for the entire summer, the only meat the small game which the women could bring down with rabbit stick and bolas. Venison and elk would be a wonderful treat for them.

Within days the camp was again on the move; only not far. Cattail Woman knew of a large cave, only in the next valley. It was big enough to shelter the now enlarged, combined camp. Now that they had men, the women were again enthusiastic about gathering and preparing food for the winter. Already the adults were eyeing one another. Soon they began to pair off. It was decided to have a celebration of 'spirit thanks', for their good fortune.

"I saw bear tracks over along the top of that ridge," Singing Water pointed, "Do you want to see if we can track it down? It would make an excellent 'spirit offering'. We could even save the claws and teeth and put them into a camp 'spirit packet'. I think that would draw the camp closer together."

"That sounds good to me," Jumping Fox answered, "I have never killed a bear. Perhaps the spirits will honor me with this one."

The hunters headed up the trail. At the top they squatted and studied the tracks. The paw marks were large, deep and wide.

"This bear is a monster!" exclaimed Jumping Fox, "So you think we should try bringing him down alone?"

"I would have at one time said yes, because I wanted the honor, but now, I think it would be better if more of the hunters were in on the kill. Especially if this bear is to be given as a 'spirit offering'. It would be more appropriate if all of the hunters participated in the kill. You stay here and I will go back to the camp and bring the others." Singing Water was already leaping down the trail toward the camp.

Jumping Fox waited. The sun was warm on his back. He settled beneath a tree and relaxed. The warm sun and quiet wrapped him in a blanket of contentment. Slowly his eyes closed...

The snapping of a branch brought his eyes open and his senses to total alertness. He had no idea how long he had slept. *Where are the hunters?* Again he heard a noise, right behind him. With fluid movement he leaped away from the tree into the center of the trail. At the same time his hand brought a dart from the carrier on his back and snapped it into the slot of his atlatl. Already the looming shadow shut out the sun.

The giant grizzly rose towering above him. He shook his head; the sun glinting off the razo- sharp teeth and the air was rent with his snarling roar. Jumping Fox had only time to glance behind him and make a choice. He cast his dart, driving it deeply into the throat of the bear. Then he bolted down the trail; ears attuned to the sounds of pursuit.

The bear roared again, this time in pain and thundered after the fleeing hunter. *There is nothing more dangerous than a wounded bear!* This advice flashed through the hunter's mind as he leaped logs and scrambled through streams. He could feel the hot breath of the angry predator on his neck. He picked up his pace. Rounding a curve in the trail at top speed he yelled and dived through the group of hunters coming to meet him. Only lightning reflexes brought darts and atlatls into position and deadly missals flying toward the furious grizzly. Hunters leaped from the path of the charging animal. It came careening through their midst, then tumbled end over end and came to a stop at the base of the trail.

The hunters crawled from the brush and gathered their hastily abandoned weapons. Jumping Fox peered from the branches of a tree where he had taken refuge, "Is he dead?" he asked breathlessly.

"I thought you were going to wait for us?" Singing Water shouted.

"So did I," Jumping Fox answered as he slithered down the tree trunk, "But the bear had other ideas!"

"What happened?"

"Well, after you left..." Now Jumping Fox blushed, "I.... Well I sort of fell asleep...."

"You what!" yelled Singing Water.

"Well, it was quiet and warm and well I didn't get much sleep last night...."

Now the entire group was laughing. Jumping Fox had just recently mated with Blue Jay. They all understood.

"So you took a nap and that bear decided to see why a foolish hunter was sleeping in his hunting ground," finished Singing Water.

"Something like that I suppose," answered Jumping Fox.

"Well you certainly lived up to your name this day," laughed Raptor Feather, "And we all got at least one dart in that fellow. It looks like you were right after all Singing Water. This bear will certainly make an excellent offering to the spirits!" He lifted a huge paw. "We will make a spirit bundle from these paws and dedicate the hide for special ceremonies. It is well that every man of the camp had a hand in the killing of this animal. Jumping Fox, you should make the special thanks to the spirits. This bear greatly honored you with the first blood."

Jumping Fox considered this, "I would, of course, be honored to do this, but there are others more deserving than I," he protested.

Raptor Feather shook his head. "The spirits have chosen you, my friend. And a better man could not be found. Come men; let's make a travois and carry this bear back to the camp. I think it would be fitting for the entire ceremony to be completed within the camp. I think everyone, man; woman and child should have a part in it. What do you say?"

"Yes!" they all shouted.

"Come on, Badger Tail help me chop down this sapling. It will serve as a pole. Elk Caller, you and Running Antelope chop down that one over there." The hunters leaped to do so. In a short while the bear was lifted onto the makeshift carrier and they chanted prayers to the spirits as they carried the beast back to the camp.

Everyone came running to see the bear. The children stood wide eyed and awed as the hunters unloaded him from the poles and lay him out in the clearing before the cave. Each hunter withdrew his dart, explaining how he came to dart the animal. The darts were set aside. They would be put in a special place and never used again. Then Raptor Feather selected his best jasper nodule and drove a fresh blade off with one expert stroke. Another followed. As they chanted, Jumping Fox and Singing Water began skinning the animal. After a time, Badger Tail and Elk Caller replaced them. So went the routine, until every hunter had taken part in skinning the bear. The body cavity was opened and the organ meat removed. The liver was laid on a wide wooden slab and sectioned into as many pieces as there were members of the camp. Even the youngest child got a portion. The heart was set aside as well. It was the spirit-center of the animal. This would be smoked and placed within the spirit packet. The hide was taken by a selected group of women. None was within her bleed. None were pregnant. They pegged the hide out and with scrapers, struck from the same jasper nodule as the blades, were used to prepare the hide. This took the remainder of the day. At dusk, the last of the flesh was removed. Every morsel was placed into a container. This bear was sacred. It would be processed and eaten only at special ceremonies over the next season. The hide would be carefully protected as well. It was decided to leave the claws attached to the hide and place the teeth and heart in the spirit packet. When the hide grew old and was no longer worthy to be revered, only then would the claws be added to the spirit packet. As they worked, every member of the camp chanted prayers to bear spirit.

Excitement ran rampant through the camp. Every eye watched each part of the ceremony. Jumping Fox left the camp, alone. He went to the stream and cleansed his body and he drank a special tea to purge his mind. He sat beside the stream and with his head reeling from the drink he called to the spirit of bear. As he waited, he chanted. Finally his head cleared and he returned to the camp. There he was careful to touch no woman. A pair of hunters accompanied him back up the trail to the very tree where he had met the bear. Here he spread a deer hide and sat to await the coming of the bear spirit. He drank the 'power' drink and settled back. The hunters stationed themselves above and below him on the trail.

*       *       *

Jumping Fox was frightened. Since his 'spirit journey' as a youth, he had not had any contact with anything even faintly resembling a 'spirit calling'. He had no idea how to even begin. So he sat and his mind called out as he chanted softly, the spirit prayers of his youth. Blackness engulfed him. There was an all-encompassing feeling of pain and anguish. It took his breath away. A chill settled into his spirit and he could not shake it. After a long time the blackness began to lighten. Then suddenly, a swirling of all the colors of the rainbow pulled him into their vortex. He felt that he was flying through the air at a great speed. Then, just as suddenly, everything cleared. He sat in a clearing on a log and in the glade beyond stood the great bear. He was shrouded in a blue glow that seemed to pulse with every breath Jumping Fox drew.

The bear rose onto his hind legs, towering above the hunter. But Jumping Fox was not afraid. The bear looked him straight in the eye. *You have given me great honor.* The bear spoke. *I came to you in a test of truth and purity of heart. You rose to meet that test with dignity and purity of spirit. Not once did you think of the glory that you could bring to yourself, only the honor that you could bring to your camp and the spirit of the great bear. Within you beats the heart of a true Man of The People.*

*The One has taken the bison away from The People. That spirit will no longer serve them. I have come to offer myself in the place of Bison. The Grisly Bear is a strong and powerful guide. Already my brother spirit has given himself to the Chosen One. Now his spirit walks in darkness. You have felt his pain and agony. The necklace made from his claws and teeth now adorns the throat of an unpure hunter. You have been chosen to lead the hunter Raven to this man. When the spring arrives you must seek out this Raven and I will lead the pair of you to Unclean One. The necklace must be returned to The Chosen One!*

I give you my protection. I will protect the camp and those within it and provide food and good health for the coming winter. You, Jumping Fox, have been chosen to be the Shaman of your camp. I will guide you in the chants, prayers and ceremonies necessary to cleanse your heart and body. So long as you serve me, I will serve you.

Then a mist began to rise and the great bear was swallowed up. Silence filled the glade and then darkness descended. Again Jumping Fox felt the anguish of the spirit bear. His heart was filled with dedication. He would find this hunter, Raven and lead him to the Unclean one. He knew who wore the necklace. Had he only known earlier, perhaps even now, the necklace would be on its way to the Chosen One. He remembered her as well and her words at the Gathering. Now he understood why the bison meat had poisoned them. He understood what the spirits meant when they said that the hearts of every single hunter must be pure. No self-glory could be allowed to live in the hearts of the hunters. The spirits must be let back into their hearts.

He heard the wind sigh in the trees and he smelled the pine and compost. Then he opened his eyes. The moon was setting. It was very late. He called to his companions. They answered and soon the three were on their way back to the camp.

*Only this morning I was no more than a hunter of the camp.* Jumping Fox's mind reeled. *Now I have been chosen by the great bear spirit to be his voice among The People. Why me? I have done nothing to deserve such an honor! I have no special skills!*

There were no answers.

In the morning the preparations for the ceremony were underway. The night before the women and men separated. A pair of women was in the blood shelter. They were not allowed to participate in the actual ceremony, but they were not left out either. The women moved to one side of the camp and the men to the other. So far, only three of the women were allowed to touch the bear hide. It had been their job to scrape it. They had been chosen because they were not mated. They had not known a man, nor were they suffering their bleed. Now the ceremony was underway they joined the rest of the women and children.

Jumping Fox rose and was amazed that in his mind were instructions. He went to the forest at the edge of the glade. Here he found growing a mass of Datura. He gathered the sacred part of the plant and returned to the camp. From this he prepared a drink. It was mild. He was instructed just how much of the plant he was too steep in how much water. To this he added other herbs, just as his mind instructed. The men watched in amazement as he went about his task. Raptor Feather nodded and sighed in relief. They had a spirit leader! He was certain that the spirits had truly called Jumping Fox.

As the day wore on, Jumping Fox asked various persons to carry out tasks for the ceremony. Finally, at dust all was ready. All night and day the heart of the great bear had been smoking. Now it was a blackened, shriveled ball. Raptor Feather had broken the canine teeth from the bear skull. These were placed beside the heart. Reeds had been woven into a container, just large enough to hold the sacred objects. Jumping

Fox tossed a handful of herbs onto the hearth. A deep black smoke rose. Through this he passed the sacred packet a number of times, chanting prayers only he and the spirit bear understood. Then he produced from somewhere within his robe a pelt. Everyone recognized it. It was from a wolf. But no one knew where it came from, except Jumping Fox who had found it waiting for him in his shelter when he returned from gathering the Datura. Now he placed the reed container on the hide and carefully wrapped it. This then was placed within a deer hide and it also was wrapped. Now the camp had a sacred bundle.

"Now what do we do with it?" asked Turtle.

"Jumping Fox is the 'Keeper of the Sacred Bundle'," replied Raptor Feather.

"Yes. But what do we do with it?" he repeated his question.

"It is the cord which connects us to our protective spirit" answered Jumping Fox. "When we need help, or answers to our problems, the spirit bundle is there to help us. It will show us the paths to take, the places to hunt, the people to travel to."

"Will it keep our enemies from attacking us?" the child looked dubiously at the bundle.

Jumping Fox shook his head, "But it will show us where the enemy is and how strong. That way we can decide if we face them, head on, ambush them, or run for our lives."

"I would never run like a coward!" Turtle strutted.

"When you are a man, the situations are not always as clearly marked as when you are a child." reminded Elk Caller.

"I still would not run," stated the child.

"Perhaps you need to examine your heart," suggested Jumping Fox. "There is a difference between bravery and vanity! Be sure that you do not practice the latter!"

"Mother made us hide in the forest like cowards!" stated Turtle. "It would have been better if we had followed. Maybe we could have freed you!"

"And maybe you also would have been captured."

"Then, at least we would have been together," answered the child.

"And perhaps you would have been dead," replied Elk Caller. "Your mother was right to take you to a place of safety."

"But we would all have died of starvation this winter if you had not found us."

"But we did find you. The spirits led us to you. So see, already bear spirit has helped us all. Now there is a complete camp where before there were helpless women and children and lonesome hunters. Now we are all happy."

"But you found us before the bear was killed!" Turtle pointed out.

"That is because the spirit of bear was leading us to you and to the sacred bear," replied Dancing Crane. "Now no more questions! If you wish to become a man, learn by example. You have a number of excellent ones to choose from."

"Where does this bear spirit lead us?" Turtle ignored his mother.

Jumping Fox started to say, then hesitated, "You have no need to know," was his final reply. Then he turned away, troubled that the youth showed definite signs of vanity.

"That is just your way of getting around the fact that you have no idea!" challenged the youth. "What kind of dreamer are you?" he scoffed, "You have only been dreamer for a day. Already you claim to know everything! I do not believe you!"

"It is true, what you say," Jumping Fox agreed, "I have been dreamer for only a day. But that day has opened my eyes to many things. If you were a man, then I would honor your words with an explanation. But you are but an impudent child who does not know his place."

"I have had to be Headman, to these women all summer," stated the youth, "I have led them well and kept them alive! Can you say as much?"

Dancing Crane yanked Turtle by the arm and dragged him protesting from the camp, "How dare you humiliate me like that before the entire camp?" she hissed at him, "You have led nothing! You have been nothing but a problem ever since we got separated from your father. I just hope that he does not punish you for this terrible breech of manners. You shame me!"

"Leave me alone!" shouted the youth, "I don't have to listen to you! Tomorrow I go on my 'spirit journey' and when I return I will never have to obey you again!" he jerked free and ran into the forest.

"Coward!" Dancing Crane shouted after him, "Running away coward!" Then she stomped back to the camp.

Elk Caller met her there, "What is going on? I hear you shouting."

"That Turtle," she grumbled, "He is impossible! No respect for his elders. Ever since the savages took you, he has been like this! He won't heed a word that I say."

Elk Caller sighed, "It was a difficult time for him. He is nearly a man and he took his place as the only male in the group very seriously. I should imagine that he felt it was his sole responsibility to see to your safety and provide for the entire group. He was of course too young and inexperienced to do so. He probably sees himself as a failure and is angry because of that."

"Still no reason to be disrespectful and you heard how he spoke to the dreamer!"

"Jumping Fox does not hold his words against him. But I do agree that he was very disrespectful and rude. I will talk to him," Calling Elk followed the path which the youth took from the camp. He found him a short distance into the trees. He sat on a log, tears running down his face. Elk Caller quietly sat beside him and looked down at his own feet.

"When I was a youth," he said quietly, "I wanted desperately to be the fastest runner in the camp. I went out almost every day to a place where no one could see me and I ran and ran and ran. When it came time for the contests, I was sure that I would win. I didn't. I was so ashamed that in my frustration I beat up another boy. My father not only made me apologize to the other boy. He actually made me promise to become his best friend for half a moon. It was a very good thing, for me. It was the beginning of a friendship which is still very important to me. That other boy was Badger Tail. I cannot begin to tell you of the number of times that man has saved my life." Then, quietly, Elk Caller rose and walked away.

Turtle watched him go. He sat on the long for a long time and then with a sigh he rose and returned to the camp. The celebration was still going on, but he watched from the outskirts of the camp.

Steaks of bear meat; stew and roast were all served to every member of the camp. The remainder of the meat would be dried and stored for special occasions. The meal was eaten in silence. Each person thought about the bear spirit as they ate. When the meal was finished, every morsel of bear meat remaining was offered to the fire. The smoke from this rose to the sky and the camp chanted as they watched. When the last of it was burned and the hearth fire smothered, the ashes were collected in a new reed basket and taken to a special place and buried. Now the spirit of bear would protect every member of the camp. The camp went to their robes in a thoughtful mood.

When the sun rose, Turtle was waiting outside of Jumping Fox's shelter. When the man stepped out, the youth bowed to him and spoke. "I was wrong to talk to you the way that I did last night. I would beg that you accept not only my apology but allow me to become your helper. I would know more about this 'spirit' work that you do."

Jumping Fox did not know what to say. Finally he looked deeply into the youth's eye and saw his sincerity. He simply nodded and Turtle fell into step behind him as he began his new life as Dreamer.

# CHAPTER 17

**Back at the valley of The Gathering...**

We are going to find the bison hunters. All of my life I have heard tales of these 'wolves of the plains'. Always I have wanted to hunt bison. Now I will! I will not follow a man who spoils women. Such a man is no man at all!" He Man snorted in disgust, "Come on Jumping Frog! There is much work for us to finish before we leave. Hunting Badger has nearly a full morning head start on us and with those lazy women holding us back, we will not be able to travel as fast as the hunters. The sooner we leave the better. Call Red Fox and Laughing Antelope. Bear Paw is already breaking camp. We have no time to waste." The stocky hunter strode toward their camp. Women and children were busy stuffing possessions into containers and folding robes. Already the hunter, Bear Paw was pulling down their shelters, making their work doubly hard as he collapsed the structures onto where they were working.

"You! Feather Robe! Get over here and help!" he shouted to his mate. She gave him a Frightened glance and quickly hurried from the conversation she was having with several women of Running Bison's camp. As she reached their hearth, Bear Paw slapped her hard across the face. "You got work to do! No time to waste giggling with that worthless sister of yours!"

Feather Robe wiped a dribble of blood from her nose and gave the departing sister one last glance. In her heart, she knew that she would never see Green Moss again. She began handing her stepdaughter, Dancing Moth, food to store in woven baskets. Sparrow, glaring hatred toward her father's back, hurried to help her mother. Feather Robe smiled gratefully at her daughter. Sparrow was the one bright spot in her life. "Here, Daughter, pack these strips of meat in that hide container. We must be sure that it doesn't spoil. Do not say anything to anyone about it though," she whispered, slipping a large packet wrapped in a woven cover. Green Moss had slipped it to her just before they parted. "Place it well under the hides still needing work. The men will not think to look there."

"Yes, Mother, I will hide it well."

Fire Weed worked alone to pack her travois. Left Hand, a man only these few days, had decided that he need listen no longer to the words of his Stepmother. He was lounging sullenly against a tree, waiting impatiently to get underway. Occasionally he took a swig from the bladder at his waist. He eyed Dancing Moth from time to time, determining whether he wanted to take her for a mate. Absently he rubbed his crotch, trying to ease the uncomfortable hardness there. There were few to choose from and although she was pretty enough, he wanted something more exciting. Dancing Moth had no imagination. She was as empty-headed as a tick. He thought back to the closing celebration, remembering the woman with the white robe. *Now there was a woman to tame!* He could almost taste her as in his mind he... He sighed. They were nearly ready to get under way. He turned his thought to bison hunting....

The men headed out into the plain, following the wide trail of Hunting Badger and his hunters. They set a fast pace. Behind them the women and children ribboned out, pulling the travois. They had no dogs so the women pulled. Cottontail rode on her mother's travois, while Toad did his best to keep up with Ash Leaf. The young mother smiled happily down at her two beautiful children.

Fire Weed walked beside her. "That worthless Left Hand," she grumbled, "Is going to be just like his father!" She shifted the straps of her backpack. "They expect me to wait on them, hand and foot! Both of them! It's, Fire Weed, do this! And Fire Weed, fetch that!" You'd think they'd help me once in a while! Huh!"

"Sometimes I think that men only mate with us to have someone to order around," agreed Ash Leaf. "I was so excited when Laughing Antelope asked for me. He was so strong and handsome and such a fine hunter! But as soon as I got pregnant with Toad he began to get abusive. Then after I was so soon again pregnant, this time with Cottontail, he has gotten worse. He does not like either child, although they are both beautiful and well behaved. He was only interested in constantly rutting between my legs and then complained when I bore the results! He said I was fat and ugly and the babies were sniveling brats."

"At least he has not given you to his friends for their relief!" Fire Weed complained, "He Man has even suggested that I 'service' Left Hand! Can you imagine?"

"But that is incest!" exclaimed Ash Leaf, "He is your son!"

"Stepson, actually," corrected Fire Weed. "But who would wish to spread their legs to that whining youth?"

"The way he keeps looking at Dancing Moth, she had better start getting used to the idea. She is of an age now and it's not as though either one of them has much to choose from."

"There is no hurry!"

"Ah! But think how giving Dancing Moth to Left Hand would ingratiate Bear Paw to He Man. He would owe He Man a brother's status. And He Man has plans to become Leader of a band. That is why we follow Hunting Badger. He Man is going to make an offer to some of those new hunters. I have heard him talking to Bear Paw about it." Ash Leaf informed the listening women.

"Have you two thought about what will happen to us once we join up with Hunting Badger and the rest of the hunters?" Laughing Water called to them.

"What do you mean," asked Ash Leaf.

"There will only be the hand of us. Those men will expect us to do all the women's work for the entire group. And the spirits alone know who will demand to use us. I do not like this at all. I would much rather have gone with Running Bison."

"You are right," sighed Fire Weed, "But there is nothing we can do about it; not then and certainly not now. Perhaps we will get lucky. Maybe the bison hunters are moving so fast that we will be unable to catch up with them. After all, none of our men are especially good trackers."

"A child could follow the trail of the bison hunters," reminded Dancing Willow.

"You are right," agreed Ash Leaf glumly. "It seems that we are doomed either way. If we don't catch up with them we will most likely get lost and starve to death. If we do find them, they will likely abuse us to the death. Either way, it does not look good for any of us."

"We could sneak off during the night and make our way back to the mountains," suggested Laughing Water.

"And then what? Have you ever killed a deer? I haven't. I wouldn't know how to even start. Besides it is taboo for us to hunt. Any hunter would kill us just for having a hunting tool," Fire Weed reminded them. "Besides, they would just follow us on the morning and beat us for running off."

"They are liable to beat us for not keeping up," reminded Laughing Water. "Come on, we are losing them!"

"I am pulling this heavy load, they are not," exclaimed Feather Robe. "Let Bear Paw beat me for that. He will find something. It might as well be for that!"

"Why did you mate with Bear Paw if you find such fault with him?" asked Laughing Water.

"I was given no choice," replied Feather Robe. "My father traded me off for a share of a bison. We were hungry. Bear Paw made the kill. He was refusing to share with anyone. So my father gave me to him for a share. The meat kept us from starving to death, but there are times that I think it would have been better for me to starve. Bear Paw is certainly not a considerate mate."

"There are those who say that Bear Paw was the father of Dancing Moth's baby," Fire Weed stated. I have heard a tale that he raped her when she was returning from her vision quest."

Feather Robe nodded, "Walking Thunder knew, but he did nothing about it. I think that Bear Paw made it worth his while to look the other way. Dancing Moth is not the first girl he has violated. I came into the shelter one time when he had another 'just turned woman' down on his robes. Had I not interrupted him, he would have raped her as well. As it is, she escaped and he took his anger out on me. He broke my nose and caused me to lose a baby I had just started. In a way, I was glad about that. I don't want any more children, at least not until these are older."

The women had picked up speed and were now catching up with the men. So their talk stopped. No one stopped at mid day to rest or eat but the hunters did call it a day just before dark. The women were grateful. They dropped the traces of the travois and quickly set up the shelters and began gathering firewood. Their path had followed a small river that provided fuel for the fires. Beyond that there was nothing. No bison chips could be found. If they wondered what they would use for cooking fuel once they left the protection of the river, no one said. They merely fixed the food; rabbits and birds that they had taken with rabbit stick or bolas as they traveled. The men were too busy following the trail of the bison hunters to concern themselves with providing food. After eating, everyone gratefully retired to their robes. In the far distance wolves set up a serenade to the full moon.

The next morning they set out again. For another pair of days they followed the river, then the tracks of the bison hunters, left it and headed out onto the empty rolling plain. The men followed. So did their families. The women had hastily secured a small supply of wood before they left the river, but there was little room on their travois for such an extra. That night they camped in an area of open moving sand. The loose sand made travel much slower. Even the men complained. There was just enough wood to cook the evening meal. Cold meat served as the early meal the next day. By now all the plants that the women had begun to learn about had been eaten by them and the children. There were no plants here at all and few on the plains that they recognized.

By mid day the temperature was becoming unmercifully hot. The children had stripped to apron, or breechcloth. The women stripped to apron and the lightest of tunics. The hunters, of course, wore only breech clot. Each individual, however, wore a reed-woven hat to keep the sun from burning them. Then the sun began to slip into a red haze. Lightly at first, then with more and more force, the hot dry wind began to pick up. By mid afternoon sand was stinging eyes and making it difficult to breathe.

"We will stop here!" He Man called, coughing and blowing sand from his nose. His eyes were watering and he was breathing hard, "I can no longer see to follow the trail. We have gone as far as we can this day. In the morning we will pick it up again.

The women gratefully dropped the traces. They were staggering from fatigue. Toad had joined Cottontail to ride the travois. Although Ash Leaf was the youngest and strongest of the women, hers was the heaviest load. She could hardly breathe at all. Blood dripped from her nose and she had a racking cough. With a sigh, her trembling legs gave out beneath her.

"Come, I will help you set up your shelter," Feather Robe staggered to lift her. "It is a bit more sheltered here against the side of the dune."

"Let me help as well," Laughing Water made her way to where the two women were struggling against the wind and loose sand. Finally the shelter was up; sort of. Laughing Antelope grunted and grabbed his sleeping robe.

"Get me something to eat, woman," He grabbed her water bladder and drank it dry, then tossed it at her feet. Ash Leaf blinked, her mouth trembling. Her precious water! She had been so careful to give the children just a sip now and then, taking some herself only when she absolutely had to. Now it was gone! Tears ran down her dirty face. By the time she got the food for Laughing Antelope, he was sprawled across the entire shelter, leaving no room for her or the children. She sighed and gratefully thanked the spirits that, at least, he was fast asleep.

Ash Leaf settled the children in a sheltered spot where the wind was less. She snuggled them into their sleeping robes and settled down beside them. She was so tired that she was asleep in a heartbeat. Gently, quietly, the sand filtered over the edge of the dune. In sculptured grace it settled softly about the sleeping people. Most of the men had followed the same route as Laughing Antelope. They took the shelters, leaving the women and children to shift for themselves as best they could. The latter were more or less bunched together in the lea of the big dune. All night the wind kept blowing, the sand kept settling. By morning, the storm grew stronger. The people huddled close, covering their heads, trying to find air to breathe which did not sear their lungs, or clog their noses and eyes. The children huddled closely to their mothers. The men grumbled and sat in the shelters.

"Fire Weed," shouted He Man, "Bring me food and water, you lazy woman! And not that putrid stuff you got from Running Bison's women. I want real food! Meat!"

Fire Weed grunted and dug into her storage container, frowning. *There was half again this much last time I looked!* She thought to herself. *Someone has been stealing my meat. Probably that lazy Left Hand! I'll have a word with him over this! He can get his own food!* She went to where the shelter was set up and handed He Man a measure of meat. While she was doing this, Left Hand, watching her all the while, slipped to her travois and helped himself to a liberal supply of the remaining food. With a shifty smile, he purloined a water bladder as well. Then he vanished into the storm,

"I said water!" He Man shouted, "Can't you do anything right? Now get me some water."

Fire Weed glared down at him and returned to her travois. She knew there was only a pair more bladders containing water. She grabbed one and took it back to He Man. Then she returned to the travois and began putting things away. That was when she realized that the second water bladder was gone. A quick check revealed that half the remaining meat was missing as well. *That Left Hand!* She took what meat remained and stuffed it into her waist bag. No one was going to get the rest of it! Then she waited and when He Man left the shelter, she scurried there and retrieved the water bladder. It was half empty. She replaced it with an empty one and hid the precious supply, affording herself one swallow. This she savored slowly.

All day the wind blew and the sand settled. Everyone was suffering both from the heat and the inability to breathe. Exhausted they drifted into sleep. Morning brought silence and clear blue skies.

Ash Leaf woke. It was just barely dawn. She reached over to check on Toad and Cottontail. Where they slept was just a mound of sand. Fear coursed through her. She began to dig frantically. Soon, one small foot was exposed, "Help me!" she shouted to the other women. "My babies!" By now she had uncovered the small limp remains of Cottontail. Soon other busy hands had found Toad. They lay side by side, hands clutched, in death, as in life, together. Ash Leaf sat sobbing, rocking the lifeless form of her little daughter. Gentle hands took the child from her and the women quietly went about the custom. They wrapped the small bodies in their sleeping robes and carried them from the camp. They helped Ash Leaf along, as the sobbing mother wailed and cut her arms with a sharp blade. It did not take long. Then they were back at the camp, loading their travois and walking away through the sand. Laughing Antelope merely grunted upon hearing that both of his children had died, suffocated by the sand. He headed out with the rest of the men, all complaining for lack of food and water. Silent shadows slipped to the top of the dune, sniffing and growling. They fought savagely for the small remains. Before the scent of the humans had disappeared from the wind, the children were no more.

Ash Leaf fell to her knees. Her legs would carry her no farther. She did not care. Fire Weed encouraged her back onto her feet and they kept her going. At Mid Day the men stopped for food. "You have eaten all of the food!" Fire Weed told them.

"What?" shouted He Man! That is impossible! When we left the valley of the Gathering, we had food enough for at least a double hand of days!"

"And you have eaten it in less," the woman replied angrily. "While we have gone without!"

"You have rabbit sticks and bolas! You tell me, that through all this time, none of you have brought in any food?"

"Since we left the river, there has been nothing to bring in!" she protested. "Not only is there no food, but there is no water either!"

"Why has no one mentioned this?" He shouted at the women, "Are you all a bunch of stupid bison cows? Could not one among you think to suggest we should hunt?" He snorted "Make Camp! We hunt!" He gathered up his weapons and stalked from the camp, followed by the rest of the men and Left Hand.

The women stood huddled in a small group, watching the men disappear into the distance. Fire Weed snorted and turned to the others. "Come on, while they are gone, at least we will get one good meal. I have a small store of meat. I will share it with you," she smiled, "See if we can find enough wood for a tiny fire."

"I will get wood," volunteered Sparrow.

Feather Robe nodded and began setting up the shelter. Sparrow wandered away from the camp, humming to herself under her breath. She picked up sticks here and small branches there, moving farther and farther from the group. A shadow fell in behind her, joined by another, silently, as more slipped around to the sides. When they were ready, the leader leaped.

"Umph!" Sparrow struck the ground; the wind knocked out of her, a searing pain ripped through her back, then blackness. They gathered as silently as they had stalked eating quickly. There was a fight over the bones, finally settled by the leader. Then they vanished into the plains. When the women finally went searching....

"I know that she went this way!" called Feather Robe. "See, here are her moccasin prints!" They followed the trail.

"Look here!" Fire Weed called, "Look at these tracks!"

The women bunched together, peering at the trail, "Wolves." stated Laughing Water. "Come on, we have no time to lose!" she started running. Feather Robe began to wail as she followed Fire Weed. Silently Dancing Willow and Ash Leaf fell in behind. They had not far to go. The bloody grass told its own story. There was nothing but a small collection of sticks for them to return to the camp. Feather Robe took out a sharp blade and began to hack off her hair as she sent up a chant of grief. She sliced her arms in mourning as well.

"My Poor Sparrow," she sobbed. "Now her spirit will never rest! She will become an evil wind upon these retched plains! Oh how I wish I had the courage to have gone with Running Bison! My baby! My poor little Sparrow!" she wailed.

"We will all join the children soon!" Ash Leaf whispered.

The hunters returned to find the camp still in an upheaval. They had found nothing; not even any tracks. Bear Paw was in a foul mood. The news that wolves had eaten his daughter did nothing to sweeten it. He began hitting Feather Robe about the head and when that seemed to bring no reaction from the grief numbed woman, switched tactics. He knocked her to the ground and kicked her several times. Then he went down on his knees and struck her with his balled-up fists. The woman made no sound. She merely stared open eyed up at him, until he closed her eyes with repeated blows. Somewhere along the line, just when no one, not the horrified, frightened women, or the encouraging men, noticed, the life withdrew from the woman. Finally, Bear Paw tired of his sport. With a last kick he grunted and walked away from the broken, bloody corpse.

The hunters followed him back onto the plain. Fire Weed was the first to react. She sighed and went to where Feather Robe lay, verifying what she already knew. The other woman was dead. Without a word the remaining women lifted their friend onto a travois and carried her out to where little Sparrow had died. It was fitting; somehow, to release her troubled spirit with that of her child. Then they returned to the camp. Before they passed from sight, the silent, hungry shadows were already closing in. The child had not filled their bellies. Before dark settled in, they were contentedly chewing on the bones, savoring the rich marrow.

With the morning, discovery that some time during the night Ash Leaf had quietly left the camp her moccasin prints headed off into the plain. There was no reason to follow. Everyone knew that by now, she also was a spirit.

They continued. The hunters had lost the trail of the bison hunters. Ever since the sandstorm they had been traveling blindly. Now they were far out on the prairie. But, in the distance, they spotted a grove of trees. Hurriedly they changed direction and headed toward it. No one had eaten in over a day and the last of the water was gone as well. Even the carefully hoarded bladder, which Fire Weed had hidden, was empty. She had shared it with the women and children.

Lips were cracked, eyes blurry and legs wobbly as they staggered into the shade of the grove. At one time a small river had flowed here. But now the only thing to greet the weary travelers was shade. "Look here!" Fire Weed dropped to her knees, "The ground is wet! Hand me a scapula and I will see if I can bring water to the surface. I have heard of it being done, although I have never tried myself."

Dancing Willow handed her the scapula. Already the men were lounging in the shade, watching. Soon sand was flying as Fire Weed excavated a hole in the sand. Deeper and deeper she went, widening the hole as she worked. Finally she was nearly deep to her waist, standing in the hole. But she gave way with a thrill of sound! Water was already getting her moccasins wet. She climbed out and watched. Within a finger of time there was water enough in the bottom of her hole to dip with a tortoise shell bowl. She did so, handing it up. Of course, the hand that took it was male. Left Hand grinned as he downed the entire amount. His pleasure was short lived, however, when He Man cuffed him along-side the head and shoved him out of the way. "Who do you think you are?" the hunter shouted at his son. "Give way to the men!" He Man glared down at Fire Weed, "Hurry up, woman, I'm thirsty!" he shouted.

"The water comes at its own speed," grumbled Fire Weed. "You are not the only thirsty one here," she added under her breath. Finally there was enough water to fill the bowl. She scooped it up and handed the bowl to He Man. Then she fell to her knees and with her mouth to the accumulating seepage, drank. The men were all clambering for their share. Finally she dug deeper and the supply of water was faster and of greater quantity. She was able to fill not just one bowl but a second as well. Eventually, everyone had drunk his or her fill. Then Laughing Water changed places with her and the women began filling the water bladders. By now someone had started a fire and so by its light, the last of the water bladders were filled. Meanwhile, the other women were digging around in the earth beneath the trees, searching for anything edible. They found a hand full of grubs and several dried-out tubers. It mattered not. They were all tossed into a watery stew.

"Look!" Dancing Willow pointed, "There is an animal up in this tree!"

"Where?" Demanded Jumping Frog, "I don't see anything."

"Up there, just at the base of that branch. See! It moved again!"

The hunter shoved her aside and took aim. The thud of dart and a squeal, followed by the sound of a falling body, told the tale. At her feet, Dancing Willow watched the creature thrash its last. Very soon, a possum was sending up inviting odors in the grove. Now that the hunters were alerted, several more of the animals were darted. That night, at least, everyone ate a modest meal.

The next morning the hunters were ready to set out once again. "I want to return to the mountains!" Fire Weed, announced, "You have lost the trail of the bison hunters. "We have all nearly died. Now we have water and there are enough possums in this grove to provide food for several days, if we are careful! There are no bison! You haven't even found as much as a dried bison turd! Yet you endanger all of our lives!"

"No one asked you, woman!" He Man shouted, "When you are Headman, then you can make the decisions! Until then, keep your mouth shut and do as you are told!" He slapped her, hard. Left Hand grinned.

"I make the decisions! And I say we keep going! Today we will hunt the remaining possums from these trees, then tomorrow we continue!" He picked up his weapon and headed from the camp to follow his words with actions. The other men followed, grinning and laughing.

"I am not staying here with a bunch of women telling me what to do!" shouted Grasshopper, "I am nearly a man! I am going hunting with the men!" He grabbed his weapons and stomped from the camp.

The women shrugged. Dancing Willow muttered, "Just like his father," as she watched the departing figure of her son.

Grasshopper went, congratulating himself on standing up like a man. He had been right to do so! Soon, as soon as there was game to be hunted, he would take his spirit journey. It wasn't right that he was relegated to the women and children. He was a man! *Well almost!* He studied the horizon. "Ah! Yes, already I see game!" He congratulated himself again. "His sharp eyes had caught just a flicker of movement, *it could even be bison!* He hurried from the grove, hot on the trail of the movement. Topping the ridge he glanced this way and that. Nothing moved. *I am sure!* Again he studied the landscape. Again, just a flicker of movement, disappearing over the next ridge. *Ah! Yes!* Quickly he trotted toward the spot. Three ridges later, again he watched. This time he was sure! Down in the bottom of a bison wallow, there was definitely movement.

Grasshopper slipped into his 'hunter' mode and began carefully working his way toward the middle of the wallow. It had not been used in a long time. Brush and even a few small trees, graced its sides. Tall grass clogged the remainder, making it difficult to see clearly. But Grasshopper was taking no chance. *This could be my spirit journey kill!* He took his time, creeping silently down into the wallow. He focused his concentration on the task at hand.

Silently, they slipped up behind him, following, making no sound. As gossamer as the shadows they resembled. They were well fed now. This human prey had provided a bounty of food. Now, again they would eat well. Yellow eyes communicated silently with brown. Light glistened off sharp canines.

Grasshopper rose slowly, his atlatl and dart, ready to cast in a heartbeat. Disappointment coursed through his veins. In the center of the bison wallow, a partially collapsed shelter stood in lonely splendor, its hide flapping slightly in the breeze. Grasshopper stood and snorted derisively.

The impact against his back sent him staggering toward the shelter. His feet tangled in the tall grass as he tried to turn and face his attacker. He went down, rolling onto his back from the glancing blow. Dart ready, his eyes widened. They stood, in a semicircle, eyes glued to him. It was as though they were frozen in time. Only the song of a meadow lark broke the silence.

The youth began to sweat. He held the dart in a defensive position. They waited. They had time. A pair of them dropped back and circled around behind. Grasshopper understood. The sun boiled down on him. The glare sent pain shooting through his head. "Get out of here!" He shouted and waved the dart. The leader rolled back her lip and growled softly. Her eyes never left his.

*The shelter! I can get to the shelter! They can't attack from behind!* He squirmed until he got his feet under him, never losing eye-contact with the big white wolf. Slowly, he eased into a squatting position, then began easing backwards. Step by step, feeling his way with his feet, he backed away from them. A twig snapped behind him. Again fear laced through his mind, as he silently began to call on the spirits. Still nothing....

*Almost there!* The big white leader stood, relaxed, watching. There was no hurry. The prey was moving nicely, just where it was supposed to. Behind the youth, the pair of wolves slid silently into the shelter. It was cooler here. They watched the leader.

*I'm going to make it,* the youth thought; a split heartbeat before he felt the feted breath on his bare neck. He started to turn, but they sprang. Grasshopper felt pain lace through his shoulder, but he rolled over and drove his dart into the throat of the attacking wolf. It yelped and faltered, then rolled over and began kicking. In a flash they moved. Like liquid they flowed down the side of the wallow and in perfect precision attacked. Grasshopper began to scream. The leader watched while a young female grabbed him by the left leg. Already he was fighting another wolf. She had his upper arm and agony laced through it as she sank her canines deep into the muscle. He kicked and the other female leaped away with a yelp. Now more entered the fray.

Grasshopper reached with his right hand and brought a handful of darts from the holder on his back. He grasped them in his left hand, forcing the muscles to work. With his right he stabbed at the wolf. She released his arm, but he could feel blood coursing freely from the wounds. He kicked with his feet and slid on his back toward the shelter. Now he could feel the brace against his back. He had lost the atlatl, so there was no way he could cast his darts. But he had them. As the wolves began to close in, he pulled the flap down, providing a measure of protection. Now he had only to protect the frontal approach.

The wolf he darted stopped moving. The leader walked over to her, sniffed and walked away. A young female tried to rouse the still form, whined and then turned toward Grasshopper. She curled back he lip in a silent snarl, hatred burning in her eyes. The dead one had been a sister. Now the hunt had suddenly become personal. Still, they waited.

Grasshopper could feel something wet against he bare rump. He reached back and brought his hand away covered in blood. The wound in his back was bleeding. Until then he had hardly noticed it. His arm was still losing blood at an alarming rate. He ripped a length of fringe from the bottom of his breech clot and tied it as best he could above the lacerated flesh. The bleeding slowed.

He blinked. His vision began to blur. He had to keep shaking his head. Funny, it had been hot. *It is almost cold now, yet the sun is still shining!* In the distance he could hear the meadow lark singing as if its heart would burst from the beauty of the day.

The leader tired of the game. The prey was nearly defenseless now. She gave the signal. All together they leaped. Grasshopper was driven backwards, toppling the fragile shelter. A shrill scream ripped from his throat, cut off, suddenly. Only silence ensued.

\*     \*     \*

"What was that?" Fire Weed raised her head, "I thought I heard something."

"I didn't hear anything," Laughing Water replied.

"I did," Dancing Willow answered, "It sounded like.... Where is Grasshopper? Have you seen him?"

"Not since before mid-day," replied Dancing Willow, "He went off on his own, remember?" She shrugged. "He will be back when he gets hungry."

"No," Dancing Willow answered, "I thought I heard someone scream. It sounded like Grasshopper! I am going to investigate. I am sure that he is in trouble."

"Wait!" Fire Weed called, "I will go with you." She picked up her bolas, rabbit stick and looking guiltily about, a pair of darts she had taken from He Man. They had no trouble following the trail. In a few fingers of time they had traveled the distance which Grasshopper had covered in two hands of time. They were not stalking. Before they mounted the last rise, an eerie howl rose from the grass nearby. Both women stopped, fear clearly written on their worried faces. Then they continued, more carefully. The first thing they saw was the darted wolf; then amongst the debris on an old shelter, the grisly remains of the youth. His throat had been ripped out and he had been eviscerated as well. One arm was nearly chewed in two. Dancing Willow gave a wail of grief and fell beside the remains of her stepchild. Grasshopper had died valiantly, of this she was certain. He had killed one of the wolves. All she had now was a chant to send him to the fires in the sky. She began the chant as she gathered him onto the shelter robe. They carried his back to the high ridge. As far as you could see in any direction, nothing moved. Here they laid him out to walk the wind. Dancing Willow sighed as she walked away. *So many deaths!*

The silent shadows assembled as the women passed from view and finished their meal.

\*　　\*　　\*

Dancing Willow was packing away Grasshoppers possessions. She had already dug a shallow pit to bury them. It was bad luck to keep personal things, the spirit could return for them. And by his death, Grasshopper was now an evil spirit on these plains. "What are you doing?" Jumping Frog suddenly demanded, from behind her, "Those things do not belong to you!"

"Now they belong to no one!" she answered, "Grasshopper is dead! The wolves killed him. You have been out having a good time with the other hunters, while your son was trying to prove himself a man! He killed a wolf for his journey! At least he will go to the fires as a man!"

"Grasshopper?" Jumping Frog said in astonishment, "My son is dead? My son is dead and you do not even grieve for him?" He grabbed her by the tunic. "What kind of mother are you?" he shoved her away, "That you do not even cut your hair and scar your arms for my son?"

"He wasn't my son!" Dancing Willow protested, "But I did what I could. It was too late by the time we found him. He was already dead!"

"It wasn't too late for you to grieve!" he slapped her hard. She stumbled backward and he advanced, repeatedly striking her with his balled-up fist. She fell, rolled away and the hunter came at her again. Dancing Willow scooted away from him, pulling herself along the ground with her hands. Still, he kept coming. Her groping hand closing on the shaft of the dart that he had carelessly dropped upon returning to camp. Still Jumping Frog advanced. Her back against a tree, with no escape avenue open, Dancing Willow brought the dart up.

The hunter roared! "You dare to defile a hunting tool?" He lunged at her, bringing his arm back to strike her yet again aside the head. Dancing Willow raised her hands protectively as he lunged forward and drove the dart directly into his throat. Jumping Frog opened his mouth, but only blood came out. It splattered over the ground and the woman, covering her in a welter of crimson. A surprised look came into Jumping Frog's eyes, and then they began to glaze over in death. Slowly, he crumpled at Dancing Willow's feet and lay still. She looked at his body and then ran her dry tongue over her lips. Then again she ran her tongue.... She looked down at the hunter, then at the other women and she smiled...

"They will kill her!" Dancing Moth whispered.

"No!" Fire Weed stated, "They will not." She looked around. The rest of the men were at the very far end of the grove, almost a hand of distance away. "Come on! We have work to do." She called the others.

"What are you going to do?" whimpered Dancing Moth.

"Prepare the racks. Dancing Moth, you help me strip the meat; dancing Willow, go find green wood for the fire, but stay close. The wolves have eaten well enough for now. Laughing Water, get a hearth started."

"You cannot mean to..."

"I certainly do. Have you any better ideas?"

"But..."

"I'll help," Dancing Willow rose, "Let Moth collect wood." She reached down and grasped the hunter by one arm, while Fire Weed took the other. Watching them silently, Sunbeam and Wildfire, carefully covered the trail of blood, Sunbeam smiled. Never again would her father force her to spread her legs for him!

Already the possum meat was dried. In short order the racks were again loaded with fresh meat. Dancing Moth made several trips for green wood and was joined by Sunbeam and Wildfire. Before long, only bones were left. Fire Weed studied them, then with a shrug tossed them onto a hide and slung the grisly cargo over her shoulder. She went a short distance from the camp, dug a hole and buried them. "There, see how you like living forever in the dark!" she kicked a last bit of dirt over the grave and returned to the camp.

She spread healing salve over Dancing Willow's bruises and cuts and bound her ribs where the kicks of the hunter had cracked them. She could do little more.

The men did not return to the camp that night. They roasted possum and sat around their fire reminiscing over old times and great hunts. When they finally returned to the camp the next evening, everything was neat and quiet. The women had food ready; the last of the possum stew. They tossed the carcasses they had bagged the previous night toward them and settled down. "Where's Jumping Frog?" He Man questioned.

"Isn't he with you?" replied Fire Weed, "And where is Grasshopper? Isn't he with you?" She glanced at each of the hunters and had a puzzled look on her face. "He left this camp yesterday to join you."

"No. He never joined us and Jumping Frog came back yesterday," Red Fox said.

The women nodded their heads. "He came back," Fire Weed waved toward Dancing Willow, "But he didn't stay! He headed back to your camp."

"Perhaps he met up with Grasshopper and they went somewhere, together?" suggested Dancing Willow.

The hunters shrugged and went back to eating.

By morning, the pair had not returned. "I don't plan on waiting for them!" He Man stated. "We have been here long enough, "It is time to move on. They can catch up. Get the camp broken and follow us," he ordered the women.

Quietly the women complied.

"There is something strange about Jumping Frog and Grasshopper going off like that," Red Fox remarked.

"What do you mean?" asked Laughing Antelope. "It doesn't seem strange to me. After all Jumping Frog has been looking at the boy for some time. And I doubt he plans to teach him to hunt!" The men laughed suggestively, rubbing his private place. "They will catch up again once Jumping Frog has him 'broken in'."

He Man merely snorted rudely and stalked off. He preferred a woman himself, but he knew that quite a few men liked boys. He had other things on his mind. Like where they were going and where the bison hunters were? *Where could they have gone? They headed directly east, but I find no sign of their trail. Perhaps I should swing in a circle and try to pick up the trail. But I was so sure that they would continue east... Why would they change their direction? Why can't I find their trail?* He glanced up at the unmerciful sun. Then as if making a decision, he turned and stalked off across the undulating expanse, gradually turning south. At least there was a large river there; there should be food and water. If nothing else, they could follow the river and look for bison near it.

Red Fox was the first to notice the change in direction. He caught up with Laughing Antelope. "We have changed direction. Do you really think that He Man knows what he is doing? I have found no trace of the trail since we left the moving sand. I think that we are lost."

"I don't think that He Man knows where we are going!" stated Left Hand, "It seems to me that we have just been wandering ever since we left the moving sand."

"No one asked you!" Red Fox glared at the youth, "Just because you are now a man, doesn't give you the right to speak your thoughts. Learn to keep them to yourself unless asked."

Laughing Antelope shrugged. "What difference does it make? Besides, in a way Left Hand is right. We have as good a chance finding the bison as they do. I doubt that crazy old Hunting Badger has any more idea where to find them than we do. I trust He Man. He is leading us well. We have not starved to death. I would not be surprised if he has not discovered that the bison hunters have changed direction. It makes sense. The bison must have water. We all know there is a river this direction. Even if there are no bison, there must be game of some sort and there will be a dependable supply of water."

Red Fox sighed and kept walking. Still, it bothered him that he had seen no sign of the bison hunters, or game of any sort. The only thing that was steady on this plain was the heat and the emptiness. He had never seen such an expanse of country with absolutely no game. Even rabbits were scarce.

Bear Paw caught up with He Man, "Why you change directions?" he asked, "You find some sign that I missed?"

He Man smiled to himself. *Thank you, stupid one!* "You mean that you did not see where the bison hunters camped? The sign was clear as day to me. Why they even left a message. They travel south."

"Where did you see that?" asked Bear Paw.

"Back there!" He Man tossed his head back to the way they had come, "I would take you back and show you, perhaps ever give you a lesson on tracking, but I don't want to lose any more time. With those lazy women slowing us down, Hunting Badger's hunters will have killed all the bison before we get there. I would rather increase our speed."

"Leave the women behind!" Bear Paw declared, "What do we need with them any way? They will catch up eventually."

"You forget; if we leave them behind, we have no shelters or food and water, or do we pull the travois ourselves?"

"I had forgotten that. Once Grasshopper and Jumping Frog catch up, you can punish them by requiring they pull the travois. Left Hand can pull as well. He is getting altogether too big an idea of his own worth. Then we can leave the women behind."

"Why do you want to leave them behind so bad?" He Man stopped, "Is there something you know that I do not?"

Bear Paw shrugged, "Nothing I know, just a feeling. I don't think that Jumping Frog and Grasshopper are out there together. I think something happened to them. I don't think we will ever see either one of them again."

"You think they are dead?" He Man studied the other man, "You think the women had something to do with their disappearance?"

Bear Paw hesitated, "I can't prove anything," he admitted. "It is just a thought. I don't think that Jumping Frog went off with the boy; that is all."

"Maybe the wolves attacked him."

"Not so close to the camp, the women would have heard something. We would have probably heard something. Besides, there would have been blood or something."

"Well it makes little difference now," He Man shrugged and started walking again. "If they are dead, then there is nothing we can do about it. But I plan to sleep with my eyes open. I agree the women are acting strange. They are altogether too agreeable all of a sudden. They are up to something."

Bear Paw dropped back to walk with Red Fox, Left Hand and Laughing Antelope. "What did you find out?" asked Red Fox.

"He Man found signs of the bison hunters. That is why we turn south."

"And Jumping Frog? Has he any idea what happened to him?"

"He thinks that Frog is out enjoying himself on the boy."

Red Fox snorted, "I tell you, Jumping Frog is dead! I just know it. And those women had something to do with it. He went back to the camp to mount his woman. It is strange that he changed his mind and beat her instead. They said he headed back to our camp, but if he did, he never made it. And those women have been up to something. You can tell it by the way they act."

"He Man doesn't think so. He is our leader. He has found signs of the bison hunters. I do not care about the women. I don't care about Jumping Frog either. He was stupid! We are better of without him. And if that sniveling boy Grasshopper has come to a bad end, it serves him right. He had far too great an idea of his own worth," Bear Paw replied. He looked Left Hand directly in the eye as he said this.

*　　*　　*

"They sense that something is wrong," whispered Laughing Water.

"What can they know?" Fire Weed snorted. "They did not even notice that the stew tasted different than the night before."

"Well, we did put a portion of the possum in the stew and the tubers could have been responsible for the difference. They ate it. But you are right. From now on they only get the possum. We will eat the 'other' meat as we travel. That will keep up our strength, for they are not likely to give us a fair share of 'their' kill," she grinned. "But we will certainly eat as much of it as we are able. Be sure that you continue to watch how they track and pay attention to the tacks. We must learn what we can by watching them."

"You are sure that this is the right thing to do?" Laughing Water questioned, "I can't believe that you think we can actually return to the mountains without them."

"Would you rather starve to death?"

"No, but still... to make food of our own mates, it doesn't seem right..."

"Does it seem right the way that Bear Paw beat Feather Robe to death?"

"You are right! I thank you for reminding me," Laughing Water smiled. "Here, have some meat. It will give you strength." She handed Fire Weed a piece of dried meat from her waist pouch. The women smiled at each other and began to eat.

That evening, a good hand of time before dark settled in Left Hand caught sight of movement just beyond the camp. He smiled to himself. Looking around the camp, making sure that no one followed him, he slipped away. He was right! A short distance from the camp he found the trail of a deer. *I will show them who is man enough to be considered a hunter! They will not again tell Left Hand to keep his mouth shut!* He trotted along the deer's trail. It led down into a slight wash, which in turn deepened and soon he found himself in a brushy gully. The deer trail was wide and clear now. *Those clever hunters!* He congratulated himself. *They did not notice this place. But Left Hand did. And there are deer here. Just look at all of the tracks! They will all be impressed when I bring in a deer all by myself!* He did not notice that the shadows were lengthening, nor that he had traveled a long way from the camp. Finally he came to a small opening.

Left Hand crouched. Just beyond him was a tiny pool of water, dug from the sand by sharp hoofs. And drinking from it was a big buck. He slowly withdrew his dart and hooked it onto the atlatl. With one quick sure cast he darted the deer.

The buck leaped, snorted and circled in confusion; the dart protruding from his side. Slowly blood began to drip from the wound. Left Hand quietly readied another dart. This one he drove into the throat. Still, the buck did not see him. He waited. The wounded animal circled again, now blood was coming from his throat as well. Soon he went down onto his knees. Now the young hunter made his move. Left Hand leaped forward with the dexterity of youth. He grabbed the deer by the antlers and quickly slit its throat.

The last shafts of day silently faded away. Left Hand gathered brush and kindled a small fire. He opened the body cavity of the deer and removed the heart and liver. *No way to make it back to the camp tonight. I'll catch up tomorrow. Right now I'm hungry.* He ran a stick through the organ meat and propped it over the fire to cook. Then he scooped more sand from the water hole and filled his water bladder. He cut the stomach free and turned it inside out. Washing it with the water from his bladder, he then reversed it and tied off the bottom with a thong. Then he filled it and his other water bladder with fresh water. These he hung from a nearby branch. He added more fuel to his fire.

When the meat was more or less cooked, he scarfed it down. Then he added wood to his fire. Soon he had the deer hanging from the tree sheltering the pool. Beyond, eyes studied his every move. Shivers crawled up his spine. Left Hand added more wood to his fire and then he started several more fires. Soon he had the entire area around the deer carcass encircled with them. All night he dosed, the jerked awake and tended his fires.

Morning found him alone in his glade. *Better to be safe than sorry!* He justified his actions, but still felt foolish that he had let the dark frighten him. He dressed the deer and made a travois from the hide and a pair of branches. Then he quartered the deer and loaded it aboard. He dragged the entire contraption up out of the draw and began following it back toward the camp. He followed it for hands of time. By high sun, Left Hand admitted that he was lost. He studied the sun, then with a nod turned and began pulling his travois in another direction. That night he cooked more of the meat, ate well and kept the fires burning. The next day again he set out, but during the days the insects had gotten to the meat and so had the heat. The meat was beginning to spoil. He looked about, but found nothing with which to build a drying rack. There was barely enough scattered brush to keep his fire going. Again, eyes watched. He dosed, jerked awake, fed the fire and dosed again. By morning he had emptied his water bladder. He shrugged and tossed it onto the travois. The meat was beginning to smell. By noon the stench was carrying a good distance.

That evening he found shelter in a small grove of trees. Here at least was enough wood to make his drying racks. He built them and then discovered that he did not need them. The putrid smell from the deer carcass was proof enough that it was no longer edible. With a grunt of disgust he kicked the travois and its contents away from him. He took the full stomach bladder and looking about the grove, selected the largest tree and climbed high into its branches.

Here he perched through the night. Below, the shadows gathered, drawn by the smell. Left hand watched, as they approached, from his perch. The big white Alpha female led them. Nearly three hands strong, they assembled. The banquet was revealed by the full moon. By morning even the hide was gone. The youth dosed toward dawn, then woke and studied his position. From the upper branches of the tree he could see quite a distance. Far enough to recognize the course of a large river, marked by a solid dark green line of trees.

*All right! Left Hand has done it! What do I need those stupid people for?* With a yelp of glee he leaped from the tree and grabbing his weapons and the deer stomach, he trotted steadily toward the river.

*      *      *

"Left Hand!" shouted Bear Paw, "Where is that boy?"

"I haven't seen him since last night," He Man replied.

"Well he must be around here somewhere! He can't have just vanished!" Bear Paw grumbled.

"Well, we aren't waiting all day for him to appear," He Man replied, "If he has been so stupid as to leave the camp and get himself lost, that is his problem. How far could he have gone since the sum came up?"

"He wasn't here last night," Red Fox said. "I thought it was funny that he missed food, but I haven't seen him since we camped yesterday. You want me to circle around and see if I can pick up his trail?"

"You can if you want to, but we aren't waiting for him either way," He Man replied.

"You mean to just leave here without him?" Bear Paw questioned.

"You go search for him yourself if you want to," He Man replied, "But I have better things to do that search for a stupid youth who thinks he knows more than seasoned hunters."

"I have found his trail!" shouted Red Fox, "You are right; he left the camp last night."

He Man shrugged, "He is food then," He looked around at the assembled people. "Let's go!" he led the way again south.

Bear Paw stood alone in the empty camp, watching the people move away. He looked toward where Red Fox has found the trail. Then he also shrugged and hurried to catch up with the camp.

# CHAPTER 18

We will set up the camp here!" He Man directed.

Quietly and with excellent organization, the women began gathering their travois together. They soon had the shelters erected and watched as the hunters grabbed their sleeping furs and took possession. At least it had not rained. The women were getting used to sleeping out in the open. Fire Weed gathered stones to create the hearth circle. Laughing Water and Dancing Willow gathered wood, while Dancing Moth and Wildflower and Sunbeam laid out the sleeping robes and then began searching for tubers, grubs and anything else to add to the stew pot. They had a hand of lizards, stunned with rocks, as they walked and a single rabbit that Fire Weed had brought down with her rabbit stick. The possum meat was gone. As they had traveled, the women and girls had nibbled on the meat they had. The men ate the possum stew, begrudging every bit to the women. They ate their share any way.

"It is time to spend a day here. I and Bear Paw are going out to hunt," He Man announced the next morning, "I need new moccasins! You might as well make all of us new ones," he gathered up his darts and atlatl and left the camp.

Red Fox glanced at Laughing Antelope, "I don't intend to spend the day here in this camp!" he also gathered up his weapons, "Are you coming?"

Laughing Antelope shook his head, "I might go later," he yawned. "But for now I'm going to rest my feet. Besides, I got holes in the soles of my shoes."

Red Fox shrugged and trotted from the camp. He had not gone far when he saw a slight movement just at the top of the rise, smiling he picked up his pace...

He Man and Bear Paw picked up the trace of a dry river bed. They followed it until mid day. They found nothing! Disgusted He Man squatted beneath the branches of a nearly dead tree. "We have gone all this way and have found no sign of game. I have not even found a track, have you?"

"Nothing beyond this rabbit," Bear Paw lifted the carcass dangling from his waist thong. "And I think we should eat it. There is enough wood here to make a fire and I am hungry."

"Agreed," He Man licked his lips; half a rabbit was better than nothing. "While it is cooking, I'll see if I can get another. There should be rabbits around here for there is grass for them to eat." He trotted quietly a short distance on down the course. "Hay! Come here!" He shouted. "There are signs of a camp here. I think we have found the trail of the bison hunters!"

Bear Paw hesitated then resumed his skewering of the rabbit. The tracks weren't going anywhere, "I will look once I have our meal cooking," he called. "Right now, eating is more important."

He Man grunted and trotted a short distance farther. A squeal and thrashing in the brush brought him about. As the pig burst into the open he darted it. The second one made it a short distance farther. With a whoop He Man raced to his kill. This was the largest game they had found since leaving the Valley of the Gathering. It was truly a time to celebrate.

Bear Paw heard the trilling shout of victory. He smiled and licked his lips. This rabbit was all his! When He Man trotted into view loaded down with a pair of pigs, he leaped up and hurried to take one of them, "Man! What a find!" he grinned.

"We might as well stay here the night," He Man stated, "It would be a shame to have this meat spoil in the heat. There is no way that it would still be good by tomorrow night."

"Why not head back right after we eat?" Bear Paw asked. "We could be back at the camp well before dark."

"And share this with the others?" He Man shook his head, "I don't think so. I'm so hungry that I could easily eat half a pig before tomorrow night. Besides, those cows back there will probably follow our trail in the morning. At least Red Fox and Laughing Antelope will. As you have said, we hunters need to eat to keep up our strength." Already they were gutting the pigs.

He Man skewered a hind quarter and balanced it over the fire. Bear Paw erected a crude drying rack and the pair of hunters began stripping the meat from the carcasses. They ate the rabbit a short time later; for it was cooked long before the pig. They were hungry. As soon as the pig meat was seared on the outside, they had stripped the done portions from the quarter. They added another ham when they realized that well before dark, this one would be consumed. So they sat around under the dying tree, swatting insects away from the drying meat, stuffing yet another piece of the partially cooked meat into their mouths and belching with satisfaction.

"This is the fullest I have felt since I don't remember when," Bear Paw rubbed his stomach. "I had forgotten how good it feels to eat until it hurts! Maybe our luck is changing. You say you found the trail of the bison hunters?"

"They crossed here, but they are headed south now. I think we are much closer. By cutting south when we did, we probably lessened the time to catch up with them considerably. I did the right thing by changing our course. Already we have found food. You will see, things will improve, from now on."

He belched again. "It is a shame to waste more time going back for the rest of the camp. We should push on and catch up with the bison hunters. We can always come back for our followers."

"I suppose," Bear Paw said half -heartedly, "But we are not equipped for a long time on the trail. We have only the water flasks attached to our waist thong and only a handful of darts. We don't even have sleeping furs."

"You are right," He Man considered his words. "It would be uncomfortable to run out of water. The stomachs of these pigs won't hold a lot. I think we must go back for the others, but not right now. The bison hunters won't get that much farther ahead and even if they do, the trail is easy to follow. One more day, or two, won't make that much difference. Hand me another piece of pig, will you."

"Besides, we have started drying this meat. We can't just leave it. Tell you what. I'll go back for the others tonight and bring them in tomorrow. By then the meat will be dry and we can get underway. If I leave right now, I can be there long before dark."

"I will wait here for you," replied He Man. "That is a good plan. I was about to suggest it myself."

Bear Paw did not loiter. He grabbed up his atlatl and darts and began following their trail back to the camp. He had no desire to be caught alone at night on the open plain, so he kept to a ground-eating trot. He arrived well before dark. Laughing Antelope was lounging in his shelter eating a bowl of watery stew. Bear Paw did not even bother feeling guilty about his own full stomach. Tomorrow Laughing Antelope would get his fill.

"Where is Red Fox?" he glanced around the camp.

"Went out right after you did, this morning; haven't seen him since." replied Laughing Antelope.

"Which way did he go?" Bear Paw glanced around, "We should go after him, it's getting dark soon. Out there is no place to be along after dark," he remembered Left Hand.

"Oh, all right!" sighed the lazy hunter. "I just thought that for one day, at least, I wouldn't have to walk."

"I'll go without you, if you prefer," Bear Paw sneered.

"I said I'll go," Laughing Antelope got up and stretched. He gathered his atlatl and darts and followed Bear Paw from the camp. The women watched them go silently.

"Do you think..." Dancing Moth questioned.

"I would say so," Fire Weed answered. "Or he would have been back long ago. He took no food or water with him."

"Perhaps we should have told them about Grasshopper," suggested Laughing Water. "I would not wish that sort of end for Red Fox, even though I detested him. After all he was my mate and he did father Wildflower."

"Well we will see when they come back," replied Dancing Willow. "In the mean time, we might as well fix a decent meal. I for one have no stomach for that stew. I'll start the water heating. The rest of you dig out some of that meat and get it to warming. I want to try these plants we collected at the last stop; they are ready to make tea."

Bear Paw and Laughing Water followed Red Fox's trail. They found where he picked up his pace. Over the ridge they went, then over another and another and another. Then they found his atlatl and darts, dumped in the trail. There were a few scuff marks, as though he was digging in his heels, then a trail. It wasn't a long trail. There was a wide area where blood and gore were splashed onto the grass; areas of bloody earth; parts of his clothing and tracks and lots and lots of tracks.

"Wow! There must be nearly a double hand of them!" Bear Paw squatted, examining the tracks. "Must be the same wolves that got Grasshopper, Left Hand and Jumping Frog as well. Certainly explains what happened to them. Come on let's get out of here! This place gives me the creeps!"

Just them the eerie wail of a wolf rose on the evening air. Both hunters glanced around then bolted back down the path toward the camp. "Red Fox was taken by wolves!" Bear Paw told the women as they burst into the camp. Laughing Water merely nodded. The women were settled in their sleeping robes and they had eaten the remainder of the stew. Laughing Antelope grumbled and went to his furs hungry. At dawn the camp headed toward where He Man waited. The wolves followed.

They arrived well before mid day. He Man had most of the meat dried and there were smiles all around as the women quickly stored it on the travois. Laughing Antelope grabbed a fist full and glared at the women. He found a place to sit and quickly stuffed the meat into his mouth.

"Where is Red Fox?" He Man looked about.

"Wolves," replied Bear Paw.

"Well we have wasted enough time," He Man stated, "I and Bear Paw will go on ahead and find the bison hunters. Laughing Antelope, you can bring the women along our trail."

"Why me?"

"Cause I said, you," replied He Man.

"Oh."

The pair of hunters picked up their weapons and the back packs with supplies which He Man had ordered the women to prepare. Then they left the camp. Slowly the women began to repack the travois. "Hurry up!" Demanded Laughing Antelope. "We have to move fast to keep up with the others."

"No need to keep up," replied Fire Weed, "You aren't going any where."

"What do you mean?" the hunter glanced around uneasily. He did not see her strike. But it gave Laughing Water lots of pleasure to bring the big rock down on his head. He felt a blinding pain, then nothing.

"I was wrong," later explained Fire Weed, "He is going with us."

"Yes, at least some of him in each of our travois and some of him in our stomachs," Dancing Moth smiled. "I will always remember how he bashed the brains of my baby against that tree. I will enjoy every bite of him!"

"That still leaves a pair of the men to go," reminded Fire Weed. "And they are the most dangerous."

"Can't we just vanish and leave them here?" asked Dancing Willow.

"They are far too dangerous," replied Fire Weed. "What we need is a plan. We can't take them both out at the same time. They are far too strong for that. At least one of us would surely get hurt if not killed."

"What about while they are asleep?"

"That might work," all the women nodded in agreement. Already they had most of the flesh stripped from the carcass and loaded onto drying racks in the blazing sun. The strips of meat were very thin, so that they would dry quickly. They did not have a lot of time to lose if they were to catch up with the other hunters. By evening they were ready. The bones were left for the predators they were certain followed. They discarded everything which was not essential, keeping one a pair of shelters and food and water. Even the sleeping furs were discarded but one each. This made the travois loads considerably lighter. They moved very fast down the trail left by He Man and Bear Paw. Somewhere in their load were packed the weapons of Jumping Frog and Laughing Antelope.

\*      \*      \*

He Man and Bear Paw ambled along, following the trail leading south. The tracks were not particularly fresh, probably over a hand of days old. And they did not number as many as they should. By close observation, they figured only about three hands of men were in this group. Bear Paw questioned that they were the bison hunters at all.

"We got nothing to lose!" reminded He Man. "Maybe they split up! Any way I am sure that Wanderer isn't with this group. He has a turned-out left foot. There are no such tracks among these."

"Well they camped here. See!" exclaimed Bear Paw, "I'll bet we are close. I think that tonight I will find a high place and see if I can spot their fires."

"Won't get us to them any faster," pointed out He Man.

"I suppose not. Wonder when Laughing Antelope and the women will catch up. I would have thought they would be here by now."

"You know how those lazy women drag their feet!" He Man snorted. "It will be dark before they catch up. That is why we have backpacks. They might not get here until morning."

Actually the women were still at the last camp, preparing to follow. And Wildflower, true to her name, had discovered something special....

"Hey Mother!" she shouted, "Look over there!" She pointed to a scrubby bush growing on the plain. It was oddly enough, covered with vines, "Isn't that morning glory?"

"You are a clever girl!" Laughing Water hugged her, "Fire Weed, we have just what we need. Look!"

They all crowded around the bush. "Quickly, everyone, get a container, your bowls will do. Gather as many of the seed as you can. Be careful not to lose any. This is a valuable find."

"What are you going to do with just seeds?" asked Sunbeam.

"They aren't just seeds," explained Dancing Willow. "They are the ingredient for a powerful sleeping drink. They are women's medicine."

"What we going to do with them?" the child wanted to know.

"We will make a special tea for the evening meal. I might even share some of it with the men. After all, they will be tired too," she smiled.

"But if it is women' medicine, should the hunters drink it? Won't it hurt them?"

"Only a little," replied Fire Weed, "So we must keep it a secret from them."

"I like secrets!" Sunbeam smiled happily. "Will it be a secret like Jumping Frog?"

Fire Weed nodded, "Very much like Jumping Frog," she agreed.

"Can I help put the meat on the drying rack?"

"Yes, you certainly can," Dancing Willow smiled down at her daughter.

*    *    *

He Man and Bear Paw camped in the middle of the trail. They put their shelter where it could be easily found. Red Fox wasn't the best of trackers, although they had left a trail that a child could follow. "They should have caught up by now," grumbled Bear Paw. "I am out of water."

"You should have been more saving with it," reminded He Man. "Go to sleep. They will be here by morning. But we aren't going to wait on them to rest. It is their own fault if they get no sleep this night. I will not be soft with them."

So, the hunters crawled into their sleeping furs and waited, but neither of them slept.

The moon rose, round and full, but still no women. "Where can they be?" Bear Paw glanced nervously back down the trail, "I am getting thirsty!"

"Well we aren't waiting for them!" grumbled He Man. But they did.

It was very late, when the women arrived. Already the moon was beginning to set. They quietly set about making the camp, only setting up a single hearth. Stew was soon bubbling in a skin and another contained a small amount of water for tea. When it was ready, Fire Weed passed out the stew, filling the bowls only about half way. There was little meat for stew. It contained a welter of tubers and grubs they had collected while they moved along. But when it was ready, He Man and Bear Paw were suddenly awake and demanding food. Fire Weed smiled softly as she handed her mate a hot bowl of tea.

"Where did you get this?" He asked suspiciously.

"Along the path," she replied, "You didn't see the Brittle Brush bushes?"

"Didn't waste time looking at plants," he snorted grabbing the bowl and downing the liquid. "Get me more," he shoved the bowl at her. "That was barely enough to wet my throat."

"Of course." Fire Weed went to the hearth and filled the bowl again.

"Bring me some tea as well!" demanded Bear Paw, "I am thirsty."

Fire Weed merely nodded and reached for another bowl. Between them, the men drained the entire supply of tea, as usual, leaving nothing for the women. They merely smiled and settled down around the hearth and slowly ate the weak stew.

Fire Weed looked at the other women and nodded. He Man was twitching and groaning, obviously on some kind of spirit journey. Laughing Water picked up a large stone from the hearth ring and Fire Weed hefted another. They went to where He Man slept. A soft squishing thud and a scrambling of feet kicking, then the smell of released urine and fecal matter told them that He Man had abused his last woman and given his final order. "I hope it was a good journey," said Fire Weed, "Seeing that it was his last."

She returned to the fire and grimaced as she noticed the blood and brain splattered on her tunic. Then she shrugged. Already Dancing Willow and Dancing Moth were closing in on Bear Paw. Soon he also was journeying to the fires in the sky.

"I will get a meal started," Laughing Water called out as she dug into the travois. "We have much work to complete this night."

Fire Weed and Dancing Willow were already processing the 'meat' for drying. "Do you think we should dry that which we brought from the last camp some more?" asked Wildflower, "We really did not dry it as well as usual."

"That would be a good idea," agreed Fire Weed. "I think it would be best if we move the camp back to the grove of trees tomorrow. So don't worry too much about things tonight. We will do what we are able. I don't like camping out in the open like this when it is not necessary. After all we are a camp of only women."

They all smiled at each other. They were bone tired, a lot of hard work faced them and there would be little sleep this night. But no one complained. Soon Laughing Water had a skin of stew bubbling. Expertly she dropped hot stones into the hide to bring the food to cooking temperature. As each stone cooled, she fished it out with a 'dipper' and returned it to the hearth to heat once again. After a hand of time the food was fragrant and done. It was a rich meaty stew, with tubers and other edible plants as well. When it was ready, everyone stopped their work and settled around the hearth to enjoy the meal.

Already there was a sizable heap of raw meat lying on a shelter hide. In the dirt beside it the bones were beginning to accumulate. They finished eating. "While we finish the butchering, why don't you go through their packs, Laughing Water and throw out anything we don't need. Keep a record in you mind of what you save. There is no sense in carrying anything we don't need."

Laughing Water nodded, so while Fire Weed and Dancing Willow completed the processing, she and Dancing Moth set about exploring the contents of the hunters' packs. "Will you look at this?" she exclaimed. "No wonder they weren't interested in our watery stew. This pack is crammed full of meat. I'll bet they had no plans for sharing it with us!" She dumped the contents onto a robe, grabbing at the artifacts that tumbled out. "Ah! They killed a pair of pigs! See, here are the tusks," she held up the souvenirs.

Dancing Moth dumped the contents of the other pack out as well. "Here is the rest of those pigs!" she exclaimed. "As well as our missing water bladders. That miserable hunter stole them from our supplies while we were working."

Fire Weed merely nodded.

Within a pair of hands of time they were finished. The travois were neatly repacked and they were headed back to the grove of willows through which they had recently passed. The observant women saw what the men had missed. Willow trees meant water. It was not yet dawn when they set up a quick camp and while Fire Weed watched, the rest slept. Later she woke Laughing Willow and crawled into her furs. Laughing Willow yawned, added wood to the fire and sat, thinking...

In due time she woke Dancing Willow and she watched the sun turn night into day.

They stayed at the willow grove for a hand of days. The meat was spread over the drying racks in thin strips. They took turns keeping insects and small thieves from the meat. Meanwhile, Laughing Water had drawn the outline of a deer on a sleeping robe they planned to discard. They stretched it between two trees and took turns casting darts with the atlatl.

"This is harder than it looks!" exclaimed Dancing Moth. "I have not hit the deer yet!"

"You would have more success if you didn't close your eyes when you throw," suggested Sunbeam.

"And now that you have hit the target, you are an expert?" tossed back Dancing Moth.

"We all need practice," admitted Fire Weed.

At the base on the largest willow they had excavated a hole as deep as Fire Weed's shoulders. In the bottom however waited a ready supply of water. They drank deeply and often, they had tea made from the plants gathered nearby. They even reaped a small container of grain and beat it on a flat stone with the blunt end of a stick. When it was well cracked, they mixed it with salt, seasoning and water and cooked the cakes on hot stones at the verge of the hearth. Wildflower and Sunbeam stripped bark from the willow and placed it in bladders.

"See these footprints," Fire Weed pointed. "There has been a group of people through here. This is probably what He Man was following. See; the trail leads south. The people who made it are probably headed toward the river that we followed to the valley of the Gathering. I think it would be a good idea if we followed these tracks, at least so long as they are headed toward the river. There will be water there and probably animals that we can hunt as well. Since I am now 'headman' of this camp, I guess it is my decision to make," she grinned at the women squatted around her.

"Do you think that the wolves will still follow us?" Dancing Willow asked, "It would do us no good if they attacked us. I would feel better if they went away."

"They follow because we have provided food for them, one way or another." Fire Weed nodded, "So, they will probably keep on following. We might have to stand guard at night or sleep in shifts so that there is always someone awake, like we did last night. I agree that our numbers are dangerously low, but that can't be helped. We will just have to be more careful."

"When do we leave this grove?" Laughing Water asked.

"We should probably leave tomorrow. We really have no reason to stay here longer. We can practice with our atlatl and darts along the way. Perhaps we will be lucky enough to reach the river before nightfall. Then we do not have to camp on the open plain. Before we go to sleep tonight be sure that all of our water bags are full and none leak. Go through things one more time and discard anything you do not have to have. Make your load as light as possible, but do not discard anything you need just to lighten the load. We need to travel fast to the river. Then we can take our time. With a steady supply of water and no one else about, we should be able to find enough to eat. But just in case, make this meat go as far as possible. Eat, but do not waste. Until we know what food there is, we must assume that what we carry is all."

Dancing Willow rose to her feet. "Come along Sunbeam, "Let's see if we can find some more off those fat grubs which burrow beneath the tree bark," she called to her daughter.

"I thought to go with Wildflower to find the last of the grass seeds down by the target." Sunbeam answered. "But we will both go with you instead. I don't like going out alone. Those wolves are probably just watching to get the chance to eat one of us!"

"Keep that thought in the front of your mind. Remember, the wolves have killed grown men, they certainly are able to kill any one of us," Dancing Moth stood, "I don't think we should do anything without the entire group doing it together. Soon those wolves are going to be hungry again. Then we will all be in danger."

"That is a very good idea," agreed Fire Weed. We will do everything together. And we will carry weapons at all times as well. There is no sense in taking chances. Now let's have a last meal and get to sleep. We will start out very early in the morning and remember, do not leave the safety of the camp even to pass water. I will take the first watch and keep the fires burning. The wolves do not like the fire." The small group busied themselves with last minute tasks and before long, each travois was neatly packed, food for morning was set aside and they had only to add their sleeping robes to the packs to be ready. Soon the camp was quiet.

Fire Weed sat beside the glowing hearth, adding occasional branches to the fire. All was quiet in the camp. Beyond the night insects chirped and sang and out on the plain, a lone wolf raised a mournful voice. Far away another answered.

*Am I doing the right thing?* She frowned into the fire. *What makes me think that I am capable of leading these people? Laughing Water is right, there are too few of us. We are in grave danger and not just from wolves and the land itself. What if men find us? What will they do to us? Where can we go that is safe? How can a hand of women and children survive the winter without men to hunt?*

"You look worried," Dancing Willow came to join Fire Weed. "You are not worried are you?"

"Of course I am worried!" Fire Weed sighed. "I wonder if we did the right thing."

"They were going to leave us behind any way," Dancing Willow reminded her. "We would have been far worse off then, for they surely would have taken all of the food and water, to say nothing of leaving us with any weapons. It is far more likely that they would simply have killed us and left our bodies for carrion. You, yourself heard them planning it."

"I know. But are we any better? We did the same thing, only they said nothing of taking us along as food."

"That just goes to show you how stupid they were. Why feed the wolves and starve yourself? We needed the supply of food. We are not yet hunters. Food is scarce any way. We could not just run away from them. They would have found us some day and then they would have killed us. At least this way we know where they are. They will never harm us again." Laughing Water sighed, "But I know what you mean. Somehow it is far scarier than I thought it would be. Funny, they abuse you, kill your youth and all your dreams, yet you still think you need them, just because it is the way you have always lived. I cannot think but that there is a better way."

"Perhaps, but is this it?" Fire Weed added another branch to the fire. "And what do we say if we come across other people."

"The men planned of leaving us. Just say that is what happened. Who is to say?" Laughing Water replied.

"Do you really think we will ever make it back to the mountains?"

"Sure, why not?" Laughing Water laughed softly. "We are as smart as those men. Look at the way they walked by a supply of water and sat in the middle of the trail waiting for us to bring them ours! We can follow a trail just as well as they can. We have been studying the animal tracks. Every one of us can recognize the animals which make the tracks."

"But can we kill an animal with the atlatl and dart? Not one of us is very good hitting the target and it stays still. What good are animal tracks if you have no way of turning them into animal food?"

"We will learn!" reassured Laughing Water. "Go to your furs. I will watch for a time and then wake Dancing Willow. Morning will make things look clearer, you will see. Besides, we have chosen our path. It is too late to change it now."

Fire Weed tossed a twig she had been worrying into the fire and rose. "You are right. Tomorrow things will look better." She walked the short distance to where she had her sleeping furs laid out. It was but a step from the hearth to anyone's sleeping place. She lay watching the ancestor fires winking in the sky. At least He Man would never reach them. There had been no prayers for his soul. No ceremony to lay him out, nor any of the other hunters they had made into meat. *It serves them right! They should never have brought us to this place!* Slowly her eyes drifted shut and she slept.

Now it was Laughing Water's turn to worry. Her words had been brave, but inside she was as frightened as a child. *What if we get lost? What if the wolves attack? What if we don't find the river, or ...* She sighed. *You only die once.* She assured herself. Later she woke Dancing Willow to take her place and retired to her furs. Still she wondered...

Dancing Willow had them up before the sun had a chance to rise above the land. They had eaten and were out of sight of the willow stand before that happened. With Fire Weed in the lead they moved rapidly along the trail, following the path of the hunters who went before them. The prints were days old, so there was little chance of their catching up with the men. Dancing Moth brought down a rabbit, Sunbeam a pair of pigeons. Then Laughing Water and Dancing Willow got a chance to try their expertise with the atlatl. An antelope leaped from the tall grass nearby. Both women cast, but the antelope was in little danger. They watched it bound from sight. Laughing Water and Dancing Willow retrieved their darts and grinned ruefully at the others.

They rested for only a short time as high sun and then pushed on again. "Look!" Willow pointed to the far horizon, "See that dark smudge? I'll bet that is the river!"

"Come on!" Fire Weed called, "Let's see!"

Everyone picked up speed and the smudge got closer and clearer and sure enough, they could all make out the trees. A long line going as far as they could see in both directions; it had to be the river!" Then the ground sloped even more steeply and they entered the breaks. Now brush and small trees blocked their way and they were slowed down.

"See if you can find a game trail," Fire Weed called out, "But stay together. Don't get separated. It would be easy to get lost here and remember that the wolves are always nearby."

"Here is a trail!" called Dancing Moth. "And it is the same one the men found, for here are their tracks." She pointed. "They went down toward the river along this trail."

"We will follow their path to the river." Fire Weed agreed.

"Look! Here is another set of foot prints and they are much more recent!" Dancing Moth squatted in the trail.

"How can you be sure?" Sunbeam squinted at the prints.

"See how the animal prints are over the top of the first bunch of footprints?" Dancing Moth pointed. "But there are none over these. That means that they were made since last night. There is at least one man out here along the river, but he is alone."

"I can see what you mean," Dancing Willow studied the tracks. "You could be right. And if there is one man, who is to say that there are not more. We must keep a sharp eye out. I will look for other tracks as we go."

"Someone made a camp here just last night," Fire Weed said. "The burned wood still holds a slight heat. It must have been the man who made those tracks. That means that he is ahead of us somewhere."

"Maybe he has gone the other way." Sunbeam stated.

"His tracks are headed the way we are going," reminded Wildflower. "That means that he is moving in the same direction, silly!"

"Well there is just one of him and more than a hand of us!" Sunbeam answered. "I'm not afraid of him!"

"What do you think we should do about this hunter?" asked Laughing Water.

"We have a choice," Fire Weed answered. "We can stay behind him, making sure that he is unaware of us, or we can catch up to him and decide if he is a danger to us."

"I would just as soon stay behind!" Sunbeam said.

"I would rather know what manner of man he is," Dancing Willow stated. "There is a chance that he is not a danger to us. But we will never know if we cower in fear. I say we follow and find this hunter. Then we can decide what to do about him!"

Dancing Moth studied the foot print. She frowned, "It is Left Hand." she stated.

"What?" Laughing Water squealed, "Are you sure?"

"I made his moccasins," Dancing Moth said. "See where the stitching is all lumpy here along the side of the print. I did that on purpose so the shoes would be uncomfortable. They should have given him blisters where that knot dug into his foot."

"But we were so sure that the wolves..."

"We never found him," reminded Fire Weed. "She could be right. And if it is Left Hand, he is a danger for certain. He will certainly question the lack of the men!"

"We decided that they left us, remember?"

"But they would not have left us food, robes, water, or weapons," reminded Fire Weed.

"Then we hunt!"

"It will be a challenge to our skills to track down Left Hand. He is a poor hunter at best. Shall we see if we are any better?" Dancing Moth rose. "I for one have no desire to fall into his hands."

A soft cheer rose as the women grinned at each other. Dancing Moth led the way, studying the foot prints. The youth was ambling along at a walk, making no attempt to cover his trail. He followed the tracks of the hunters ahead of them. It took Moth a short time to get used to looking for the moccasin prints, then she fell into a pattern and they moved swiftly along the trail. It was not necessary to see every print, just the distinctive track every so often. Just to be sure they were still following the right trail. They found where he had rested beneath a tree and passed water.

"It will be dark soon," remarked Fire Weed, "We will rest here until then. If he is nearby we should be able to see his fire."

They settled down in a tight circle, resting against the travois or the base of the tree under which they waited. Darkness fell. Still, they waited.

"Something is not right about this," whispered Laughing Water. "He should have camped by now. We should be able to at least smell his fire."

"Unless he didn't make one."

All eyes turned toward Dancing Moth. "He told me once, in bragging, how he slept in trees sometimes," she offered lamely.

"Well if he is sleeping in a tree, we are not likely to be able to sneak up on him!"

"Maybe, maybe not," Fire Weed replied, "Remember the possums?"

"You are right. He would stand out sharply against the moonlight."

"But the moon will not be up for hands of time!" reminded Sunbeam, "And then we will have to wait until it is going down to be able to see him. That could take all night!"

"We could set a trap for him." Dancing Willow suggested.

"What do you have in mind?" Fire Weed asked.

"We planned on sneaking up on his camp. Let him sneak up on ours instead. I know Left Hand. If he smells a fire, or sees it, he will come to investigate."

"You mean just let him walk into our camp?" Sunbeam squealed.

"Sure, why not! There is just one of him. He will have no fear of us! He is too used to ordering us around. It is far more likely that he will demand food," Dancing Moth snorted. "We need only offer him a share of our special tea and wait!"

"Only we haven't any left," Fire Weed reminded her. "We gave it all to He Man and Bear Paw."

"Well he can't stay awake forever!" Dancing Willow said. "Hide the weapons. Let him think he can order us around. Don't let him get suspicious. Our time will come. The first time he goes to sleep will be his last!"

"I can't believe that the wolves didn't get him!" Laughing Water mused. "He is smarter than I thought. Such a simple plan might not work."

"He is no thinker! I assure you," Fire Weed said. "Laughing Water, start a hearth and Dancing Moth, strip down to your apron. Then sit by the fire."

"What!"

"You heard me. The way that youth has been watching you ever since the Gathering, it will be like a bee going to honey."

"But...!"

"We will all be here! What can he do, rape you in front of us?"

"Well... if you are sure...." Slowly Dancing Moth began to remove her tunic.

Laughing Water started the hearth and soon there was a savory smell of food cooking. Dancing Moth sat by the fire, keeping watch that the food did not burn. The rest lounged around the hearth and they waited.

"Do you hear that?" Sunbeam whispered to Wildflower.

"Yes!" She replied, "Something is moving about in the brush behind us. Do you think it is him?"

"I hope so. I would rather it were Left Hand, than wolves." Wildflower answered.

Soon the rustling stopped. The women waited: but not for long.

"Hello, the camp!" a voice called from the darkness.

All heads turned.

"Who goes there?" called Fire Weed.

"It is I, Left Hand," he stepped into view. He glanced about the camp. "Where are all the hunters?"

"They left us," Fire Weed stated. "What happened to you? We thought the wolves ate you."

"Nah! I'm smarter than that!" the youth bragged. "You got any food left?" He licked his lips, watching Dancing Moth. She rose and filled a bowl with stew from the pot and handed it to him. He came into the camp and found a place to sit.

"So how did you get here?" he asked, "A bunch of dumb women!"

"We just kept walking," Dancing Moth shrugged, watching him eye her bare breasts, as he licked his lips in anticipation. "We thought we were following the tracks of the men, but I don't think so. There were too many moccasin prints."

Left Hand grunted, "Of course there were!" he shifted to a comfortable position against the tree. "There are at least three hands of men in the group. I plan on catching up with them myself, perhaps joining them, perhaps not. I might take this camp on my own way, instead though; now that I am Headman."

Fire Weed raised an eyebrow at Dancing Willow. "The next thing you know he will be demanding one of us spread herself for him," she whispered. "We had better be careful. He is sneakier than I thought. I was sure the wolves got him!"

"You! Women! What are you whispering about?" He glared at Fire Weed suspiciously.

"Nothing more than discussing our surprise at seeing you again." She replied evenly. "Here, my Son, let me refill your bowl." She came with a dipper of stew and dumped it into his nearly-empty, bowl. Then she retired to her former position on the other side of the hearth. Sunbeam and Wildflower sat beside her. Wildflower whispered something to Sunbeam and handed her a packet, which she in turn, handed to Fire Weed.

"What is this?" murmured Fire Weed.

Sunbeam merely smiled sweetly as she winked at the woman beside her. Fire Weed unobtrusively opened the packet within the folds of her tunic and let her fingers investigate the contents. She smiled and reached for a water bladder. She poured some into a large tortoise shell and added a hot stone from the hearth. As it cooled, she removed it and added another, which brought the water to steaming. Then she added a pinch of herbs and the contents of the packet to a stone and with another ground them into a fine powder. These she dumped into the hot water. A fragrant odor wafted from the bowl.

"What is that?" Left Hand sniffed.

"Just some tea," Fire Weed answered. "Nothing special."

"Give it to me!" he demanded.

"I will make some for you, if you wish," Fire Weed answered, "But this is for Dancing Moth."

"Make her more! Give that to me!" he demanded.

Fire Weed glared at him, but grudgingly told Sunbeam to take the bowl to him. Meanwhile she dug out another bowl and made more tea, this time without the 'special' additive. Left Hand greedily slurped down the tea and wiped his mouth with the back of his sleeve. Then he tossed the bowl down and turned to Dancing Moth. "Take yourself to the shelter!" he ordered, "I have a man's need."

Dancing Moth gave a frightened glance to Fire Weed who nodded slightly. Slowly the girl rose and, Sunbeam ran to meet her with the bowl of tea. "This one is for you," Sunbeam said, "The other was 'special'" she added in a whisper. Dancing Moth glanced quickly at Fire Weed who again nodded slightly. The girl smiled and sauntered slowly to the only shelter. There she lifted her hair behind her shoulders, making sure the watching youth saw the rise of her firm young breasts.

"More tea?" asked Fire Weed, Offering another bowl to Left Hand. He grunted, squinting slightly and took the bowl. It was very hot, so he had to sip it. Fire Weed watched his eyes and was relieved to see them dilate. She wanted to make sure he did not go to the shelter too soon. By the time he finished the tea he was weaving drunkenly toward the shelter and as soon as he reached it she heard his stagger, fall and mumble. He pawed Dancing Moth for a few breaths and then became limp.

Dancing Moth shoved his groping hand off her breast and crawled from the shelter. "Quickly, before he wakes up!" she called.

"He won't wake up," assured Fire Weed. Not now, not ever! We must weep and rend our clothes, for our young 'Headman' has just come to a tragic end." She brought a large rock down on his head. A squishing noise and the now familiar odors of urine and fecal release wafted on the air.

"Now we are truly free," she rose.

"This accounts for every single one of them," Dancing Willow smiled. I'll set up the drying racks." She rose and methodically began assembling the rack. Meanwhile Fire Weed and Laughing Water dragged the limp carcass from the shelter and stripped off his tunic. This they tossed onto the fire. His weapons and tools were stored aboard the travois and the pack he had set down upon entering the camp was emptied onto a sleeping robe.

"Look here!" exclaimed Laughing Water, "My missing blade! And here is your awl," she tossed an object toward Fire Weed." What a little thief! Look at all the things he has hidden in this pack. He has been stealing from everyone for seasons!" She lifted a leather bag, "Here are those blanks which He Man beat you for losing!" She handed them to Fire Weed.

"And My obsidian Mirror!" Dancing Moth squealed. "I thought it was stolen at the Gathering!"

"So it was," replied Fire Weed. "He even has Sunbeam's missing doll." She lifted a rabbit skin shaped like a human figure. "Probably just took it for spite." She handed the doll to Sunbeam, who smiled, a little embarrassed that a 'nearly a woman' still played with dolls.

"It was a gift," she explained, blushing, as she tucked the doll quickly into hr sleeping fur.

Fire Weed and Laughing Water returned to their task, blades flashing in the firelight. Before they retired to their furs, the drying racks were loaded and the bones broken and tossed into the stew pot. Dancing Moth took Left Hand's head and drove a sharp branch up into the neck hole, then she jabbed the other end into the dirt in the middle of the trail. There she left it. "Now see how you like watching me!"

They stayed at the camp the next day, drying the meat. Then they were ready to move out. Fire Weed Led the way and they followed the river westward. As they traveled, they became more proficient with the atlatl and dart. Before long they were able to hit the target regularly. One day Laughing Water brought down a pig. A few days later, Dancing Moth killed a deer. Before cold weather arrived they had reached the mountains and found a snug cave to spend the winter. They went out and gathered provisions, killed deer and elk and when the snow fell, they were ready for winter. Then one day, not long after that, a pair of hunters came into their valley and moved in the cave with them.

# CHAPTER 19

The wind whistled through the trees, whipping their branches back and forth. The rising moon cast grotesque shadows across the faces of the somber men, hunched closely about the hearth. The remainder of the band slept. As branches creaked and moaned, the elders discussed their most pressing trouble.

"What are we going to do about it?" Questioned Beaded Lizard.

"I have made my recommendation!" Green Parrot retorted. "Are we men, or a bunch of whining women? He has covered the land with blood! When it was the blood of strangers, I did not agree with the practice, but when he sacrificed my Humming Bird, he crossed the line! When Shaking Earth spoke out against him, he was the next sacrifice! What are we going to do, wait for him to find fault with each and every one of us? Do we go to the alter as quietly as Shaking Earth? I say he must be stopped and the sooner the better!"

"Fine!" Iguana countered, "But how?"

"Kill him!" Beaded Lizard cut in, "He would not hesitate to kill any one of us!"

"But how?"

"He is only a man! We are more than a hand of men. He sits up there," He pointed to the ridge, "Communicating with his bloody spirits! I say send him to them! Right now! Get your war clubs and follow me! I am not afraid of Quinquel, or of his spirits! If you are not men, then I will go after him by myself." He rose and stalked to the shelter where his mate and children slept. Bending over he picked up his war club and turned to face the elders. "Are you with me?" he cried.

"I'm with you!" Green Parrot rose and called to Walking Man, "Come on, I agree, this has gone on long enough! Beaded Lizard is right. Now is the time to strike, when the dreamer is in a trance."

"What if he 'sees' us coming? Quinquel has powerful spirits. They could strike us dead where we stand."

"I haven't seen any sign of that," Iguana snorted! "For all that he has commanded us, has said his spirits call, I personally, have never seen him do anything which even would indicate that he truly is a dreamer. Remember back! When we were living in the southern valley Quenquel was a tracker! What proof did he offer that day when he walked into the camp and proclaimed himself Dreamer? We were fools! Blindly we took his word for it and just stepped aside and let him lead us down this bloody path. I have nightmares when I sleep! The angry spirits of all those which we have sacrificed to Quenquel's alter rise up and demand justice."

Indignant agreement came from all around the council hearth. "Are you with me?" Beaded Lizard pointed toward the path leading to the summit. "The 'Great Dreamer' awaits! I for one will not disappoint him! Death to Quenquel!" he shouted.

"We are with you!" Green Parrot lifted his war club and Whistling Elk did likewise. Within a few heartbeats, the wind blew past an empty hearth. Shadows flickered in and out along the trail, as the men made their way to the summit.

Green Parrot was in the lead. His blood pounded in his ears and his breath came in hurried jerks. Then the moon passed from behind a cloud and he found himself standing before the dreamer.

Quenquel sat very still. He was naked but for the white breech cloth he wore when he communed with his spirits. He sat with his legs crossed and his eyes closed, so still his beautiful face could have been frozen in ice.

Green Parrot stopped so abruptly that Beaded Lizard ran into him. They stared at the hated dreamer for a full heartbeat, before, with a blood curdling war cry, Green Parrot brought his war club down against the dreamer. Beaded Lizard was not to be left out. His club struck the dreamer on the right arm. It broke with a resounding 'crack!' Already the still body had begun to collapse. The entire right side sagged and without a sound the great Quenquel lay crumpled upon the ground. Iguana kicked the limp body several times and grunted, in frustration. It was too easy!

"He is finished!" He waved his club in the air. "We have vanquished the rot from our midst. Come on; let's get out of here!

"It's time to celebrate!" Yelled Beaded Lizard. "Wake the women and children. We will greet the new day with prayers and offerings to the old spirits!

As quickly as they came, the men left the summit.

"I have a skin of beer." Whistling Elk stated. "Has anyone else something to bring to a celebration?"

Several of the others grumbled or offered to contribute something. By the time they had finished waking everyone up and throwing more wood on the hearth fires the entire camp was alight with a golden glow. Beaded Lizard began to dance around the central hearth and sing the saga for the celebration. "The Evil One is dead!" He pranced, yelped and then turned around, "Green Parrot struck the first blow!" Again he yelped. Now Green Parrot joined in.

"Beaded Lizard struck down The Evil One!" He yelped, "He led the hunters, brave!"

Soon the entire council was dancing and telling their part of the story. The women and children watched wide-eyed. It had been a long time since they had heard the 'old chants'. Quenquel had forbid these. Fermented beer flowed freely among the men. Finally, near dawn, Iguana shouted, "One last offering!" he staggered and nearly fell, regained his footing and swung his bladder in the air. "Let us color the bloody alter one last time! I say we give the spirits of Quenquel something special."

Beaded Lizard whooped, "I say we offer them the heart of Quenquel!"

"But he is already dead!" reminded Whistling Elk.

"You sure?" Iguana asked, "Did anyone really check?"

The silent hunters all shook their heads.

"We had better make sure!" Beaded Lizard slurred, "I will go back and bring him down, but I can't do it alone. Whistling Elk, will you come with me?"

"I will," answered the equally drunk Whistling Elk.

They staggered from the camp and wobbled and stumbled up the trail, running into branches and nearly falling backwards. But finally, breathing heavily, they reached the top of the trail and lurched onto the flat rock. Beaded Lizard blinked, "Where is he?" he looked stupidly about. "We left him right here. Didn't we?"

"Right here!" agreed Whistling Elk, "Got to be here somewhere." He glanced fearfully around. "Don't think his spirits came and got him, do you?"

"Maybe he wasn't dead! Come on, we got to find him. Iguana will be really pissed, if we don't bring back the body. You look over there, I'll check here along the edge." The hunters staggered and stumbled about in the dark, only the light from their torches showing them the ground. They found nothing. They searched the entire ridge. "Come on, let's get out of here!" Beaded Lizard backed toward the trail. "I don't care what Iguana says! I'm not staying up here any longer."

"What we going to tell him?"

"The truth is that he isn't here."

Quickly the hunters retraced their steps.

Iguana looked fearfully about after hearing their news. "Get the camp broken!" he called to the people. "We are leaving this place, just as quickly as we can. If you don't need it, don't take it! We leave at dawn."

"What about our celebration?" asked Green Parrot drunkenly.

"Forget it!" answered Iguana.

As the sun touched the eastern sky with light, the camp filed quickly from the glade. Only the smoldering fires and one lone shelter remained.

*     *     *

From far away he heard them coming. Faintly, fear trickled along his spine. Quenquel had been expecting something like this, but not yet. He had his plans made; Iguana would go to the alter next. He was getting too suspicious. It was time to make him an example. Without Iguana, the others would be too frightened to stand against him. Soon! Now he realized that it was too late. But it was also too late for him to escape. His body was atop the ridge, but his spirit was floating on the wind.

The first blow, stuck by Green Parrot brought him back! Pain shattered his dreaming, as the blow broke his shoulder. Luckily, Green

Parrot had missed his head in his eagerness to strike the first blow. With a snap his right arm broke with the second blow. He felt no more. Pain drew him into oblivion.

Pain also brought him back. He lay in a broken heap on the cold earth. Blood seeped from his shattered nose and he had to breathe through his mouth. But pain also cleared his head. They were gone, but soon they would realize that they had not made sure of his death. If he was to survive; and above all else, Quenquel was a survivor, he must hide. When he tried to move, he realized there was no way he could escape the ridge. He tried to think. *Where?* He shook his head to clear his vision. Just an arm's length from him was the mouth of a deserted wolf den. *Yes!* With utmost care, slowly, painfully slowly, he dragged himself into the den. Once deeply enough inside, he used his feet and kicked lose dirt toward the opening. With it were several large rocks. He did not stop until nothing remained of the opening. Then with a sigh of pain, he collapsed into unconsciousness. So he lay as the drunken hunters searched. Had it been light, had they been sober, he would surely have been discovered. But his spirits protected him. When again he became aware of his surroundings, the birds were calling cheerfully outside and all else was quiet. He tried to move. Oblivion again claimed him.

The next time he regained consciousness, he was careful not to move his right arm and shoulder. Rather he fingered his waist pouch with his left hand and found the packet he sought. He slowly eased his hand up until he could shove the contents into his mouth. With a sigh he chewed the herbs. His head began to spin, but he was able to bear the pain. Kicking his way out of the wolf den was slow and excruciatingly painful work. He was barely aware when finally he lay on the stone in the sunshine. His head reeled and his stomach rolled. The herbs were strong medicine and he had put no food in his stomach since high sun the day before. He was breathing hard. Beside him lay a broken Branch. He had no idea that it was the very thing that broke his arm, but it was suitable for a support to bind it. He lost consciousness several times before he finally got the arm realigned and bound to the branch with cords from his waist thong. The shoulder would be far more difficult. But he was able to crawl to the edge of the ridge and look down into the glade. He gave a huge sigh of relief. The glade was empty. The camp had left. Nothing moved but the flapping hide of his shelter. He lay his head down on the warm stone and tears slid from his eyes. He rested there for a long time.

Traveling down the path from the ridge was difficult in the extreme. Time and again he barely saved himself from pitching forward head first. The sun was about to set when he staggered to his shelter.

Angry hands had destroyed almost all his possessions. He had stashed food and his medicine bag beneath his sleeping furs. The hunters of the camp had overlooked them. He crammed food into his mouth and barely chewed it. His water stomach lay a short distance away, but he could see that it would never hold water again. An angry hand had slashed it open from top to bottom. However, kicked beneath a bush was a smaller stomach that a child had discarded, and he was almost grateful for the carelessness that had given it to him as he swallowed a few mouths of tepid water. Then he curled up on his sleeping fur and gave in to the pain. His head pounded and when he closed his eyes a kaleidoscope of vibrant colors exploded. He cried out!

*   *   *

Bear Claw Woman moaned in her sleep and thrashed free of the fur. Guardian immediately whined and nosed Raven. The hunter alerted, in the blink of an eye. He turned to Bear Claw Woman and shook her. The woman whimpered but did not awaken. Again and again he tried to waken her.

"Woof! Woof!" Guardian leaped into the air and grabbed Bear Claw Woman's staff. She shot into the dark.

Raven held his mate in his arms and rocked back and forth, sending prayers to any spirit that might be listening. He felt so helpless! After what seemed forever, a scrambling of claws told him that Guardian was returning. She dropped the staff and nudged it against Bear Claw Woman. Immediately the blue glow began to envelope the woman. Finally she sighed and opened her eyes.

"What happened?" Raven questioned.

"Pain!" she whispered, "Unbearable pain!" She began to shiver.

Raven wrapped her in her sleeping fur and pulled her back into his arms. "But from where?"

She shook her head, "I have no idea," she settled back against him, "It is gone now." She pulled the fur closer about her shoulders. "Is there anything to eat?"

Raven chuckled, the tension released. "I will get you some meat from the hearth and tea as well. It always amazes me that so small a woman can eat so much after one of these events."

"I am totally drained. Who or whatever was pulling power from me was very strong. I could not break free, even when you tried to waken me. I hope we find a power source nearby, for there is no way that I can go very far."

"Woof!" Guardian nudged Raven. Then she whirled and leaped in the air.

"I understand," Raven nodded, "As soon as she eats, we will follow you." He settled Bear Claw Woman against the shelter pole and went to the hearth. Very shortly he had hot tea and a plentiful supply of food. She ate ravenously. When she finished, Raven lifted her into his arms and picked up her staff. Guardian led the way. Luckily the moon was up so he could see to follow. There was no way he could carry a torch as well.

Guardian led him some distance down a side path. Eventually they found themselves beneath the spreading branches of a huge oak tree. Its gnarled trunk rose far above their heads. With a sigh, Bear Claw Woman reached out and touched the trunk. The blue glow spread immediately. Raven settled her against the tree and quickly lighted a small fire. They stayed there until first light.

"I feel much refreshed," Bear Claw Woman yawned as she shifted position. Raven had sat keeping watch. "But I am afraid to go to sleep again."

"You cannot travel all day and get no sleep at night," the hunter protested.

"Then we had better find a place to camp at night which is at a power place. If this happens again, I cannot guarantee that I will wake up. But for your quick thinking, I would have been completely drained."

"Not my thinking," Raven nodded toward the wolf, "Guardian's."

Bear Claw Woman looked at the wolf, which grinned and wagged her tail.

"Yes, Guardian would know what to do." She ran her fingers through the thick fur on the animal's neck. "But be careful that she does not touch me under any circumstances when I am in one of those 'mind talkings'. It would kill her if I drew on her power. She is still too young to be able to withstand such a thing and she would gladly give her life if she thought I needed the power. Never let her do that!"

"I would gladly give my life if I thought it would help," admitted the hunter.

Bear Claw Woman frowned and shook her head. "we had better get back to the camp. I am sure the others are wondering where we are." She rose with help and followed Guardian up the trail.

Bull Elk was looking at their deserted shelter with a puzzled expression on his face when they entered the camp. "Where you been?" he questioned. "I woke up and got the meal ready, we have already eaten. I was just about to go out searching for you!"

"I'll explain it to you as we travel," Raven answered. Quickly he collapsed their shelter and loaded the travois. In a few breaths they were ready to go.

\*     \*     \*

Quenquel awakened feeling stronger and refreshed. His head was clear. *What happened?* He thought to himself, *I must have come in contact with some kind of power. I feel strong!* Pain laced through his shoulder. *Must find a way to bind this broken shoulder.* He made tea and heated some of his food. Then he sat, thinking. Eventually he made his way to the stream. The muddy bank almost sent him into the stream. He sat down and picked up a handful of mud. *Clay hardens when we pack meat in it to cook. I wonder...*

He packed several handfuls of clay against his shoulder. It promptly fell off. He frowned. *It has to work! What am I doing wrong?* The clay had fallen into the grass. When he tried to pick it up, grass came away with it. He packed it into a ball against his thigh with his left hand and noticed that the grass held it together. With a slight smile he set to work. Back at the camp he found the remains of a net which some woman had discarded. He managed to spread a thin rabbit skin over the broken shoulder. Then he maneuvered to spread the net over it and then packed the back and top of his shoulder with wet mud mixed with grass. Then he took a stick and forced the broken clavicle back into place. He felt the bones go into place, but it took his breath away and pain almost made him lose consciousness. He gritted his teeth and packed the wet mud around the stick and the rest of his shoulder. Already he had strapped the broken ribs and arm to keep them in place. Now he packed the shoulder to hold it immobile.

When he had this smoothed and shaped to his satisfaction, he wrapped the remainder of the netting over the entire thing. Then he sat is the sun. He was very tired. Propped against the side of his alter rock, Quenquel slept. His mind reached out....

*    *    *

"He is trying again!" Bear Claw Woman stopped dead in her tracks, "I can feel his mind searching for me!"

"Can you stop him?"

From trying? No! From succeeding; yes." She shook her head. *Who are you? Why to you take what doesn't belong to you?* Again and again she asked her question. But she received no answer. The contact was broken. But in those brief heartbeats that the contact existed, she was drained of an enormous amount of power. She sagged against Raven.

"Come!" he lifted her onto the travois.

"Young Wolf is strong. You go with Bull Elk and Calling Wolf. I am going ahead with Guardian. We will find a powerful place to spend the night. Try to sleep, if you can."

"I am afraid!" she whimpered, "What if he steals my soul while I sleep?"

"Can such a thing happen?"

"I have no idea! But I don't want to learn that it is possible after it has happened."

"Why don't you ask your spirits?" Bull Elk suggested, "They should be able to tell you, shouldn't they?"

"I don't know."

"What do you need to do in order to ask them?"

"Take a 'spirit journey' I suppose. This is how I have contacted them in the past. But I haven't done that since I was in the land of the dead."

Bull Elk shifted uncomfortable at the mention of the land of the dead, but gamely he kept on. "Do you have everything that you need to take such a journey?"

"I think that she should regain her strength before attempting such a risky thing!" Raven cut in, "Surely it can wait until we have found a 'power spot', can't it?"

"All right! You go on ahead and find this spot and we will follow your trail. Go now, we are wasting time just standing here," Calling Wolf directed.

Raven and Guardian took off at a trot. Young Wolf whined, but he was hitched to the travois and carried Bear Claw Woman. The three fell in behind Raven and moved at a much slower pace. From time to time, Bull Elk or Calling Wolf checked on Bear Claw Woman, to make sure that she was still awake and no harm had come to her.

Guardian led Raven down the trail at a full run until the hunter called out in protest. "Slow Down!" he stopped and gasped for breath. "How far can this place of power be?"

Guardian leaped into the air, "Woof!" she answered and shot down the trail until she was nearly out of sight. Then she again leaped into the air "Woof! Woof! Woof!" she came running back to him.

"All right I get the message. We are nearly there. So go on, I will follow. But just remember, you have four feet, I have but two!"

They left the main trail and followed a steep narrow path down into a gully. Here Guardian slowed down and waited for the hunter to guide him through the heavy brush. After a time they emerged into a deep canyon glen. A stream bubbled merrily through the lush grass. A doe raised her head and before he thought, Raven had sent a dart into her. The animal fell where she stood.

"Well we will have fresh meat any way!" Raven grinned at the wolf.

She wagged her tail and led him to a huge boulder resting at the base of the cliff. Upon its surface, long ago, someone had carved figures into the soft stone. Raven reached out to touch the stone. A shot of 'power' leaped from it to his finger. "This is truly a powerful place," he agreed with the grinning wolf, "You have done well." He pointed back to the trail. "You go and bring them in, while I make camp and butcher this deer. We will stay at this place for several days. Bear Claw Woman can absorb a lot of power from that boulder and we will process this deer while she does it."

Guardian shot up the trail and vanished. Raven walked to the deer and removed his dart. He went down on one knee beside the animal and made a short prayer to the spirit of Deer, thanking her for the gift of her daughter. Then he told her of the uses that he intended for this gift. Nothing would be wasted. Then he opened the body cavity and removed the organ meat. He made his hearth close to the magical boulder. From time to time as he worked, he studied the markings. They showed a group of people, he suspected a camp of The People. A big man wearing a bison headdress led them. Behind him walked a dreamer, eagle feather cloak and staff. Behind them walked a group of people, women and children as well as hunters. Then below them was the drawing of a single woman, with a wolf and beside them walked a creature that he could not even imagine had ever walked the land. It was so huge that it towered over the figures. He ran his fingers over the stone, the deer forgotten. Then he saw a group of hunters throwing darts at the creature. From that time on, the numbers of the camp began to dwindle. In the end only the woman and wolf remained.

Raven rose, pondering on the story which the boulder told. Just beyond where the deer lay, a pond swelled out, surrounded by reeds. The hunter knew that his woman was partial to the crispy bulb roots. He grinned and pulled off his moccasins to wade into the water and collect her some. As he separated the reeds, however, he found himself rooted to the spot. There, in the center of the pool rested the remains of an animal such as he had never seen. It was huge. The body was mostly mired in the mud of the pond. But the head rested partially upon the upright leg bones and the rest upon the huge curves teeth that grew from its upper jaw. Of course only the bones remained, for this surely was the monster, Thunder Giant, of legend. It had not walked upon the land in more generations than a man could count.

Raven backed from the pond and returned to his deer. He dragged the carcass over to where he had set up the hearth and went on with his processing. Bear Claw Woman would understand more about such things than he. It was better to leave it to her. He did not wish to take the chance of interfering with 'power'. Barking in the distance alerted him that soon the others would be joining him. He grinned and skewered the organ meat to cook. When the small parade filed into the glade, he was already loading drying racks.

Young Wolf hurried up to him, dragging the empty travois. Bear Claw Woman walked slowly behind. When Raven frowned, she explained, "The path was far to steep for the travois. It was better that I walk. Young Wolf has carried me far enough. What have we here?" she sniffed, "Fresh venison! How thoughtful! We have been eating trail meat ever since leaving the landslide."

"Look over there," Raven pointed. "The boulder has a story to tell you and tomorrow I will show you something even more wondrous!"

Bear Claw Woman made her way to the boulder and sank to her knees. She placed her hands against the rock and the blue haze enveloped her strongly. Softly she began a chant of thanks. The hunters set up the camp and finished processing the meat. After they had finished processing the meat, Raven helped Bear Claw Woman settle against the boulder. She was totally exhausted, even after her time drawing power. Very shortly she was sound asleep.

Raven sat and watched. Guardian lay beside him. Finally, the hunter dozed off. Bear Claw Woman began to moan and whimper. His eyes popped open and Raven was totally alert. He made sure that she was in contact with the boulder. The blue haze pulsed strongly around her. He had tried to wake her on the previous occasion. This time he did not even try. The moon rose and traveled across the sky. Then, just before it set, she sighed and drifted into a natural sleep. Only then did Raven sleep. Guardian watched.

Morning arrived all too quickly. After eating Raven took her to the pond.

"What do you think it could have been?" he asked her.

Slowly she removed her amulet and opened it. Onto her palm tumbled two small figures. One was a bison, Raven recognized that. The other, however, bore a remarkable resemblance to the skeleton sitting in the pond. "It was called Mammoth!" Bear Claw Woman said softly. "It was the spirit animal of the Ancient Ones. They are all gone to walk the wind."

"Does it have 'power' for you?"

"I have no idea. But I can certainly find out." She removed her moccasins and waded out into the pond. Raven watched from where he stood. As Bear Claw Woman approached the great skeleton seemed to shiver. When she reached out to touch it, he could almost swear that it gave forth with a thunderous roar of greeting. He covered his ears. Softly she began to sing a chant as she stroked the curving teeth. He watched for a long time. She ran her hands over the domed skull and down the forehead. Then she returned to the long curving teeth. Finally, at sun high, he called her to come away. Reluctantly Bear Claw Woman left the pond. Raven caught his breath. She was glowing with perfect health. Bear Claw Woman merely smiled at him and taking his hand led him back to the camp. . .

Calling Wolf and Bull Elk saw them come into the camp. They stilled for a breath when she walked into the camp, but then resumed their chores. This 'power' thing was beyond Bull Elk but Calling Wolf could hardly wait to find out what had happened.

As they sat around the hearth eating, Bear Claw Woman told them the story of the boulder. "When the Ancient Ones walked the earth, they had a wondrous spirit animal. It was so tall that a man could walk right beneath it and never touch its belly. The canine teeth had grown to such proportions that they curved outward and swept the ground, while its nose grew so long that is was like another leg, but it could move freely in any direction."

"What happened to it?" questioned Calling Wolf. "I have heard of the Thunder Giants."

"Would you like to see one?"

"What?" he leaped to his feet and looked fearfully around.

Bear Claw Woman laughed, "Relax, brave hunter. It has been dead for all these generations that you speak of. It will not hurt you. But I can promise that you will find it interesting."

"Where?" again he looked around.

"I found it while I was waiting for you," Raven explained, "I wanted to show it to Bear Claw Woman first"

"So that is what...." Calling Wolf began and then cut off his sentence. "Who wants more meat?"

After we finish eating I will take you to the remains," Raven offered, "But do as Bear Claw Woman tells you. I do not know if it could hurt you."

Calling Wolf turned to Bear Claw Woman. "You have communicated with the creature, haven't you?" he glanced toward Raven." You are refreshed. Like when I first met you last season at the cave. Whatever has been draining your strength has not affected you here."

"The strange force did attack me last night. But the power of the stone is great. It was able to give me more power than was taken from me. But finish eating and come with us. You will see for yourself, the great Thunder Giant of the Ancestors!

"I have had enough!" he wiped his hand on the grass and rose to his feet, "I wish to see this wondrous thing."

"Are you sure that it is safe?" Bull Elk was slower to rise. "I mean, it couldn't attack us could it?"

"It has been dead for a very long time," Bear Claw Woman replied. "I do not find any danger from it. I only sensed a greeting."

So the hunters followed her and Raven back to the pond. Calling Wolf was excited, pulling off his moccasins to wade into the water. But he did not touch the bones. He walked in awe around the skeleton. He approached closely, to peer into the eye cavity and down into the water to see the rest. Bull Elk was satisfied to look from dry land.

"I wonder what it looked like with flesh on it?" Calling Wolf murmured, "You can't really tell from just the bones."

"Here," Bear Claw Woman held out her hand, "This is what the living animal looked like."

"Where did you get that?" Calling Wolf stepped back.

"It was a gift from the spirits upon my 'becoming a woman'," Bear Claw Woman replied, "I carry it in my amulet bag."

"Then return it there! Such things are not for the eyes of simple hunters! There is no telling how much danger you have put me in!"

"Absolutely none," she replied dryly. "You wanted to know how the animal looked alive. I showed you. You did not touch it. Nor would I have let you. It is, as you say, a sacred object. But there is no harm in your looking at it."

"Do I dare touch it?" he nodded toward the skeleton.

She studied the man, then the skeleton. "You did say that you were training to be a dreamer, did you not?"

"Yes, but I never finished my apprenticeship. Our dreamer died and there was no other to teach me. But I have already told you this."

"Well, if you intend to continue to learn the arts of the dreamer, this is a perfect opportunity to touch the 'spirit'. Come. I do not feel any anger from it; curiosity yes but nothing more."

"You can feel that?" Calling Wolf stepped back.

"Certainly and so will you, if you find the courage to reach out."

Slowly Calling Wolf stepped forward and touched the curving tusk. He jerked his hand back, looked at it; then again lay his hand on the ivory. For several heartbeats he stood quietly. Then he smiled and removed his hand. "That was a memorable occurrence," he said quietly, "I understand what you mean. Thank you."

"Do you think it would be all right if I touched it?" Raven stood beside Bear Claw Woman.

"I see no reason why not," she replied.

So he also laid his hand on the great tusk. He could feel the thrill of greeting run up his arm, just as he thought he had heard it earlier. He came away with a feeling of deep peace in his soul.

The hunters returned to the camp but Bear Claw Woman remained with the skeleton in the pond. She explored it's every surface absorbing the 'connection' with its spirit. Her fingers found an object driven into one of its ribs. Carefully she worked it free and brought it to the surface. In her hand lay a stone tool. It was not a knife, but a dart point, like the ones that were used on the ceremonial darts at the gathering. But it was unlike any of those. It was nearly as long as her hand and made of the familiar jasper that they carried. But no dart that The People used could carry such a tip. She started to return it and then something changed her mind. Instead she placed it into her waist pouch. "I will put it with the sacred teeth." She murmured. A deep feeling of rightness filled her. She knew that was the right thing to do. As she ran her fingers along the curving surface of the tusk, a sliver broke off and fell into the palm of her hand. She looked at the skeleton, at the sliver and then nodded. "I thank you great spirit of my Ancestors. I will keep this in my amulet," she placed it there, with the figurines of the bison and mammoth. It just felt right to do so.

They stayed in the canyon for a hand of days. Every day Bear Claw Woman spent either at the boulder, or with the skeleton in the pond. The men explored the canyon and became familiar with the area surrounding it. Each night the strange 'power thief' attacked Bear Claw Woman. Only the presence of the boulder for her to draw from and the addition of the sliver of ivory now in her amulet bag, saved her from being completely drained of power. The power of the boulder began to drain and each night it became weaker. "We must leave this place and go on," Bear Claw Woman told the hunters.

"How can we leave it?" Raven exclaimed, "Without the power you draw from the boulder, surely you could not live!"

"The boulder is dying!" she replied. "I am only able to sustain by drawing heavily from the skeleton. Soon, it also, will have lost its power. We must go on!"

"But what will happen to you?" Raven questioned.

"I must either stay awake and fight off the mind attachment or find another source of power to draw upon. Trust Guardian. She will lead you to another source."

"I agree with Bear Claw Woman," Calling Wolf spoke. "I have noticed the loss of power from the boulder. Another night and it will be useless to her. We must take the chance of finding another source. Either that, or one or the other of us must stay with her and keep her awake."

"Then we should leave immediately," Raven frowned. He rose and began packing their things onto the travois. The meat had been dried and packed away, the stomach was now a water skin and the hide had been tanned and folded away as well. Even the hoofs of the deer had been used. Now Calling Wolf carried his own staff, topped with a pair of eagle feathers he had found and the deer hoofs fashioned into a rattle. It dangled from his staff. As they left the canyon, he sang a prayer from his childhood. The others joined in off and on.

*     *     *

Quenquel wakened from his rest against the boulder. The clay had begun to harden. He could tell that when it had done so, provided he did nothing to break the dry clay, it would hold his shoulder in place. But it was heavy and he was sure that once it dried it would be hot as well as uncomfortable. But it held the shoulder immobile. Other things were beginning to concern him. The power he was drawing from this strange source left him strong and alert upon waking, but it did not take long to fade. He needed to be making plans and decisions. First and foremost, he needed food. He had scavenged throughout the campsite but had found little of use. A discarded net had proved useful. He had been able to capture a number of fish from the stream, but although they supplemented his food supply, they would not provide enough to live on. His injury was such that it would be impossible for him to hunt for at least another moon. He knew that even eating sparingly; he did not have enough food. He was lefthanded and it was his right side that was injured but moving his upper body at all was impossible. He had no strength to cast the dart in any case. This left plants. Even men knew something about which plants were edible. At least plants did not try to escape.

He also needed shelter. When the camp destroyed his shelter, they did a good job of it. It would provide no shelter from rain, or cold. He needed somewhere secure, dry and warm. But where? *There must be a cave around here somewhere! Think!* Then he grinned, *yes!* It took him only a short time to collect what he would take with him. He dumped everything on his sleeping fur and tossed it onto what was left of his shelter hide. With difficulty he was able to fashion a handle which he could use to pull the hide behind him with his left hand.

Then Quenquel headed up the stream and into a canyon along a wide path. Ahead, at the base of the cliff, within easy reach of the stream was a cave. It was not large, but certainly big enough for one man. There were cattails growing at the edge of the stream and numerous edible plants both along and within the stream. As he glanced about the canyon, he noted even more plants. Also, there were tracks of a small herd of pigs. He studied the possibility of constructing a snare but could figure no way without both hands. Rather, he settled for stretching the net across the trail and waiting to herd a covey of quail into it. This worked! He brought down several rabbits with his rabbit stick as well.

So far the cast he created to hold his shoulder in place was working. However, even dry it was heavy, itchy and irritating. He had to sleep sitting up, because he couldn't take the chance of lying down and breaking the clay. It was hot as well. Even the slightest exertion caused the flesh within to sweat. He also had to be careful not to get it wet. Then it began to rain. Quenquel was holed up in the cave for nearly a hand of days. He ate the last of the rabbits before the rain stopped.

Each night he closed his eyes and let his mind travel...to the power! At the dark-of-the-moon he decided it was time to move on. The cave would not be suitable for a winter shelter. There were no large game animals in the area and the 'power' was growing weaker. He decided to follow it. It was highly unlikely that who or whatever its source; was traveling on the plain, so that only left the mountains. He was far from recovered, but daily grew stronger. The day he finally managed to construct a snare and caught one of the pigs made his decision final. Once more he set the snare and before dark, heard the enraged squeal of yet another pig. He hurried to kill it before it broke the snare and escaped. Now he had meat. He smoked the two animals and packed them onto his newly constructed travois. He had fashioned a harness that could be attached around his waist so that his left hand was free to throw the rabbit stick if opportunity presented. He took only what he absolutely needed; a water bladder, his sleeping fur, food and of course his weapons. The part of his shelter would keep him dry if it rained.

He set out at dawn, following the canyon westward. For days he traveled, each night feeling that the 'power' was getting stronger. Then one day he came upon a place where the earth had slid and blocked the trail. He studied the area and with a thrill of excitement recognized human foot prints.

He studied the prints; *three men and a woman, no, three men and a woman and several dogs. A small party. I wonder if one of them is the one with 'power?'* He found where their trail led around the landslide. *They passed here after the rain so that means that they are no more than a moon ahead of me. Perhaps I can catch up. Maybe it is Iguana. No. Iguana had no dogs. But perhaps they will lead me to Iguana.* He dragged his travois after him up the trail and found where they had camped.

*Someone is injured.* He smelled the discarded dressings and smiled to himself. *This will slow them down.* He picked up his pace. So far he had managed to kill a rabbit or two each day as he traveled. Or perhaps squirrels or grouse; always something so he saved his dried meat for when there was no fresh meat. This also happened on several occasions after leaving the landslide. He studied the travois tracks, one dug deeply into the earth. The trail led south and finally down and into a large valley.

Quenquel found where they had camped. *They spent a long time here.* He found their trail out of the valley and smiled to himself. *Ah! So the man is recovered!* He recognized a fourth pair of moccasin tracks. He picked up speed. *They can only be days ahead of me now! The power is stronger every night!* Each night he settled against a tree and concentrated on the 'power'. Each morning he wakened stronger and more refreshed. Each day he picked up speed and endurance. Finally, as the moon turned full once more, he discarded the heavy clay cast. He was amazed that the shoulder and arm seemed to be completely healed. Stiff and sore, yes, but healed! Fully a half moon before they should have. *Truly this is powerful 'spirit medicine' which I follow!*

He discovered where they had defecated. It was fresh! *I am right behind them!* He smiled. Then he discovered where they left the main trail and headed down into a canyon. Here he discarded his travois, hidden deep within brush. Carefully he slipped down the trail, mindful to keep down wind. Dogs would alert them. Hidden in the deep brush, he watched as they prepared to leave their camp. *Almost missed them!* But they were not of Iguana's camp. No! These were of The People. He recognized their dress and they walked with wolves, not dogs. *But what are these 'wolves of the plains' doing so deep in the mountains? They should be far south and east of here, well onto the Llano by this time of season! This merits further investigation! Perhaps yet, they will lead me to Iguana.*

He watched them leave the canyon and then slipped into their deserted camp. He gave the drawings on the boulder only passing consideration. But he gathered cattails from the pond and he found the skeleton. *What manner of creature was this?* He waded into the water and circled the skeleton. When he touched it, a spark of 'power' sizzled up his arm. *Ah! So this is the source!* He retrieved his travois and belongings and moved into their deserted camp. All day he stood by the skeleton and drew 'power' from it. By nightfall, he felt as recovered as though the attack had never happened.

\*       \*       \*

"Here, Bear Claw Woman, have some more meat. You have had a long day. Rest here and I will get you some tea as well," Raven settled his woman against a tree.

"I feel much better than yesterday," she protested, "Really, I haven't felt the 'pull' at all today. Perhaps it is gone!"

"I wouldn't trust that!" the hunter replied dryly.

"No! Really! I think it is finished. There has been no sense of pain for quite a while; just a 'draw' of power. Perhaps who or whatever it was has healed and has no further need. I think it is finished."

"We will see."

"How far do you estimate we are from Running Bison and the camp?" she asked Bull Elk.

"Perhaps half a moon, maybe no more than a double hand of days," he shrugged. "It is hard to say, for we do not follow the same trail. We are farther south. Why?"

"I just wondered," she replied, "I think perhaps it would be best if from now on we covered our trail."

"Why?" Raven questioned, "Do you think someone follows us?"

She nodded, "The 'power-seeker follows us," she answered. "Perhaps a day or so behind, but no more than that."

"What?" Both he and Bull Elk leaped to their feet and exclaimed, "Why did you not say something? I would have found this 'thing' and killed it!"

"That is exactly why," she answered. "You are a strong hunter, my mate, but this is 'power' you are dealing with here. Power can be very dangerous. I would not see you injured, or either of you!" she turned to the other men.

"Well, if it is human, it can be killed!" Bull Elk stated.

"And what if it only 'looks' human?" she smiled as the hunter turned white as hot ash. "It is best left alone, my friend. Leave it behind! Let's just vanish! With no trail to follow, whatever it is will be left behind. We have been traveling west, now Calling Wolf tells me it is time to turn toward the north. This is an excellent opportunity to lose our follower."

"I could leave a false trail for a time, then cut over the mountains and rejoin you," Bull Elk offered. Calling Wolf nodded and so it was decided. They were on rocky ground any way, so it was easy to select the hard, rocky surfaces and where the travois or their feet or paws left tracks, a whisk from a branch removed all trace. Meanwhile, Bull Elk purposefully left travois marks and foot and paw prints as he led his wolf down the main trail for a long distance. Then, when he reached a place where again rocks dominated, he simply vanished! He packed the wolf and hefted his own backpack, from which stuck the travois poles. Then, again with the use of a branch, he simply removed their trail. They hiked over several high hills along a narrow path, then onto another and yet another, before catching up with the others. But from then on, they were careful to remove all trace of their passage. They dry camped, leaving no ashes. For over a hand of days they followed narrow trails, until finally, they came upon a wide, easily traversed path once again.

"See that mountain over there; the one which has snow on it," Calling Wolf pointed to the north. "The valley where Running Bison is camped is at its base."

"We are that close!" Bear Claw Woman exclaimed.

"No, we are not close. Distance can be deceptive in this clear mountain air. It will take us nearly another hand of days to reach that mountain."

"But it looks to be just beyond the next valley!" Bear Claw Woman protested.

"You will see that it is not," Bull Elk chuckled.

"I was not paying attention to such things when first I crossed these mountains," she admitted. "I have never been in this particular area any way. When I lived with the Gatherers, we were farther north."

"You lived with the Oak Leaf Camp, didn't you?" Bull Elk asked.

"Yes."

"I know where they lived. It is much farther north. But you should have been able to see the snow-capped mountain from there."

Bear Claw Woman frowned, "Oh! Yes! I do remember a snow-capped mountain, far to the southwest of our valley. You mean it is the very same mountain? It doesn't look the same."

"That is because you are seeing it from a different direction."

"It is still hard to believe that it is so far away," she laughed, "But I am willing to take your word for it. Besides, if you say it will take us a hand of days, then that is how long it will take. You have not been wrong yet!"

Bull Elk laughed, "I have been wrong, more times than I care to remember, but fortunately, not yet while with you," he still chuckled as he continued down the trail.

\*     \*     \*

Quenquel scratched his head. He again squatted and studied the trail. Yes! It was the same footprints. But the ground was so rocky that he had been having difficulty finding them. But he had studied the trail for some distance ahead. And there were no further prints. Clearly, this group knew that he followed. Somewhere along the trail, they had left the path he was now on and one of them had deliberately misled him.

*I can either take a great deal of time and find where they left the trail, or I can guess where they are going and go there. Either they went to the south, headed to the Llano Escarpment, or they went north farther into the mountains. They are bison hunters. The Llano!* He decided. *But Iguana would stick to the mountains! Do I follow these people, or do I seek Iguana?*

For some time he sat there, still squatted over the foot print, thinking. Then he rose, dusted off his hands and studied the terrain. He knew that the valleys to the south lead to the Escarpment. He also knew the lay of the land to the north. They had raided the Gatherers who lived in that direction. There was a plentiful harvest of plants and good hunting there as well. The Llano could be chancy. He needed a secure supply of food. So, he headed north.

\*     \*     \*

A trill of sound rent the air. The travelers stopped dead in their tracks, and then Calling Wolf threw back his head and answered! Soon a pair of hunters trotted into view.

"Running Bison said you would probably show up any day now!" Thunder Cloud slapped Calling Wolf on the back, "I see that you have found them!"

"We were at the cave," admitted Raven.

"Well you have arrived none too soon. The sky has been promising snow for the last pair of days."

"We have been watching it," replied Bull Elk.

"Just then, as if in answer to their words, fat white flakes began to drift gently down.

"Is she with them?" called an out-of-breath female voice from the trail beyond the pair of hunters. Then Whispering Wind came running into view. With a squeal she threw herself into Bear Claw Woman's arms. "I have missed you!" she sobbed.

From a ridge, high above, a lone figure studied the meeting. *Humming Bird!* A stunned Quenquel announced to himself, as he studied the new arrival. *How can it be?*

# CHAPTER 20

Huffing and puffing, another woman came into view down the trail. She carried a squealing infant in her arms and was followed by a pair of wolves carrying packs. "You silly girl!" she accused Whispering Wind, "Your child needs feeding!" She shoved the baby toward Whispering Wind. "You should have stayed at the camp. This is no place to bring a baby. What Running Bison is thinking to allow it, I can't imagine!" grumbled Robe Maker.

"He knows how important Bear Claw Woman is to me," replied Whispering Wind. "Besides, you didn't have to come along. You could have stayed warm and safe in the cave."

"And let your take my precious babe into danger!" protested the old woman.

Whispering Wind merely shook her head. "This 'Grandmother' is worse than a new mother! She will not allow me to do anything but care for my child as if I would hurt a hair on his precious head!" She crooned to the baby, who merely sucked lustily from the nipple he had hungrily attached himself to.

"Come on!" Thunder Cloud led the way, "We had better get moving. It is still a long way to the main camp. We have set up a temporary camp at the top of the trail and it is getting colder by every finger of time that passes. Besides, that storm is moving in fast," he glanced toward the sky.

He led the way back up the trail, followed by the hunters and then the three women. They were involved in the baby. None saw the shadowy figure slip closer...

\* \* \*

Quenquel had followed his own path and had been more than surprised to see the groups meet as he topped the final ridge. In a flash he had hidden from sight and watched. He did not recognize any of the men, but when the woman came running down the trail it took his breath away. *Humming Bird!* He was stunned. *How can it be?* He slipped closer.

But the closer he got, the more convinced he became. *It is her! I know that I sacrificed her, yet here she is alive and well and she has given birth to our child! Truly, the Spirits have rewarded me well for my service.* He was shaking, he knew not if from cold or the surprise of his discovery. Either way, however, the weather did not encourage squatting on the exposed face of a hill. He had to find shelter and very soon.

He scanned the area, finding nothing that would be suitable. So he followed the people at a discrete distance.

\* \* \*

Thunder Cloud led the group over the narrow pass and down into the valley. As the storm settled in they could no longer see even their hands before their faces. The wind screamed and tore at their clothing, cutting through and chilling the flesh. Whispering Wind had her baby wrapped in a rabbit fur robe, then bundled in warm wolf-hide as well. He at least, was warm. Finally, over the last hand of time, they were totally dependant on the wolves to lead them to the caves.

The man following lost them somewhere just beyond the pass. But he found the small cave they had been waiting in. And inside, they had left a careless few provisions. Over the last moon, always there had been someone at the cave, watching for the travelers. Thunder Cloud had not bothered taking the last few supplies with them. They were in a hurry to beat the storm. But only this fact saved Quenquel from freezing to death on the trail.

The temperature plummeted to far below freezing. But a hide attached to the opening was soon put back in place and a fire rekindled in the minute hearth. In rapid succession, another robe found its way around his shoulders and food onto skewers over the fire. The cave was small, but that meant easier to heat. There was a meager supply of branches stacked against the back wall. And a pile of extra sleeping furs as well. The fuel would heat food, but there was not enough to keep the cave warm on a constant basis. But with the entrance covered, at least when the temperature outside dropped even lower, the cave stayed relatively the same.

\* \* \*

The storm raged for days on end each one more stressful on the lone man. The fuel was soon consumed. The blizzard made it impossible to search for more. So he bundled up in the sleeping furs and depended upon his own body heat to keep from freezing to death. He even considered the option of seeking out the camp, so desperate was he. But he also knew that beyond the cave, even a few steps, death awaited. Essentially, he was trapped.

\* \* \*

Thunder Cloud and his group stumbled into the first cave. They shook snow from their clothing and welcomed hot tea and food. Bear Claw Woman was greeted by Running Bison and Crooked Spirit, who was visiting him. Room was made for Raven and Bear Claw Woman, Calling Wolf and Bull Elk in the cave. They were placed at a hearth near the back of the cave against the wall. It suited them very well.

"Why didn't you 'call' to me?" Whispering Wind questioned once the pair of women were settled comfortably, munching of grain cakes.

"We decided it was safer not to, remember?" Bear Claw Woman answered. "But I was tempted a time or two. You will hear all about our journey after we have gathered everyone here to hear it. Raven says that Running Bison has arranged a celebration this very night."

"But tell me, what really happened to you!" she nestled her baby into his sleeping basket and relaxed.

So Bear Claw Woman told her of her murder and return from the 'land of the dead' and her discovery of Raven's love.

"I find it hard to believe that creature is our beloved Obsidian!" Whispering Wind nodded to Guardian, as she lay at Bear Claw Woman's side. Guardian merely grinned and thumped her tail. "I have never seen a wolf that looks like her!"

"Her kind have not walked this land since the great Thunder Giant's did so," replied Bear Claw Woman.

"She is so big! Even bigger than Obsidian and she was the largest dog I have ever seen."

"When she is full grown."

"What do you mean, 'full grown'!" Whispering Wind squealed, "Don't tell me that she will get bigger!"

"Well, not much," Bear Claw Woman ruffled the animal's fur, "She is nearly half a season old now. Perhaps she has gotten her growth early. But from the drawings that I saw in the canyon, unless the women were much smaller than I, she will gain at least another hand in height."

Whispering Wind merely shook her head in amazement.

Raven came to interrupt them, "Crooked Spirit wishes to talk with you," he told Bear Claw Woman. "He is most apologetic but insists that it is very important."

Bear Claw Woman nodded, "I will be back as soon as I can," she sighed and went to where the dreamer waited.

"You are well?" he asked after the formal greeting.

"I am," she replied, "You have a request to make of me?"

He nodded, "The celebration tonight; I want to take the opportunity to return the Ancient Relic Bundle to you at that time. I just wanted to make sure that it would be acceptable to you. I realize that we should probably make a special offering or something, but I want that thing back in your hands as soon as possible. I have been very uneasy with the responsibility of its care, all these moons."

"We can make the transfer easily. Simply return it to my care before all the camp. There is no need to make a special sacrifice. That will be done at the spring ceremony, which must be held at the sacred spring. I have a special offering to be given at that time, but it must be made there and no where else."

"As soon as everyone arrives, we are ready to begin the celebration," Running Bison called to Crooked Spirit.

"I must bring something from my cave," the dreamer answered, "So don't start without me. It is most important!" The old man bundled his hands into mittens, wrapped another fur about his head and slipped through the slight opening between hides, out into the storm. Cords had been strung between the caves during the previous winter, so that people could travel from one cave to another without getting lost in storms such as this. Before the storm struck, they had been strung once again. Crooked Spirit followed the cord, passing others along the way, headed toward the first cave. He was glad that his cave was second. It was brutally cold outside and the wind savagely cut into even the minutest access. His nose burned from breathing in the air, even though it was filtered through fur first. He added fire to his hearth once inside the cave, then searched out the Sacred Bundle. He had it stashed safely in a basket at the very rear of the storage area. Even handling it now made him nervous. This was 'women's magic! He wrapped it in an additional hide and attached this securely to his waist thong. Then regretfully, he faced the blizzard once more.

Running Bison had the hearth fires burning hotly when he slipped once again into the first cave. He was greeted with cheers from his cave-mates. Spits were groaning with food and bags held stew into which women were methodically and expertly adding hot rocks and removing cool ones. Already the food was aromatic as it finished the final stages of cooking. The third cave had brought baskets of grain cakes and plant foods. The second cave had added elk roasts, now completing the final stages of cooking over the first cave hearths. Honey, tea, dried berries and nuts were passed around as people waited for the ceremony to begin. Now that Crooked Spirit was back, it was time.

Hollow Bone blew his whistle. Bear Man beat on his drum and people became quiet. Running Bison, his official headdress in place rose and stood before the assembly. "We have been living in this valley for an entire season now. But we have not, in all that time, had the blessing of the spirits to make this our home. Now, with the arrival of Bear Claw Woman, Keeper of the Sacred Relics, at last we can give proper thanks to the spirits for the bounty of their gifts to this camp. In her absence, Crooked Spirit, Dreamer of the Wolf Camp, has been given charge of these objects. But it is time they are returned to their proper Keeper. It is time that we send prayers of thanks to the spirits and beg for their continued care."

Crooked Spirit stepped forward. He carried the Sacred Bundle gingerly to the middle of the cave. Here he stopped and called for Bear Claw Woman to come forward and receive it back into her keeping. "Come forth, Bear Claw Woman, Woman of The People, Keeper of the Sacred Relics," he called.

Bear Claw Woman had been waiting at the rear of the cave. While Crooked Spirit had been gone, she also had been preparing. Now, as she stepped forth, breaths were drawn in. She was naked but for her apron. Her entire body had been covered with white ash and about her shoulders she wore once again, a cape of white feathers, made for her by the women of the camp in anticipation of her return. She carried her staff and at her side walked the near-white wolf. She came and knelt before the dreamer. She bowed her head, said a few prayer words and then rose.

"I take back the care of the Sacred Relics," she said in a voice that carried to all parts of the cave, even though it was softly spoken. Then she unwrapped the bundle and lifted wolf-hide-bundle for all to see. Already the eerie blue glow was beginning to build around her and Guardian. A deathly silence filled the cave, broken only by the occasional exploding of sap particles. She knelt and laid the wolf bundle on a bare rock and untied the cord holding it together. As the coverings fell away, the Ancient Relics glowed softly in the firelight. Slowly Bear Claw Woman lifted them out, one in each hand. She threw her head back and called out... "Spirits of our Ancestors hear our plea! Give us guidance and protection. Look into our hearts and find pureness and devotion to you! If one of us fails to please you, take him or her from us! Lead us in the paths you wish us to trod and we will walk them with thanks on our lips and in our hearts."

The blue glow seemed to shimmer then in the blink of an eye it vanished. Bear Claw Woman gasped! She returned the relics to the wolf-hide with a whimper of pain. Then she froze and did not move. Everyone held his or her breath... Then with a groan, she opened her eyes. Bear Claw Woman was as pale as the ash covering her body. She rose and faced the cave, slowly turning so that she met all eyes. In a voice which was not her own she spoke.... *There are others who do not follow the path trod by the Wolf Camp. Until every man, woman and child belonging to people, follow the dictates of the spirits, they will not bless The People. You must seek them out and cleanse from among them those who have greed in their hearts, those who claim the greatness of the spirits as their own. It is not enough that this camp follows; all must follow. The bison will not return until then. No more will the spirits look favorably upon this camp if they do not seek out others and unite all people. There is unspeakable evil lurking nearby. It must be cleansed from the land! I, Wolf Spirit, have spoken."* As if a cold wind struck her, she began to shake. Then, as suddenly as it had vanished, once again the blue glow shimmered to encase her. She drew a deep breath and blinked. She shook her head and knelt to replace the covering over the Sacred Relics. Then the ceremony was over. Slowly people began to move about and make final preparations. Food was handed around to the children as Bear Claw Woman returned to the rear of the cave. There, with the help of Robe Maker and Whispering Wind, she removed the ash and thankfully pulled on her tunic and leggings. Even though the cave was well warmed, she was chilled to the bone, but she was sure it was not from the lack of heat in the air.

"What did I say?" she asked, "People are looking strangely at me!"

"Don't you know?" Robe Maker asked.

"It wasn't 'me' speaking," Bear Claw Woman explained.

"You said that we have to seek out the rest of The People and reunite them again. That we must drive the non-believers out and that there is evil nearby," Whispering Wind answered.

"Wow! That is quite a lot; no wonder eyes do not greet mine with welcome!"

"I suppose this means that with the spring we will leave this valley," Whispering Wind sighed, "I have liked living here."

"We must leave any way," Bear Claw Woman replied, "I must make an offering at the Sacred Spring, if not at the Spring Ceremony, then at Mid-Summer."

Robe Maker broke in, "You did not say,' unite all of The People again', you said, 'unite all people'. I wonder if the spirits mean even those belonging to the Gatherers, the Raiders and even the Savages."

Bear Claw Woman frowned, thought for a moment, then nodded, "I believe that you are right Robe Maker. The spirits do not mean merely the Bison Hunters; they mean all the people with whom we come in contact with. We are to unite everyone into one tribe and teach them the ways of the spirits. Only then will we see the bison return. Only then will the spirits truly bless us with plenty. This is the task I have been given."

"It is impossible!" Robe Maker shook her head, "No one could do that! and certainly not a woman!"

"The spirits made it very clear at the gathering. Those who do not return to the ways of the Ancestors will suffer. The men will watch their women and children die before them. They will suffer greatly. Already some of this has happened. Look at how the raiders attacked the camps of the Gatherers and then how the Savages attacked them. So many people have died, not just the Bison Camps, but all the peoples. And they will continue to do so unless we find them and take them in. We must show by our example."

"But how do we find them?" Whispering Wind questioned.

"The spirits will lead us," Bear Claw Woman replied.

Raven approached, "Come and eat, others are waiting for you." He smiled at the women as he led them to their places. Then once they were seated, everyone was handed food and when all were served, they began to eat. There was much speculation as to the meaning of Bear Claw Woman's words. But now was a time of celebrating. Later was time to think upon the words.

Bear Claw Woman felt complete again. She had the Sacred Relics once again in her care. Now she would be able to learn the extent of her 'power'. Now she could begin to help others as she knew the spirits wanted. Still, she did not feel 'ready'.

The blizzard raged for days. Then during the final night, the winds died down, the snow stopped and with the morning, blue skies and bright sunshine greeted them. The snow was deep, but snow walkers were kept handy just outside the caves. Soon youths were out with the wolves and children were making designs in the snow. The adults sighed. With the addition of so many people to the camp, the caves were much more crowded that the previous winter. With the cold, those who had camped in the open were now living in the caves as well.

*     *     *

In the small cave up in the pass Quenquel was still alive, barely. He crawled to the opening, shivering violently. The sun was bright, but there was no warmth in it. He staggered a short distance and managed to find some deadwood. He struggled through the knee-deep snow back to the cave and with frost-bitten fingers, got a fire started. He dug pig meat from his pack and started a bag of melted snow to heating. Into this he dropped the pieces of meat. His stomach was cramping from hunger. He had run out of water, it froze in the container, so he was forced to eat snow. This had dangerously lowered his body temperature. Now he huddled close to the fire and tried to thaw out his frozen fingers and toes. Too soon, the wood was burned. Again he had to struggle through the snow for more. He dragged it into the cave and tossed it against the back of the wall. He was surprised when one piece struck something other than stone. He lighted a branch from the fire and examined the spot. A deer- hide had been stretched over another opening, leading into another part of the cave. Inside, he found an ample supply of wood. There had been no need for him to freeze nearly to death. He explored further and found a basket containing an odd assortment of clothing. He did not care. Warm leggings and moccasin liners and a winter tunic were soon pulled on. Gradually, as his fire warmed the small cave, he thawed out. His fingers and toes were painful. One toe had turned nearly black. He was afraid that it would have to be amputated. The little finger of his right hand was totally black. It had no feeling at all. With a sigh he dug out more of his herbs and as the fire heated a smooth rock very hot, he searched among his things and found a newly struck blade. He chewed the herbs and when he could feel their power take hold, he laid his hand on a rock and with the blade, hacked and sawed through tendon, flesh and bone, until the finger lay severed on the rock. Then he watched as blood came from the wound. Only when the dripping blood was clean and fresh did he place the open wound against the hot stone. The stench of burning flesh rent the air and he nearly fainted from the pain. But the bleeding stopped. The wound was closed. He applied an ointment to the stub and wrapped his hand in a piece of rabbit fur. The toe pained badly. At least the pain meant that the toe was not dead as well.

Again he searched the back cave, but he found only a few scraps of food. He still had some of the pig meat left, for he had used it very sparingly. But fact was fact; it would never last all winter! It was highly unlikely that anyone from the camp below would venture up here. He was safe from detection as far as they were concerned, but he needed food. He needed plant food as well and meat, but mostly he needed meat. He had left the hide off the cave opening, so that he could see better to remove his finger.

A scuffling sound at the mouth of the cave alerted him. Whirling around he dived for his atlatl and darts, he had been wrong! Already he had been discovered and hunters were about to kill him! He braced his back against the cave wall and waited to dart the first one. A grunt was followed by the twitching nose, then the rest of a grizzly bear, drawn by the odor of his burning flesh. He almost cried out in joy as he watched the bear rise on his hind legs and growl as it smelled the fire. Then he cast his dart, followed by another and another. Each drove deeply into the bear's chest. With a umph of pain, the animal collapsed in the entrance. He had food.

Quenquel butchered the animal where it dropped. He had not the strength to drag it further into the cave. He skinned it, quartered it and stashed the quarters in the back cave. Then he skewered the organ meat and relighted his fire. The hide he stretched out, covering most of the remainder of the cave floor and after he replaced the opening cover, he began to scrape the hide. This would make a set of winter clothing that would keep out the cold.

His hand slowed him down. It was clumsy wrapped as it was. Finally, he removed the bandage. He would have to take a chance. After all it was only a little finger. The wound was seared closed. It did not bleed. But it hurt! He chewed more of the herbs.

The sun set. and he sat at his fire and ate the heart of the bear. With sinew taken from the carcass and wood from the back room he managed to produce a crude set of snow walkers. With them he would explore this end of the valley. Perhaps, there was a chance to make a raid on the food supply of the camp below. He would wait and see. But now he was content to hole up in the little cave and heal.

*I wonder if I can still draw on the power?* He smiled to himself.

\*     \*     \*

Bear Claw Woman jerked upright. The furs fell away from her and her movement wakened Raven. "What is wrong?" he was instantly awake. "It happened again!" she whispered.

"What?" he frowned.

"The 'power' stealing!" she crawled from under the furs. 'But I will show whoever it is just what they are dealing with! She dug in her storage basket until she found the packet, "See how he likes this!" She quickly unwrapped the Sacred Relics and took one in each hand. Then she closed her eyes and let her mind flow. A surge of blue shot up into the air. Bear Claw Woman smiled.

\*     \*     \*

Quenquel sat at his fire and let his mind search. *Yes!* He could feel the contact. Then it was broken. He frowned, settled more comfortably and closed his eyes and searched again. Suddenly a bolt of power struck him and knocked him clear across the cave. He lay stunned against the back wall, a knot rising on the back of his head. *What happened?* Dazed he shook his head then tried again. Wham! He flew through the air like a dart. Slowly he rose to his feet. *What is happening?* He looked all around the cave, but nothing was different. *The power is doing this! But why? It never has before.* He thought about it for a time and then decided to try once more. Only this time he kept his eyes open. It made no difference. His body was lifted like it weighted no more than a feather and cast with such force against the back wall that for a time he thought that his back was broken. Very slowly he moved, testing each arm and leg to be sure. *Leave me alone!* The thought came unbidden to his mind from another. Then he felt the cold and noticed that his hearth fire was scattered all over the cave. Coals were burning holes in the bearskin. Quickly he scrambled to his feet and kicked them off. Smoldering from his sleeping furs alerted him to a fire there as well. *So it has learned how to fight back!* He smiled *we will see! My time will come!* But he did not try to touch the mind again.

\*     \*     \*

Bear Claw Woman smiled, "I don't think he will try that again soon!" She rewarded the relics and put them away.

"What was that all about?" Raven questioned.

"Oh, just a little 'game'," she replied. "I told you that with the Sacred Relics I could stop the 'theft'. Well, I just did. It will be some time before he tries that again."

"What did you do?"

"I'm not sure, but whatever it was, the power convinced him to leave it alone. I could feel his body moving through the air and I think the power hurt him. But it didn't kill. I only intended to warn, not really injure."

"You can do that? I mean actually cause injury with your power?"

"I'm not really sure if I can actually kill with it, but I can certainly cause serious injury. I am sure that with time and practice I should be able to kill, but why would I want to do such a thing?"

"I had no idea that those relics were so powerful! Even in the crystal room you couldn't control the power in such a way."

"I never tried until now. It is possible, I suppose, that I could have done so at any time, but until tonight, I hadn't gotten angry. I think I had better think more carefully about this power of mine. I had no idea that I could do anything except guide another mind."

"Of course you can. Look at how quickly you healed Bull Elk's injury. But I thought that your power was only for good."

"Well, perhaps the power thief is the evil that the spirits spoke of. Whatever it is has followed us. Even wiping away our trail did no good. Perhaps what we are dealing with 'is' an evil spirit. I never thought of that! It would explain everything. Why the draw was so strong, why it kept following us, even after we left no trail. Why it is here now," she shivered.

Raven pulled her back beneath the furs and wrapped his strong arms about her. "Whatever it is, I will not let it harm you!"

"I am not sure that there is anything which either of us could do to stop that. But 'power' can. You see, the Sacred Relics have little power in the hands of another and I have little power without them, but together, well, that is the difference! But there is a price to pay. Without an offering at the Sacred Spring either at the Spring Ceremony or Mid-Summer, they will begin to lose power. And it would do no good if one other than me made the offering."

"That makes sense. You are, after all 'Keeper of the Sacred Relics'. But you do not always carry them with you."

"No, usually they are kept in a safe place within the cave, provided we have one. Other wise I keep them on my travois. When we travel, that is always where they are, which is why I have my staff. It is really a link that connects me to the relics, or another source of power if necessary, such as when we were traveling. But another source is only necessary when I have been cut off from the Relics."

"You mean that when you gave them to Crooked Spirit at the Gathering, he was supposed to give them back?"

"Absolutely! That was merely a 'ceremony' thing, where I was symbolically returning not just the Ancient Relics, but myself as well, back to The People. Had not Angry Bull taken a hand in the events that followed, Crooked Spirit would have handed the relics back the next day. He was never intended to have care of them. Had he known, he would have been better off to trust them to Whispering Wind. They are not happy in the care of a man."

"Wouldn't Crooked Spirit know this? After all, he is a dreamer."

"He is also a man. The spirits of the Ancestors which inhabit the Relics will not communicate with a man, although if one were to steal them, they would be forced to comply with his commands in some way, but not necessarily the way he commands."

"You mean a stranger could 'steal' the relics' power?"

"Only if he stole the relics themselves, but a man would not know the drink to use, nor would it work for him as it would for a woman if he did know. But if he made a direct demand of the relics while they were in his hands, yes, they would release power, but it could just as easily be directed at him as at his enemy. If a woman stole them however, things would be much different. She could control them much better." Bear Claw Woman yawned and snuggled down into the furs and against Raven. He grinned and pulled her close. Very soon both were asleep.

The next morning Bear Claw Woman found Calling Wolf, Talking Shadow and Crooked Spirit deep in conversation at the main hearth. She grinned. The big hunter was setting himself up as an assistant to the dreamers, just like Hollow Bone. The four of them were almost inseparable, making numerous trips from the second cave and into the forest. This was very good. There would be need for more dreamers when the Wolf Camp set out come spring.

*     *     *

"It is mine!" screeched Little Doe.

"You stole it from me!" countered Mountain Quail.

"What is going on here?" Demanded Robe Maker as she hurried to the front of the cave.

"She took that cougar fur which I was planning to make into a tunic for Grasshopper!" answered Mountain Quail. "I told her days ago that I had plans for it. Now she has taken it and cut it for her own use! It isn't right!"

Robe Maker turned to the belligerent woman clutching the hide. "Is this true? Did you know of Mountain Quails plans?"

"She didn't say 'for sure' only that she thought she might!" replied Little Doe, "And she didn't do it! As far as I am concerned that meant that she had changed her mind!"

"Is this the only cougar hide in the camp?" asked Raven.

"As far as I know," Mountain Quail grumbled. "Crying Coyote could tell you for sure."

"It is the only one," Hollow Bone answered. "But there is a cougar up at the north end of the valley which has been stalking the smaller children all fall. We have discussed going after it on a number of occasions, but just never did."

"It is not that cougar which is the problem. It is this one's hide. Both these women claim it belongs to them," Crooked Spirit stepped in and explained. "How do you suggest we settle this problem?" he turned to Calling Wolf.

The hunter frowned, knowing that this was a test for him. As a dreamer, he would be required to make these kinds of decisions on a regular basis. He studied the hide. It had already been partially cut, making it useless for Mountain Quail's purpose. But she had a prior claim. He thought for a time and then made his decision. "For now, this hide will go to Crooked Spirit for safe keeping. Tomorrow Calling Wolf and I will go after the other cougar. If we kill it, then the hide will be turned over to Little Doe to process. When she had done this and given it to Mountain Quail, then she will have this hide returned to her. Until then, neither woman will have a cougar hide."

Crooked Spirit nodded; Calling Wolf had made a wise decision. Robe Maker nodded; this would be her answer as Cave Elder.

But this sort of petty bickering began to break out in all three caves on a regular basis. There were just too many people crammed into too small a space. And winter was just beginning.

"There is another cave toward the north end of the valley," Running Bison stated, "It would take quite a lot of work to make it livable, but perhaps we should consider such a task. There is little to do during the cold, perhaps it would lighten the stress as well as give us something to concentrate upon besides getting on one another's nerves." He glanced around at the council gathered beside the hearth, "You know the cave that I mean." He turned to Thunder Cloud, "We sheltered there during a storm several moons ago."

Thunder Cloud nodded. "It would indeed take work. If I remember right, part of the roof caved in and most of the floor is nothing but a pile of rubble."

"That's the one!" Running Bison nodded, "But once the cave in is cleared, it is even a larger cave than this one."

"But it is so far away!" Robe Maker protested.

"Do you have any other suggestions?"

She shook her head, "I suppose that this cave provides the only solution," she sighed.

# PART 3
## THE FULFILLMENT

# CAST OF CHRACTERS

## (in order of appearance)

Chapter 21
**Bear Claw Woman:** The Chosen
**Raven:** Her mate.
**Running Bison:** Headman of the Wolf Camp
**Whispering Wind:** His mate.
**Guardian:** Dire Wolf, protector of The Chosen
**Crooked Spirit:** Dreamer of the Wolf Camp
**Hollow Bone:** Acolyte to Crooked Spirit
Women of the Wolf Camp
*Robe Maker    Laughing Water    Little Doe    Dancing Reed*
*Dancing Star    Mountain Quail    Elk Woman*
Men of the Wolf Camp
**Thunder Cloud    Calling Wolf    Running Antelope    Elk Caller**
**Crying Coyote    Jumping Fox        Bull Elk**

**Young Wolf:** Raven's wolf
**Quenquel:** Savage Dreamer outcast by his camp

Chapter 22
**DaNu-Calf:** Whispering Winds son.

Chapter 24
**Raptor Feather**: Headman of the Bear Camp
**Jumping Fox:** Dreamer of the Bear Camp

**Sun Catcher:** Acolyte to Jumping Fox
Women of the Bear Camp
*Cattail Woman   Dancing Crane CiCi*
**Badger Tail:** Hunter

Chapter 25
**Prairie Grass**: Hunter
**Bull Elk:** Hunter
**Deer Camp**
**Spirit Dancer**: Dreamer
**Two Bears:** Headman
**Bison Robe**: Woman
**Rosebud:** Girl

Chapter 26
Hunting Badger's Cave
**Hunting Badger:** Headman of cave
**Bull Elk**: Hunter, the only other man
Women of the Cave
*Dancing Willow   Laughing Water   Dancing Moth   Fire Weed*

Chapter 27
**Sky-Ash Branch: Blue-eyed Healer of Gatherers**
**Harry Man:** Her stepfather
**Soft Robe: Her Grandmother**
**White Eagle: Quenquel in hiding**
**Yellow Bird**: Ash Branch's friend.

# CHAPTER 21

The firelight cast flickering shadows against the roof of the cave. Bear Claw Woman lay beside Raven wide-awake and finding whimsical imaginary figures within the shadows. Winter had set in and those living in the valley were beginning to get on each other's nerves. Running Bison had made several suggestions, but the only solution seemed to be to move part of the camp to a large cave some distance up the valley. Raven had suggested that they be among those relocating. Bear Claw Woman was not completely happy about this. She had just been reunited with Whispering Wind, her only real connection with The People. She sighed and tried once again to find sleep.

"We are going to investigate the new cave," Raven finished eating and drank the remainder of his tea. "You might as well stay here and keep warm. I don't know when we will be back, but it will probably be tonight after dark."

"Do you think trying to move the debris from the floor is a practical idea? What if more of the roof caves in? Someone could be hurt!"

"I hope this doesn't happen. We will be sure to check the roof before we begin. Until we get there and look things over, there is no way we can know if it is possible. But you must agree that something has to be done before there is blood-shed among us."

Bear Claw Woman sighed and nodded. "Who would have thought that trouble would come from the women of the second cave? To fight over such ridiculous things as a fur! It isn't as though there are not more animals to provide!"

"I know, but both women claim ownership of the cougar hide and we were unable to provide another. But these are the sort of silly things that happen when people are forced to live too close for too long. They get on each other's nerves. Ordinarily these two women are probably the best of friends and would even die for each other. But winter has put them at war. I have seen it happen before. The best solution is to separate them for a time. This we have done, but still they are too close. Now the only answer is to move them apart farther. The cave at the end of the valley does this. I know that you are not happy about the separation from Whispering Wind and the baby, but you will see that tension all around will be less. There are those here who are uncomfortable with you living so near."

Bear Claw Woman nodded, "I knew this would happen. Any time that 'power' is involved, people get nervous. I am used to it now, but at first it did bother me." She finished eating and rose to walk with him to the cave entrance, "I will miss you while you are gone. It will seem strange. This is the first time that we have been separated since I awakened in the cave in the canyon. Sometimes I wish we had just stayed there!"

The big hunter shook his head, "It was time to move on. Life is for living, even if at times that living is unpleasant. Right now, the important task is to investigate this cave. If it isn't habitable, then perhaps we should look beyond the valley for another. Wait until we know for sure before you begin to worry farther."

Bear Claw Woman watched the hunters as they attached their snow walkers and headed north becoming smaller and smaller, until they disappeared around a point of rocks. She shrugged and let the flap fall back into place. Whispering Wind came up behind her, "They will be back well after dark if I know that group!" She sighed and shifted the baby, "Come on and have a bowl of tea with me. I want to talk to you about something."

"Is something wrong?"

"I am not sure. I want your opinion," Whispering Wind poured the tea and the women settled comfortably beyond the general noise and chatter of the cave.

"What is bothering you?" Bear Claw Woman asked.

"I can't really put my finger on it," Whispering Wind admitted, "It is just that every time I leave the cave I have the feeling that I am being watched. It is eerie! I know there is no one around, but still the feeling is there!"

"Only when you are outside?"

Whispering Wind nodded, "The feeling goes away as soon as I step inside any of the caves."

"How long has this gone on?"

"Ever since you arrived; before then there was no such feeling. But ever since you arrived, it has been there."

"We were followed," Bear Claw Woman admitted, "It would not surprise me if 'he' is the one, watching you!"

"But why? And who is 'he'? And why haven't you mentioned it before now?"

"I have, but only to Raven. He doesn't know for sure, that the follower is here in the valley, but there hasn't been time, or opportunity for him to go 'hunting'."

"What do you think followed you? Was it a person, or dare I ask?"

"I don't honestly know," Bear Claw Woman admitted. "At first, I thought it was a person, someone who had been badly hurt. All during the trip from the cave here, every night something stole 'power' from me. But when Bull Elk looked, he found no trace and then it went away. But during the first blizzard again I felt the pull. That doesn't mean that who or whatever it is, is here in the valley, but I am beginning to suspect that it is. And now you say that it watches you! Something must be done!"

"But what?"

"I think that it is time for me to take a walk on my snow walkers."

"You are going after 'it' by yourself?"

"I don't know what to do!" Bear Claw Woman admitted. "But if it is now focused on you, then it is my fault and my responsibility!"

"You could be in danger."

"As could you, every day that this 'thing' follows your every move. What if it is an evil spirit and has decided to steal you?"

Whispering Wind shivered and hugged her baby closer, "You don't think..."

"I don't know what to think. Do we tell the men and let them handle this, or do we take care of it ourselves? There was a time that we would have done just that. In the meantime, if you are against my going out and facing this creature, then the alternative is that you do not ever leave the cave alone. Always go in a group."

"That is what I have been doing," admitted Whispering Wind. "But promise me that you won't do anything rash! I should not even have mentioned it to you and I certainly would not have if I had thought, for a single heartbeat, that you would go out and put yourself in danger!"

Bear Claw Woman sighed, but gave in, "I won't do anything stupid," she promised, crossing her fingers within the folds of her robe. A short time later Whispering Wind and another pair of women headed toward the third cave to work on spring tunics; Bear Claw Woman waited until they were inside, then called to Guardian and slipped from the cave. She followed the path to the third cave and then making sure no one saw her, continued toward the southern pass. Guardian was nervous and kept circling and whining. Finally, she stopped crossways in the path and refused to let Bear Claw Woman proceed farther.

"Come on Guardian! You know there is something up there! Get out of my way!"

"Woof!" The wolf replied softly but refused to let her continue. Finally, Bear Claw Woman realized the wolf was not going to let her pass. With a disgusted snort she gave up and turned back to the caves. She fretted the rest of the day. The men returned late; determined that the clearing out of the big cave was feasible. They had removed a great deal of rubble. Although there was one piece of the roof which was too big for any number of them to move, it was flat on top and could be left right where it was and with little effort the floor built up to match it. They were gathering supplies and returning in the morning. They expected to be gone for at least a pair of days and then with luck, people could begin moving in. The good thing was that with all the traffic, there would be a wide easy path between the two parts of the camp. Bear Claw Woman said nothing about her conversation with Whispering Wind. Whispering Wind said nothing either, not wishing to bother Running Bison with more problems than he already had.

In the morning the men left. Whispering Wind went back to the third cave to complete the tunic work. Bear Claw Woman was grimly determined to discover the identity of the watcher. She tied Guardian securely to a peg at the rear of the cave and ignoring her pitiful whimpering, donned snow walkers and retraced her path of the previous day. Then she followed the trail toward the high pass, sure that the watcher was somewhere near. She was puffing and panting with exertion long before she entered the thick pine forest at the base of the upward trail. Here she rested for a time before pushing on.

The shadows closed in on her once she entered the forest. The path twisted and turned, and she was forced repeatedly to clutch as branches to keep her balance. She passed close to a large boulder and felt a blinding pain in her head, then nothing...

\*     \*     \*

Guardian tugged desperately at the thong; but Bear Claw Woman had attached it securely. She tried to dig up the peg, but it was driven securely into a crack in the rock, she couldn't dig it free. Finally she elected to chew the thong. The leather was tough and it took a long time, even with her sharp teeth. Finally, she was free and as she leaped from the cave, she howled and called to several other wolves. Seven shadows streaked after her as she flew up the trail in pursuit of Bear Claw Woman.

Guardian reached her first. Already her body was cooling dangerously. Someone had removed her outerwear and left her to freeze to death in the cold. Guardian huddled against her, lending something of her own body heat. Another wolf and yet another did the same. The remainder followed the trail. They saw the figure ahead of them, but as they got close, darts began to strike. One wolf yelped and flopped onto its side. Then it lay still. The other three stopped, sniffed and whined, but could not rouse the fallen one. They circled and turned back.

Guardian raised a mournful howl. Far below, in the valley, Whispering Wind heard. She raised her head. "Did you hear that?" she asked the other women, "It sounds like one of our wolves."

The women looked around. "There is a pair of wolves missing," Robe Maker stated. "But what one is howling; and from where? It sounds far away. Are you sure that it is one of ours?"

"I am sure and I know which wolf it is further!" stated Whispering Wind as she rose and began to run to the entrance. "She promised!" she wailed.

"Who?" Robe Maker asked, "and what did she promise?"

"Bear Claw Woman, replied Whispering Wind. "I just know something awful has happened to her! And it will be all my fault!" She struggled to pull on her snow walkers and finally stood upright, "I am going after her!"

"What about the men?" Robe Maker questioned, "If she is in trouble, shouldn't we let the men handle it?"

"Where are the men?"

"At the new cave, you know that!"

"Exactly! There isn't time. If she is hurt, time is essential. She could freeze to death very quickly in this cold. You don't have to come with me if you don't want to, but no one is going to stop me! Laughing Water, you take care of my baby. I'll be back as soon as possible." With this Whispering Wind headed up the valley following Bear Claw Woman's trail through the snow. Grumbling, Robe Maker and three other women followed her. The howling of the wolves was getting nearer and soon Whispering Wind was able to call out and the women caught their breath as they watched the animals streak down the trail to meet them. Guardian was not among them, but one was wounded, blood dripped from a dart wound in its shoulder, but the cast had been glancing and although the shoulder was cut open, the dart itself had not imbedded.

"I told you there was trouble!" Whispering Wind struggled again up the trail. When she rounded the boulder and nearly stumbled over Bear Claw Woman's cold still body, she screamed out in concern. Quickly the other women joined her.

"She is so cold!" Whispering Wind stated. "What on earth is she doing out in this weather without outer clothing?"

"Look! Here is one of her mittens!" Robe Maker called, "She didn't set out that way; someone took her clothing so that she would die of the cold." If we don't get her warm, they will have succeeded! Who could do such a thing?"

"Come on, help me get her to her feet, here, wrap my robe about her!" Whispering Wind shrugged out of her own robe and handed it to one of the women. The others helped raise the stricken woman and get the warm robe beneath her.

"Now what?" Robe Maker asked.

"Get a fire started," Whispering Wind instructed. "We have to find out how badly she is hurt and get her warm. Did any of you bring a blade or anything with which we could construct a travois with?"

"I have a hafted knife," Little Doe offered, "But what good would it do to cut travois poles? We have no thongs from which to make a harness and no hide either?"

"We have our robes!" Whispering Wind replied, "Here, cut one into strips. I have my awl still in my pouch. I'll punch holes in the edge of the robe, the rest of you find wood, get a fire started and get those traces chopped! Quickly! We haven't time to waste!"

Little Doe and Dancing Reed set out to cut the traces, the recent animosity between them entirely forgotten with this emergency. Robe Maker expertly got a fire started beneath the branches of a spreading pine provided a bit of shelter from the wind. Guardian whined and got repeatedly underfoot until Whispering Wind gave her sharp instructions to stay out of the way. They dragged Bear Claw Woman to a place beside the fire and the wolf resumed her position against the inert form. Whispering Wind was satisfied that they had done what they could for the present to help Bear Claw Woman. She turned her attention to the construction of the makeshift travois. Remembering the pig hunt, many moons previously, she thanked the spirits that now she knew what to do to save her friend's life.

Little Doe and Dancing Reed dragged the poles up to the fire and quickly they stripped the twigs free. Now spread one of your robes over the poles," instructed Whispering Wind.

"But we will freeze if you take all of our robes! And from the look of the weather, we had better be doing just that and as fast as we can. So hand over those robes. Huddle close to the fire until I get this attached then we will be on our way. I am far more worried that Bear Claw Woman has not moved at all, than I am that we will freeze. Without her to intercede with the spirits you can bet your life we will all be dead soon!"

With no more protest the women handed over their robes and watched as Whispering Wind expertly and rapidly constructed the makeshift travois. She wrapped Bear Claw Woman with what remained of their robes and they started down the trail, taking turns dragging the travois.

Half way to the cave they were met by a group of women who had seen them coming and brought warm robes.

"Take the bottom edge of the robe, several of you and help us carry her up and into the cave!" Whispering Wind ordered, as she and Robe Maker and Little Doe carried the other end. Quickly they transferred the still unconscious woman to her bed furs. Again, Guardian snuggled close to her. A blue glow again developed. Whispering Wind had seen it before and again on the trail earlier. Quickly she ordered the wolf away. Then with deft fingers she dug in the storage basket and found the deer hide covered Sacred Bundle. This she undid and then lay the relics against Bear Claw Woman's flesh, wrapping each limp hand about one of the teeth. Again the blue mist spread, this time very strongly. Then Whispering Wind went to where the exhausted wolf lay on her side. She found Bear Claw Woman's staff and settled it against the animal's forehead. With a sigh Guardian closed her eyes and let the power flow from the staff into her body.

Whispering Wind settled down beside her and ran her fingers through the wolf's fur. "You would give your life for her as well, I know. But when she returns to us, I don't wish to be the one to have to tell her that I did not take care of you and that you are again dead. We are taking the best care of her I know. Now it is up to 'power'."

The group of women huddled about the hearths in the first cave. They nibbled disinterestedly on food and drank copious amounts of tea as the day wore on. Outside the wind howled angrily and whipped snow into a driving frenzy. Night settled in. Children were nestled into furs and put to sleep. Eventually youths and girls retired to their furs, but the women kept their vigil. With the aid of hot rocks wrapped in rabbit fur nestled against her cold body, gradually they returned Bear Claw Woman's temperature to normal. Now she lay wrapped within her very own sleeping furs, the Sacred Relics clutched in lifeless hands. She had an egg-sized lump on the back of her head where she had been struck with a branch. It had been found lying beside her. Nothing else seemed to be damaged, but after the attack by Angry Bull it was possible that any head injury would always react severely with her.

"What will happen to us if she dies?" Little Doe asked as she handed Whispering Wind another bowl of tea.

"She can't die!" Whispering Wind replied, "Don't even think that! Without Bear Claw Woman and the Sacred Relics to protect The People, we are lost. No matter who else dies, she must not perish! If she does, the circle of life will close, and we are all doomed. The spirits promised this at the Gathering. We all heard! Angry Bull tried to end her life. Actually he succeeded. Bear Claw Woman died, she went to the land of the dead and chose to return so that the spirits would not wipe The People from the face of the land. We are responsible for making sure that nothing happens to her. Obviously, her word is not good! She promised me only yesterday that she would not do anything foolish! Now look! And it is all my fault!" Finally Whispering Wind began to sob, "If I hadn't spoken to her about..." she wailed.

"There is nothing more that we can do now," Robe Maker patted Whispering Wind on the shoulder. "We can ask the spirits... if you think that would help?"

Whispering Wind nodded. "At least that gives us something to do except wait and watch."

Robe Maker nodded. "Come with me Little Doe and help me find some ingredients that I need to make a special tea which will open our minds to the spirits. I know that it is here somewhere in these baskets!"

\*     \*     \*

The form blended well into the blizzard. The tall figure was bent nearly double fighting the driving wind. But he had followed the women returning to the caves. No one had bothered to watch behind. He slipped from tree to tree, keeping them in view. Then he huddled beneath the spreading branches of a huge pine and watched as they all gathered in the far cave. This was his chance! As the wind rose and howled, closing the women into the sheltering warmth of the first cave, Quenquil slipped silently into the third. He knew it was unlikely that anyone would be returning there this night. They were all worried about the fate of the woman he had bashed over the head. Unfortunately, it had not turned out to be Humming Bird, but the one he had followed to this valley.

He took his time plundering the supplies of the cave. He took furs and food stores and carried them into the forest where he stashed them to retrieve later. Then he returned for more. While scouting the valley from his perch at the pass, he had noticed a dark blotch at the base of the canyon wall, in a sheltered area. Here he found a small cave much more to his liking. Now he was preparing to move into it. Already his wood supply and food had been transferred. He did not plan to return to the high cave again. The second and third load of plunder he carried to the small cave and then returned for the first. He chuckled to himself as he added the finished cougar tunic to the last bundle: it was just his size.

The blizzard would remove all trace of his trail and since he was certain that as soon as the men returned they would go search the high cave, he had left it as nearly as he had found it as possible. They would not know he had ever been there. He had even left the mangy robe behind.

Now he had a fresh wolf pelt to make into a hood for his outdoor clothing. He huddled down into the robe that he had taken from Bear Claw Woman, thankful for its warmth. The fire soon warmed the small cave and Quenquil took his time arranging his plunder and settling in. Now all he had to do was survive the winter. He began arranging the boulders across the front of the cave, closing all but the very upper part of the opening. No one would ever find him here. And he was safe until spring. He had food and wood for his fire. The small opening to the cave would be easy to clear when he had needed to go outside. He lay on his newly acquired sleeping furs and watched the smoke spiral lazily toward the roof. Then he slept.

\*     \*     \*

"Here, take this hide and see if you can attach it to that wall by using pegs into that crack!" Running Bison instructed. "We are going to be in trouble if we don't get this entrance closed off before the storm strikes full-force. Have you men gathered all the wood you could find?" he shouted to the three hunters, staggering into the cave looking like misshapen giants, carrying huge piles of wood upon their backs.

"We have enough wood to last at least a moon," protested Thunder Cloud. How much more do you think we need?"

"Right!" Running Bison laughed, "There! That should block the entrance!" He stood back and surveyed the covering with satisfaction. "I am not happy that we are going to be stranded here for the duration of this storm, but at least we know that our women are safe in the home caves. This storm can't last forever, and it gives us a chance to explore and decide if the cave is suitable."

"I think there is a passage leading deeper!" shouted Calling Wolf, "Someone help me clear the rubble away!"

Running Antelope and Elk Caller went to his assistance. Soon a whoop of excitement echoed through the cave. "Will you look at this!" exclaimed Calling Wolf, "I think we have found the solution to all of our problems. There is more than a hand of large caves leading from this passage; plenty of room for the entire camp!" He lifted his torch, "And it keeps going farther as well."

"Let's explore this place," Running Bison called. "Come on men, get torches, but be careful! We don't know the condition of these roofs and floors. Don't take chances!"

Crying Coyote and Jumping Fox led the way deeper into the mountain. Their excited voices echoed back to the other, on their own paths of discovery. The storm rages outside, but the men were more than pleased with their find. Finally they all returned to the main cave and settled about the hearth built on the flat stone.

"I think we should move the entire camp here," Crying Coyote stated. "There is plenty of room for everyone, even if each hearth wants their own space. And the front cave is large enough for everyone to work together and not get underfoot. We could bed the wolves down there as well and even in the worst weather we would be safe and warm."

"I agree," Running Bison nodded. "So, as soon as this storm stops, we will begin moving the camp. Besides, this cave is closer to the trail from the valley. It will make watching it, much easier and when we are ready to leave, we can store the supplies we aren't taking with us until we return."

"I watched the pull of the smoke from our torches. There is another opening to this cave and I think we should find it. Most of the side caves will fill up with smoke if much of a fire is kept going in them, but the main passage still draws the smoke deeper," Thunder Cloud noted.

"There is little need to heat the side caves," Running Bison said. "They will not get any colder and mostly they will be used for sleeping and storage. We will be living in this cave, which we have discovered is much larger than we first suspected. Our work clearing the rubble has opened it up considerably. Now all we need to do is transfer the camp and get settled in. You men might just as well decide which caves you want to claim for you hearths. I plan on taking the first one, so that I am closest to the main room, but we should decide how to organize the rest."

I think it should go on standing in the camp!" Thunder Cloud stated. "Crying Coyote and his family should get the second cave and Crooked Spirit the next one and so on."

"Where would this place us?" Raven asked. "We are the most recent to join the camp, yet my mate is a powerful member."

"You are correct," Running Bison nodded. "I think that your mate should have the cave next to Crooked Spirit. It will also make the teaching of those wanting to learn more of the spirit world easier. I know that a number of women are interested in the healing plants and Bear Claw Woman has promised to begin teaching them."

"I also would like to learn more of these," Calling Wolf replied. "But we would be doing this in the main cave. I don't see that it much matters how we set up the sleeping caves. Perhaps it would be a good idea to ask the women how they want to do it."

"Then we will wait. First, however is to get everyone and all our supplies moved from the three caves to this one." Running Bison closed the discussion. "Now we might as well go to our furs and rest. Tomorrow will be a busy day even if the storm keeps us here."

\*　　\*　　\*

Whispering Wind sat next to Bear Claw Woman. It was nearly dawn, but her friend had not moved since they brought her back to the cave. They had drunk the special tea that Robe Maker had prepared and made prayers to the spirits. Now all they could do is wait.... Bear Claw Woman's breathing was steady, but shallow. Wind just didn't know what more she could do. She castigated herself for not insisting on learning more of the healing plants since Bear Claw Woman had joined them. There had just been so much to catch up on! She rose and fetched more hot tea and when she settled again in her furs, she noticed that Bear Claw Woman had moved. She had dropped one of the Sacred Teeth. With trepidation, Whispering Wind picked it up. A thrill of 'power' shot up her arm. She nearly dropped the thing in fear.

However, instead, she closed her eyes and called out to the spirits. *If you can hear me, please, help me to help her!* She pleaded.

There, of course, was no answer. She sighed in resignation, but suddenly remembered a conversation from seasons back. Bear Claw Woman had explained to her how to make a special herbal compress to lessen swelling. She frowned, but thinking through their plant gathering, realized that she had everything needed.

"Robe Maker, wake up!" she whispered as she shook the other woman, "I have an idea."

"What is it?" Robe Maker blinked sleep from her eyes.

"Help me find where we stored the Nacodo leaves. I am going to make a poultice to bring down the swelling in Bear Claw Woman's head."

"Do you know how to do that?" Robe Maker asked.

"Yes, I do," Whispering Wind answered. "Bear Claw Woman taught me herself."

"Then why are we just talking about it, let's get to work!" Robe Maker scrambled to her feet. Soon the women were searching through the storage baskets.

"I found it!" Robe Maker shouted.

"What is going on?" Little Doe sat up.

"Oh! Sorry! I didn't mean to waken you," Robe Maker apologized. "We have decided to try to decrease the swelling in Bear Claw Woman's head. I just found the herb we needed."

"Really? Is there a way that I can help?"

"You could see if there is any dry clay still stored in those baskets over there," Whispering Wind nodded toward the back of the cave. "We can cover the poultice with clay and then wrap it with rabbit skin. This will hold in the heat which the Nacodo generates."

"I will do that," Little Doe pulled on her tunic and made her way to the far end of the cave. She filled a bowl with dry clay and returned. Quietly the three women heated water, steeped the plant and then mixed it with mustard before applying it to Bear Claw Woman's wound. They covered the area with clay and wrapped it with a bandage of rabbit fur. Then they sat back and waited.

"Do you think this will work?" Little Doe questioned.

"I have no idea," admitted Whispering Wind, "But it was the only thing I could think of. We can only wait and hope that it does."

They settled again and waited. The wind howled outside and shivers ran down their spines, even settled warm and secure as they were. "I hate this time of night!" Robe Maker pulled her fur closer, "It is the time of Death Stalker!"

Just then Bear Claw Woman groaned and opened her eyes. The three women froze.

"What happened?" she asked, looking about with puzzlement. "I don't remember returning to the cave. I was following the path to the pass."

"So you were," Whispering Wind sighed, "That is where we found you. After you promised not to do so foolish a thing! Had not Guardian found you and howled until she got our attention, you would be a frozen memory now!"

"Guardian! I left her tied in the cave," Bear Claw Woman admitted.

"Well she chewed through the thong, thankfully!" Whispering Wind replied. "Due to your foolishness, we have lost one wolf, another is wounded and everyone is worried to death about you!"

Already many women had wakened and were grouped around them, anxious about Bear Claw Woman.

Yipping beyond them alerted Whispering Wind to the fact that Guardian was still tied out of reach. Quickly she released the wolf who promptly rushed to Bear Claw Woman and made sure she was all right. "I had to take her away," Whispering Wind answered the unasked question. "She was depleting her 'power' to help you. I placed the Sacred Relics," she nodded toward Bear Claw Woman's hands, "In you hands and tied her up. Then I replaced her power from the staff. I hope that I did right?"

Bear Claw Woman nodded, "I could have done no better myself."

"Now, tell us what happened!" Robe Maker asked.

"Bear Claw Woman frowned, "I don't really know. I was following the path to the pass, but just beyond the big boulder I think someone struck me from behind. He must have been waiting there to ambush me."

"Someone?"

"At least we now know that the watcher is human," Bear Claw Woman frowned and put her hand to her head. "What is this?" she felt the bandage.

"As you say, someone struck you from behind," Little Doe answered. "When we found you, you were unconscious, lying in the snow clothed only in your tunic and leggings. The wolves went after whoever did this to you. One of them was killed and another wounded. We brought you back here and Whispering Wind treated you."

"I apologize for the trouble which I have caused all of you," Bear Claw Woman bit her lip, "I only wanted to discover who was watching."

"Watching?" Little Doe frowned.

"I felt that someone or something was watching me every time I left the cave," Whispering Wind admitted, "So Bear Claw Woman took it upon herself to investigate! Even though she promised me that she wouldn't do anything so foolish!" Wind reminded Bear Claw Woman.

"I thought it was just my imagination!" Little Doe exclaimed, "You mean you also have felt that someone was watching you every time you stepped out of the cave?"

"I have also noticed it!" another woman exclaimed.

"Well at least we do know that there is someone out there and whoever it is isn't friendly!"

Robe Maker stated. "So from now on, it would be best if we only go out in groups. When the men return, they will find out who this is and deal with him!"

"How can there be anyone in the valley we don't know about?" Dancing Star asked.

"Someone followed us to the valley," Bear Claw Woman admitted, "I wasn't sure before, but now I am." She took the bowl of tea that Whispering Wind handed her and sipped hungrily. "He is clever, whoever he is, but I did not sense danger from him, at least not until about a moon ago. He tried to attack my 'power' and steal it. I thought that I had discouraged him. Even then, however, I didn't know that he was here in the valley. Only when Wind told me about the feeling of being watched did I begin to realize how close he was. That is why I set out to challenge him."

"Well now we will let the men deal with 'him'," Whispering Wind stated. "I don't intend to let you out of my sight until they return."

"You have nothing to worry about," Bear Claw Woman assured her, "I have learned my lesson." She rubbed the bandage on her head. "Believe me, the headache I have is enough to discourage any more attempts to do things independently."

Whispering Wind's baby began to cry, others wakened and soon the bustle of the cave brought the security of a normal day. A meal was served to all and finally the squabble between Little Doe and Mountain Quail seemed to be ended. Once again they were best of friends.

The storm raged on, convincing them all to remain together for yet another night. But the next morning brought clear skies.

"I am going back to the second cave," Basket Woman announced. "The hearth has certainly gone out and the cave will be cold. I will be back shortly, just as soon as I have started the hearth fire."

"Someone should also light the fire in the third cave," suggested Elk Woman, "I suppose it might just as well be me." She rose and began bundling against the cold. "It is a good thing we all brought our snow walkers here for there is no other way we could get through all this snow!" She exclaimed once the hide was drawn back from the cave entrance. "This storm had almost doubled the snow on the ground!"

"I will go with you and help," Dancing Reed called to Elk Woman. "Two can do the work much faster!"

Soon, a hand of women, were headed back to the second and third caves to get the hearth fires started and gather things to bring back to the first cave. Elk Woman grunted in disgust. "Someone left the hide loose! Look at all the snow that has blown into the cave! We will have to sweep it out before we can get the hearth fire started!"

"Wait!" Dancing Reed put her hand on the other woman's arm, "Something is not right here! I was the last one out and I am certain that I securely closed the entrance. Besides, things are not where we left them. Look at those storage baskets. Did we leave them out in the middle of the cave? And were those over there dumped over?"

"You are right!" Elk Woman agreed, "Furs that we had stacked against that wall are gone as well. Someone has been stealing our supplies while we were gone. Come on, we had better see what else is missing."

"The cougar tunic for one thing," Dancing Reed exclaimed in disgust, "After all the hard feelings it has cost! I left it folded on my sleeping furs. Even they are gone!"

"Do you think we should wait for the men to return? Maybe it would be better if we didn't disturb anything," suggested Elk Woman, "They will be back before sun-high."

Dancing Reed nodded, "Let's just get the snow swept out and the hearth fire started. Then return to the first cave. This place causes goose bumps to crawl up my spine!"

\* \* \*

"Are you certain?" Running Bison questioned the women.

"Of Course!" Elk Woman snorted, "We are neither stupid, nor blind. Things are missing. Food, furs, tools; weapons! We did not count it all because we were waiting for you to return. But these things are gone."

"I know you are not stupid," Running Bison ran his hands through his hair, "But the wind could have..."

"No, the wind could not have!" Dancing Reed cut in, "My bed furs are missing, as well as the contested cougar fur tunic. The storage baskets are all pulled out into the middle of the cave and things are just gone!"

"We will see what can be done," Crying Coyote cut in, "But it matters little, for we are all moving from these caves to the new place. There will be no more going out in storms to get from one cave to another. There is plenty of room for everyone!"

"All in that one cave?" Robe Maker asked.

"It has turned out to be a very large cave. There is room for all of us, plus many more! And each can have their own private space. The cave system extends far into the mountain."

"So we should begin moving right away," suggested Thunder Cloud. "We will also investigate the theft, but the sooner everyone is moved, the better I will feel. These caves have been invaded. It is time to leave them."

"No one feels safe here anymore," admitted Dancing Reed.

Raven was kneeling beside Bear Claw Woman. "Who did this to you?" he grated as his fingers explored the lump on her head.

"I think it was the 'follower'," she admitted. "I think he is here in the valley, in fact I know that he is. It was probably he who stole the supplies from the third cave. At least we know it is a man and not a spirit."

"The wolves will soon hunt him down," Raven stated, "And he will be sorry for all the grief he has caused."

"Tell me about this new cave," Bear Claw Woman changed the subject. "Is it as nice as Running Bison would have us believe?"

"I think so," the big hunter nodded. "It is big and there are many small side caves."

"Someone had better stay here until the last load has gone," she sighed.

"We will be the last to move," Raven assured her. "I want you to rest as long as possible before making the trip. I intend to stay right here with you to make sure that you do nothing more foolish. I leave you for a pair of days and return to find that someone has tried to kill you while I was gone; never again!"

"I have learned my lesson!" Bear Claw Woman protested, to no avail. The big man merely shook his head stubbornly.

In a flurry of activity travois were loaded, wolves placed in the traces and storage baskets strapped securely. The first group headed for the new cave. Thunder Cloud led them. The next were from the third cave. Crooked Spirit marched just behind, then Hollow Bone. Of this group, only Thunder Cloud would return with the wolves. Another pair of trips and the third cave would be empty. This suited them all. Before dark they were standing uneasily about in the big cave. Finally Dancing Reed marched to a place against the far wall and began unpacking food supplies. Soon others began to settle in as well.

"That is the last of it," Bear Claw Woman stood, hands on hips, her lower lip stubbornly stuck out. "There is no way that I am riding on that travois!"

"Then we will be here until spring!" Raven replied evenly, stretching and yawning as he leaned negligently against the wall.

"Fine! Then you might just as well unpack our things," she stomped back to where they had settled their hearth and planted her backside firmly on a rock.

"You are keeping the others waiting out in the cold," the big hunter reminded.

Bear Claw Woman merely glared back at him. Suddenly with a swoop he scooped her up in his arms and carried her from the cave and deposited her on the travois. "And stay there!" he admonished. "Or I will show these people how a man of my people controls a wayward mate!"

A laughing cheer rose from the amused onlookers. Bear Claw Woman bit her lip, considered leaping to her feet and stomping off, but she really did not feel recovered. With a sigh she relaxed into the furs and accepted her fate. Young Wolf trotted strongly down the trail and Bear Claw Woman rode the travois. When they reached the new cave, Raven grinned from ear to ear as again he scooped her into his arms and carried her up the path to the cave. To her chagrin even Guardian was grinning from ear to ear!

Several days passed. The camp was settled into the new cave and everyone seemed content. "I think it is time that we went 'hunting!" Raven stated as he and several hunters sat around a hearth late one night.

"Where do you suggest we begin?" Running Bison asked.

"I think he hid out in that small cave up on the pass," Thunder Cloud stated, "That is where we should start."

"Is there anywhere closer?" Raven questioned, "I doubt he made the trip clear from the pass to raid the cave and then carried his stolen goods back up there, not in a blizzard!"

Running Bison thought for a time, then shook his head. "If there is, I don't know of it," he admitted.

"I suppose it is futile to expect the wolves to pick up his trail?" Crooked Spirit asked.

Running Bison nodded. "But if he has been living in the little cave on the pass, they will certainly be able to pick up his scent and remember it."

"We could spread out in several groups and scour the entire valley," Crying Coyote suggested.

"I suspect 'he' has gone to ground like the fox he is," Bull Elk stated. "With all of this snow it will be impossible to find him. With the supplies he has stolen from the third cave there will be little reason for him to come out again, particularly if there is but one man."

"You think there could be more?" Thunder Cloud asked.

They all shook their heads. "There is only one man," Raven assured him. "Eventually we will catch him. He can't hide from us forever!" Raven clinched his big fists in frustration, "I will personally tear him limb from limb!"

"He has evaded us for moons," reminded Bull Elk.

"Sooner or later he will make a mistake," Raven replied, "And when he does, I intend to be there."

"I can understand that you want him badly." Running Bison reminded, "But don't let it cloud your judgement. We have no idea how dangerous this person is, if indeed he is a danger."

"What about his attack on Bear Claw Woman?" protested Raven, "Don't you call that dangerous?"

Running Bison shook his head. "He made no attempt to attack anyone until she went after him," reminded Running Bison. "Chances are he would have kept his distance and we wouldn't have even known of his existence if she hadn't stumbled onto him."

"She didn't 'stumble'," protested Raven. "This creature has been following us for moons, draining power from her time and time again. We had hoped to find safety here, but perhaps we were wrong, there may be no safety for us anywhere, but I will not sit idly by and let anyone attack my mate and do nothing about it."

"No one is asking you to," replied Running Bison. "Only use you head and don't let your strong emotions cloud your vision. Work with us as part of a team. Together we have a far better chance of catching this fellow. More eyes and more time will bring faster results. As Thunder Cloud suggested, the place to begin our search is at the cave on the pass. Tomorrow a group of us will go there and decide what path to follow next. I am as anxious as you are to catch this thief. He is a threat to all of us. Stealing food and supplies is about the worst thing anyone can do to a camp, particularly in the depth of winter. Had he come into the camp and asked to be taken in, that is one thing, but to steal is not acceptable!"

"You talk as if the theft was a greater threat that the attack on Bear Claw Woman," protested Raven.

"Certainly not!" Running Bison quipped, "But if you were thinking with a clear head, you would realize that even the death of one person is less serious than the death of many. Had we not gathered far more food than necessary, the theft of so much of it would have been very serious indeed, perhaps even life-threatening, to the entire camp!"

"You are right," Raven sighed, "I am not thinking straight. I have never before had someone I care for so much as Bear Claw Woman, but I have to do something!"

"And so you shall! Tomorrow, I promise you. You can lead the group to the pass. Perhaps that will take some of the edge off your surplus energy. I also agree with Crying Coyote that we should spread out over the entire valley. Keep your eyes sharp for anything. Anyplace someone could hide; anything out of place. When we have the information gathered from these excursions, we will talk again. In the meantime, get some sleep. Tomorrow will prove to be a hard day on all of us."

"She did it for me, you know," Whispering Wind explained to Running Bison later, as they snuggled in their furs. "I told her that I felt someone was watching me every time I left the cave. She went there to face this creature and make him leave me alone."

"Why didn't you say anything to me before now?" Running Bison almost exploded, "Do you expect a woman to do my job for me? How long has this been going on?"

"Calm down," Whispering Wind whispered. "You will wake the whole camp! Just this response is why! And you call Raven unreasonable! Haven't you enough to worry about? I only thought to spare you more. Bear Claw Woman promised me that she wouldn't do anything. We were going to wait until you returned, but she didn't. Now everything is crazy! We have some demented thief out there hiding, just waiting to strike another of us down. Every woman in the camp is frightened. It is as well that we have all moved into this one cave, for none of us would have found the courage to venture outside alone. At least here there is no need."

"Did you really feel someone watching you?"

"Of Course and I am not the only one. The other women felt it as well."

"Yet not one of you thought the presence of some stranger in the valley important enough to mention it to me?"

"It was just a feeling," Whispering Wind sighed. "I had no proof. None of us did; you would have only laughed at us and blamed an over active imagination or too much crowding. I just didn't think it was that important."

"Any time a stranger is involved it is important," Running Bison answered. "And I have too much respect for your level head to blame such a thing on over active imagination." He rolled over and pulled her close. "Next time you have such a feeling, please, just tell me and let me deal with it, all right?"

"All right," she sighed and gave herself up to more pressing issues.

"I don't understand it!" Thunder Cloud scratched his head. "I was sure that our thief must have been here." He glanced about the cave. "But everything seems to be just as we left it. No one has been into the store room and this one is just as we left it."

"I don't think so!" Bull Elk shook his head. "This wolf doesn't think so either." The animal he referred to carried a fresh wound on her shoulder. She curled back her teeth and growled as she moved about in the cave. "She smells the stranger. Look at her!"

The others studied the wolf's actions. "I agree with Bull Elk," Crying Coyote said. "She is on to something! Bring the others over here. Let them get the scent. Maybe one of them will be able to catch it again and we will find our thief."

"If it is a thief, it is certainly an odd one," Thunder Cloud sighed, "He certainly didn't steal any of the things from here."

"I wouldn't be so sure," Crying Coyote knelt near the hearth. "This hearth has had a fire in it very recently. I can still detect the wood smoke. Yet you say that no one has been here in over two moons." He shook his head, "I would say that someone has been here within a hand of days, no more."

"Perhaps we should check closer," Thunder Cloud nodded. "I don't remember what we left here, to be honest. My best recollection is that old robe and some firewood in the back room. I collected it the very day Raven and his group arrived."

"There is no wood back here!" Raven called, "If there was, it's gone now."

Thunder Cloud went quickly to the hide door cover. "You are right. I am sure that I left a huge pile of firewood back here. And I never left that basket there either!" He pointed to where a dilapidated reed basket leaned drunkenly against the far wall. "Someone has definitely been here. If the lack of wood is any indication, he spent quite a while here, yet tried to leave the place exactly as he found it. That is curious!"

"Almost as if he knew we would check here first," Crying Coyote nodded, "This man is not stupid!"

"But where could he be?" Raven shouted, "We have all agreed that there is no other place someone could hide in this valley."

"Then we are all wrong," Crying Coyote answered. "We have missed something. Now all of you: think! We know that someone was here. That someone attacked Bear Claw Woman and took her outer clothing and left her to die of exposure. That same someone killed one wolf and wounded this one." He pointed to the fretting female beside him. "During a storm, while the women were all gathered in the first cave, he entered the third one and stole supplies, a large quantity of them. Now how far could one man, even a strong one, carry such a load, during that savage storm? Certainly not clear back to here!"

They all agreed, but no one could remember any other place a person could shelter, certainly not one which would not be readily obvious. "The only thing I can think of to do is cover the entire valley again and again, until we find him. If he is still here, sooner or later, we will catch him." Raven answered. "If he isn't up here, then he is down there, somewhere." He nodded toward the valley. "And as long as our families are there as well, we are all in danger."

33 *Stachys palustris:* Woundwort.- Swamp hedge-nettle. The leaves were bruised and probably mixed with other plants to make a poultice to stop bleeding of wounds and open sores. The leaves and roots were also used in poultices to reduce pain and inflammation of the head. **Kershaw:** 152

# CHAPTER 22

The hunters scoured the valley for days on end. They found nothing. No sign of the intruder. The wolves picked up no scent. Another blizzard swept through the valley. Finally they gave up and accepted the idea that the intruder had outsmarted them. With the wolves sheltering in the outer cave and all snug and contented within, there was little to worry about. The hunters were always nearby.

"I am sure that I remember where to find it," Whispering Wind was adamant.

"You know where? You are certain?" Bear Claw Woman questioned her.

"Of course; look, it will only take me a couple of hands of time to go there, collect it and be back here. No one will even know that I have gone!"

"You know what Running Bison said about leaving the cave!" Little Doe reminded.

"He isn't here, he is out hunting," Whispering Wind replied, "Robe Maker is very ill. You said that this plant will help?"

Bear Claw Woman nodded. "It will make all the difference," she admitted.

"Then it is settled! I will leave immediately," she rose and began to pull on her outer clothes.

"Where do you go?" Crooked Spirit asked sharply, "You know what Running Bison said about going out alone!"

"Robe Maker is ill and I know where the plant is that Bear Claw Woman needs to make special medicine. Somehow it got left behind in the move. I am going back to the cave and I will collect it and return."

"You had better take Tall Bear with you," Crooked Spirit called for the youth, "Go with this woman to the old caves and see that she is returned to us safely."

I will," promised the youth. He grinned with pleasure as he donned outer clothes and then snow walkers. He called to his wolf and they followed Whispering Wind down the trail.

"There is no need for you to watch me so carefully!" Whispering Wind protested. "I know that Crooked Spirit said not to let me out of you sight, but he didn't mean it quite so genuinely. Now I need to concentrate on where I saw those herbs and I can't do it with you breathing down my neck." She was scrambling among a welter of discarded baskets and strewn trash. "I certainly don't remember leaving this place is such a mess either!" she muttered as she tossed yet another tattered empty basket out of her way.

"Well, if you are sure!" the youth bit his lip, "I think that I left something in the second cave. If you don't mind, I will just go search for it."

"Go ahead," she flapped her hands at him, "Give me some peace here!"

He nodded and slipped from the cave.

Whispering Wind watched him go, then sighed and returned to her task. Nothing seemed to be where she remembered. Containers, which had been against the north wall, were now in the middle; things that had been stored were strewn all about. It looked like the place had been searched thoroughly for something! She sneezed as dust tickled her nose and wiped tears from her eyes as they smarted as well. She was still down on her hands and knees searching when Tall Bear returned.

"You can at least help me look!" she called over her shoulder. "I know that they were in a small tall basket!" The youth did not respond so she finally turned to tell him again. Her voice caught in her throat and her heart nearly stopped beating. Before her stood, not the youth she expected but a tall, wild eyed, stranger. Fear trickled down her spine as she scooted back away from him. His eyes never left hers and he followed her step for step, finally trapping her against the far wall.

"Who are you? What do you want?" she finally managed to whisper.

He merely smiled and kept moving toward her. Whispering Wind opened her mouth to scream for Tall Bear, but she was too late. He clamped his hand over her mouth and covered her nose with a fur soaked in something. Whispering Wind tried to breathe then knew no more. She sank limply to the floor. The tall man lifted her swiftly and strode from the cave. In the blood-soaked snow lay the body of the wolf, darted through: beyond it, the still form of the youth.

He studied the sky and then smiled as he quickly followed his trail through the trees. It would be dark before they began to worry, probably fully dark before anyone would get really concerned. Long before then the storm would have obliterated his tracks. He had watched for nearly two moons for his chance. Now he had what he came for. There was no reason to return to the caves again. He had plundered them of every useful thing left behind, including the basket containing the herbs which she had come for.

He was barely breathing hard when he crawled into his cave and pulled her after him. He deposited her carefully upon the furs and quickly closed the entrance. Now that he had his prize, he would be more careful. They would be searching for him now harder than ever. He smiled to himself. "But you will never find me!" he whispered.

Tall Bear groaned and flopped over in the snow. His hand came into contact with the fur of his wolf, sticky and cold. He blinked snow from his eyes and shivered. He was so cold that his body shook uncontrollably. Squinting he studied his hand. It was covered with a dark-red sticky substance, blood. With a sinking heart he ran his hands over the still form. His wolf was dead! The dart still protruded from her side. Tears filled his eyes. Then, suddenly, he remembered the woman! "Whispering Wind." he muttered, "What has happened to her?"

He struggled to his feet, head swimming and staggered into the cave. As he feared, it was empty. "Whispering Wind." He called again and again, as he stumbled about the cave. Fear ran in trails up his spine, leaving him filled with dread. "What will I tell Running Bison?" he asked himself. Sobbing with frustration and fear, he nearly fell down the steep path from the cave. Snow was beginning to fall. Regretfully he staggered past the body of his wolf, realizing that he had neither the time nor the strength to take her back to the cave. It was essential that he reach the hunters as quickly as possible.

*    *    *

It was beginning to get dark. "Where is she?" Bear Claw Woman bit her lip and paced the floor. "She should have returned long ago! I knew we shouldn't have let her go!"

The wailing of Whispering Wind's infant son added to their concern. Finally Laughing Water put him to her own breast and he quieted. She had enough milk for both him and her own son.

"Should we send someone for the hunters?" asked Crooked Spirit.

"They should be back by now as well," Reminded Hollow Bone. "Someone is coming from the direction of the caves!" he shouted, "But it isn't Whispering Wind. It must be Tall Bear, but from the way he is staggering, I would say that he is injured." Already Hollow Bone was pulling on his snow walkers. "Come on, something is wrong!" he started down the valley.

"The hunters are coming down the trail from the pass!" Dancing Reed called.

"Tell them what has happened," instructed Crooked Spirit over his shoulder as he hurried to follow Hollow Bone toward the distant figure.

Dancing Reed met the hunters as they dragged heavily laden travois up the trail and into the cave. "What's wrong?" Running Bison frowned as he greeted the anxious woman.

"Whispering Wind hasn't returned!" Dancing Reed whimpered tearfully, "She should have been back long ago!"

"Back? Back from where?" he snapped.

"From the old cave," Dancing Reed answered.

"What!" Running Bison shouted, "She went there; by herself?"

Dancing Reed shook her head, "No, Tall Bear went with her. But Hollow Bone just saw him returning and he is alone. They have gone to meet him."

"They?"

"Hollow Bone and Crooked Spirit."

"Come on men! Leave the meat!" he turned and headed back down the trail, as fast as his snow walkers would take him. The rest of the men followed close behind.

Hollow Bone reached Tall Bear first. The youth all but collapsed into his arms, his breath coming in rasping jerks. "Whispering Wind," he blurted out between gasping breaths. "She is gone! My wolf was killed and I was struck from behind as I bent over her. When I woke up, Whispering Wind was gone! Just vanished!"

"Where were you when this happened?" Crooked Spirit panted.

"I.... Well, I was coming from the second cave," admitted Tall Bear. "Whispering Wind said I was under foot and well.... I wanted to find my hafted knife. Somehow I left it behind! But it wasn't there. The cave was a mess! It looked like someone had gone through everything. I was returning to warn Whispering Wind when my wolf yelped. When I looked, she had been darted. Then something hit me from behind. When I woke up, my wolf was dead and Whispering Wind was gone."

"Here comes Running Bison and the men!" Crooked Spirit remarked, as he glanced back toward the cave. Within heartbeats they reached the three apprehensive figures waiting for them.

"Crooked Spirit, you and Hollow Bone take Tall Bear back to the women. We are going on to the cave! I don't know when we will be back, but no one is to leave the cave! Understand?"

The three men nodded.

Without another word, the hunters swept past them and down the trail. Slowly, the dreamer and his apprentice helped the injured youth reach the cave and the waiting women. The only good news to greet them was that Robe Maker's fever had broken and she was much improved.

"This cave is a mess!" Running Bison held up his torch, "Someone has systematically ransacked it."

"The others will probably be in the same shape!" Bull Elk muttered, "This fellow is really starting to irritate me!"

"He is like some spirit which is always one step ahead of us," admitted Thunder Cloud.

"He is no spirit!" angrily, Raven stomped about the cave, lifting his torch to examine the damage. "But he certainly seems to know just what we are thinking!" He stopped. "Bear Claw Woman! Why didn't I think of it sooner?"

"What?"

"I am not sure," he admitted, "Just a thought."

"What is it?" Running Bison was visible shaken. "Come on man! Anything might help!"

"Remember how Bear Claw Woman can communicate with her mind." The others nodded, "well, what if this stranger can hear her thoughts?" He frowned. "He could know our every move."

"Is such a thing possible?"

"I have no idea," Raven admitted, "But it could explain a lot of things. Like how he knew just where to hide and attack her and that Whispering Wind would be returning to the cave. Only, why Whispering Wind? And what has he done with her? Obviously he didn't kill her, for we haven't found her body. There was no struggle here, yet she would not go with him willingly. None of this makes any sense. Why nearly kill Bear Claw Woman? If all he wanted was a woman, why not take her?"

"You think he was after Whispering Wind specifically?" Running Bison Questioned.

Raven shrugged, "I don't know. None of this makes any sense. We have found no trail from the cave, because the snow has covered it. Now the storm has settled in and we are stuck here until it lifts. By then, once again, there will be no trace of this fellow."

"At least we know it was he," Bull Elk remarked, "This wolf has told me so." He was squatted beside the wolf with a dart scar on her shoulder. The animal was growling low in her throat.

"Do you think there is a chance she could find his trail?" Running Bison asked hopefully.

"We can try," the hunter replied, encouraging the animal. The wolf circled, sniffed, whined and shook her head. Then she backed away toward the entrance and sniffed again. With a woof she leaped from the cave and streaked toward the second cave. The hunters followed. They followed to the third cave and then the trail became cold. Try as she might, the animal could not find another sign of scent.

"There is no way we can search in the dark with this storm," Raven stated. "We might just as well spend the night here and start with the dawn."

"We have already scoured the valley with no luck," reminded Calling Wolf.

"Then we will scour it again! And again until we find her!" Running Bison ground out.

And they did for days on end; from one side to the other, back and forth, with absolutely no luck.

"He has to be here somewhere!" Running Bison ground out.

Quenquel held his breath. The hunters stood but a short dart-cast from the tiny opening, which is all that showed, of his hidden cave. The snow had blown and drifted and covered all but the very top of the opening. It was no larger than a rabbit hole. Then he relaxed and smiled as they tromped away. A slight sound behind him alerted him that Humming Bird was waking up again. Quickly he placed the skin against her nose and she sighed and returned to sleep. From time to time he had allowed her to waken slightly, but only long enough to give her food and allow her to take care of her person. Never did he let her come far enough out from under the soul-stealing influence of the plant that she would cause him trouble. It puzzled him that she did not seem to recognize him, but just at the present he had more pressing matters to worry about. These hunters just wouldn't give up! They had searched again and again, each time passing within an arm's length of his hiding place. But they never found it.

*     *     *

Images wove in and about and out of the wobbling haze. A face appeared, frightening, the intense eyes peering deeply into her own. Questions bombarded her ears, but the words did not make sense. Someone pressed food upon her and she managed to eat it although her hands did not seem to be part of her. Her breasts hurt. The milk built up within them and she did not have coordination enough to be able to release it with hands that refused to follow directions. She cried. As time wore on, she began to accept her hazy world, even wait in anticipation for the release of the drug.

Voices called in her head, but she could not understand them. The stern-faced keeper called her Humming Bird. Yet, it did not feel like her name. The voices in her head called Whispering Wind. She tried to answer, but another, more powerful force, would not let her. Something was missing. Again and again she reached out for something, but what? She did not know. Time ceased to matter. Finally, the pain in her breasts subsided. Her milk dried up. Gradually, the keeper spoke to her for long periods of time and she began to understand his words. He told her that her name was Humming Bird and that she was his mate. They had been driven away from their camp and were hiding here in this valley. He said that if the hunters ever discovered them, they were both dead. She quivered in fear but had no thought to disbelieve him.

She had memories of capture, frequently faces flitted through her mind, but just as she was about to make a connection with them, they vanished. She wakened one night, her mouth open, ready to scream. The howls of the murdering attackers still echoed in her head. Images of bodies, spread on the ground in a hideous mockery of life, were so real she could almost smell the acrid smoke of their burning flesh. Then her keeper soothed her fear. He gave her the wonderful drink and with a sigh she sank into welcome oblivion.

Another time her visions were of rape and murder. Not her rape, nor her murder, but somehow they tugged at her soul. She tried not to let them go, but as usual.... They slipped away.

\*　　\*　　\*

"I don't know what else we can do!" Crooked Spirit sat beside Running Bison, "He must have somehow taken her beyond the valley and escaped us."

"How! We have had men stationed at the only ways out of the valley."

"Then he must have done it before we were even aware that she was missing. I don't know!

But we have been over the valley again and again and have found not so much as a footprint which was not our own."

"I have tried repeatedly to 'talk' to her," Bear Claw Woman added. "I get a sense that she is there, but something keeps me from contacting her. I have touched her mind, but then not really. It is hard to explain, but I get no sense of where she is. Always there is a feeling of darkness and confusion. That is all. And a strong presence beyond"

"Well at least that means that she is still alive," Raven replied.

"We have done everything that we can to find her," Bull Elk said, "Now we must go on with life. There are things that we have neglected; now we can put them off no longer. Soon it will be time for the spring ceremony, yet other than a token tunic; nothing has been prepared for the new hunters and new women. Crooked Spirit tells me that Bear Claw Woman's spirits have declared that we must make the offering at the Sacred Spring. If we are to be there before it is time, we must leave now, before the snow melts and traps us."

Running Bison raised tormented eyes. Raven felt his heart bleed for the other man. He did not say anything, merely nodded his head. Quietly the men went about preparing to leave. They cut fresh traces for the travois, repaired or replaced harnesses. Women watched the headman silently. Laughing Water handed the baby of Whispering Wind over to Bear Claw Woman. She had taken over caring for him. Now that he was weaned, the task was easier. Soon he would be old enough to be given a name. Already he tried to stand on wobbly legs, clutching at skirts and leggings and the ever-present finger.

Robe Maker was completely recovered, but she heavily blamed herself for the loss of Whispering Wind. Bear Claw Woman also carried the guilt, but no one bore so heavy a load as Tall Bear. Once the decision was made, within a hand of days, the camp filed over the southern pass and from the valley.

*     *     *

He watched them go. To make sure he gave her a stronger-than-usual dose of the drug, then slipped carefully from the cave and followed them. He watched from the top of the pass as they passed from view. Then he returned to the cave, checking to be sure that she was still 'sleeping' before continuing to the big cave. It was empty. They were alone in the valley, safe at last.

"Come on, it is safe!" he encouraged the frightened woman, "The enemy has gone. It is warm outside. The snow has almost all melted."

"No!" she whimpered and pulled back, "It isn't safe! You may think so, but I know!"

"Of course it is safe," he encouraged softly, nearly losing his grasp on his patience. "Haven't I told you so?"

She nodded and shaking, barely able to stand, wobbled to the mouth of the cave. The valley spread out before her, calm, peaceful, safe. She sighed and sank onto a nearby boulder. She let the sum warm her face, closing her eyes because the light was so bright. The tall beautiful man watched her with intense eyes. Slowly he smiled.

"See, Humming Bird, nothing bad will happen. As I said, it is safe here. Those who seek to kill us are far away. Rest now after a while we will go to the lake and wash."

"The lake?" she blinked, "Yes, I remember the lake.... We gathered cattails there...."

"Yes, there are cattails. We can gather them in you like. Perhaps you will make baskets from the reeds, like you used to. Iguana always said that you made the finest baskets in the camp."

"No," she shook her head. "Robe Maker's baskets are the finest." Confused, in her mind she could see the older woman, yet the name Iguana brought no such images.

"So you have always insisted," the man nodded, careful as always. "Are you ready?" he held out his hand and she hesitantly placed hers within it. They walked slowly down the path and shortly were looking down at a small lake. "See, perfectly safe!" he again reassured.

"Yes, safe...." she sighed.

While she sat on a rock and attempted to weave a basket from the reeds he brought her, the man slipped into the forest and purposefully began to gather the tubers of specific plants, expertly slicing off the tops and popping the root into a hide container attached to his waste thong. Finally, satisfied, he grunted and returned to the lake. She sat just where he had left her, on her lap sat a lopsided, loosely woven basket which would shame a child. He frowned and called her to come with him back to the cave. She rose, letting the forgotten basket fall to the ground, where it immediately fell apart.

"What are you doing?" she sat on their sleeping furs watching him shave slivers of tuber into a bowl.

"Preparing your medicine," he replied.

"Why?"

"Because you were nearly out," he answered.

"Why do I have to take medicine? Have I been ill?"

"You don't remember?" he asked.

She shook her head. "I can't remember much of anything," she confessed. "Sometimes I almost do, but always it seems to slip away!"

"Well, that is why you must take the medicine," he answered. 'Without it you will have the dreams which cause you to scream and plead with me."

"I don't remember them...." she sighed.

"Of course not, that is why you take the medicine. You don't want to remember them, do you?"

She shook her head. "I guess not." she frowned. "But why do I have these dreams? Did something terrible happen to me; something so horrible that I am unable to face it?"

Now he paused for a moment and then smiled slightly. "Yes, so horrible that you cannot face it; dreams where you are killed, where your heart is cut from your still living body."

She shuddered and moaned. "My baby?"

He frowned. "Dead," he replied. "The men who raped you killed it; you set it out yourself to walk the wind." He had listened carefully to her words as she rambled in her drug-induced haze. This death of an infant figured heavily in it, as did the rape. "Oh! Yes, I remember that.... When did it happen?"

"Some time ago," he answered.

"And I have been like this ever since?"

"Don't you remember?" he asked.

"No, not really. Time seems to play tricks on me. I wake up and expect to find myself somewhere else. It is odd, but it always surprises me when I wake up and find you beside me. Always, it seems that there should be someone else."

He shrugged. "I was not your first mate. It is probably him you expect."

"Will I ever get better?"

"I don't know. That is why the camp drove us out. The dreamer declared that you were possessed of evil spirits. That is why they were hunting us down to kill us. But I sneaked you from the camp during the dead-of-night and we fled. They followed us to this valley and very nearly caught us, but we were able to fool them and hide in the secret cave."

"But they have gone now?" she glanced fearfully about.

"They have gone now," he agreed. "But we must be very careful of strangers. If they should ever hear of where we hide, they will be back. That is why we must avoid all strangers, no matter who they are."

"Why do they think evil spirits live in me?" she leaned slightly forward.

"Because you are always talking to the dead., he answered.

"She sighed, "I don't remember...." She lay back on the robes. "Perhaps you should leave me and return to the camp yourself. It cannot be pleasant for you to be taken away from those you care about."

"You are all that I have left," he said bitterly. "Everything else has been taken from me; but one day.... Yes one day, I will get it back... all of it..." Angrily he brought the blade down, barely missing the stub where once his little finger had been.

Pains began to build in her stomach. Anxiously she watched, running her tongue across her lower lip in anticipation. As soon as he had the medicine prepared, greedily she grabbed the bowl and drank it down. Then with a sigh she slipped back into the haze.

"Why do you have to go?" she whined. "I want you to stay here with me!"

"Do you want to eat?" he snapped at her.

"Take me with you then."

"You would only get in the way! Women are useless when hunting."

"I am not!" she shot back. "Sage and I killed a full hand of pigs, to say nothing of a grizzly bear!" She gasped, clasping her hand over her mouth.

"I thought I told you never to speak of the dead!" he shouted at her.

"I am sorry..." She whimpered. "I don't even know who Sage is. I don't know why I said that...." She began to tremble, "But for a heartbeat it seemed so real..." she whispered.

He shook his head. "Only in your mind!" This Sage person you speak of, she never lived, at least not outside of your mind. She is merely another of the 'spirits' with whom you always seem to be living. Sometimes I wonder if you are not a spirit yourself, merely deceiving me that you are alive. Now stay here and if I have not returned by nightfall, stay in the cave and don't forget to take your medicine!"

He shouldered his pack and picking up his atlatl and darts strode off down the trail. She watched him go and then wandered over to her favorite spot, the big rock just outside the cave. "They do seem real, my spirits!" She whispered. "Far more real than the people you say I know." Restlessly she picked her way down the well-worn path to the lake. She closed her eyes and could hear the laughter of women as they worked beside the lake. She opened her eyes and they vanished. Aimlessly she followed an old path and it led her to a place she had never been. Slowly she crept up the path to the cave.

He had forbidden her to ever come here every single time she has asked what lay up the trail, but she was drawn to the place. Slowly she felt the familiar path beneath her feet. Everything felt familiar, as if she had lived here. With trembling fingers she traced the surface of the wall. Shivering with something just beyond the grasp of her mind, she bit her lip and as images began to crowd into her head, she clasped her hands over her ears and ran, crying out in terror, from the cave. She was covered in sweat and gasping for breath when she stumbled into the cave and with shaking hands prepared and then bolted down her medicine. He was right! She should never have gone to that place! Ghosts lived there and they had tried to steal her soul! She sighed as the mist took over.

He returned late, frustrated with lack of success. That meant that tomorrow he would have to go out again. But everything was in perfect order. The woman lay as she did every night, in a drug-induced stupor. He was even losing interest in mating with her limp unresponsive body. In fact nothing was turning out as he had expected. But he knew that soon she would be convinced that she was Humming Bird. Then he could begin to withdraw the 'medicine'. Eventually, she would accept that she was who he told her and although she would be confused, at least he could fool himself and when he closed his eyes, she did become Humming Bird for him.

For several days he was forced to go out hunting. She did not return to the cave, no matter how the spirits in her mind called to her. Day after day she trembled and stayed inside the cave. Her mind called, but she closed herself to it. With trembling hands she made the medicine and drank it.

Then she sank shaking all over onto her furs, hands clasped over her ears, shouting for the ghosts to leave her alone.

He did not return that night.

She woke and immediately vomited the contents of her stomach. Then she clutched her stomach and moaned. With trembling legs she staggered to the container where the medicine was kept. She scooped inside with her hand and then dumped the entire thing upside down. Nothing came out. She scrambled to where the man had stored the root. That container was empty as well. Then she curled into a tight ball and clutched her stomach. For hands of time she lay there, pain taking control of her whole world. Again and again she vomited, even though there was nothing more to come up. She began to tremble and sweat. All day she lay there in utter misery. Finally she crawled into her furs and tried to block everything out.

He did not return that night.

Birds chirping outside woke her. She opened her eyes slowly and saw only bright sunlight playing in shadows on the stones. She frowned. Tentatively she moved. Nothing bad happened. Slowly she sat up. Her head felt light and her stomach was empty. In fact she was starving. She made her way to the hearth and started a fire. Soon she had a bag of food cooking. It seemed to take forever and she ate ravenously as soon as it was ready. Then she sat back and looked around. The whole place was filthy. Vomit puddled on the floor and she smelled bad! Wrinkling her nose, she rummaged through an accumulation of baskets until she found some soap berries. Then she grabbed a couple of rabbit skins and headed toward the lake. There was a fresh breeze and the air was warm. She wadded into the icy water and quickly crushed a handful of berries bringing lather to her hair. Then she scrubbed the rest of her body. She was shivering violently from the cold before she finished, but she was clean and it was worth it! Her clothes smelled just as bad as she had. With a grimace of disgust she pulled them on and headed for the cave. *I wonder if the old tunic I left in the cave is still there?* automatically she followed the old path and was soon climbing the path to the cave. It was a mess! But she did find an old tunic and it was far cleaner than the one she wore. Quickly she pulled it on and headed back to the lake, the other in her hand. A good-sized rock and another handful of soap berries improved it greatly. She spread it out to dry and began searching for mustard and leeks. Then she wadded out and pulled a hand full of cattails, smiling as she cut the reeds and kept the root. It did not take long to start a fire and soon she had her meal cooking as she dropped hot stones into the skin that had carried the soap berries. As her tunic dried she worked the leather to keep it supple. *I wonder what else I could use from the cave* she frowned. *I am not supposed to go there! I wonder why?* She frowned, then gave up and enjoyed the sunshine. Late in the day she started back to the cave, then stopped and pulled off the old tunic she had found in the cave. She pulled on the one she always wore and hurried up the old path. Quickly she tucked the old tunic back where she had found it, then smiling skipped back down the trail. She was back in the cave, straightening it when the man returned.

"So, have you been here all the time?" he asked, frowning at her. "You cleaned up."

She nodded. "I went to the lake and bathed and washed my tunic," she replied, twisting her hands in the leather nervously.

"Well, you can start getting this elk meat ready to dry!" He said sharply. "I had better go out and find more of the tubers for your medicine. You are nearly out."

"I just took the last of it before you returned." She said nervously. "It can wait until morning surely." She backed away from him and began gathering up branches to construct the drying wrack. She was so nervous that she dropped them and then stumbled and fell. As she untangled her feet from the branches, he struck her full across the face with his hand.

"Liar!" he shouted. "You haven't had medicine for days, have you?"

Her head rang. "I don't know what you mean!' she scrambled away from him. "I told you, I just took the last of it!"

"Well that is strange, because I only left you enough for one more day and I have been gone nearly a hand of days! So how do you explain that?" Again he struck her, knocking her to the ground.

She crawled away from him, whimpering. Blood dripped from a split in her lip. Her head was swimming and nausea gripped her stomach. "I didn't take it all because I didn't know when you would return," she whimpered. "So I saved some. But I hurt so bad that I couldn't stand it any longer, so I took all that was left." She scooted back against the wall. "I needed to do something, so I cleaned the cave."

"You are still lying!" he glared at her. "But tomorrow I will make sure that you have the medicine again and I will make sure that you do not run out again. Now, however, I have a man's need!" He roughly shoved her to the sleeping furs and began pulling his clothing off. She didn't know what to do! In the end she did nothing. She lay there and let him have his way. It seemed to satisfy him.

Afterwards she worked far into the night, processing the meat. He watched her for a long time, then he dosed off. She waited until she was certain that he was asleep and then she slipped over to where a stout branch lay ready to be put on the fire and picked it up. With shaking insides she crept quietly to where he lay and raised the branch. She was ready to bring it down upon his head when suddenly he opened his eyes. With a lunge he grabbed the branch and ripped it from her hands. Then he threw it away and grasping her wrist cruelly he began beating her, all the while cursing at her. "So, you think that you can kill me, do you?" He slapped her hard. "I do not sleep! I am aware of every move that you make, even when I am not here! You can't fool me, stupid woman!" Again he struck her. "I can see the thoughts in your mind!" Again and again he hit her, until with a moan she slid unconscious at his feet. He gave her one last kick and left her where she lay.

When she woke in the morning, he was gone, but she knew he had not gone far. Soon he would return and she knew, without thinking about it, that he would make more of the 'medicine' and force her to take it. Not for a moment did she believe that he could really know her thoughts, but he was an extremely good judge of character and he had known that she would retaliate for the beating he had given her earlier. He had just pretended to be asleep, giving her the chance to act.

Now, while he was gone, she studied the cave. There had to be a way that she could avoid taking the medicine. She knew that it took longer to take effect on a full stomach. So, while he was gone, she ate and ate, until she could hold no more food. When he returned she watched silently as he prepared the concoction, then pretended to be far more hurt than she was. He forced some of it down her throat, but she had managed to let most of it dribble out the sides of her mouth and when he wasn't looking, spit out more of it. In the end, she avoided more than she took in. Then, as was her custom, she left the cave to relieve herself. Here, she stuck her finger down her throat and vomited up the contents of her stomach. With a grim smile, she set herself to play a part. When she returned to the cave, she forced a lax uncoordinated movement to her entire body. She slumped onto the sleeping furs and closed her eyes. Evidently he was convinced. He watched her for a short while, then picking up his atlatl and darts left the cave. She watched him go.

Once she was sure that he was gone for the day, she found the container containing the 'medicine' roots. She studied them carefully, until she was sure that she would recognize them. Then taking her digging stick, she quickly made her way into the forest. She recognized the plant and knew another place where it grew. Here she expertly dug up several them, not knowing when she would have another chance. Back at the cave, finding a place to hide them was more difficult. The cave was small and there were few places to hide anything. She shredded the root, just as she had seen him do. Then she put a good amount of it into her waist pouch. The remainder she stuffed into another pouch, one she had found in the forbidden cave and hid beneath the rock upon which she sat most of the time.

Then she left the cave and made her way to the forbidden caves. Here she searched diligently, putting things she could use into a basket. This she hid, in a place scooped out, near the cave. When he returned, she was exactly where he had left her, rocking back and forth and weeping. He tossed the carcass of a pig down and ordered her to get food prepared. She did so, making a strong dish of stew heavily seasoned and dropped a good amount of the 'medicine' plant into it. Already she had eaten, having gathered plants and prepared food for herself while he was gone.

Again he forced her to take the medicine. She dribbled most of it out of the side off her mouth, soaking it up in a rabbit-skin she had wadded up in her hand. He was satisfied, so he went and filled his bowl with stew. He cursed at the taste. "You put far too much seasoning in this!" But he ate it.

She followed her usual routine. After the meal, of which she ate very little, she left the cave and once out of sight, vomited up the remainder of the medicine. After two doses of it, her head was still clear. She smiled as she made her way, laxly, back into the cave. She flopped down of the sleeping furs and pretended to sleep, leaving him to process the pig himself. She smiled into the furs as again he cursed her.

He did not finish the pig. He began to weave about and finally slumped to the floor of the cave and began to snore. She nudged him several times with her toe, assuring herself that he would not waken and then she quickly finished processing the pig. He would not remember who did it. She was making plans, but she wasn't quite ready to make her move. When she did, she would simply vanish. Humming Bird would cease to exist! Without the medicine, her thinking was crystal-clear and she knew exactly who she was and what had happened. He had tried to convince her that she was this Humming Bird and had nearly succeeded, but Whispering Wind was made of stronger stuff than he had anticipated.

Her season living alone with Sage had prepared her to be far more self-sufficient than this hunter had anticipated. She would prepare carefully and when she was ready, when he was gone from the camp, she would slip away and hide in the far cave. She knew it well and he had never set foot inside of it. There were passages they had discovered which would give her places to hide, for he would surely go there to search first. But again, she planned to lead him astray. Before she finally retired to the sleeping furs, leaving him lying on the cold cave floor, she again ate as much food as she could, not from the tainted stew, but from a bladder she had prepared containing plants and meat. She ate it cold, but that wasn't important.

When he wakened in the morning, he was still groggy. He muttered and shook his head, trying to clear his brain. He gave her several suspicious glances, but again Whispering Wind pretended to be asleep. He made her take the medicine, as usual and as usual, she vomited it up when she went to relieve herself. But always, she did absorb just enough of it to give her eyes a glassy look and allow her to relax her muscles and stagger about in a stupor. When she returned to the cave, he had thrown out the stew. She shrugged and stumbled to her furs, leaving him to do all the work that day. He did not leave the cave, but sat about drinking copious bowls of tea, purging the drug from his body. She couldn't judge if he realized that she had purposefully put the plant into their food, or thought it to be an accident, but she was certain that he recognized that he had ingested it. She would have to be very careful in the future.

She ended up taking more of the drug than she anticipated the next day and the slovenly stupor was not a fake. Slowly, they returned to the former relationship. Again she became confused and once more, he gained control over her. For over a moon he stayed near the camp. Then, again he was forced to hunt. Humming Bird was an obedient mate. She took her medicine, just as she was instructed. The fleeting freedom of Whispering Wind was forgotten.

*     *     *

"So that is the Sacred Spring!" Bear Claw Woman stood beside Raven on the slight ridge above the pond. "Look! There is the skeleton of one of the Sacred Beasts within the pond!" She glanced around. People were busy setting up the camp. "Do you think it would be all right if I went down to the pond?"

"I don't see why not. I will set up our shelter. Go ahead. I know that you are anxious to commune with the spirit of the creature."

"Thank you!" she smiled happily and slipped the harness from Guardian. Together they followed a faint path down to the pond. As she approached, the stench of rot nearly overwhelmed her. From above, the pond looked clear and clean, but close, it was a festering bog! She was almost convinced not to wade out into the murky gunk but gritting her teeth did so any way. She sank to her knees in the slim and nearly lost her balance. Carefully she eased to the skeleton. Guardian danced along the edge, refusing to put foot in the water. As Bear Claw Woman laid her hand on the darkly stained tusk she could feel the spirit of the beast call to her. She did not stay there long. When she regained dry land, she did her best to wipe the slime from her legs. She got most of it washed off, but still the smell clung to her. "Some Sacred Spring!" she muttered, "More like a slime bog!" She glanced along the verge. "No wonder the animals do not come here to drink. I wouldn't either. Come on Guardian; let's go back to the camp. The sooner this spring offering is done, the sooner we can leave this place."

"Whew! What happened to you?" Raven raised an eyebrow at her as she joined him in their shelter.

"The pond," she replied, "It is a stink hole!"

Raven frowned. "We are nearly out of water. Running Bison assured me that we would find fresh water here."

"Well there is none, at least none that I could find. But I didn't look for fresh water," she admitted, "I was only interested in the skeleton. Perhaps there is a place where the spring comes to the surface, but there are no animal tracks."

"You are sure?"

"No, like I said, I didn't look for water, but I didn't see any tracks either and Guardian wouldn't go near the place."

"Running Bison," Raven called, "We have a problem!"

"What is it?" Running Bison hurried to where they stood.

"We had best see if we can find good water," Raven told him.

"The pond is right down there!" Running Bison frowned.

"The water is bad!" Bear Claw Woman informed him, "Just smell me and you will understand. I waded out into it."

Running bison frowned, "If that is the case, we are in trouble! There is not enough water to make it to the caprock. We were expecting there to be a plentiful supply here. Come on Raven, we had better get down there and investigate. Calling Wolf, stop setting up the camp!" he shouted," Come here and help us!"

"What's wrong?" Calling Wolf loped to join them.

"No fresh water!" Running Bison answered, "The pond is putrid."

"Maybe we can clean out the spring."

"That's what I intend to find out."

The men hurried down to the pond and circled it, stopping at the north end. Here they spent some time discussing and gesturing. Bear Claw Woman watched them from where she stood. Suddenly a thought came into her head. She frowned, studied the area below and then dug in her supplies. She came up with a deer scapula and with it in hand, made her way down to the pond. She selected a spot below, where a stream would flow from the pond, if there were an active spring there. Here she began digging. Soon the hunters joined her.

"What are you doing?" Raven questioned.

"Digging," she replied.

"I can see, that, but why?"

"Did you find fresh water? Can the spring be cleaned?"

"We don't know yet." Running Bison replied.

"Well, if there is fresh water, I should find it soon."

"Digging here?"

"It was just an idea that popped into my head. I can't explain it, but yes, right here!"

Raven nodded. He was used to the way her spirits contacted her. "Then there will be fresh water soon. Why don't you let me help? I can dig a lot faster."

She grinned and climbed from the shallow hole. He widened it considerably and was soon tossing shovel-full batches of dirt from the hole. After a time, Calling Wolf replaced him and it was he who shouted. "Wet dirt!'

This speeded up the digging and finally, after another hand of time, they were standing around their hole and watching the bottom of it filling up with clean, clear, water. They whooped and leaped and slapped each other on the back. Then they called for people to resume setting up the camp and to bring their water bags down, a few at a time. Before dusk, all of them were filled.

"How did you know to dig for water?" Raven asked, much later, after the camp had settled into quiet. They were sitting, side-by-side before their fire.

"It just popped into my head," she replied. "Probably another 'message' from the spirits. I have been nervous about this ceremony. Now that we are here, I really do not feel good about it. I am supposed to make an offering, but it would be an insult to the spirits to do so into that stink hole!"

"But the spirits are what instructed you to do so," he reminded. "Perhaps there is a reason."

"There is always a reason when the spirits are involved," she replied. "I just hope that I am doing the right thing."

"You always do," he answered. "Have you tried to contact Whispering Wind recently?"

"I don't know," she sighed. "I thought so, but it is so hard to understand what is going on with her. I know that I have reached her, but the response that I get makes no sense. Then something powerful always cuts the contact. I am sure that she is still alive, but the 'power thief' still has her. He won't let me talk to her."

"Have you spoken to Running Bison about this?"

She shook her head. "As you asked me, I have said nothing to him. As far as I know, he has accepted her death. Are you still going forward with your plan?"

He nodded. "Calling Wolf, Bull Elk, you and I leave right after the Spring Ceremony."

"Have you told him?"

"No, we decided to wait. It is best that way. If he merely thinks that we have decided to leave the camp it is better. I do not wish to get his hopes up. We are certain that they are still in the valley. Moving fast, we can be there in half the time it took us to reach this place. If we are successful, we will catch up at the valley of the Gathering. Until then, it is best that you do not try to contact her, in fact, it would be best if you did not 'mind talk' at all. We do not know what powers this man has. So far, they have been considerable. We also do not know what condition Whispering Wind may be in. If he has abused her, we may have to carry her out on a travois!"

"I will be ready," Bear Claw Woman sighed. "I have worried so... as we all have. I am glad that we are doing something positive. Running Bison could not jeopardize the entire camp for the sake of one person, no matter whom, but we can do this, I am sure of it. In my heart, I know that she is still in the valley and I know that we will find her. He will not be so careful now that we are gone from the valley."

"But you can be certain that he will be watchful!"

"This bothers me. How do you plan to sneak into the valley?"

"During the middle of the night; besides, he will expect the south pass to be used and we will slip down the north one and into the cave. It would be suicidal if we didn't know the path so well!"

Calling Wolf slipped into a seat across from them. "Are we still going?"

Raven nodded, "Just as soon as the ceremony is completed. I have even thought of an excuse. I will tell Running Bison that it is essential that Bear Claw Woman return to the cave, that the spirits have directed this. He will not question that!"

Calling Wolf nodded, "We will be ready." He rose and faded into the night.

The day of the Spring Solstice arrived. Bear Claw Woman nervously paced the ridge. She was ready, but as always was filled with a feeling of being unprepared. The people gathered around the stinking pond as sun-high approached. She waited, set apart within the shelter. Raven had moved in with Calling Wolf the day before. She was dressed, covered with white and the Sacred Bundle was ready to be picked up. The drumbeat began. It was time.

As she stepped from the shelter, a freshening wind ruffled the feathers on her robe. She glanced to the north and noticed clouds building. The people fell silent as she followed the path first down the ridge, then north to where at one time, the spring issued forth. Here, where the hunters had dragged several large rocks, she stepped up on their prepared platform. It brought her just high enough to enable her to see where to toss the offering. She waited perfectly quiet until the drums worked to a crescendo, then abruptly stopped. The silence was absolute. She raised the Sacred Bundle and showed it to all and then she untied the wrappings and revealed the wolf hide within. From this she raised the teeth. A blue glow spread and enshrouded her and the wolf at her side. The wind flipped the feathers on her cape and made it dance as if alive. "The spirits of The People have instructed that we make the Spring Ceremony offering here, at this Sacred Spring, where long ago our ancestors gathered to do just the same. We are here, to establish the same bond with the spirits as they shared with those ancestors! Over the many generations, we have drawn away from the spirits. They are not happy! They have taken away the bison and led us into the mountains! Now they instruct that we are to gather all the people, not just those we call 'brother', but even those whose language we do not understand, together at the Valley of the Gathering! It is the task of this camp, which has named itself after the great wolf guide, to bring all these people together. It is our task to tell them of the spirit and to unite them all as brothers! Today, I make an offering to the spirits. It is a very sacred object that I give. Special; made by our ancestors!" She now raised the object that she had discovered imbedded in the skeleton of Great Thunder Beast, far to the north. "With this offering, I implore the spirits to guide us on our assigned task! To bring us to these peoples and help us bring them to an understanding of our ways." She raised the object for all to see, then wrapped it in the special rabbit fur. "Clunk!" She whapped it with her wand. It broke into two halves. These she raised and then cast into the putrid pool. The waters rippled slightly, then again became mirror smooth. Behind her, the wind picked up and within a few breaths, clouds rolled in and thunder boomed. Lightning streaked from the naked underbellies of the billows and then rain slashed down. Not a gentle rain, but a torrential downpour. People squealed and ran for the ridge and their shelters. Raven helped Bear Claw Woman down from her perch and they joined the others.

"What kind of an answer was that?" he shouted in her ear.

She turned and looked back. "Look!" she cried, "The pond!"

Others shoved past them and soon they stood alone on the ridge. From the upper end of the pond, the water rolled, as if some giant monster moved restlessly beneath its surface, then water shot into the air, in great gushes. It danced and cavorted on the putrid pond and filled the slight depression to overflowing. Before their very eyes, the feted waters were swept away, the bottom and sides of the pond scoured clean. Then, fresh water spewed forth from the spring, filling the pond with clear, clean, pure water.

"I am not sure what kind of an answer that is, but it is not bad!" She nodded toward the pond. Suddenly the clouds rolled away toward the south and within a few breaths, the sun shone and a rainbow cut across the sky, complete and brilliant. People crawled from their shelters and all marveled at the pond. The spring rolled forth and a good-sized stream meandered from the lower end of the pond. Within it, the skeleton of the Great Thunder Beast reflected in the ripples of the surface.

The Spring Ceremony went on. There was dancing, the telling of the beginning of the people and naming of new hunters and women. Whispering Wind's son was given a name. Running Bison named him DaNu, Calf. When it was all over and the camp was preparing to move on, Raven and Calling Wolf approached Running Bison and told him that they would be leaving the camp for a time and returning to the cave in the canyon. They would join up with the camp at the valley of the Gathering. Then they loaded their travois, waved farewell and as the camp went east out onto the Llano Estacado, they headed north, back into the mountains.

34 Blackwater Draw, near Clovis New Mexico. Here within a layer of white 'spring' sand were excavated numerous artifacts. Among them were several Agate Basin points.

# CHAPTER 23

They pushed hard, traveling from before sunrise and until they could no longer see after dark. But they made it back to the valley in less than a half moon's time. Now they waited, just beyond the top of the trail into the north end of the valley. Their plan was simple. They would slip into the valley under the cover of darkness and hide in the cave. From there they could watch and survey the entire valley. If Whispering Wind was still there, they were sure to see her. Then they would make their last-minute plans to sweep down and snatch her back. Then they would head for the gathering!

It wasn't a brilliant plan, but it should work. The sun went down and they rested finally and munched on cold trail food. Only when it was totally dark did they move to the top of the trail.

"Here," Raven whispered, "Tie this securely about your waist. It is so dark that we do not want to take the chance of one of us losing our footing and falling. Keep close to me and do exactly as I say."

"Wouldn't it be easier to slip from shadow to shadow? Why must we do this in total darkness?"

"Do you want to take the chance that 'he' could be watching?"

"No," she sighed, "You are right. I will keep close and be careful. At times like this I wish that I could see as well as the wolves. They have no problem with the darkness." She tightened her grip on the leather leash attached to Guardian. Each of them would let the wolves lead them over the pass. The attaching of the line was merely an added precaution.

Calling Wolf led. When he tugged on the line, Bull Elk followed. When the signal came, Bear Claw Woman stepped carefully out after Guardian. Raven brought up the rear. So they traveled over the pass, a short distance at a time. But it worked. There were no incidents. Not even a stray rock rattled down to alert anyone below of their presence.

Bear Claw Woman, however, heaved a sigh of relief when they entered the cave. At least there they could have a fire. They lighted a torch and followed the passage deeper into the mountain. Then Calling Wolf unshouldered his pack and set it against the wall. Bull Elk handed him the torch and gathered up wood for a fire. Soon they were all settled comfortably. There was nothing to do now but wait until morning.

They waited far longer. Daily, the men watched the valley. Nothing moved. At night they searched for a fire. They found none.

"I am going to go down into the valley tonight and make my way to the old caves," Raven paced restlessly across the cave. "We have seen no movement from them, so it should be safe. At least it will be action!"

"Do you think you should go alone?" Bull Elk asked.

"It would be safer for just one of us," Raven answered.

"It would probably be safe for the entire camp to run screaming at the top of their voices, form all the activity we have seen. I am beginning to think we were wrong after all!" Calling Wolf barked in frustration.

"She is here! I just know it!" Bear Claw Woman protested, "I can feel her!"

"Well she is certainly nowhere visible!" Calling Wolf grated in exasperation. "I expected to find her days ago and here we sit!"

"We all knew that it might not be easy!" Raven reminded his impatient friend, "We are all primed for action. That makes the waiting all the harder.

"I think that I should go." Bear Claw Woman said suddenly.

"What?" Raven shook his head, "No way! It is far too dangerous!"

"She is my friend. Besides, Guardian knows her scent. Even if we can't find her, Guardian can!"

"She makes sense," admitted Calling Wolf. "The wolf might be able to lead us to her."

"I can agree with that, but no way is Bear Claw Woman going down there! That madman has already made one attempt on her life! I don't intend to give him a chance to make another!"

So it was decided, but Guardian refused to go without Bear Claw Woman. In the end, Raven went, with Young Wolf, hoping he would remember the scent and follow it. They wasted another day. That night Raven returned, shaking his head.

"I am going down there!" Bear Claw Woman stuck out her chin. "The longer we wait here, wasting time, the more danger Whispering Wind is in. I tell you, Guardian can find her, if she is here at all!"

"All right," Raven gave in, "But I go with you!"

"Fine, we are wasting time! Come on, we can be there before dawn!" Already she was scrambling down the path just behind Guardian. They reached the cave without incident. Guardian wandered about sniffing here and there, then wagged her tail and whined.

"She has found the scent!" Bear Claw Woman whispered excitedly. Dropping to her knees beside the animal, Bear Claw Woman hugged her. "Where is she?" She whispered. "Take us to her!"

Guardian circled, sniffed the air and put her nose to the ground. She sniffed, wagged and moved slowly down the trail toward the lake. They followed. At the edge of the forest, Guardian stopped, she growled softly deep in her throat and looked toward the cliff. Then Raven saw it! At the very base of the cliff, a small fire flickered from within a tiny opening.

"I see it!" he whispered to the wolf, "You have done well!" They eased back toward the cave and then hurried back up the valley.

"We found her!" Bear Claw Woman said excitedly.

"We found someone!" corrected Raven. "They are in a cave on the far side of the forest, at the base of the cliff."

"There is a cave there?" Calling Wolf asked in surprise, "I have not ever seen it!"

"With good reason; but I assure you it is there. We have walked within a hand's throw of it countless times. Were it not for the evidence of my own eyes, I would not believe it!"

Calling Wolf began to chuckle, "All of our stealth! Sneaking about in total darkness and hiding out by day! What a waste!"

"But now we can make a move!" Bull Elk stretched. "It is about time! I am ready for action!" He grinned. "What do we do next?"

"We have to move to a place where we can actually observe the cave. Then we wait." Raven glanced apologetically at Bull Elk.

"Where would you suggest?" The big hunter nodded with acceptance.

"Wherever we go, we can't settle in. The best place would be the forest beyond the lake, but that is certainly a far-from-safe location. We dare not have a fire there, nor even put up a shelter."

"What need have we of a shelter, unless it rains?" Bear Claw Woman replied impatiently.

"Then it is settled!" Calling Wolf nodded, "We will head there at dawn."

"We might as well have a hot meal now, because by the time we have finished, it will be time to leave." Bull Elk, always practical, suggested, "We wouldn't sleep any way."

"We are not going to do anything until we are absolutely sure what we are dealing with here. It that fully understood?" Raven addressed only Bear Claw Woman.

Reluctantly she nodded. "Then let's go!" he turned and led the way. They left everything but the absolute essentials; food weapons and water. Raven led them through the forest until he reached a place from which the cave was visible, but they were not. Here they settled down to watch and wait, but not for long. Just after sunrise, a scrawny, filthy figure, clothed in a tattered, grimy tunic, made after the fashion of The People, left the cave. She wobbled drunkenly to the edge of the forest and relieved herself.

"That isn't Whispering Wind!" exclaimed Bear Claw Woman in disappointment. She watched the figure return to the cave. A short time later a man emerged. All three men sucked in their breath.

"Quenquel!" they whispered.

"Who?" Bear Claw Woman asked stupidly.

"The Savage dreamer," Raven replied. "No wonder. That explains a lot!"

"You all obviously know this man, why don't I?"

"It was from him that Running Bison saved us," answered Bull Elk. "That man is leader of those bloodthirsty Savages who have been terrorizing everyone. They have put to death more people than you even know! We watched him cut the hearts out of living people and laugh about it!"

Bear Claw Woman shivered.

"What is he doing here, hiding out in our valley then?"

"A good question," Calling Wolf replied, "I'd like to know the answer myself."

Later, the man they recognized as Quenquel came out of the cave and with gathering bag in hand and a digging stick headed directly toward them. Quickly they slithered deeper into the forest and took to the shadows.

Their prey seemed unaware of them. He did not even glance about but went directly to a patch of plants and began digging. As soon as he had as many as he wanted, he headed back toward the cave, stopping at the lake only long enough to jerk up several cattails and chop off the reeds. He dropped them carelessly on the ground and stuffed the tubers into the bag. Then he continued to the cave.

"I'm going to see what he dug up!" Calling Wolf rose from his crouched position, "I'll be right back.

They watched him sneak to where the dreamer had dug, pick something up, scratch his head and head back.

"This makes no sense!" he whispered, "This is what he dug up!" He handed a tuber to Bear Claw Woman. She turned it over in her hand and shook her head.

"What is it?" Raven asked.

"The juice from this is a mind-stealing drug," Calling Wolf replied, "No one would eat it!"

"Perhaps he uses it to take dreamer-trips!" Bull Elk said.

"Or fed it to someone he wanted to keep confused." murmured Bear Claw Woman. "It is beginning to make sense. Poor Whispering Wind! She must be nearly as demented as that poor creature we saw earlier." Tears ran down her face.

They waited. The man went in and out of the cave countless times, but the woman did not emerge again until evening, when once again she wobbled to the edge of the forest and then returned. They waited, taking turns, all night. The next day was a repeat of the previous. That night they returned to the cave and slept.

"What do you think we should do?" Bull Elk swallowed the last of his tea.

"There is only one man," reminded Bear Claw Woman, "There are three of you, plus the wolves."

"You don't know him!" Calling Wolf reminded.

"Are we going to spend the entire summer here?" she scoffed. "If so let me know and I will go down there and challenge him!"

"Now is not the time to make stupid mistakes!" Raven replied angrily, "And you are NOT going anywhere to challenge anyone!" He glared at her. "The man is a snake! He kills without thought or consideration! If Whispering Wind is his captive, he will show her no more mercy than he would a wild doe. Do you want to have come all this way, only to set her out to walk the wind?"

Tears stung her eyes as she shook her head. "No," she whispered.

"Then we will do this the way we planned!" He looked around at each of them. "We wait until he leaves the cave! Sooner or later he has to get meat! To do that, he must hunt! That is when we make our move. Not until. It that understood" he looked at Bear Claw Woman. Silently she nodded. "We let him get far enough from the cave that he can't hear if that hag screams. If necessary, we dart her before she can raise the alarm. Then we get Whispering Wind. That is how we planned this and that is how we will proceed. Knowing the identity of the man does not change anything, except we know what we are dealing with."

All agreed. Glumly they settled down to wait. Dawn saw them settled again in the woods, watching. "He is leaving the cave!" Calling Wolf hissed.

"He leaves the cave every morning," Bull Elk reminded.

"This time he has his weapons," Calling Wolf replied.

"Finally," Bear Claw Woman sighed. "I am really worried. We have seen no sigh of Whispering Wind. Only the dreamer and the hag! What if she isn't there?"

"We will soon know!" Bull Elk was already stashing his food.

They watched as the hunter headed away from them toward the southern end of the valley. When they judged that he was out of hearing range, they began to move. They had made their plan. They would move to the base of the cliff and follow the trail along it to the cave. Once there, they would rush the cave and rescue Whispering Wind. It was simple. It would work. They had only the hag to deal with and as Raven said; if necessary, they would dart her.

"Ready?" Raven whispered.

They were crouched just out-of-sight of the cave.

"Ready!" They all answered. The hunters had darts nocked ready; Bear Claw Woman held the wolves back, out of the way. Then the men rose and rushed the cave. At that same instant, Guardian leaped forward, snapping the lead and rushed after them. There was a gurgling scream and Bear Claw Woman followed the men. She stumbled into the darkened cave. It took a while for her eyes to adjust. Before her stood the three men, darts ready; and before them crouched the terrified hag, with Guardian braced before her, growling at the men.

No!" screamed Bear Claw Woman, "Its Whispering Wind!" She leaped forward to take her friend into her arms. The frightened woman turned terrified eyes to them and tried to crouch farther away. Bear Claw Woman stopped. "What's wrong with her?" she turned to the hunters.

"How can that be Whispering Wind?" Calling Wolf stared, his mouth hanging open.

"I don't know!" Bear Claw Woman answered, "But Guardian made no mistake! We might not recognize her, but believe me, it is Whispering Wind."

"Then why doesn't she recognize us?" Bull Elk asked.

"That is what he has been using that tuber for," Calling Wolf muttered.

"You are right!" Bear Claw Woman agreed, "It would mix her mind up so badly she would not recognize anyone. What do we do now?"

"If we take her out of here screaming and fighting, it will alert the dreamer," Raven stated. "And we don't have much time. Any suggestions?" He turned to the other men.

Guardian took the situation in hand. She went down on her belly and flopped onto her back, squirming and grinning. The frightened woman watched the animal. There was a flicker of recognition in her confused eyes. Bear Claw Woman softly spoke to her. "Whispering Wind, it is Sage. You remember Sage, don't you?"

The hag shook her head, "Sage doesn't exist! She lives in my head."
"Is that what he told you? Well it wasn't true! I am here, standing right before you, see? Touch me, prove for yourself! Sage is real. She lives. Go ahead, no one will hurt you."

Uncertainty replaced terror. "You are real?" She blinked, then reached out a shaky hand and touched Bear Claw Woman. Quickly she jerked it back.

"See, I am real! And so are these hunters. You remember them don't you?" She nodded behind her. "Raven is my mate. Calling Wolf is your friend, as is Bull Elk. We have come to take you to Running Bison. You remember him don't you?" A flicker of memory clicked in her eyes. "Running Bison is waiting for us; Running Bison and your son."

"My son...?" She licked her lip, "He said my son was dead."

"Not so!" Bear Claw Woman reassured. We named him at the spring ceremony. He misses you! But we must hurry and we must leave this place quickly, before the dreamer returns."

The hag crouched away again. "No! It is a trick! Like the last time! You aren't real! None of this is real! My name is Humming Bird! Quenquel is my mate! Go away! Before he returns and beats me again!" She began to rock back and forth and sob quietly.

Calling Wolf shook his head. "It's no use," he said softly. "Until the drug wears off, she is living under his influence." Then swiftly he reached out and with a doubled-up fist, struck the weeping creature on the jaw. Like a sack of sand, she collapsed. "Sorry," he turned to the others. "but this is the only way." He reached over and lifted the unconscious woman into his arms and strode from the cave. Almost he expected a dart to pierce his chest, but nothing happened. They followed him toward the lake, past it and into the forest. He stopped only shortly, to instruct Bull Elk to dig up and bring along several the tubers, explaining, "We will need to take her away from the drug slowly or it will be very painful for her. Until they have released her mind, she will be as you see her." Then he continued to the cave.

Meanwhile, Raven remained behind and carefully erased every trace of their trail. When he joined them in the cave, they were ready to leave. Whispering Wind was strapped securely to a travois, a gag in her mouth. Her frightened eyes followed them as she struggled futilely to escape.

As they left the cave, Raven scattered fresh dust over their foot prints. All the way over the pass he did so and then they moved with well-oiled precision down the trail. Before dark they were far from the valley. Only then did they release the gag from Whispering Wind's mouth. But she was far to frightened to scream. They stepped into the waters of a creek at the base of the trail and kept to the water as it joined a larger waterway and it another, until they reached the river. They followed it until the headwaters vanished. By then a double hand of days had passed and the hag, whom Bear Claw Woman had cleaned up at the first opportunity and clad in fresh clothing, was beginning to look more like Whispering Wind. She was pitifully thin. And withdrawal from the drug was being taken slowly, but she was beginning to respond. She seemed to recognize Guardian, although she insisted on calling her Obsidian. She seemed to recognize Bear Claw Woman from time to time as well.

They were camped high up in the mountains, not far from the canyon cave.

"I think it would be a good idea if we stopped at the cave," Bear Claw Woman suggested. "I want to see if she recognizes the cave. Perhaps it will help jog her mind. I really hesitate to return her to Running Bison in her present condition. It wouldn't be fair to her. She needs to gain some weight and get her mind straightened out. I think that I can do that at the cave. We spent a lot of time there and she should recognize it. Besides if all else fails, I will take her into the crystal room and see if I can use power to help her."

"You know that we discussed the idea of using power and decided that it would be too risky!" Raven reminded her. "What if the dreamer is 'listening'? He would know that we have her, after all the work we did to make it look like she merely vanished on her own."

"You are right, no power," Bear Claw Woman agreed. "But I still want to go to the cave. Like I said, we spent a lot of time there. I just can't figure out how to take this Humming Bird from her mind."

"He spent moons putting her there so perhaps it will take the same time to remove her," Bull Elk suggested. "After all, she is a long way from recovered. We have still been giving her the drug and that makes her think that she is this other woman. We could stop giving her the drug. It would be painful for her, at least for a day or so, but I think that in the long run, it would speed up her recovery."

"What do you think, Calling Wolf? Would it be very painful for her to do without the drug completely? You know much more about its use than any of us."

"She has been taking it for a long time. Withdrawal is going to be painful in any case. We could try it and if it is too hard on her, resume it, I suppose," Calling Wolf nodded in agreement.

"How long will it take us to reach the cave from here?" Bear Claw Woman asked.

"About another day," replied Raven.

"Then why don't we wait until we get there? One more day will not make that much difference," Bear Claw Woman suggested. "At least we will be in a more controlled situation there."

Whispering Wind listened carefully to their conversation. She was very confused. The woman whom they called Bear Claw Woman was familiar to her, she flitted in and out of her memory, but then again, she was the enemy, for she had helped the hunters steal her from her mate. He would be furious and she was absolutely certain that he would catch up to them at any time. This thought alone kept her from trying to escape. Surely he would not blame her? She shuddered to think what he would do to these hunters and the strange woman with them. But so long as he understood that she was the victim and had nothing to do with running away from him, she should be safe from his wrath.

They arrived at the cave the next evening. Now Whispering Wind was really confused. This place she recognized. It had been her home, hers and the strange woman. She wandered about, touching this and that, refreshing her memory. Yes, this place seemed safe. She even found tools that she recognized as her own. She had the first restful night since they kidnapped her. She woke up refreshed and her mind was a bit clearer. After eating, Bear Claw Woman suggested they go to the underground stream and bathe. Whispering Wind remembered the stream. She went with Bear Claw Woman and was pleased to bathe in the warm water. Then Bear Claw Woman suggested she show her the crystal room. Whispering Wind was hesitant, but it seemed harmless enough, so she nodded.

"It is just here," Bear Claw Woman motioned to the wall. "You don't even have to duck your head, just walk beneath the rock. Go ahead and I will be right behind you with the torch!"

"All right but promise that you will not leave me in the dark." Whispering Wind replied.

"Why would you think that I would do that?"

"You did before," reminded Whispering Wind.

"You remember that?" Bear Claw Woman was excited.

"I don't know!" Whispering Wind bit her lip, "But it seems to be a memory."

"It is!" Bear Claw Woman nodded smiling. "I left you and Running Bison in the dark, but that was seasons ago! You really are getting better!"

Whispering Wind frowned. She shook her head but followed the directions that Bear Claw Woman had given her. Somewhere in her mind, she knew that she wanted to see the crystal cave. Why she had not ever been there before, she did not understand. But she stepped beneath the rock and sucked in her breath as the light from the torch illuminated the walls. "They are beautiful!" She murmured.

"That isn't all!" Bear Claw Woman replied. "They are magical as well! Reach out and touch the crystals and you will see." She smiled to herself as she casually rested her staff against the wall. Whispering Wind did not hesitate. She walked right up to the wall and placed her hand against the crystals. Immediately, the blue mist began to surround her. Bear Claw Woman watched her and was amazed to see the changes taking place. Within only a few fingers of time, she took her staff again in hand and the blue mist faded. But Whispering Wind turned and smiled.

"Bear Claw Woman; how I have missed you! What happened? I am so confused. Where are we? And where are Running Bison and my baby? Why do I feel so funny?"

"It is a long story!" Bear Claw Woman sighed, "But I am very glad to have you back! I just hope that Humming Bird is gone forever!"

"Who?"

"That is the best answer I could hope for!" Bear Claw Woman nearly shouted. "Come on, you are probably starved! Let's get back to the living cave and get something to eat!"

"Of course; this is the crystal room! But why have you brought me here? I didn't think that it was allowed for anyone but you to come here!"

"You have been ill. I brought you here to cure you. That is what the power of the crystals is for. And they have worked. You are better! You remember that you are Whispering Wind and you recognize me."

"Of course I know who I am! What silliness is this? Why wouldn't I recognize you? You have been truly my sister for seasons!"

"I will explain it all to you, but right now, I am starving!"

"Now that you mention it, I am very hungry," Whispering Wind nodded. "Come on, let's get back to the living cave and fix some food."

"It will be ready, but I agree, we need to hurry."

They passed beneath the wall and climbed from the water. It did not take them long to pull on their tunics. "Why on earth am I wearing this old thing?" Whispering Wind wrinkled her nose in disgust, I thought that I threw it away!"

"Well, it was far cleaner than the one which we found you wearing, and I haven't had time to make you another. This we will do, this very day!"

"I hope so! I certainly don't wish to be seen in this rag!"

Bear Claw Woman chuckled, "It is so good to have you back!" she exclaimed.

"Funny that you should say that for I was thinking almost the same thing. Have we been separated?"

Bear Claw Woman nodded. "But we will go over that later. Right now it is more important that you are back!"

"Guardian old friend, how are you?" Whispering Wind squatted down and hugged the wolf. "It seems like a long time since I have seen you as well!" She rose and led the way back to the living cave, only to come to an abrupt halt as she entered. The three hunters were lounging about, repairing harnesses and relaxing.

"Where is Running Bison?" she glanced about. "Did he and the others go out hunting?"

"Whispering Wind has returned to us," Bear Claw Woman smiled. "We took a walk to the crystal room. She found it quite fascinating!"

"You promised?" Raven growled.

"I did nothing!" Bear Claw Woman replied, "Nothing which could be listened to. The crystals did it!"

Whispering Wind glanced around, "Where is my baby?"

"He is with Running Bison and the remainder of the camp," Calling Wolf replied.

"What?" Whispering Wind began to become frightened. "How can that be? He needs me, to nurse!" She felt her breasts and became even more confused. "What has happened to me? Why do you all look so strangely at me?"

"You were taken from the camp many moons ago," explained Bull Elk. "We only just found you and we are going to meet the camp. But we stopped here on our way. You will be reunited with your son, just as soon as possible, but for now, it was more important that you remember who you are."

"None of what you say makes any sense to me!" Whispering Wind was nearly in tears. "I do not understand!"

"Don't worry about it right now. DaNu is fine! He is growing and even walking and when you see him again, I am sure that he will remember you." Raven tried to calm her.

"Who is DaNu?" She blinked.

"That is the name that Running Bison gave your son, at the Spring Solstice. He is a fine boy!" Bear Claw Woman answered.

"Just how long have I been gone? And why don't I remember?" she turned to Bear Claw Woman, "Please, explain this to me."

"You were stolen at the very first of winter," Bear Claw Woman replied. "And it is the moon before the Mid-Summer now."

"That long! Why that is half my son's life! There is no way that he will even recognize me! Someone else has become his mother!" she wailed. "And for the second time I have lost him!"

"No, I promise you, he will remember you!" Bear Claw Woman replied, "I will make sure of it!"

"You can do that?" Whispering Wind whimpered.

"I will do what I can," Bear Claw Woman promised.

Raven handed Bear Claw Woman a bowl of food while Calling Wolf did the same for Whispering Wind. Both ate ravenously.

Afterwards they explained what had happened. Whispering Wind shuddered! "How could so evil a person have slipped into the valley without our even knowing of him?"

"I knew of him!" Bear Claw Woman replied, "But I didn't know he was so close. That is the problem with the 'mind talking' there is no way to tell where the other person is, unless they wish you to know. By the time we realized that he was so close, it was too late. And we searched and searched for you. But he was very clever! We walked right by where he had you hidden, but we did not find you. Finally Running Bison was forced to take the camp to the Sacred Spring for the Spring Solstice Ceremony. Just as soon as it was over, we headed back to the valley to find you."

"Running Bison didn't want to come?" Whispering Wind bit her lip.

"We did not tell him of our plan," Raven admitted. "It would have only upset him more! As it was, he jeopardized the entire camp, leaving so late, in his desire to find you. He is heartbroken at your disappearance. We only told him that it was necessary that Bear Claw Woman return to this cave. He accepted that. Running Bison is a good leader, but he nearly put his own desires before the safety of the entire camp. Had we told him of our idea, he would have insisted that he come along and that would have been impossible. He must, foremost, lead the camp. As it is, he will be not only very surprised that we have you with us but will be very angry at us as well!"

"What if he has taken another mate?"

Bear Claw Woman shook her head. "Laughing Water is caring for your son and as you know, she is Running Bison's cousin. There can be no mating between them, besides which your mate is so besotted with you; no other woman could ever replace you. I think he has secret plans to return to the valley and search for you again. I know that he would never give up, until he either found you or was assured that you were dead, even if it meant giving up leadership of the camp."

"You think that he would do that for me?" Whispering Wind gasped. "Running Bison is above all the leader of his people! He would never allow a woman to interfere with that!"

"It was all that we could do to convince him of that." Raven said dryly. "And I am not sure that we did so even then."

Outside ravens gave voice, alerting them that something or someone had entered the canyon. The three men leaped to their feet and lunged to the door of the cave and then they gave forth with whoops and laughter, shouting to someone outside. They were answered and Whispering Wind shivered as she heard the voice. She leaped to her feet and before anyone could stop her, darted from the cave and flew up the path with joyful voice. She threw herself into the arms of the hunter running to meet her and he lifted her and whirled around and around whooping in delight.

"I decided to join you here and see if I could convince you to go back to the valley with me to search for her." Running bison admitted later, as they were settled about the fire.

Laughing Water greeted both Whispering Wind and Bear Claw Woman gladly and proudly displayed a healthy, chubby little boy to a delighted Whispering Wind. "This is your Mommy," Laughing Water told the toddler.

He peeked shyly from behind her leggings, then with a wide smile, said. "Mommy? I is a big boy now!" Then he proceeded to take a few hesitant steps, only to sit down suddenly, a surprised look on his face.

"Indeed you are!" Whispering Wind laughed as she scooped him up into hungry arms. He squealed to be put down, but she ignored him for a few precious heartbeats, before reluctantly releasing the inquisitive child again onto his feet. "They grow up so fast," she sighed.

"So tell me, how is it that you found her?" Running bison could not take his hungry eyes away from the woman. She may be gaunt and look haggard, but to him, she was the most precious sight in his world.

So the hunters related their kidnapping spree. Raven was more worried about the camp.

"Crying Coyote is doing a fine job of leading them." Replied Running Bison. "He almost drove me from the camp because he was so tired of my long face and distracted leadership. He simply told me finally that the only thing for it was for me to come here, gather you and go back to search again for Whispering Wind. I agreed; he was right. With my mind half on her, I was useless as a leader. I was no good to myself or the camp."

"We decided that before we ever left the valley," admitted Calling Wolf. "Which is why we returned there straight from the Spring Ceremony and even then, it took us a hand of days to locate where he had her stashed."

"You killed the kidnaper. Right?"

Calling Wolf frowned then shook his head. "No, we were just glad to be able to snatch her away while he was out hunting. I do not want to have to go up against that man again, unless I am forced to."

"You are certain that it was the Savage dreamer? You could not be mistaken?"

"No mistake! It was he all right! I could never mistake him!"

"But, where were his people?"

"I have no idea!" Raven replied. "But if it was he who followed us last fall he was badly injured to begin with. Perhaps he was injured in a hunting accident and was lost, or maybe they got tired of his bloody ways and cast him out! Either way, they were no where around. I am absolutely certain, however that it was Quenquel!"

"You realize that he is far too dangerous to be allowed to continue to live?" Running Bison spoke quietly, "It is too bad that you did not complete the job at the time, for now we must return to the valley and make sure that he is a danger to no one ever again."

"I am not returning there!" Bear Claw Woman protested.

"That is right!" Running Bison agreed, "You women stay here at this cave and wait for us to return. Then we will rejoin the camp. They will be waiting for us in the valley of the Gathering."

"What makes you think that he is still there?" Bear Claw Woman shook her head. "I think he has left that place. Once he discovered that Whispering wind had escaped him, there was no reason for him to remain. He will either be trying to follow her, which means you could run straight into him and lead him directly to her, or you will be wasting your time and he is long gone elsewhere. Either way, returning to the valley is a bad idea."

Raven studied her words, then nodded. "She is right! We would be wasting our time. He is not going to sit there and wait for us to find him. I am sure that he has realized that Whispering Wind did not vanish without help. Even though we left no trail for him to follow, he will know that someone was there. He will also know that the camp would not just sit back and allow him to go unpunished. If he is any way near as cunning as I think he is, he will be long gone from the valley."

"I won't just walk away from this!" Running bison ground his fists, "The man must pay!"

"And he will, some day," Calling Wolf answered. "In our time and our way, he will pay. But now is not the time. We have more important things to do. Remember we have people to find and bring together. That must be our task for the immediate future. If we are to ever regain the bison, we must first unite all people."

"That could take more than a lifetime!" protested Running Bison.

"Then we had best get started!" added Bull Elk.

"How do you suggest that we begin?" Running Bison leaned forward.

"I will tell you where they are," Bear Claw Woman answered.

"How will you do that?"

"Easily," she answered. "I merely close my eyes and seek them out!"

"Of course!" The men nodded; the question that they were all secretly asking themselves, answered so simply.

"What of Quenquel? What if he intercepts your 'mind talking'?"

"Then he will come to you and save you the trouble of seeking him out," she replied calmly.

"One of the reasons I wanted to come here, was that this is an excellent place for me to seek the others from. I have a ready supply of power and it is safe here as well. No one, even this Quenquel you are all in fear of, could sneak up on us. Besides even if a full force of enemies came down the trail, we could easily escape them," she reminded them.

"How will you go about finding the other groups?" Calling Wolf questioned.

"I plan on a 'spirit' journey," she replied. "Since Whispering Wind is reunited with her mate and son, there is nothing to stop me from beginning immediately, now that my mind is clear of worry."

"Do you think that perhaps I could join you on that 'journey'?" he asked.

Bear Claw Woman frowned, "I have never tried to take anyone with me. I don't know if my spirits would allow it."

"Would you mind trying?"

She thought for a time, glanced toward her mate and finding him nodding his head in agreement, said, "I will try."

That evening she and the shaman went to the underground stream and cleansed their bodies. Then she prepared the 'spirit' drink and they shared it. She led the way into the crystal cave and lighted the oil bowls. Then they seated, not touching and waited....

# CHAPTER 24

They could feel the mist forming. It swirled about her, sending icy trendels along her arms and down her spine. Then the brightness behind her closed eyelids alerted her to changes. Slowly she reached out and took the shaman's hand. Then she opened her eyes. It had been a long while, but she recognized the meadow where she stood. Just beyond them was the log upon which she had sat and conversed with the ancestors. She looked around. The meadow was empty.

"I don't know if they will come since you are with me," she said.

"At least I am with you," he looked about with keen interest, "Where is this place?"

"The land of the dead, I think!" she replied.

He shivered, "I hope not!" he answered, "I can think of places I'd rather be.

"They have always been here before." Bear Claw Woman sighed. "I am not sure what to do next."

"Perhaps we could look around," he suggested.

"You think there is more to this place than the meadow?" She asked in surprise.

"I have no idea, but one way to find out is to look."

"But what if we get lost and can't find our way back? I don't know if I can return to my body from anywhere else!"

"I wish you hadn't said that!" he replied, "But I am going to have a look around any way. Are you coming?"

She nodded and followed him across the meadow. Just as they were about to enter the forest, someone stepped out of the trees and walked toward them. Bear Claw Woman recognized Ancestor Basket.

"Greetings," Bear Claw Woman called out.

The woman stood silently for a moment, then stepped forward. *"You bring someone with you." she remarked. "Why?"*

"This man is called Calling Wolf. He is a shaman, something similar to a dreamer. He wishes to help with uniting the people. He asked to come and meet you. I did not know if this was possible, or right, but I felt that if it was wrong, he would not be allowed to join my journey. Since he is here, I can only assume that it is acceptable."

*"The spirits which guide you are women's spirits. They do not feel comfortable with a man. But he has been allowed to come for they have looked into his heart and found it pure. You are not exactly welcome, Calling Wolf, but you may be allowed to stay."* She turned to the shaman. *"I know why both of you are here. You wish to know where to find the people. Come, I will show you where they are. Take my hand."* She held out one to each of them.

With Bear Claw Woman on her left and Calling Wolf on her right, Ancestor Basket lifted them into the air and soon they were soaring like birds over the land. Bear Claw Woman was fascinated! Below she recognized their canyon and the burned area where she and Whispering Wind barely escaped with their lives. Then they were above the mountains and looking down into a valley at the edge of the plains. Here a small group of women worked, while two men lounged lazily. Bear Claw Woman gasped as she recognized Angry Bull, still wearing her necklace about his thick neck.

*"You must retrieve the necklace."* Ancestor Basket reminded her. *"Before you can proceed farther with uniting the people. You have need of its power. It was not meant for that hunter. Great Bear Spirit is most unhappy!"*

"I am not happy about it either," Bear Claw Woman replied. "I will make sure that it is returned to me somehow."

*"Leave it to your mate."* The ancestor told her. Then they were over the plain, moving south along the river. Soon they reached a great stone quarry and here was another group of people. Calling wolf recognized several of the hunters form the Gathering. They saw their own camp,

moving along yet another river to the south of the quarry. Then they looked into a deep canyon, where another group of people was gathering and hunting. None of these were recognized. And so it went. They swept the land to the east, south west and north, locating group after group.

"How will we find them when it is time?" asked Calling Wolf.

*"These are the places where they will be."* replied Ancestor Basket.

"What of the man called Quenquel?" he asked.

She swept them far to the west, beyond where Calling Wolf had ever been. Here, among a small group of gatherers, with whom he was totally unfamiliar, he recognized the unmistakable figure. *"He must be eliminated!"* Ancestor Basket said through stiff lips. *"He soaks the land with blood! Yet is not the time, but soon! Before the next Gathering you must contact those in the valley, in the canyon and at the quarry. Bring them to the Gathering and teach them the ways of The People. From the Gathering, move to the north and make a great circle. Contact the groups whom I have shown you along that route. Bring them to the winter valley. There you will all be safe and the spirits will provide well for you. During the winter, teach them also. In the spring, go again to the Sacred Spring for the offering. A special offering will again be given to you. As before, you will recognize it. After the offering, go to the far southwest group. There, the dreamer will be found. He must be given to the spirits in the same way that he has offered so many! His blood will free those trapped spirits he has denied release! But be wary, for he is very clever! The Dreamer, Hollow Bone, must make the sacrifice!"*

"Hollow Bone?" Bear Claw Woman questioned. "But he is but a child! Do you not mean Crooked Spirit?"

*"The dreamer is to join us soon."* Basket replied." *The youth you recognize as Hollow Bone will be a great Dreamer! It is he and only he who can make the sacrifice of Quenquel! Only the hunters Elk Caller, Running Antelope and Bull Elk, along with you, Calling Wolf, will be able to capture the elusive renegade. He must be brought back to the place where he took the life of the woman Humming Bird!"*

"You mean there really was such a person?" Bear Claw Woman asked in surprise.

*"Indeed and she was the image of the one you know as Whispering Wind. This is why he kidnapped her! But he changed the path of the people*

*when he took the life of Humming Bird. The spirits had a purpose for her. This purpose has now been shifted, to the shoulders of the one known to you as Whispering Wind. She will be the mother of the future leader of The People!"*

Soon they were back at the meadow and Ancestor Basket bid them farewell.

"Will we remember this journey?" Bear Claw Woman asked.

*"You will, but the shaman will not!"* She replied as she vanished into the forest.

Bear Claw Woman and Calling Wolf were left standing beside the log. "Why can't I be allowed to remember?" He asked regretfully. It was the most wonderful experience he had ever had.

"These are women's spirits," Bear Claw Woman answered. Then the mist began to form and soon all was quiet. Then she wakened....

\*      \*      \*

"I didn't go with you!" Calling Wolf said regretfully. "Did you go?"

Bear Claw Woman merely smiled. Let him wonder from where came, the sudden insights he would have!

"Indeed," she replied, "And it was very enlightening."

"You know where to find them?"

She merely nodded and stepped into the water.

"You go and I will follow," she told him as they pulled on their clothes. "There is something I must do first and I will be along shortly."

He nodded and headed down the passageway. Bear Claw Woman seated herself beside the water and called out.... *Crying Coyote, are you there?*

*Bear Claw Woman?*

*It is I. We have found Whispering Wind; she is reunited with Running Bison. We go to the Valley of the Gathering. You must turn back to the west and go to a secret canyon. There you will find a group of people. Bring them to the Valley. At the big river, follow it north, to the quarry. There you will find another group of our people, some of the hunters who went with Hunting Badger. Bring them as well.*

*How will I find this secret canyon?*

*You will find it! Close your eyes and concentrate!* She closed her own and sent the picture to him. *Do you see it?*

*I see it!*

*See you at the gathering!* She straightened up and followed Calling Wolf.

"So, did you take the journey?" Raven held her close. Only the embers of the hearth cast a faint light.

"I did and Calling Wolf went with me, but he can't remember," she chuckled.

"What is so funny?"

"I was just thinking of the frustration that I suffered when thoughts just popped into my head. It will be enjoyable watching that hunter cope with them."

He is a very good man!" Raven protested.

"Yes, he is. And it was a great honor that the spirits allowed him to accompany me, but he is a man, so they did not allow him to remember the trip. But the knowledge is still his and it will pop into his mind when he has need of it, but that is most frustrating." She sighed, "I certainly should know."

"What did you learn? Or is it information forbidden to me?"

"One thing I did learn is that the dreamer Quenquel is long gone from the valley. We will go in search of him one day, but not yet. Our first task is to find Raptor Feather and his camp and then join Crying Coyote at the Valley of the Gathering. He will be bringing others in."

"Angry Bull," Raven muttered. "I wonder where he is, if he is still alive?"

"Jumping Fox will lead you to where he is," Bear Claw Woman replied with a yawn.

"What?" Raven questioned, but already she slept.

He lay awake long into the night, going over in his mind the many possible ways he could deal with Angry bull, each one of them giving him much pleasure.

*     *     *

They stayed for another hand of days at the cave in the canyon. Whispering Wind blossomed.... She was absolutely delighted with Calf, who found an equal fascination with her. It was "Mommy this" and "Mommy that" as he struggled to make his word understood by the adults. But his sturdy little legs began to carry him with increasing efficiency, constantly into mischief. Whispering Wind was delighted! Laughing Water and Bear Claw Woman made her a new tunic, for she forgot entirely about the ragged one she wore. Running Bison seemed content to just sit and watch his little family. He couldn't get enough of them.

The other three men went out and hunted, bringing in a pair of deer.

"I think that I saw Sister Cougar," Raven commented to Bear Claw Woman one night.

"Really? How could you tell?"

"I don't know, perhaps the way she came close and then yowled. Then she followed us all the way back to the canyon. I am sure that it was she."

"You think she would remember you?"

"I am quite sure," he was adamant.

The next morning they found cougar tracks all about the trail before the cave.

"I am going out and see if she is still about," Raven blushed.

"Go ahead," Bear Claw Woman encouraged, "She was your friend."

The hunter went a short distance from the trail and called out softly. From the brush nearby, the plaintive call of the cougar answered him. Then slowly, she stepped out into the trail. He waited, holding his breath. She came closer and then stopped. He held out his offering, a rabbit, something she would remember. She yowled again and then lay in the trail and rolled onto her back. Raven smiled, remembering the many times she had done this as a kitten. "Here, my friend, have a meal on me. And walk in peace," he called softly, tossing her the rabbit. She leaped into the air and grabbed it, just as she had done seasons ago. Then she vanished like a ghost. Raven was satisfied.

The next morning, when the hunters stepped to the opening of the cave, they found the carcass of a nearly grown deer, left there.

"Where did this come from?" Calling Wolf questioned, as he walked around it, noticing the cougar tracks all about.

"From a friend," replied Raven smiling.

Calling Wolf raised an eyebrow. "You have some strange friends, is all that I can say." was his answer. "I wonder if she could be tamed like the wolves?" He mused.

Raven shook his head, "She is a wild animal," he replied. "We got the wolves when they were very young. She was far too old when I killed her mother. Yet she was too young to make it on her own. Her brother was killed. I merely fed her and showed her how to hunt. I doubt we will ever see her again."

"Still, it is a thought," Calling Wolf murmured.

\*   \*   \*

"Is everyone ready?" Running Bison stood at the head of the group. Everyone nodded and so he turned and headed up the trail out of the canyon. Soon they were over the high narrow pass and the hunters shivered as they hurried past the valley where Quenquel had held them captive, until Running Bison released them. They were nearly to the Valley of the Gathering when suddenly Calling Wolf halted and called to Running Bison. "I think we should turn south here."

"Why?"

"I don't know," Calling Wolf replied, "It just came into my head."

Running Bison looked suspiciously at Bear Claw Woman who merely chuckled and looked innocent. "What is going on here?" he questioned.

"Oh, nothing!' she replied, "But I would suggest that we do as he says. There is sure to be a reason!"

"And I'll bet that you know what it is! Running Bison wasn't fooled.

Bear Claw Woman merely smiled and continued past him. They turned south, following a small river. It joined another and they followed it as well. A hand of days later they moved down into a valley and could hear voices.

"There are people living in this valley!"

"Perhaps it would be a good idea if we waited here and you went to meet them." Calling Wolf paused and frowned.

"Running Bison nodded and then he trotted down the trail, soon to call out before entering the camp. "Hello the camp! We come in peace!"

\*   \*   \*

Raptor Feather raised his head from the tool he was crafting. That voice was familiar. Quickly he placed it in his memory, *Running Bison!* He rose and hurried to meet the big man waiting in the middle of the trail.

"What brings you to our valley?" Raptor Feather asked.

"We come to bring all the people to the valley of the Gathering for the Mid-Summer Ceremony," Calling Wolf answered. They were settled comfortably in the camp. Several of the children and young people were eyeing the wolves with fascinated eyes.

"Crying Coyote is bringing others," Raven added.

"It will be a wonderful celebration, one such as we have never before experienced!" Bull Elk added.

"Will the bison return?" Raptor Feather asked.

"One day." Running Bison replied. "That is one reason for this gathering. We have been given the task of uniting all the people, not just those of The People, but everyone. The spirits are calling us to gather and become One People. This is one reason that the bison have been taken from us."

"Well I personally don't care if I ever see another bison," Raptor Feather muttered, "One experience with them was enough!"

"You have found them?" Bull Elk questioned.

Raptor Feather related their experience with the Bison and told them of banishing Hunting Badger and Angry Bull from the camp.

"I wish I knew where they were!" Raven Muttered, "I would give much to place my hands about the neck of Angry Bull and strangle the life from him!"

"You will get that chance," Jumping Fox smiled, "I will take you to him."

"You know where he is?"

"When it is time, I will lead you to him. My spirits have promised me this!" He nodded. "The Great Bear will show us the way."

"When?"

"Not yet," Jumping Fox sighed, "But soon."

With this Raven had to be satisfied.

Cattail Woman and Dancing Crane brought food and offered it to their guests. Beyond Jumping Fox sat a youth that hung on their every word. He had been introduced as acolyte to Jumping Fox, son of Dancing Crane and Elk Caller. The youth had just been named a man at their spring ceremony and he was called Sun Catcher now. He did not speak but listened very carefully. Everything he heard he tucked away in his agile mind. He was learning very quickly what was needed to be of service to his people. No more did he dream of personal greatness. Grizzly Bear had spoken to him on his spirit journey and told him that he was called to be a dreamer. At first it had disappointed the youth, but now, it was all he yearned for.

Dancing Crane was delighted. A dreamer was safe. Hunters were constantly in danger; at least her son would probably live to become an old man. Elk Caller on the other hand was disappointed that he would not become a hunt brother. Yet, what did it matter, so long as the youth was satisfied.

"Jumping Fox, tell them of your meeting with the Spirit Bear!" Badger Tail suggested. "I am sure that they will find it interesting."

"Well," started the embarrassed dreamer. "I was sleeping beneath a tree beside the trail...." He began, as other men chuckled. "And that is how I became Dreamer of the Grizzly Bear Camp" He concluded. "It is surprising, you think that you understand the path which your life will take and then suddenly, in the blinking of an eye, all is changed! The spirits call and you answer."

Beyond, Sun Catcher nodded.

Calling Wolf frowned, "I have been trying for seasons to find the path to the spirits. I call, but they have not answered."

"Perhaps it is not your path," replied the dreamer.

Calling Wolf nodded. "I am beginning to believe that is true. Since becoming a man and even before, I prepared. On my spirit journey I was not enlightened, yet still I have continued to seek the way." He signed. "Perhaps you are right and my path leads elsewhere."

"Your path leads where you have always been seeking," Bear Claw Woman whispered to him quietly, "But not yet. You must be patient. The time will come."

"You are sure?" he whispered back.

"The people to the west are your destiny," Sun Catcher murmured to him.

"How can you know this?" Calling Wolf asked excitedly. "I have had no indication! People to the west, you say?"

Sun Catcher nodded, "I have seen it."

"You have? Why haven't I?"

The youth shrugged "that is the way of the spirits. When they are ready, you will be called, until then, all that you can do is wait."

"I am getting very tired of 'waiting'," muttered Calling Wolf.

"Perhaps that is why," Bear Claw Woman answered. "You must learn patience."

The hunter gave her a sour look but was silent.

"You say that you made a special offering at your Spring Ceremony, at the Sacred Spring?" Jumping Fox asked. "I have hard of this place but I have never visited it. Is it true that there is a vast oak forest only as high as a man's knee, yet yielding a plentiful harvest?"

They all nodded. "I would see such a wonder." Sun Catcher said.

"Wait until you see the remains of Great Thunder Beast!" Calling Wolf spoke to him. "It is magnificent! Impossible to believe that once such a creature walked this very land!"

"Really; you have seen this?" Sun Catcher's mouth fell open.

"Not only have I seen it, but I have touched it and heard its voice!"

"Was it magical?" Yearningly the youth questioned.

"Very magical," Calling Wolf replied, "I could nearly feel him breathing when I placed my hands upon the tusks."

"Do you think..."

"If we go anywhere near the place, I promise that I will take you there, if not, you will surely get the chance at the Spring Ceremony."

"I can wait," Sun Catcher's eyes glittered.

The next morning, the group was gathered about the various hearths finishing the early meal. "We are about to make an offering to Grizzly Bear." Jumping Fox mentioned. "The preparations are well underway. You are welcome to join us. I am sure that Bear Spirit would be honored to have the Chosen One attend." He glanced questioningly toward Bear Claw Woman. She nodded. "It is to be tomorrow night."

"Then there is time for all of us to purify before the ceremony," she became thoughtful. "Perhaps I could ask the women of your camp to accompany me tomorrow to find some special plants?"

Dancing Crane nodded. "We would be honored to go with you. All of us are quite familiar with the plants which grow here if you could describe what you seek we can lead you to it."

"They are not difficult plants to find." Bear Claw Woman replied. "Whispering Wind and I merely found them to be very good eating. Others make a fine tea. We would show these to you, if you do not already know them."

Dancing Crane chuckled, "We have tried to eat every plant that we came across, during the last season, before we found these men, plants are about the only thing we were able to catch. But I will certainly be more than happy to accompany you."

Several other women nodded in agreement. Later, near dusk they led Whispering Wind, Laughing Water and Bear Claw Woman to a place along the stream where they could wash and relax. All the camp women joined them, leaving Running Bison and Raven in charge of Calf. Since he was a male child, they would care for him until after the ceremony. As of mid day, the men and women had kept separate from each other.

"This is a very pleasant valley," Laughing Water trickled water down her throat, rubbing it with a handful of bison berries to make suds. Then she washed.

"We have spent a wonderful season here in this valley," Dancing Crane sighed. "I will be sad to leave it."

"The valley where we will spend the winter is also wonderful." Whispering Wind assured her. "There is even a lake there. Bear Claw Woman taught me to swim and I really enjoyed that place. I even swam completely across the lake. The water is cold, but during the hot summer that is pleasant."

"I have never lived around a large enough pond to learn," Dancing Crane admitted. "And this is something that I want very badly. I lost my sister to drowning in a spring flood and if I had been able to swim, there is a good chance that I could have saved her."

"Or drown with her," Cattail Woman said dryly. "I remember when Willow drowned; that river was raging and if your recall; a pair of grown men also drown trying to save her. You would have only made one more tragedy that day. I hope that you haven't blamed yourself all of these seasons for her death!"

"I have felt guilt," admitted Dancing Crane. "But I have also realized that I could not have saved her. Remember one of those men who drowned was my uncle. I missed him nearly as much as I missed Willow."

"Well, if we get to the valley early enough, I will gladly teach you how to swim," Bear Claw Woman smiled at the other woman. "Or if I don't have the opportunity, Whispering Wind is as capable."

"I doubt that we will reach the valley much before snowfall." Laughing Water stated.

"You are probably right. We must travel to the north and locate the people living there." Whispering Wind nodded, "And Running Bison has never changed his mind once it is made up. I wonder that the hunters were able to convince him to leave me behind and go to the Sacred Spring."

"They left you behind? Dancing Crane asked, "Why?"

"That is a long story. We haven't time for it now." Whispering Wind waded from the stream and began to dry herself. "Did you remember to bring the cones to comb our hair?" She asked Laughing Water.

"They are here somewhere." The other woman glanced around. "Look over by our clothes; that is where I think I left them."

"Here they are!" Whispering Wind lifted the cones and then sat down and began removing the tangles from her long hair.

CiCi was looking curiously at Bear Claw Woman. Finally she got close enough to touch her softly.

"What is it?" Bear Claw Woman turned to the child.

"You have eyes the color of the sky! So does your funny looking dog. Why?"

"It is very rude to ask such questions!" Dancing Crane grabbed the child by the arm.

CiCi began to cry.

"It is all right that she asks me," Bear Claw Woman reassured the upset woman. "I hear that question all of the time. You see, CiCi, I am called The Chosen One. My mother and my grandmother had eyes like mine, as have all the grandmothers before them. And my wolf is very special. There is not another one like her living. Once there were, but that was a very long time ago when the Great Thunder Giant walked the land."

"Oh!" CiCi said softly, "Do they hurt?"

"What?"

"Your weak eyes."

They all laughed, breaking the tension. Still Dancing Crane talked seriously to the child as they walked back toward the camp. Once there, the women were very aware.

Just beyond the camp, on their side, they prepared a smoky fire and each one of them, from the smallest to the oldest, passed slowly through the smoke to purify them for the ceremony. They were careful to keep to their own side of the camp and not break any taboos. They even ate separate food.

Meanwhile, the men were performing a similar cleansing. The men of course were partaking of the flesh of the spirit bear, where as the women were eating only plant food. But they sat late around their hearth visiting and telling tales from their past. Whispering Wind told them of the flood that scoured the valley and made it a bad place to live. Dancing Crane told of the Savages attack on their camp and how they escaped only because they were out gathering berries at the time. "Then we had to live on what we could find until Raptor Feather found us." She concluded her story.

Bear Claw Woman told the story of her flight from the gatherers camp and Running Bison.

"Why would you wish to run away from Running Bison?" Dancing Crane asked, "He is one of the most honest and honorable men I have ever met."

"I didn't know that?" Bear Claw Woman protested. "I didn't even understand his words, only that my grandmother was very frightened. She died there in my arms!"

"Your grandmother was Clover Blossom?" Cattail Woman asked. Bear Claw Woman nodded. "I remember her when I was a girl. She saved me from dying. She was a wonderful healer!"

"She was a wonderful person," Bear Claw Woman said softly. "She saved many people and she taught me the healing plants until she became too ill. I have tried to continue to learn on my own and Talking Shadow, our dreamer, taught me more. But still, I feel that there is much that I do not understand."

"There is a healer living with the gatherers to the far west, she is very wise."

"Really?" Bear Claw Woman was interested. "You know of this person?"

Tuber Woman shook her head. "I have only heard of her. I have never seen her with my own eyes. But I have heard that she has very powerful healing medicine. I have heard that from people whom she has healed. Like you, they say that she has eyes the color of the sky."

"What is her name?"

"She is called Ash Branch."

"I will remember that name. Bear Claw Woman said.

"How could she be a more powerful healer than you?" Whispering Wind asked puzzled once they were alone.

"I am not the only healer," Bear Claw Woman protested. "Even with the help of the spirits, there are things which I do not know, plants with which I am unfamiliar. I would very much like to speak with this Ash Branch."

"Then why don't you?"

Bear Claw Woman stopped dead in her tracks, her mouth open in surprise. "You mean...?"

"Why not? Isn't that what the spirits gave you the power for; to use it to help people. If you can speak with this woman, not only can you help our people but possibly hers as well. It makes good sense to me, if she will talk to you, that is."

"I will think about it," Bear Claw Woman promised. "Perhaps it would be best if I consulted Spirit Wolf or even Ancestor Basket first. She was not at all happy when I took Calling Wolf on the spirit journey."

"I can understand that! I am only surprised that the spirits allowed it at all. What were you thinking; to take a man along on a women's spirit quest!" Whispering Wind shook her head.

"You will have another son." Bear Claw Woman suddenly said.

"What?"

"That is what Ancestor Basket told me. You will have another son, who will be leader of the people."

"But, what of Calf; is he not to follow Running Bison as leader?"

"I did not think to ask! Perhaps it is he that she was referring to. After all, it would be logical. He is Running Bison's son. But the leader was to be born to Humming Bird." Whispering Wind shivered violently at the name. "But Quenquel killed her, so the task was passed on to you, for you are very near the spirits."

"Me?"

"That is what Spirit Wolf told me. If I must leave the Sacred Relics again, for any reason, they are to be placed in your care. Had you thought, they would have been much happier with you than with Crooked Spirit before."

"I had no idea!" Whispering Wind replied, "I thought that he was to be 'Keeper' once you returned them to him."

"As you have just reminded me, they are women's objects; they are not comfortable in the care of a man. The return was merely symbolic any way and I had intended to get them back the next day. Crooked Spirit knew that. But well... you know the rest."

Whispering Wind nodded.

"What do you think of the woman, Dancing Crane?" She asked Bear Claw Woman.

"She seems a level headed, good woman, why?"

"I thought the same. I think that she will be a good addition to the camp as a whole. She kept their group together and no one died after their camp was captured. It takes a strong woman to do that, particularly when she had no knowledge of leadership."

"We do what we must," Whispering Wind nodded. "Who would have thought that we would learn to hunt and become independent the way that we did? Even if I never am forced to hunt again, at least I am confident that I could if I had too."

"We had better join the others. I think that the food is about to be passed around," Bear Claw Woman remarked. They hurried to where the women and children were waiting and joined them. Dancing Crane passed around the food; proud of her ability to make the plants taste good. She explained what each dish was made from and Laughing Water and Whispering Wind nodded. Bear Claw Woman frowned, then she dug in her pack and brought out the salt. The Grizzly Bear Camp women exclaimed in delight when they tasted the difference.

"You mean, the white substance which the deer seem to like to well is this?" Dancing Crane was amazed. "I never thought to try to eat it!"

"I did," Cattail Woman said, "But I did not think to use it as a seasoning to add to the food. It is not very good by itself."

They all laughed.

"I have used it to preserve meat as well." Bear Claw Woman added. "It keeps the meat from spoiling just as well as smoking and it gives a different flavor to the food. Plus, when you add the meat to plant dishes and cook it, the salt is already there."

"We will certainly remember that!" Cattail Woman grinned. "There is a lot of this 'salt' around here. I think that before we leave this valley I will collect an ample supply of it. Perhaps we all should." She glanced around at the other women of the 'Bear' Camp. They nodded, smiling.

Just then the drum began to sound and quickly they finished their meal and made their way to where they would watch the ceremony. They had arranged rocks and logs where they could sit comfortable and not interfere with the men. A pair of women was relegated just outside the 'blood' shelter for they were having their 'women's bleed'.

The night was very dark. Later the moon would rise, but now, only the flickering 'ancestor lights' shone in the sky. The hearth fire cast flickering light that threw dancing shadows against the trees. The men were arranged similarly to the women on the opposite side of the camp, only Jumping Fox and Sun Chaser were absent. Then from the forest rose a ferocious roar! Spirit Bear was approaching!

\*     \*     \*

Again he roared, much closer now. Everyone held their breath, shivers running up and down their spines. Then with the flick of a hand, Calling Wolf sent something into the flames and sparks of blue, green and red shot up into the air. Oooohs and Aaaaahs rose from the watchers. Then into the camp the Great Spirit Bear exploded.

He stood nearly as tall as a pair of men, his great head raised and his mouth open is an angry roar! Again it sounded! Then the spirit danced around the hearth, bowing and rearing all the while. Behind him came Sun Chaser, wearing only his breech clot and his entire body covered with red ocher paint. He carried a bone whistle from which he steadily blew short blasts of shrill sound.

Again Calling Wolf sent colored sparks from the fire, smiling happily, for he had been included in the ceremony. Then the spirit bear turned and danced toward the woman's side of the camp. The children shrieked in fear and excitement; the women squealed as well. Then the spirit turned and danced from the camp. Sun Chaser followed.

Everyone held his or her breath. What would happen next? Then with a blood-curdling yell, Jumping Fox, true to his name leaped into the camp. He also was painted with red ochre. He danced about the fire once for each direction, chanting as he did so, explaining each move. He made offerings of food to the hearth to honor spirit bear, then he fell to his knees and Sun Chaser brought forth the sacred objects.

"The heart of this great spirit bear gives us strength and courage!" Jumping Fox shouted as he held up the blackened, shriveled heart of the animal. "The canine teeth of the great spirit bear guide the aim of the hunters of this camp, that they may cast straight and true!" He held the teeth up with his other hand. "The spirit bear is pleased with the honor bestowed upon him by the people of this camp." Again he shouted.

Sun Chaser blew on his whistle and whirled about in tight circles. Then Jumping Fox rose and faced the men. "This afternoon I went to the place where first I met the Sacred Bear. There I went on a 'spirit journey' and spoke with him. This is what he has told me."

"The people of the Grizzly Bear Camp are to join with the people of the Wolf Camp. They are to become two parts of a New People. The hunters of this camp are pure of heart and they have learned, painfully, that it is not they, who are the great hunters who provide for their people, but the spirits of their ancestors. This camp understands! This camp venerates the spirits and pays them the proper respect, from their hearts as well as from their mouths!"

Bear Claw Woman was amazed. This man had not attended the Gathering, yet he was following the instructions given her exactly! Yes! The spirits were working their magic!

Jumping Fox continued. "We will join with Running Bison and help him to collect all of the peoples living in these mountains and elsewhere and bring them together, to form the New People! We will teach them the ways of the mountain people and learn from them the ways of the plains and desert peoples. We will share our knowledge and live in peace with each other. The Dreamers and Shaman of the camps will gather regularly and share what they have learned. The people will gather as well, to exchange knowledge and renew friendships. This is what the spirits of our ancestors have told me!" He threw himself flat on the ground before the fire, spread-eagle. Sun Chaser did a complicated dance about him then leaped and whirled and ran from the camp, still blowing shrilly on his whistle. Jumping Fox lay absolutely still during his dance, then leaped to his feet and followed him.

Now Raptor Feather called the men to begin their dance. The drum resumed its steady beat, hypnotic in its boom, boom, boom! As they danced, the hunters called out prayers to their individual protective spirits, asking them to honor the humble hunter and abide with him. Each made a personal offering to the fire, one known only to him and his spirit. All-the-while everyone sipped on a special tea prepared for them by Jumping Fox, or for the women by Dancing Crane, as directed by the dreamer.

\*       \*       \*

Shadows shimmered. Bodies leaped and whirled. Jumping Fox and Sun Chaser, cleansed of their ceremonial paint and dressed again in the traditional garb of the camp, slipped quietly in and joined the celebration. Bodies swayed the drum beat. The special tea began to take effect and soon everyone was swaying in time to the drum, prayers became chants which all joined in with and majestically, the moon rose, full and shimmering. On and on they continued. Children began to yawn and were snuggled into furs beside the parents. Then the moon traveled across the sky and sank from sight. Slowly the drum beat slowed and then stopped. The ceremony was over.

Quietly hunters wrapped in sleeping furs, settled down about their hearths. Women did likewise. Silence and dark settled over the Grizzly Bear Camp. Beyond, just at the verge of the forest, a large shadow rose and sniffed the air. With a soft grunt the magnificent creature shook his head and shuffled away, satisfied.

# CHAPTER 25

Is everybody ready?" Raptor Feather shouted.

"We are ready!" People shouted back.

He nodded and led the way. They filed from the valley, headed north and east toward the Valley of the Gathering. Running Bison led the way, his wolf walking at his side. The other wolves pulled the travois. Even Guardian was fitted to the contraption. She was not happy, but if Bear Claw Woman wanted her to pull it, then she would. The women of the Bear Camp were fascinated with the wolves. They had once had dogs, but none as magnificent as these creatures. During times of famine, they had, unfortunately, eaten the dogs. Now, they had nothing to pull their travois, except the women.

"You say that when your camp joins us at the Gathering, there will be wolves to trade for?" Dancing Crane questioned Whispering Wind.

"I cannot promise, but there were many pups born during the winter, if they survived, they should be old enough to have begun training. But Crying Coyote will be bringing in an additional pair of camps with him. They may trade for the extra pups. But I will see what I can do, to at least get one for you."

"What about the rest of us?" Cattail Woman asked, "Our backs get just as tired!"

"I said I will do what I can!" Whispering Wind repeated, "That is all that I can do."

"You are Headman's Woman," Cattail persisted, "If you insist, the animals will be offered to us."

"But I do not 'insist' of my people." Whispering Wind replied evenly. "The people of the Wolf Camp work together, they do not work against each other. That is why we get along so well. There is seldom strife amongst us and when there is, it is dealt with fairly."

"Then what good is it to be Headman's Woman?" Cattail shook her head.

"It is not a position to be used, but one of service to others. It is a responsibility, to make sure that the women of my camp are happy and no one is treated unfairly."

"How can you do that? The men treat us as they will. No woman can tell them how to treat another!"

"The men of the Wolf Camp are hunters. They provide the meat for the camp. The women are in charge of the hearths. They are responsible for the distribution of the food, the hides and the hearth placement. Each cave has its own Head Woman. She is responsible for the food stores, organizing gathering expeditions and distribution of hides and other supplies."

"I have never heard of such a thing?" Dancing Crane's mouth dropped open. "You are indeed fortunate! I would wish that we had such organization!"

"You will have," Bear Claw Woman promised her, "That is one reason we gather this summer. To show each camp how well this works."

"The men do not protest?"

All three women shook their heads and laughed. "The men are happy with the arrangement. It takes much responsibility from their shoulders, allowing them to concentrate on the important tasks of hunting and protecting the camp. The women are happy, because they finally have a say in their own lives. They have status, they have security. We have an unmated-women's hearth where all gather and work on projects. We go out with our rabbit sticks and bolas and bring in small game; we collect plants, nuts and berries and prepare the food. But all get a share in it."

"You think that our men will accept such an arrangement? Dancing Crane shook her head. "They are proud! They have always held control. I do not think that they will give it up easily."

"Then Running Bison will speak with them. I am sure that once they see how well this works for our camp, they will be willing to give it a try."

"Head Woman! I have never heard of such a thing!" Cattail Woman muttered, shaking her head. "Next you will be telling us that there is even a woman elder!"

"There certainly is!" Whispering Wind laughed. "One from each cave, ours is Robe Maker."

"Robe Maker," squealed Cattail Woman, "Why she is my sister! How can this be? I did not even know if she still lives! She mated with a man of another camp and left. I have not heard from her in seasons."

"Well you will be seeing her again, just as soon as Crying Coyote brings the camp to the valley."

"Can you imagine that; Robe Maker, an elder!" Cattail Woman kept repeating to herself.

*    *    *

They camped that evening beside the river leading north toward the valley of the Gathering. Here Bear Claw Woman slipped quietly from the camp, with Guardian and found a sheltered place. Here she spread her robe and seated herself. She called upon Spirit Wolf. The mist began to swirl and once again she was seated on the log is the meadow.

*You have come to ask about the healer, Ash Branch.* Spirit Wolf said as soon as Bear Claw Woman opened her eyes.

"You know?"

Spirit Wolf nodded. *I have been expecting you to find out about her and ask.*

*Who is she?*

*She has sky colored eyes.* Spirit Wolf replied.

*You mean she is related to me?* Bear Claw Woman asked in amazement.

*You are my direct granddaughter, many times over.* Replied Ancestor Basket, from Bear Claw Woman's other side. *But I had a twin sister, one who also carried the mark. She did many things with me. This Ash Branch is a grand daughter of hers. She also carries the mark of the spirit, but she is not 'chosen'. Her gift is healing. When the time is right, the pair of you will come together. She is to help you by bringing the 'gift' of healing to all the people, teach at least one from each camp, the healing ways. Your path is to intercede with the spirits.*

The pair of you will work together, just as my twin, Star Child and I did, traveling from camp to camp, you and Ash Branch, together will help guide and teach others. There is a special place where you will go to rest and regain your power. The cave in the canyon is that place. The waters there have healing powers, the crystal cave, spirit power.

"When will we go there?"

*The time is not yet. There will be many seasons of traveling, bringing the messages of the spirits to all the camps; sharing the healing knowledge with others. Then you will rest in the cave in the canyon.* Spirit Wolf answered.

First the people must be brought together and then they must learn the new-old ways. The men must purge self-greatness, from their thoughts. This will not be easy and they will not be given much time to do this. The spirits will eliminate any that refuse. Many have been taken already. The spirits give only one chance to change. It will take many seasons to merely gather all the people under the shelter of the spirits. Running Bison has begun the task, but he will not live to see it ended. None of the people walking now will do this. Generations will pass before there is peace among all.

"The bison will not be returned in our lifetime, will they?"

They will cease to be important in your lifetime. Disease rages through the herds. They are not good meat. Most of them will die from the disease. Those that do survive will need time to replenish the herds. But the Shaman, Calling Wolf, who you brought to me, he will meet with the Great White Spirit Bison. He will tell the people. This is not your task! You will speak at the Gathering, make the offerings and protect the Sacred Relics. You will intercede with the spirits on behalf of the people and you will work with Ash Branch, but beyond that, you are free to make a life for yourself and the hunter Raven. You will bring forth a daughter and she will carry on the line. This is your task. The mist gathered and Bear Claw Woman found herself seated on her robe.

\*　　\*　　\*

"Where did you go?' Raven had searched all over looking for her.

"I spoke with Spirit Wolf and Ancestor Basket," She replied.

"We are doing something wrong?"

She shook her head. "I heard of a woman from the 'Bear' camp women. I wished to know more of her."

"And Spirit Wolf gave you this information?" He was surprised.

"She did."

"And, as usual, it is not something which you can share with me?"

She merely nodded. "I do not really remember what she said, but inside I can feel 'right' about things. It is hard to explain. What they want you to know, you remember, but the rest is stored up in your mind for when you have need of it. Just like Calling Wolf 'journeying' with me. He cannot remember, but the knowledge is there for him to draw on. I only know that after talking with Spirit Wolf and Ancestor Basket, I feel better. Somehow, my questions were answered."

"Spirits move in their own way," Raven said in agreement.

Bear Claw Woman did not like to lie to him, but some of the things revealed to her were only for her to know. Besides, she hadn't lied. She did not remember everything! But she did remember about Ash Branch. Somehow, she knew that one day they would meet. With this she was satisfied.

They traveled for a double hand of days and arrived at the Valley of the Gathering. Running Bison and Raptor Feather scouted the valley before they settled in. No one seemed to have been here since they had vacated it. Bear Claw Woman walked with Raven to the stream.

"It was right here, that I found you," he pointed. "Obsidian was farther up the trail."

"I remember Angry Bull darting her and leaping at me. But that is all," she admitted. She ran her hand around her throat, remembering the feel of the necklace.

"You are not complete without it, are you?"

She shook her head.

"I will find him. One day I promise you."

"Let's go back to the camp. This place holds bad memories for me," she shivered and turned away. Guardian fell into step beside her, growling deeply and softly in her throat in agreement. They left.

"Have you any idea when Crying Coyote and the camp will be here?" Laughing Water asked Running Bison.

"I have no idea. Why don't you ask Bear Claw Woman?"

"How would she know? She left the camp at the Spring Ceremony! You left only a little over a moon ago."

"Ask Bear Claw Woman," Running Bison again replied. "She can tell you far more accurately."

Laughing Water sighed and turned away. Finding Bear Claw Woman was equally difficult. She was no where to be found. Laughing Water asked about, but no one had seen her, or the hunter Raven, nor Guardian. Finally she glanced toward the stream and saw them approaching the camp. She felt very foolish asking Bear Claw Woman her question, but she was anxious to know the answer.

Bear Claw Woman frowned for a moment and then told her. "I will answer your question shortly. I need some time first."

This also made no sense. Laughing Water had promised Cattail Woman that she would find out when Robe Maker could be expected. Since she knew that her sister was with the Wolf Camp, Cattail Woman was nearly beside herself with excitement.

Bear Claw Woman went a short distance from the camp, to settle beneath the very tree where she had sat upon her first 'mind talking' trip. *Crying Coyote, are you there?*

*Bear Claw Woman?*

*Yes, it is I. How is the camp?*

*All is well. We have located the secret canyon. The people here are very mistrusting of us. We are having difficulty understanding their language and convincing them that we mean them no harm. They fear the Savages and their dreamer. We cannot convince them to come with us.*

*Who is their leader?*

*A man named Colored Fox. He has reason to fear the Savages. They took his camp captive. But for the intervention of a pair of strangers, they would all have been sacrificed.*

*Tell him that the stranger who freed him is called Running Bison. Tell him that he leads your camp. Tell him that the hunters Raven and Bull Elk walk with Running Bison. Tell him that his camp is welcome to come and walk with Running Bison also.*

*I will try.*

*We are at the valley. When do you think you will arrive here?*

*We are over a moon travel from there! I cannot say.*

*Tell Robe Maker that Cattail Woman waits impatiently.*
*Cattail Woman?*
*They are sisters.*
*Ah!*
*Let me know how it goes with the headman.*
*I will.*

Bear Claw Woman blinked and reached for her staff. She tucked the Sacred Relic bundle securely into her waist pouch and headed back to the camp. Raven waited for her there and handed her a heaping plate of food. She ate ravenously.

"Tell Laughing Water that is will be nearly a pair of moons before Crying Coyote arrives."

"That will be barely in time for the ceremony!"

"He is having problems. The headman distrusts him. It seems that this group is the one that Running Bison rescued and released along with you and Bull Elk."

"Colored Fox?" Raven exclaimed.

"You know him?"

"We spent nearly half a moon locked in a cage together. Actually we became quite good friends, baring the fact that we could not understand a word which the other spoke." He grinned.

"Well if Crying Coyote has more trouble with him, perhaps you should speak to him. At least he should remember you."

"I could speak with him?"

"Of course! You need only take my hand to do so."

"That 'mind talking' makes me very nervous. But if you say it will help, then I will do as you ask. When do you speak again to Crying Coyote?"

"He will 'call' if he needs help."

"I will go and give Laughing Water your message." He rose and left the hearth.

Laughing Water nodded and turned to Cattail Woman. Raven left.

"How can she know this?" Cattail Woman questioned suspiciously.

"You forget, she is The Chosen One. She has special powers."

"I do not know this 'Chosen" which you speak of, so tell me how she can know where my sister is!"

"She can 'talk' to people with her mind," Whispering Wind explained. "I have experienced it with her myself. It is as though she is separated from you by nothing more than a hide."

"I do not believe such a thing!" the woman exclaimed. "It cannot be done! Such a thing must be guided by evil spirits!"

Whispering Wind was quick to spot trouble. "Come with me. I will prove it to you. You shall speak with Robe Maker, yourself; right now!" She pulled the protesting woman to her feet and all but dragged her to where Bear Claw Woman was seated. "This woman wishes to speak to Robe Maker!" She signaled 'trouble' with her eyes. Bear Claw Woman frowned; nodded and led the pair away from the camp.

"Where are you taking me?" Cattail Woman pulled against Whispering Wind's grip on her wrist.

"To speak with Robe Maker," Bear Claw Woman replied, "I cannot do so with the noise of the camp. I must be able to concentrate."

"So please, be quiet!" Whispering Wind added.

With much trepidation and a good portion of suspicion, Cattail Woman complied.

Bear Claw Woman seated herself and closed her eyes. *Robe Maker!* She called.

*Bear Claw Woman?* Robe Maker glanced all about and then shivered. This 'mind talking' made her nervous.

*Yes! I have someone here who wishes to speak with you.* She took hold of Cattail Woman's hand and held tightly as the frightened woman struggled to be released. Then suddenly she stopped.

*Robe Maker, is that really you?*

*Cattail?* Robe Maker nearly lost her balance. *You are with Bear Claw Woman?*

*I am. I can't believe this! Am I really talking to you?*

*It takes a while to get used to, but she really can 'mind talk'. But tell me, how do you come to be with her? I thought that you were with Great Thunder's camp.*

*I was. The Savages attacked. I was out with several women gathering plants. When we returned, the camp was burned and all taken captive. We wandered in the mountains for moons before Raptor Feather found us. Then*

*Running Bison and those with Bear Claw Woman walked into our camp.
We came with them to this valley and I wait here for you!*

*I will be there! Bear Claw Woman, thank you for doing this for my sister
and me. I realize what a strain it is on you.*

*You are welcome, Robe Maker!*

Bear Claw Woman released Cattail Woman's hand. She sagged
against the tree and breathed shallowly. Two such long contacts so close
together had drained her completely. Not even the Sacred Relics could
replace power that quickly.

"What is wrong with her?" Cattail Woman asked Whispering Wind.

"Her 'gift' does not come without consequences! To help you, she
went earlier and spoke with Crying Coyote. Now, unselfishly, she again
goes, so that you might talk with Robe Maker and not cause upset within
the camp. But each time that she 'mind-talks' it drains her strength. Now
she must draw power and rest. We will go back to the camp and send the
hunter Raven to her. He will know what to do." Whispering Wind escorted
the excited woman back to the camp.

"I still cannot believe that I actually talked to Robe Maker, yet I know
that it is so. I feel wonderful!"

"As does everyone who is involved; everyone comes away from the
experience feeling wonderfully refreshed, at the outlay of Bear Claw
Woman. It will be days before she will be returned to her normal level of
energy and Crying Coyote will probably contact her again yet tonight."

"Will she be able to talk to him?"

"Raven will do what he can to protect her," Was all that Whispering
Wind could offer.

She left Cattail Woman at the edge of the camp and went to where
Raven waited a worried look on his homely face. "She is waiting for you
at the old oak tree," she nodded in the direction of the tree. "It would
be best if you take her to the ring of trees where we found Obsidian. She
will find the power she needs there and others will perhaps not bother
her foolishly again, as I just did."

"I am sure that you had a good reason. You are familiar with what
this does to her."

"The woman Cattail was about to cause trouble. It was the only thing
I could think of to divert it."

Raven nodded. "We will return in a pair of days or so. He went to where Bull Elk sat and spoke to the hunter. He nodded and began packing up his shelter and Ravens. Then he spoke to Calling Wolf. That man nodded. Raven hooked Young Wolf to the travois and headed toward the old oak. Bull Elk broke down the shelters and loaded them onto his travois and Calling Wolf went in search of Running Bison. Then he also headed out the trail to the west. He soon caught up with Bull Elk. They in turn fell in behind Raven shortly thereafter. The group halted in the jasper quarry for the night. Early in the morning, the men replenished their supply of tool blanks, then headed again west to the valley of the circle of trees.

They arrived well before sun-high and set up their camp. Raven carried Bear Claw Woman to the flat boulder and spread a bear hide. He settled her there leaving Guardian with her. Bear Claw Woman settled with the Sacred Relics and a weak blue glow began to form. Guardian studied her for a time, investigated the ring of trees to make certain that it was safe and then she returned to Bear Claw Woman. She was restless. She whined and dug about at the base of the boulder, unearthing several moldering bones. These she nosed about and fretted. Then she dug a much deeper hole and dropped them in. She did not stop until she had buried the remains of her old body to her satisfaction. Then with a leap, she joined Bear Claw Woman on the boulder.

The hunters settled around their hearth and knapped tools for the better part of the day. Then they took a quick trip toward the far end of the valley. Here they flushed a pair of turkeys, which they expertly darted. Back at their camp they plucked the birds, saving the feathers in a reed basket. Then they skewered the turkeys over the hearth and once again the men had little to do, except wait. Before dark Raven went to check on Bear Claw Woman and discovered that she and Guardian were just where they had been early that morning. The blue glow still pulsed about them, much stronger now. Satisfied, he quietly retreated.

*Bear Claw Woman!*

*Crying Coyote! How did it go?*

*You were right. Once that I told him that I was part of Running Bison's camp they joined us eagerly. We have already left the canyon. Our next stop is the place of stone. I do not anticipate much trouble convincing the people there to join us. After following Wanderer out on the plain, they will be happy to see familiar faces once again.*

*If you run into trouble let me know. Otherwise, we will see you when you arrive at the gathering.*

*Take care! Give Raven my regards and tell Running Bison that everything is going well.*

*I will.*

The blue mist faded once again barely visible. On and on she sat, the glow gradually rebuilding some. Finally, Bear Claw Woman stretched and rubbed the back of her neck. Guardian licked her face and wiggled joyfully on the fur. Bear Claw Woman grinned and scratched the animal's exposed stomach. Guardian groaned and made scratching kicking movements with her hind feet.

A movement beyond alerted her to the arrival of Raven, but her nose had already picked up the scent of the cooking meal. She leaped gracefully to the ground and raced to meet him, tail high in the air. The hunter carried food for himself and Bear Claw Woman. They sat together at the base of the boulder and ate their meal, tossing the bones to Guardian and Young Wolf. The latter shot away from them and expertly ran to ground a rabbit. Not to be outdone, Guardian leaped into the air and went in search of her own rabbit. Very shortly she returned and the wolves lay companionable side by side and ripped into their own meal. Raven laughed at their antics.

"Crying Coyote contacted me again, a short while ago," Bear Claw Woman told him. "The headman was actually eager to join us once he realized that Running Bison led the camp. They have already left for the place of stone."

"I hope that is all of the 'mind talking' that you must undertake for a while. At least until you have recovered from this. I hope that Whispering Wind did not endanger you just to impress Cattail Woman!"

Bear Claw Woman shook her head. "It could have broken down into serious trouble. Cattail Woman was about to make trouble. She did not understand about the 'mind talking' and had already begun to mutter 'evil spirits' and you know where that can lead. Whispering Wind did exactly right. Now instead of a troublemaker or an enemy, we have a staunch friend. She will never forget that I suffered physical pain just so that she could speak to her sister. You will see."

"I hope so. It is not good to have doubters in a camp. But I still wonder if it was necessary."

"I felt that it was."

"That is all that I need to know. Do you dare return to the camp tonight, or would you prefer to stay here?"

"I think that it would be safe for me to return and share your shelter. It will be another day before the power has been restored and I will be tired for several more days, but I feel that we can return to the camp after one more day and night here. At least I can concentrate at this place. This boulder is a strong power place. Each time it is used, it gains in strength. It is like the Sacred Relics. They build power while I possess them and they give me more power each time that I use them. I must be very careful not to misuse them. Too many times and the power they contain would be beyond my control. It could actually become dangerous."

"But what if you need a large amount of power? Would the relics be able to supply that?"

"No, but then I would not expect them to. At such a time I would use them only as an umbilical cord to the spirits. They would answer directly, just as they did when the Ancestor Chosen battled their enemies. That is very dangerous. Ancestor Yel was killed during her battle with evil and it took both twins working together when Ancestor Basket faced the Spirit Dreamer. I am fortunate that I do not face such a task."

"What of Quenquel? You will not have to face him?"

She shook her head, "He will be dealt with by others." She did not mention who the 'others' would be. It was information for her only. "I am a pathway, but I am not the only way. The dreamers are also connected with the spirits. When the fate of Quenquel is to be fulfilled, those responsible will know. Until then, he is safely far away from here."

"Come, I will carry you back to our shelter." He lifted her easily in his arms and as the wolves streaked ahead, on their own paths of interest, he carried her to their shelter and happily joined her there, holding her close. Darkness settled close and the night insects began to sing. At some time the wolves slipped quietly into the camp and settled.

\* \* \*

Calling Wolf opened his eyes. He had been sound asleep, but suddenly, now, he was wide awake. He keyed his ears to the sounds. Nothing was out-of-place. He shifted onto his side and closed his eyes. It was no good. He was wide awake! With a sigh he quietly rose and added wood to the fire. He sat on a log and watched the moon rise. He wondered about his path in life. For so many seasons he had searched.... to no avail. He still had no answers! A flicker of movement caught his eye, out beyond the camp. Something was moving.... He rose and reached for his weapons. Guardian appeared at his side and slowly, he let them slip from his fingers. As if in a dream, he stepped away from the fire and followed the big wolf away from the camp.

As they walked, the moon rose higher and shed its light on the valley floor. Calling Wolf paused, his eyes adjusting to the light, yet he was unable to believe what they told him.

Beyond where he stood, perhaps a double dart cast, grazed the largest bison he had ever seen. But it wasn't the size that made him catch his breath! This bison was pure white! As he approached, the animal raised its great head and looked his straight in the eye. Calling Wolf halted.

\*　　\*　　\*

*Greetings Shaman! Come and lay your hand on my forehead.* The animal spoke to him.

"Who are you?" Calling Wolf asked in a stunned whisper, "You speak to me!" He unconsciously followed the directions, thrilling as his hand contacted the soft fur of the animal.

*I am the spirit come in answer to your prayers. I bring you a message to take to the people. My kind are dying! Disease rages through the herds. Their meat is poison for the people. The people are to move into the mountains and not eat of the meat of bison. The dreamer, Crooked Spirit carries the tattered remains of the white bison robe. You are to take it and bury it at the base of the 'power rock' where Bear Claw Woman has rested. One day, when my kind have recovered and the people have united, I will come again to one chosen to carry the message and the bison will be again returned to the people. The spirits are pleased with you, Shaman. Your prayers have been heard.*

\*　　\*　　\*

Then, in the blink of an eye, Calling Wolf and Guardian were alone. The hunter stood there, stunned, unable to quite believe what had just happened. Were it not for the wolf at his side and the residual tingling in his fingers, from stroking the fur, he would have claimed the whole incident a dream. Slowly he unclenched his hand, to find that in the palm, lay a tiny charm. It was shaped just like the horn of a bison. With shaking fingers, he placed it into his amulet and returned to the camp. He lay awake for the remainder of the night, reliving the experience and seeking to understand its message. Finally, the sun rose and so did he. Guardian lay beside Bear Claw Woman and when he looked toward her, he could have sworn she winked back at him. He was very quiet that day, as they crafted tools beside the fire. The next night he slept soundly. In the morning they returned to the camp.

Later, that same day, Calling Wolf sought out Crooked Spirit.

"I would speak with you, Dreamer," he requested formally.

Crooked Spirit frowned, for such a request meant something unusual was afoot. He led the hunter away from the camp and to the old oak tree. Here they seated and Crooked Spirit waited for the other man to make his request. This was formal etiquette.

"I have a request to make," Calling Wolf began, "And I do not quite know where to begin. A pair of night ago, I was visited by a spirit. This creature told me to come to you and request the Robe of the White Bison. I am to take it and return it to the spirits in a proscribed way. It is no longer to be used by or for the people. It has been called back by the spirits."

Crooked Spirit sighed and nodded, "The White Bison..." he murmured.

"You have seen it?" Calling Wolf asked excitedly.

Crooked Spirit jerked alert. "You have seen the Spirit of White Bison?" he questioned.

"Isn't that what you asked?" Calling Wolf responded.

Crooked Spirit shook his head, "No, I was merely thinking to myself. There are of course, legends of those who have actually seen the spirit, but the robe is so old and it seems to have lost any power it once carried. You actually saw the Spirit of White Bison?" he asked in awe.

Calling Wolf nodded, "I even touched him," he fingered his amulet absently.

"When do you want the robe?"

"I will come to you when I am ready," the shaman replied. "First I must cleanse and pray. When the moon is full, I will come for the robe."

Crooked Spirit again nodded and they returned to the camp. It was a hand of days before the moon would be full. Calling Wolf gathered a few things and he and his wolf left the camp, quietly. Those who saw him leave, did not question.

When he returned, Crooked Spirit was watching. He met the Shaman at the edge of the camp and gave him a deer hide wrapped parcel. Then Calling Wolf left the camp again.

Traveling swiftly he reached the stone well before high-sun. He had a deer scapula in his backpack. He set the parcel on the stone and began to dig a deep hole, on the far side of the stone. Once he was below the stone, he dug back beneath it, enlarging his hole to a size that would accommodate the parcel. When he was satisfied, he carefully inserted it and packed earth all around it then filled in the hole. He even replaced the sod plug over it. When he was finished, there was no sign of disturbance. He nodded in satisfaction. Then fingering his amulet, he sent a prayer up to White Bison Spirit. A feeling of well-being indicated to him, that his prayer had been heard. He smiled and returned to the camp. No one asked where he had been.

\*       \*       \*

"People are coming!" Prairie Grass hurried into the camp from where he had been hunting to the north. He had seen them, as mere specks at great distance, but had wasted no time in alerting the camp. Running Bison called his hunters together and they left the camp, going out to meet these strangers.

"How many?" Bull Elk asked.

"At least as many as we are," he replied. "I didn't stop to count them. I just hurried back to warn the camp."

"I wonder if they are people we know?" Crooked Spirit questioned.

"We will soon know the answer to that!" Running Bison stopped his group. Beyond, settling into a camp beside a stream was a sizable group of people. The hunters quickly hid and watched. It was a large camp. There were many women and children, laughing and calling back and forth as they unloaded their travois and released the dogs. The men seemed content to let them do the work. They settled in the shade of trees and called for food and drink. Their requests were hurriedly complied with. Running Bison frowned. There was only a hand of men. "I don't think this is the entire camp!" He whispered, "Besides, they seem to be waiting for something!"

"I think some of us had better go back to our own camp!" Prairie Grass inched back from where he peaked over a slight verge. "While we are here, they could be attacking our camp!"

Running Bison nodded and most of the men quickly and silently eased from sight and headed back toward the camp. He and a pair of others stayed and watched. It was nearly dark, when a disturbance from the camp below alerted them. Soon a large group of men trotted into the camp. They carried quartered carcasses on their shoulders, or dragged them on travois behind them. They dumped the kill in the middle of the camp and flexed aching shoulders. Running Bison sucked in his breath, "Bison!" he whispered.

"What do we do?" Calling Wolf whispered back, "They will surely die if they eat that meat! The spirits have told me that it is poison!"

"We must act quickly!" Prairie Grass nodded, "But how?"

"Follow my lead!" Running Bison rose and strode clearly into view of the entire camp. Declaring loudly, "Hello the camp; we come in peace!"

*       *       *

The camp became silent. People froze where they stood

Running Bison halted in plain sight, his hands clearly visible, holding no weapons. Again he repeated his greeting. "Hello the camp! We come in peace."

A pair of men at the edge of the camp spoke hurriedly and quietly to each other, a puzzled expression clear on their face. Raven stepped up beside Running Bison. "They do not understand the words of The People. Let me try." He cleared his throat and said clearly some words that Running Bison did not understand, but by their expressions, those within the waiting camp did. You could see relief spread over the worried faces. The pair of men at the edge of the camp came forward. "We will walk to meet them and I will explain then," Calling Wolf told him.

"We come from the camp of The People, settled at the far end of this valley," Calling Wolf told the pair.

"We have been sent by the spirits to find you." Replied the wizened old one. I am Spirit Dancer, Dreamer of the Deer Camp. This man is Two Bears, Headman."

"You say that the spirits have sent you to us?" Calling Wolf questioned.

The old one nodded solemnly, "I took a Spirit Journey, at the beginning of the last moon. The Great Grizzly Bear Spirit directed me to take this camp to this very valley at this time, to meet with a great people with whom we are to join. Our people have been living to the far north of here. There all of the bison have been dying." He motioned toward the carcasses that the women were busily processing. "These are the first bison we have seen since leaving the lands with which we are familiar."

"We have hurried to greet you for just this reason," Calling Wolf answered. "The bison are poison. They carry a terrible disease and any that eat of their flesh will suffer a gut-wrenching agony. I myself have experienced it. Many who ate of them then, now walk the wind. Gift the meat to the spirits in fire and come into our camp and eat. We have food to share with you."

"What are you telling them?" Running Bison wanted to know.

"Told them not to eat the bison," Calling Wolf answered, "And offered them good food instead. The Bear Spirit sent them to join us."

Running Bison nodded and made the hand sign for peace and welcome. The pair of men nodded and waved them into their camp. Calling Wolf walked beside the dreamer, exchanging news of the gathering. As soon as they entered the camp, the headman called out sharply to the women, who stopped working, looked worriedly at the strangers, at the bison and at the fires. They shrugged and tossed the meat in their hands into the fires. It sizzled, burned and sent up a black, evil-smelling smoke. The women wrinkled their noses and backed away, looks of fear and unease clear on their faces. They called among themselves and soon all the meat was being fed to the fires.

"I wondered about this meat," Two Bears mentioned to Calling Wolf, "It does not smell right and there were creatures living within the liver. I have never seen such things before.

Calling Wolf nodded, "That is how is was with us, only we were very hungry and we ate the meat any way. We were doubled over for days with terrible pains in our guts and several of our number died. Our dreamer called to the spirits, but they did not answer. Only this moon have they spoken to us regarding the bison. Great White Bison Spirit himself spoke to me."

"You are a dreamer?" the old one glanced sharply at him.

Calling Wolf shook his head, "Among my people I was called Shaman! It is similar to a dreamer, yet different. Among The People, I am still learning the ways of a dreamer."

"Ah! That is how you understand our words!" Spirit Dancer nodded.

"I have traveled far and lived with many peoples over the last several seasons. I have tried to learn the words of each group. Your words are similar to others with whom I have lived. But come, call your people to load again their travois, it is but a short way to our camp. You will be made welcome there and we have food to share which is not poison."

"Do you also have the one called The Chosen, with you?" Spirit Dancer questioned excitedly, "It is he we seek."

"She," Calling Wolf corrected, "Yes, she is with us."

"She?" Spirit Dancer stopped dead.

"The Chosen is a woman," explained Calling Wolf. "A most powerful woman, we are pleased that she is with us."

"You did not say The Chosen was a woman!" Two Bears glared at the dreamer.

"I did not know, Head Man," the dreamer protested. "My spirit said to find The Chosen One and join with The People, there was no mention that this was a woman!"

"Come to our camp and meet her for yourself. If you do not find her special, you are free to leave," Calling Wolf offered.

"Is there a problem?" Running Bison asked.

"They have just found that Bear Claw is a woman," replied Calling Wolf. "Their spirits said to find The Chosen, but did not specify. Now the Headman is uneasy."

Running Bison merely nodded and sighed. It was the same with everyone, until they met her. As the men talked, the camp had repacked their travois and once more put the dogs into harness. When they were ready, Running Bison and Calling Wolf led them toward the camp. They noticed when hunters slipped unobserved from hiding and circled to beat them back to the camp. When they led the new people in, there was already ample food to share with them. They were directed to a very good place to set up their camp and the women of the Grizzly Bear Camp hurried to help the newcomers to set up their shelters. Then they brought food to them.

*　　*　　*

There were planks filled to overflowing with deer, bear, turkey and rabbit and bladders of steaming vegetables and stew. "What is this?" a matron sniffed the plants.

"Taste it!" suggested Dancing Crane. "You will find it wonderful! I felt just the same the first time I had it, but it did not take me long to realize what a wonderful food this is. Why, all last winter, I did not have a single sore gum."

"What is it?" another woman sniffed with interest.

"Just a variety of plants which we have gathered and prepared," Laughing Water said. "We eat them all of the time and it has made a great difference in how we feel and this food is much easier to find than animals, because it does not run away."

"I don't know...." the first matron backed off.

"Oh, come on Bison Robe! I'm certainly going to try this food, it smells wonderful!" the second woman reached for a shell bowl.

"You would eat anything once!" Bison Robe snorted, "Probably bison dung if you didn't know what it was!" But she also reached for a bowl.

"Mother, may I also try it?" a small tidy girl asked quietly from beside Bison Robe.

"Ah! Rosebud! There you are," Bison Robe smiled. "I wondered where you had gotten off to. Honestly child! The way you slip around, I can never know exactly where you are!"

"I am right beside you, Mother," the girl smiled. "But you have not answered my question. Might I try this new food? It really smells quite delicious."

"I see no reason why not. But if the taste does not live up to the smell, you must still eat it. It would be most impolite not to," Bison Robe warned.

"Then I will wait until you have tried it," the child said seriously. "I would rather that you ate something which tastes bad, then I. If you say it is good, then I will also eat it."

"She is old beyond her seasons," Bison Robe frowned at the child, shaking her head.

Dancing Crane merely smiled. "I can understand how she feels. I remember the same doubt when first I was offered this food. But it did not take long to get used to eating these plants. Now I cannot imagine how I got by before."

"I heard you say that these plants keep away the bleeding gum disease?" the other woman was already scooping up a portion of the plant food. "I am called Yellow Leaf," she smiled at Dancing Crane. "Bison Robe and I are sisters."

Dancing Crane introduced Laughing Water and Whispering Wind who had just arrived with more food. The women were formal at first, but soon began to relax. Bison Robe tasted the vegetables cautiously, then smiled and nodded. Rosebud, noticing that her mother found them good, immediately took a very small portion of her own. Caution seemed to be second nature with this child. She tasted just as carefully and then smiled. Soon she was asking for more.

"I was amazed when no one in our camp suffered from bleeding gums this last winter," Dancing Crane replied. "The only thing different in our diets were these plants. I cannot imagine how we lived for so many seasons eating only Bison meat. Now we eat many kinds of food and every meal is something to look forward to. It amazes me that our ancestors did not discover these plants and how good they are to eat."

"They did know of them," Whispering Wind said, "But over the generations, the knowledge of them has gone from us. So long as the camps followed the bison herds, these plants were not available to us, for they grow in the forests. Only the grasses grow on the plains and it takes such a long time to gather them that there has never been time, always on the move as we have been. But now we have moved into the mountains and our men hunt other game and we gather the plants and since we have joined with The People, our camp has begun to learn new ways as well. You cannot believe all of the wonderful things we are learning!"

"Is that how you can understand our words? You also are new to The People?" Bison Robe asked.

"That is so," Dancing Crane nodded, "Whispering Wind can understand your words because she was taken captive by people who speak as you. I grew up in the camp led by Great Thunder."

Bison Robe nodded, "I have heard of him, but not for a while."

"He has gone to walk the wind," Dancing Crane answered. "The Savages captured our camp and sacrificed him to their spirits."

"They are near here?" yelped Yellow Leaf, "I will not sleep a wink!"

"There are no signs of them anywhere," replied Dancing Crane. "Our headman, Running Bison believes that they have left this place and that their dreamer is no longer with them. They have returned to the peaceful ways they lived before he came into their lives. I hope this is true!" she shuddered, "Were it not that Bear Claw Woman has assured us this is so, I also would hesitate to be here."

"Who is this Bear Claw Woman and how would she know this?" Bison Robe questioned.

"She is The Chosen," answered Whispering Wind. "Just wait until you meet her!"

"Mother, is their leader a woman?" whispered Rosebud, "Father will never allow us to stay!"

Whispering Wind assured the child, "Running Bison is our leader," she said proudly. "And he is a wonderful leader!"

Dancing Crane chuckled, "He is also her mate." she said smiling, "But she is right, Running Bison is an excellent leader, as far as I have seen. Our camp has been with him for nearly a double hand of days and so far I am truly impressed." So the women settled down comfortable and got acquainted, as the men did, not far from them, exchanging greetings and struggling to understand the words which each other spoke. Gradually, as he listened, Running Bison began to recognize a word here and a word there which were so similar to his own, that he was able to follow the general drift of the conversations. Of course, Crooked Spirit was instantly able to communicate with Spirit Dancer in the ancient formal language that the dreamers had always used. He had spent a lot of time teaching this to Hollow Bone, so the youth was also able to understand. Actually, Running Bison, Prairie Grass, Laughing Water and

Bear Claw Woman seemed to be the only ones who could not converse freely with the new camp.

"I think it is time that I began to learn the words of others," he told Calling Wolf later that evening as they sat drinking tea just before retiring for the night, "I know that you know them, would you teach me?"

"I know the words of this group, because they are quite similar with those spoken by the camp I grew up in, but there are many groups of people and it seems that each one speaks differently and how we are to unite them it beyond me."

"The dreamers seem to have no difficulty."

"I know, but they have a special way of speaking, using much symbolism and their hands. I have learned much of this from Crooked Spirit."

"Why could we not use something similar? I mean, there must be hand signs which would represent the same thing in any group."

Calling Wolf frowned and nodded, "It should be possible and then the spoken word would become less of a barrier. Of course, the best answer is for all to speak the same, but that is not practical. We do not have time for that! If we are to gather the tribes together and become One People, then we are going to have to find ways to communicate. We were just lucky this time that some from our group did understand their words."

"You understand these people, Bear Claw Woman understands the gatherers and the dreamers seem to understand each other, but this is not much to have when faced with people that none of us can speak to. We must study on this problem and find a solution to it. I was absolutely amazed when their dreamer said that their spirits had directed them to find us, what do you make of that?"

Running Bison sat thoughtfully for a time, "I suppose it might mean that Bear Claw Woman's spirits are helping in our task, but why their own spirits would guide them to join us, this I do not understand."

"Perhaps they are the same spirits," Calling Wolf mused. "I suppose it is possible that at one time we were all the same people and have wandered away from each other through many generations. Maybe that is why the spirits want us to be united. I have noticed in my travels that there are words in almost every tongue which sound the same or nearly so and have similar meanings. These are the words that logically; we should begin with to build this common manner of communication. A few spoken words would help a lot. I will think on this idea and we can discuss it more later," he rose and bid Running Bison good night.

# CHAPTER 26

I would speak with you," Jumping Fox sat beside Raven. He had watched the hearth unobtrusively, until Bear Claw Woman left with Whispering Wind on a task of their own; now he approached the hunter.

Raven offered him a horn of tea and they drank companionably for a time. "You had not yet joined us when Great Bear Spirit came to me and spoke," Jumping Fox began. "He gave me a task to aid you with. Before the Mid-Summer Gathering, you must retrieve the spirit necklace taken from your woman."

Raven clutched his big hands into fists, nearly snapping the horn he held. "I want nothing more than I want to place my hands about the throat of Angry Bull!" he grated through clinched teeth.

"The Spirit Bear charged me with the task of guiding you to him. Now is the time to do this."

"I am ready!" Raven leaped to his feet, tossing the last of his tea into the hearth fire.

"We will go as soon as we are ready," Jumping Fox nodded.

"I am ready NOW!"

Jumping Fox frowned, "We must not rush into this task, my friend. Unless you wish to get yourself darted through! Angry Bull is not the brightest man, but he is one of the more dangerous ones. Success can be jeopardized by rashness. We need to form a plan and be sure that we do not make foolish mistakes. I have thought about the best way to accomplish this task and it does not include losing lives, especially not yours."

Raven sighed and slumped back down onto the log. "It is just that I have wanted for so long to avenge Bear Claw Woman's death at his hands...."

"We will get the necklace back, my friend, do not doubt that. I have been studying the men who travel with you and I have made my selection of a group to go with us. But let me tell you of my idea and let us discuss it calmly and logically." He sat down again as well. "The hunter Bull Elk and yourself from your group and myself and Black Cloud from my camp should be enough. What we need is a small, fast moving, well-organized group. After all, Angry Bull is but one man. Still, it is best not to underestimate him."

Raven nodded.

"It is also best if none besides ourselves has any idea where we are going."

"Is there really any need for such secrecy?"

"Do you think your mate would let you go without her?"

Raven shook his head, "You are right! she would insist on coming as well and I want her no where near when I meet Angry Bull. I need to have a clear head and be able to concentrate. This would be impossible with Bear Claw Woman along. So we will sneak out of the camp and she will not even know where we have gone. Of course, I will hear about it when we return, but hopefully, she will so glad to have her necklace back that she will find forgiveness in her heart. How long will it take?"

"Probably about a hand of days."

Raven nodded, "I will say that Bull Elk and I are going hunting. That will arouse no suspicion on her part. Besides, women are not welcome on hunting excursions."

"We will meet up at the knapping quarry," Jumping Fox added. "From there we can make our plans in a general way and after we study the layout at Angry Bull's camp, we can make the final decisions. This is a good plan."

"What of the other men in that camp? They will not just sit there and let us kill Angry Bull."

Jumping Fox grinned, "There are no other 'men' in that camp. We drove him and that old woman, Hunting Badger out. I don't expect any trouble from him!"

"You mean they are alone?"

Jumping Fox shook his head. "They are with a group of women and girls. I do not know them, but perhaps you will recognize them when you see them. I have only seen what the spirits wanted to show me, but only the pair of men seemed to be in the camp. After the way those men acted, I doubt that these women will protest if Angry Bull is lost to them."

Then I will see you at the quarry," Raven rose and hurried to his shelter. Now was as good a time as any to begin getting his things together. He called to Bull Elk when he saw the other man heading past the hearth. Elk turned and they spoke quickly for several breaths, then Bull Elk nodded and went to his own shelter just beyond their hearth. While Bull Elk loaded their travois and made their excuses to Running Bison, Raven went in search of Bear Claw Woman.

"Bull Elk and I are going hunting," he explained, not really looking her in the eye. Bear Claw Woman was busy and not really paying close attention any way. "We will probably be gone a hand of days."

"On a simple hunt," Bear Claw Woman frowned.

"We are also scouting for signs of others," Raven quickly added. "There is little to do while we wait. I am too restless to just sit around camp. I'd rather be out hunting."

"I will finish here shortly and help get our things packed," she answered.

"Ah... Just Bull Elk and I are going...." he scuffed his toe in the dirt.

"You don't want me...?" Bear Claw Woman looked closely at him, "What is going on?"

"Nothing! We are just going out hunting! What is the problem with that? Besides, you are busy with the new people and doing your things. I am just under foot. So I am going hunting and Bull Elk is going with me. We will be back when we get here!" He answered gruffly, then swung around and stomped back to their hearth. *You really handled that smoothly!* He castigated himself, *why didn't you just shout out loud that you were about to do something she wouldn't approve of? Now she is going to be suspicious! And you probably hurt her feelings as well!* He glared at a pair of boys who were playing and ran into him. "Why don't you watch where you are going?" he shouted at them. Then he stomped on toward the hearth, muttering to himself.

Bull Elk waited beside the loaded travois. Young Wolf romped excitedly beside and then ran to meet Raven. at last, the warm welcome of the wolf softened Ravens glum mood some. He ruffled the animal's thick fur and soon the hunters were striding away from the camp.

Bear Claw Woman watched her mate stride away from her, his encounter with the boys and frowned. *Something is up.* She thought. *Raven is acting very strangely.*

"Bear Claw Woman," Whispering Wind called, "We need your help!" She turned and hurried to where the women were working and soon forgot all about Raven's strange behavior.

Raven and Bull Elk arrived at the knapping quarry long before the other pair of hunters. Raven was restless. He paced back and forth, sent rocks hurling through the air with his powerful cast and prowled. Bull Elk frowned. He certainly hoped that his friend got himself under control before they reached Angry Bull's camp. In his present mood he was not only a danger to himself, but others as well. Nearly a hand of time had passed before the other hunters joined them. Then they set off at a fast pace, Jumping Fox leading the way. Raven had gotten acquainted with Black Cloud on the trail to the valley and he was very impressed with the strong quiet hunter. This was a good man to have beside you in a time of danger. They moved at a fast pace all day. Their camp that evening was merely a banked fire beneath the open sky. Here they began planning.

"What is their camp like?" Bull Elk asked.

Jumping Fox drew a diagram in the dirt with a stick. "This is how the valley is shaped." He drew the outline. "And here is where the cave is located," he added it. "Along here are stands of thick forest," he outlined an area along the entire side of the valley opposite the cave. "We will be able to travel to this point, directly across from the cave, without being detected," he marked a spot on his map. "From there we should be able to study the camp at our leisure. When we have decided upon our final plan we will act. Are there any questions, or suggestions?" He looked at the three hunters. "All right then, we might as well get some sleep, we must be back on the trail at first light." They all nodded and soon were rolled up beside the hearth. Silence settled in. The wolves were off on a task of their own and after a time Young Wolf silently settled beside Raven.

The big hunter reached out and ruffled her fur. Raven was far from sleep. His mind was seething! Almost he could taste the victory of his hands closing about Angry Bull's throat. He could imagine looking the hated foe directly in the eyes as he squeezed the life from them. He could imagine them silently pleading and then fading into sightlessness as death took him. *I'll be the last thing he ever sees!* Again and again he replayed the scene in his mind, as he had a thousand times before. Finally, long after the moon had set, he slept.

"Come on, man!" Bull Elk shook him awake, "Time to go!"

Raven leaped to his feet and shook the sleep from his brain. "Didn't sleep well," he muttered as he strapped his sleeping fur to the travois. Bull Elk handed him some food and a horn of hot tea and they set off following Jumping Fox. Late that day they slipped into the valley where Jumping Fox claimed they would find Angry Bull. They had a dry camp, with no fire. Once again that night Raven had trouble sleeping. He was so close... finally though, his eyes drifted shut.

Young Wolf licking his face wakened him. Silently he accepted the trail food handed to him.

"We will go along this side of the valley," Jumping Fox indicated in soft voice and watch the cave from a good vantage point. No rash moves!" he glanced sternly at Raven. "Is that understood by all?"

Raven nodded.

"Then follow me," he led them of along a faint game trail threading through the heavy brush. After nearly a double hand of time he began easing toward the valley floor. They could catch the scent of wood smoke on the air. Finally they reached the edge of the forest and just across from them, as Jumping Fox had drawn on his map, lay the cave. There were several women and girls working about in the open. There was no sign of any men. So they settled down and watched. Late in the day, nearly at dusk, one single man came into the cave. Raven clutched Bull Elk by the tunic. "Angry Bull!" he muttered softly.

\*     \*     \*

Dancing Willow straightened, her back aching; the last moon of her pregnancy very obvious. She glared toward the hunter who had just shouted for her to fetch him water. She sighed; *it is time we got rid of these worthless hunters!* She thought to herself as she went to fetch him the water stomach. Angry Bull was getting impossible! Both she and Laughing Water carried his children. And she was suspicious that Dancing Moth did also. He had certainly lain with her enough times. At least old Hunting Badger was beyond the lust to couple. He only wanted to be waited upon hand and foot.

Fire Weed watched the exchange. She frowned. It was time! They had needed the hunters during the fall to provide meat for them, then during the winter for protection against predators. But now it was well toward summer and they had no need of them anymore. They had learned from watching and when the men were not around, they had practiced. Now Angry Bull drank his fill, rose, stretched and scratched his crotch. He was bored.

"I am going hunting!" he reached for his atlatl and darts. "You coming?" he called to Hunting Badger.

"You go ahead!" the old headman ordered, "I am going to take a nap." He yawned, scratched his bulging stomach and ambled toward his sleeping furs. The women watched. Soon, Hunting Badger was snoring loudly and Angry Bull far from the cave.

Fire Weed nodded to Dancing Moth and Laughing Water. Each of them picked up a good sized rock. "Wait!" Fire Weed halted them, "I want him to know!" She kicked the old headman sharply in the leg.

"What?" he rolled over sleepily, he eyed them suspiciously; understanding slowly dawned in his eyes just as she gave the order. He tried to dodge but was too late. His skull popped with a satisfying sound and they watched smiling as his body twitched and then, finally, became still.

"What do we do with him?" Dancing Moth asked, "Same as the others?"

"Why not?" Fire Weed nodded.

Dancing Willow watched from the comfort of her furs as the others stripped and prepared the meat. When they had finished, Fire Weed loaded the bones and head onto a hide and dragged it away from the cave. She found a deep ravine and dumped it in, watching with satisfaction as the head tumbled into a deserted animal den. "Serves you right!" she muttered and then tossed the hide after the grisly remains. "May the predators feast on what is left of you!"

Angry Bull returned to camp late, just before dark, empty-handed. "Where is Hunting Badger?" he asked.

Fire Weed shrugged, "He went out just after you did, returned with this meat a short time later, then said he was going looking for you. Didn't he find you?"

"Would I be asking where he is if he had?" Angry Bull glared at the woman.

"I have no idea," she replied, "He went out and he hasn't returned. That is all that I know." She turned her back on him and returned to her tending of the curing fire.

Dark came, but still Hunting Badger hadn't returned. Angry Bull shrugged. He didn't really care if the old tyrant never returned. Hunting Badger was far too fond of ordering him around. He'd had a lifetime of it and it was wearing very thin. Morning came, then another day and another. Finally Angry Bull understood that the older man wasn't going to return. He smiled to himself with satisfaction. He was now in charge and he intended to stay there.

Dancing Willow went into labor and he left the cave, taking a several-day hike into the forest. He returned to the cave, to find that the child had been born dead. He shrugged and went about his daily routine. It was nothing to him!

Fire Weed had made the decision. There would be no male children allowed to live. They all understood this. So it came to Fire Weed to strangle the baby when he was born. They took him out and gave him a proper funeral, setting him out to walk the wind in a sheltered pretty glen. Dancing Willow sighed with acceptance. After all, she still had Sunbeam!

As summer drew closer, Laughing Water went into labor. Again Angry Bull left the cave. When he returned this time, it was to the angry squeals of an infant girl. He merely grunted and demanded food. When it wasn't quick enough coming, he lashed out at the nearest target. This was Dancing Moth, now obviously pregnant. He struck her across the face, then twisted her arm behind her back and shoved it upward. He smiled as she screamed out.

\*     \*     \*

"What was that?" Jumping Fox halted. They were at their temporary camp, if one could call it that, a short distance from where they had set up watching the day before.

"Sounded like a woman screaming!" Raven replied as he pushed past the dreamer and began running up the trail.

"Wait!" Jumping Fox called, "You have no idea what you might be rushing into!" He took off after Raven, closely followed by Bull Elk and Black Cloud. They all burst into the open meadow in time to see Angry Bull shove the struggling woman away from him, then kick her in the stomach.

Dancing Moth writhed in agony, clutching her stomach. Soon there was blood on the ground. The hunters raced across the meadow and burst into the camp whereupon Raven charged Angry Bull. Angry Bull glanced up just in time to recognize Raven before the big hunter was upon him, the Bull leaped back. Raven rushed at the burly hunter and in his anger, ran right past him. Angry Bull did not hesitate, He raised a large handy branch and was about to bring it down on the hunter's head, when suddenly, the necklace around his neck tightened, so fast and hard that it cut off his breath.

\*　　\*　　\*

"What is going on?" Bear Claw Woman turned to Running Bison. "Where have the men really gone? And don't tell me that weak story about hunting!" She had finished working with the women and returned to their hearth with Whispering Wind. Something just didn't feel right. Then her mind flashed back to the farewell and she remembered that Raven had not met her eyes when he told her about the purposed hunting trip. Now her instincts were in full control.

Running Bison looked guilty for a flashing breath, but it was long enough.

"I demand to know what is going on!" Bear Claw Woman stormed. "You know as well as I do that Raven could get himself into grave danger. He has gone after Angry Bull, hasn't he?" She demanded and gained the satisfaction of bringing a guilty look to his face.

"Guardian!" she shouted, "Find the trail! We must hurry! They have hands of time head start on us." She grabbed up her staff and the sacred relics, stuffing them into a backpack to which she added a sleeping fur and several packages of food.

"You can't mean to go after him!" Whispering Wind exclaimed, "Not all alone!"

"If I have to! If no hunter will come with me." Bear Claw Woman never hesitated.

"You cannot go alone," Calling Wolf said. "Be reasonable Bear Claw Woman! He is a grown man, well able to take care of himself."

"And I am Chosen of the Spirits and I can feel that he is in danger!" She replied still packing. "You can stay here, if you like!" She glanced around, "You can all stay here, but just remember, Raven is your friend. Can you sleep well at night if something should happen to him?"

"I have seen her like this before," Whispering Wind began grabbing some of her own things and stuffing them in her backpack. "I am going with her. Someone must try to control her. Let her go off on her own and she is only going to get into trouble."

"And you won't?" Running Bison raised an eyebrow.

"I can't let her go alone!" Whispering Wind began to cry, "Can't you see?"

"I can see that you are determined," Running Bison sighed. "So I might as well send a pair of hunters along to keep you out of trouble."

"I think perhaps, I should go along as well," Crooked Spirit rose and hurried to gather his own provisions."

"I will be glad to escort them," Calling Wolf rose as well. Raven and Bear Claw Woman are my best friends. If anything were to happen to either of them, I would always blame myself if I did nothing to stop it."

Running Bison nodded, "Try to be back before the ceremony time, if you can. We cannot start it without Crooked Spirit." In a few fingers of time they had left the camp, following Guardian. He watched with increasing frustration as the four grew smaller and smaller. *Why must I always have to choose the people over my mate?* He wondered gloomily.

\*     \*     \*

"Where do you think they are headed?" Whispering Wind panted beside Bear Claw Woman, who was nearly running as she followed the trail that Guardian tracked.

"After Angry Bull!" Bear Claw Woman replied angrily. "I just know it! He couldn't let me handle this! He had to go off and get himself killed!"

"He didn't go alone. Bull Elk is with him. Bull Elk won't let him do anything stupid!" Whispering Wind assured her.

Bear Claw Woman merely snorted.

"They are not alone," Calling Wolf studied the signs on the trail. There are four men. One of them is Raven, see his moccasin prints? The other two are from the Bear Camp. I wonder why they go on such a mission; Raven hardly knows them. If he was going after Angry Bull, surely he would ask me," he sounded truly hurt.

"Jumping Fox!" Crooked Spirit muttered.

"What?"

"The Bear Camp Dreamer is one of the men," Crooked Spirit repeated. "There are spirits at work here."

"Nonsense!" Bear Claw Woman snorted. "There is only one stubborn-headed hunter at work here!" She glared at the dreamer, "If it were spirits, don't you think I would know it?"

"Not necessarily," Crooked Spirit replied. "You would know only what the spirits wish you to know. I think it would be best if we turned around and left these men complete their task."

"You may return if you wish," Bear Claw Woman glared at him, "You may all return! But I'm going after them!"

"I said I would go with you," Crooked Spirit puffed up in hurt response, "So go with you I will, but I still think it would be best left to others. These men know what they are doing! We could even get in the way and cause someone to get hurt, or even killed. I do not have to like it."

So they followed the hunters, resting only when they were so tired they could go no further and it was too dark to see. They ate well the next morning and once again followed Guardian as she led them after the men. Bear Claw Woman was not worried about her decision, for Guardian would not permit her to go where there was danger. Evidently, they were either getting closer, or the men were a long way from their destination. Either way she kept after her wolf.

The second night they camped just below the top of a pass. It was dark, as the clouds masked the moon. They had only a tiny fire to heat tea and ate cold trail rations. Well into the night, Guardian slipped silently from the camp. She trotted over the pass and down into the valley there. She wagged and greeted the pair of wolves who met her there, then returned to Bear Claw Woman.

They were in thick brush, about half way down the side of the valley when they heard a woman cry out in pain. Voices sounded just ahead and Bear Claw Woman's heart raced as she recognized Raven's. When they rushed into the camp, however, it was empty. In a few heartbeats, they released the wolves from the travois and rushed after the hunters. As they burst from the forest, they were just in time to see the hunters rush into the camp. Bear Claw Woman was running for all she was worth, her mouth open to grab a few ragged breaths. She saw Raven rush Angry Bull, saw the other man pivot from his path and at the same time grab a large broken branch from the top of a pile of fire wood. He raised it and at that instant, Bear Claw Woman sent a silent scream to her spirits!

*　　*　　*

Angry Bull raised the broken branch, intent upon bringing it crashing down on Raven's head, when suddenly, the necklace around his neck tightened, so fast and hard that it cut off his breath. He was forced to drop the branch and twisted around clutching his throat. Beyond him stood the woman he had killed. She was wild-eyed and breathing hard, but very much alive. He went white, sure that he was seeing a spirit, then the need to breathe took over and he again began struggling with the ever-tightening loop. She merely smiled as he tried in vain, to loosen the thong. Then she allowed it to loosen, just long enough for him to take a single strangled breath, before again it drew taunt. The hunter, Raven had regained control of his headlong rush and had returned to glare at the spirit woman.

Others gathered around her. Angry bull recognized the dreamer, Crooked Spirit, Calling Wolf and Bull Elk. Traitors! All of them! Again breathing was becoming difficult, but he grabbed a dart from his holder, still on his back and with all his strength cast it at the hated woman. She did not move, but the dreamer, Crooked Spirit did. With a strangled sound, he leaped in front of the woman and Angry Bull cursed silently as the dreamer took the dart, full in the chest. The old man made a surprised gasp and fell to the ground.

Angry Bull struggled with the cord now growing ever tighter as it cut into his neck. He struggled, going to his knees. He groped about in his pouch, reaching for his blade. But it wasn't there. It was on the ground beside the bleeding woman. He scrambled on his hands and knees to it and clutched it in desperate fingers. He tried to cut the cord, but only his flesh yielded to the blade. In his desperation, he sliced open the jugular vein in his neck and as his life-blood pumped, running over his fingers, he dropped the blade. His eyes clouded over, his tongue protruded from his mouth and he fell to the ground. His last thoughts were regret. Regret that he had obviously failed to kill her. Then there was nothing....

Raven leaned over and lifted the necklace from where it slithered from around the dead hunter's throat. Then he rushed to where the rest were crowded around Crooked Spirit. The old man lay on his back, Angry Bulls dart protruding from his chest. Bear Claw Woman was crouched over him, sobbing and pleading for him to open his eyes. Finally, Whispering Wind gently drew her away and let the hunters tend to him. Jumping Fox began a low death chant.

"It's all my fault!" moaned Bear Claw Woman, "He told me someone could die! Why! Oh why!"

Raven stood silently watching all that went on around him. He was shocked! He still held the bloody necklace in his hand. At his feet lay the body of Crooked Spirit, while just beyond Bear Claw Woman crouched with Whispering Wind, crying. Behind him, the women of this camp were tending to their own. Finally, he forced his legs to move. He raised the necklace, cause of all of this. He carried it to the stream and washed the blood away, then carried it to where Bear Claw Woman crouched. With an apologetic frown, he placed it about her neck. A blue glow emanated from it and then vanished. She rose and went to where Crooked Spirit rested. With deep regret she reached out and lay her hand on the bloody wound where the dart had entered his body.

"Go to the spirit world, my friend," she whispered. "I shall mourn your life and carry the guilt for the remainder of mine! You gave your life so that I might not die. This is a debt which I will never be able to repay." She spoke at length to the spirit of Crooked Spirit.

Meanwhile, Whispering Wind and Fire Weed were helping Dancing Moth into a squatting position. There was a great deal of blood, then something else, an unformed, bloody mass. Bear Claw Woman hurried to where they toiled and quickly produced an herb that she instructed Dancing Moth to chew. The young woman recognized the new comers and did as she was instructed.

Much later, the hunters dragged the body of Angry Bull away from the camp and left it for the predators. They saw no reason to give this man a proper rite to walk the wind. Then they returned to the camp. Quietly, the entire camp, even Dancing Moth, carried on a liter, followed Jumping Fox to a high place where they laid the dreamer, Crooked Spirit out to walk the wind.

Over the next several days, while they tended Dancing Moth, they learned the tale of how the six females came to be living in this valley with Angry Bull, when they had last seen them following their families after the bison hunters. There was no mention of how the men of their camp had come to end their lives, or of the death of Hunting Badger.

But the women were treated kindly, cared for and looked after. They sighed in finality. It was over! When they left the valley, going with Jumping Fox and his group, nothing of the meat went with them.[1] Dancing Moth recovered and Laughing Water's baby girl died unexpectedly. But she was not upset, for she still had Wildflower. All things, which were connected to their ordeal, had vanished. Soon, it had even left their minds. The spirits were kind to them.

\*     \*     \*

The camp was stunned when they heard of the death of Crooked Spirit. Hollow Bone trembled in fear. *I am not ready!* He wailed silently, *how can I ever walk in the prints of the Great Dreamer Crooked Spirit? I am not worthy!* He went out alone into the mountains. He was gone for days, but when he returned, he was a different man. Gone was the unsure youth. In his place walked a confident man. He went about the tasks of preparing for the Mid-Summer Ceremony with a calm, unruffled, poise. Speaking with Jumping Fox had helped. He now understood that all along the spirits had intended to take Crooked Spirit. It gave him confidence that the spirits felt he was ready, even if he did not.

As the days passed, bringing the ceremony ever closer, small groups of people began to arrive unexpectedly, all with the same tale as the

Deer Camp. By the time that Crying Coyote led his combined bands into the valley, it was rapidly filling up. Oddly enough, the communication problem that has so worried Running Bison turned out to be no problem at all. It seemed that someone always understood the words of others. His idea of developing a common sign language grew into being. Soon even he could 'talk' with this sign, to strangers who's words he could not comprehend.

Then the day of the beginning of the Mid-Summer Ceremony arrived. The valley seemed to be bulging to overflowing with people. Jumping Fox, Hollow Bone, Calling Wolf and many other dreamers were gathered in a special shelter built in the very center of the valley. From there, acolytes hurried on special missions. Hunters were busy providing food for the many people, but strangely, there seemed to be an abundance of game. Women went out on gathering expeditions, chattering excitedly as they learned of the wonderful possibilities of plants.

Through all the excitement, only a pair of people seemed isolated from the excitement. Bear Claw Woman had increasingly taken to staying within their shelter and then finally, she and Raven had left the camp. They were sheltered within the ring of trees, a pair of valleys away.

Raven watched, Young Wolf hunted, Guardian lay at the base of the flat boulder and watched and Bear Claw Woman sat quietly on top, her necklace around her neck, her staff beside her and the Sacred Relics clutched in her hands. The blue glow pulsed strongly around her. Then, on the morning of the ceremony, she climbed down from the boulder and ate a tremendous meal, the first in a hand of days and smiled at Raven, keeping a safe distance away.

"We must return to the camp now. I am ready!

Raven nodded and began loading their shelter onto the travois. Soon he was leading Young Wolf back toward the valley of the Gathering. Bear Claw Woman followed behind, making several short excursions from the trail, while Raven waited for her. Well before sun-high they were back at the main camp. But Bear Claw Woman did not stop at their hearth, but rather headed toward the stream followed by Guardian.

She followed the same path as she had seasons before, to the gnarled cottonwood. Here she spread out her potions and paints and began the laborious task of preparing herself for her part in the ceremony.

She would not attend this day, or the next. But on the final night, she would once again ceremonially present herself and the ancient relics to the tribe. She also had a message from the spirits, but this time not as terrible as the last. She settled in the bowl of the tree and listened to the drums start.

Talking Shadow called the people together. From all directions they came. Once they were gathered, he began the tale of The People. He explained the legend of the Sacred Relics and told the story of the Chosen Ones. He explained how they balanced the power of the Dreamers and how the spirits favored them. On and on he talked, gradually informing the newcomers of each special relationship between the humans and their guardian spirits. Many of the new people nodded, for this was similar to their own beliefs. At one time, they thought to themselves, we must have all been One People. It was right that they be united again.

The Dreamers had gathered and exchanged knowledge earlier. They had divided up the various parts of the ceremony, making sure that each had an important part and none were left out. They had also discussed how they could meet periodically, sometimes with one, at other times with others, so that there would be a continuous exchange of information. They also decided that every hand of seasons they would have a major gathering, one time here, the next at the Sacred Spring, then again elsewhere. This way all the people would feel that they were united. They would not lose contact with groups that lived far away and there could be an exchange of new ideas as well. The ceremony began early in the day for there was much to go over. It was completely dark before the various story tellers had completed their part. It had also been decided that from now on the naming system would follow that of The People, with children given one-word names and adults given two-word names. Some of the adults had chosen to select new names, to follow this new tradition. So the naming ceremony lasted far into the night. In fact, before the last child had been identified, the sun was beginning to tinge the eastern sky with pink.

The second day's ceremony began early as well. Already hunters had gone out and returned with hands of deer, elk and antelope; all ready to be lowered into pits to cook. At dawn the next day they would be coated with clay and then buried between two layers of hot coals to cook all day.

Today was the day for the hunters to tell their story. As they each called out their totem animal and related dreamers drew their clan and kindred lines in the dirt, declaring the taboos of each. These relationships were very important and the dreamers were in charge of making sure that no mating broke them. Both the blood-lines and the clan lines were to be observed from now on, so the dreamers had a considerable task before them.

They had chosen to take hides and mark these relationships upon them, indicating by a symbol each individual; be it man, woman, or child. With the addition of so many new people, there were also new clans added as well. Once the men had completed their naming of totem and kindred, the women began. Again it was dawn before the last child had been recorded. Since Bear Claw Woman had not attended, Whispering Wind stood in for her. Until they took a spirit journey, children followed their mother's camp. This was how The People had always traced the kindred of a child. With so many changes in mates, due to death mostly, it was sometimes hard to trace lineage through the father, but a child stayed with its mother. Once a boy was old enough to begin learning to be a hunter, his father at that point, or an uncle took over his education and upon taking his spirit journey, he moved from the family into the unmated men's hearth. Here he remained until he set up his own hearth.

Little of this practice had changed; only that the hunter would now move to the camp of his mate rather than the other way around. This would make keeping track of the kindred lines much easier. Totem lines were set at puberty when they were acknowledged. It had taken quite a lot of talking to get all the dreamers to agree on this. They had equal difficulty persuading their individual camps to this as well. Amazingly, no groups had left the valley. All had agreed. Truly, they were becoming One People.

Also, several hunters of The People had mated with women from the new clans. It would fall upon their shoulders to help the new ones continue to follow the proper ways. Again, these matings brought the people closer. Everyone retired, sleepy, yet filled with anticipation. The final day of the celebration was when the spirits told of their relationship with the humans and the Chosen One gave her special message from the spirits, as well as the dreamers, if a message they had.

Jumping Fox opened the ceremony, about a hand of time before dark. The sun was just touching the western horizon as the drums began to beat. Flasks of fermented brew were being passed around to those taking part in the ceremony. There could be anywhere from one to a handful of participants in the telling of the totems. The Eagle Clan opened the ceremony. With a flourish of fast beating drums, the spirits danced into the huge opening set apart for this. In the very center was a huge bonfire. All the people were gathered around the outer circumference, leaving plenty of room for the dancers. As the spirits entered, a story teller narrated their tale. There were now nearly fifty clans so it took a long time. The moon rose full before they finished.

Bear Claw Woman waited in the shadow of an old oak tree, for her turn. She pulled the white feather robe close about her as a breeze whipped it about. No one was paying the least attention to her, for the dreamers were making their announcements. She was amazed at what they revealed. It seemed that the spirits had indeed been busy. Besides the Deer Camp that had first joined them, nearly a double hand of other small groups had ambled into the valley over the past moon or so. Now Hollow Bone rose and stepped forward. He would receive the Ancient Relics form Bear Claw Woman. As he spoke the drum sounded softly. When it was time, it became silent. Then Bear Claw Woman stepped forward and the mass parted for her. In absolute silence she made her way to where Hollow Bone waited. She carried the Sacred Relics before her in both hands. As she approached, Guardian at her side, she began a low chant that gained strength as she stopped before him. She spoke of the Ancient Ones and the pledge they had made to the spirits. As she spoke she unwrapped the relics. She turned and held them up for everyone to see and as she did so the blue haze began to engulf her and shimmer. "The Spirits made a pledge to our ancestors!" she began. "They promised their protection and guidance so long as the people gave them proper prayers in their hearts. Over many generations, time and again, the people have forgotten this. Again and again, the spirits have sent one, such as I, to remind the people. Now the spirits have said we are to change our ways again. No longer are we to be hunters of bison. Why; because we have abused the privilege of this food. Because hunters have been wasteful! they have killed many more animals than we could eat.

They have taken the honor of the kill upon their selves and bragged about their feats of strength, cleverness, and abilities as hunters. We did not give credit to the spirits who made these kills possible. We did not give prayers to the spirits of bison for the gift of their flesh. So now the spirits have taken the bison from us. They have sickened the animals and made their flesh poison"

"But the spirits have not just taken from us. They have also given. They have given new ways, new foods, and new relationships! A new way of life for the people, and with this new way of life, they have given new demands as well; demands which we as people, are expected to follow. We have been charged with gathering all the people together to make a New People; a people who will learn from each other and share with each other and pledge to bring no violence to each other.

We are also instructed to bring the spirits back into our hearts. The spirits will take any person who does not do this. There will be no second chances!"

"We are given the task of uniting all of the people into One People. So far, the spirits have smiled down upon us. They have given much and asked only that we take them into our hearts. The dreamers have made arrangements among themselves to gather at regular intervals. The healers are charged to do the same. The people are encouraged to share their knowledge with each other, to help each other and gather together at regular intervals as well. When we all leave this valley and go our separate ways, each of us has a task to contact other new groups and invite them to join One People. It seems that the spirits have already made the path open for this. This is the message which the spirits bring to you." She lowered her arms and the blue haze faded away.

She turned to face Hollow Bone and knelt before him. "I bring to you the Sacred Relics of the One People," she held the relics out to him.

Hollow Bone blew on his sacred whistle and bowed his head. Then he reached out and carefully took the deer hide offering from her, careful not to touch the Sacred Relics themselves. Then he raised it and made a prayer offering to each of the six directions; north, south, east, west, up and down. All the while, he blew on the whistle and Talking Shadow muttered prayers. When they had finished, Hollow Bone returned the Sacred Relics to Bear Claw Woman just as carefully as he had accepted them. She wrapped them again and returned them to her carrying pouch. Then she bowed to the Dreamers, to the people, to the directions and with Guardian at her side, left the gathering just as suddenly as she had entered it. A deep silence followed her departure and then a sigh rippled through the crowd. Her message had not been as bad as many feared. Soon people began whispering to each other, then talking out loud; the spell was broken.

People began to shout and jostle each other. Now the ceremony was to the point many had been waiting for, the feast! Soon hunters were digging the meat from the pits, women were bringing skin after skin of plants and stews and nut cakes and berries. Planks were soon groaning with food and fermented drink was being passed around in liberal quantities. By the time that Bear Claw Woman had cleaned her body and washed her hair, careful not to spill any of the water, for it must be buried in a special place, known only to her, she returned to the camp. There she joined Raven and Whispering Wind and Running Bison and all the others of their camp to complete the celebration.

"Here, I have saved this for you!" Raven presented her with a bowl overflowing with succulent treats.

"Thank you," she smiled and was glad that now the taboos were over and they were together again. Guardian savored her own special treats and settled beside Young Wolf. All around the valley hearth fires twinkled and sparked and people danced and ate and drank. The feast continued until no one could possible hold another bite. They continued to dance and send payers until the sun again began to show a faint pink in the eastern sky. Only then did they retire to their furs. Mates greeted each other joyfully, for they had remained separated for the entire hand of days before the beginning of the Mid-Summer Ceremony.

"Where do we go from here?" Bear Claw Woman asked Raven, "I suppose that Running Bison has a plan."

"We are headed north and through the mountains, gathering groups as we go, ending up at the winter camp. There we will begin by teaching those with us the plants and their preparation and the legends and ways of One People. Hopefully we will also learn useful things from them."

"In the spring we are heading south and west, into new land and meeting new groups. After the spring offering we will head into land which none of us have ever seen. It will be a great adventure!" Bull Elk smacked his lips; eyes alight with excitement at the prospect.

"What of Quenquel?" Bear Claw Woman questioned.

"When the time is right we will find him," Raven replied. "Until then we will do as the spirits direct."

"And Ash Branch; will we meet her soon?"

"I do not know when, but if not this season, surely the one following," Calling Wolf answered. "You know how vague the spirits are about time. They only said that when it was time we would be led to the evil one and that when it was time, Ash Branch would be united with you. But until they are we must continue to do the tasks set forth for us. This is a great adventure! Think about it! All the people we will meet, all the places we will see!"

"Right now," Raven yawned, "The only thing I can think of is shutting my eyes and not opening them again until the sun is well down tomorrow."

"Where is your soul of adventure, man?" Bull Elk snorted.

"It is asleep!" replied Raven, "Just as I will be, if you will go to your furs and let me!"

The hunters had a few choice comments to say, joking and casting eyes toward where Bear Claw Woman waited for the big ugly hunter and then they all retired gratefully to their furs to sleep well into the afternoon of the day.

A pair of days later the last of the people were leaving the valley, the only sign of their occupation, the ashes from their fires and the flattened grass where they shelter stood. Running Bison's camp was the last to leave. They waited, ready, in a line, travois loaded and with a final satisfied glance at the valley, he led them north, on the first leg of the 'great adventure'.

1. There are a few archaeological finds which indicate some cannibalism was present at this time. I hope that I have treated the subject in a tasteful manner.

# CHAPTER 27

**Far to the west much earlier**

Sky was returning to the camp after completing her Spirit Journey. She had her water flask and the rabbit skin pad clutched to her flat chest and because one of her straps had broken, the left moccasin was flapping loosely and causing her to trip. Sighing she finally set her various articles down on a handy rock and stooped to add another knot to the worn strap.

Pain flashed through her back. She grunted as the wind was knocked from her lungs and she found herself flat on the ground, her face in the dirt of the trail. Atop her she could hear the panting and grunting of a man and with terrified heart she knew it was her mother's mate. She could smell him! And she could feel his huge hands grappling for her private parts. Feebly she struggled to throw him off, spitting dirt from her mouth and begging him to stop. His only response was a cuff aside the head which set her ears to ringing and then she screamed as he penetrated her tender orifice with his huge organ. Again and again he pumped into her frantically wiggling body, to finally relieve himself and with a satisfied grunt, disengage.

Then he rose and grabbed her hair in his huge fist, dragging her painfully off the ground. "You say anything to anyone of this and I will see you dead!" he snarled and then shoved her from him. With a snort of disgust he shoved his bloody organ back into his filthy breech clot and staggered away toward the village.

Sky dropped again to the ground, hurting, bleeding and filthy. She had expected this. Fear had kept her from mentioning the possibility to her mother. Harry Man already hated her. This was just another in a long line of ways he had tortured her ever since mating with her timid mother three seasons ago. Sky cried out to her long-dead father. *Why! Why did you have to leave us? We were so happy together! Mother is no match for Harry Man! He treats her as poorly as he does Waterbug and me.*

She struggled to her feet and gathered her pathetic little bundle of belongings and turned away from the village. Blood and other body fluids were running down her shaking legs. She struggled toward the small stream that ran through their village. Up here there would be privacy to clean herself up. Harry Man had come a long way from the village to waylay her. Even her screams could not be heard from here. Sky dumped her things beside the stream and not even bothering to remove her tattered apron, she waded into the shallow water and began to frantically wash the signs of rape from her body. Dully, she realized that this was all she had to look forward to, again and again, if not by Harry Man, then by some other man of the village.

It had only been by her mother's tearful pleading that she had not been cast out long ago, at her father's death. Sky was true to her name! The eyes that looked out from her face were as blue as the sky for which she was named. No one else in the village, indeed in the entire tribe, had ever seen eyes like hers before. It made them uneasy! Every other girl, upon reaching puberty, was given a warm welcome into the village society, now as a participating adult. Her family would throw a feast, inviting the entire village and there would be presents, celebrating, a naming ceremony and then courting by eligible youths. But this was not what was in store for Sky.

She had told her mother of the 'first bleed' and had taken the traditional 'Spirit Journey", but this, as everything else in her life, had been a failure. She had taken no journey and the only thing she found upon waking, was a white owl feather laying on the ground before her and she could feel a sore spot on her breast. She had shrugged and put the feather in her pouch before cleaning the paint from her face and burying it as she had been instructed. She supposed that she would be given and adult name, but Mother hadn't mentioned anything about it, or a celebration. She had merely looked about with frightened eyes and instructed Sky not to mention this to anyone. She hadn't, but evidently Harry Man had, either overhead their conversation, or figured it out.

Wearily, Sky removed her apron and washed the blood from it as best she could. Then, with a sigh she climbed from the stream.

She did scream then! A high thin wailing moan! For standing before her was the wild woman of the mountains! She knew now that she was to die! She had heard of this vile creature, but as with every other child of the village, had been careful to avoid any place where she might be.

Once, seasons ago, she had seen the Hag slipping through the rush at the edge of the camp. She had been so frightened that she had not left the camp for an entire moon and even then cast fearful glances over her shoulder at every step.

Now, the worst apparition of her life stood before her! Her hair was a tangle of rats and knots, crating a wildly moving halo around her ugly wrinkled face. Tiny eyes sparkled from above a huge twisted nose. Sky suddenly stopped screaming, sucking in her breath and holding it. Those eyes which looked at her! They were the same color as her own.

"Hush!" the old woman whispered, "Or they will hear you and come! We haven't much time. I have been watching and waiting! I saw what he did; the filthy pig!"

"Wh...What do you want?" Sky gulped down her fear. "Please! Don't hurt me!" she whimpered. I have been good! It wasn't my fault! Please, just let me return to the village." She pleaded.

"Hurt you! Now why would I want to hurt you? My very own Grand Daughter!" The old one gave a toothless grin. "I haven't come to hurt you! I have come to take you away from that man and others like him, to keep you safe and teach you the old ways and the healing secrets of the Ancient Ones!"

"You are my Grandmother?" Sky stared, open mouthed.

"Haven't I just said so?" the old crone waved her hands. "Hurry, we haven't time to waste! It is a long way to my cave!" She chuckled gleefully, "We have a naming ceremony to perform and a celebration as well! Quickly! We must be gone before anyone misses you!"

Sky looked more sharply at the old one. Upon closer examination, she wasn't so frightening. The eyes sparkled with kindness and the voice was soft and soothing. *What have I got to lose?* She thought. *Surely, a life alone in the wilds with her could not be worse than living in the village at Harry Man's mercy.* She smiled shyly at the old one and took the hand offered. Quickly she scrambled from the stream and wrapped her wet apron about her slender hips. Then she gathered up her meager belongings and followed the old woman through the forest. She never looked back!

This is how Ash Branch first met her Grandmother. The seasons that followed were rich in many things. Old Soft Robe, for that was her grandmother's name, was a wonderful, loving woman. She told Ash Branch many things that had always confused her. It had been her own blue eyes which had finally driven her from the village, but not before seeing her only son safely cared for by a dear friend. Then she had waited, all these years, sighted occasionally by the villagers; to fulfil the promise made to her by the spirits. She would have a granddaughter, born to her son, with eyes as blue as her own. It would come to her, the task of teaching this one the many skills of the healer.

And she did. Ash Branch frequently reflected on those seasons of learning. They had flown by, filled with love and kindness. The spot on her breast had begun as a bruise, but before long developed into a tiny wolf. Soft Robe had merely nodded and sighed when she saw it. When Soft Robe had died, only Ash Branch had been there to mourn her, but she had tended the old one and buried her beneath a stone slab in the back of their cave. Alone now, Ash Branch had continued to live in the cave and increase her knowledge of the healing skills. Eventually, however, she had given in to the pressure of the spirits and made her way back to the people, not, however, to her old village.

Surprisingly, she was accepted. Not only accepted but revered for her knowledge. And she put this to good work. Rapidly, she became known for her healing skills. Far and wide, people came to her for help and most of the time she had been able to give it. Now she had just passed her twentieth season.

The peoples of the southwest deserts were facing a great drought. It had not rained in seasons and even the plants that were used to little rain were dying. Then, a pair of seasons ago into their village had walked a dreamer, a handsome man with a long thin scar marring his beauty. He claimed that he could bring the rain and he had done so. Now White Eagle was a hero to the people. He had gained immediate status within the desert culture. He lived in their own village and surprisingly had begun to court Ash Branch.

She was flattered. This man was tall, handsome beyond belief and powerful. Why would he want a simple healer? She hesitated. He waited. Every time she wondered if she should accept his offer, the tiny wolf upon her breast would pulse painfully. She had come to understand, over the seasons, that this was a sign. Something was wrong here. So she continued to hesitate. Her best friend, Yellow Bird could not understand!

While still living with her grandmother, they had rescued a pair of wolf pups from the den after their mother had died tragically, mauled by a bear. So now, Ash Branch wore a tunic and apron trimmed with wolf fur, from the hide of the mother and by her side walked her faithful companion, Fina. The she-wolf went everywhere with Ash Branch. The brother, Fana, had grieved himself to death after Soft Robe had passed on to the Ancestor Fires in the Sky and now lay beside her in the old cave. Only Ash Branch knew this.

*Soon!* Wolf Spirit whispered; *soon they will come! Then you will know what to do!* She sighed and turned in her sleep. Fina whimpered and snuggled closer. Beyond them the hearth fire crackled and sap sent up sparks. Beyond, White Eagle sat and frowned into the fire.

*Why does she hesitate?* He tossed a stick impatiently into the fire. *I can't wait forever! I must keep moving, but I need this woman! She isn't Hummingbird, but she had great power! Must I sacrifice her also, to gain that power?"* He rose and paced away from the village. It had been two seasons since he had left the valley to the east, fleeing from the hunters he knew had found Whispering Wind, even though they had left no trace. Now he was settled among these desert gatherers, riling against every moon that passed. His spirits had deserted him and if Iguana and the camp ever found a hint that he was still alive, he had no illusion that they would come after him. He had heard of peoples to the west, living along a great salt sea. Among them he should be safe. But he needed this woman. Her abilities would smooth the way for him. With her at his side, he would once again become a powerful dreamer. But she hesitated! He ground his teeth in frustration.

\*     \*     \*

The men hunkered down behind the screen of brush. They watched the man pace from the camp. We could take him now!" Calling Wolf whispered, "There is not likely to be a better chance."

"We will wait," Bull Elk stated.

"Why? We have been watching this village for three days now. We know that it is safe to capture him! It is unlikely that the villagers will come to his aid!"

"I am more interested in the woman," Bull Elk sighed. "If anything were to happen to her, our plan will have been in vain." He placed his hand on his impatient friend's arm, "You know how important this is. It seems that he has become very close to this Ash Branch. You know as well as I do that we are to bring her back with us. Do your spirits tell you as a prisoner?"

"You know that they say she comes of her own free will. But how else are we to capture Quenquel? You know as well as I do that he will not come freely!"

Why don't you ask those spirits of yours what to do next?" Bull Elk suggested, "It would be more productive than lying here doing nothing!"

"A good idea! Calling Wolf slipped quietly from his vantage point. "Perhaps they will tell me!"

He hurried a good distance from where they watched, slipping quietly into their hidden camp. Others of the groups slept until it was time for their turn at watch. He could hear Prairie Grass snoring softly in his shelter. Running Antelope and Elk Caller lay just beyond, rolled up in their sleeping furs beside the minute fire. They had come, a hand of men, armed for battle if necessary, to capture Quenquel and return him to face the wrath of the spirits. But he was also instructed by his own spirit, that of the white bison, to return with the healer, Ash Branch.

He settled beyond the camp and concentrated on the spirits. He could only hope they would answer. Slowly, the tingling began in his finger tips and the journey started. He found himself in a strangely familiar glen, seated on a log. Toward him loped the great gray wolf spirit of the One People.

\*　　\*　　\*

*What are we to do?* Calling Wolf asked, *do we take him, or do we wait?*

*The woman hesitates!* The spirit answered, *she is unsure! Take him now, tonight. Ask her to go with you. Explain to her. She will understand! She is one of our own, you forget! Call upon Bear Claw Woman. She will talk to this woman and sooth her fears if she has them. But take the dreamer tonight, least he escape!* The blackness swirled about Calling Wolf and suddenly he was again sitting beneath the sparkling sky. He sighed and rose, calling to the others as he passed through their camp. Quickly and soundlessly they followed him, a group of shadows, slipping through the night.

*       *       *

"Where is he?" Calling Wolf whispered to Bull Elk, as they joined him, "We are to do it now! The spirit has told me."

Bull Elk nodded and pointed to a shadow standing beneath a pine at the far edge of the village, "He waits there!"

"We can slip around the village on this trail and sneak right up behind him," Prairie Grass whispered. "We will be on him before he even knows it!"

"Follow me!' Calling Wolf slipped along the path skirting the village. In his hand he carried a stout club. Behind him flitted the shadows of the others. Silently as death they approached and with an anticlimactic thud, the dreamer, Quenquel crumpled to the ground.

"Quickly, stuff the gag into his mouth!" Calling Wolf whispered. "Hand me the thongs!" Someone thrust them into his hand and expertly he trussed the unconscious man tightly. "Now let's get him back to our camp!" They grunted as they hoisted the inert weight onto Calling Wolf's shoulders and they moved around the village and back to their camp. Before getting there, Calling Wolf could feel muscles tightening and he knew that the dreamer was awake. He dumped him roughly onto the ground beside their hearth and was rewarded with a flicker of fear threading across the handsome features.

"Put a noose around his throat and tether him to the tree!" Calling Wolf instructed Prairie Grass. "If he tries to free himself, he will only tighten the noose and strangle himself!" he grinned down at their captive, "But be sure to keep an eye on him, at all times, after all we don't want anything to happen to him!"

"What about the woman? Do we take her as well?" Running Antelope asked.

Calling Wolf shook his head. "Tomorrow we will go into the village and explain ourselves. At that time I will invite the woman to accompany us. If the spirits are correct, she will come willingly. But, just in case she comes in hopes of freeing her friend here, keep an eye on her as well! I don't trust either one of them!" He stood and straightened his shoulders, "Right now, however, we might as well get some sleep. Did you wipe our trail?" He questioned Bull Elk.

"I did." The hunter answered. "But I think it would be a good idea if one of us returned and watched the village just in case."

\*     \*     \*

*Ash Branch....* A voice in her head called to her. At first her heart leaped with joy! *Grandmother?* But then she realized the voice was that of a much younger woman. In her sleep she moaned and turned.

*Who calls me?* She questioned.

*You do not know me, but I have eyes the same color as your own. Many generations ago, our grandmothers were sisters, twin sisters. My name is Bear Claw Woman and I bring you a message. Men will come into your village; they will ask you to go with them. The spirit of wolf has called you to come to me. On your breast you carry his mark, just as I do. Remember the words of Soft Robe and have no fear. I await you with open arms!*

\*     \*     \*

Fina whined and nudged Ash Branch. "What is it?" the woman asked. The animal wiggled, washed her face and urged her to rise. "Is something going on?" Again the animal whined and wiggled. "All right I'm getting dressed," Ash Branch, shaking off the remnants of her strange dream, quickly pulled on her tunic and followed the wolf into the night. Through the seasons, she had learned to trust the wolf completely.

She saw the hunters slipping like silent shadows away from the village. Ash Branch and Fina followed. They crept after the hunters and watched and listened to their words. Ash Branch frowned. *What is going on here? Why have these hunters taken White Eagle prisoner? Do I go back and alert the village or wait and try to understand what is going on?* Then she remembered the dream.

Fina took the decision out of her hands. With a soft "woof" she stepped into the camp, alerting the hunters. As Ash Branch stepped out, she faced a full barrage of dart points; all of them ready to cast at her. Quickly she turned her palms forward to signify that she was unarmed and no danger to them.

"I am called Ash Branch." she stated. "I live in the village from which you just captured this man. I think you owe me an explanation!" She straightened her shoulders and took a deep breath, realizing the foolishness of her present situation.

Calling Wolf stepped forward and motioned the hunters to put down their weapons. "We can explain," he said. "This is not what you think!"

"How do you know what I think?"

"Well, I realize that this does not look good, from your point of view. But we mean you no harm. Look, we have lowered our weapons," he glanced around the camp. Beyond watched a hand of wolves. He smiled. "You do realize that your wolf has already told you that you are safe. She would never have brought you into our camp other wise."

Ash Branch frowned at Fina, who was wagging her tail with complete friendliness. She understood exactly what this hunter was referring to. She sighed, "All right, so I am in no danger. But what has White Eagle done to you that you have him trussed up like this?"

"White Eagle? Who is White Eagle?"

She pointed, "That man right there, he is the dreamer, White Eagle. Everyone among the desert people will tell you that!"

"That man has lied to you!" Bull Elk snorted. "He is a dreamer all right, but his name is not White Eagle! His own people would be very interested to know that he still lives, for they think that they killed him seasons ago!"

"I do not understand!" Ash Branch frowned. "This man is well known! How could he be someone else?"

"Have you ever heard of the Savages?"

She shivered, "Who has not heard of them? They terrorized the land for seasons! But they have not bothered anyone for seasons now!"

"That is right!" Bull Elk answered, "For they turned against the man responsible. They think that they killed the dreamer, Quenquel. Not so! He sits before you, trussed to that tree."

"You are sure?" Ash Branch paled.

"Absolutely," Calling Wolf replied. "I was myself a prisoner and watched many go to the alter beneath his blade. Somehow, he escaped the camp when it turned against him, but the spirits know him! They have instructed us to come to this village, where he has been living and capture him and return him to face his fate."

Ash Branch moved into the camp and walked to where the man she knew as White Eagle sat. One glance at his face confirmed that what these men said was true. Again she shivered. Now she understood why she had hesitated... this man was the culmination of all that was evil! She turned to Calling Wolf. "Obviously you tell the truth. I will speak to the headman of the village as soon as it wakens. I will bring you into the village and clear the way for you to take him away." She gave White Eagle one last disgusted glance before turning and calling Fina, left the camp. Fina trotted ahead of her, totally at ease. This told her more than any assurance that the hunters had given her. Fina was never wrong.

Ash Branch stirred the hearth before her shelter. Then she set a container of water to heat and searched out another to begin cooking food in. She sat in thought as the water heated, wondering about the events of this night. *Men will come and take you away from the desert people.* She could almost hear the sound of Grandmother's words as she had heard them seasons ago. *Go with them! You have a greater destiny!*

At the time, holding her dying loved one in her arms, she had paid scant attention to her words, but now she remembered them. *Grandmother, how can I know if these are the men you spoke of? What should I do?*

Almost as if she had answered, thoughts filled Ash Branches head. *Trust these men. Go with them. Do not look back!* She sighed and added hot stones to the cooking bags. For hands of time she tended her fire and sipped tea. Just as the first sleepy birds began tweeting to usher in the dawn, she completed the food cooking. Then she went in search of the village headman.

"Scorpion, I would have a word with you," she said quietly. "Please, walk with me a short distance from the camp."

"Something wrong?" the old man yawned, scratched his head, setting his hair on end and followed her from the camp.

"Last night men came into the village..." she began.

"You did not alert anyone?" he snapped back, suddenly wide awake.

"They meant no harm to us," she assured him. "But they will tell you this as soon as I go and bring them in."

"How can you know that?" Scorpion jerked about and glanced worriedly about the sleepy village. "You are a woman! What do you know of such things? Where is the dreamer, I need to talk to him!"

"He isn't here," she replied, "That is what I am trying to tell you."

"Not here!" Scorpion questioned. "What do you mean not here? He go off to commune with the spirits or something; just when we need him!"

"No, he hasn't gone anywhere," she tried to answer.

"But you just said..."

"Will you let me explain? When I have finished, then I will gladly tell you anything more that I know," she replied.

"Very well, but hurry! I may need to alert the men of the village!"

She shook her head and began her tale. "The dreamer, he isn't who we thought. He is not the man White Eagle at all, but an imposter. I have no idea what became of the real White Eagle, probably he is dead."

"Not White Eagle, you say? Then who is he?"

"His real name is Quenquel," she answered.

Scorpion shuddered. "Don't even jest such a thing!" he protested.

"I am absolutely serious," she responded. "These men who will soon come into the village have been hunting this man for seasons. His own camp thought they had killed him, but somehow he escaped. The spirits have sent these men to capture him and take him back."

"Who told you this?"

"A man who calls himself Calling Wolf; he leads the group. But I had only to look into the face of the man we knew as White Eagle, to know they were telling the truth. But they are here now, come and I will introduce you to their leader," she led the way to where the men waited to be invited into the village.

"This is our headman, Scorpion," she introduced and then turned to the elder, "And this man is known as Calling Wolf. He will explain the situation to you."

"Calling Wolf," the headman frowned. "Related to Pinecone of the Deer camp?"

"The very same," Calling Wolf nodded. "Pinecone is my Aunt. My mother was Needle."

"Ah! Needle! Now there was one beautiful woman!" Scorpion said softly.

Calling Wolf raised an eyebrow, "My mother was nearly as broad as she was tall!" He protested. "As far as I know, she was such all of her life."

Scorpion blushed as he nodded, "You are as you say," he grinned. "Can't blame me for making sure!"

Calling Wolf nodded. "I would have done the same," he assured the headman. "But we are who we say and our mission is as we tell you."

"Ash Branch tells me that you are here to capture the dreamer, Quenquel," Scorpion said.

"We have him," Calling Wolf admitted.

"You are certain?"

"Absolutely," Calling Wolf replied. "I spent more than a moon as his prisoner. His is a face I am not likely to ever forget! Besides, Ash Branch tells me that he has been calling himself White Eagle. Have you ever met White Eagle?"

Scorpion shook his head.

"You would recognize him instantly. He has a gash across his head, from here to here." He made a motion across the top of his head. "And his hair is completely white along it. Besides, he is one of the ugliest men I have ever laid eyes on. He is hardly taller than Ash Branch here and weighs much less."

"Quenquel, on the other hand, is one of the most striking of men. He is tall, pleasing of features, much younger, lean and strong."

"That certainly describes the dreamer we have been following," Scorpion nodded. "But I would speak to him, myself, if you don't mind. I should like to know why he lied to us when we took him in and offered him shelter."

"That you may do, as soon as we remove the gag from his mouth," Calling Wolf agreed. "In the meantime, he isn't going anywhere. I have left him securely tied up and a man guarding him as well. Don't intend to take any chances with this man."

"If he is the one known as Quenquel, then it is understandable. I would do the same," admitted Scorpion. "But come, it seems that our healer, Ash Branch has prepared food. Eat, and then we will talk." His sense of hospitality deemed that this be so. The hunters settled around the hearth, ironically the very one that Ash Branch had shared with the dreamer, as well as another family. Soon the news spread like wildfire through the village. Many curious individuals came to catch a glimpse of the newcomers.

"What is to be his fate?" Scorpion asked, more curious than worried.

"The spirits demand that he suffer the same fate as those poor souls which he has trapped, never to reach the ancestor fires in the sky. His own death will give them release. This we have been selected to do. We will return him to meet with the camps he claimed sacrifices from. All will be invited to attend, even his own camp. This time however, we will make sure that he does not walk away alive."

"It is hard to believe!" Scorpion muttered, "I would have trusted that man with my life, in fact did in many ways. He seemed so caring, so honest!"

"That is how he tricked people. He gained their trust; then when he was secure, he began to change. Before he became a dreamer, he was a valued member of the hunting society. Men trusted him. It was easy to convince them that he had suddenly become a dreamer. I doubt, however, that such trust lasted. I haven't spoken to any members of that camp, but I have heard tales!" Bull Elk stated.

"Well, if you have finished..." Scorpion rose. The hunters did also. Calling Wolf led the headman and several curious onlookers back to where Running Antelope guarded their captive. Scorpion studied the man keenly, even asked him a few questions once the gag was removed. White Eagle however, was silent. He glared angrily around, realizing that there was little hope for support from these stupid desert dwellers. They were easily tricked and he could expect nothing from them in the way of help. However, his eyes did touch on those of one member of the group, only for a flicker of time, but it was enough, at least he had that fragment of hope.

Calling Wolf sent Running Antelope off to eat and Bull Elk took over in his place. Ash Branch returned to the village and began gathering up her things. When the hunters left, she needed to be prepared to go with them. Meanwhile, she had much work to occupy her. There were several persons from neighboring villages here, hoping to find release from pain from her potions and remedies. She applied a salve onto a burned arm, rebandaged a boil which she had lanced the previous day, changing the poultice which had done an excellent work of pulling the rot from the wound. She gave a mother-to-be a tonic for strength and an ancient matron one for painful joints. So went her day! Before she realized it, dusk was settling in.

As was the custom of the village, the visitors were welcomed with a feast, complete with dancing and storytelling. As the ceremony came to an end, Calling Wolf found an opportunity to inform Ash Branch that they would be leaving very early the next day. "I am ready," she assured him. "If you would rather, I can move to your camp tonight. My travois is packed and Fina and I are ready to leave. I have already said good by to those who matter to me."

Calling Wolf nodded. "It would be best if you move to our camp," he agreed. "But not necessary. We will be leaving just after dawn."

"I will be there," she assured him.

As the festivities closed, Ash Branch retired to her last night in her shelter within this village. It had been a good three seasons. She had made several friends, but only one really close, for she was very reserved. After the experiences of her young life, making friends was hard for her. As always, she settled next to her wolf and slept soundly. As usual, the animal was alert to everything that went on about her. She flicked an ear as someone moved quietly past the shelter, but recognized the smell and merely yawned and settled more comfortably.

Just before dawn, she nudged Ash Branch and the woman rose and folded her sleeping fur and tucked it onto the loaded travois. Harnessing the wolf, quietly she left the village, hurrying to the camp beyond.

They were still finishing up a hurried meal when she arrived. She accepted a bowl of hot tea and some roasted meat. The dreamer was already prepared to travel. His feet had been untied so that he could walk, but the noose around his neck had been joined by another and each was attached securely to the hunter who would walk in front of and behind him. His hands were tied behind his back, attached to yet another noose. No mater how he should try to escape, he would only end up strangling himself.

Calling Wolf nodded and Running antelope took up one line, while Bull Elk secured the other. With Elk Caller in the lead and Calling Wolf bringing up the rear, they set off. Ash Branch walked behind the hunter Prairie Grass. They moved at a steady pace all day, stopping to drink from their water bags occasionally, but not really stopping for any length of time. Well before dark, however, Calling Wolf called for a halt for the night. The prisoner was secured again to a tree. He was allowed to eat and relieve himself only with the assistance of a hunter. His hands remained securely tied.

Ash Branch was tired. She had not traveled extensively for seasons and she was out of shape. Her legs ached and her back felt like the backpack she carried weighed considerably more than it had early in the morning. The straps had raised blisters on her shoulders and she had more on her heels. Application of salve and pads helped the blisters, but nothing helped the aches. She crawled gratefully into her furs and drifted off to sleep almost before her head settled.

\*     \*     \*

She slipped from the sleeping village well into the night. No one saw her go and no one would miss her in the morning. The women knew she was leaving very early for a neighboring village. Before anyone discovered otherwise, she would be long gone and so would her lover. They were heading to the far west, where no one would ever find them. She traveled wide of the enemy camp and cut onto the trail well beyond their camp. Here she waited, watching, until they passed. It was a simple task to fall in behind them, well out of sight and follow. They stopped early; picking a campsite that was ideal for her task. She hid in the thick brush and when the hunter prepared to feed the animals, she easily slipped close and added something to their food and likewise, for the guard. Even the general stew had something special. While everyone was busy, she expertly tossed a neat ball of food into the skin. Smiling, she slipped into deep brush and waited and waited.

The only thing still awake in the camp was Fina and she would not raise the alarm. She merely thumped her tail in greeting and took the offered treat. Almost, the woman regretted that she should treat a trusted companion thusly, but then there would be no lasting effects. The rescue of her lover was far more important. She expertly cut his bindings and turned to leave.

"Wait!" he called, "I will only be a few moments!"

"What are you going to do?" she whispered, "We have to hurry, before they wake up!"

"Thy won't wake up!" he snarled, "I'll see to that!"

"You don't mean..." she gasped, "No! Not Ash Branch! She is my best friend! I can't stand by and let you kill her!"

"Would you rather see me dead?" he snarled, "Get out of my way!"

"No," she pleaded. "Please! We will be far from here before any of them waken. I promise! I put so much of the sleeping tonic in their food that the sun will be up before they are."

Just then Calling Wolf stirred in his sleeping fur and rose. "Come on!" she urged.

Having no choice, Quenquel followed her. They quickly left the camp behind, but it was completely dark and they stumbled and fell countless times.

"Stupid woman!" he muttered as she whimpered in pain from a sprained ankle. Finally, sweat pouring from his brow he could hear the wolves calling behind them. "Stay here!" he ordered, slapping her so hard across the face that her head nearly snapped off her neck. An angry red weal appeared on her cheek and new tears of pain and disillusion sprang to her eyes. "Don't worry," he sneered, "They won't hurt you!"

"What are you doing?" she whispered, "Where are you going?"

"Where no one can follow," he snarled, leaping over a cliff into the rushing water below. Yellow Bird crawled to the edge and glanced down. She could see nothing, but the sound of the angry river told her everything she needed to know. She still sat there, crying, when the hunters found her.

\*     \*     \*

Fina watched. A friend came quietly to her and gave her a treat. Happily she swallowed it, thumping her tail in thanks. Soon her eyes began to close and after a short time she was snoring gently beside Ash Branch.

Already Prairie Grass snored softly beside his captive, a quick additive to his tea when he went to relieve himself, saw to that. Now that the entire camp was asleep, with help, a shadow slipped silently to where Quenquel was tied. Sharp obsidian made easy work of his bindings and he followed the shadow into the forest.

Calling Wolf yawned. He had need to relieve himself. It was time to check on the captive as well. He trotted to where Quenquel should have been trussed to find cut bindings, a snoring guard and the captive long gone.

"Prairie Grass!" he roared, kicking the snoring man's feet. Groggily, Grass wobbled to his feet, shaking his head to remove the fuzziness, "What's wrong?"

"He's gone! Men!" Calling Wolf shouted.

"Gone?" Prairie Grass looked to where he had last seen the dreamer, tightly trussed to the tree. Now only the cut bindings remained. "I don't understand! How could I have gone to sleep? I wasn't even drowsy! I know how important this is!"

"You were drugged!" Calling Wolf replied. "We all were. Probably put in the stew. But I didn't eat any. That's why it didn't affect me. Come on, we have to wake up the men and get after him!"

"But who would drug us? I don't understand!"

"Someone must have followed from the village."

The entire camp seemed to be suffering from the same effects as Prairie Grass. Even the wolves staggered on their feet. Calling Wolf hurried to where Ash Branch rested. Shaking her awake he demanded. "Do you have any remedy to remove the effects of whatever drought we have been given?"

She blinked, tasting the dryness in her mouth and nodded, "I will prepare something," she sighed, "I suppose he is gone?"

Calling Wolf nodded. "Someone drugged us and while we were asleep, let him free," he answered without need. It was already obvious to Ash Branch what had happened. She even knew what had been given to them to cause the unnatural sleep.

"Can you tell how long...." Bull Elk stomped to where Calling Wolf waited to hand out the remedy. "Even the animals have been given something!" he grumbled.

"Here! Give them this," Ash Branch handed him several pieces of meat coated with something she took from a flask on her travois. She gave some to Fina as well and then handed portions around to the men. "This will take effect almost immediately," she assured them.

"Get the wolves onto his trail just as soon as they can follow!" Calling Wolf shouted.

"I'm coming too!" Ash Branch scrambled to her feet.

"Suit yourself!" Calling Wolf whistled to the wolves and set them on the trail. With woofs of understanding, they streaked off into the dark. The hunters followed for hands of time. They had no idea how much head start Quenquel had, any more than they knew how he had escaped.

Ash Branch struggled to keep up, panting; a stitch in her side. When the wolves suddenly became silent, she shivered and picked up speed. She rushed so fast she nearly went over before Calling Wolf stopped her. She was astonished to find her best friend sitting on the grass, with a badly sprained ankle, tears pouring down her red and swollen face.

"He's gone..." Yellow Bird sobbed.

"Where," shouted Calling Wolf.

She nodded to the precipice and the hunters went to stare down. "What do you think?" Calling Wolf asked.

"I know this river," Bull Elk replied. "It makes a big curve, all rushing water here, but a man could live through it. Beyond, down there, it widens out. But there is no way out of the canyon anywhere near here. If we hurry, we can be at the place where it widens, before he could possible get there! Come on men, follow me!"

"Go ahead," Ash Branch nodded to Calling Wolf. "I'll get Yellow Bird back to the camp and see to her ankle. I am sure this is all a big misunderstanding."

Calling Wolf merely raised a disbelieving eyebrow at her and turned to rush off after the others.

"Yellow Bird, how could you?" Ash Branch groaned.

"We were going away!" the other woman whimpered. "He promised to take me back to my own people! We were leaving in just a few days!

Nearly everything was ready," she sobbed. "Now I have nothing! No people, no way to ever get home again and the man I love is dead!"

"How could you love such a one as he?" Ash Branch muttered as she bound the swollen ankle. He has repeatedly made advances toward me right in front of you!"

"He explained that!" Yellow Bird sniffled. "He knew you would never take him seriously and it was the perfect cover for us!"

"And you believed him?" Ash Branch rocked back onto her heels; her mouth open in amazement. "He would have dropped you like a hot stone if I had even shown the slightest interest in him! We went over that, numerous times! I was sure that you finally understood what kind of man he is. I told you that I didn't trust him! I told you that there was something about him..."

"Oh, I know that! But he made promises to me. And you told me often enough that you had no interest in him; so why not? I had a chance, finally, for something that would make ME happy for a change! So I took it! Now of course, after I have made a complete fool of myself and set a dangerous killer free, I see that he was just using me. But now is too late and when those hunters return, they will kill me!" again she began to wail.

"Oh, shut up!" Ash Branch retorted. "There, try to stand," she finished bandaging the sprained ankle and stood up. She helped her sobbing friend to her feet. "Here, take this broken branch and use it as a crutch. We should just about make it back to the camp before the men do. And once there, you had better have some heart-felt apologies to all concerned, particularly if they do not recapture the dreamer. I just do not understand how you could do something so stupid! Why on earth didn't you come to me?"

"Oh, sure and hear the same old tale over again! How many times have we gone over this? I tell you; I was in love with the man! I couldn't see straight! Not until he left me and jumped into that river did I understand that he was just using me!"

Well, it is over now! I don't know how we will get you back to the village, what with your injured ankle and all. I am sure that none of these men will be willing to accompany you especially if they do not recapture the dreamer."

"I don't want to go back to the village!" Yellow Bird whimpered. "If I can't return to my own people, I'd rather go with you. But I am sure that these men will just kill me for letting White Eagle go and leave my remains for the predators!"

"Nonsense; even if they do not recapture Quenquel, they will offer you no harm! I will see to that. But do not blame me if you find your welcome less than warm!" Ash Branch helped her limp down the trail.

*　　*　　*

"Come on men!" Bull Elk headed down a wide trail at a dead run, "We can still capture him if he still lives!"

The men followed, wolves racing ahead with Bull Elk. They cut away from the gorge and across country, following a well-used game trail. A hand of time later the trail began to drop steeply toward the river below. Just as the sun rose, they reached the place where the river widened out into a smoothly flowing sheet of water. Here they spread out along the shore, studying the river for signs of a floating body, or the still-living man. They saw logs, even the carcass of an unfortunate deer that had somehow fallen into the raging torrent. But there were no signs of a man.

"Wait!" Elk Caller shouted."

*　　*　　*

Quenquel leaped into the gorge in desperate flight. He struck the water hard and pains shot through his entire body. It felt as if the water had ripped the skin from his body. Boulders and sharp rocks bruised his flesh as the water tumbled and tossed him. He struggled to keep afloat barely able to do so as the swift current carried him along. Desperately he kicked and stroked with his arms frequently choking on water as his head went under. The water was icy, swift and deep. The cold began sapping his strength and his struggles became weaker. Then he snagged on a tree trunk that was wedged in the bank. With his last bit of strength, he grabbed it and pulled himself from the freezing water. Shivering uncontrollably, he crawled onto the tree trunk. From there he found hand holds and slowly drew himself up the side of the canyon. Then he could go no further. He was trapped! Roots from trees above had held the soil and rocks, while below the river had gouged away the soil. All he could do was work his way up into the root mass and hope to be hidden from view. There he crouched, battered, beaten and bleeding.

# CHAPTER 28

What do you see?" Bull Elk squinted upriver.

"I think I see him!" look, about half way up the cliff on the opposite side clinging to that root!"

"I see him! Your right! But what do we do now? We are on this side of the river and he is on the other! The water here is still too strong to cross!"

"Even so, how do we reach him?" Elk Caller asked.

"I have an idea!" Calling Wolf looked thoughtfully. "Bull Elk, you and Elk Caller help me get that log afloat! You can use it to kick your way across the river. Once there, climb the cliff and lower a rope to the dreamer."

"What makes you think he'll take it?" Bull Elk asked.

"What choice does he have?" Calling Wolf answered. "He is stuck where he is. He can't get any further up without our help. His other choice is going back into the river. If he does that, we are on both sides of the river. Either way he goes; we have him! It's recapture or drown. He is a chance-taker! It's my guess that he will choose recapture over death. As long as he is alive there is a chance of another escape. Death is very final. Let's go!"

They shoved the log into the water and the pair of men strongly paddled across the river. From his perch, Quenquel watched. He screamed silently in frustration! He fully understood his predicament. He couldn't get any farther up the cliff. He was bone tired from fighting the whitewater had taken all his strength. He was trapped. There were few options open to him. With a sigh he took the only path offered to him. He waited.

Bull Elk and Elk Caller pulled the log safely up onto the bank. Then they studied where the dreamer was stuck. When they reached just above him, they lowered a rope and he took it. They pulled him to safety and with him between them, made their way back to the log and paddled back across the river.

Calling Wolf trussed the dreamer again and they all headed back to the camp. Quenquel glared at his captors but said nothing. The sun was hot by the time they reached the camp. The women were not yet back, but then with the one injured, Calling Wolf hadn't expected them to be. The hunters returned Quenquel to his tree and began preparing food. Bull Elk grinned as he saved the last of the contaminated stew for their captive. At least this day he would give them no more trouble!

*     *     *

"I have to rest!" Yellow Bird whimpered, "I just cannot go further!" She halted her awkward hopping motion and stood drooping tiredly in the middle of the trail.

"Fine we will rest!" Ash Branch sat down on a handy log after helping Yellow Bird to settle there, "But the longer it takes, the hungrier you will be. I haven't any food with me."

"Oh!" Yellow Bird reached into her waist pouch, "I do." She handed some dried meat to Ash Branch. "We can share what I have. That is the least that I can do, considering all the trouble I have caused. How could I have been so stupid?" She sat glumly on her log, her injured ankle stretched out before her. "Now, of course, I can see it all clearly! You are right! He was just using me. How could I not know that a man like him would never be interested in someone like me! It was just too good to be true! There is nothing about me that a man would find attractive!"

"Not at all," Ash Branch replied. "Don't be so hard on yourself! You are a good woman. You just haven't had much luck as far as men go." She stretched and chewed thoughtfully on her meat. "Why don't you let me teach you the healing plants?"

"What good would that do?"

"Perhaps none, but at least it would give you a value, apart from a man. You wouldn't really need a man to make your place in any camp. A healer is welcome everywhere."

Yellow Bird frowned, "I wouldn't be any good at that," she sighed. "I can't recognize one plant from another!"

"You certainly recognized enough to make the sleeping potion!" Ash Branch reminded.

Yellow Bird blushed. "I didn't do it; the dreamer did."

"When?"

"I told you, we planned to leave the village in a few days. He didn't want us to be followed. That potion was made to put in the food at the moon celebration, just enough to make everyone sleep soundly," she said lamely.

Ash Branch shook her head, silently wondering how Yellow Bird could have been so stupid! It was obvious to her that White Eagle had something very different planned with the sleeping potion. There had been enough to make the entire village sleep for days! She had no clear idea of what the dreamer really had planned, but she had few doubts that Yellow Bird had figured in those plans. She shivered as her mind turned to the possibilities....

"Come on, we had better get back on the trail," Ash Branch rose and helped Yellow Bird to her feet. "It is still a long way back to the camp and you had better hope that they got the dreamer back!" She stomped off down the trail following the lead set by Fina. Yellow Bird hobbled slowly after her.

It was well after sun-high before they reached the camp. Ash Branch was relieved to see the dreamer once again securely trussed to the tree. Yellow Bird glared at him angrily and refused to go anywhere near him. When Calling Wolf said nothing about her presence in the camp, she relaxed some, but the less-than-friendly looks from the rest of the hunters kept her close to Ash Branch.

"There is hardly a reason for us to move on today," Calling Wolf said after everyone had eaten and the dreamer was snoring loudly from his meal. "How is her ankle?" he asked Ash Branch.

"She needs to keep off of it for a few days," the healer answered. "But other than that, there was no great harm done to it. She can share my shelter and if need be ride on a travois. Fina can pull that and I can pull my own. She has decided that rather than return to a village where she has no connection, she would rather come with me, as I am her friend."

"What about him?" Calling Wolf nodded toward the sleeping dreamer.

"She has realized that he was only using her. You have nothing to fear from her. She will certainly not free him again!" Ash Branch replied. "He tricked her into helping him."

Calling Wolf nodded, "It is as we thought. Bull Elk said as much."

Again Yellow Bird flushed. She looked down at the ground and refused to meet the eyes of the men. *I will never trust another man!* She gritted her teeth. *They are nothing but trouble!*

The hunter Bull Elk watched the woman color. He was fascinated with her, something strange for a man who had never really had an interest in any woman. She had completed a daring rescue single-handed! This certainly impressed him. *This woman is worth looking into!* He smiled to himself. *I am getting to an age where family and children are more and more attractive, and this is just the sort of woman I need.*

Later he went to Calling Wolf. "What do you think about taking this woman with us?"

"We do not seem to have much choice," Calling Wolf answered. "She doesn't wish to return to the village. It seems that it wasn't her village. She comes from the far west coast. The only reason she was helping the dreamer was because he promised to take her back to her own people. Now she has decided to go with her friend, Ash Branch. I do not have a problem with her so long as she stays away from the dreamer."

"I think she has learned that he is not to be trusted," Bull Elk replied. "I will be pleased to keep an eye on her though, just in case," he flushed.

Calling Wolf looked closely at his friend and then smiled. "Well, well, well!" he grinned, "At last!" He slapped Bull Elk on the back, "Good luck!"

Bull Elk blushed even redder and then hurried away.

The camp settled down for the night. Bull Elk kept wide-awake, watching the dreamer sleep. His mind was alive with thoughts. He had studied the woman, Yellow Bird all through the afternoon and evening. He admired the graceful way she moved her hands and she seemed to be very pleasant as well. Calling Wolf had already arranged that she would travel on his travois over the next few days. This would certainly give him opportunity to get to know her better. Finally, Prairie Grass came to replace him well into the night and he went to his furs still thinking about the woman.

They set out again the next day. Yellow Bird rode Bull Elk's travois, much to her embarrassment. Ash Branch watched the pair of them and smiled. Yellow Bird had little to fear about her future. So far, Ash Branch was very impressed with the hunter, Bull Elk. He had an ingrained kindness that would be perfect for her friend.

The dreamer was watched very carefully. His escape put them all on their toes. Yellow Bird made sure that she did not go anywhere near him. He pleaded with his eyes, but she was not drawn in again. As they moved along the trail eastward, Yellow Bird talked with the hunter Bull Elk. The man impressed her, but she refused to be drawn in. She rode his travois, was polite to him, but escaped back to Ash Branch the moment they stopped.

After a double hand of days they left the desert and entered the mountains. Now the terrain became much more difficult. They traveled up and then down, along twisted snaking trails, beneath towering trees and through stream after stream. Yellow Bird felt a weight lift from her heart as they entered the forest. She was forest born and bred. She had hated the openness of the deserts.

They traveled for over a moon through the forest. Bull Elk explained to her where they were headed, pointing out landmarks and slowly easing into a friendship with her. Now she walked with him laughing and relaxed. Ash Branch watched, smiling. They were headed for a canyon where some spiritual leader was waiting. It was here that the dreamer would be held until the camps drew together. This group of hunters was charged with guarding the dreamer and once the man had been dealt with they were joining up with the main camp. Calling Wolf would be going on to join up with a man named Running Bison. But Ash Branch and Yellow Bird were going to be part of the traveling camp that Bull Elk was going with. This fitted with what she knew from her own sources. She was to join some dreamer named Bear Claw.

Late one evening they eased down a steep narrow path into a deep canyon. Ravens welcomed them and a small group of people stood at the mouth off a cave watching them. They had arrived! Calling Wolf sent out a piercing whistle before they began the descent. Ash Branch was glad.

She was tired of all this traveling. She looked around with increasing interest as they followed the trail down into the canyon. This was some place! From above it was nearly invisible. The weather would treat it gently. There was even a nice stream flowing through it. In the meadow beyond the cave a small herd of elk grazed unconcerned. A shiver of excitement ran down her spine.

The hunters all seemed very at home here. Obviously, this was not their first visit. Yellow Bird also watched the men thoughtfully. Or rather, she watched Bull Elk thoughtfully. Ash Branch smiled to herself. Then she followed the men up the trail and into the cave. Here she came to an abrupt stop, almost forgetting to breathe. Before her stood a small plain woman and beside her stood a nearly white wolf, the largest Ash Branch had ever seen. And they both had eyes as blue as her own!

The woman stepped forward, "I am Bear Claw Woman," she introduced herself.

A shiver ran down Ash Branch's spine. She groped for words, but the only ones that came were. "You have blue eyes!" Funny feelings were running all through her body. This was someone very powerful! This was someone very important! This was someone she felt that she knew as well as she knew herself!

Bear Claw Woman smiled, having an idea of what was going through the other woman's mind. "We are connected." She said gently, "You will get used to it after a time."

"Connected? Ash Branch stuttered.

"Related," Bear Claw Woman added, "We are cousins."

"How can that be? I have no relatives!" Ash Branch shook her head.

"You have this," Bear Claw Woman answered, revealing the tiny wolf on her breast, identical to the one which adorned Ash Branch's.

"How did you know?" she stuttered, "I mean, no one knows about it! I don't know what it means," Ash Branch confessed. "Perhaps my grandmother did, but if so she died without telling me. I have wondered, however. At times it burns and at other times it throbs with pleasure." Bear Claw Woman merely nodded.

"Come into the back reaches of the cave. We have a place prepared for you and your friend."

"You knew she was coming?" Ash Branch stopped.

"Calling Wolf told me about the escape and the part which Yellow Bird played in it. He also explained that she has been a great help since."

"But you haven't even greeted Calling Wolf!"

Bear Claw Woman shook her head, "We communicate in a way I will show you. But right now come and get settled into your new home. I am very pleased to have another woman here. Sometimes I get very lonely with only the men. My mate, Raven is wonderful, but there are still many times that I yearn for a woman's point of view. The spirits have promised that we will be very close. This thrills me, for I have not had anyone of my own family since my grandmother died, seasons ago. But come, we have many things to speak of, but right now let me make you and Yellow Bird comfortable and get food served for all of you."

Ash Branch realized, now that she mentioned it, that food was waiting. Somehow these people knew exactly when they would arrive. It was uncanny!

The men settled the dreamer in a room beyond the living cave and a guard was with him at all times. It was virtually impossible for him to escape, but they were taking no chances. After everyone had eaten, the men sat around sharing news. Ash Branch and Yellow Bird stayed beyond the hearth, letting them relax. Women were seldom welcome when men began to reminisce. Bear Claw Woman had disappeared, along with her wolf. No one seemed concerned.

"This place is strange," whispered Yellow Bird. "Did you see that woman? She acted like she was on a level with the men! What do you make of that? And that wolf! Never have I seen such an animal!" She shivered, "She gives me the creeps!"

"Perhaps she is close to the Spirit Leader who lives here."

"The men say this Bear Claw is very powerful!"

"What did you say?" Ash Branch jerked around.

"The men say."

"No! What name did you say!"

"Bear Claw; that is the name of the Spirit Leader," Yellow Bird replied.

"I don't believe it!"

"Well, ask them yourself!" Yellow Bird replied in a hurt voice.

"I don't mean that you are wrong!" Ash Branch hurried to tell her. It is just that the blue-eyed woman is named Bear Claw. I just can't believe that their spirit leader is a woman! I have never heard of such a thing!"

Yellow Bird's mouth dropped open, "Are you sure?"

"That is how she introduced herself to me. She said her name is Bear Claw Woman. Surely there cannot be two so closely named."

Both women glanced around. "I don't see her anywhere or that odd wolf," Yellow Bird said. "Perhaps she is feeding the dreamer. I cannot believe that a woman could serve in so high a position in any camp, but if it is so, that is the camp I want to live in!"

Just then Bull Elk came over to where they were sitting. "I brought you fresh tea," he said his face flaming with embarrassment.

"Thank you," replied Yellow Bird. "Perhaps you can answer a question for us."

"If I can," he answered.

"The woman..."

"You mean Bear Claw Woman?"

"Yes."

"She has gone into the inner cave to commune with her spirits," he said softly, almost as if he were uncomfortable with the idea. "She will return when she is ready."

"Then, you mean that she really is your Spirit Leader?"

He shook his head, "Bear Claw Woman is not a dreamer. She is much more than that. She is The Chosen One, sent by the spirits to lead The People back to the proper ways. Bear Claw Woman answers to no one; not even her mate, Raven. But she is very powerful indeed. Had I not seen it with my own eyes, I would not believe some of the things that I have seen her do. I was there when she strangled the hunter Angry Bull with nothing but her mind! He had stolen her necklace, the one that you saw her wearing. We went to get it back, but she followed. Just when Angry Bull was going to dart Raven, she caused the necklace to tighten about his neck and the man slit his own throat and bled to death right before my own eyes. Once he was dead, the necklace just let go and fell to the ground. That is how powerful she is! And that is not all! She can talk to people with her mind! People anywhere! Why, on our way here she was in contact with Calling Wolf at least a hand of times!"

"So that is how they knew exactly when we would arrive," mused Ash Branch.

Bull Elk nodded, "As much time as I have spent in her company she still makes me a little nervous. Not that she acts pushy or anything. She is as nice as any proper young woman, but it just isn't natural... those eyes..." He glanced suddenly at Ash Branch and blushed. "Sorry! Didn't mean anything..."

"I understand," she cut in. "I am used to comments about my eyes."

He squinted, thinking rapidly. "You not related to her, are you?" he asked excited.

Ash Branch frowned and shrugged, remembering the very words spoken by Bear Claw Woman only a short time before. "If we are, I am not aware of it," she answered quickly.

"Well, you both have blue eyes and you're both healers. I just wondered..."

"She is a healer?" Ash Branch perked up.

"Best one I have ever come across. I'll tell you, I got caught in a landslide, broke my leg and a few ribs. Why she placed her hands on me, that funny blue glow spread around us and I could almost feel the bones grow back together. Within a moon I was walking as good as new and not even a limp. Why you'd never know this leg was ever broken." He slapped his thigh, "And not a single twinge of pain have I ever had from it!" He grinned, "And she was being drained of her power by that dreamer in there at the same time! That's how powerful she is!" He nodded his head enthusiastically. "Why she can cure anyone of anything and doesn't even have to be there to do it. She even guided the hands of a girl to turn a baby that was coming out feet first. I know this is true because I have spoken to both the girl and the woman who had the child. And they were well over a moon's distance away!"

"How can this be?" Yellow Bird blinked, "Surely it is not possible!"

"Yet Bear Claw Woman did it!" Bull Elk was adamant.

Ash Branch frowned thoughtfully. If even half of what this hunter had just said was true, then Bear Claw Woman was truly a gifted healer. She had never heard of anyone communicating over distance with their minds, but she supposed such a thing could be possible, if the spirits were involved. It was not difficult to imagine that Bear Claw Woman was very involved with spirits! She shivered with excitement. Just to contemplate that she just might be actually related to one so powerful, nearly took her breath away! And she was a healer!

Gradually the initial excitement of their arrival quelled, and the hearth fire burned to coals. Still Bear Claw Woman had not returned, but no one seemed concerned. The hunters yawned, finished their final drinks and prepared to retire for the night. The women made one last trip from the cave to relieve themselves and then sought their own furs. Ash Branch lay far into the night, her mind racing. Finally she drifted off to sleep.

Bear Claw Woman hurried down the passageway, leaving the excited travelers to settle down. She glanced in at the dreamer as she passed his cell, noting that Young Wolf lay watching every move the man made. The dreamer was still trussed with his hands behind his back attached to a noose around his neck. He was also tethered to a post securely buried in the floor. She had no doubt that if he made a wrong move Young Wolf would rip his throat out. She was also certain that the dreamer knew it as well.

Meeting Ash Branch had been a jolt! She had never felt such an instant connection to another person in her entire life. She needed to speak to Wolf Spirit. She needed to know! Almost without thought she dropped her clothes and slipped into the stream, letting the water carry her beneath the ledge into the crystal room. Climbing from the water, she dried off and slipped into a waiting tunic. Then she seated herself and reached out to place her hands against the wall.

The blue glow swirled around her and she sighed. She opened her eyes. She was in the meadow and Spirit Wolf stood before her. Beyond, other spirits waited, watching silently, as usual.

\*       \*       \*

*She has arrived?* Spirit Wolf asked.

*She is here, just beyond, in the living cave.* Bear Claw Woman replied. *I am surprised. I had not expected to feel such a strong connection to her. Yet I do not feel anything of the spirit in her.*

*No, she has no spirit powers.*

*Yet she carries your mark!*

*Had you chosen to remain dead, then she would have been called. You chose to return, so she was not needed. But she had already been marked, just in case. Still, she has much knowledge of healing; she knows the plants of the deserts. You know those of the mountains. She reinforces your power and you her strength. Healers will come from far and wide to learn from the pair of you. Bring her to me and I will explain to her. She is still afraid. I will ease her fears.*

*I will bring her to you tomorrow.*

\*        \*        \*

Spirit Wolf nodded and Bear Claw Woman opened her eyes to see the flame flickering in her oil bowl. Guardian yawned and stretched. Bear Claw Woman ruffled her fur and pulling the tunic over her head folded it neatly beside her mat. Then she slipped into the stream and swam beneath the wall. Guardian splashed after her, choosing to cavort in the stream, splashing and playing happily for the time it took Bear Claw Woman to dry off and don her tunic. Then Guardian climbed from the water and shook, spraying water all over. It was a game they frequently played. Bear Claw Woman squealed in mock alarm and leaped clear of the shower. Then she picked up the torch and they headed back to the living cave.

The fire was out in the hearth and only the sounds of sleeping people reached her ears. Guardian settled in her usual place and proceeded to squirm into a comfortable position. Bear Claw Woman slipped silently beneath the furs and cuddled up against Raven. He reached out and pulled her close, not waking. With a deep sigh she closed her eyes. Then she jerked bolt upright.

"Umph!" Raven woke up. "What's wrong?"

"He is at it again!" she whispered. "The dreamer! He just tried to...."

"Well he won't," Raven began to rise.

"No! It is all right. I'll deal with him," Bear Claw Woman replied. "It was just a surprise."

"You sure?"

"Yes. But I wouldn't turn down some food. I'm awake now. Sleep is far away and I'm starving!"

Raven chuckled, "What is new? Actually, I have saved you food. It should still be warm. I'll get it for you."

"No, that's all right. I can get it myself. Go back to sleep. I didn't mean to waken you."

"Like you, I am wide awake now. I'd rather keep you company. But just to be sure, I think I'll go check on our 'guest'." He rose and lit a torch. Bear Claw Woman filled a bowl of food from the bladder still hanging beside the hearth and settled down to eat. Raven headed down the passageway to where the dreamer was held.

Young Wolf lay watching the dreamer with steady unblinking eyes. The man glared at Raven when he entered. Raven smiled back. "Leave her alone!" he advised. "Or she will prove to you again, just how powerful she is. Don't forget what happened to you the last time you tried to steal from her! That is just a taste of what will happen if you try again!" He checked the bindings and ruffled the fur on the wolf's neck. "Don't turn your back on him!" he whispered to Young Wolf," He is not to be trusted."

"Woof!"

Raven, satisfied that the dreamer was still safely their captive returned to the living cave. Bear Claw Woman was just finishing up her meal. She set aside her bowl and the pair of them slipped silently from the cave, Guardian at their heels.

"What do you make of this healer that Calling Wolf brought to us?" he asked. "Is she all you expected?"

"That and more," she answered. "Did you know that had I chosen to remain dead, she would have taken over my place?"

"Really? Good thing the spirits didn't tell you that at the time. I might not have had the richness of our time together."

"No! It was the promise of this time that brought me back; that and our daughter."

"Daughter? What daughter?" the hunter stopped.

"The one which I carry," she replied.

"You...are sure?"

She smiled at his dumbfounded expression. "Of course I'm sure! It doesn't take spirit powers to know such a thing. I'm a woman! I have known for a while, but I just wanted to find a special occasion to tell you.

Now seemed perfect; just the pair of us, the night sounds and the moon bright overhead."

"A daughter," he frowned. "I can understand knowing that you carry a child, but how can you be so sure that it is a daughter?"

"I have spoken to her," Bear Claw Woman replied.

"Spoken...." Raven looked shocked. "How can you do that? No! I don't want to know! Your spirits still make me uncomfortable!"

Bear Claw Woman chuckled. "Not now, while I carry her in my body. I spoke with her while I was in the land of the dead. It was she who convinced me to return. It was she who promised the joy we share!"

"Humm! Perhaps I will thank her someday for that." He led her to a place where the grass was deep and soft and here they lay together, exploring, enjoying... Much later they returned to the cave and slipped unnoticed back into their sleeping furs.

The smell of food cooking awakened them. Yellow Bird was scurrying about, fixing the meal, a bright flush to her face and Bull Elk watched her, with a funny wistful look on his. Ash Branch was folding their sleeping furs neatly against the back wall of the cave. Calling Wolf and Elk Caller were nowhere to be seen. The remaining men were stretching and yawning. Birds called cheerfully from beyond the cave and the noise of the wolves playing filtered in.

Bear Claw Woman reached automatically for the seed cakes she had stashed beside her furs. Before even trying to rise she ate a couple. This was not missed by Ash Branch. *Ah! She is pregnant!* She noted. She smiled to herself and headed to where Yellow Bird was serving up the food to men who magically appeared at just the right time. She poured hot water into a bowl and added a generous portion of herbs from a packet she had already dug from her supplies. This she carried to Bear Claw Woman. "This will help," she smiled as she handed the bowl to her. "I have found that this calms the queasy stomach very well."

"You are very observant," Bear Claw Woman raised an eyebrow. She took the bowl and sipped the tea. "I recognize deer foot and goosefoot." She replied, but there is something else, with which I am totally unfamiliar."

"That is because it only grows in the desert," Ash Branch replied smiling. "It is ground root of desert torch. I have found that it really aids the strength of the other herbs."

Bear Claw Woman nodded, "We have much to share with each other. But first, once we have finished eating and getting things arranged here in the living cave, I have been instructed to introduce you to Wolf Spirit."

Ash Branch paled. "Wolf Spirit..." she asked hesitantly.

"Do not be afraid. You will find the spirits fascinating! Besides, they are anxious to meet you, not harm you!"

"Oh!" she replied, at a loss for words.

"Thank you very much for this tea," Bear Claw Woman smoothed over her confusion. "It has really helped." She rose and began settling their bedding. She had her own 'tea' which she drank every morning now to settle her stomach, but the kindness of the other woman made her reluctant to mention it. Raven had risen and left the cave to relieve himself. Yellow Bird brought them all food and the three women settled comfortably to eat.

"I must congratulate you," Bear Claw Woman smiled. "I have never seen Bull Elk so rattled!"

Yellow Bird flushed, "I do not know what you are talking about..." she protested.

"Oh no!" Chuckled Ash Branch, "No idea what-so-ever!"

"I told you, I am finished with men!" Yellow Bird tossed her hair back over her shoulder. "They are nothing but trouble!"

"Ah, but what trouble," Bear Claw Woman rolled her eyes and wiggled her hips!

"You're shameful; both of you!" Yellow Bird turned a fiery red.

"You could do well to change your mind," Bear Claw Woman told her. "Bull Elk is a fine man. He is dependable, honest, gentle and kind. What more could you want?"

"I keep telling Ash Branch that I am not interested in men! But she refuses to listen."

"I can understand how you feel. When I was just turned a woman I was savagely raped by three renegade hunters. They took turns! It was many seasons before I was able to put that experience behind me. Raven has made all the difference! I think that Bull Elk might do the same thing for you."

"Oh I have put the rape behind me," Yellow Bird replied. "But the lying!" she wiped away a tear. "That I cannot forgive!"

"She is still hurting because White Eagle, excuse me Quenquel, used her badly. He made promises, which he knew she couldn't resist and then convinced her to risk everything to release him. She is hurting more from this betrayal than anything. In time, she will realize that not all men are bad."

"So far none in my life have treated me any way but poorly!" Yellow Bird snorted. "I am not likely to give another the chance to hurt me."

Bear Claw Woman did not reply, but already she was busy figuring out ways to help her old friend Bull Elk and her new one Yellow Bird, to find happiness together. Whispering Wind was right! You could always tell a woman who was happily mated, for she invariably wanted all of her unmated friends to find the same happiness."

Guardian nudged Bear Claw Woman's arm and whined. "All right you are right. Come on, I'll take you for your run!" She rose and smiled at the other women. "I suppose that I spoil her, but we always go out every morning so that she can get some exercise. Otherwise she is always by my side and at least recently I have not been as active as usually I am. Now I just watch where once I ran with her!"

"Why do we not all go out?" Suggested Ash Branch. "I would welcome some fresh air myself and gentle exercise will do you good. It is not good for your health to just sit around. Moving about is healthy for both you and the baby."

"You are pregnant?" Yellow Bird questioned.

"Nearly four moons," Bear Claw Woman replied. "I am just beginning to show. Actually I have felt wonderful but for the sickness in the morning and I know what to do for that. Actually, other than my mate, you are the first to know."

"The sickness will pass any time now," Ash Branch told her. "But of course, you know that. I forget, you are a more talented healer than I."

"You are a healer?" Yellow Bird again was surprised. "I thought you were the Spirit Leader!"

Bear Claw Woman laughed. "I can just see men allowing a female dreamer! Not in our lifetime! But I am in contact with spirits; women's spirits. In fact, very shortly I will be introducing Ash Branch to the Wolf Spirit."

Yellow Bird shivered, "I am glad it is her and not me! Spirits make me feel very uneasy! I am finished with them and dreamers as well!"

"Ah! So you have dealt with our handsome Quenquel! I can't blame you. That man is worse than a snake! He will use anyone to reach his own ends. Remind me to tell you how he used my best friend, Whispering Wind and me. I will rest easier when that man has been given back to his evil spirits! I certainly didn't want him here, but this was the most secure place to hold him till the camps are called together. I just hope that isn't long. Running Bison said within the moon. It won't be too soon for me!"

"Well I never wish to lay eyes on him again!" Yellow Bird sniffed, "He made a complete fool of me. Looking back, I can't believe that I was so gullible! But that is the way of a man! He struts and promises, but in the end, all that a woman gets is used and disappointed."

"Not all men are like that." Bear Claw Woman protested. "Now take Bull Elk, for example. Any woman who was lucky enough to capture his heart would be lucky indeed. He is a fine man."

"Already you are in league with Ash Branch!" Yellow Bird squealed, "All she can say is the same thing!"

"Then perhaps you should listen to us," Ash Branch said her nose in the air.

Bear Claw Woman laughed and led them down to the stream. Once there she spent several fingers of time throwing a stick for Guardian to retrieve. They all freshened while they were there and then returned to the cave.

"Come with me and I will show you more about our cave," she offered both women.

"You aren't doing that 'spirit' thing now are you?" Yellow Bird stopped.

"Yes, but you need not be afraid. I will leave you to enjoy the underground stream while we do that."

"I don't like water!" she shook her head, "I'd rather stay here."

"Perhaps then you will keep Bull Elk company," Bear Claw Woman said smoothly. "The rest of the men have gone hunting and he is stuck here keeping an eye on the dreamer."

"On second thought, that underground stream sounds rather interesting," she flounced after Guardian down the passageway. Both women chuckled.

As it turned out, she did find the stream interesting. The warmth of the water was wonderful and it was shallow enough that she could stand up and not be swept under. So she paddled about, careful to stay away from the deep pool which Bear Claw Woman pointed out to her. She watched with shivers, as they passed under the ledge and out of sight. It was almost as if they vanished by magic!

"Just place your hand in mine," Bear Claw Woman instructed. "You will find that it isn't frightening at all."

Timidly, Ash Branch did, resisting the urge to pull free. She felt a funny tingling all through her body and then light struck her closed eyelids. She opened them. They were in a grassy meadow, sitting on a log. Bear Claw Woman was seated beside her. She glanced around. All over the meadow, animals stood studying her with calm, interested eyes. There were deer, elk, wolves, antelope, rabbits, badger and many others. Then a voice spoke right beside her and she jumped nervously.

*　　*　　*

*You are Ash Branch, the healer?* A huge wolf, very similar to Guardian spoke just at her side.

"What?" She stuttered.

*You are Ash Branch, the healer* repeated the wolf. *I remember you as a child. I led Soft Robe to you and I provided food and shelter for the pair of you, watched over you and when it was time led you to the village where you began to practice the healing secrets. When you became a woman, I put my mark on you, just as I did with Bear Claw Woman.*

"Oh!"

*I have brought you to this place as well. Here you will be safe from those who would do you harm. Here you will share and learn from your kin, Bear Claw Woman. Here the pair of you will share the combined knowledge that you possess for the betterment of all the people. You have been given special talents, do not abuse them and do not waste them. Soon the pair of you will begin traveling to all the camps. You will learn from other healers, the plants and potions! These you will share with healers on your travels. But this cave will by where you always return, to rest, to study and to renew your strength.*

*I have not had time to explain everything to her yet,* Bear Claw Woman said quietly, *but soon I will and once she understands I am sure that she will agree with our hope and task.*

*Come, Ash Branch, healer of the people, let me introduce you to the other spirits.* The wolf turned and trotted out into the meadow. Ash Branch reluctantly followed. Soon however, she forgot her fears. As she was greeted by each of the animal spirits and learned a little about them, she realized that she had nothing to fear from them. All too soon she was back at the log and Bear Claw Woman had taken her hand once again. Then she opened her eyes and found herself once again in the crystal cave with only the flickering oil bowl for light.

\*     \*     \*

"That was unbelievable!" she whispered.

Bear Claw Woman merely grinned. "Over the next several days you will learn more about the task we have been called upon to complete. Actually, it is quite simple. We are to live here and share the healing knowledge with those who come seeking it and heal those in need of our help. Part of each season we will travel to various groups and learn from them and share with their healers our knowledge. This is a good place to live. It is safe, this cave is huge and there is a special escape route from the canyon if needed. The elk herd remains in the canyon most of the winter and we take only what we must from them."

"How many people will be living here?" Ash Branch liked what she had heard so far. She had always felt like an outsider in the desert villages. Here she felt as at peace as she had while living with her grandmother, hidden away in their little cave in yet another secret canyon.

"Myself and Raven of course plus Bull Elk and if he can convince her Yellow Bird; yourself and if you should so choose; your mate. Prairie Grass and Elk Runner and any mates, children and extended family we bring into the camp. I think eventually, this will be a real camp, but just now we are only a small group. The idea, however, is that there is plenty of room for visitors, places for sick and wounded to recover. The mountains around here abound with healing plants and when we decide to, we will take journeys to the desert people, and others as well."

"So, this canyon and cave is to be our home?"

"That is what the spirits have indicated," Bear Claw Woman nodded, "But of course that can also change at the whim of the spirits. Just now, however, the most important task we have been given is to keep the savage dreamer isolated from doing harm. He also has mind powers and he has no hesitation in using them. That is why Young Wolf guards him. He cannot trick the wolves. I can tell you; I will be glad when Running Bison comes and takes him!"

Ash Branch shivered, "I know what you mean." They pulled themselves from the water and began drying off. Already Yellow Bird was dressed and poking about with a stick.

"Well, how was it?" she asked Ash Branch.

"Unbelievable!"

"Really" Yellow Bird blinked, "You actually enjoyed it?"

"I have never had such an experience before! I feel absolutely wonderful!"

"Yes, I can see that, that you do, on the other hand, you look worn out!" she nodded toward Bear Claw Woman.

"These sessions always do that to me. It is different if I go alone, but taking another with me draws heavily on my powers. Particularly now while I carry her!" She rubbed her belly.

Yellow Bird frowned, "It is bad luck to suggest the gender of a child before it is born!"

"So my mate tells me!" Bear Claw Woman grinned at her. "But I will not mention it again, just so that everyone is comfortable about it." She patted her stomach again. "We won't tell!"

"I could make you a tonic..." Mused Ash Branch.

"It has nothing to do with my pregnancy," assured Bear Claw Woman. "It has always happened. Every time that I take one of the Mind Talkings everyone else is wonderfully refreshed and I am exhausted. That is what dealing with spirits is like. You are given one thing and something else is taken away. I can also draw upon spirit power to heal, like I did when we were traveling and Bull Elk broke his leg. But while he healed much faster, I could hardly keep on my feet."

"Then why do it?" questioned Yellow Bird.

"That is my task," she replied. "I was born to the line of The Chosen, just as Ash Branch was. The spirits have more control over our lives than the lives of others. I did not want to be 'chosen' and I fought it for a long time. But finally I came to realize that while I had some choice, when I was stubborn and fought the spirits, bad things happened to me and when I did as they wished, I was richly rewarded. For example, when I was running away and hiding from The People, I was raped and nearly killed. Once I gave up fighting, I found Raven," she smiled softly, "he has been the most wonderful thing in my life!"

Yellow Bird merely snorted.

Ash Branch picked up on Bear Claw Woman's words. "You have said before that we are related. How can you know that? Even Wolf Spirit spoke of it."

"Lone ago.... Bear Claw Woman told the legend of the ancestors and of The Chosen. She mentioned the blue eyes, the special wolves and the mark.

"You have a mark?" Yellow Bird stared at Ash Branch, "I have never seen it."

"It is not something which I show," she replied. "My grandmother said it was very important that people did not know that I had the mark. She even tried to alter it a number of times. But nothing she ever did changed it. It is still just as clear as ever. Luckily it is not in a place where it is readily visible." She flushed, "At least not to anyone but a mate. Since I am a modest woman and the villagers do not think it odd that I do not go about with only my apron, no one has had cause to question it."

"I want to see it!" Yellow Bird frowned. "We are best friends. I cannot believe that you have kept such a thing from me! Don't you trust me?"

"Of course, I trust you. Actually, it has become such a habit not to expose the mark, I never even think about it anymore." She pointed to the place just over her heart, "It is right here."

"It can prove to be very dangerous to bear such a mark," Bear Claw Woman said. "My own mother was murdered because she bore it. That is why my grandmother took me and ran from The People. We lived for seasons with the gatherers and I never knew they were not my people. That is how dangerous the mark is. Of course, now everyone knows about it, but I have Raven to protect me. Until I bear a daughter to take my place and she survives, I am the last of the line, except for Ash Branch, of course. The spirits have brought her to this place so that she can be safe as well."

"Safe from what," Ash Branch stopped.

"There are those people out there who see a woman such as we as a threat. I have been attacked because of it and only the help of the spirits brought me back so that I could complete my task. Had I not returned; you would have found yourself in my place."

As Branch shivered. "I am glad you returned. I do not envy you your task. This 'mind talking' frightens me. I suppose you do other things equally dangerous as well!"

Bear Claw Woman grinned, "Not really! I make offerings and give The People messages from the spirits. Beyond that, I live here and now will bear children to my mate. That is what remains to me of my task, that and working with you to share the healing secrets. Actually this is one of the big tasks we have been given. Once the people are all united into One People, healers will come to us to learn. We will make journeys of course, to gather supplies and meet other healers from far away, but for the most part, this canyon and cave, will be our home."

"But don't you miss village life?" Yellow Bird asked.

"I miss Whispering Wind," Bear Claw Woman admitted. "We spent seasons together and she is my best friend. But she is mated to Running Bison and I do not see much of her anymore. Running Bison is taking the message of the spirits to far away groups. Sometimes I have been lonely for another woman, but now that the pair of you are here, I will be less lonely."

They entered the living cave to find it deserted. Bear Claw Woman showed the other women where things were stored and they settled down to enjoy a bowl of hot tea. Suddenly, Guardian growled low in her throat and streaked down the passage and Bear Claw Woman grabbed her staff and followed her heart leaping with fear.

She reached the room where the dreamer was being held to find Bull Elk on his knees holding his head in both hands, moaning in agony. Guardian crouched before the dreamer and her hackles were raised. She growled deep in he throat and then suddenly a bolt of blue light shot out from her and struck the dreamer.

35  *Ceanothus* spp. Buckbrushes. These shrubs are famous tea substitutes. Dried leaves and flowers were steeped to produce a pale-yellow mile sweet tea. **Kershaw:** 80

36  *Gaultheria* spp. False-wintergreen. Dried leaves make a fragrant wintergreen-flavored tea. **Kershaw:** 94

37  *Yucca.* Spanish bayonet. Ground root added for flavor. **Elias:** 134

# CHAPTER 29

The dreamer jerked, his whole body going rigid. Then he slid forward and his body went limp. Bear Claw Woman knelt beside Bull Elk, who was now shaking but seemed to no longer be in pain, "What happened?"

"He used some kind of spirit trick on me!" Bull Elk muttered. "Caused really bad pains in my head."

"I see!" she glared at the dreamer, noticing that he was leaning into the noose that held him and it was cutting off his breath, but she didn't really care. "Come on, sit down over here," she helped Bull Elk to his feet.

"What happened?" Yellow Bird hurried to the injured man. "Are you hurt?" she began stroking the hunter's face tenderly.

"Hurts here," he pointed to his brow. Yellow Bird, oblivious to the others in the room, pulled his head to her and placed her lips against the spot, then cradled his head against her chest. "And here," he pointed to his cheek. She ran loving fingers over it. Bear Claw Woman and Ash Branch looked at each other and grinned.

"We had better release the pressure of that noose, or he will end up dead," she nodded to the dangling dreamer, "And then everyone will be mad at us." Bear Claw Woman muttered. "I'd just as soon let him strangle." She approached the dreamer and went to shift his limp body.

In a flash he had her, gripped in a painful hold, with both hands. One held her arm high behind her back, while the other was around her throat in such a manner that one quick move and he would snap her neck. "Make any sort of move to stop me and I will kill her!" he snarled at the startled silent group. "And order that obscenity back!" he motioned toward Guardian, who was bristling and balancing on her toes, ready to attack. "Do it! Or I'll kill you!"

Bear Claw Woman, trembling with fear, motioned Guardian to back down. Holding her tightly, the dreamer ordered Bull Elk to bind the women and then forced Bear Claw Woman to bind him. Quenquel took no chances. He inspected the bindings to make sure they were tight and then he made her place the noose around Guardian's neck and then grasped the only lighted torch in the room. He grinned maliciously at the three captives and shoved Bear Claw Woman roughly into the passage. Guardian howled and lunged against her tether, only causing the noose to tighten cruelly about her throat. Frantically she fought it, until Bull Elk yelled for her to stop.

"Chew the bindings!" he called to her as he struggled against his own. Guardian quickly sank sharp teeth into the leather tether and in very short order it gave way and she leaped across the room and Bull Elk held out his hands so that she could sever his bindings as well.

"A good thing you can see in the dark!" he muttered to the wolf, shaking to overcome his fear of the dark. "Otherwise we would never find our way out of this place!"

Bull Elk felt around in the dark, his hands finding the stack of unlit torches. He quickly ignited one with his fire stick and once he could see again, immediately released the women. "Come on, he's getting away!" he dived from the room and started down the passage following the floating dust left by Guardian.

Quenquel shoved her arm painfully up her back, his other arm holding the torch. "Is there any other way out of this cave?" he snarled.

"Not one that you will escape from alive!" Bear Claw Woman retorted.

"Don't mistake me, woman! I have nothing to lose! You either get me out of here, or you die; is that clear?"

"You will never get away!" she retorted. "They won't stop until they have you again! Even if you kill me! And if you do, then my mate Raven will hunt you down like the vermin you are. He won't rest until he kills you!"

"What do I care? No stupid hunter will ever capture Quenquel again! Now show me the way out!"

"There is no other way out! Only through the living cave! And the men won't let you pass through there! You may be free of your bonds, but you are still just as much a prisoner!"

"So, I was right! There is a way out going this direction! And you will show it to me! I have ways of making pain that will compel you to do anything to make me to stop!"

Bear Claw Woman thought frantically! Then, suddenly, she quit struggling against him. "All right I'll take you out of the cave!" she could smell the underground stream. Once they got there, she nodded to the ledge; "it is beyond the stream. That ledge leads you over it. Once beyond, the cave leads through the mountain and exits on the far side."

His reply was to shove her roughly onto the ledge. A silent streak of deadly wolf was about to launch into the air. *No!* Bear Claw Woman stopped her.

"Oh yes!" the dreamer snarled, "Get on across!" He pushed her onto the far side of the stream. Bear Claw Woman led him along the passages and into the big room where she had found her staff. Her mind was whirling, she understood that he had heard her unspoken command to Guardian, but he hadn't realized what it was. Had the animal toppled them into the water, she had no idea what would have happened, but now she had a plan! She was careful now, to guide him deeper and deeper into the inner cave. She couldn't see the torch, but she didn't have to. Any time now, it would sputter and go out. Then they would be plunged into darkness so deep that there was not even the tiniest bit of light. Just as she was thinking this, the torch sputtered, flickered and went out.

"You Bitch!" the dreamer snarled, jerking and shoving her about. "You want to play games, do you? Well Quenquel is very good at playing games! Where are more torches? And don't tell me that you don't know where they are! You wouldn't be such a fool as to lead me in here and risk being left in total darkness!"

Bear Claw Woman made her move. She was small and of slight-build so it made it easier for her to bend, ignoring the pain in her arm and thrust her leg between his. Then throwing all her weight forward, she jerked him off balance. They went down. He snarled, then grabbed, but she was too quick for him. Bear Claw Woman broke free and on hands and knees scrambled forward. She knew exactly where she was. Just in front of her was the root. She felt frantically about. Her fingers brushed against it and she lost no time climbing.

Once perched safely out of reach, she closed her eyes and directed all her power toward the dreamer's mind.

A blue glow lightened the spot where the dreamer lay, his entire body thrashing in agony. An ear splitting scream issued from him. Then silence. Bear Claw Woman stayed where she was. Already she could hear Bull Elk and the women entering the room. The glimmer of their torch was like the sun on a bright day.

"Woof!" Guardian whirled about at the base of the root. Beyond, the dreamer groaned. *At least I didn't quite kill him* she thought. *Running Bison wouldn't have liked that!*

Where are you?" Bull Elk shouted through the echoing cacophony of wolf barks.

"Hush! Guardian," she called softly. "Over here, along the wall to your left! The dreamer is about a finger's distance beyond. Get him first, I am fine!" She began scrambling down, Guardian licking and nuzzling her all over in greeting.

"What did you do to him?" Bull Elk held up the torch, studying the dreamer's still body.

"Be careful! He is full of tricks!" Yellow Bird shouted.

"You didn't kill him, did you?" Bull Elk asked worriedly.

"I don't think so. but Yellow Bird is right, don't trust him!"

"Don't worry!" muttered Bull Elk. "I've had enough of his tricks for one day." He kicked the limp form, then handed the torch to Yellow Bird to hold and jerking several thongs from his waist pouch he tied the dreamer again.

"I nearly refused to believe my eyes when Guardian went this way! Where did he think he was going?"

"Bear Claw Woman stepped up beside him, massaging her sore shoulder. "Out the back way," she answered grinning.

"There's a back way out?" he asked surprise obvious on his face.

Bear Claw Woman shook her head. "Not that I am aware of, but he seemed convinced!

"You mean that you could have gotten lost in here in the dark and we'd never have found you."

"Guardian would have," Bear Claw Woman reminded him. "Besides, just how far was he going to get with one torch?"

Just then Quenquel groaned again and began to move. "On your feet!" Bull Elk jerked on the bindings. "I've had enough trouble out of you. You will be sorry for this!"

The dreamer glared at him, but with another jerk he got to his feet. Bear Claw Woman led the way back, Guardian growled and glared back at the dreamer all the way back to the stream. Here Raven and the other hunters met them, Young Wolf leading them at a furious pace.

"I think we must do something about him!" Bull Elk stated. They sat around the hearth well after dark, discussing the escape. "He pulled sort of 'pain spell' on me! I couldn't move. It is dangerous for anyone to be in there with him!"

"What can we do? Running Bison was very explicit. He wants him alive!"

"Why don't you feed him the sleeping drought which he prepared for me?" Yellow Bird offered, from her place beside Bull Elk.

"I have a better idea, Raven said, "Do we have any of those tubers he used to control Whispering Wind?"

"No, but I think I can find a place where they grow," Bear Claw Woman offered. "Why didn't I think of that? That is the perfect solution."

"I still like the idea of putting his eyes out with a burning stick!" Elk Caller muttered.

"But he could still use his mind," Bear Claw Woman pointed out. "With the tuber he won't have one."

"How long will it take you to find the tubers?" Calling Wolf asked. "I don't remember seeing any around here."

"There is a place, about three valleys east of here, where they grow. I know because accidentally I dug them and put them in our food. Whispering Wind and I suffered the consequences of that meal for days. This is how I knew their effect when we found Whispering Wind. If I leave early in the morning, I can be back before dark with an ample supply."

"I don't like the idea of you making such a strenuous trip in your condition!" protested Raven. "Calling Wolf is just as capable."

"Nonsense!" Bear Claw Woman sputtered. "There is nothing wrong with me! Besides, Calling Wolf doesn't know where these plants grow and explaining it to him would be difficult."

"Then I am going with you and you are riding on a travois!" Raven said stubbornly. "You will not take any chances with yourself or our child! Already you have acted foolishly! That maniac could have killed you, or worse! No more!"

"You are welcome to go with me." Bear Claw Woman answered. "I never thought that you wouldn't. But the walking will be good for both of us. And I will go carefully. It is not a difficult journey. We will take Ash Branch as well and she can be getting familiar with the healing plants of these mountains at the same time."

Raven studied her suspiciously for a time, but eventually gave in. They left just after sunrise, Guardian, Raven and Ash Branch accompanying Bear Claw Woman. The weather was fine, the sun bright and the sky clear. Beneath the tree where Bear Claw Woman had slain the Great Spirit Bear, she directed Ash Branch and Calling Wolf to where the tubers grew. They collected enough to keep the dreamer's mind muddled far longer than entire turning of the moon. Then they returned to the cave in the canyon.

By the next evening, the dreamer was no longer a threat to anyone! Another moon passed before Running Bison began heading toward where the camps would gather. He was presently with Iguana and the former Savage camp, now peaceful gatherers in their valleys to the far south. By Mid-Summer, all the camps would once again gather in the valley beyond the quarry. Before that, they would have another 'special' gathering, where Humming Bird died.

*   *   *

*We will be there in a hand of days. Is everything ready?* Running Bison asked tiredly.

*Everything is ready. I have been in contact with Laughing Water and the other groups. Everyone should arrive within a pair of days of each other.* Raven clutched Bear Claw Woman's hand tightly. He still did not like this mind talking, no matter how frequently he did it and lately it had been almost daily. There were nearly two double hands of camps that were to converge on the site selected for the sacrifice of Quenquel. So far all would arrive nearly at the same time.

*Has the dreamer caused you any more trouble?*

*None!* Bear Claw Woman replied. *Calling Wolf has made sure that he was given the tuber every day. He is docile as a baby. When it is time for the sacrifice, however, the men have decided that he will be aware of exactly what is happening. A hand of days before Calling Wolf is taking away the drug, so both the withdrawal and the sacrifice will be suffered with complete awareness. I will tell him so that he can begin right away. We will be careful to keep him well guarded.*

*Do that! I realize that he has caused you a great deal of trouble with his attempted escapes, but guard him carefully, even more so now! Raven, perhaps it would be best if the men made a cage to hold him, one similar to how the savages made those pole enclosures. Then leave the wolves to guard him as well as a pair of hunters. No matter what it takes! Once on the trail he will be doubly dangerous.*

*Whatever happens, Bear Claw Woman, it is imperative that he is brought successfully to the altar. If this sacrifice is not made, I fear that the spirits will turn away from the people completely! It is that important!*

*We all know that! The hunters are doing the best they can. We will see you at the appointed valley in a hand of days! I hope the rest of the camps will be there already or soon after! At least with so many, there will be more to share the watching. Until then...*

Raven called to the hunters, "Running Bison suggests that we cage the dreamer so that he is unable to escape while we are on the trail, but I have a better idea!"

"What?" The hunters crowded close.

I purpose that we cover his eyes so that essentially, he is blinded. Then not only will he be off balance and unable to get away, even should he find a way to cast a spell on us, but he will also not know where we are taking him. So far he realizes; I am sure, that we are saving him for something, or someone, but he has no idea what really is in store for him. By blinding him, he can have no idea."

"That would mean that we need not keep him in a moving cage. But wouldn't it be simpler just to keep him on the drug until we get there? He is mindless while on it!"

"It would mean a longer wait at the other end. Running Bison was very specific; he wants him to be completely aware of what his fate will be. That is important."

"So, how do we cover his eyes so that he can still breathe and yet not see? We can't place a bladder over his head," Bull Elk frowned.

"I suggest that we pack his eyes with a poultice and bind it in place with a strip of breech clot. The leather is soft enough to conform to his face and the poultice would mean that he is forced to keep his eyes tightly closed."

Raven nodded, "That is an excellent idea, Running Antelope! He will be forced to keep his eyes closed or suffer getting pieces of the poultice in them. He can have no idea where we take him and if everyone is careful not to speak of it within his hearing, there is no way that he will."

"Besides, with him blinded, he cannot try his 'mind tricks' on us!" muttered Bull Elk.

"No matter how important this sacrifice is, we will not hesitate to kill him if he tries to escape!" Calling Wolf rose. "I don't care what Running Bison says!"

"Then we had better make sure that he does not. For Running Bison was very clear about that! We must deliver him both alive and unharmed." Raven rose, "You and Bear Claw Woman had better get together with Ash Branch and come up with a poultice!"

Calling Wolf nodded and rose. He had his own ideas of what should be in the poultice unfortunately, Raven had indicated that the dreamer was to arrive unharmed! He sighed in frustration. It had been a hard moon for the hunters. There had been little to do beyond watch the dreamer and since the tuber, that had not been a problem. Still, they had been careful. But they were all keyed up. A pair of quick hunting trips; one for the first shift of watchers and one for the second group helped. The rest of the time they had been cooped up in the cave day and night. Everyone was restless for action of some kind.

"Do you think he suspects?" Bull Elk questioned.

"Not unless someone has told him what we intend," Running Antelope replied. "I don't think either of the women know and even if they did, I doubt they would tell him. I know that Yellow Bird was sympathetic with him at the beginning, but she has stayed as far from him as possible since they got here. She even refused to take his food to him."

"She wouldn't help him!" Bull Elk said angrily. "Just because in the beginning he had her fooled! That doesn't mean she would do anything to help him now!"

"Easy!" Calling Wolf calmed his old friend, "No one was implying that she would. Only that she is frightened of him. That is mainly why I have made sure that only we men go near him. It isn't that we don't trust the women; we don't trust the dreamer! There is no telling what kind of tricks he would try and the women are all too small to be able to deal with him."

"If you remember, Bear Claw Woman dealt with him quite well," Raven reminded them.

"But it shouldn't have been necessary!" Bull Elk flushed very red. "If I had been doing the guarding like I should have, it wouldn't have been necessary for her to endanger both herself and your child. I would never be able to forgive myself if she had been injured because of my carelessness!"

"As it turned out, she was probably better suited to deal with him than any of us. That power bolt she shot at him nearly killed him!" Raven replied. "I have learned that those who try to hurt her usually suffer. But I am glad that she was a fast thinker. I like the idea of the blinding of the dreamer. It will confuse him and make him easier to handle. Also, we will be moving before the effect of the drug wears off. He won't know how far we have traveled or where he is. Therefore, if he can't see, he can't recognize familiar landmarks. I am sure that if he saw people whom he recognizes, he would understand what we are up to. Then he will surely try to escape, no matter what!"

"I also suggest that no one speak to him, except to give him simple direct orders," Calling Wolf offered.

"I think it would be in order if no one talked at all," Bull Elk said. "That way no one will accidentally give away what we are up to. Also, it will further confuse him."

"An excellent idea," Calling Wolf nodded. "Now if we are decided, I will prepare the poultice and we will be ready to leave at dawn. We may be required to get him there alive and unharmed, but no one said he had to be in perfect health! I have no intention of feeding him before we leave. He can have water along the way, but only enough food to keep him walking!"

"There is no need to starve him," Raven sighed. "Much as I would like to. We will be moving at a punishing speed, at least for the women, but he will need to keep up with us. I have no intention of his riding a travois. It worked well when you brought him to the cave to use the double noose method. I see no reason to change that. And if he tries anything and I mean anything, Bear Claw Woman will hit him again with a power bolt. So now let's all get some sleep. Morning will be here soon enough!"

Calling Wolf shook Bull Elk awake well before the first light of dawn. "Come and help me get the dreamer ready," he whispered.

"Yah! Just let me pull on my clothes and I'll be with you," Elk Yawned sleepily. "Did you get everything ready?"

Calling Wolf nodded. "I have the poultice and blindfold ready and checked the nooses to make sure they are strong. I wanted to make sure that he was trussed and ready before we took him from the deep cave. That way he will have no idea which way we go other than from the warmth of the sun. I do not know how to do anything about that, but he should be so confused for a few days that he won't even be thinking about which direction we go. The pain from the drug withdrawal should keep him occupied for a pair of days at least. After that he will be disoriented for a pair more before he is really aware and by that time we should be nearly to the valley."

Bull Elk merely grunted. He followed Calling Wolf down the passage, rubbing sleep from his eyes. He had lain awake far into the night and then slept soundly. Had not Wolf wakened him; he would have slept for at least another hand of time.

Calling Wolf lighted the torch inside the cave room and sent the guard wolf to the living cave, relieved of duty. Then he fed the man, keeping his hands tied tightly behind his back. As Bull Elk held the dreamer to the ground; Calling Wolf placed the poultice over his eyes and tied the blindfold tightly. The men spoke not a single word. When they were finished, Calling Wolf doused the torch and they returned to the living cave where everyone else was now up and completing the preparations both for a last meal and leaving. The travois were already loaded except for their sleeping furs and now the wolves were put into harness. As soon as a quick meal was eaten, the hearth fire was smothered and Calling Wolf went to lead the dreamer from his prison. He was looped with the nooses and one hunter took either end. Throughout, not a word was spoken. Raven led the group down into the canyon and up the trail.

*     *     *

Quenquel was confused. He realized that his food was laced with the dreaming tuber, but there was nothing he could do about it. So, he ate it. He drifted mindlessly in a stupor. How long he did not know. Then he realized that something was happening. First, he was blindfolded, and then his food was no longer laced with the drug. He could feel the first feathering of withdrawal along his nerves. He clinched his teeth together and fought it. He needed to have his wits with him. Even now he began to fight the floating feeling from the drug. Something was taking place and if he was to escape, he had to be able to concentrate and take advantage of any opportunity. His ears were his only weapons of defense at the moment. He felt the stone beneath his feet, then dirt, then heard the birds calling. He knew they were once again on the trail. He felt the rise in the trail and then they turned east at the top of the canyon.

As the day wore on, Quenquel could tell that they were traveling east and then turned south. But this did him little good because he had no idea where they were to begin with, other than in the mountains. Perhaps they were traveling to the plains. He had no idea. This whole capture had him confused. *Why didn't they just kill me? What are they up to? Where are they taking me? Why?* He stumbled along feeling the nooses tighten and loosen on his neck. It was eerie that no one said a single word. He was given water and food at regular intervals. He was not really mistreated. But there was no doubt what-so-ever that he was their prisoner. As the day began to cool, they stopped and he was tied to a tree for the night. He was allowed, with help to complete his bodily functions, but still, not a word.

He slept little that night. The air cooled and he was forced to shiver for body warmth. No one cared to drape a robe about him. The withdrawal of the drug was quite painful now, his muscles jerking as nerves protested. He knew that it would take several days before the drug was completely out of his system. Actually, the stress of the day had helped pump it out from his body, but now, with no activity, his muscles twitched painfully.

At dawn, again he was given food and water, then as the day before, they moved, all day. That night he was less cold, indicating that they were at a lower elevation. The downward tilt of the trail also suggested this. That night he did get some sleep. The effects of the drug were all but gone from his body. His senses were nearly returned to their normal levels. But he was careful to act confused and more disoriented than he was. His ears picked up the sounds of streams, various bird calls and his nose detected various odors, of trees, flowers, forest must. He could almost visualize the terrain through which they traveled.

Secured to a tree, that third night he began working actively at his bonds. His wrists were slippery with blood before he gave up. There was no way he could wear through the tough leather. He could not get enough leverage to rub the bindings against the rough tree bark and even soaked with blood, the leather did not give. He nearly pulled his arms from the sockets in an effort to break free. Morning found him still securely in place. Even his spirits had deserted him, no matter how he pleaded and called to them in his mind.

At the end of the fourth day he sensed the tenor of excitement from his captors. They stopped earlier than previously. Although he was tied just as securely, activity in the camp was far less. It was almost as if there were fewer people moving about. *That's it! Most of them have gone from the camp! But why? We stopped early, are they meeting with others and if so, where? I haven't heard a spoken word in days!* This was enough to double his efforts toward freedom. Each evening and morning, someone had inspected his bindings, adjusting them. This night he had tightened his wrist muscles, forcing them to expand with the might of his mind. Now, they were looser than they had ever been. He had also swelled his body when they attached him to the tree. Now he had a bit more space. Frantically, but with controlled purpose, he worked. He rubbed the bindings against the bark of the tree; even the continuous itching of the poultice on his eyes was not allowed to distract him from his task. Footsteps alerted him and he stilled, pretending to sleep. As the hunter checked his bindings, he tightened his muscles again and satisfied, the hunter retreated.

Quenquel waited... Finally, convinced it was safe, again he went to work on the bindings. Finally the leather began to yield. Then it snapped and he was able to free his hands. He worked the bindings away with his fingers, careful to remain quiet. Then slowly he brought his hands around to the front and silently removed the blindfold and hated poultice. He rubbed his eyes with his tunic sleeve then cautiously opened them.

The moon was almost blinding in its brilliance! Coals glowed dully from the campfire. Just beyond a sleeping figure snored within the confines of a hide shelter. Quenquel looked no further; there was no time to waste. With a smooth nearly liquid movement he leaped to his feet, now free of their tether and making no more sound than a shadow, melted into the deep shadows beneath the trees. Almost with his first move, an ear-splitting howl shattered the night. The sleeping hunter leaped to his feet and already the wolf was lunging into the deep shadows in hot pursuit! Running Antelope was fast on his heels.

Quenquel did not have time for stealth. He crashed blindly into the brush, branches grabbing his tunic sleeves, tangling in his hair and wrapping around his legs. Brambles snagged, vines hindered and with a solid thud, the wolf landed on his back, driving him off balance onto the forest floor and knocking the wind from his lungs. *No!!!!!!* Silently he wailed.

Kicking, he tried to dislodge the wolf. But the animal had a firm grip on his tunic with her teeth. Within heartbeats, the hunter was there, grabbing his arm and jerking him rudely upright. Then a strong right fist crashed into his jaw and with a grunt, Quenquel slithered to the ground. Running Antelope muttered under his breath and then dragged the unconscious culprit out of the brush and hefted him onto his shoulder. He staggered back to the camp with him and dumped him unceremoniously onto the ground beneath the tree. Angrily Running Antelope trussed him viciously back around the tree and slapped the blindfold with poultice back into place and jerked it tight. Finally, he retied the feet.

Then with reaction setting in, he gathered up the severed bindings and disposed of them with shaking fingers.

*So close! What would I have done if he had succeeded in this escape? How could I have explained it? What justification could I have presented for being asleep?* Running Antelope tossed his faithful wolf a generous helping of fresh venison and gave her a thorough petting. Then once again, he checked the bindings of the dreamer and made a bladder of hot tea. The remainder of the night he sat at the fire, keeping it alive and himself wide-awake. He worried about how he would explain the bruise which was sure to appear on the dreamer's face come morning, but that was nothing compared to the explanation he would had to have given were the man gone.

*     *     *

Running Bison was tired. His whole camp was tired. They had been traveling nonstop for moons it seemed; going from one group of strangers to another, delivering their message. Most were glad to hear that the Savage dreamer was a captive and would pay for the deaths he had caused. Some groups could hardly wait to head for the designated valley, others merely shrugged. Their loved ones were dead, nothing Running Bison or anyone else could do would bring them back. What was the point? They put it all behind them and went on with their lives. Many groups, particularly those of the Gatherers, were so shattered and scattered there was no one to deliver the message to.

Iguana and what had once been the camp of the Savages were ashamed. They had botched the task themselves and now it had fallen to someone else. Iguana, himself, was too old and infirm to make the trip, but several men of the camp elected to travel back with Running Bison. Among them were Broken Branch, Green Parrot and Walking Man. Over the three moons they had been with Running Bison, they had become firm friends with the man and many of his hunters. It was, in fact, unlikely that they would ever return to their former camp. They had left no family behind and it was a long distance to travel just to return to that camp. Green Parrot's mate was happy traveling with Running Bison's camp. She and Robe Maker had become fast friends.

Now Running Bison's camp was settling into the very place where once Quenquel had erected his altar and sacrificed so many, including some of their own. Green Parrot searched around and found the scattered altar stones. With the help of several others, he rebuilt the hated edifice. Many other small groups were already in the valley when they arrived. Now they waited for those bringing in the dreamer. It was almost a celebratory mood that spread through the camps. They had not long to wait. Running Bison had arrived at sun-high. At evening Raven and Calling Wolf and their group trotted into the valley from the north. They had the dreamer trussed not far away!

Now all was ready. The next night signaled the arrival of the full moon! Green Parrot had made replicas of the obsidian knife, the head dress and the cloak. It had been decided to forgo the fermented blood drink. But every member of every camp would be waiting, silently, until it was time. Then they would cheer!

Very late, well after the moon had risen when Calling Wolf, Raven, Bull Elk and the women slipped into their camp. Raven checked the bindings on the dreamer, finding all well. Running Antelope greeted them with a cheerful smile and shrugged when Bull Elk offered to take over, but he shook his head. He was wide awake. So he remained on his lone vigil while the others slept. Quenquel was awake, but unaware the others had returned. As far as he knew, only the one hunter was in the camp. It made little difference. He realized he had lost his chance, probably his last chance, to escape whatever fate awaited him. He was beginning to have bad feelings about that! His one glimpse had assured him of where he was. He already had a pretty good idea. His imagination supplied the rest.

The next morning, once again, most of the people left the camp. This time, however, it was Bull Elk in charge of guarding the dreamer. Running Antelope got some sleep, until sun-high and then he also trotted off to the main gathering. He was glad to turn responsibility over to Bull Elk. That man was taking no chances! He checked the dreamer's bindings at regular intervals. He set his wolf just beyond the captive with instruction to alert him if the man so much as wiggled wrong! He stayed within sight of the man at all times. The day passed slowly.

The June sun was unseasonably warm. Bull Elk had stripped down to moccasins and breech clot and settled in the shade of a huge oak tree. Here he sat whittling on a stick to pass the time. Late in the day several men from the main camp filed quietly in and settled beside him, talking in mere whispers.

"Everything is ready," Raven squatted next to Bull Elk. "When the moon begins to rise we will escort him into the camp. When everyone is in place, then and only then, will the blindfold be removed."

"Do you think he will fight?" Crying Coyote asked.

"He won't go without!" Bull Elk replied. "He has tried repeatedly to escape," he sighed. "I will be glad when it is over. This is bloody business. I can't say that I like any of it!"

"Would you rather we just let him go?" Crying Coyote raised an eyebrow.

Bull Elk shook his head, "Of course not! But I still don't like it. Leaves a bad taste in my mouth, if you know what I mean."

Everyone nodded. They sat studying the trussed man beyond the camp. Each had their own thoughts, remembering those dead friends and loved ones that had suffered at the dreamer's hands. No one really liked what they were about to do, but they were determined to go through with it. They were each grateful that it was Hollow Bone who had to do the actual deed.

Back at the main camp, Hollow Bone was preparing himself for the grisly task before him. It was not within his nature to take human life. Only the knowledge that this death was necessary, made it possible for him to comply. He had eaten nothing since the previous night. He had isolated himself from all others since. Now he made his way to the stream and thoroughly cleansed, washing with the sacred soap. Then he used a stick shredded with his teeth to pull the tangles from his hair. He left it hanging free so that the headdress would fit. Then he oiled his body as Green Parrot had instructed. In his shelter lay the head dress; cloak and white breech clot that he would wear. He had been instructed about the signs to be painted on his face and the paint was also waiting. He returned to his shelter.

The entire valley seemed to be waiting with breaths held. The sun slipped from the sky and people moved restlessly about their camps. From the north came a delegation, bringing the dreamer in. A final hush fell over the valley. Not a human sound could be heard. And they waited...

The moon began to rise; a huge orange orb. Slowly, majestically it slipped full above the ridge. Hollow Bone donned his regalia, picked up the unfamiliar obsidian knife and slipped into his position before the altar. Then the drum sounded. Quenquel jerked once. Calling Wolf removed the blindfold and washed the dreamer's face with clean water. He frowned, noticing the dark bruising on the man's temple. Shrugging he cut the ankle tether so the man could climb the altar steps. Then with Bull Elk on his other side they ushered their captive toward the altar.

Quenquel struggled! "At least give me the drink!" he shouted.

They ignored him, dragging him kicking and fighting toward the altar. At the base he managed to throw Bull Elk off balance and they all went down in a welter of bodies and legs. But the hunters quickly sorted themselves out and jerked him erect once more, "Act like a man!" Calling Wolf snarled.

Now the drums beat in frenzy. People were shouting and dancing about freshly ignited fires. Green Parrot and Broken Branch leaped to the base of the altar and screamed in his face, causing Quenquel to jerk back. Then he was hustled unceremoniously up the steps. He jerked free and threw himself from the altar, landing with a bone-jarring thud driving his shoulder into the ground. Before he could even catch his breath Calling Wolf and Bull Elk were beside him once again and they yanked him upright and with impatient curses hauled him back up the steps.

They called for help and Green Parrot and Broken Branch leaped to their aid. Now each man grabbed an arm or leg and held the struggling dreamer down. They stretched him cruelly across the altar stone, holding him there with brute strength. Still, he struggled. He bunched his muscles and tried to break free. To no avail! Then he began shaking. Sweat poured from his body. He gritted his teeth and spit hatred at those holding him. Then Hollow Bone stepped forward. Quenquel's eyes grew round with surprise and then filled with hatred. There was absolutely nothing he could do.

Through his mind passed all those he had sacrificed. It was all very clear. One by one he replayed them, just as they had happened. The very first sacrifice had given him a tremendous thrill. To hold the still-beating heart of the strong hunter in his hands and let the life blood run down his throat. The entire camp was cheering madly! They had been celebrating for hands of time and everyone was falling down drunk.

That hunter had been followed by another and another all enemies of the camp, all strangers. And when he ran out of strangers, anyone who had criticized him quickly came under scrutiny. Then Humming Bird had become a danger and he had dealt with her the only way he knew. He closed his eyes.

Hollow Bone stood before the altar. Inside he was shaking. He was not sure that he could do this! He glanced out across the waiting crowd. Now the drums were silent, as were the people. Holding their collective breaths, waiting.... for him to continue. Running Bison stood closest. Beside his was Whispering Wind. He remembered what this man had done to her. He stepped forward.

Hollow Bone raised the black obsidian serrated knife and held it out for all to see. It was beautifully made, sharper than anything he had ever held. With quivering hands he started to bring down the blade. Then stopped and raised it to begin again. Quenquel took that moment to open his eyes. Hollow Bone nearly lost courage. He had practiced the movement time and time again; but never on a living victim. Suddenly it was as if something took over control of his arms. With a sure decisive downward drive, the knife flashed in firelight as it whistled through the air. There was hardly any resistance as it entered the warm flesh. With a quick twist, again coming from beyond Hollow Bone, the knife sheared vessels and veins and he lifted the still-beating heart into the cool night air. He did not drink of the blood however. He merely showed the heart to those waiting.

The night was absolutely still, not a single breeze; yet leaves on nearby trees rustled, almost like voices speaking. Warm breezes caressed Hollow Bone's face and lifted his hair. They played through the flames of the nearby fires and then as quickly as they came, they vanished. Twinkling ignited in the clear night skies as new fires were kindled. And a single star fell, trailing fire to the ground.

The hunters released the limbs of the dead dreamer. He wasn't going anywhere now. They didn't feel the elation that they had expected. Green Parrot had a bad taste in his mouth. He discovered that he had bitten his own tongue. Hollow Bone was shaking so badly he nearly dropped the bloody knife. As it was, he threw the repulsive thing as far from him as he could and then rushed down the steps, nearly stumbling in his haste. He ran to his shelter and ripped off the hateful cloak, head dress and breech clot. He wiped the oil from his quivering body with a handy rabbit fur. Falling to his knees, he crouched into dry gut retching heaves.

It was then he saw the blood. It was on his hands, had run up his arms and now was all over his face. He staggered from the shelter and ran to the stream, throwing himself in. He scrubbed and washed the filthy brand from his body. Then and only then, did he crawl from the water and return to his shelter. He dried his body and then pulled on his old familiar tunic and breech clot. He still did not feel clean and free of the taint, but he felt better.

Green Parrot and Broken Branch dragged the corpse from the altar and far from camp. They left it there for predators. When they returned, it was to find others already dismantling the altar. One group of hunters was already breaking the altar stones into pebbles, not stopping so long as there was a piece larger than a closed fist. Calling Wolf had collected the cape and headdress and they were smoldering in a nearby fire. The obsidian knife had been collected and given to Bear Claw Woman. She wrapped it in her ceremonial rabbit skin and tucked it away on her travois. As the camps settled down for the night, not a single clue remained of the grisly offering.

Well beyond the valley, scavengers fought over a carcass. Coyotes dragged the viscera into the underbrush and gulped hasty bites. A cougar screamed as it claimed an arm and a giant grizzly bear huffed and drove it away. The coyotes reclaimed the leavings when he finished. By morning there remained a few strands of hair still clinging to the skull. Ravens and vultures feasted on the head, picking out bits of brain and tags of flesh.

\*     \*     \*

Hollow Bone staggered to the top of the nearby bluff. He felt that he still had blood on his hands, no matter that he had washed them repeatedly. He had not slept all night. Again and again in his mind he replayed the 'act of sacrifice'. He was sure that a spirit beyond himself had taken his hand and completed the grisly deed. His legs were still shaking and his head ached so badly he could hardly think coherently.

He found a flat rock and settled his hide there, climbing tiredly into position. He had made the drink earlier. But now, just as the sun rose, he needed to contact his spirit helper again. He swallowed the drink in a single gulp and then sighed. He waited...

The spiral of color lifted him and carried him into the dark void. Then as usual the light appeared and he found himself floating above the land. *Where am I?*

*You are in the place where the spirits have gone, those that you released.* A voice answered at his elbow. Hollow Bone jerked, startled. He had not noticed that he was not alone. Beside him floated the translucent image of the great Wolf Spirit clearer, than he had ever seen him. They seemed to be walking, but there was no ground beneath their feet. Beyond, however, Hollow Bone could see the faint images of people. Many people!

Have I released all of them?" he asked in surprise.

*Yes, all these people. They were trapped in the darkness, unable to escape to the land of the Ancestors. Now they are free. No one honored them with a 'walking the wind' ceremony. Their spirits have been very unhappy here!*

"Is that why we sacrificed the dreamer; so that their spirits could be free?"

*They were victims! They did not choose to be sacrificed! They were given no honor with their deaths; their bodies were tossed away like carrion!*

"But isn't that just what we just did with the dreamer?

*It is! That is a fitting fate, don't you think? His spirit for theirs! He will, of course, be an unhappy spirit and will probably cause trouble in the future, but to free all of these, it was a fair exchange! He cannot leave this place, the valley where he died, so people should avoid it from now on. There should be a marker left behind, something to warn others to stay away. And of course, spread the word among the camps.*

"I will do that," Hollow Bone nodded. Then he watched as gossamer images of people, some he even knew, slowly moved away and faded as they were lifted by an invisible hand, toward the ancestor fires in the sky. Suddenly he felt much better. Then the clouds began to swirl and he opened his eyes to find himself still sitting on the rock atop the bluff. The first sleepy birds were just waking and twittering to greet the sun. He gathered up his things and followed the path down into the valley.

\*       \*       \*

Already camps were loading shelters onto travois. People were quiet. Hollow Bone went to where Running Bison and Calling Wolf were sharing an early bowl of tea with several others.

"We need to put up some sort of marker, something which will warn people not to come into this valley anymore," he said.

"What sort of a marker?" Calling Wolf asked.

Hollow Bone shrugged, "I have no idea!" he responded. "The spirit said people should not come here anymore. The spirit of the dreamer is imprisoned here. It is no longer a good place for people to be!"

Running Bison nodded, "I have an idea of what is needed. I have seen markers beside places of bad water. I think we can erect something like that at either end of this valley before we leave. Already others are anxious to be gone from this place. I can understand. I don't want to linger here either. Come along," he motioned to several men. "We will get this task completed and leave this place ourselves!" He led the way, followed by a hand of hunters.

They moved swiftly to the far end of the valley. Here Running Bison instructed them in building a monument to warn others that the valley was a bad place. While they lugged huge stones and built up a carrion he used a sharp graver on a large piece of sandstone. He carved deeply into the soft stone the open hand and below that a drawing of a dead deer. He only hoped that others understood his message! Then they moved to the near end and repeated the process. While they were doing this, the remainder of the camp was loading the travois and harnessing the wolves. A somber gloom had settled over the place, even though the sun was shining brightly.

It was still a moon until the Mid-Summer Gathering and that valley was less than a hand of days, walk. Some of the camps were going hunting in the surrounding mountains. Others were heading farther north. But all would gather at the next full moon, to renew their bonds and to hear what the Chosen One had to say.

# CHAPTER 30

I intend to go directly to the valley and get the camp set up," Running Bison announced to the hunters waiting for his signal. "There is much to be done before the ceremony. We can hunt in the mountains there and it will give the knappers plenty of time to craft tools and gather blanks for the next season. Also I am sure that the women will enjoy hunting small game there and resting before the long trek back to the winter valley."

"I wish to make a journey to pay respect to Crooked Spirit: Hollow Bone said.

The silent hunters merely nodded. They understood that dreamers walked a different path. After the way Hollow Bone had just accomplished his grisly task, they felt he probably wanted to cleanse his spirit. What better place that where the venerable old dreamer had passed. For Hollow Bone, it would be a 'spirit' place.

Whispering Wind and Bear Claw Woman were nearly inseparable during the day when the men were involved with their own tasks. Bear Claw Woman was fascinated with Wind's newest child; a little girl only a hand of moons old. Bear Claw Woman could hardly wait until Morning Star was born. But she wisely said nothing about her knowledge. "What is it with Bull Elk?" Whispering Wind asked quietly, "He is acting really odd!"

"That is because he has found a woman," Bear Claw Woman replied. "Yellow Bird has him all tied up in knots inside. She can't decide if she wants to run away, or after him. You can hardly blame him for being confused from her conflicting signals."

"Yellow Bird; isn't that the woman from the desert camp?"

"Yes, she came with Ash Branch. They were friends there and she had no one else so she came along, or at least that is what she tells me. The hunters have a slightly different story."

"Do you think she is good enough for Bull Elk?"

Bear Claw Woman nodded, "She has a very good heart. She might have made mistakes, but then so have we all. Now tell me about Calf. I don't see him with the camp."

"No, he is traveling with Green Moss and Crying Coyote. They left earlier and are hunting for a few days before joining us. Calf wanted to go hunting with Uncle Coyote. He is crazy about hunting. It is all he can talk about and he carries that ridiculous atlatl and dart which Coyote made for him, even to his furs at night."

"It is hard to imagine that he is more than a hand of seasons old. Soon we will be giving him his adult name and he will be gone!" Bear Claw Woman sighed, "Where has the time gone? It seems that only last moon we were living in the cave in the canyon. Now look at us! You have a pair of beautiful children and soon, I will have one as well. I always knew you would catch Running Bison's eye without even trying, but who would have ever thought that I, plain old Sage, would find at mate as wonderful as Raven?"

Whispering Wind gave a most un-matronly snort, "Plain old Chosen One. Quiet little Keeper of the Ancient Relics! You have always underestimated yourself. Look at me! All I have to commend me are my looks and already they are beginning to fade!" She patted her well-rounded posterior. "I will never regain the slenderness I had before babies. But you have always been special. It took courage to go into the mountains the way you did with only Obsidian as company. And it took courage for you to come into that death camp and search for me! If you hadn't..."

"Raven would have found you and returned you to the Bison Camp and you would have been mated with Running Bison much sooner," Bear Claw Woman reminded her.

"Perhaps, but then who would have taught you the ways of The People?" Wind smiled. "I am pleased that the spirits chose me for that task."

Then they entered a new part of the mountains and Bear Claw Woman called Ash Branch to her and began teaching her the plants and their uses. Slowly the camp meandered toward the valley. The mountains were very dry. Hot winds swept down from the north, but no rain fell. The grass sprouted green and fresh, but in a few days was burned dry and brittle. There was little food for the grazers. The browsers faired little better. Trees and shrubs were late to leaf out and they only put on the minimum number of leaves, conserving the precious water their roots were able to draw. Few elk calves or deer fawns had been dropped this spring. And even the predators seemed to understand that it would be a lean season. Wolf packs that ordinarily would have whelped a hand of cubs only dropped one or a pair. All-of-nature seemed to be in-tune with itself.

When they reached the valley of the Gathering, they were amazed. Where once a wide swiftly-flowing stream had been, now all there was is a weed-choked trickle.

"We will have to clean out a section of the water before we can even bathe and it hardly looks drinkable!" Winter Rain wrinkled her nose.

"There has been little rain this spring," Bear Claw Woman said, "It is a shame. This was a beautiful valley the last time I was here. Now the grass is spotty and already brown and dying. I can even see a sand dune beginning to form at the far end of the valley. The plants, which once grew along this stream no longer, live her. They have been replaced by these noxious weeds!" She wrinkled her nose.

"Do you think there is enough water provided by this stream to support the Gathering?" Ash Branch asked.

"Perhaps we should ask Running Bison," Whispering Wind bit her lip. "Although I have no idea what we can do about it if there is not."

"Move the site of the Gathering closer to the Muddy River," Bear Claw Woman replied.

"But how can we contact all the camps?" Wind exclaimed, "Oh! I forgot!" she rolled her eyes. "Just close your eyes and call out a name!" She grinned at Bear Claw Woman, "There are times that 'mind talking' of yours is most convenient."

"Well if there is a chance we aren't staying here, I'm not clearing the weeds," Winter Rain sat back, a hand full of weeds dripping from her fist. She threw them onto a pile she had already pulled.

"We won't have long to wait," Ash Branch motioned to the west. "The hunters are coming in right now and if I'm not mistaken Running Bison is the one under that big buck."

Shortly the hunters joined the women beside the stream. Thunder Cloud frowned and kicked at the pile of weeds. "Waste of time trying to clean that!" he muttered. "Water's gone bad. Not fit to drink. See, even the wolves won't touch it." He glanced at Running Bison, "What do we do now?"

"We have enough water with us for tonight," Running Bison unloaded his deer. "But this meat has to be processed quickly in this heat or it will rot. We all know that. I can't see leaving it. There is little game in these mountains as it is. I think it would be best if we sent a group with the water stomachs and they carried drinkable water from elsewhere. Who can remember how far it is to a clean source of water?" he called to the entire camp.

"There was a stream we passed about sun-high yesterday," Raven replied.

"It is nearly that far to the Muddy River," Calling Wolf added. "If we left with the wolves and carried the travois poles and water stomachs on our backs, we could make it and back well before dark in one day. We can all move quickly with a light load. But water is heavy so the return trip would be much slower. The question we must decide is whether it is easier on the animals to go to the Muddy River."

"The breaks for nearly a hand of distance from there are very rough. It would be hard going pulling heavily loaded travois," Running Bison remarked.

"Then it's back to the last stream we passed," Calling Wolf nodded. I will go and take my wolf. Who will go with me?"

"I'll go," Thunder Cloud volunteered.

"I will as well," Raven added.

"Then count me in as well," Bull Elk offered.

"I think a pair of men will be enough," Running Bison said. "The rest can help with the meat. The sooner we get it stripped and drying, the less will spoil. But as soon as it is done, we had better search for another place to hold the Gathering.

"The valley beyond the canyon has good water," Raven said, "And there is better hunting there as well. I would suggest we move there. It is not too far out-of-the-way for any camp to go there rather than here."

Running Bison stood, "In the morning I want to take a quick trip out toward the plains. I want to see what changes have occurred to the plains since the last time I traveled there. If so much has happened here, it must be far worse there." Raven nodded.

"We had better get busy cutting racks!" Whispering Wind rose and dusted off her hands, "I see a few willows over there. At least they haven't died yet."

Soon everyone in the camp was busy. Water was set to make tea, but there was none for washing, or for making the usual vermin killing douse. People grimaced as they pinched fleas and pulled ticks from their bodies. At dawn Thunder Cloud and Calling Wolf headed back with all the empty water skins, while Running Bison and Raven ranged out toward the plain at a ground-eating run. The sun was well up when they reached the crest of the last ridge and the plains lay spread far below them. They just stood and looked. As far as they could see, there was little or nothing living. Certainly there was no lush grass, nor bison. Several dead trees attested to the lack of rain. And as far as they could see, nothing moved, except the wind flicking bits of sand from the tops of the moving dunes and a flock of lazily circling vultures.

"Let's get back to the valley. This place is worse than even I had imagined. There is nothing there for any animal to eat! When I think back to my childhood and the waist-high lush grass and huge spreading oaks, it is hard to believe that this is the same plain," Running Bison turned away.

They returned quickly to the valley and told the camp of their findings. "I think that Raven's suggestion of moving the Gathering to the valley beyond the canyon is a good one. Bear Claw Woman, I realize I have frequently discouraged you from using the 'mind talking', but if you would, I would greatly appreciate your contacting the other camps and letting them know of our findings and where we will meet."

Bear Claw Woman merely nodded. Already she had discovered the ancient cottonwood she had previously found to be a 'place-of-power' had died and with its death, the power had faded.

"I will have to go to the circle of trees where Obsidian was left but I will do it."

"If you leave now, when can you be back?"

Raven stepped forward, "I don't like this idea! Every time she uses this 'mind talking', it drains her strength. She is pregnant, man!"

"Have you another suggestion as to how we can contact the other camps?"

Raven shook his head. "I don't have to like it!" he muttered, "Even if I know it is the only way."

"When would you like us to leave?" Bear Claw Woman asked.

"As soon as you are ready," Running Bison replied with a heavy sigh." I agree with Raven, I'd rather you didn't do this thing either."

"I'll be careful. I won't over-tire myself."

Within a few fingers of time Raven was leading Young wolf and Guardian, followed by Bear Claw Woman toward the valley. When they arrived, both of them studied the valley. They were amazed at the changes here as well. They already expected to see the grass dry and desiccated. The stream here had all but dried up completely, leaving only a pair of small stagnating pools; both heavily used by the animals. There were prints of a few large animals and numerous smaller ones, but only large predators were represented.

"What do you make of this?" Bear Claw Woman asked Raven.

"The large animals cannot find food. They have either moved elsewhere or have died. Look at the trees! They are showing the strain of no rain as well. I remember this place being a cool shady spot to rest. There are barely any leaves on the trees. I suppose they are dying also."

"What will happen to the 'power place'?" Bear Claw Woman asked. "The tree beside the stream no longer holds power. Do you think the same thing will happen here?"

"What if all of the power places you have located lose their power how will you renew yourself?"

"The crystal cave should not be affected by any changes in the rainfall."

"What if the underground stream stops flowing? Do you think that will have an effect?"

"I hope not. We will be forced to leave there if the water dries up. But we just left there less than a moon ago and that area doesn't show the devastation of the plains and these mountains. And we have had some rain there; it looks as though none has fallen here. Come on, I need to check on the sacred place. I hope there is still a power source there otherwise I don't know what I'll do about contacting the other camps to tell them of the change of location for the Gathering. There is no way that I can contact all of them by mind talking unless I can pull power from something. The Sacred Relics are not enough by themselves, not for as much mind talking as I need to do."

"Can you make it short?"

"That will help some, but it is hard to tell. I have not had to look for power places for a long time. There must be others around. The lack of rain can't have killed them all. Besides, it is the stone within the circle that holds the power! We might as well find out! Standing here talking about it isn't going to answer our questions. There is no sense in looking for obstacles. Let's see if the stone still is, a sacred place before we worry about other problems."

They dumped their packs where they would make camp and gave the wolves permission to go about their own exploring. Then they walked side-by-side into the circle of trees. There they stopped and looked around.

"It doesn't look so bad," Raven said hopefully.

"Only one way to know for sure," Bear Claw Woman replied. "I might as well see if I can tell if there is any 'power' left here." She walked to the stone and climbed atop it. She sighed, because already she could feel the 'power' pulsing through her body.

"It is strong," Raven said; the relief clear in his voice. "You stay here and I'll get the camp set up and see to food and water. Perhaps the wolves will have found something to eat. If not, I'll scout around. There were plenty of small animal tracks at the pools so surely something will come in to drink this evening."

"We do have other food, don't we?"

"Yes and I brought some of the deer meat to cook. Come to think of it, I'd better do that before it starts to spoil in this heat. I'll check on you later." He turned and left the grove, sighing in relief as he stepped into the bright sunlight. No matter how long he was around it, 'power' still left him uneasy. He set up their shelter, carried stones to make a hearth, carefully clearing the dry grass from near it so that a fire couldn't get started. Then he found branches to skewer the meat and started it cooking.

Bear Claw Woman reached out, one by one to the leaders of the various camps. After a hand of contacts, however she was totally exhausted. She curled into a ball on the stone and slept. Quietly, Guardian settled at the base of the rock and absorbed her own 'power' from it.

In the valley of the Gathering, everyone was busy. Racks were erected; meat cut into thin strips and set to dry in the burning sun. It didn't take long. Winter Rain made reed hats to shield heads from the sun and near evening Calling Wolf and Thunder Cloud returned with full bladders of water and everyone had a good deep drink. As soon as they returned, the hunters headed to the place of stone and quickly gathered as much of a supply of it as they could load on their travois. They would refine it later.

"As fast as the sun is drying the meat, we should be able to move toward the canyon some time after sun-high tomorrow. We can fill the bladders again as we pass the stream. So everyone, drink deeply! You have earned it!"

"I saw vultures flying just to the north!" Calling Wolf said, "I think I'll check it out."

"I'll go with you," Running Bison replied and soon the pair of hunters passed from view of the camp. "I found signs of many dead animals on the way to the stream." Calling Wolf told him. "I scouted one way and Thunder Cloud another. He discovered the same. There are no tracks even of large animals."

Running Bison nodded. "I feared as much. Look how far we had to go for those deer and they were in such poor condition, there is no fat on them at all. I just hope this drought has not spread to the winter valley. If so, we will have a hard winter. But, I think we had better head straight there as soon as the Gathering is over. We will need the extra time to bring in enough food for the winter."

They topped a ridge and glanced down. Below them was a rather largish pond. In and around it lay the dead, rotting remains of numerous animals. The only things alive seemed to be the vultures circling lazily above. A putrid stench greeted them as they approached. They found the remains of antelope, deer, bear and wolf. Some carcasses were at least a moon old, others much fresher.

"There must not be another source of water for a long way!" Calling Wolf knelt beside the edge of the pond and smelled the water. "It even smells bad! Look at all the rotting carcasses in it! No wonder it is putrid! I'm going to see if I can at least drag some of them out."

"Don't bother!" Running Bison shook his head. "At least they will warn other animals not to drink here!"

Regretfully, the hunters turned and retraced their path back to the camp. Everywhere they looked, it was the same; dead and dying vegetation and blowing sand and as far as the eye could see, more and more of the same.

True to his words, by sun-high they were ready to leave. "We will go and pick up Bear Claw Woman and Raven on our way." Running Bison led the way.

Raven had cooked the sun-high and evening meals, taking them to where Bear Claw Woman rested. She contacted more of the camps late in the day, near dark and then rested on the soft fur that Raven brought to her. He slept at the base of the rock beside Guardian and Young Wolf, both of whom had managed to find their own meal. After the morning meal she contacted the remainder of the camps and again rested, exhausted.

"People are coming!" Raven called to her. "I will see who it is, but it sounds like the whole camp!" He trotted toward the noise and then returned. "I was right, it is the entire camp. Running Bison has decided to move on toward the canyon now rather than wait any longer. Water is a problem for everything!"

Raven broke his camp, loaded the travois and then carried Bear Claw Woman to ride upon it. She had finally learned not to protest when he insisted on her riding, but she still didn't like it!"

Late that night, Hollow Bone rejoined the camp. For a half moon they traveled through the mountains toward the west. To the north, at night, they could see a red haze light the sky. "A big fire," Raven stated, "Not surprising, as dry as the forests are. If we aren't careful we could start one ourselves and then be trapped by it."

"I have already told everyone to be very careful with the cooking fires," Running Bison nodded.

When they started across the place where Raven and Bull Elk had been rescued by Running Bison, they picked up their pace. By evening everyone was settling into the canyon cave. It was strange to have so much activity and noise in their quiet canyon! Part way through the next day Crying Coyote and his hunting party joined them.

"Mama!" Cried Calf as he ran on stubby legs to Whispering Wind. "I killed a rabbit!" He held the prize up for her to admire. "Just now and I gotted him with my dart!"

Whispering Wind admired the kill. "What a good hunter you are! I don't remember any boy bringing in food so young! Surely you will be a great hunter!"

Calf looked at her thoughtfully, the said solemnly. "Uncle Coyote says that only if my heart is clean, will I ever be a hunter! What does he mean, Mama, is my heart dirty?"

"He means that you must always thank the spirit of any animal that you kill. This rabbit gave its life for you. Unless you thank the spirits from your heart, I mean really mean it, this rabbit's spirit may decide not to return and make another rabbit. After a while, if no hunter thanks the rabbits, the rabbit spirits will not return to make another rabbit. Pretty soon there won't be any more rabbits. That is why thanking the spirits of every animal is so important."

"How do I thank rabbit for giving himself?"

"Ask your father!"

Calf sighed deeply, "Father just told me to ask you. He said you could splain it better."

Whispering Wind frowned, then sat beside Calf and took the rabbit from him. She laid it on the ground before him and told him. "Close your eyes tight."

He did. "Now think real hard how much you enjoyed getting that rabbit."

He screwed up his face, concentrating. "Now think about how good it will taste when you eat it." He smiled. "Now tell that rabbit how grateful you are for his giving his life so that you could be a hunter and that you would have food to eat."

"Rabbit," he began, "I is really happy that you gived yourself so that I could be a hunter. You is my first kill. I will never forget you. And I is going to eat you, so I won't go hungry. I is really happy that I won't be hungry. I hope that you will come back and make lots more rabbits cause I really like rabbit!" He opened his eyes and looked up at her. "Do you think that was all right? I really meant it!"

"Whispering Wind wiped a tear from her eye. "That was the finest hunter's prayer of thanks I have ever heard!" She hugged her son. "Now let's go and fix this rabbit so that you can eat him."

"I want you to eat some of him. Father, also. Maybe even Aunt Bear Claw Woman and Uncle Raven." Then he looked hopefully at the rabbit. "Maybe he will make more rabbits before we eat?"

Guardian was lying near. Quietly she slipped from the cave and found Young Wolf and Traveler. Soon the three were seen headed out of the canyon. They weren't gone long. Quietly they slipped back in and laid several more rabbits beside the one that the child had brought in. He had gone to fetch green plants to go with the rabbit. When he returned he squealed! "Mama! Come quick!" Whispering Wind hurried from the next cave, "Look!" He pointed with eyes wide with wonder; "the rabbit made more rabbits! I must have gotted it right! Now we can all eat rabbit!" His eyes shone with pleasure.

The woman's mouth fell open and she looked around in confusion. Then her eyes lighted on Guardian. She would swear for many seasons that the animal actually winked at her.

Bear Claw Woman and Raven and Whispering Wind and Running Bison enjoyed the best roasted rabbit they had ever eaten. Praise was heaped on the child. *I will always remember to say thank you!* Calf thought to himself.

Within a double hand of days, people began to trickle into the canyon. Running Bison took them to the valley and they began setting up their camps. The stream ran clean and fresh. Before the moon was full, the valley was overflowing with people. Bear Claw Woman withdrew to the crystal cave and prepared. She shivered when she received the message from the spirits.

The day before the ceremony arrived. Hunters had been out into the mountains hunting, women had scoured the nearby area collecting plants and the dreamers huddled together, making plans. The sun set with a cool breeze blowing from the north. A flicker of light sprang up from a coal left from the sun-high campfire, a pair of valleys to the north. The breeze lifted it, breathed new life into it, and gently laid it in the dry grass. Greedily it grew. While the camps slept, flames spread. The wind picked up and they leaped from spot to spot. They licked the bases of the tall pines then flowed up the trunks to the dry needles, hanging from desiccated branches. Sap popped, sending showers of sparks to light even more fires. Soon that valley was aflame. The wind quickened, lifting thick billowing black clouds. When the sun rose, the sky was hazy, but people were busy. Women were laughing and sharing tasks, there were many tasks to be completed before the naming ceremony began. Mothers were putting last touches to tunics for daughters. "Stand Still! Stop twitching!" Fathers were giving sons final instructions for their part in the ceremony. "Be sure to keep your dart high! Don't forget to leap at this place!" No one was paying any attention to anything but their own task.

"Fire!" A hunter stumbled out-of-breath into the camp. "The whole mountain's aflame!" He gasped. "Get out of here! We're all going to burn!" Then he staggered to his shelter and began knocking it down, dumping everything hurriedly onto his travois. He called to his mate and children and within breaths was leading them rapidly from the valley.

People began screaming; pandemonium reigned. Wolves howled. Children cried. Women ran here and there. The flames topped the ridge and started down the north end of the valley.

"Stop!" Running Bison shouted. No one paid any attention to him. "Don't panic!" he tried to calm people. It was too late. The fire was sweeping down the valley, faster than the people could run. Some began choking, other were knocked to their knees. Mothers grabbed children and ran dragging them, away from the fire.

"Whispering Wind, get those children to the stream!" Running Bison shouted.

She nodded and herded a double hand of youngsters quickly to the stream, adding their frantic parents as she went. "Come with me. I know a place where you will be safe! The fire can't reach us there!" More people joined her. She led them to the stream and beneath the wall, and then instructed them to follow the stream and go to the cave. Then she went back.

. "Get Hollow Bone and Calling Wolf to help you." Bison Man was urging another double hand or so of people into the stream. "Get as many as you can into the canyon!"

"You're crazy man!" one hunter jerked free as Running Bison tried to direct him and his family to the stream. "We'd die there! The fire won't stop cause of that little stream of water!" He turned and grabbing his mate rushed her toward the south end of the valley.

Some listened. Crying Coyote and Calling Wolf gathered an entire camp and led them to the stream. Hollow Bone, Raven and Bull Elk gathered more. They hunkered coughing and blinking from the smothering smoke. Running Bison joined them with most of several more camps. One whole camp and about a double hand of individuals more found their own way to the stream by accident. Raven showed them how to pass beneath the wall into the canyon. Once there, breathing was easier, but even in the canyon the smoke was getting thick. The hunters hurried their pathetic group up the path and into the cave. Here the air was fresher. Once everyone was inside, the hunters blocked the entrance with the hides. People moved into the rooms beyond the living cave. They were shaking with fear, only their trust in Running Bison keeping them from total panic. They were trapped and they knew it. The wolves tucked their tails and crowded silently against each other. Running Bison lighted torches and settled people. Even in the cave, they could hear the roar of the fire as it swept everything before it. For the rest of the day they waited.... Calling Wolf and Raven crouched at the mouth of the cave, watching.

"Did you hear that?" Calling Wolf tilted his head.

"What? Is there someone out there still alive?" Raven leaned forward.

"There! I hear it again!"

"It can't be!" Raven unhooked the hide and covered his mouth with a rabbit fur. Again he heard it, closer now. He called out, "Sister Cougar, over here!" Then he stumbled down the trail and squatted at the base. "Help Me!" he called to Calling Wolf. "She is burned badly!"

The other hunter hurried to his side. The big cat lay on her side at the base of the trail. She could go no farther. Her paws were burned to the bone; the hair on her hide singed and patches of raw flesh bled on her back and side. She looked up at Raven and from beneath her, with the last of her strength, lifted a singed bundle. She laid it at his feet and again mewed, then shuddered and died.

Calling Wolf lifted the bundle. It wiggled, coughed and looked up at him with wide frightened eyes. He cuddled the small animal into his tunic and laid his hand on his friend's arm. "There is nothing more you can do for her. Come on, at least maybe we can make her sacrifice have meaning. Look!" he held up the kitten. "She came to you, trusting you to take care of her little one! She never forgot your kindness."

Raven knelt for a few more heartbeats, his hand on the big cat's head then he rose and followed Calling Wolf back into the cave.

All night long people huddled in the darkness. Even in the cave the air began to fill with smoke. "Lay close to the ground. It is fresher there!" Bear Claw Woman went from group to group, encouraging, tending to hurts and calming the frightened ones as best she could. Ash Branch and Whispering Wind and Green Moss did the same. Gradually, the women of the Bison Camp settled and soothed and provided food for those trapped there. The morning brought black billowing clouds of smoke filtering down into the canyon, as the fire raged on. Seasons of drought had set the conditions. Now the mountains were ablaze. The fire in the immediate area had burned itself out, but the flames were spreading in every direction. The smoldering skeletons of mountain giants groaned and crashed to the ground as the wind rose to a shrieking pitch. It whipped ash and still burning cinders and threw them angrily at the ground. Toward evening clouds built to the north and thunder tried to outdo the wind. Lightning forked from the sky and finally, rain fell. It didn't just fall, in coursed down in sheets. The scorched earth sizzled and whole trees exploded in a shower of heat-driven missiles. Angry torrents of black muddy water rushed and cut along the paths of least resistance. Whole hillsides were gouged into the rolling boiling mass. All night the rain came down.

"Mother, what will happen to the rabbits?" Calf worried, "Who will say prayers for them?"

"I don't know, son. Perhaps we should all send prayers for all of the animals and the people who are out there...." she glanced toward the mouth of the cave. "Why don't you go and ask Calling Wolf to show you the cougar kitten?" She suggested. He went off and she searched out Bear Claw Woman.

"What are we going to do?" she sighed. "The whole world has gone insane! What do your spirits say?"

"Those who are worthy will survive." That is all that Wolf Spirit would say. I suppose that mean those of us huddled in these caves. But there are entire camps missing! There is no way they could have survived the fire!"

With the dawn, the rain slackened and by sun-high the clouds were drifting away and patches of blue sky could be seen. The heat returned and steam began to rise.

"We need to spread out and see what we find." Running Bison collected the hunters. There is enough food stored in the caves for now, but we must discover what has become of the others." He sighed, "at least we should try to recover their bodies."

"Most of them ran toward the south," Calling Wolf said. "I'll go in that direction with Bull Elk and Raven. Perhaps Crying Coyote and Thunder Cloud could scout to the west."

"Take at least a hand of hunters with you. I'll take more and see if we can find any food." He picked up his atlatl and darts; "if you come across anything that is edible...." he looked around at the hunters and sighed. Quietly they all left the cave.

The path to the rim was nearly impossible to traverse. Rubble and mud clogged the trail. Once they had toiled to the top, toppled trees and smoldering stumps amid a sea of black land, cut through by angry channels had changed the landscape. The devastation was complete. Not a single blade of grass or twig had survived the fiery inferno. Silently they split and headed in the designated directions.

Calling Wolf and Bull Elk were working along the east side of the stream while Raven and Young Wolf scouted the west. "Wait! I think I heard something!" Calling Wolf held up his hand. "Listen!"

"I hear it also!" Bull Elk nodded, "Raven, over here, we have found something!" he shouted.

Raven forded the stream and Young Wolf lifted his head. He let out a woof and headed into a pile of thick burned brush. Once the hunters had shoved their way through as well, they were amazed for crowded into a tiny glade, no bigger than a bison wallow was a group of women and children. The smoke blackened them and some had suffered burns as well, but they were alive!

"Come, we will take you to the others," Calling Wolf reached out his hand. "It is not far. If you need help, we will help you."

"Please," A woman with a badly burned arm called. "My baby, I think she is dead!" She wept.

Raven went to the woman and gently lifted the blackened bundle. There was a feeble movement in one leg. "She is not dead, but I fear the worst if we don't get her to the cave quickly."

"Please, go ahead with her! I don't care about myself, just save my baby!" She wept. "My leg is broken as well. There is no way that I will make it anywhere. Just give my baby to a woman who will love her."

"No other woman could love her as much as you do," Raven knelt beside the injured woman. "So it would be best if you lived to care for her yourself. Come now. It is going to hurt when I lift you, just put your good arm around my neck and I'll be as gentle as I can. There are healers at the cave. Your leg can be set and your child given the breath of life as well." He lifted the woman, whom immediately slumped into unconsciousness. "It is probably just as well," he sighed. "There is no way to make her passage less painful." He stood and looked around. "I cannot believe that anyone could survive here! The spirits truly must have blessed these."

"I'll take her and the child and the rest of these people, back to the camp and catch up with you. Keep looking, there might be more!" Raven led the way back to the wall. "It is much faster to go this way," he said. "It is only a short walk to the cave once we have passed beneath this cliff. Just hold hands and follow me." He handed the infant to one of the women and lowering himself and his burden into the water he sank beneath the surface and traveled the short distance through the cliff. When he rose to his feet he let out a piercing whistle and as soon as his group was all accounted for, he led them toward the cave. They were met and helping hands took over. He explained what they had found and turned them over to the people waiting to take them to the cave. Then he dived back beneath the cliff wall and joined Young Wolf for the run to catch up with the others.

Amazement set in. They searched and found other small enclaves of survivors. The Bear Camp had sheltered in a big cave. They had suffered smoke inhalations and most were very hungry.

"My wolf led us here," Jumping Fox explained. "We went as far as we dared into the cave. There was enough good air."

A pair of children was found wandering confused through the blackened land. Crying Coyote came in with the same results. No one could understand how anyone could have lived through the fire and storm, but they had. "The Spirits have protected us!" Jumping Fox insisted.

When the searching was over, only one in every three was unaccounted for. It was possible that some had outrun the fire. Bear Claw Woman insisted on 'searching', although Running Bison was against it. Whispering Wind had told him that Bear Claw Woman was spotting blood. It was far too soon for her child to be born. She needed to rest! But Bear Claw Woman being Bear Claw Woman, she made her way to the crystal room, Whispering Wind for once insisting on going with her and let her mind roam.

"The Fox Camp is to the south and east of here. They cut back behind the fire, but the flood cuts them off from us. There is a hand of hunters trapped in a deep crevasse beyond that ridge. One of them is injured badly. That is all," she sighed.

"You hear her. We will need ropes to reach the hunters. The Fox Camp will take care of itself. Meanwhile, I think we should all rise thanks to the Spirits! We are alive!"

"May I make a suggestion?" Hollow Bone rose.

"Go ahead," Running Bison stopped in his preparations.

"I think that when you have returned, those of us here should hold the Gathering ceremony. There are children to be named, hunters and new women to be recognized and prayers of thanks raised for our lives."

Running Bison nodded, "And then we are leaving this burned out area before we run out of food and drinkable water. While we are gone, see how many of the supplies in the storage areas of the cave can be put to use. I know there are spare travois poles and stacks of hides. The injured will have to ride, but no one can stay behind here." He looked directly at Bear Claw Woman, "If you have extra water stomachs, food, anything which we can use...."

She nodded, "Of course, there are plentiful supplies. Not perhaps, for so many, but with luck and speed, we should pass beyond the burned-out forest before we run out of food and water."

"We will be back as soon as we can. Calling Wolf, perhaps you could be of assistance to Hollow Bone. We don't need you on this rescue. You have done enough."

Hollow Bone turned to Bear Claw Woman, "I know that you should be resting. Why not let Whispering Wind and me organize the supplies. She is familiar with the cave and perhaps some of the other women would be better occupied with working and organizing rather than worrying."

Raven stepped forward. "Bear Claw Woman is going to stay in her furs until we leave. It is not good for her to be moving about. A healer is always the worst person to treat! If she doesn't rest, she is going to lose this baby!"

Bear Claw Woman opened her mouth to protest but looking from Raven to Whispering Wind she simply closed it and lay back on her furs. They were right, she knew that she had foolishly risked Morning Star's life with her activities the last several days, but she didn't know what else she could do. Ash Branch had dealt with the heavier work of setting broken bones and treating the worst of the burns. Still, she was spotting blood and had even felt a cramp or so. It was too early for the child to be born. Raven was right. She settled back and tiredly accepted people waiting on her. It was then that she realized that it was helping the other women to have something to do. So she began asking them to organize small things and soon the packing was going smoothly.

Late in the day the hunters came in with the remaining people who had survived the fire. It was amazing! Only a few hunters had actually perished in the fire. Bear Claw Woman thought back to her message from the spirits and in her head went over the names of the hunter who had died. She realized that these were probably the last hold-outs against the spirits. Now perhaps, the people could begin living again.

*　　*　　*

Hollow Bone rose and walked slowly to the fire, keeping time with the beat of the drum. "We are gathered here to add the names of people to the Camps of the Wolf. Bring forth the young so that they may be recognized!" He called in a soft but steady voice.

Several women came forward. Whispering Wind carried the baby girl belonging to the one with a broken leg. "This child is named Rosewood!" she lifted the child, "She belongs to the woman Shifting Sand, of the Bear Camp."

Hollow Bone drew a line with black ash down the child's forehead. He then stepped back. "Rosewood, Daughter of Shifting Sand, you are recognized." Then several more women came forward with season-old children to be named. After that the youths that had completed their spirit journeys were given adult names. Young women were recognized.

There was only a brief 'hunter recognition' ceremony and then Hollow Bone called forth Bear Claw Woman to give the message from the spirits. Whispering Wind and Raven sitting on either side of her helped her rise.

"The spirits have already fulfilled their message," she said quietly. "They have called the unworthy hunters from our midst. Now they bid us to move to the western mountains and make a life there, living in peace amongst ourselves, keeping them in our hearts and learning from each other. They are pleased with those of us still living. The circle has been kept open." She let Raven and Whispering Wind settle her once again and she sighed. It was done! Hopefully the death and pain were over. She glanced around at the people in the canyon, remembering back to the time she had joined the Bison Camp. Many faces were absent, but these remaining, all held a look of reverence in their eyes. She sighed in relief.

In the morning they filed from the canyon. There was little left in the cave and Bear Claw Woman knew that it was unlikely that she would ever return there. Guardian pulled the travois upon which she rode. Raven and Bull Elk walked beside her. Whispering Wind and her baby were always near. But the land through which they traveled had been raped! It was desolate! Nothing had been left alive. They traveled all day and another and another, still nothing changed as far as the eye could see. Only blackened burned land. The sun beat down on them unmercifully! Day after day, already drying up all traces of the rain and once again the forest was bone-dry.

There were no sources of fresh water. All the stomachs had been filled before they left the cave and people were using it sparingly, but still Running Bison was becoming worried. "Do you think it would be worth it if a small band of us went on ahead and tried to find a source of fresh water?" Calling Wolf asked, as he sat feeding chewed meat to the baby cougar. She had bonded to him to the extent that if he left her in the care of anyone else she yowled pathetically until he took her up again. But she was growing! It would not be long before he could no longer carry her in the sling that Whispering Wind had fashioned for her. But she brought him endless satisfaction. He felt that he owed a debt to Sister Cougar to raise this kitten which she had given her life to bring to Raven.

Running Bison sent a fast-moving group ahead to find water. They met up with the main camp several days later, with the uneasy information that they had not found water, nor had they found the end of the burned forest. They had, however, seen fires raging to the south.

Raven sat thinking and then he rose and went to Running Bison. "I wonder if it would work to dig for water," he suggested. "We have crossed several places where once rivers ran. Perhaps there is still water beneath the surface. I was listening to Fire Weed talking last night. She is right. We might be able to dig for water."

"Where would we dig?"

"I will ask her." he rose and went in search of the woman. When he returned, he frowned. "They dug at the base of willow trees."

"Well how can one recognize willow trees among these burned stumps?"

"I think if we locate a river bed, then dig in the middle of it, perhaps we could find standing water. I don't know, but I have no other ideas. How bad is the shortage?"

"Not critical yet, but it soon will be. I have encouraged everyone to be very sparing."

"When we stop tonight, I think I will try to dig for water," Raven sighed, "We have already traveled half the distance to the winter valley and still have found no end to the fire-burned area. What if it has burned all of the mountains? What if the winter valley is like this?" he motioned around them.

"I don't know," Running Bison frowned, "I have been worrying about the same thing. I guess we keep going until we find a place to settle."

They made a dry camp, beside what once was a wide beautiful river. Now it was a dry, scoured raw scar on the land. Raven, Calling Wolf, Bull Elk and Prairie Grass got out scapula diggers and began digging near the base of a large stump. For a pair of hand time they took turns digging. The hole got bigger and deeper. Finally, the men were over their heads in the hole.

"Wait!" Raven squatted. "I think I have found damp sand!" he took a handful of it and handed it up to Calling Wolf. "What do you think?"

Calling Wolf felt the sand, sniffed it and then handed it to Bull Elk. "I don't know," he replied, "Perhaps it is damp."

"It is definitely damp now!" shortly thereafter, Raven called up excitedly. "I can almost squeeze the moisture out of it!"

Calling Wolf jumped down into the hole with him and took up a handful of sand. "You are right! This is wet! Let's keep digging."

"Throw down a water bladder!" Raven soon shouted to those standing above. "There is enough water to fill it and slowly all of the others as well!"

All night hunters took turns in the hole, slowly filling the water bladders, until, by morning, all were brimming once again. Running Bison sighed in relief. No longer was water a problem, but it was only replaced with food. They had found nothing alive in the forest. He had no idea how much farther the fire had reached. But if they did not get fresh food soon, people would begin to suffer most cruelly.

"I want a pair of hunters to find a high place and see if they can find an end to this devastation!" He called together the men of the camp. "If we do not find food soon, we will be forced to eat the wolves!"

"I will go out tomorrow!" Raven said, "Perhaps Jumping Fox and Prairie Grass could come with me. I know of a high place to the north, perhaps a hard day's travel. From there we should be able to see a great distance."

Running Bison nodded, "We should be turning north any way. We will be following the same trail we have traveled before. You will find us along that route."

At dawn, several men set out at a fast pace, they pushed hard all day, always uphill. Just at evening they toped the last ridge. But it was too dark to see. They had a dry camp, eating frugally of the last of their trail food. Well before dawn they were up, pacing restlessly along the west-facing ridge. The sun rose and with the faint rays of early morning, they saw it. Green forest!

# CHAPTER 31

Look!" Raven Shouted, "Have you ever seen anything so beautiful?" He took a deep breath of pine tanged air.

"Do you think we should find meat and take it back to the camp?"

Raven shook his head, "We haven't the time. This heat would rot any meat which we could bring back."

"What about plants? It would not take us more than a pair of hands to be there! We could gather tubers and green plants and carry them back to the camp. At least it would be food!" Bull Elk said.

"I have an idea!" Prairie Grass suggested. "Why don't we go and gather the food. It would only take one of us to go back and bring the camp. That person could bring the camp toward us. We could meet everyone along the way with whatever we can find."

So it was agreed. Bull Elk was the swiftest, so he elected to fetch the camp. The remaining hunters hurried into the green forest. They worked hard for the rest of the day, digging tubers, pulling cattails and cutting off the roots, tossing them into waiting receptacles. They cut green leafy plants and collected ripe berries and nuts. When they reached the camp, their backpacks were bulging and each pulled a travois piled high with tubers and fresh plants. The camp was staggering with hunger but not for long. They stopped right there and had a celebration. The fresh plants were wonderful! It was not enough to fill every stomach to the fullest, but no one went hungry. Already another group of hunters were headed toward the green forest and they would bring in meat as well. They had made it! Silently heads were raised toward the sun. Tears streamed down tired, dirty faces and many hearts sent up prayers of gratitude.

With the coming of the next full moon, the burned-out-forest was behind them. The camps began to go their separate ways.

And so it went. For Running Bison and his camp, the winter valley brought a feeling of home-coming. Bear Claw Woman was barely settled into the big cave before her labor began in earnest. With Ash Branch and Whispering Wind in attendance and the pacing, concerned Raven not far away, she prepared for the long-awaited birth. Within pair of days she held her daughter in her arms. She was a perfect, beautiful baby and Bear Claw Woman knew that she had been right to return to the land of the living. Throughout the coming moons, she and Raven dotted on the child and when it came to her naming day, Bear Claw Woman was finally able to tell everyone the name by which she would become known as a child. Sunrise was the center of her parent's lives.

Over the seasons that followed, Sunrise and all the children flourished. The camps had formed a kinship bond during their 'trial of fire'. Frequently now, small groups of people traveled to nearby camps. Over the next pair of seasons, Ash Branch learned the healing of the mountain plants. She became restless, however and when Daughter Cougar had turned her second season, Calling Wolf decided to escort her back to her own desert people. It was a sad day when the Wolf Camp bid them goodbye. Everyone knew that it was unlikely they would ever see them again. Calling Wolf led the way, Daughter Cougar at his side and a small band of followers behind. He found his destiny as well, in the desert camps to the west.

The Wolf Camp now stayed year-around in the winter valley. Once in every hand of seasons they trekked to the Sacred Spring. Bear Claw Woman made the offering and they spent the late summer gathering acorns and grasses on the Llano and then returned to the winter valley. So the seasons passed. During them, Whispering Wind gave birth to a hand of children and Bear Claw Woman presented Raven with a pair of sons. With great satisfaction they sat back and watched their children grow. The adventure of their youth gave way to the responsibilities of maturity and then, much later, the infirmity of age. Sunshine came of age and Morning Star became a woman. Bear Claw Woman wondered where the time had gone.

Traveling groups of people eventually became known as traders. They carried goods and news from one camp to another. They developed a sign language that could be understood by all. Stone, mountain plants carefully preserved and nuts and berries were carried as trade goods to the desert camps. Obsidian and desert plants were carried to the mountain camps. Information and news of loved ones were exchanged and these traders became an integral part of the lives of every camp.

The seasons passed in a welter of living. Morning Star mated and in turn, gave birth to her own children. One day Whispering Wind and Bear Claw Woman sat on the wide stone in the front cave, sewing tunics for their grandchildren. Bear Claw Woman looked at Whispering Wind. Lately she had felt the long-ago familiar pull of her mark.

"When did all of this gray grow in our hair?" she sighed. "It seems only yesterday that we were young and living on our own. Look at us now! There is more white in my hair than brown!"

"I know. It seems that the time has passed very quickly, but still, it has been a good life!" Whispering Wind sighed. "When I think of all those who have gone to walk the wind, it reminds me that soon it will by my time. I am glad that we no longer move from place to place all the time. It is good to live in one place. Did you listen to the trader last night? Calling Wolf has become a great Shaman, he is known far and wide as 'Man Who Walks with Cougar'".

"I noticed that they repeatedly mentioned that Ash Branch has become well known as a healer. It is well that the spirits have directed us these seasons."

"Do they still contact you?"

Bear Claw Woman shook her head, "It has been many seasons since my mark has alerted me. I think that perhaps my task is finished. I have turned the tasks of Keeper over to Morning Star and soon she will hand them down to her own daughter. I do not miss the trips to the Sacred Spring, but then, only recently, I have been feeling the mark calling me. It urges me to return to the cave in the canyon."

"At your age!" Whispering Wind shook her head. "It would be nearly an impossible trek!"

"Don't you ever wonder what it looks like now? It has been many seasons since the fire, far more than I like to think about. Surely the land has recovered!"

"There has been little rain though, during any of those seasons. Look at the changes here! These mountains look more like a desert than mountains! Think of the plants that once we gathered which no longer live here. And look at the ones that do! The land has changed. The traders say that little grows in the burned-out-mountains even now. I doubt there are many plants growing there, much less game. Besides, who would take us?"

"Us?"

"I would never let you go without me. I know that at our age, it would be a one-way trip. We would never return here. Besides I miss Running Bison and I know that you miss Raven. It is hard to believe that it has been more than a hand of seasons since they went to walk the wind. But at least we have our children and grandchildren."

"Young Elk has wanted to take a journey," Bear Claw Woman mentioned her grandson. "He is at that restless age. I have been thinking, perhaps he and Black Wolf...."

*       *       *

"Hurry up Grandmother!" Young Elk called impatiently, "It is time to go!"

"Ah, youth!" Bear Claw Woman muttered. Already Whispering Wind was standing beside Black Wolf, waiting for her. She picked up her staff, no longer merely a symbol of her station, but an essential part of her getting around and hobbled to where they waited.

Already the group had bid loved ones goodbye. With a last hug, Bear Claw Woman looked for the final time upon the beloved face of Morning Star. Tears ran down her face. "Don't cry for me Daughter," Bear Claw Woman whispered, "I am going home!"

"But why do you have to go there?"

"Because my spirits call me," Bear Claw Woman replied calmly. "Much of my life is at that cave, it is only right that my spirits call this body there."

"But why won't you let me come with you?"

"You have responsibilities here. This valley is your home. The cave is only a place that you have heard about in stories. But in a way, it is where my life began. It is where I finally accepted that I was chosen and it is where you were conceived. It is where I came to love your father and it is where I wish to close my eyes for the last time. I will take good care of Summer Blossom and she will return to you."

They traveled slowly, the old women frequently riding the travois, pulled by descendants of Guardian and Young Wolf. The burned-out-forest was nearly as barren as if the fire had just occurred. Few green shoots had pushed their way up through the blackened ground. But as they traveled, more and more green could be seen. Long before they reached the canyon, the land had recovered. There were tall pines and lush undergrowth. The streams ran fresh and clean.

"Is this the place where the path goes beneath the cliff?" Young Elk asked.

They were resting beside the stream. "It is," Bear Claw Woman admitted. "But I think we will go around by the trail. I am too old to be swimming under that wall."

Both old women had made the journey surprisingly well. Before dark they were waiting at the base of the trail leading up to the cave. Within, they could hear the racket of barking and snarling. Whispering Wind smiled. "Remember..." Just as Bear Claw Woman said. "Remember..."

Just then, a snarling, spitting angry cougar leaped from the cave, followed by a pair of furious wolves. The old women merely smiled happily. They were home!

Bear Claw Woman unpacked her belongings, frowning as she lifted out the Sacred Relics. The old spirits were tired. They wanted to give way to younger spirits. In a way, this was Bear Claw Woman's last task for them. They also wanted to go home. She sighed. It was still a long way to the place where they wished to be returned and she was glad that it would wait until spring, because she knew that she still had not reached the end of her journey.

The small group settled into the cave. Whispering Wind and Bear Claw Woman spent many hours soaking in the warm stream waters, looking out at the elk herd grazing in the canyon and remembering all the times of their lives lived in this place while the younger women gathering and the men hunted. When the first snows of winter softly settled in the canyon, they were well prepared. The men hunted elk in the canyon and deer in the surrounding forests. Sadly, one morning, toward spring, it was discovered that old Whispering Wind had died quietly in her sleep. Bear Claw Woman mourned her 'sister in spirit'. So many had gone on before, but with the passing of Whispering Wind, she felt truly alone. With the coming of spring however, her spirit became restless. Time was drawing near. The spirits were closer.

*    *    *

"You are sure?" Young Elk frowned. "It sounds like a long distance, Grandmother. Are you sure that you can make it?"

"It matters not if I make it or not!" Bear Claw Woman grumbled, "The Relics must be returned to the Sacred Circle of Trees. I have explained that to you!"

"Yes, I understand, but why must Summer Blossom do this thing? She is barely a woman! Surely I could be entrusted...."

"A man entrusted to fulfill a woman's spirit task? I think not!" the old one sputtered. "Don't worry about me, Grandson! I'll make it! Just follow my directions and let's get going, the sun is already up!" She settled more comfortable onto the travois.

Young Elk shook his head and led them up the trail into the forest. Bear Claw Woman was right; he had no place messing around with 'women's spirits'. They made him nervous. Summer Blossom, on the other hand, merely smiled that superior smile and shrugged. "Men!" she murmured under her breath.

It was the full moon of mid-summer, when they arrived at the valley of the sacred circle. Bear Claw Woman could hardly believe it, the trees were still alive! Eagerly she tottered to the great stone within their center. She placed her hands on the smooth surface of the boulder and felt the familiar tingle. It was just as she remembered it. "See, right there," she pointed out to Summer Blossom. "That is where you are to dig the hole, deep and back beneath the stone itself. Be sure that you dig under the stone itself."

"You have told me repeatedly, Grandmother. I will do it just as you instructed!" Summer Blossom replied patiently, "You can sit right there and make sure!"

"No, I won't be able to tell you. The spirits are close; they are calling for me. Lay me out on the stone and make sure that my staff is beside me and my amulet about my neck. And take care of that necklace!" the old one sighed.

Late that day, she felt the pains begin in her chest. Her eyes closed and her breathing became shallow. Shadows crept closer. Just as the sun vanished beyond the mountains, she gave up the spirit. The wolves gave forth with a mournful howl.

Bear Claw Woman looked down. Her old worn-out body lay on the palate beside the fire. Summer Blossom sat beside it crying softly. With the dawn, the young woman followed her instructions. The hunters reverently lay the old grandmother out on the sacred stone. Already Summer Blossom had dug and buried the Sacred Relics. Now she laid the staff beside the old one and wiping tears from her eyes she stepped back.

"Walk in peace with the spirits, Grandmother," she said softly.

A breeze sprang up and it rustled the leaves of the trees, as the people left the sacred circle and returned to their camp. It was done. The great Bear Claw Woman, Spirit Woman of the Wolf People, had been laid out to walk the wind. The wind picked up and clouds formed to the north.

"There is a storm coming in," Young Elk tossed another log on the fire. "In the morning I want to go farther east and see what is there. Many say that once there was a great plain filled with grass. I would see it if this is so."

Just then a blinding flash of lightning struck so close it raised the hair on their heads, followed by a deafening roll of thunder.

A whirling sound assailed their still-ringing ears. They whirled toward the trees and watched as a blue mist rose from the sacred circle. Then, as quickly as it had come, suddenly the storm was gone. The sky cleared and birds began singing as though nothing had happened. "What was that?" Young Elk asked, "It came from the circle. Come on!" He headed there at a run, Summer Blossom right on his heels.

"Look!" They both halted, mouths hanging open in surprise. "The Sacred Stone, it's gone! Grandmother is gone as well! There is nothing but a deep hole!"

*     *     *

Birds were singing in the meadow. Bear Claw Woman sighed. It was always such a beautiful place.

"Woof!" She glanced up and braced herself as Guardian threw her paws onto shoulders suddenly young and strong. The raspy tongue joyfully washed her face and she buried her face in the luxurious fur.

"Oh Guardian" she cried as she fell to her knees and hugged the animal. "I have missed you so!" Tears of joy ran down her face.

"And me?" asked a deep voice beside her.

"Raven!" she rose and melted into the powerful arms of their youth. Laughing and strong she walked beside her wonderful hunter, running the last few steps into the arms of those who had gone before her. Whispering Wind, young and beautiful again stood nearby, within the protective arms of Running Bison, smiling softly. Sage had come home.

**THE END**

# BIBLIOGRAPHY

**Barnett, Franklin:** Dictionary of Prehistoric Indian Artifacts of the American Southwest.
1991: Northland Publishing

*Blackwater Locality #1 Site, A Brief Scenario of Life at..*
2002: Eastern New Mexico University Department of Anthropology. www.google.com

**Brown, Lauren:** Grasslands: The Audubon Society Nature Guide.
1989: Alfred A. Knopf Inc. Publisher.

**Densmore, Frances:** How Indians Use Wild Plants for Food, Medicine & Crafts.
1974: Dover Publications, Inc., New York

**Elias, Thomas S. and Peter Dykeman:** Edible Wild Plants: A North American Field Guide.
1990: Sterling Publishing Co., Inc. New York.

*Geology Fieldnotes:* Alibates Flint Quarries National Monument:
1997: National Park Service, Texas. www.google.com

*Glendo State Park:*
2000: Wyoming State Park Service. www.google.com

**Kershaw, Linda:** Edible & Medicinal Plants of the Rockies.
1951: Lone Pine Publishing. Renton, Wa.

**Kirk, Donald R.:** Wild Edible Plants of Western North America.
1975: Naturegraph Publisher, Inc. Happy Camp, Ca.

**MacMahon, James A.:** Deserts: Audubon Society Nature Guides.
1988: Alfred A. Knopf, Inc., Publisher.

**Malcomson, Scott, L:** Kennewick Man: the Battle Still Rages.
1998 Journal of Indian Justice

**National Geographic Society:** Field Guide to the Birds of North America: 2nd Edition.
1989.

**Telford, Gregory L:** Edible and Medicinal Plants of the West
1997: Mountain Press Publishing Co. Missoula, Montana.

*Texas Parks & Wildlife*: Edwards Plateau. www.google.com

**Wendorf, Fred and James J. Hester :**Early Man's Utilization of the Great Plains Environment.
1962: *American Antiquity, Vol 28; No. 2.* Salt Lake City.

**Wormington, Marie H.:** Ancient Man in North America.
1957: Denver Museum of Natural History.